SELECT EDITIONS

Selected and Edited by Reader's Digest

SELECT EDITIONS

Selected and Edited by
Reader's Digest

 New York · Montreal

FROM THE EDITORS

Our mission for each volume of Select Editions is simple: find the best four books possible. We take into account plot, characters, genres, and settings, always aiming for a nice mix. Sometimes we notice an unexpected theme cropping up. That was the case this time around. Let's call it the "Missing" Volume. In each book, someone or something needs to be found.

Leading off is *The Wild One* by Nick Petrie, an exceptional thriller filled with atmosphere and . . . bad weather. Tough and smart former marine Peter Ash tracks down a missing child in snowy, cold, and dangerous Iceland. You can practically feel the biting wind as Peter confronts bad guys right and left.

Second up we've got *Dachshund Through the Snow* by David Rosenfelt, a longtime favorite SE author. With his trademark wry humor, Rosenfelt sends his lovably grouchy series character, Andy Carpenter, on the hunt for a missing father—with dogs, of course.

In book three, the missing person is a husband. *No Bad Deed*, a terrific tale of suspense, comes from debut author Heather Chavez. We're super excited to share this talented newcomer with you.

The final slot is filled by another perennial SE author, Richard Paul Evans, with *Noel Street*. What's missing here? Why, true love. And you can bet RPE knows how to find it again.

So if you've been missing good books lately, we hope we've found a solution. Enjoy!

Inside
SELECT EDITIONS

NICK PETRIE

THE WILD ONE

ONE

A
PETER ASH
— NOVEL —

Chapter 1

Twelve Months Earlier

Óskar wakes them both by jumping into their bed, a warm and wiggly bundle of excitement. Erik groans, and Sarah buries her head under the covers. It's barely dawn, and the Air and Space Museum doesn't open until ten, but Óskar doesn't care. He wraps himself around his father's neck. "Happy Sunday," Óskar whispers loudly, seven years old and unable to contain himself.

Sunday is Family Day, when Óskar gets to choose an activity they will all do together. For more Sundays than Erik cares to think about, the Air and Space Museum has been Óskar's choice. But Erik is still mixing batter for Family Day pancakes when Sarah's phone rings with a work emergency. She gives Erik an apologetic look and runs upstairs to put on work clothes.

Erik can't face yet another Sunday fighting the tourists without her. Instead, he drops to his knees on the kitchen floor. "Óskar," he says, "what would you say to a Viking adventure in Rock Creek Park?" They've been reading Norse mythology together, and the park has plenty of wild sections and epic landscapes.

Óskar cheers and jumps around the house while Erik stuffs a backpack with sandwiches and extra clothes and a thermos full of hot chocolate, knowing that Óskar will happily wander all day if he's warm and fed. December weather in Washington, D.C., is nothing for a pair of real Vikings.

AFTER a long and muddy day of exploration, they arrive back home at the last unrestored town house in Adams Morgan. Óskar sprawls on the floor amid a chaos of LEGOs while Erik stands at the open refrigerator, waiting for Sarah to text him back.

It is unlike Sarah to ignore her phone. Erik reminds himself that his wife runs her own small cybersecurity company, and a client emergency could well be a very serious thing. She might not be home until midnight or later, and dinner won't wait with a hungry boy in the house.

Erik has chicken thighs braising and a green salad coming together when, to his surprise, Sarah bangs through the back door, her scuffed leather bag slung over one shoulder.

As usual, Sarah's crisp, professional look has come undone during the course of her workday. Her sandy hair falls free from its ponytail. Her good wool coat is unbuttoned. He steps in to press his lips to hers, but she holds him back with a hand on his chest. Her eyes remain dark.

"I need to show you something." She slips her bag off her shoulder. "Where's Óskar?"

"Busy." Erik tilts his head toward the tinkle of LEGOs and Óskar mumbling numbers in the living room. "What's up?"

Sarah sets her laptop on the counter and types in her long and complicated password, automatically positioning her body to shield her keystrokes from prying eyes.

Then she steps sideways to make room for him at the counter but keeps her torso angled to block the view from the door to the dining room. The door Óskar would come through. She hits a key, and a paused video frame comes up on the screen.

It shows a dim room, two bodies entangled on a leather couch.

She presses Play. The bodies begin to move. Erik can tell immediately that something is profoundly wrong.

The body on top is significantly larger than the body on the bottom. One is a grown man, his pants down to his knees. The other is just a girl. And she fights to get free.

Erik turns from the screen. "Sarah, what is this?"

Sarah's voice is calm. "Look at him. Do you recognize him?"

Erik blinks. He looks. He does recognize the man. He fumbles for the remote and turns on the small television in the corner of the kitchen. And there the man stands, as he does so often, on a futuristic set with his crisp haircut and a fresh shave and a microphone on his lapel, wearing a midnight suit and a bloodred tie.

The same man in the video with the girl.

That same face. Mouth moving, charming his viewers. Erik feels sick to his stomach. He unplugs the TV and looks at Sarah.

"Where on earth did this come from?"

Chapter 2

Present Day

PETER ASH WOKE, gasping for breath, from a dream of gunfire. He could still feel the desert heat on his skin, and the memory of spent powder lingered in his nose.

Beside him, his elderly seatmate strained upward, one finger stabbing the call button overhead.

Peter blinked away the nightmare, wondering what he'd said or done in his sleep. He was a tall, bony man with shaggy black hair, a tired face, and the thoughtful eyes of a werewolf five minutes before the change. His green hiking pants were frayed at the seams, his T-shirt ghosted with old stains.

A beefy male flight attendant advanced up the aisle, broad face expressionless, hands open and ready. Peter could tell the man had some physical training and was probably tasked with controlling unruly passengers on this packed transatlantic flight.

Peter caught the man's eye. "Sorry." It was hard to get the words out, his throat choked with the panic raised by the memories still burned into his brain. "Just a bad dream. Give me a minute, I'll be fine."

He bent to his bag stuffed under the seat and dug for his pills. His seatmate had shrunk himself against the window. Passengers across the aisle were looking anywhere but at him.

"Sir." The flight attendant was almost on him. Peter's fingers closed on the prescription bottle, and he straightened up.

"I'm all right." He tried to believe it. "I just need my meds."

He fumbled the top off and shook four of the small pink circles into his hand. Then he found the last intact mini bottle of Reyka vodka in his seat pocket, twisted it open, and swallowed hard, pushing the pills down.

The dreams were new. He'd come back from Iraq with claustrophobia bad enough to make living outdoors seem like a good idea. For more than a year, he'd slept under the stars or under a rain fly, above the tree line of one mountain range or another, barely able to manage resupply in small-town grocery stores.

The post-traumatic stress came from kicking in doors in Fallujah, he figured. All those weeks of fighting house to house, room to room, clearing insurgents one doorway at a time.

Along with everything else he'd done.

He called it the white static, that feeling of electric overdrive that sparked up his brain stem. Nerves jangling like electrodes under the skin, his fight-or-flight reflex gone into overdrive. When he first mustered out, he could only handle twenty minutes indoors before the static turned into a full-blown panic attack.

In the time since then, he'd found a way forward. He'd made friends with the static, in a way, and a start at a new life. He'd found a veterans' group. He'd met a woman he didn't deserve, a woman named June Cassidy.

But he'd never had dreams, not like this.

In retrospect, this trip was a bad idea. He'd been in a hurry, had booked his tickets for same-day travel. The schedule was brutal. He'd started in Portland, Oregon, changed planes and airlines in Minneapolis, then done it again in New York.

Long hours spent in the stale fluorescent clatter of airports. More long hours with his oversize frame jammed into undersize seats, trapped in a cigar tube at thirty-five thousand feet.

His only exercise was pacing the aisles, his only sleep a few fitful naps. He'd hoped the Valium would help keep the white static at bay, but he'd been stuck inside for too long.

He touched the little screen on the seat back. The plane icon was over Greenland now. Only ninety minutes to Reykjavík, Iceland, in late December. Where it snowed for days at a time and the sun never truly rose, only brightening the sky for a few hours at midday.

He told himself he'd quit the Valium once he got off the plane. He'd pick up his rental, find a place to park outside the city, and sleep it off. He had plenty of practice sleeping in a vehicle.

For now, he closed his eyes and drifted.

THE airport's long, narrow halls were packed with people. Peter walked with the crowd to get his heavy pack and duffel, jumping out of his skin with the need to stand under the open sky and feel the wind on his face. Eight in the morning and still dark outside. Daylight wouldn't come for hours.

At customs, the female agent behind the glass ran Peter's passport under the scanner. He heard a beep, and her cool eyes flickered up at him. "Please wait a moment."

In less than a minute, two uniformed agents appeared as if from thin air, a man and a woman. The man collected Peter's passport from the scanner. "Sir, please come with us."

His English had just a trace of an accent. He was older than Peter, early fifties but slim. His crisp black uniform had two tags, one in Icelandic on the right breast, LÖGREGLAN, and one on the left that read POLICE.

The woman was younger than Peter, but not by much. Her tag read CUSTOMS.

Peter took a deep breath and let it out. "What's this about?"

The man saw Peter's rising tension but seemed unconcerned. If he'd known what Peter was capable of, the things Peter had done, he would have been worried as hell.

The woman smiled with professional warmth. "Your name is Peter, right? I'm Sigrid. This is Hjálmar. Come with us for a moment, and we'll explain everything."

Peter bent to pick up his duffel. He already wore the big pack slung over one shoulder.

They walked him down a hallway to a bright yellow door that opened to a plain white room. It was furnished with a long laminate table and six plastic chairs. Inexpensive stuff, but elegant.

The man, Officer Hjálmar, held the door against the spring, and the woman, Officer Sigrid, ushered Peter politely inside. He set his duffel on the table, then the pack. Officer Hjálmar followed, and the door closed automatically behind.

Peter thought about how hard it would be to kick his way through the wallboard. With his heavy leather hiking boots, not hard at all.

Officer Sigrid gave him the smile again. "Please, have a seat." Everything was designed to put him at ease. It didn't work.

Peter leaned against the wall. "Why am I here?"

"I'm told you had some trouble on the airplane," Officer Hjálmar said. "You were agitated. You shouted."

"I had a bad dream," Peter said. "I think I'm still having it."

"You're sweating," Hjálmar said. "Are you nervous?"

"I have claustrophobia." Peter hated the weakness it implied. "I get panic attacks in small spaces."

The man looked at Peter. "I'm sorry." Maybe some sympathy there, but he was still a cop. "Is that what the medication is for?"

Peter pushed back the shame that washed over him. Eight years a recon marine, more deployments than he cared to remember. He was proud of his service, but it had changed him.

"The medication is none of your business," he said calmly.

There was a knock on the yellow door. A female officer leaned in and said something in Icelandic. It was a beautiful language, sinuous and sibilant. Then she left, and a new man stepped in.

He was plump, pink, and balding, one of those men who'd been middle-aged since he was seventeen. He wore a gray suit with a blue windowpane pattern that matched his pocket square and tie.

He tucked both hands in his pockets. Not police or military, Peter thought. A civilian. Peter could tell by the careless slouch of his shoulders. His soft, useless slick-soled shoes.

The civilian nodded at the officers. "Please. Continue."

Sigrid spoke. "What is the purpose of your visit?"

Peter waved at the big pack filling a chair. "Hiking."

"In winter?" She turned on the smile. "You must be part Icelandic. You are signed up with a tour operator?"

"No. I'm renting a car."

Hjálmar shook his head. "This is not like"—he consulted Peter's passport—"your Wisconsin. Iceland can be quite dangerous, especially in winter."

"Don't underestimate Wisconsin." Peter smiled for the first time. "And I don't mind dangerous, either. What's the problem?"

The civilian spoke a second time. "Let's see what's in his baggage, shall we?" He didn't sound Icelandic. He sounded American, from the East Coast. Several generations of private schools and private clubs distilled into a smug, nasal honk.

Peter said, "Who are you?"

The civilian looked amused. "That's not important," he said. "The luggage, please."

The customs officers glanced at each other.

The woman went to Peter's pack, popped the buckles. She began to lay out his things on the table. Tent, poles, fly. Stove and pot. Sleeping bag and pad. All the things he'd need to survive alone in open country. She left the folded emergency blanket and fifty-foot coil of Kevlar-core rope in the top compartment.

"The duffel as well."

The woman set her jaw but moved the bag to a chair and opened the zipper. There was something odd here, Peter thought. These cops were annoyed. They didn't like taking this soft man's orders.

Sigrid pulled out more hiking gear, along with town clothes and a simple day pack with his laptop and charger, a thin insulated jacket, a Ziploc bag of homemade granola bars, his travel documents, his pills, and a few books.

Inside his guidebook, she found a photo of a man holding a

mop-headed boy in his arms like a sack of potatoes. The boy was seven, loose-limbed and cheerful. The man was thirty-three, with a bushy blond beard and a face as empty as a stone. His deep-set eyes seemed too blue to be real.

The civilian stepped forward and tapped the photo with his index finger. "Who's this?"

"A friend," Peter said. "Cute kid, isn't he?"

The civilian's frown deepened, his lips like squirming pink worms. He held out his hand. "Give me your phone."

"I don't think so. I'd like some answers."

The civilian was definitely unhappy now. "Here's an answer for you," he said. "You are not welcome in Iceland. Unfortunately for you, there are no available seats back to the States until late afternoon, the day after tomorrow." He took an envelope from his jacket pocket. "Here is your ticket. You will be on that plane. These officers will see to your safety and comfort until that time, and they will escort you to your seat."

Peter felt the static crackle and rise. He ignored the ticket envelope. "On whose authority, exactly?"

"It's unofficial." The civilian gave Peter a tight smile. "But real nonetheless. You are persona non grata here. Go home."

Peter looked at the customs cops. "He can do this?"

They glanced at each other again.

Officer Hjálmar said, "In fact, that is a bit unclear. There are procedures for these things. Forms must be filled out."

Peter suppressed a smile. Insistence on standard procedure was the most elegant form of bureaucratic resistance.

Anger and frustration radiated off the pink civilian. The envelope trembled, just slightly, in his manicured hand. "This request is unofficial. From one nation to another."

"It is *extremely* unofficial," Officer Hjálmar said. "We will honor your request that he leave the country. But lacking written orders from our superiors, Mr. Ash will not be detained today." He took the envelope with the ticket. "We will collect his rental car and hotel information. If he does not report here four hours before the flight, we will dispatch officers to collect him."

Officer Sigrid turned to Peter. "Perhaps you should pack your things."

Peter tucked his equipment back into place with the efficiency of long practice. Sigrid took out a notebook and pen. Her smile was still professional, but now it held true amusement. "Your contact information?"

Peter gave her his cell number. "I don't have a hotel room yet." Or plans to get one.

The pink civilian was turning red. "Do you know who is behind this request?"

"Unfortunately, no. Not officially." Hjálmar turned to Peter and held out his passport and the envelope with the plane ticket. "I will walk you out."

Hjálmar led Peter into the airport's modest main hall. Through the glass walls of the atrium, Peter could see snow swirling bright under powerful lights.

It was after ten in the morning, and the sky was barely beginning to brighten. Peter was exhausted and hungry. He wanted badly to walk outside. But he knew they weren't quite done yet.

Hjálmar watched Peter carefully. "I hope I haven't made a mistake."

"You haven't." Peter stuck out his hand. "I'm Peter. What do I call you?"

"Hjálmar, please." They shook hands. "We are informal here."

"Who's the guy in the suit?"

"Someone connected to your embassy." The man adjusted his shoulders, as if working out some kink in his back. "There is some weight behind the request. Eventually my government will be forced to honor it. If you do not return when you are due, we will collect you. And we will not be gentle."

Peter nodded. "I'll try to behave myself. But I still don't get why I'm not in a holding cell."

A smile flickered across Hjálmar's face. "Icelanders are independent people," he said. "We do not like being told what to do."

"Huh." Peter watched the snow blowing sideways, drifts gathering in unlikely places. "Me neither."

"You were in the military." Not a question.

"I was a United States marine," said Peter. "Still am, I guess. It's not something that leaves you."

Hjálmar nodded. "I was a ground observer with Norway in the first Iraq war. Why don't they want you here?"

"Honestly? I have no idea." For the moment, it was the truth. "Are we done?"

"Yes. I'll see you in two days."

Peter smiled. "Not if I see you first."

Then he stepped forward, and the double glass doors slid wide, and he walked into the biting, sunless cold.

DESPITE the weather, Peter wasn't ready to get back into a vehicle just yet. He fished his phone from his pocket and sent a text.

Landed in Reyk. Someone from U.S. embassy wants me sent home, won't say why. Any ideas?

It was 6:00 a.m. in Maryland. He wasn't expecting a response. But his phone buzzed immediately.

My husband is well connected at State. I'll look into it. But please don't let anyone stop you.

Will do.

Peter walked to the taxi stand and knocked on the window of a Renault station wagon. "Iceland Four-by-Four Rentals? On, uh—"

"*Já*, I know it." The driver started the motor without looking at Peter. The rear cargo hatch floated up. "Thirty minutes."

Peter stowed his gear. The static didn't like the enclosure of a back seat. So Peter climbed in and stuck his face to the window, getting as close to the world as he could.

The blowing snow and limited visibility didn't slow the driver. He had his wipers on high and the pedal down. The landscape was flat and white and barren of trees. The sky had begun to brighten slightly, as if dawn was coming, but was still some way off. There wasn't much traffic. Iceland felt blissfully empty.

Peter had skimmed the guidebook on the plane, trying to figure out what to expect. The island nation was the size of Maine, but with a quarter of the population: only three hundred thirty thousand people. More than two hundred thousand of those lived in and around

Reykjavík, the capital city, in the southwestern section of Iceland.

Reykjavík itself was fairly temperate, because the Gulf Stream's North Atlantic Current carried warm ocean water up from the Caribbean to northern Europe. Iceland also sat at the junction of two tectonic plates, which helped warm the island further and created a surplus of hot springs and volcanoes.

The northern part of Iceland, on the other hand, could get snow year-round, and the high mountain interior was filled with glaciers. Big sections were accessible only a few months a year. And Iceland's weather was unpredictable. Powered by strong Arctic winds, major storms could develop in a matter of hours.

The driver made a right into a rambling industrial park. The rental agency was a dented steel shed with a variety of four-wheel-drive vehicles parked around it. The taxi meter read fifteen thousand krónur, which was about a hundred twenty dollars. Peter was glad it wasn't his money. He paid the driver, then dragged his gear out of the car. The driver pulled away.

The rental office was stifling and close. A door opened to a big garage section where an air wrench shrieked. The static filled Peter's head. It took everything he had to stay at the counter.

The rental agent was a young guy in an Iceland World Cup stocking cap and a quilted flannel shirt. He wiped grease from his hands with a rag as he talked Peter through the paperwork. The agency provided coverage for gravel damage, he said, but river crossings and wind damage were Peter's responsibility.

Peter raised his eyebrows. "Wind damage?"

"Yes. Always park facing into the weather so the wind doesn't bend the doors back. That's an expensive repair." He handed Peter a single key on a ring. "Your vehicle is outside," he said. "The white Mitsubishi Pajero. Remember that it requires diesel fuel." He gestured toward the door. "Safe travels."

REYKJAVÍK proper was crowded with traffic and pedestrians. A small cluster of glass-clad towers crowded the waterfront, and a cruise ship sat in the harbor. Modern new apartment buildings grew on the lower reaches of the old city. Packs of tourists wandered aimlessly through the snow, standing in curious clumps with their shopping bags. Peter parked the Mitsubishi on a busy street and walked uphill into the old city.

The snowy streets were narrow and clogged with traffic. The buildings got smaller and older as he climbed the hill. Heavily customized 4x4 vehicles lined the side roads, often parked halfway up on the skinny sidewalks. With the low heavy clouds and the snow, the sky hadn't gotten any brighter. He wondered if this was all the daylight he would get.

He walked through a maze of narrow side streets to a hand-lettered sign on the side of a building. SNORRI'S RAVE CAVE. Below the sign, stone steps led down below street level. At the bottom, a dented steel door, electric green, glowed faintly in the shadow. A sign screwed to the door gave the hours: 20:00–??? That was 8:00 p.m., six hours away. He tried the knob, but it was locked.

He found an outfitter's shop, where he bought a better sleeping bag, good to twenty below. His old gear was still sound, but Iceland seemed to call for an upgrade, and his choices would likely narrow significantly once he left Reykjavík.

His stomach growled, and he realized he hadn't eaten since the day before, so he stopped for a bowl of Thai noodles and chicken from a take-out window and ate standing in the street. Finally he walked down to the Mitsubishi and drove along the harbor road until he found a half-empty parking lot sheltered from the traffic noise by a wide earthen berm. It had been too long since he'd had a full night's rest without gunfire dreams.

The Pajero was a full-size SUV with the boxy feel and diesel rattle of a truck. The rental company had removed the back seats and converted the vehicle into a kind of camper, with a slim plywood storage shelf, a hinged tabletop, and a little couch that unfolded into a bed. It was a small space, but there was enough room for Peter to stretch out comfortably. He cracked the windows for ventilation, then kicked off his boots and rolled into his new sleeping bag. The view was of the swirling snow and dimly lit sky. The wind howled in his ears like something wild.

He closed his eyes, hoping he was too tired to dream.

Chapter 3

THE DREAM WAS ALWAYS the same.

Peter stood in a dusty street, binoculars fixed on the face of a small brown man with sad eyes and a thick black mustache. The man sat behind the wheel of a faded blue Toyota Camry rolling toward a makeshift checkpoint at the edge of Sadr City, an impoverished Baghdad neighborhood at the heart of the insurgency.

The afternoon air was still and thick. Four of Peter's Marines stood sweating by a pair of Humvees parked in a V, blocking the road, waving at the Camry to stop.

This was a year into the insurgency, and the sad-eyed driver should have known to slow down.

When the driver was a hundred meters out, Big Jimmy Johnson stepped from behind the hood of his Humvee, M4 slung and hands held palms out, knowing the riflemen and turret gunner behind him would have his back.

The sad-eyed driver got closer. He said something, nobody knew what. His eyes got wide. But he didn't slow down.

Big Jimmy shouted. Raised his rifle. Made it clear that the man should stop or there would be consequences. A voice came through Peter's earpiece. "Lieutenant? Do we fire?"

The sad-eyed driver became more agitated. He waved his arms. He shouted. He didn't slow down.

Behind his own Humvee, Peter kept his binoculars on the man's face. A car bomb had hit an army checkpoint the day before. Another had blown up a Sunni market that morning. "He's too close," Peter said. "Okay to fire."

The Marines fired their M4s, but the dusty Camry kept coming. When the turret gunner let loose with the fifty-cal, the deep thumping sound was almost physical in the thick, foul air. The Camry shook on its springs. It wasn't until the tires were shreds and the engine died that the car finally lurched to a stop.

There was no bomb. It turned out that the Camry's brakes didn't work. Later, Peter discovered that the driver was a Sunni facing death threats from his Shia neighbors. He was fleeing his home, scared out of his mind, reacting poorly, in a car that, once started, didn't want to stop.

His young wife and two small children were huddled out of sight in the back seat. Probably so his neighbors would think he was just going to work and not frag everyone in the car.

They had died anyway.

Peter had given the order, and a family had died.

It was a righteous call, by the book. Nobody had questioned it. Until the dreams started, Peter had barely remembered it.

How many calls like this had he made? How many more innocents had died in that war? How many children?

The honest truth was that Peter hadn't hated the war when he was fighting it. It became a place to test himself, to improve his skills. He'd signed up to fight for his country, but then his mission became to protect his men. Get them home alive.

The *real* honest truth was that, more often than not, he'd loved the war. Standing with his brother Marines, armed and armored before an assault, amped up and focused and ready to take the fight to the bad guys. High as a kite on terror and adrenaline.

He'd felt alive then. Well and truly alive. But that was then.

Civilian life wasn't the same. Not at all.

A VA doctor had prescribed him the Valium. It helped until it didn't. It was easy to build up a tolerance. It was also addictive.

Now he woke sweating in the cold, dark truck, wondering how many more faces would swim out of the past to visit his dreams.

THE snow was falling faster when Peter left the Mitsubishi to walk the winding streets of Reykjavík. The wind pulled on his coat, but a warm yellow glow poured through shop windows and restaurant doorways.

The sign above the steps to Snorri's Rave Cave was lit now. Black lights in the concrete stairwell made the painted walls glow more vividly with each descending step. Peter tried the handle of the steel door again. This time, it opened.

He found a low, darkened vestibule with an unmanned coat check and an empty doorman's podium. A red velvet rope hung from two metal stands, blocking the entryway to the club. He stepped over the rope and went down another flight of stairs.

From the entrance, Peter had thought Snorri's Rave Cave would be small, but at the bottom of the steps he found a large, high-ceilinged space. Stand-up tables ringed the room. Rope lights hung from the ceiling in wild, tangled loops.

The dance floor was huge. At the far end, a DJ with a shaved head assembled his equipment. The insistent rhythms of electronic dance music poured from speaker towers.

A pair of bartenders in white tuxedo shirts chatted with early customers at a long wooden bar that ran down one side of the room while two barbacks methodically stocked the coolers. Peter put his elbow on the polished oak and caught a bartender's eye.

"I'm looking for Bjarni," he called over the music.

"There are many Bjarnis." The square-shouldered young bartender reminded Peter a bit of the well-fed farm boys he'd grown up with. Except for the stylized black tattoos peeking out from under the rolled-up sleeves of his tuxedo shirt. His square, clean-shaven face was polite and uninterested. "Which one?"

"Bjarni Bergsson. He works here, right?"

Peter only had a year-old photo of a face blond-bearded to the eyeballs and half hidden in a long tangle of hair. He'd looked on social media for others, but there were half a dozen Bjarni Bergssons in Reykjavík.

"Why do you want this Bjarni?"

"It's personal. About his family."

The bartender glanced over his shoulder down the bar, then turned back to Peter. "You are American?"

Peter nodded. "Is Bjarni here?"

"He's late. But he should be here soon." The bartender had

the same soft, sibilant Icelandic accent. "If you are staying, cover charge is two thousand." About twenty dollars. "The club will fill soon. Beautiful women, great music. Dancing."

"Sure." He took four of the colorful Icelandic bills from his wallet and held them out. "Two thousand for the cover charge. Another six for you to point out Bjarni when he gets here."

The bartender slipped the money into a pocket and walked down the bar to the taps. A minute later, he came back with a pale, foaming pint. "Our special Icelandic bitter," he said. "No charge."

"Thanks." Peter took a sip. It was definitely bitter, but also pretty good. Peter took a longer sip. He was hungry and thirsty. The beer would help with both, for a while.

There was a noise at the entrance as a dozen people clattered down the stairs. The women were dressed in sleek skirts and glittery tops, and the men wore tight jeans and shiny shirts. A doorman in a white tuxedo shirt and a bow tie met them at the velvet rope to collect money and stamp their hands. The music got louder.

The house lights dimmed, and the hanging ropes lit in a chaos of color. More people crowded in, talking and laughing.

Peter had never been a young adult, not really. He'd worked construction for his father and uncle all through high school. After that, he was a scholarship student at Northwestern, working during the summers to make food and rent money for the year. Then he'd signed up for the Marines after the towers came down and spent the next eight years in the fight.

No wonder he was having trouble figuring out what to do with himself now that it was over.

He drained his beer. The bartender brought him another, just as bitter and foamy. Peter looked at him with raised eyebrows. The bartender shook his head. "No Bjarni." Peter could barely hear him over the sound system.

The music got louder still. The house lights faded to black, and lasers flickered on, narrow beams strobing across the ceiling. Peter put his back to the polished wood of the bar and watched as the growing crowd began to edge onto the dance floor. The DJ called out, and the music changed, speeding up.

Then everyone began to dance.

Somewhere near the bottom of his second beer, Peter realized he was feeling better. The static was still there, but its pressure had receded. His head was lighter than it should have been from a few pints of beer, although not in a bad way. He felt clear as a window-pane. He probably should get something to eat.

The club had gotten warm. Peter shed his coat and found an empty stool at a corner table. He draped his coat over the stool. Blinking at the lights, he felt the beer in his bloodstream.

He was still too warm, so he peeled off his fleece and laid it over his coat. A young woman at the corner table locked eyes with him. She wore a green necklace doubled up as a headband. She stood and took his hand and led him onto the dance floor.

She was blond and pale and slender as a reed. In her early twenties, she was way too young for Peter, but she pulled him into the crowd like an electromagnet. Her skirt was short and loose and filled like a bell when she spun on her toes. Her dark pupils filled her eyes. Peter had never been much of a dancer, but he found himself moving to the rhythm.

The press of people should have set the static raging and driven him out of there, but it didn't. The static rose, yes, but instead of feeding the urge toward fight or flight, it extended the boundaries of his senses. He felt connected to the crowd like he never had before. The static merged with the music and lifted him. His feet and hips and shoulders flowed like liquid.

He was part of a group now, all swirling together in the pulse of the music. He felt warm and strong and graceful.

He took off his T-shirt and threw it high over the raised arms of the multitude of dancers. His feet were slower than he wanted, so he took off his boots while he danced. The magnetic young woman, laughing, took them from his hands. She went away, and he slipped around the glittering floor in his hiking socks, his entire body floating high and humming with joy.

Eventually he was barefoot, naked but for his white feather-weight long underwear slung low on his hips. Under the strobing LEDs, in the center of a circle of glittering young women, he danced like a wild man, a beautiful ecstatic primitive released from his darkened cave into the bright world for the first time.

WHEN the tuxedo-shirted bartender pushed his way into the circle of dancers, it took Peter a while to come back to himself.

The young bartender took Peter's arm and pulled him close to shout into Peter's ear. "Bjarni."

"Oh," said Peter, remembering. "Where?"

"Outside. Having a cigarette." The bartender towed him, dancing, through the crowd. "Where are your clothes?"

"I don't know. Somewhere. Do I need them?"

"This is Iceland. December. You need clothes."

Peter pointed to the chair with his coat and fleece, but although the dancing girl had put his boots next to the chair, his shirt and pants were gone. Peter had thrown them into the crowd. The bartender said something in Icelandic, shaking his head. He pushed Peter's bare feet into his boots and pulled the coat around Peter's shoulders. He didn't tie the boots or zip the coat, but Peter didn't mind. He was still too hot.

The bartender gestured toward a rear exit. "Bjarni is there. I'll show you." They set off, Peter's loose boots sloppy on his feet.

They climbed endless stairs into a narrow dead-end alley. The night air was cool and refreshing, and the snow fell in fat, heavy flakes. Perfect white mounds piled high on the lids of trash cans and the windowsills of the stone buildings around them.

One of the barbacks leaned against the stone. He was short and wide in a wool sweater and jeans. Smoke trickled up from a cigarette held between his thumb and forefinger. His hands were the size of soup bowls. Peter said, "You don't look like Bjarni."

The barback pushed himself off the wall.

"That's Dónaldur," the bartender said. He finally smiled.

The short barback flicked away his cigarette.

Still feeling the love from the dance floor, Peter didn't quite understand. It must have showed on his face.

The young bartender rolled his thick shoulders. "I am Bjarni, you stupid American." Then he stepped close and swung a low, heavy fist toward Peter's stomach.

Peter danced sideways without conscious thought. The punch didn't touch him. He wasn't understanding. "You're Bjarni? Why didn't you tell me that from the start?"

Bjarni came at Peter again with a long roundhouse to the chin. Peter did an elegant shuffle and watched the knuckles pass.

"Why are you upset?" Peter asked. "I just want to talk. I'm looking for your cousin Erik. I'm trying to help."

Dónaldur moved in from the side and tried to hit Peter in the kidney. Peter deflected with a forearm and pushed the shorter man back with a hand to the chest.

"You know what happened to Erik." Bjarni's face was twisted with anger. "You people are responsible."

"I don't know what happened," Peter said. "I just want to help Erik do what's right. What's best for his son, Óskar."

Bjarni came at him in a rush.

Peter tried to slip to the side but had somehow stepped on his own untied bootlace, so his foot couldn't move. He felt his center of gravity shifting irrevocably toward the snowy street.

He tried to turn the fall into a roll, but a jumble of trash cans got in the way, and he couldn't find his feet in his loose boots.

Then Bjarni kicked him in the stomach hard enough to knock him off his knees. Dónaldur stepped in and caught him in the hip. Peter covered up as they took turns, grunting with each deliberate blow of their heavy-soled rubber boots.

When they stood away, breathing hard, Peter lay curled into himself on the snowy pavement, his thin long underwear soaked with melt. A bottomless growl grew somewhere deep inside him.

As a short pair of legs wound up for a field goal, Peter caught the kicking boot with both hands, then twisted Dónaldur off his feet to a hard landing by a recycling bin. He put a bony knee into the fallen man's thick chest and launched himself off the cobblestones. He looked at Bjarni with blood in his eye.

Bjarni blinked, startled. He scooped up a stone doorstop and came at Peter with it. Peter was slower than he should have been, but he stepped inside the blow. He caught the man's thick right wrist with one hand and locked his elbow with the other. When

Peter broke the man's arm, it made a *snap* that he felt in his teeth.

Bjarni made a sound like a trapped rabbit.

Peter heard the dull scrape of thick bottle glass rising off rough pavement. Dónaldur among the recycling.

Peter released Bjarni and was half turned toward the sound when he felt a bright starburst at the back of his head. His knees evaporated, and he fell face-first into the snow.

Now a frenzy of wild boots from both sides. Peter got his knees under him, but a steel toe to the ribs knocked him sideways.

Then the kicking stopped. They leaned in. Peter could only see from one eye. The other was swelling shut.

Bjarni didn't look happy. His arm hung at a strange angle.

"This is Iceland. Outsiders do not mess with Icelanders. Forget Erik. Forget Óskar. Go home. Do not come back."

Then they were gone. He heard the slam of the club door. Flakes of snow floated down from the sky. An empty vodka bottle lay by his head. He imagined a dent in his skull the shape of its base.

THE wind came up and raked across his chest. His long underwear bottoms were soaked through. It was embarrassing enough to get a beatdown by a farm boy in a tuxedo shirt. Even worse to die from it. He grunted and made it to his hands and knees.

Footsteps came softly in the snow-muffled night.

"Mary and Joseph." A voice rose and fell. He felt a hand on his shoulder. "Can yeh stand, laddie?" Then a quick laugh. "I see you're a bit worse for the drink. But I've got you now."

A musical accent. Irish. The hand found his underarm and pulled him up with surprising strength. "Be proper criminal behavior to leave a man in this weather."

Peter forced himself to stand, taking census of the damage.

A pale, black-haired face peered at him. "That's quite the punch-up you've had. Got a name?"

Did he? "Peter." He hawked and spit blood.

"It speaks. I was gettin' worried. I'm Seamus Heaney, like the poet." Pronounced *Shay-mus*. Dark eyes under thick black eyebrows, the shadow of a black beard beneath pale skin. "Did you see who jumped yeh, lad? Shall we call a copper and make a complaint?"

Peter shook his head, then stopped. It hurt too much.

"Ah, we're peas in a pod, we are. I'm not so fond of the coppers myself. How about a doctor?"

"No doctor," Peter said. "Sleep."

"You Americans, cowboys every one. Where's your hotel?"

"No hotel. Car."

"You must be joking. It's gone midnight. And well below freezing." He peered at Peter's grim face. "Perhaps not." The Irishman looked around at the toppled trash cans. "Is there nothing else you were wearin', lad?"

"Clothes in the club." How had Peter gotten this drunk on just two beers? Unless there was something else in those foamy brews.

The Irishman put a strong arm around his shoulder and turned him. "Come on, lad. Where's your car?"

THEY limped slowly down the alley. Gravity pulled them down toward the bay, Peter's mind blown wild with the wind.

By the time they found his car, the parking lot was nearly empty, and the still falling snow had erased all footprints and tire tracks. The Mitsubishi loomed out of the darkness like a boulder.

The door was locked.

Peter reached for the key in his pants pocket, then remembered he'd lost his pants. That explained why his legs were so cold.

He patted his coat. No key. No wallet or phone, either. All in his pants. His brain definitely wasn't working right.

"Lad, you'll stay with me, all right?" The Irishman put a hand on his shoulder. "Just the one night. I can lend yeh some clothes."

Peter shrugged off the hand, then turned and slammed the back of his elbow into the Mitsubishi's slightly open rear passenger window. Dull pain bloomed. The glass cracked. He hit it again, and it spider-webbed. Once more, and it buckled inward. "I'll be fine." He pushed his hand inside and unlocked the door. He cleared his throat. "Thanks. I owe you one."

He climbed inside while the Irishman watched. The man's eyebrows furrowed. "You're sleeping in your hire car?"

"You don't know a thing about me." Maybe said with more force than he'd intended.

The Irishman shook his head, then turned and walked away. Peter climbed into the back and shook out his new sleeping bag to let the down loft. A diffused light filtered through the clinging snow. Wind pushed more snow through the broken window.

Shivering, he knelt and dug into his duffel for dry tops and bottoms. Stomach tight, he crawled into his sleeping bag and waited for his heat to fill the down.

He found the pill bottle and shook two into his hand. Then two more. He gulped them down dry.

Chapter 4

Twelve Months Earlier

THEY EAT SUPPER TOGETHER like any other night, even if Sarah is unusually quiet and the food grows cold on their plates. Erik tries without success to wipe the video from his memory while Óskar tells his mother tall tales of their adventures in Rock Creek Park. Recitations of pi are not allowed at the dinner table.

After Óskar has cleared the plates, Erik and Sarah remain. In the living room, Óskar sprawls on their big white couch, boneless as a squid and spellbound by a game on the family tablet. He knows something is up, but the game sucks him in anyway.

Quietly, Erik says, "Where did that video come from?"

Sarah's lips are pale at the edges as she presses them together. "The Prince's server got hacked last night."

"The video came from the hacker?"

She shakes her head.

Of course, Erik thinks. The video came from the Prince.

Most of Sarah's clients are nonprofits. She does, however, have one corporate client, the client who helped get her one-woman firm off the ground. Although she would like nothing more than to free herself from him, the client won't let her go. He is too influential, too connected. A few quiet whispers in the right ears would ruin her business. Her career.

In private, when she talks about him, she refers to him as the Prince. A kind of shorthand.

The Prince is the rare Washington power broker with no media presence, because he prefers to work in the darkness. He has no ideology or political affiliation and is dedicated only to the cause of filling his pockets and broadening his reach. He has been investigated many times but never indicted. He has somehow managed to avoid the laws that regulate the lobbying industry. He's an attorney and a consultant, so his clients remain secret.

Sarah keeps a private catalog of his sins, gathering ammunition for the day when she might slip his grasp. But this sin is of an entirely different magnitude.

The video confirms every suspicion Erik might have had about the Prince. He thinks about how somebody was behind the camera. The same person who set up the whole thing. Erik can only imagine its value, evidence of a public figure's crimes.

He says, "Did you catch the hacker at least?"

She shakes her head. "Lost him in the Maldives." She means the hacker came in through a series of proxy servers, hiding his tracks with each step.

"Did the hacker find the video?"

"I don't think so," she says. "He didn't even get past my secondary firewall. The file was on a hidden drive I found when cleaning up the mess." She looks at Erik. "Although, if the video got out, that wouldn't be so bad, would it?"

"You're not considering—"

"I am. That video should be in the hands of the police." Her voice is low but fierce.

Through the door to the living room, Óskar looks up.

"It's more complicated than that," Erik says. "You have a nondisclosure agreement. Your business will be ruined."

"Are you kidding me?" Sarah can no longer contain herself. Her glare could spit a lamb and roast it. "That man goes on television every night and tells half of America what to think. What to believe. What's *moral*. That's reason enough. But to know that the Prince has it? And what he might do with it?"

Sarah's emotions are contagious. This is part of why Erik loves her, the deep currents of her passion. Nonetheless, he keeps his voice calm. He puts his hand in hers. "There's a lot at stake." He angles his head at the living room. "It's not just us."

She squeezes his hand. Her grip is astonishing.

"I'm with you," he says. "We want the same thing, okay? To do the *right* thing. We need to talk with an attorney, someone who specializes in these things. Agreed?"

He glances at the living room. Óskar's eyes are glued to his parents. The boy has been listening, of course. He is only seven, but he misses nothing.

"Why don't you go for a walk?" Erik tells Sarah. "While I put the tiny Viking in the bath and to bed."

Óskar speaks up. "I don't want to take a bath."

Erik smiles at the boy. "Tomorrow is Monday. And Monday means school, yes?"

"Yes," Óskar says grudgingly. Despite the fact that he's skipped two grades because of his photographic memory, he still finds school boring beyond belief.

"Then tonight, a bath," Erik says. "And in bed, I will read you the story of Thor and the sea serpent."

Sarah squeezes Erik's hand again, but more gently. "A walk is a good idea," she says. "I'll do bedtime tomorrow."

But, of course, she won't.

Because by ten the next morning, she will be dead.

Present Day

FOR Peter, it began three days before, when Tom Wetzel called, looking for a favor. Peter's first question was how Wetzel had found him.

Wetzel answered, "I won't ask your secrets; don't ask mine."

Peter and Wetzel had been new lieutenants together in

Afghanistan. Wetzel was capable but hard for Peter to respect because he twisted himself into knots finding reasons to stay inside the wire. It wasn't enough to protect him, though, and he got sent to Germany with mortar fragments in his ass. An undiscovered knack for paperwork manifested itself during his recovery, and he ended up commanding a desk at Pendleton for the rest of his tour. Now he was some kind of corporate hotshot, and he wouldn't tell Peter what the favor was, not until he'd signed a nondisclosure agreement.

It was sensitive, Wetzel said. Peter would have to travel internationally. There might be some heavy lifting, but nothing Peter couldn't handle. The money would be better than good.

Peter didn't care about the money.

THE morning he left, he'd sat with June Cassidy on the sleeping porch he'd built onto the back of her farmhouse in Washington State. Since the static had gotten worse, they didn't sleep together there, although they still did the other things they used to do. The unmade bed was a tangle of sheets.

Outside the floor-to-ceiling windows, it was clear and cold. The ground was almost frozen, and soon the snow would start to pile up. June wore a fleece vest and a wool hat and thermal leggings. Peter wore a threadbare T-shirt and faded mountain pants. He could see the high valley walls from every spot on the porch. The walls had felt sheltering once. They didn't anymore.

"Tell me you're not going to do it." June wouldn't look at him.

"I'm not going to do it."

"But you want to."

He felt the spring wound too tight inside him. "I want a lot of things," he said. "World peace. The Packers in the Super Bowl. A perfect breakfast burrito. Will I get them? Maybe, maybe not."

"Peter, what *are* you going to do?"

He didn't answer. It was a conversation they'd been having for too many months. June had been after Peter to find work outside the valley. "Start roofing houses," she'd said. "That'll let you stay outdoors. Or find a job with one of the local outfitters, take people on backcountry expeditions. Make some new memories."

How to explain to her that none of those ideas felt much like living. Nothing could compare to the relentless, dread-filled thrill of a firefight. But the addictive, overwhelming dopamine rush of combat was inextricably tied to the suffocating guilt of surviving it. It was an ugly feedback loop, and he was stuck in it.

"You're not talking to me," she said, "not like you used to. That's what worries me the most. You're locking it down when you need to be letting it out. Please. Just let me help."

He wished she was mad at him. Anger he could deal with. Hell, he was *good* at anger, especially lately. Instead she felt sorry for him. And there was nothing worse than pity.

He didn't tell her that he'd started thinking about going back. There was plenty of overseas contract work for someone with Peter's experience. Executive protection, corporate mercenary stuff. Maybe he should stop fighting it. Maybe armed conflict was in his blood. Maybe it was all he had left.

He found himself standing on the cold plank floor without any recollection of getting to his feet. He felt her eyes on him. As always, when June looked at him, he knew she was really seeing him. More clearly than anyone ever had.

Early that morning, she'd watched through the kitchen window as he packed his truck.

She reached out to him now. "Peter, please. Sit with me. Just a few minutes."

The long muscles in his legs ached with the need to move.

"Are you going to Death Valley?"

"Just for a few weeks. Maybe the desert will remind me of Iraq and knock something loose."

"Is that a good idea? To spend all that time in your own head?"

"I'll be stuck with myself anyway," he said. "You're leaving for D.C. the day after tomorrow."

June was an investigative reporter, and she was working a side angle on some bombings in Venezuela.

"You're not meeting that corporate guy, Wetzel," she said.

"Oh, no. Definitely not."

She got to her knees and crossed the bed toward him. She bunched his T-shirt in her fist and pulled him close. "You'll come back to me. I need you to promise."

Peter scooped her up into his lap. "Woman, will you please stop talking?"

"Never." She grabbed him by the ear, pulled him close, and bit his lip. "This conversation isn't over, Marine."

PETER never made it to Death Valley.

He was on I-84 headed west from Hood River, low dry hills to his left, the Columbia River wide and shining on his right, when his phone rang again.

It was Tom Wetzel. Peter considered letting it go to voice mail. Instead he turned up the volume to hear Wetzel's voice over the big V-8. Wetzel was so wound up he didn't even say hello.

"There's a woman coming to see you. She's on a plane now."

"Wetzel, I'm not doing it. I told you already."

"Tell her yourself. She lands in Portland in forty minutes."

"Wetzel. Whatever it is, I'm not doing it. I have other plans."

"Fine. Tell her that. After you listen to her story."

"I thought you weren't giving me details without a nondisclosure."

"For now, I'll trust you. We'll talk after, okay? She'll meet wherever you like."

Peter sighed. "There's a place called Lardo in Portland, corner of Southeast Twelfth and Hawthorne."

"Corporate money and you pick a place called Lardo?"

"You called me, remember?"

LARDO was a low-key pork-oriented sandwich place set in a funky corner building across from a gas station. Along with a dozen sandwiches, it served local beer on tap and dirty fries made with crispy chunks of pork. It also had wide windows that helped tamp down the static, even on a dark and wet winter afternoon when the clouded sun had fallen past the horizon.

Passing the place in search of parking, Peter saw a black sedan at the curb, a thin plume of exhaust curling from the tailpipe. An angular man in a black suit stood on the sidewalk under a wide umbrella, watching Peter's truck as it drove by.

Peter left the Chevy around the corner and walked back in the rain. On Lardo's covered patio, a woman waited. Slim and poised, she wore a long coat the color of midnight, unbuttoned to the weather. Beneath it he could see a strand of pearls as big as marbles.

She stood with her back to the interior light. Rain hammered the patio cover. He couldn't see her shadowed face. "Mr. Ash?"

Pending the nondisclosure agreement, Peter didn't know her name. He held out his hand. "Please, call me Peter."

She took it and didn't let go. Her hand was thin, but her grip was strong and tight, like that of a pond skater fallen through the ice. "I'm Catherine Price. Thank you for meeting me."

He smiled. "Tom Wetzel is very persuasive." Her face was still hidden in the darkness. "Shall we go in?"

Catherine Price hesitated. A car came around the corner, sweeping the patio with its merciless headlights, and now he saw her ravaged face. Lines of grief carved deep as canyons, heavy bags under her eyes that carried everything her makeup and elegant clothes tried to hide. She'd been a classic beauty once, until some disaster had crash-landed into her life.

The disaster she'd come a long way to tell Peter about.

She didn't waste any time.

"Twelve months ago, my son-in-law murdered my daughter and abducted my grandson," she said. "They've never been found. The boy is now eight years old. His name is Óskar."

Behind her, the restaurant glowed with warmth and light. Couples sat across from each other, holding hands.

Three minutes before, Peter had wanted nothing more than a cold beer and a hot sandwich and to get back on the road. Now, though, he couldn't remember why he was headed for Death Valley. He said to Catherine Price, "Let's talk in your car."

He owed her that much, at the very least.

THE angular man with the black umbrella opened the back door for Catherine Price, eyeballing Peter as he walked around to the far side of the enormous sedan. Peter opened his own door. The man with the umbrella stayed outside in the rain.

Inside, it was warm and dark. The back seat was bigger than Peter's childhood bedroom. He felt the unruly static slowly begin to rise in the enclosed space. "Tell me about it," he said.

Catherine Price pulled her coat around herself more tightly. A black satchel handbag sat open beside her like a hole on the seat.

"Do you have any children, Mr. Ash?"

"No."

"Once upon a time," she said, "I had two."

He saw it then, the bottomless ocean of her grief.

"William, my oldest, died four years ago," she said. "Black ice on the highway; his car went through a guardrail. His wife was with him. She died, too. She was pregnant." A vein pulsed in her forehead. "A year ago, I lost Sarah, my daughter, at the hands of her husband, Erik." She turned to look at Peter. "But it's possible I haven't yet lost my grandson."

"Surely, the police—" Peter said.

"The D.C. detectives tell me they believe my son-in-law took my daughter's life. They have physical evidence and no other suspects. He left the country immediately, taking my grandson. He bought two one-way tickets to Iceland. He grew up there, has family there. And the D.C. police have no jurisdiction."

"But the Icelandic police," he said. "Interpol—"

"They can't find him. It's possible his family is protecting him. We asked a Norwegian private security firm to investigate, but their person spent weeks in Iceland and got nowhere. He filed his final report after he was injured badly enough to end up in the hospital. That was ten months ago."

"Something new happened," Peter said. "That's why you're here now."

She nodded. "Three days ago, Óskar's schoolbag turned up in Reykjavík Harbour. It was a LEGO backpack. Sarah bought it for him before he started first grade. When it washed up in the harbor, it still held his stuffed bear and his collection of little LEGO people. He kept them in a plastic peanut-butter jar with a lid, along with his membership card for the LEGO Club. His name was on the card. The air in that jar is the only reason the backpack remained afloat."

Her grief rose in her like a breaking wave. He watched her struggle for control.

"The day I heard, I called the security firm we had hired before. They were sympathetic, but instead of seeing a sign of hope, they saw it as a confirmation of my grandson's death. They suggested I simply accept what had happened and try to move on." She caught herself again. "I spoke with a dozen more security companies. Large international firms. None of them would do the job." She looked down at her hands. "It sounds ridiculous, but I believe that he's alive. I can feel it. I *know* it."

She looked up at Peter. "Will you help me?"

"I'm not sure I can," he said. "I don't know what Tom Wetzel told you, but this isn't what I do."

"Tom tells me you were a marine officer, among the best. He says he's seen what you can do."

Peter closed his eyes. "I'm not qualified," he said. "I have no credentials, no authority. I'm not a policeman."

"I've tried all the policemen," she said. "I need somebody else. Someone who won't stop until he finds my Óskar."

She took a brown cardboard folder from her purse and reached inside. She didn't have to fish around to find the photograph. The heavy paper was soft at the corners. It showed a serious bearded man holding a smiling blond boy in his arms.

"That's my Óskar," she said. "And the man who murdered my Sarah. Please bring little Óskar back to us."

Peter put his knuckle on the picture. "That's Erik?"

She nodded.

"I have to ask. Are you looking for revenge? I won't kill him."

"Dear God, no," she said. "I want you to find Óskar, that's all. I'll do what's needed to bring him home."

She held out the folder. Her hand was shaking.

"My family has more money than we'll ever need. My late first husband had a knack for it." She pushed the folder toward him. "This is fifty thousand dollars to start, in cash, along with a credit card for expenses. The card has no limit. Anything you need, buy it. The police report is in here, along with everything from the other investigators. Start with his family. His family is the key."

"Mrs. Price," Peter said. "I really don't—"

"Please." Her voice cracked in the quiet car. "Just look at the police report, that's all I ask. Both my children are dead and gone. And that man has taken my only grandchild."

Peter watched as a tear slid down her ruined cheek. He thought of that child's backpack adrift in the bay. With only the air in a plastic jar to keep it from sinking to the cold, rocky bottom.

He reached out and took the heavy folder from her hand.

WHEN Peter got out of the car, the angular man with the umbrella walked around to meet him in the street. He had long, narrow limbs and a pale hatchet face pocked with acne scars. "Are you going to do what she's asking?"

Peter tucked the folder under his coat.

"I don't know," he said. "Probably."

"Another guy tried. It didn't go well. You any good at this?"

Peter raised a shoulder. "Guess I'll find out."

The angular man leaned toward him almost imperceptibly.

"I been with Mrs. Price almost ten years," he said. "Before that I was twenty years a D.C. Metro street cop."

"I figured," Peter said.

The other man gave Peter a hard smile. "What I'm saying is, you better not just be taking her money."

"I'm not taking any money," Peter said. "Not yet. And if I do, it'll just be for expenses."

The angular man processed this information. "How come?"

"Somebody has to." Peter didn't mention the other reason. The thrill at the prospect of being useful again.

The angular man held out a card between two fingers. "I'm Novak. You get in trouble, call me."

"Does Mrs. Price always take you with her when she flies?"

Novak nodded. "Where she goes, I go."

Peter nodded, took the card, then turned and walked toward the restaurant, feeling the weight of the brown folder under his arm. He hadn't even opened it and already he had questions.

Why did this guy, Erik, kill his wife?

Why did Catherine Price need a bodyguard?

And what the hell was he going to tell June?

Chapter 5

PETER FOUND A TABLE in the rear where he could get his back against a wall. After the waiter took his order and brought back a Jubelale, he opened the folder and laid out the contents. Along with the worn photo of Erik and Óskar, there were two sheaves of paper held together by binder clips and a fat padded envelope.

He upended the envelope over the table. Five banded stacks of crisp new hundreds spilled out, along with a matte-black credit card and a tiny thumb drive. The name on the credit card was Price Consulting. He reloaded the padded envelope and tucked it back into the folder.

The first binder clip held police information about the murder of Sarah Price, at least a hundred pages. Skimming, Peter looked at the initial incident report from the first officer on the scene. The evidence inventory, which included a .44 caliber revolver with three spent shells and two intact rounds. The coroner's report. Purchase records for the revolver and the plane tickets, showing that Eiríkur Grímsson and Óskar Eiríksson had left the U.S. on Icelandair.

The last page was a printed copy of an email from a detective Philip Moore. He regretted to inform Mrs. Price that the investigation had reached the limits of the MPD's jurisdiction. The case had been referred to the Icelandic arm of Interpol. He'd included contact information at the end of the email, everything from Iceland's Interpol office to Moore's own cell.

Peter looked at the time. Three hours later in Washington, D.C. He picked up his phone and dialed.

"Phil Moore here. Who the hell is this?" A voice like a scrape.

"Detective Moore, my name's Peter Ash. Catherine Price said I could call you. I'm trying to find her grandson, Óskar Eiríksson. She said his backpack washed up on the beach in Reykjavík, and she asked me to go to Iceland and take another look. Do you remember the case?"

"Yeah, she called me about the backpack." A sigh came over the line, long and thin as an unraveling thread. "Listen, Catherine Price is a great lady. She's been through a lot. But this is my first night off in two weeks, so make it quick. Whaddaya need?"

"Did you ever figure out why Sarah Price was killed?"

"We never found anything like a motive." The sound of ice rattling in a glass. "Sometimes motive is overrated. Sometimes you never find out why. It's all about the evidence."

"And the evidence pointed to Erik Grímsson."

"Absolutely. We found the gun at the scene, registered to him, with his prints all over it. The ballistics match the rounds we dug out of the wall. His prints were on the shell casings. And he shot her three times in the face, which is a very personal way to kill somebody, by the way."

"You're convinced he killed her?"

"I'm sure of it." Peter could hear Moore breathing through his nose. "I've been a cop a long time, and I'm telling you, he's guilty as hell. Plus, he ran where we couldn't follow. Why would he run if he didn't do it?"

Peter wasn't doubting; he just wanted to know more. "Why would he take the boy with him?"

"Maybe it was for protection, like a hostage. To get his in-laws to back off. You know we think the kid was with him, right? When he did it?"

"Wow."

"You said it, buddy."

"Well," said Peter. "Thanks for your time."

"No problem. Now I'm gonna hang up and finish getting drunk, then fall asleep on the couch. Don't ever become a cop."

PETER WENT BACK TO Catherine Price's papers.

The second sheaf came from the Norwegian investigator, who had done a fair amount of work before he ended up in the hospital. He'd begun by making a list of members of Erik's extended family, including photos lifted from social media. Then he'd used public records to create a detailed profile of everyone he could find. The profiles included home and work addresses, property and vehicles, occupations, and any criminal history.

The histories were interesting. Scanning the paperwork, Peter found a robust multigenerational tradition of physical assaults going back to Erik's great-grandfather, Thorvaldur, who was ninety-six. Thorvaldur's last criminal complaint came at the age of ninety-two, when he assaulted another farmer with a hayfork.

Clearly, the family was a problem.

After the background work, probably all done from his desk, the Norwegian had gone into the field to interview the family members. He'd started with Erik's cousin Bjarni Bergsson because he was the only family member Erik was known to have made contact with after the murder. But Bjarni had been uncooperative. He'd broken the Norwegian's nose.

Next the Norwegian talked to Erik's mother, Greta. She was a vulcanologist at the Institute of Earth Sciences, and she lived in Selfoss, an agricultural community an hour's drive from Reykjavík. But when the Norwegian arrived at her house, she slammed the door in his face. Unfortunately, it happened before the Norwegian managed to get his face entirely out of the way.

It occurred to Peter that the Norwegian investigator, while great at digging up information on the internet, might not be suited to fieldwork. At least not with this family.

Another cousin ran a high-end guesthouse outside of Skaftafell. She'd set her sheepdogs on him, then pulled rocks from her yard and pelted his car as he drove away. The medical paperwork noted twelve stitches in the Norwegian's calf and a rabies shot.

Between these pleasant home visits, the Norwegian had called Erik's relatives who were living abroad. Icelanders often left home to gain work experience overseas. Erik's father lived in London, his sister lived in Edinburgh, and a brother lived in Toronto. None of them had returned the Norwegian's calls.

The Norwegian's last stop was Seydisfjordur, where two of Erik's uncles docked their fishing boat. But the boat was gone when he arrived, and after waiting for three days, it hadn't returned. Either they were fishing in the North Atlantic or their boat had sunk, because the Norwegian never found them. He never made it to the family farm, either.

The farm was more of a compound, Peter realized. Catherine's documents included a Google Earth photo blown up to blueprint size, and when he unfolded it, he saw green hills and fields that stretched from the mountains to the sea. The Norwegian had marked the farm boundaries in different colored pens.

Outlined in red, the main farm stood at the base of a high, rocky promontory. Founded more than two hundred years ago, and owned now by Erik's grandmother, Yrsa Thorvaldsdóttir, it had grown to cover a wide, fertile plain, then jumped the main road and continued down to a broad, open bay with a gray beach. Peter saw braided streams, a wandering gravel driveway, and the long, straight lines of ditches draining the meadows.

Wrapping around the promontory on each side, two more farms spread out like wings, their borders drawn in black and blue. The farms were owned by Erik's grandmother's brothers, and although the fields stretched away from the headland, each farm's buildings stood fairly close to one another. An easy walk, Peter figured, from one farm to the next. A close-knit family.

The Norwegian had been on his way to the compound when a jacked-up silver SUV came up behind him and ran him off the road. The Norwegian didn't recognize the make or model. The license plate had been smeared with mud.

When the rented Volvo rolled down the rocky slope, every airbag had inflated. Still, the resulting injuries forced the doctors to put the Norwegian in a medically induced coma for five days.

In his final report, the investigator fired his clients and made note of his final invoice, which was not included in Peter's papers and must have been enormous. The Norwegian had made an effort, Peter thought. And paid for it.

How was it that Wetzel thought this was something Peter could do? More troubling, why did Peter want so badly to try?

Unfortunately, he already knew the answer to the second question. If he went to Iceland, someone might try to kill him. In fact, it seemed likely. Peter didn't want to admit that the prospect of dying made him feel more alive than he'd felt in months.

He finished his dinner and was going through the papers again when his phone rang. It was Tom Wetzel. "You met with Catherine Price," he said. "Tell me you're going."

Peter didn't remember Wetzel being this relentless. His battalion nickname had been Wetzel the Pretzel. Maybe corporate life had stiffened him up.

"I haven't decided yet. I'm still reading the file she gave me. Mrs. Price has legal custody of the boy?"

"Absolutely. I'll email the paperwork if you want to see it."

"I do," he said. "Tom, what happened with Sarah Price? Does anyone have any idea why Erik might have killed her?"

"I don't know. When you find him, you can ask. I'm running point on this for Catherine, but I actually work for Jerry Brunelli, Catherine's husband. Can we get back on task here?"

Peter looked at the name on the black credit card. "What kind of work does Price Consulting do?"

"We're a political consulting shop. People hire us to get stuff done. Why are you asking?"

"I was wondering why Catherine Price has a bodyguard."

"In this town, perception is everything. A bodyguard is a D.C. Lamborghini, the ultimate symbol of importance."

This was classic Wetzel the Pretzel. "Has there ever been a threat?"

"We're a small shop, but we do a serious business. We pull the levers, you know? But some levers don't like to get pulled."

"You didn't answer my question."

"If everyone liked us, we wouldn't be doing our job."

Peter looked at the finger-worn photo of stone-faced Erik and little Óskar propped against his half-empty beer glass.

He said, "Do you know anything else that isn't in the report?"

"Did you see the video?"

"No." Peter fished through Catherine Price's envelope. "On the thumb drive?"

"That's it. You should take a look. You'll get a sense of Erik. Maybe provide some motivation."

PETER packed up and walked back through the rain to his truck, where he fired up his laptop, found the video file on the thumb drive, and hit Play.

The screen showed Óskar on his mother's hip, arms around her neck. His face was dreamy, half buried in her hair, his lips moving as he talked to himself. Peter could see the straps of a backpack over his shoulders, sky blue with the yellow LEGO logo.

"Such a lover boy." Catherine's voice. She must have been holding the camera.

A smile quirked the corner of Sarah's mouth. Her glasses were perched atop her head; her sandy hair was blowing in the wind.

The camera closed in on Sarah's and Óskar's faces. In that simple act of observation, Catherine's love was evident.

With the camera closer, Óskar's voice was loud enough to be understood. He wasn't talking to himself; he was reciting numbers. "Three point one four one five nine two six five three five eight nine . . ." The digits kept coming, spilling out of him.

Sarah raised one arm and pointed. "Hey, Óskar, look at the trees. Aren't they pretty?"

The boy turned to look. "Wow," he said. He released his mother's neck, slid from her arms, and hit the ground running, dumping the backpack to the grass as he ran toward the trees.

The camera tracked him across a lumpy green field backed by a row of trees wearing fall colors. A park. The screen bounced as Sarah and Catherine hustled to catch up.

The boy sprinted from tree to tree, skinny arms and legs pumping. "What kind is this tree? How about this one? And this one!" After all his time in war zones, Peter had almost forgotten what it was like to watch a child run without fear.

Óskar stopped at a flame-orange maple with broad, spreading limbs and wrapped his arms around the trunk in a hug. No, not a hug, he was climbing up the tree like a monkey.

The camera jolted, forgotten but still taking video. "Is that a good idea? What if he falls?" Worry clear in Catherine's voice.

"Hey, kiddo?" Sarah sounded calm, a good mother. She held his backpack in her arms. "Be careful, please. Not too high."

"He's fine." A man stepped under the tree, looking up into the branches. Erik, his face almost invisible under a thick blond beard. His voice was deep. "How's the view up there?"

"I can see forever!" Óskar's voice was high and excited.

Then a soft *crack* and a panicked yelp. A thrashing of branches, the slow ticking fall of leaves knocked loose.

Sarah's voice stayed steady. "Óskar? Are you okay?"

"A branch broke. I sorta slipped?" A quiet but rising panic. "Now I'm stuck. I can't get down."

"You're doing fine," Erik called. "You're a Viking, remember? Hold tight with your hands and find a place for your feet."

"Sarah," Catherine said, "he's seven."

"He'll figure it out," Erik said. "How else will he learn?"

"This isn't Iceland, Erik." Sarah dropped the boy's backpack and reached for the lowest branch. "Sometimes kids need help."

She wore a cardigan and high-waisted jeans and ballet flats. She did not appear particularly athletic. Yet she pulled herself up onto the first branch, then the next. "I'm coming, Óskar."

Limb by limb, she climbed until she vanished into the flame-colored leaves. Erik remained on the ground, his expression hidden under the heavy beard. Then the video ended.

Peter couldn't stop seeing Erik's face. The depth of feeling in his eyes was startling. The eyes of a man who would do anything.

Peter uploaded the data stick from his laptop to the cloud, then used Catherine Price's credit card to make reservations for the first flight to Reykjavík, leaving that evening.

He spent the next few hours on his laptop, learning everything he could about Iceland's culture, geography, and winter weather.

In the end, he didn't tell June. He didn't even call her.

He told himself that she thought he'd be off the grid in Death Valley. She wasn't expecting to hear from him for weeks.

He just got on the plane and left.

BY THE time Peter woke in the back of the Mitsubishi, the storm had softened. The Reykjavík curbs were piled high with thick, wet snow, and everything inside the 4x4 was damp from the weather that had blown through the broken window.

Peter's head throbbed painfully. His right eye had swollen completely shut. Blood clotted his hair where Dónaldur had clocked him with the vodka bottle. His back and ribs and legs ached where each boot had hit its mark.

Losing his pants, with his phone and wallet and key, was obviously a setback, too.

The truck's clock said it was after noon, which meant he'd slept something like twelve hours. The midwinter sun was hovering somewhere near the southern horizon.

He gulped ibuprofen from his first-aid kit, then unwrapped alcohol wipes to clean his swollen eye and the split skin on the back of his head. He was probably too late to actually sterilize the wounds, but the sting of the alcohol got him focused. The hardest part of getting dressed in the car was putting on his socks.

In his still damp coat and boots, he walked up the hill into the old city, feeling his stiff body begin to loosen up. He wondered why Bjarni and Dónaldur hadn't simply killed him. Maybe the family didn't want to risk any more attention.

It didn't matter. Peter had a job to do.

He stopped at an apartment building with a covered entrance where he could stand out of the snow and keep his good eye on the stairway to Snorri's Rave Cave. It wasn't supposed to open for hours, but Bjarni would have to come to work eventually.

The snow came softly down. He was hungry and cold and long overdue for coffee. But the white static was strangely silent.

He found that he missed it.

He didn't want to think about what that meant.

THE SNOW HAD MOSTLY STOPPED, and shopkeepers were shoveling their sidewalks when Bjarni came around the corner in a dirty red coat and familiar rubber boots. The white static finally woke, sparking high.

As Bjarni passed the apartment entrance, Peter stepped out behind him, grabbed his hood, and slung him around to slam him face-first into the building.

Bjarni said something guttural in Icelandic, then pushed off the wall with one hand. When he spun to meet Peter, his eyes widened in recognition. One sleeve was empty, his right arm slung under his coat. Even with just one good eye, Peter had no trouble thumping Bjarni in the temple with his sore elbow.

Bjarni's eyes fluttered, and his knees buckled. Peter caught him under the armpit and held him up.

Bjarni started thrashing, so Peter popped him on the broken arm. He wore a cast inside the sling, but Peter's hands were hard, and the break was fresh. Bjarni froze, paralyzed by the pain.

"Where's your wallet?" Peter said.

"You are crazy."

"Yes. Where's your wallet?"

Bjarni shook his head. "Back pocket."

"I'm going to take it now. If you try anything, I'll break your other arm. Got me?"

"*Já.*" Yes.

Peter fished out the man's wallet. It was a thin leather envelope with his national ID and a bank card and a few high-denomination krónur folded between. The ID didn't have an address. Peter put the wallet in his own pocket.

"Give that back."

"Maybe later."

Peter put a knuckly hand on Bjarni's bad arm. "Where are my things from the club? My phone and wallet and key? My pants?"

He watched Bjarni weigh his options. To help him along the path to truth, Peter drummed heavy fingers on the cast. Bjarni's eyes tipped down. "At my home."

"Then that's where we're going. Do we walk or drive?"

"I cannot be late for work," Bjarni said.

"Look at my face." Peter pointed at his swollen eye, his cheek gone black and blue. "You think I feel bad for you?" He scooped up Bjarni's bag. "Now, do we walk or drive? Or should I break something else?"

Bjarni had a banged-up little Škoda hatchback parked just down the hill.

THEY drove along the Saebraut, snow piled waist-high beside the road. Bjarni turned right on Snorrabraut, which cut back up the hill and through town. It was a major thoroughfare, four lanes packed with cars and trucks and enormous yellow-orange buses. The buildings were mostly concrete, three or four stories tall, built right up against the sidewalk and each other.

Peter already had the city map in his head, so he knew where they were, but he didn't know where they were going, and he didn't speak the language. Bjarni could be taking him anywhere.

"Give me your phone."

Bjarni looked at him, astonished and offended. "No."

"Really?" Peter rapped his knuckles on the other man's cast.

Bjarni fished his huge smartphone from his coat pocket and handed it over.

Peter woke the phone and saw a photo of three men in a snow-field, wearing winter gear, their arms around each other's shoulders. Two enormous men with cropped hair and graying beards flanked a younger man, clean-shaven and handsome, with empty eyes and a wool hat pushed back on his head. Erik Grímsson was the man in the middle. Maybe the two others were his uncles, the fishermen? Bjarni would have taken the picture.

Peter held up the phone. "What's your security code?"

Bjarni made a face, but stuck his thumb on the button and the phone's main screen came up.

The phone's language was set to Icelandic, but Peter recognized the app icons. Global capitalism at work. He found the map function. "What street do you live on?"

Smirking, Bjarni rattled off an impossibly long word. Peter shook his head, opened the glove box, and unearthed the car's paperwork.

It had Bjarni's name and what looked like an address. He held up the paper. "This?"

Bjarni made a sour face and nodded once.

While Peter tweaked the phone's settings and put the address into the mapping app, Bjarni drove into a tree-filled neighborhood on a small peninsula sticking out into the sea. The app identified it as Karsnes. He stopped at a modest single-story home with a low roof. Tire tracks showed in the snowy driveway.

Bjarni didn't move from his seat. "What do you want?"

"I told you," Peter said. "My phone, my wallet, my car key, my pants." He gave Bjarni a smile. "And your cousin Erik."

Bjarni just looked at him. He was trying for empty eyes but couldn't quite manage it.

Peter took the keys from the ignition, unlatched his seat belt, and opened his door. He still hurt all over. "Come on, I can't wait to see your place. What's for dinner?"

Bjarni muttered what sounded like a potent Icelandic curse and followed Peter to the house.

AT THE narrow entrance, Peter handed Bjarni the keys and hung back while the big man unlocked the house. Peter didn't know what might be waiting inside, so he bumped Bjarni off-balance and slipped past to turn on the lights.

He saw an open-plan living area decorated in Icelandic Bachelor Pad. The wide front windows might be nice when the sun was out, but in the midwinter darkness, they reflected the pale lamplight back like mirrors. The static didn't like any of it.

Bjarni came in, and Peter pointed at the low couch. "Sit."

Broken arm or not, square-shouldered Bjarni looked bigger indoors. He glared while Peter poked around. A kitchen area separated by a counter and stools. Coats and trekking packs in a closet by the door. Plastic crates in the corner held climbing gear—crampons and harness and rope and a short-handled folding shovel. An excellent tool for a marine on the loose in Iceland, Peter thought.

The blade's black finish had worn away, leaving the curved tip shining and polished by use. One edge was serrated, for chopping roots, branches, and, if you ran out of ammunition, the enemy.

He locked eyes with Bjarni. "Let's start with something easy," he said. "Where's my stuff from last night?"

The Icelander nodded at a wall unit on the far side of the room, bookshelves over cabinets.

There Peter found his phone and wallet and car key. His cash and the black credit card were still in the wallet. His pants, belt, and fleece were folded neatly on a shelf.

Peter transferred his things to his pockets, put his clothes by the front door, then picked up the shovel and twirled it in his hand, the weight comfortable and familiar.

He turned back to Bjarni. "Next question. What did you put in my beer last night?"

"I don't know what you're talking about."

Peter tested the shovel blade with his thumb. Recently sharpened. Then he kicked away the coffee table and swung the shovel, the blade coming closer to Bjarni's face with each orbit. The Icelander's eyes got wider. "What did you dose me with?"

Bjarni's breath came back. "*Já*, okay. I gave you some Molly."

"I don't know what that is."

"Ecstasy," Bjarni said. "A party drug. Synthetic, very good quality. Medical grade. It made you feel good, I think?"

Ecstasy was the classic club drug. It was supposed to lower your inhibitions and increase your feeling of social connection. And Peter *had* felt pretty good.

He poked at Bjarni's chest with the sharp tip of the shovel. "Did somebody give you the drugs? Tell you what to do?"

Peter was thinking about the embassy man who wanted Peter to go home so badly he'd gotten him kicked out of the country.

Bjarni raised his palm and gently redirected the blade. "Why would anyone do that? I sell Molly at the club." He gestured at the house. "You think I afford this place as a bartender?"

"Then why dose my beer with that stuff?"

"You asked about my cousin." Bjarni glared at him. "The last time someone asked about Eiríkur, two men broke my jaw. I had nothing but beer and smoothies for two months."

Two men? That incident wasn't in any of the reports Peter had seen. "Where's the rest of your dope?"

Bjarni opened his mouth, then closed it again. "In the freezer."

Peter took a backward step toward the open kitchen. "If you move off that couch, I'll break your head. You got me?"

Bjarni raised his hands. "*Já, já,* I got you."

With one eye on the Icelander, Peter put the shovel on the kitchen counter, then dug under plastic bags of frozen fish parts until he found a yellow DHL mailer filled with thumb-size clear plastic Ziploc bags. Inside each was a small pile of pale powder.

He put the mailer on the counter and opened the fridge. A lonely block of cheese, a moldering cabbage, a few cans of beer. Also three cardboard cartons of milk, which seemed like a lot.

The first carton was almost empty. The next was unopened. The third, tucked way in the back, was stuffed with money.

He carried the mailer and the milk carton to the living room.

Bjarni looked sourly at Peter. "Tell me what you want."

"I want your cousin Erik. Tell me where he is and I'm gone."

Bjarni shook his head. "Why do you continue to ask about Eiríkur? He is dead."

"Wait. What?"

"He is dead. Your people killed him. Last winter."

Peter watched the Icelander's face. "My people?"

"Who else? The men who broke my jaw. Your people."

Peter hadn't seen anything about that in the Norwegian's report, either. Something wasn't adding up.

"Do the police know about Erik?"

"Please. My family, we do not talk to police. Eiríkur is family. We buried him on the home farm."

Easy enough to claim, Peter thought, and unprovable without digging up the body.

"How about Óskar? His mother and father dying must have been pretty traumatic. Is he okay?"

Bjarni glowered at him. "Óskar is also dead. What kind of men kill a child? What kind of man are you?" Bjarni leaned back into the couch and folded his good arm across his broken one. "Some things are sacred. I say nothing more."

Peter still didn't know whether to believe him. If Erik and Óskar were dead, why was someone trying to send Peter home?

Changing tactics, he pointed at the DHL mailer with its cargo of little powder-filled bags. "How many doses in there?"

Bjarni blinked. "About two hundred."

"How much for one?"

"Forty euros each. Five thousand five hundred krónur."

"So you've got about eight thousand euros in product." Peter picked up the milk carton and spilled the contents across the coffee table. Euros and krónur and dollars in neat rubber-banded folds. "That's gotta be another ten thousand euros at least."

The look on Bjarni's face told Peter he was underestimating.

"That's a lot of money," Peter said. "Tell me where Óskar is and I leave now. Your money and dope stay here."

"I told you, Óskar is dead." Bjarni leaned forward, shifting his weight. "Money is just money. Family is everything."

"So you said." Peter stepped into the kitchen and took the folding shovel off the counter. When he came back, Bjarni was rising off the couch, looking at an ice axe in the crate of climbing gear.

Peter shook his head, the shovel resting on his shoulder. "Stay down, stupid. You're going to get hurt."

Bjarni made it to his feet and moved forward, scooping up the ice axe with his free hand. His arm had been broken, but he was still on the attack. Peter almost liked the guy.

Bjarni brandished the axe and came at him.

Peter snapped the shovel around at the end of one long arm and smacked the Icelander in the side of the head with the back of the blade. But gently, more or less.

Bjarni did a few knee-wobble dance steps. Peter stripped the axe from his hand and caught the cast at the crook of the elbow, then eased the other man back to the couch.

"You're okay." Peter was fairly sure it was true. He went back to the kitchen and returned with two tall cans of Viking Beer. He popped the tops and held one out. "Are all Icelanders like this?"

Bjarni grabbed the beer like a lifeline. He drained it without appearing to swallow, then looked at Peter with one bleary eye.

"*Já.*" Bjarni jutted his chin at Peter. "It doesn't matter what you do to me. Family is everything. I give you nothing."

Peter didn't know whether Bjarni was telling the truth or just telling a story to protect his family. Either way, Peter wasn't going to get anything more out of him.

Damn Vikings.

Chapter 6

Twelve Months Earlier

AFTER A BATH AND A STORY, Óskar snores in his bed. Erik and Sarah sit again in the dining room, a cheap phone on the table between them. It's nearly midnight.

Erik hoped Sarah would calm down during her walk. Instead she found a market that sold disposable phones, bought one with cash, then used the mobile browser to research attorneys. She used the same phone to leave a message with the answering service of Ginger Mulanax, a California whistleblower specialist.

Mulanax calls back an hour later. She is on speaker now, explaining how the federal whistleblower statute works.

"There's a huge amount of personal risk involved," she says. "Whistleblowers have to cooperate with prosecutors, secretly record business conversations, obtain company documents."

Erik looks at Sarah. He wants to make sure she understands the weight of this. The muscle in her cheek is twitching.

Behind Ginger Mulanax's voice, they hear the low murmur of voices. The attorney is calling from a dinner party.

"Resolving a case can take years. It can be incredibly stressful. Your role will almost certainly be known to the company. You'll be fired. You'll likely be named in a countersuit. It may be very difficult to find another job in your field."

"That does not sound promising," Erik says. "We have a young son."

"It's not for everyone," Mulanax says. "But the federal government wants to encourage people to come forward, so the statute sweetens the pot a little. Whistleblowers have the right to anywhere from fifteen to thirty percent of any fines levied and monies recovered. That can be millions of dollars."

"What if we don't care about the money?" Sarah says.

"You just want the people caught?"

"I want him punished," Sarah says.

If Erik had any doubts before, he has none now.

It's personal for her.

"I can't advise you on a path outside the law," Mulanax says, "but many jurisdictions have a pipeline for anonymous tips. Any tipster would need to assemble enough documentation to compel the prosecutors to begin their own investigation. It's harder than most people think."

They talk for a few more minutes; then Ginger Mulanax returns to her dinner party. Sarah powers off the phone and removes the SIM card. Her face is flushed red. Erik's heart sinks.

"We already have the documentation," she says. "We have the whole hidden drive. We can release everything and pretend the hackers did it."

"What do you mean, you have the hidden drive? I thought you just had that single video."

"There's more than one video," she says.

"What? How many more?"

She isn't listening. "I already made a backdoor into the server. And we don't need to find a prosecutor, either. We just copy the drive to an offshore server and send a link to reputable journalists. That or publish the video online, along with the drive address and the password. The internet will do the rest."

Erik cannot believe what he's hearing. "You were planning this all along," he says.

She puts her hand on his arm. It is hot to the touch. "We can do this," she says. "Don't you want to see him punished?"

"It's not that simple," he says. "What if something happens to us? What about Óskar?"

But Sarah isn't listening. She's already reaching for her laptop.

Present Day

PETER left Bjarni on the couch with false assurances that he'd leave his car keys and phone at Snorri's Rave Cave. He took the money from the milk carton, along with the shovel and the ice axe, but he left the tiny envelopes of medical-grade Molly.

The storm had eased, but the temperature had dropped. The wet snow had frozen into a hard crust. He wanted to check his phone but drove the little Škoda a mile before pulling over to the side of a busy road. Peter had two texts and four voice mails.

The first text was from Catherine Price. *My husband is talking to his contacts at the State Department and trying to solve your problem. He will call you when he has something.*

The second text was from June. *Drive safe.* Then a smiley face.

She still thought he was driving to Death Valley.

Peter closed his good eye and felt the little car rock in the wake of the tractor trailers flying by. It occurred to him, not for the first time, that he didn't deserve her.

The voice mails were all from a number the caller ID identified as Commissioner Hjálmar, followed by the Icelandic word *lögreglan*. Police.

In the first voice mail, left the afternoon before, when Peter was sleeping off his jet lag in the Mitsubishi, Hjálmar had invited Peter to dinner at his home. "I promise, I will not serve fermented shark or dried fish, just a hearty Icelandic meal of lamb with brown sauce."

In the second voice mail, left at eight o'clock the night before, when Peter was walking down the steps to Snorri's Rave Cave, Hjálmar had invited Peter to an after-dinner drink. "I invite you to a drink at Ölstofan. They have excellent Icelandic beer."

The third call came at midnight, when Peter was getting the stuffing kicked out of him in a snow-covered alley. The commissioner's tone was much more businesslike. "I call to remind you that you must report to the airport within thirty-two hours for your flight back to the United States."

The fourth call came just a few hours ago, while Peter was waiting for Bjarni by the apartment entrance. The commissioner's voice was again cordial, even cheerful. "*Halló*, it is your friend Hjálmar. I invite you again, dinner tonight. I will text you the restaurant to make it easy to find."

The commissioner's persistence was not a good sign.

PETER parked Bjarni's Škoda in a snowdrift behind an ancient Volvo camper, then walked through the white streets toward the rented Mitsubishi with his clothes rolled under his arm, the ice axe in one hand and the folding shovel in the other.

He kept Bjarni's keys and phone. When the big Icelander had unlocked the phone with his thumb, Peter had taken the opportunity to change the passcode and the language. He could use an extra phone. At the very least, it might take longer for Bjarni to alert the rest of the family.

He drove to the Grandi Mathöll, an industrial building on the waterfront, and parked outside. The structure had been converted into a large, well-lit space with counter-service food stalls on three sides and a wall of windows on the fourth. Long family-style tables and benches took up the center of the hall. Through the tall windows, Peter could still see glimpses of the illuminated city across the harbor.

He was acutely conscious of his swollen face, but nobody looked at him twice. Either folks were very polite or brawling was a national pastime.

He ordered a giant grilled sandwich from one stall, lamb chops and roasted new potatoes from a second, and a Viking Beer from the bar. Peter sat alone by the window, angled toward the harbor, and fell on his supper like a wolf.

As Peter saw it, he had two challenges. The first was to talk with Erik's family without getting killed. The second was to deal with the Icelandic police. The embassy man's demand required that

Hjálmar put Peter on a plane back to the States in less than twenty-four hours. Peter needed more time than that.

He thought about his conversation with Bjarni. He didn't know whether he believed that Erik and Óskar were dead. If they were, he owed Catherine a confirmation of that fact. If they were still alive, he'd find them. Either way, his task was much the same.

Then there was the question of Sarah Price. As Detective Moore had noted, shooting someone in the face was a very personal way to kill. Most murders, even premeditated murders, had simple, personal motives. Jealousy or greed. Anger or fear. It would be nice if Peter could figure out what it was.

When his supper was finished, Peter opened his day pack, set Bjarni's phone on the table beside his own, then reached into the pack's laptop sleeve for Catherine Price's folder.

He leaned the photo of Óskar and Erik up against his empty beer glass, then paged through the Norwegian investigator's report. The Norwegian had been on his way to the family farm when he'd been run off the road. It had happened right after he'd tried to find Erik's uncles on their fishing boat.

The Norwegian was a much better researcher than Peter would ever be, but he seemed more comfortable on the internet than in a hostile environment. Peter wasn't about to get chased off by Vikings with snowballs.

"There you are."

Peter turned his head to see Hjálmar standing in what had been Peter's blind spot. "I see that you ate your supper without me."

He wore a short black jacket, blue jeans, and snow boots. Civilian clothes. No bulge at his belt, no sag in his coat pocket. The police didn't carry guns in Iceland, Peter reminded himself.

"I was too hungry to wait." Peter felt the heat radiating from his eye. "I was about to call you. How'd you find me?"

Hjálmar tried to hold back a smile. "It is my work."

"You found the agency where I rented the car," Peter said. "I assume my rental has a GPS, but those only ping every few hours. So why didn't I see you watching?"

The Icelander had the grace not to gloat. "I left my personal car in the parking lot with a cellular-linked camera on the dashboard. I had a coffee watching live video on my laptop."

Hjálmar was better than Peter had expected. Peter began to gather his papers. "Please, sit. Can I buy you a beer?"

"Unfortunately, I cannot. I am on duty."

The gusting wind pushed against the glass like a giant's hand. Peter felt the pressure change inside the building. "Wow."

"The coming storm will be worse. A big one."

Peter raised his eyebrows. "This isn't a big one?"

"Not really," Hjálmar said. "Our weather people compare the coming storm to our last large one, five years ago. In East Iceland, we measured winds at two hundred sixty kilometers per hour."

"That's too bad," Peter said. "I was hoping to get out of town for a few hours."

"I do not recommend you attempt to leave Reykjavík. With this storm, it is possible to die from exposure. And I must mention, your flight to America leaves in twenty hours."

"You know, I had almost forgotten." Peter tucked his things into his pack. "I could really use a few more days."

"I am sorry. That is not possible."

Peter nodded. "How many officers do you have outside?"

"None," Hjálmar said. "We are civilized human beings, so we take the civilized path. I offer you my guest bedroom for the night. Tomorrow, after coffee and breakfast, I drive you to the airport."

Peter stood from the table, shrugged into his coat, and shouldered his pack. He walked around the table toward the other man.

Hjálmar stood almost formally, feet apart, hands clasped behind his back. "I have no baton or pepper spray," he said. "If you leave now, I will not attempt to stop you. But the civilized path will no longer be possible. Only the barbarian's path. Perhaps you are familiar with it."

"You checked up on me."

"I run also Iceland's Interpol office." Hjálmar was apologetic. "We have a good relationship with your FBI. They confirmed that the request to send you home did not come from them."

"I live a simple life. There's nothing else to know."

"So why does someone at your embassy want you to leave Iceland?"

"If you tell me his name, I might be able to answer that."

"The name on his credentials was David Staple. When I called him at the embassy today to follow up, I was told they had nobody there by that name. When I spoke with the ambassador, she told me she could not comment on State Department personnel."

"Huh." Peter considered the options. "So where did the order to kick me out of Iceland come from? The embassy or Staple?"

"The ambassador would not comment on that, although she was diplomatic about it. Either way, someone does not like you."

"What if I told you I came to Iceland to find a child? The American son of an Icelandic man who apparently killed his American wife, then fled to Iceland with his young son?"

"Ah." Hjálmar nodded. "You are looking for Óskar Eiríksson. The boy's backpack came ashore in the last storm. You work for Mrs. Price, like the Norwegian before you."

"You know about this case?"

"Of course," Hjálmar said. "We are a small country."

"Do you think the boy and his father are still in Iceland?"

"We continue to search but have not found him. We have spoken with Erik's family members and friends many times. We also watch his finances, but he has not attempted to access his accounts. We believe someone shelters him, most likely a relative."

"What can you tell me about his family?"

"Rich in land, not krónur, and a long history of violent behavior," Hjálmar said. "We believe two brothers who own a fishing business are actually smugglers, using Iceland's location between Europe and America."

"But the family wouldn't have the money or connections to influence David Staple."

"I do not believe so. And it is not their way. They are more, ah, direct." Hjálmar scratched his chin. "But who knew you were on your way to Iceland to find Óskar?"

Peter was a little embarrassed that he hadn't thought of it himself. When the backpack was found, Hjálmar had called Catherine Price. Had Hjálmar called someone else? Had Catherine?

He changed the subject. "What if I told you Erik and Óskar were dead? Murdered, their killers never found?"

"I would ask for the source of this information."

"His cousin Bjarni."

"Ah." Hjálmar permitted himself a modest smile. "This explains your bruises. Do you believe him?"

"It doesn't matter. I'll keep looking either way."

Hjálmar regarded Peter for a moment. "Bjarni is just a pup. The smugglers, Eiríkur's uncles, are quite dangerous. If you find Óskar, what will you do? You are one man."

"I have your cell number," Peter said. "I guess I'll call you."

"If that is the case, perhaps we should have a coffee." Hjálmar extended a hand at the table. "Surely you have other questions?"

Peter smiled. The commissioner was stalling for time. But Peter asked, "If you had to guess, where do you think he might be?"

Hjálmar frowned. "The farm in Nordhurland Vestra is a possibility. He would have work and shelter and family. But we have been there many times and have not found either Eiríkur or the boy. I think Seydisfjordur, to the east, is more likely. Eiríkur's uncles own a fishing boat and a small processing facility there, and we are told that Eiríkur is close with them."

Outside, the sound of the wind rose and fell. Peter was running out of time. He adjusted the pack on his shoulders. "It's been nice talking with you," he said. "But I've got to go."

"Please," Hjálmar said. "Come with me. As my guest."

"I can't." Peter took a backward step toward the door. "I'm sorry, Hjálmar. You've been very civilized." He turned away.

"This is an island," Hjálmar called after him. "Every person, on every airplane and every ship, departs Iceland only with the permission of the customs police. Unless you are a very strong swimmer, you will not leave."

When Peter walked outside, he heard sirens on the wind, coming closer. The pack thumped on his back as he ran for the car.

HE DROVE the Mitsubishi too fast, the engine wound up, tires slipping on the snowy pavement. He was certain Hjálmar had told the dispatcher what Peter was driving, including the plate number. Time to get rid of the big 4x4.

He steered through the tight maze of streets, small apartment buildings built right up against the narrow buckled sidewalks. He passed groups dressed for the clubs, laughing despite the snow and wind. Almost eleven and they were just getting started.

Bjarni's dented little Škoda sat at a snowy curb, right where Peter had left it.

It was a narrow one-way road with parking only on the left. Peter bumped the Mitsubishi up the opposite curb. The sidewalk was so skinny that the truck was tight to the wall of the building yet half in the road. He shouldered his heavy pack and duffel, his day pack hanging from one hand. He still had Bjarni's keys.

A dirty mountain bike leaned against the Škoda's back end. A square-shouldered man in a red coat pulled open the driver's door and folded himself awkwardly into the small seat.

Peter didn't have time for this. He dropped his gear and grabbed the man's arm to pull him from the car. Through the coat, he felt the hardness of the cast. Bjarni turned, mouth open to speak, until he saw Peter's face and froze in place.

Peter said, "You rode your bike here? With all this wind, on these icy streets? With a broken arm?"

"Taxis are expensive." Bjarni was indignant. He jutted his chin at Peter. "You said you would leave my things at Snorri's, but you did not. I am glad I brought my extra keys."

Peter held out his hand. "Give them here."

Bjarni turned away, trying to protect his cast. "No."

Peter grabbed Bjarni's ear and pulled. "Keys. Now."

Reluctantly, Bjarni held out the keys. "Where is my phone?"

"Get out."

Peter heard sirens. The big Mitsubishi would grab the eye, parked with two wheels on the walkway. Time to go.

Bjarni pulled away and rubbed his ear. "Why do you want my car? You have one already."

"You can have it." Peter held out the 4x4 keys. "Think of it as an upgrade. Take it."

Bjarni scowled. "I want my own car. I *like* this car."

Peter didn't have time to debate the merits of the brown Škoda. The sirens were getting louder. But if he left Bjarni behind, he was likely to tell the police what Peter was driving. Hjálmar could add car theft to Peter's growing list of offenses.

"Fine, you can give me a lift. But I'm driving." He pushed Bjarni's shoulder, shoving him across the transmission hump.

Peter threw his gear into the back, then jammed the mountain bike into the cargo bay for good measure. The tire hung over the bumper, and the hatch wouldn't close. It didn't matter. He climbed into the driver's seat and got out of there.

He found his way to the Saebraut, the shortest path out of town. He used his turn signals and kept to the speed limit. The cold winter wind swirled through the open rear hatch.

Bjarni looked concerned. "Where are we going?"

Peter saw a bus station at the end of a monolithic strip mall. "Right here." He turned left and pulled into the parking area.

"Buses will not run in this weather," Bjarni said.

"I'll spend the night in the station." Peter opened his door. "You've only got one good arm. Let me help get your bike inside the car. It's too cold to drive with that hatch open."

"Thank you, but I have it." Bjarni climbed out and walked around to the back. He shoved the bike inside one-handed. "See? All is good." He closed the hatch with a thud.

Peter hadn't left his seat. He popped the clutch, hit the gas, and the car jumped forward, the movement slamming his door shut.

In the rearview mirror, he saw Bjarni standing on the asphalt, mouth open, coat blown wide by the wind, watching him go.

Peter really wished he didn't feel sorry for the guy.

HE DROVE until he saw an ocean of cars and trucks surrounding a big white building, part tow operation, part auto shop, part junkyard. The brown Škoda would look right at home. He parked out of sight from the street and sorted through his gear, trying to ditch the duffel and fit the essentials into his heavy pack. He wanted his hands free. How much crap did one man need?

Then he dropped the keys on the floor, hauled the bike out of the Škoda, shouldered the sixty-pound ruck, and pedaled away.

In the time it took him to ride two kilometers, the wind knocked him over four times.

He left the bike behind a glass-fronted Land Rover dealership and found a secluded spot in the lee of a slope under a copse of evergreens, where he used Bjarni's folding shovel to dig himself a shelter in the frozen snow. The dealership opened in nine hours.

He lay in his sleeping bag, rolled into his ground cloth like a burrito, wide awake in the middle of the night. He took out his phone and pulled up the video Catherine Price had given him. Óskar reeling off random numbers in his mother's arms. Óskar dropping his LEGO backpack to run across the grass and climb the maple. Óskar stuck in the tree. His mother climbing up to save him.

Peter watched again and again. Trying to lock Óskar into his memory. By the third time through, he thought to wonder about Óskar's numbers in the beginning of the video. By the fifth time through, Peter was pretty sure Óskar was reciting the first twenty-seven digits of pi.

He looked at the time. Four hours earlier on the East Coast. His phone battery was almost drained. He called Catherine Price. She picked up on the second ring.

"Have you found Óskar?" Her voice was filled with hope.

"Not yet," Peter said. "Although I did get a name on the embassy guy, David Staple. Has your husband made any progress with the State Department?"

Her voice dropped from the weight of her disappointment. "He's still waiting to hear from his contacts there," she said. "I'll text him the name; maybe that will help."

He asked about Óskar's numbers.

She said, "Óskar has a photographic memory, just like his grandfather—like his genetic grandfather, my first husband, I mean. And he's in love with pi. Do you know pi?"

"I do." Pi was the mathematical constant that described the ratio of a circle's circumference to its diameter. As far as mathematicians had determined, pi went on forever without repeating or demonstrating a pattern. In the seventh grade, Peter had memorized the first hundred digits. He'd since lost all but the first six, 3.14159, until Óskar's voice brought them back.

"Well, Óskar knows the first four thousand digits. He'll recite them at the slightest provocation." Her voice roughened, and he knew she was pushing down tears. "He's quite a brilliant boy."

Peter pictured her face, the lines carved with grief. "When they found Óskar's backpack, who else did you talk to, before me?"

"My husband, because of his connections. He told me to talk to Tom Wetzel. And Tom sent me to you. Why do you ask?"

"I don't know," he said. "I'm just trying to figure out who the players are."

"Peter, I need you to call me." He could hear the strain in her voice. "Every day. I need to hear what you're doing, what progress you're making. Can you promise me that?"

"Catherine, I can't," he said gently. "I'll be traveling cross-country soon, and the weather is going to get bad. I don't know what kind of connection I'll have."

"Do what you can," she said. "Promise me that?"

"Yes," he said. "I will."

Then his phone went silent. The battery had died.

He found his headlamp and pulled out the photo of Óskar. Peter held up the photo by its thin, worn corners. He lay there amid the howling darkness and looked at the photo for a long, long time.

Chapter 7

THE SLOUCHING SALESMAN clearly didn't believe Peter could afford to buy a Land Rover, even a used one.

Peter didn't blame the man. His eye was still swollen shut, and the cut on the back of his head felt raw. He hadn't showered since he'd left Portland three days ago. Standing by the dealership windows, he could smell himself through the open neck of his coat.

But when Peter held out Catherine Price's black credit card, the salesman flashed a smile and carried the card reverently to the manager's office, where they stood in hushed consultation. The manager then came out and shook Peter's hand.

He ended up with a seventeen-year-old blue Defender 110. With serious four-wheel drive and seating for nine, the utility vehicles were legendary for their toughness and durability. Peter's Defender had a powerful engine and oversize tires with good rubber remaining, and the previous owner had tricked it out with a winch on the front bumper and a cargo basket on the roof carrying four spare gas cans and a substantial snow shovel.

The salesman was happy to sell Peter a pair of sand ladders and a bumper jack for crossing roadless areas. Then Peter pulled into an empty service bay, where he borrowed a wrench from a tall mechanic in black overalls.

The mechanic scratched his beard as he watched Peter remove the second- and third-row seats to make a sleeping bay in the back. He didn't mention Peter's swollen eye or his pained grunts as he contorted his aching body to get to the seat bolts.

When Peter returned the wrench, he noticed the mechanic's safety-yellow work coat hanging from a hook on the side of his toolbox. The coat was worn and dirty but Swedish-made and designed for Nordic weather. "Nice coat."

"*Já.*" The mechanic shrugged. "It is warm."

"May I see?" The mechanic nodded. Peter picked it up and pulled it over his fleece. It fit him well enough. The mechanic clearly didn't like Peter wearing the coat. Peter took it off.

"Can I buy this one? I need to drive north, but I don't think my coat is good for working in this weather." He took out a fat wad of Bjarni's krónur. "What do you think?"

The mechanic didn't answer.

"Why don't you try my coat?" Peter laid his own across the hood of the Defender. "Not so durable, but warm."

The mechanic stepped forward cautiously, as if Peter were

playing a trick on him, then pulled Peter's coat over his overalls. "It looks good on you," Peter said. "Keep it." He held out the wad of krónur. "And the money. Please."

The mechanic shook his head at the extravagance. "Okay."

He took the bills, and they shook on the deal. Peter put on his new work coat and climbed into the Defender. The mechanic came over and put his hand on the doorframe.

"I do not want to give advice," he said. "But this weather is bad, even for Iceland. There is a storm coming. It will get worse. You should not go. Maybe instead go to the doctor?"

Peter smiled. "Thanks for the coat." Then he threw the truck into reverse, backed out of the service bay, and headed out into the snow. He had officially gone native.

It was oddly bright out, probably because the previous night's wind had wiped the clouds from the sky. The Defender's heater was working hard. There was no thermometer in the vehicle, but the previous owner had epoxied one to the side mirror. In Celsius, it read twenty below zero, which was about zero Fahrenheit.

Of course, it was only noon. Things would get a lot colder when the sun went down.

Driving out of the city center, Peter plugged Bjarni's phone into the cigarette lighter to charge. His own phone's battery was so dead that the phone wouldn't even turn on.

He parked in front of a strip mall in a busy commercial area, then went surfing on Bjarni's reviving phone. He found a nearby hostel with an open room and made a reservation on the website with Catherine Price's black credit card. He didn't like using the card, because it could leave a trail for Hjálmar to follow, but he really needed to take a shower.

He couldn't check into the hostel until four, but that was fine.

He had a few other things to do first.

First, he went to Bónus, a big grocery store. He paid cash for several weeks' worth of food he could eat without cooking, like bread and butter and cheese and cured sausage. He also bought a roll of tinfoil, although he wouldn't be cooking with it.

At a gas station that doubled as a convenience store, he filled his tank and his spare gas cans and picked up a handful of preloaded gas cards. He also bought a new smartphone with a front-loaded data plan and a wool hat with earflaps that partially covered the sides of his face. He'd seen a lot of locals wearing them.

In his hat and safety-yellow coat and six-day beard, nobody gave him a second look. Peter Ash, master of disguise.

THE United States embassy was a three-story concrete office block set in a snug neighborhood among small apartment buildings and single-family homes on Reykjavík's central hill.

Peter parked a quarter block away. The sun had gone down, and the streetlights had come on. The building's blank face was bright with security lighting.

Iceland was a small, low-risk posting, which explained why the building was set right on the street, with no gated compound, barbed wire, or guard tower. Still, an array of cameras watched the street, and a pair of armed men were stationed by the door.

A busy thoroughfare paralleled the embassy, with a historic church and the National Gallery on one side and a small lake on the other. From there, it was a half kilometer to the highway.

The snow had been cleared, although some ice remained on the uneven sidewalks. Peter could see the embassy entrance from the driver's seat. The truck's previous owner had rigged the cigarette lighter to work when the engine wasn't running, so he unplugged Bjarni's phone from the charger and plugged in his own.

When it collected enough juice to wake up, Peter tore off a rectangle of tinfoil, folded it in half, then in half again, and laid it on the passenger seat. Then he called Hjálmar's cell phone.

"*Halló,* my friend Peter Ash. Your timing is perfect. I have not yet had lunch. May I invite you?"

"Thank you, Hjálmar. First I was hoping you'd give me the cell number for David Staple. I have some questions."

A pause. "Why would I do this for you? It would only make trouble for me."

"You don't like him, either. He's using you. Icelanders are independent people, remember?"

"Okay," Hjálmar said. "I will text you David Staple's information. After you finish with him, you call me back. We will have lunch; then I will take you to the airport."

"Sounds great—thanks."

Peter figured the only reason the police hadn't found him yet was the fact that he'd drained his phone battery. But they'd had the overnight hours to get themselves ready.

Hjálmar's text arrived. Peter made the call.

"Who the hell is this?" Definitely Staple. Peter could practically see his outraged pink face.

"Hi—it's Peter Ash. We met at the airport a few days ago."

"You? Son, you better be there now, or on your way. Your flight leaves in, what, four hours?"

"About that," Peter said. "My rental car got towed. Any chance you can give me a lift?"

Staple sighed loudly. "Where are you?"

"Do you know that big modern church on top of the hill? It's not far from the embassy. That's where you are, right?"

The embassy was a wild guess. He could have been anywhere.

"Yeah, but I'm in the middle of something," Staple said. "Give me an hour. Meet me at the statue out front of the church."

It was a ten-minute walk. The hour would give the police time to get set up.

"Great," Peter said. "Thanks so much for your help."

Then he called Hjálmar back. "All set. Where do you want to meet for lunch?"

Hjálmar seemed to be in a chatty mood. "What kind of food would you like to eat? We have traditional Icelandic, of course. Thai food is always good. Let's see, there is Gló . . ."

Clearly Hjálmar would talk until Peter's phone gave them his location. Peter laid the phone atop the quadrupled rectangle of tinfoil while Hjálmar yammered on: ". . . sushi, steak, fish . . ."

Hjálmar kept talking as Peter folded the foil around the phone. When he crimped the edges tight, the sound cut off as the improvised Faraday cage blocked the signal and killed the connection. Next thing, Peter'd be making himself a tinfoil hat. Crazy, maybe, but even the paranoid have enemies.

Peter wondered again exactly who Staple was.

He was sure that Hjálmar, as the local head of Interpol, made it his business to know the players in the staff of every embassy, especially the American embassy. But Hjálmar didn't know him.

Which meant that Staple either wasn't on the embassy staff or was new on the country team. Which still didn't account for the ambassador's refusal to acknowledge that Staple worked at the embassy. Or to confirm the request to refuse Peter's entry.

The embassy's front door opened, and Staple appeared. He carried a paper cup of coffee but nothing else. He wore his slick-soled dress shoes and topcoat but no gloves or hat. He turned up the sidewalk toward Peter and a row of angle-parked cars.

Peter tugged down his new hat with the earflaps and put Bjarni's phone up to further hide his face.

As Staple passed, Peter watched his eyes flick across the Land Rover. But Staple didn't break stride—just pulled a key from his pocket. A black Renault flashed its lights at the end of the row.

Peter left the Land Rover and hustled after Staple. He carried a hiking pole in one hand, the other hand held to his ear as if he were still on the phone.

"Já, já." He spoke loudly. "Nei. Reykjavík. Já. Björk. Takk fyrir. Oh, já." That was pretty much all of Peter's Icelandic.

Staple didn't notice, just took a big slug of coffee. Peter closed in from behind, watching where the other man stepped.

When his right foot landed on a smooth patch of ice, Peter stuck the spike of the hiking pole into the leather back of the man's expensive, slick-soled dress shoe and pushed.

Staple's right foot slid forward on the ice and flew into the air. His arms pinwheeled. He was, for a moment, fully airborne.

He landed first on his left hip, then his elbow and shoulder. He lay there unblinking, trying to process what had happened. Peter tucked the hiking pole under his arm, woke Bjarni's phone, and took a few photos of the man's face.

The shock of the fall faded, replaced with confusion and pain. Staple raised himself onto his elbow. "What the— Who are you?"

Peter put away the phone and pulled off the earflapped hat. "Hello, David."

Recognition dawned. "You?"

"Yep." Peter reached down and yanked open Staple's topcoat, then dropped a heavy knee onto the man's soft chest.

Staple grunted and twisted on the ground, but he couldn't dislodge Peter. "You are in deep trouble. You'll be living in a cardboard box by the time we're done with you."

Interesting that the guy didn't threaten him with federal prison. Peter smiled pleasantly. "'We'? Who's this 'we,' exactly?"

Staple pushed at Peter without effect. Not a physical guy.

Peter slapped him hard across the face. The blow shocked Staple into stillness. Peter tore open the man's suit jacket and searched the pockets. He found a big smartphone, a passport wallet, a State Department ID, and the envelope with Peter's plane ticket. He flipped through the documents. The passport and other ID all gave his name as David Staple.

Peter tucked everything into his safety-yellow coat. "Why do you want me out of Iceland? Who's running you?"

Staple only pressed his lips together. Peter slapped him again. He didn't have a lot of time.

Staple was shaking. Anger, adrenaline. And fear, too. But of Peter, or someone else?

"I could kill you right now," Peter said. "Give me a name."

Staple's shakes got worse. Definitely fear. His voice was hoarse. "He will squash you like an insect."

"Hey." A voice behind him. "Hey!" The embassy guards stood on the sidewalk, not half a block away. They hadn't seen what happened but were responding to the shouting. Still bent over the man, Peter took up his hiking pole and cracked Staple on the temple with the butt of the handle. Staple's eyes fluttered like a geisha's. Peter pressed the man's pink thumb into the phone's button, but it was the wrong kind of phone for that.

"*Já*, I see him," Peter called over his shoulder to the guards, trying to sound like a local with poor English. "He falls on the ice. He does not wear boots."

One man walked toward Peter. "What happened?" He had his coat open and his hand on the butt of his sidearm.

Peter pulled the earflap hat low on his head. "Tourist." He shook his head, disgusted. "You help." He rose and turned back to his truck, grinding Staple's phone into the sidewalk as he did.

He backed out of the parking spot, but instead of driving forward past the embassy, he continued in reverse until he hit an intersection—the simplest way to avoid the embassy cameras.

He didn't want the Defender to become a siren magnet just yet.

PETER parked outside the Litla Guesthouse, an odd little building on a busy corner across from a bus stop. According to the website, it was a European-style hostel for budget-minded travelers, which meant that the bedrooms were private, but the bathrooms were shared, along with a common kitchen. The manager had already emailed him his room number.

The main door opened onto a tiny unheated landing with a narrow stair leading up. The overhead light was out, and the rough-plastered walls reminded him of the concrete construction in Iraq. The static reacted immediately, sparking up his brain stem.

The only way out, he told himself, is through.

The bathrooms were at the top of the stairs. He locked the door, stripped off his clothes, and let the scalding torrent pound his shoulders. If he closed his good eye, he could pretend he was standing under the waterfall in June's little pocket valley.

He wondered what it meant that he didn't want to tell June where he was and what he was doing. But he knew already.

He hadn't called her because he didn't want to lie to her. Because that would be crossing a line. An important one.

Peter lived a life outside the boundaries of society. He worked no regular job. He lived on the dwindling remains of his combat pay. He was afraid, lately, that he could no longer remember the man he'd been before the war. But who had he become?

A man who lived only by the rules he made for himself. Because without them, he was truly an outlaw. Capable of anything.

And lying to June would be breaking the rules.

Under the burning flood, Peter scrubbed until his skin was raw. Then he turned off the water. He was glad the mirror was steamed over and he couldn't see himself more clearly.

The bathroom opened onto a central hallway, bedrooms on three sides, the common kitchen on the fourth. Peter came out in clean pants, a fresh thermal top slung over his shoulder, trying to dry his hair with a towel without reopening the cut on his scalp.

A man with a swimmer's build in an Ohio State sweatshirt and a woman with a plastic spatula in one hand stood in the kitchen doorway. Silver bracelets jangling, the woman rested her other hand on the man's arm. But she was staring at Peter, shirtless and sweating from the steam, eye still swollen shut, bruises turning green on his ribs. "Wow," she said. "What happened to you?"

At the table behind her sat a man with midnight hair and the dark shadow of a beard on his pale face. "The lad was jumped," he said. "Behind a nightclub." The Irish accent was clear. "Do yeh remember me?"

The man who'd picked Peter off the ground and gotten him to his car. "I do. Seamus Heaney, right?"

A smile creased the Irishman's face. "'Tis, indeed, just like the poet. And you're Peter. Come in, let's have a look at yeh."

Peter stepped into the Irishman's searching gaze. "I'm afraid I was rude to you that night," Peter said. "I owe you an apology."

"Nah." Seamus waved it away. "I'm sure I'll do you far worse before we're done. Because tonight, you're buyin' the whiskey. You can tell me how you came to be in that snowy place."

"I'd like that," Peter said, "but I have to go. I've got to get to the Eastfjords, and I'm trying to beat the storm."

"I'm about done with Reykjavík myself," the Irishman said. "Would you care for company on the Ring Road? I've got a good vehicle. Be safer in this weather if we made a convoy."

Ohio State looked at the girl with the bracelets. "Actually, we were thinking of leaving ourselves. What good is coming all the way to Iceland if we never leave Reykjavík?"

Peter wasn't going to endanger anyone else. Plus, he didn't want to have to explain himself. "Sorry. I've got to meet somebody. I'm already packed."

The Irishman nodded. "See you down the road, then." But he wasn't done. "Listen, boyo, yeh might want to get some antibiotics on that." He tipped a knuckle at Peter's swollen eye. "Don't want to get yourself an infection."

The first flakes of snow hit Peter's windshield as he pulled onto the highway out of town.

Chapter 8

Twelve Months Earlier

It's AFTER THREE in the morning when Erik spoons coffee into the filter, turns on the machine, and waits for the familiar gurgle. Their third pot since midnight.

Sarah sits at the dining room table with her laptop, her fingers flying across the keyboard like a concert pianist's. She is finalizing the configuration of a mirror server at a cloud farm in Iceland. They both know that the physical location of the hardware is irrelevant, yet Erik is comforted by the connection, however tenuous, to his family.

The mirror server will be a secret, remote, real-time copy of the Prince's server, including the hidden drive, with all the data intact. The mirror server will also track all changes across the original system and keep a copy of all files. Even hidden, deleted files. The mirror server will be invisible, Sarah swears.

Erik is still unsure whether they're doing the right thing.

He slides Sarah's second laptop toward him. It, too, is invisible, untraceable, layered with multiple security protocols. He clicks the drive icon.

A row of folders appears. They are named GOVERNMENT, INDUSTRY, OPERATIONS, and PROJECT.

He opens the GOVERNMENT folder and finds a long row of video files, recognizing most of the names.

The files are in chronological order. He clicks on the newest.

It's a wide-angle video of a doughy man standing in a hotel room. He picks up a leather overnight bag and upends it over the bed. Bundles of banknotes tumble out. He looks in the direction of the lens, annoyed. "What do I look like, a city councilman? You want your issue to come up before my committee, I need to see six figures. And put it in a numbered account like a professional." He pushes past the camera. "We're done here."

The man is a member of the House of Representatives. He is a senior member of the Committee on Armed Services.

Erik navigates to the OPERATIONS folder. He clicks on the most recent file.

The video starts. Another hotel room, as seen from a fish-eye lens somewhere high in a corner. Four men stand around the bed. "It'll be the easiest thing in the world," says a small man with his back to the camera. Erik spent a year at Oxford, and he knows an Irishman when he hears one.

A man with a shaved head and a heavy beard speaks. "Easy enough for the man staying on dry land." Also Irish, Erik thinks. "Where do we get the goods?"

"If hard men like yourselves can't find high explosives somewhere between Miami and Maracaibo, I've got the wrong lads for the job." The small man lifts an athletic bag and drops it on the bed. "Operating expenses and a plan of the vessel. The first half of your fee will be wired tonight. Are we agreed?"

"Aye," says the man with the heavy beard.

The other two men nod. "Aye," they say.

Erik feels a hole in his stomach that has nothing to do with the amount of coffee he has drunk. "This is bad," he says.

Sarah doesn't look at him. "I know." Her hands keep moving.

"Sarah." He puts a hand on her keyboard to still her fingers. She finally looks at him. He can't read her expression. He says, "What about us? I'm scared."

"Me too." She moves his hand away. "I'm almost done."

Present Day

PETER drove alone across a white treeless plain punctuated by dark rocks. The wind gusted unexpectedly, a drunken giant shoving the Defender from its lane. The snow was up to his wheel hubs. The sun was a distant memory.

Highway One was called the Ring Road because it circum-navigated the island. If he drove far enough around its fourteen-hundred-kilometer length, he'd end up back where he started.

The only other traffic was the occasional tractor trailer running fast toward the safety of Reykjavík. When they passed, the heavy Land Rover shuddered like a toy. Peter kept both hands on the wheel.

The coming storm had both complicated and simplified his plans. Before he left Reykjavík, he'd pulled up Iceland's weather website—www.weather.is—on Bjarni's phone, trying to decide which direction to drive. Hjálmar had told Peter that the most likely places to find Erik and Óskar were the farm and the fishing boat. The farm was on a peninsula jutting out into the Greenland Sea, about three hundred kilometers north of Reykjavík, but the weather website showed the north road closed by snow in five places. Peter didn't want to get stuck.

Seydisfjordur, where the fishing boat docked, was seven hun-dred kilometers to the east, and the road was still clear, even if the weather map showed the rising storm as a giant white spiral howl-ing in from that direction.

Hjálmar had no reason to think Peter was dumb enough to run into the teeth of an arctic hurricane. He'd figure Peter was hun-kered down in Reykjavík. He certainly wouldn't mobilize officers during a storm with no good cause. Or so Peter hoped.

Bjarni, on the other hand, was dumb enough to come after him. In that brown Škoda. With one good arm.

Peter liked the fishing boat as his first stop because the Norwe-gian had been run off the road after visiting there. Besides, if Peter didn't find Erik and Óskar in Seydisfjordur, he could keep driving the Ring Road and approach the farm from the opposite direction.

It was six at night when he left Reykjavík. He hoped to get to the fishing dock by six the next morning.

THREE and a half hours and 180 kilometers later, he stopped outside the town of Vik, his last guaranteed chance for gas until Höfn, almost 300 kilometers away. The roads weren't recently plowed, but the fat-tired Defender was making reasonable time.

Peter parked at the pump with the windshield facing into the gale. The sound of the wind against the skin of the truck was a low, eerie song played on a strange instrument. As he got out, the wind tore the door from his grasp and slammed it shut. The flying snow felt like bird shot on his exposed face and hands.

While the thirsty Defender guzzled, he fired up his new Icelandic phone to check the roads. The route north to the farm was still closed, and the route east to the uncles' fishing dock in Seydisfjordur was still open. So far, the weather wasn't too bad by northern Wisconsin standards.

Then he checked the forecast and saw that the giant white storm spiral had slowed offshore. It hadn't even made landfall yet. Maybe Peter wasn't giving Icelandic weather enough credit.

When the Defender had drunk an entire gas card, he climbed back in the truck and found the Norwegian investigator's number in Catherine Price's papers. The time was an hour later in Oslo. He wondered if the Norwegian was the type to keep his phone on after work.

"*Halló*, Kristjan Holm."

"Mr. Holm, my name is Peter Ash. Can we speak English?"

"It's very late. What do you want?" Holm's voice was thin and reedy, his accent faintly British, his irritation clear.

"I'm working for Catherine Price. Looking for her grandson, Óskar, in Iceland. Do you remember the case?"

Kristjan Holm didn't say anything for a moment. Peter heard a mechanical clatter in the background.

"Yes." Then Peter heard the flare of a match and an intake of breath. Holm had just lit a cigarette. "How far have you gotten?"

"Not very," Peter said. "I found Erik's cousin Bjarni. I'm on my way to Seydisfjordur to talk with Erik's uncles."

The Norwegian took an impossibly long draw on his cigarette. "How many people do you have?"

"Just me," Peter said.

Holm gave a chopping laugh. "Did you not read my report? Are you this unintelligent? Or perhaps you simply like pain."

"Bjarni told me Erik and Óskar were dead."

Silence for a moment. Maybe he was blowing smoke rings. Then, "Do you believe him?"

"The police have been looking for a year. It might explain why they can't find them. What do you think?"

"If you are asking if they are good policemen, I would say yes. You have met Hjálmar? The other police I have met are like him. Very professional."

"Hjálmar thinks the best places to look are the fishing boat and the farm."

"There are more places to hide than the police might consider. If you look, you will see many abandoned farm buildings still holding back most of the weather. The police don't have the manpower to search every broken-down farmhouse or caravan."

"Neither do I," Peter said. "So if Erik and Óskar are alive, the farm and the boat are my best bets. But if they're dead, who'd have killed them?" Peter heard the mechanical clatter again.

Holm said, "Normally I would think the family. But every member of Erik's family defended him to me, denied that he was involved with his wife's death. So maybe it wasn't the family."

"Or maybe you didn't talk to the right person."

"Correct. Maybe it was Erik's uncles. He brought the police to their doorstep. Hjálmar believes they are smugglers, by the way. Maybe that's why they came after me, too."

"Or maybe it wasn't the family," Peter said. He told the Norwegian about David Staple from the State Department, trying to keep Peter out of the country, and Bjarni's claims of two men looking for Erik. "Maybe it was someone else. That would change things."

"Yes. It would mean that Erik didn't kill Sarah."

"I talked to Phil Moore, the Washington, D.C., detective," Peter said. "He's convinced Erik killed her. Although he couldn't give me any kind of motive for the murder."

"Detective Moore only thinks about his retirement," Holm said. "You have to find Erik. Maybe he's dead, maybe he's alive. But if you find Erik, you'll find the boy."

"Do you think they're still alive?"

"I hope so," Holm said. "Besides, if they are dead, why would someone want you out of Iceland?"

"Good point." It was helpful, talking to the Norwegian about this. Better than just bouncing ideas around in his own head. "Listen, why don't you join me here? You must want to hit back after they ran you off the road like that."

"You have no idea what these people are like."

"I'm learning," Peter said. "But you've already met them. I could use the help. How long would it take you to get here?"

"Most of my work is on the computer," Holm said. "Background checks, security interviews. After what happened in Iceland, I'm not leaving my desk again."

"The pay is good," Peter said. "Double your normal fee. Triple if you want." The thought of an actual trained investigator with knowledge of the family was appealing. "Don't you want to get back at these guys? Or have you forgotten about the boy?"

"I haven't forgotten anything." Holm's thin voice was flat. "The auto crash damaged my spinal cord. I'm paralyzed."

That explained the sound. Holm's wheelchair. "I'm so sorry. That must be difficult."

He heard another match flare. "I should feel lucky. I can still use my arms. Anyway, I can't help you."

Peter thought again about Holm's written report and how much information he'd found on the Icelanders. "I have another idea," he said. "Would it be okay if I sent you something? You won't have to go anywhere, just some computer work. Charge me what you like."

Holm sucked in another lungful of smoke. "Do what you wish, but you won't hear from me. I'm done with that family."

Then he hung up.

Peter had already sent himself the picture he'd taken with Bjarni's phone, the close-up of Staple lying on the sidewalk. Now he took pictures of Staple's passport and the plane ticket home. He texted them all to the Norwegian with a note.

This is the man from the State Department who told the police to remove me from Iceland. What can you tell me about him?

Then he sent one last text. *If you don't want to help, I understand. I'm sorry for what happened to you. I'll make them pay.*

HE ARRIVED at the harbor village of Seydisfjordur just after eight in the morning. The sky was still dark, but the snow shone with ambient light. His body ached from the tension of driving through the gusting wind and snow. Still, the roads had remained passable. The worst of the storm had not yet arrived.

Seydisfjordur sat at the innermost point of the fjord, where an empty parking lot waited at the ferry terminal for the weekly boat to Denmark and the Faroe Islands. The houses were painted in bright, cheerful colors. The sheer stone walls of the valley rose around the village and channeled the wind into a steady gale.

Peter found the uncles' address at the edge of the village. A boxy red building crouched midway between the road and the shore, the corrugated metal siding loose and humming in the wind. Behind the unlit building, partly hidden from view, a fishing boat lay against a plain concrete pier. The boat was festooned with lights, and the pier was edged with yellow paint. Safety first.

Peter drove the Defender down a narrow gravel access road and parked in partial concealment between two faded shipping containers, where he could still get a good look at the boat.

She was bigger than Peter had expected. Maybe twenty meters long, she had a high, oceangoing bow followed by a pair of tall crane masts for hauling nets and off-loading fish, then the long working deck with the cargo hold beneath and a rounded two-story superstructure at the stern. On the overhang shielding the curved windows of the wheelhouse, someone had hung a wood plank with *Freyja* painted in bold blue letters.

The *Freyja* was definitely not a new vessel. Her graceful curves spoke of an earlier era, when the vast, capricious power of the ocean was something to be negotiated with rather than overcome by sheer mechanical might.

A slender gangplank with rope rails angled down from the high gunwale to the pier, where a heavy four-door flatbed truck with disintegrating door panels waited beside a newer black Dacia station wagon. Neither vehicle's engine was running, but the snow had been scraped from their windows the night before.

The vehicles and their plates matched what the Norwegian had found registered to Eiríkur's uncles, Ingo and Axel Magnusson.

Peter sat and watched the *Freyja* while his brain cried out for coffee. He ate some bread and cheese and tried not to think about a hot breakfast. The back of his head still throbbed where the vodka bottle had hit him. He touched it with his fingers. Did it seem warm, even a little puffy? He tried not to think about that, either. Instead, he thought about where Erik and Óskar might be.

Bjarni had told Peter that family was everything. If that was true, they'd want what was best for the boy. Which would probably mean getting back to the comfort of family and the familiar routine of school.

The red building certainly didn't look like any kind of home. The wind would blow right through that siding. The boat must have cabins and some heat, but it looked ready to sink at any moment. Either way, this was no place for a child.

Peter's Icelandic phone buzzed. The number began with +47, the country code for Norway. It was Holm.

"Staple is a staff attorney for the American State Department in Washington. So he does not work for the ambassador."

No hello, no good morning. "You've been up all night."

The Norwegian's voice was flat. "I no longer sleep well."

"Me neither," Peter said. "How did you find out about Staple?"

"I have access to six databases of current American government employees. It's public information."

"So it's not the ambassador trying to kick me out of Iceland."

The scrape of a match, the start of a cigarette. "Staple should not be able to do so, either. He is a low-level functionary."

"He didn't act like one," Peter said.

"Perhaps that is an old habit. I found his employment history. When he was twenty-eight, he was an attorney in your White House. After that he was a partner in a multinational law firm. Then he worked for a U.S. senator. Then back to the law firm."

"And now he's a low-level lawyer at the State Department?" This wasn't the typical D.C. revolving door. Something had happened to Staple.

Peter looked out the window at the red shed and the two parked vehicles. "I was thinking about the people that drove you off the road. Did the police ever find them?"

"No. And I couldn't help. I didn't see the driver's face. They could only search for a large silver SUV. The police were certain it would be damaged. They went to repair shops. They spoke with tow drivers. They reviewed insurance claims. They reviewed every silver SUV registered in Iceland. All such cars were accounted for. They found nothing. As if it didn't exist."

"You didn't imagine the car, right?"

A deep inhalation of tar and nicotine, the crackle of burning paper. "Icelanders love their automobiles, and they have many amateur mechanics. It would be possible to get the SUV repaired without reporting the accident."

Peter scratched at his growing beard. "Do you think the police have stopped looking?"

"Perhaps not. They take their work seriously."

"They're not the only ones," Peter said. "I thought you were done with this."

"I told you, I no longer sleep well." The *clink* of a mug on a countertop. "Also, I need the money. But let me ask you a question. When I took the job, I did not know how dangerous Erik's family was. You do. You risk your life for this boy. Why?"

"Somebody should," Peter said. "And I like to be useful."

He didn't mention the dead he saw in his dreams.

On the boat, two men stepped through a door in the lower superstructure.

"I have to go," Peter said. "I'll call you in a few hours."

ON THE *FREYJA*, THE MEN walked to the waist-high rail and down the gangplank, which sagged beneath their weight. They wore dirty orange coats unzipped and flapping in the wind. No gloves or hats, the white stubs of cigarettes poking from their bunched fists. Faces hidden beneath unruly gray beards.

The men in the photo on Bjarni's phone, standing with Eiríkur on a snowy slope somewhere. Ingo and Axel Magnusson. Erik's uncles. Neither one looked much like him.

They looked like NFL linemen. Only bigger.

From the Norwegian's file, Peter knew the uncles were on the far side of middle age, but they were no less powerful for that. Thick-shouldered and barrel-chested, these were men who had done hard physical labor for decades, who thought of getting drenched and frozen and hurt as a normal part of the workday.

Just watching them, Peter found himself shrinking into his seat. Ingo and Axel were going to be a problem.

The enormous uncles somehow managed to shoehorn themselves into the little black Dacia wagon, which settled deep on its springs. Peter watched as it lurched around the corner of the warehouse, strained up the hill, and turned on the road into town. He didn't know how much time he had, but he meant to make the most of it.

Peter left the Defender in a parking lot on the far side of the road, dug a flashlight out of his pack, and walked up the gangplank aboard the *Freyja*, trying to look like he belonged.

The boat's working deck was stacked with empty gray bins. Vicious-looking fish gaffs lay clipped in easy reach below the side rails, varnished handles gleaming in the floodlights. The wind was bitter. The pilothouse windows were bright. Peter undogged a round-cornered hatch and listened at the opening. He heard nothing. He took a deep breath, then stepped inside.

He stood in the ship's galley and common area. Built-in benches flanked a dining table, the wood finish and upholstery reminding Peter of a suburban breakfast nook from the 1970s. Lockers held cans and boxes of easy-to-prepare food. Despite the substantial supply of Reyka vodka, everything was clean and in good repair. The steel stove was polished to a high shine.

Tick tock. Peter ducked down a ladder, static flaring, to a small landing with two doors, one to each side. He opened the left door and saw a wide bunk built into the curved side of the hull, with storage for personal things below and a narrower bunk above, with no mattress. There was just enough space for a grown man to change his clothes. The porthole was the size of a dinner plate.

The cabin to the right was the same, only messier. Both cabins had pictures taped to the bulkheads, tropical beaches and swimsuit models and family snapshots. Very homey. The only things missing were a half-knit sweater and a ship's cat.

Peter opened lockers and held up clothes. Everything was sized for giants, both cabins. No kids' clothes, no LEGOs. No Erik or Óskar. No sign of anyone living aboard except the uncles.

The static climbed Peter's spine. He couldn't hear anything outside the boat. He imagined the uncles climbing out of their clown car, then tried not to think about it. Down a half ladder, he found the engine room, all heavy metal and color-coded paint, but not a spot of rust. Cabinets full of mechanical tools, lockers loaded with spare parts. No pallet on the floor, no sleeping bag.

Tick tock. One last possibility. Moving quickly, he climbed back up the ladders, past the cabins and the galley to the pilothouse. He found a spoked ship's wheel and a sagging leather captain's chair flanked by banks of elderly marine electronics. A chart table with rolled maps in a rack and a built-in bench.

The brass and chrome gleamed. The broad, curving windows looking out over the harbor were clean.

Outside, the black Dacia station wagon rolled down the gravel drive and onto the pier.

Peter didn't like how easily big Uncle Ingo and Uncle Axel unpacked themselves from the small car. They were quicker and more limber than anyone their size had a right to be.

He dropped to his knees and peered under the chart table and pilot's controls. If this were his boat, he'd have a shotgun stashed somewhere. Nothing. He opened drawers looking for a handgun and found nothing but an orange-handled fishing knife in an orange rubber sheath. He shoved it into his back pocket.

He clattered down the ladder and pushed open the hatch just in time to see the uncles step from the gangway to the deck, fresh cigarettes in their fists. They stared at him.

Peter felt like a seal at a polar bear convention.

Up close, the uncles looked very much alike. Their round, wind-worn faces were creased by years of squinting into wind. Their hands were huge, thick from years of cleaning fish. Their stomachs would have the hard kind of fat.

The slightly smaller uncle said something in Icelandic. Peter felt the adrenaline rise in his blood, but he just held his hands up, palms out. "Sorry, I don't speak Icelandic. English?"

"*Já*, I have some English," said the same uncle. He had a voice like an idling bulldozer. He wore a gray hand-knit sweater under his coat and a gold pirate hoop in his left ear. "You are the American. You broke Bjarni's arm."

"Bjarni started that fight," Peter said. "I could have done much worse. You are Ingo and Axel?"

In Icelandic, the one with the gold hoop said something to the other. Peter thought he caught the Icelandic word for "farm."

"I am Ingo." The talker jerked his head at his silent brother. "He is Axel. What do you want?"

"I'm looking for Óskar Eiríksson. I just want to know if the boy's all right. I'd like to see him, to talk with him. Then I'll go."

The uncles looked at each other, then back at Peter. Neither man spoke. Their massive hands flexed restlessly.

"Bjarni told me Erik and Óskar are dead," Peter said. "Is that true?"

Ingo dropped his cigarette to the deck and stepped on it. Axel rolled his shoulders like a boxer between rounds.

Peter said, "If something happened to Erik or Óskar, it had nothing to do with me. Has anyone else talked with you?"

Ingo's lips twitched in the tiniest of smiles.

"So many questions, Mr. American. But I have a question for you." The smile grew wider. "Can you swim?"

Behind him, Axel gave a rhythmic grunt. Peter realized the bigger brother was laughing.

Axel stepped left to block the gangplank, still holding his cigarette.

Ingo stepped right and slipped a two-foot fish gaff from its clips under the rail. The sharp steel tip shone bright under the floodlights. Two on one was always hard, but these two would be harder.

Peter's open coat flapped in the wind. He still had the orange-handled fishing knife in his back pocket, but he'd have to get inside their reach to use it. If they didn't smash him down first.

For men of their size, the uncles were impossibly fast. Even as Peter reached for the knife, Ingo stepped into Peter's blind spot and caught the windblown open front of the safety-yellow coat. Peter spun backward and counterclockwise to slip his grip, but Axel was already there to meet him. He caught Peter's lower sleeve in one thick fist and held him.

Peter didn't wait for the other fist. His back now to both brothers, Peter raised his open arms in a gesture of surrender. But before they could improve their grasp, he dropped to his knees and slid his arms from the slick sleeves of the coat. Then he angled right, took three fast steps, planted a firm hand on the cold steel rail, and vaulted over the top and into thin air.

It was a long drop, eight feet or more. Off-balance, Peter landed hard on the snowy dock but managed to push his momentum into an ugly forward roll. Still, he hadn't hit his head or sprained his ankle, so he called it a win and popped to his feet.

On the *Freyja*, the big Icelanders stared at him over the rail. They were too big to jump. Instead, they boiled toward the gangplank, shouting as they came.

Peter turned and ran.

The black Dacia and the four-door flatbed were parked at odd angles on the dock, nose in toward the gangplank. The Dacia was closer, and the driver's side would give him some cover. Running, he put his hand to his back pocket, pulled out the orange-handled knife, and cut into the soft sidewall of the Dacia's front tire. He was rewarded with a quick blast of air as the tire went flat. Without slowing, he did the same at the back wheel. Nobody carries two spares.

He heard the uncles bellowing over the sound of the wind. They were behind him somewhere, probably on the dock by now.

Staying low, he ducked across the gap to the flatbed and jabbed the knife into a truck tire. The blade wouldn't go through the side-wall. The thick rubber was hard with age.

Axel ran past the front of the truck, saw Peter, but skidded on the too slick snow, which gave Peter a few extra seconds. Pushing harder, he wiggled the blade back and forth and finally heard a hiss. The tire wasn't flat yet, but it would be.

He reversed away and around the back of the flatbed. He jammed the knife into the next tire, got it in far enough to stick, then stepped down on the end of the grip. The tire began to hiss.

Ingo came around the rear of the truck, and Axel came around the front. The gaff hung negligently from Ingo's hand. Peter tried to pull out the knife, but it was stuck.

The storm was loud in his ears, and the snowfall had accelerated again. Without the good yellow coat, Peter's fleece was heavy with moisture. Ingo and Axel came closer. Peter stepped on the flat of the knife handle, hoping to free it. The hiss turned to a soft *pop*, and the tire sank, but the blade snapped at the hilt.

When they saw the blade break, Ingo and Axel ran at him, one from each side, tilting forward in their rush. Peter dropped flat to the slippery snow, and the fishermen's thick torsos crashed to-gether. Before they could grab hold of him, he pushed off the dead tire with his legs and squirted out onto the dock.

Then he was off, legs sprinting strong across the pier and onto the uphill drive. When he made the top of the rise, he glanced over his shoulder without stopping. Ingo and Axel were coming hard, the gaff still in Ingo's fist, but Peter was a runner, and the uncles were smokers, and he was thirty meters ahead.

He ran across the road and up the low hill to the Defender, keys already in his hand. Thankfully they'd been in his pants, with his wallet and phone, and not in his coat.

The Defender started without a hiccup. He threw it in gear and bounced down the snow-slick slope, slewing sideways onto the road just as the uncles made it, breathing hard, to the top of the drive. Ingo threw the gaff overhand, and it hit the passenger side with a thump. Peter put the hammer down.

He had a moment of panic as the four tires spun. Then rubber grabbed the road, and he shot forward into the worsening weather. Man, he was going to miss that coat.

PETER fled up the high-walled river valley. The wind dropped heavy new snow into the road, narrowing the two-lane to a single track. There were no other tire marks. The Defender slewed sideways on the curves and wouldn't go faster than eighty kilometers per hour. It had also developed a new and unpleasant rattle.

When he reached the top of the valley, he stopped the truck and walked around to the passenger side, where the rattle came from. He found the gaff's hook caught in the door hinge, the bright steel still vibrating. He worked it free and threw it into the truck, then looked behind him, his swollen eye throbbing in the cold. The sun had come up behind the clouds, and Peter could finally see farther than the limits of his own headlights.

Another vehicle was halfway up, a white plume in its wake. It was too far to see the kind of car, and he didn't want to take time to dig out his binoculars, but it could have been a silver SUV. Maybe the same one they'd used to force the Norwegian off the road the year before. Maybe hidden in a barn for a year, waiting until it was needed again.

Peter wasn't going to wait around to get a closer look. Without any weapon more serious than the fish gaff or Bjarni's folding shovel, direct confrontation was out of the question. For now, he could only outrun them.

He thought about what Ingo had said to Axel on the boat and the little bit of Icelandic Peter thought he'd understood. The word "farm." With little else to go on, Peter decided that single word meant that Óskar was at the farm. He had four hundred kilometers to figure out the rest of it.

He pushed the Defender hard back toward Egilsstadir, watching in his rearview as the other vehicle faded ghostlike into the snowy distance. In town, he estimated his lead at fifteen minutes, then burned three of those minutes when he stopped to top off his tank. While the pump ticked off the liters, he took the tinfoil off his American cell and waited for it to find the network. He didn't know how much longer he'd have service.

His phone showed six texts. The first five were all from Commissioner Hjálmar, with time stamps going back sixteen hours. The tone was polite but increasingly insistent.

Mr. Ash was accused of assaulting an American citizen and government employee, which was a serious offense. He should contact Hjálmar immediately to tell his side of the story.

Mr. Ash would be late for his flight to America.

Mr. Ash had missed his flight.

Mr. Ash was out in the largest storm in twenty years. Hjálmar was concerned for his well-being.

Mr. Ash had not responded to any messages. He should contact Hjálmar immediately.

The man was relentless. In fact, Peter was counting on it.

He texted back. *Sorry I missed our lunch, but your country is too beautiful to leave. I'll buy you dinner when I get back to Reykjavík.* He didn't mention that he was going the long way around.

With that message, he hoped the commissioner's tech people would learn his nearest cell tower and get Peter's rough location. He didn't want Hjálmar entirely in the dark. He was going to need the police to get Óskar free from Erik's family.

Peter glanced at the road. No sign of the silver SUV.

He opened the last text, from an unknown number. *This is Jerry Brunelli. You're looking for my grandson, Óskar. We need to talk. I'll meet you at the Hotel Borg in Reykjavík at four p.m. local time tomorrow.*

Catherine Price's husband was coming to Iceland?

Peter replied, *On the other side of the country, can't get back. Please call.*

Brunelli responded immediately. *Too sensitive for phone. The restaurant at the Hotel Kea in Akureyri, seven p.m. tomorrow.*

Brunelli was flexing his muscles. Peter had no idea why, but he hoped the man had found something. Akureyri was the second largest city in Iceland, about three hundred kilometers away, and Peter had to pass through it on the way to the farm.

He'd planned to stop anyway. He needed to pick up a good coat, along with a few other things. He texted back: *See you then.*

He wondered about Brunelli's motives. What had he found that he needed to talk about in person? Or had Hjálmar asked him to set the meeting? Was Brunelli even coming to Iceland?

It occurred to Peter that he didn't know enough about Jerry Brunelli.

BACK on the Ring Road and headed north through deepening snow, Peter called the Norwegian, who sounded almost cheerful.

"*Halló.* I have made no progress. Only breakfast."

"Norwegian pancakes?" A staple of Peter's Wisconsin childhood, served with powdered sugar and jam. He was hungry.

"French breakfast. Coffee and a cigarette."

"You're a gourmet. I have another request. Would you take a quick look into Jerry Brunelli, Catherine Price's husband?"

A short, rasping laugh. "A quick look is all that is possible. I tried last year, when my legs still worked. I found very little."

"He runs a political consulting business. There must be some public information, disclosure requirements, that kind of thing. He worked with Catherine's first husband, right?"

"Perhaps you know more than I do. His online presence is minimal. The company's website is very small, just a few paragraphs of text. Not even a photo. Why do you want to know?"

"Catherine said he had connections. He's coming to Iceland and wants to meet in person. It makes me wonder what his connections are." Although now Peter was wondering why a political consultant would want a low profile. Wasn't visibility one of the metrics of success in politics?

"I'll look deeper," Holm said.

After Peter turned off the phone, he rewrapped it in foil, then checked the rearview mirror again. He hadn't seen another car since he'd left town.

The silver SUV could still be back there, the driver biding his time. Peter wouldn't be hard to follow from a distance, with his tire tracks the only man-made marks on this snow-covered highway. It didn't take a genius to figure out where he was headed.

He was more worried about Ingo and Axel than he was about the weather. So far, Peter wasn't terribly impressed by what Icelanders considered to be a big storm. Sure, they had some pretty good wind, but Peter had grown up on the shore of Lake Superior, where winter came early and hit hard.

But an hour into his drive, he began to see what an Icelandic blizzard was all about. The snow came in wind-blown clouds that made it hard to see. Where the road ran across open sections, it was often scraped clean by the gale. In those sections, slick black ice was indistinguishable from pavement. More than once he found himself turning a slow pirouette on the road. Still, the Defender was capable as hell. Peter had plenty of gas. There were no head-lights behind him. He was slow, but the uncles, if they were still behind him, were slower. He drove on.

After three hours' driving, the storm had become unlike any-thing Peter had ever experienced. The wind rattled the wipers, and the defroster was losing the battle with the ice.

He came to a turnoff leading to a small picnic area. This wasn't exactly picnic weather, but a snowplow had cleared the drifts, so the turnoff was passable. Peter needed to put some food in his belly, maybe close his eyes for a few hours. If the plow driver had managed to turn around and get back to the road, Peter figured he could do the same. The dashboard clock read 13:27.

The parking lot sloped gently downhill and away from the access road. Peter pulled around in a slow circle and parked at the highest, flattest spot with a straight path back to the highway. The wind came from the same direction, so he didn't need to worry about his door getting bent back. He left the engine running. Before get-ting out, he made sure every door was unlocked. It would be pretty stupid to get stuck outside in this weather.

When he tried to open the door, the force of the storm pushed back like something alive. He shifted his center of gravity, put his shoulder to the metal, and stepped outside. The wind blew the door shut and pushed him toward the rear of the truck. He caught himself with a hand on the roof rack and looked down. The park-ing lot was covered with black ice.

This was not a good place to stop. He wrestled the driver's door open and hopped inside. That shift of weight, along with a blast of wind, was enough to start the truck moving. Sliding backward, an inch at a time, down the modest slope and away from the highway.

The weight of the vehicle created a thin layer of melt, which acted as a lubricant under the tires. The truck was dead weight on four rubber ice skates. With a slow, stately grace, it began to pick up speed. Peter watched through the window as the Defender approached the downhill edge of the parking lot. Soon, he thought, the tires would hit snow or exposed gravel and the truck would lurch to a stop.

But the Defender slid faster. Peter peered out. The dark ice extended onto the rough shoulder without losing any slickness. Beyond that was an equally smooth transition to a steeper slope that dropped twenty meters down to an empty snowfield below.

The shoulder got closer. The wind rose to a prolonged howl.

Outside the window, the world turned white.

The truck slid down the long embankment and into the deep, drifting snow.

Chapter 9

Twelve Months Earlier

THE EASTERN HORIZON GLEAMS crimson through the living room windows. Neither Erik nor Sarah has been to bed.

While Sarah sits at the dining table and reverses course through the Prince's system, erasing the evidence of her work as she goes, Erik roams the house until Óskar's footsteps thump overhead. He thunders down the stairs in his Batman pajamas and announces that he is starving. "Like, to death, Dad."

Erik leaves Sarah at her laptop and makes breakfast. He finds a temporary calm in the simplicity of feeding a hungry boy.

Sarah's fingers dance across the keyboard. Across from her, Óskar licks the wreckage of eggs and sausage from his plate.

"Óskar," she says.

He looks up at her. "Mom. It's the best tool for the job."

She smiles too brightly. "I know, honey. Hey, can you do something for me? I need you to take a picture of these." She walks around to slide the laptop in front of him.

Erik comes from the kitchen to look over her shoulder. Her screen shows the URL for the hidden drive on the mirror server, a web address almost two lines long.

"Click," Óskar says. "Got it."

Sarah opens a new window. This one shows a sixteen-by-sixteen grid of three-digit numbers. The server's access code.

"Is this a good idea?" Erik says. To involve Óskar, he means.

"You wanted security," Sarah says. "If we keep no electronic or physical copy of the passcode, it prevents any kind of side-channel attack. Without it, 256-bit encryption is essentially unbreakable. The mirror server data will remain intact even if they physically destroy their own server."

"It's okay, Dad." Óskar glances at the grid of numbers, then turns to look at his parents, one by one. "This is a secret, right?"

Erik feels the breath go out of him right then.

"Yes, honey," Sarah says. "It's a big secret."

"Then I'll put it with pi," Óskar says. "I already had four thousand." He turns back to the screen. "Click. Now I have more."

While the pit in Erik's stomach turns into a black hole, he fills two travel mugs with coffee, then loads Óskar's lunch in his LEGO backpack while Óskar gets dressed and brushes his teeth. Sarah fusses with her laptop for a few more minutes, erasing the night's work, then changes into a fresh work outfit.

At the door, she says, "It won't look right if I don't show up."

"Call me afterward," Erik says. "I want to know you're okay."

Sarah nods and heads for her car.

In two hours, someone will shoot her three times in the head.

Present Day

THE Defender landed almost softly, with its nose pointed uphill. The wheels turned slowly on the slick slope, and the boxy rear end was jammed firmly in the high drifted snow.

Peter put the truck in neutral and climbed out his door and up to the roof rack, where he unstrapped the burly snow shovel and jumped off the back and into the bottomless drift. Up to his waist in the snow by the rear bumper, the big truck looming over him, he began to dig. Without the protection of the safety-yellow coat, he wore only a thick fleece top that was anything but waterproof.

He attacked with the shovel, but the blade was too wide for this thick, dense drift. He tried to take small bites, but it was taking too long. Trying to take a bigger bite, he felt the telltale crack through his gloves as he overleveraged the fiberglass handle. Damn. He climbed back into the Defender to grab the folding shovel he'd taken from Bjarni.

When he climbed out, the wind's wild, unearthly cry was like a screaming choir of demon sopranos who couldn't carry a tune.

He jumped into the hole and began to dig again, working to clear the drift from under the car and behind it. He quickly realized that, while the folding shovel was tough enough to take any punishment he could dish out, he wasn't making much progress. The blade was barely larger than Peter's cupped hands, and fresh snow blew into the hole almost as fast as he could take it out.

Breathing hard, he leaned against the drift and watched the hole he'd made fill again. He had enough food and gas to stay fed and warm for a few days. Eventually a plow driver would pass through and either stop to help or call one of Iceland's famous rescue crews.

He jammed the blade of the broken shovel into the snow to act as a windbreak for the exhaust, then climbed the icy slope to the driver's seat, where he turned the heat up as high as it would go. He stripped off his wet things and hung them over the passenger seat to dry. Shivering in the cold, he pulled on fresh long underwear and laid out his sleeping bag in the tilted back. He wouldn't be comfortable, but he'd survive. The storm couldn't last forever.

The wind was so loud it was like standing inside a cymbal's crash. The only thing he could see outside was swirling snow. He might as well be locked in a small white room. The static rose, sending sparks up his brain stem.

He cracked a window but felt the temperature plummet and rolled it back up. The static rose higher.

Screw it. He riffled through his groceries and found the small bottle of Reyka vodka he'd bought. He cracked the seal and washed down four Valium from his dwindling stash.

Only four pills left.

He needed sleep without dreams—that's all he wanted.

HE WOKE shivering in the early morning, aware of some change in his environment. It took him a moment to realize that the world outside was silent.

The wind had died. The sun was nowhere in sight, but the night was bright. The clouds had washed away, and a billion glittering stars shone in the sky. On the other side of the windshield, a shimmering green curtain stretched across the northern horizon.

He pulled on clothes and boots, checked the gas gauge, and climbed out into the still, frozen night. The air was crystalline. The milky spray of stars and the electric waves of the northern lights felt close enough to touch. Low, dark mountains made a jagged line against the sky like torn edges of the world. As if this small, high place had somehow ripped away from everything solid to rise into the sky and float through the universe.

It was profoundly cold. Peter's nostrils froze shut with each inhalation of breath. His eyeballs hurt, leaking tears that turned to ice on his lashes. Every bit of exposed skin felt scraped raw.

He had to get out of this place.

Back in the tilted truck, he stuffed himself with bread and cheese and chocolate while he ransacked the car for the warmest clothes he could find. No coat worth a damn, but yesterday's fleece had dried. He layered up like a polar explorer. When he pulled on his hat, he felt a wet spot on the back of his head.

He touched it with his fingers. The wounded skin was spongy and weeping, definitely infected. He needed antibiotics. No wonder his head hurt.

He climbed back outside, filled his gas tank from the cans on the roof, and began to dig.

He made it down to solid ground to set the jack and stabilize the truck, then started excavating the rear tires. He laid the sand ladders behind them and reversed the truck six feet to the edges of the ladders while the front tires sank into the snow. Then he jacked up the rear bumper and moved the ladders and did it again. And again. Six feet at a time. He'd managed to move the truck forty-two feet, maybe a hundred more to go, when he heard the sound of a diesel engine on the road at his back.

He climbed up the drift to look, hoping for the snowplow.

Instead he saw a pale SUV, slowing to a stop on the highway. Was it silver? It looked like the Mitsubishi he'd rented and abandoned in Reykjavík. It came from the southeast, just like Peter.

He took the fish gaff from the back of the Defender and waited.

The SUV door opened. A figure got out and looked at Peter.

Then he gave a big wave. He wore a puffy white coat with a fur-trimmed hood that hid his face. Avoiding the skating rink pretending to be a parking lot, the figure walked nimbly down the embankment. As he came closer, he threw back the hood.

It was Seamus, the Irishman, his black hair and unshaved face dark against the clean, bright snow. He nodded at the fish gaff in Peter's hand. "Are yeh catching any?"

Peter stepped forward to shake his hand. "Not a damn thing."

THE Irishman was good in the snow. He drove his pale rental SUV another quarter mile down the highway until he found a place where the embankment was slightly less steep. He angled down the crusted verge, slowly but in total control. On the wind-scraped plain below, he navigated the scattered rocks and uneven ground to the deep drift where the Defender sat idling.

After that, it was a simple matter to hook the Mitsubishi's winch cable to a tow hook bolted to the Land Rover's bumper. With the winch, it didn't take long to haul Peter's truck out of the drift. They made it up the embankment and stopped on the road.

Seamus stepped out into the cold. Peter did the same, looking over his shoulder at the highway. He'd lost sixteen hours to that snowdrift. The wind had scoured the pavement clean.

Despite the temperature, Seamus stood with his puffy white coat unzipped, showing the black sweater and jeans beneath.

"Where'd you learn to drive like that?" Peter said. "You don't get this kind of snow in Ireland."

"I've been all over. You pick up a few things along the way."

Peter was tempted to pull out his stove and make coffee, but he didn't want to linger. "That storm's not done. Let's keep moving."

"Agreed." Seamus climbed back into his SUV and roared off.

Closing the distance, Peter saw the Mitsubishi's license plates.

They were from Great Britain, not Iceland. Which meant the Irishman's milk-white SUV wasn't a rental after all.

THE sun rose low in the light blue sky as they dropped down from the high plateau. Ahead and behind, the cliffs stood caked in wind-sculpted white. Seamus drove more slowly than Peter would have liked, but Peter didn't mind keeping the Mitsubishi where he could see it. By early afternoon, they'd curved north around Mývatn Lake, shining like a tarnished silver plate.

The Mitsubishi looked strange through Peter's windshield, and he couldn't figure out why. For some reason, it reminded him of a three-legged dog the platoon had briefly adopted at a combat outpost along the Pakistani border. The dog had run with its hips slightly out of line with its shoulders, as if whatever event had taken its back leg had also somehow bent the entire animal at a slight angle only detectable at speed.

The sun was long gone by the time they saw Akureyri, Iceland's second largest city, climbing the hills across the dark fjord. After three days in the wilderness, the bright-windowed buildings seemed like something out of a dream. It was midafternoon, but it felt like midnight.

At the end of a long causeway where the river drained into the sea, they came to an N1 station with a few cars filling up before the storm returned. Peter tapped his horn and flashed his lights. Seamus turned off the road and stopped at an open pump. Peter looped around to the far side of the island. Diesel gurgled through the hoses, its fumes sweet in the cold air.

Peter looked across the pumps at the Mitsubishi. He still couldn't figure out what was strange about it. It looked normal enough from the side. Seamus had his door open, head down, collecting food wrappers and crushed coffee cups for the trash. Peter walked around for a better view.

The Mitsubishi wasn't a camper conversion like the one Peter had rented, just a regular SUV. He glanced down at the front passenger tire. It was worn unevenly, the tread almost gone on the outer edge. Which meant the front end was out of alignment. Which might be why the vehicle looked off, the front end rolling slightly out of line from the back. Like a three-legged dog.

He ran his hand along the passenger-side fender. Instead of a smooth, clean curve, he felt the telltale ripples of a hurried repair.

Peter looked closer at the milk-white paint. It wasn't opaque but translucent. A cheap spray job, not a factory finish. Along the inside of the open door, he could see the original color. Silver.

On the driver's side, Seamus straightened up with his hands full and saw Peter standing there. "I believe we're due a meal, lad. I'm thinking whiskey and red meat."

"Sounds perfect." Peter walked toward him. "I have to run a few errands and meet a guy at seven. How about eight o'clock?"

"Another meeting?" The Irishman looked at him. "I'm starting to believe you're not truly on holiday."

"What makes you say that?"

"The beating you took, a real tourist would have gone to the clinic," Seamus said. "Instead you braved a hurricane to make your meeting in Seydisfjordur and again to get here. Also, you've changed cars. But I can't tell if you're the fox or the hound."

"I'm a little confused myself." Peter took out his Icelandic phone and thumbed open the camera app. "Listen, you really saved me, digging me out of the snow. How about a selfie?" He went to sling an arm around the Irishman, thumb already on the button.

"Lord, no." Seamus knocked the phone down and almost out of Peter's grasp. The Irishman had extremely fast hands. "I'm old-fashioned. Graven images and all that. No offense."

"None taken." Peter turned off the camera and tucked his phone away. "For the record, I wasn't trying to steal your soul."

The Irishman's smile was bright, but his eyes were dark. "I've no soul left to steal, boyo. I was ten years a copper, a black bastard from Belfast. I've seen things a man can't unsee."

Peter heard the whine of an airplane engine coming from the north and glanced up at a small turboprop. Then he caught movement in the corner of his eye and turned to the road.

Two cars appeared under the lights of the causeway, headed into Akureyri. A black Dacia, followed by a brown Škoda.

HE MADE a plan to meet Seamus for dinner, then set off toward town, hoping he didn't see anyone he knew, not until he was ready. The streets were full of cars, a busy shopping day before Christmas. Peter realized he didn't even know what day it was.

He turned off the sea road into a long municipal parking lot, where he passed an unoccupied police Volvo. He angled into the next row of spots, and there they were, the black Dacia Duster and the brown Škoda, side by side. Also empty. No Bjarni, no Ingo, no Axel. No cops. They were all in town, on foot.

He drove out of the lot and past the Hotel Kea, where he was supposed to meet Jerry Brunelli at seven, then up a long curving hill to a tall gray modernist church overlooking the city. He left the Defender on the far side of the church's parking lot, snug between a minibus and a rusty Ford F-350.

He wasn't hiding, he told himself. He was being strategic.

Peter didn't want the police to find the Defender. He'd need it for a few more days at least. He was still waiting for Kristjan Holm's report on Brunelli.

But he had another question for the investigator. He found the stealth video he'd shot while attempting to set up the selfie with Seamus. Most of it was useless, but somewhere between sky and pavement, he'd managed a quick, clear capture of the man's face.

He isolated the image and sent it to the Norwegian, along with the Mitsubishi's license plate number. *Who is this guy? Says his name is Seamus Heaney. Irish? Police?*

Then he pulled his fleece hat down low, grabbed his day pack, and walked to the edge of the church parking lot, where a wide pedestrian stair dropped down the hill.

At the bottom of the steps, the beige bulk of the Hotel Kea stood across from a street that had been narrowed to one lane as a kind of pedestrian mall. He slipped through the crowd, his eye peeled for Bjarni and the uncles. A thin, cold rain began to fall.

Head on a swivel, he went shopping. First he bought a new orange-handled fishing knife because he felt naked without some kind of weapon. Then he went to a 66°North store, where he found a waterproof coat and winter bibs that had been designed, according to the serious young salesman, for the Iceland rescue teams.

As he paid, he looked up at a pair of vintage steam-bent snowshoes hung on the wall as decoration. The wood frames, rawhide webbing, and leather bindings looked in decent shape. He pointed and tried to look rich and stupid. "How much for those?"

It took a great deal of Catherine Price's cash, but Peter left the store wearing his new coat with the bibs in a shopping bag and the big snowshoes tucked under his arm.

Watching for familiar faces and safely camouflaged among the tourists in his spotless, high-end outerwear, he realized he still had an hour to kill before his meeting with Brunelli. He walked until he found a *bakarí* with a row of damp tables under an awning. Inside, waiting to order, he glanced at the television.

He saw Commissioner Hjálmar being interviewed in front of a shiny building. The date was noted in the bottom corner of the screen, indicating the footage was from the day before. The day after Peter had left Reykjavík. The sound was off.

The video changed to uniformed police on a city street. Beyond them, a glimpse of what could only be a body covered with a plastic sheet. The snow was dark red around it.

The screen changed again, this time to a photograph of a man's face, probably from a passport. A passport Peter had taken from the man and stashed in the glove box of the Defender.

On the crawl, David Staple's name.

Next came Peter's own passport photo. His name on the crawl.

Peter didn't need to speak Icelandic to know the news. Staple was dead, and the police thought Peter had killed him.

He looked around. People were talking and eating. Nobody was watching the television.

In Peter's passport photo, he was clean-shaven and impossibly young. Now his face looked like a punching bag, and his unshaved scruff was dark and rough.

He got back in line and ordered two large cappuccinos. When his coffees came, he carried them outside to a chair under an awning and sat with his back to the shop window and his hood pulled low and his good eye on the street. Hiding in plain sight.

He took out his phone and found an English-language Icelandic news site. Staple's murder popped up as the lead story. It was a huge deal, the nation's first murder in three years. The police believed Staple, an American tourist, was killed with a knife, stabbed from behind. He was found stuffed under his car almost twenty-four hours after Peter mugged him outside the embassy.

Someone had asked Staple—had almost certainly paid him—to keep Peter out of Iceland. Why kill him now?

To shut him up, Peter assumed. Unless they'd killed him to throw suspicion on Peter, to give the police a more urgent reason to find him and put him out of commission.

It didn't matter. What mattered was that Hjálmar would be actively working to locate and arrest Peter. That was a problem.

Most of all, it mattered who'd taken the man's life. Because Staple's assassin had been bird-dogging Peter this whole time.

He stood abruptly, looking up and down the street. He had to walk. He had to keep moving. Then he knew. It was the Irishman, of course. But who was behind the Irishman?

He called Holm and got no answer. The rain turned to sleet.

HE CROSSED the street to a narrow pedestrian path that angled up the hillside. The snowshoes were awkward under his arm. He climbed to a winding road that ended above the hilltop church where he'd left the Defender. His binoculars showed no police cars, no black Dacia or brown Škoda, so he walked down to the parking lot. The minibus was gone, but the pickup was still there.

He unlocked his truck and off-loaded everything but the orange-handled knife and his binoculars, then started down the long diagonal steps toward the concrete hotel where he was to meet Brunelli.

The sleet stung Peter's battered face. He raised the binoculars and scanned down the stairs, which ended at the corner of the hotel. He had no view around the corner to the entrance. He wondered if Brunelli had caught the news and called the police.

Through the lenses, he saw a small, faint cloud appear briefly against the line of the hotel wall. It vanished, then came again. A plume of breath in the cold air. Someone was standing on the far side of that corner, waiting.

Peter slipped laterally across the slick hillside, trying to get a glimpse around the corner of the hotel. He stopped behind a sparse evergreen tree, still not far enough to get an angle on the corner, but now he had a good view across the street. At the mouth of an alley, a man leaned against a red Jeep and watched the hotel entrance. Something familiar about him, that athletic slouch. Peter raised the binoculars again.

He'd seen the man before, in the hallway of the Litla Guesthouse in Reykjavík. The grad student with the swimmer's build in the Ohio State sweatshirt.

Peter scanned farther, looking for stillness in the thinning sea of pedestrians, and found Ohio State's friend, the young woman with the spatula and the silver bangles. She wore a dark parka and stood at the back of the raised hotel patio, sheltered from the wind, with views down both sides of the intersection.

Peter dropped to the snow and slid farther across the hillside until he came to a concrete retaining wall. Sheltered in the wall's shadow, he could finally see around the corner of the hotel. A third figure stood out of the light, a large man almost invisible in a watch cap and a gray jacket. Peter had never seen him before.

The sleet came down hard, dampening the sound from the street. Ohio State and Spatula Woman weren't Hjálmar's people. They'd been with Seamus at the Litla, so Peter assumed they were with Seamus. But who the hell was Seamus with?

Peter dug out his phone and called Holm again.

The phone rang and rang. When the Norwegian finally came on the line, he was abrupt. "Tell me you didn't kill David Staple."

Peter kept his voice quiet. "I didn't kill David Staple."

"I shouldn't be talking to you. Interpol could charge me for assisting in a crime. I should hang up right now."

"So hang up," Peter said. "But first let me tell you about this SUV I found."

Holm didn't say anything, but he didn't hang up, either.

"It's a big white Mitsubishi," Peter said. "Recently painted. Used to be silver or gray. It's had some repair work done on the front end, like it was in some kind of collision."

The cheap cell gave off the eerie silence of a digital connection. Then the Norwegian lit a cigarette, and the crackle of the burn came over the line. "Okay," Holm finally said. The wheelchair rattled softly. "That's the plate number you sent earlier?"

"Yes. And the photo of the man driving it."

Fingers clacked across keys. "The plate is for a Mitsubishi Pajero. Silver. Registered in the UK to a Seamus Heaney. Like the poet." More keystrokes. "A citizen of Ireland? He is not Icelandic?"

"He says he's Irish. He dug me out of a snowdrift this morning. Says he was a cop in Belfast. Maybe you could find out more."

Holm took a long drag on the cigarette. "*Já.* I will." He exhaled. "Thank you, Peter."

"My pleasure. Did you have time to look into Brunelli?"

"Ha." The laugh like a bark. "First let me tell you about David Staple. Remember how he started at the White House, worked his way up to a nice law partnership, but somehow ended up as a low-level attorney at the State Department? I found out why. He resigned from his partnership when the *Washington Post* revealed that he was a person of interest in an FBI investigation into money laundering. For something called the True IRA."

"Oh, wow," Peter said.

The original Irish Republican Army was a separatist group responsible for many decades of political bombings and assassinations throughout Ireland and England. But the most violent element of the IRA had formed a splinter group called the True IRA, which pursued everything from gunrunning to bank robberies to murder for hire, all over the world.

"David Staple never went to trial, of course. Lawyers never go to jail. But I wanted to learn about his early career," Holm said. "Do you know who Staple worked with at the White House? Someone whose career turned out very differently?"

Suddenly it fell into place.

Peter thought about the boy, reciting pi to four thousand places. What other things did he carry in his head?

On the steep and slippery slope, the sleet turned into snow.

Chapter 10

Twelve Months Earlier

MONDAY TRAFFIC IS WORSE than usual. Erik gets Óskar to school on time but is stuck on the Beltway, still miles from his office, outside of Rockville. When Sarah calls, it's automatically sent to the car's speakers.

"My key card didn't work," she says. "Tom Wetzel was there, but he wouldn't let me in. He said they're releasing me from my contract. They found a new cyber provider." Her voice is hollow.

"Did Jerry say anything yesterday?"

"Yeah," she says. "He thanked me for coming in on a Sunday."

The only thing that changed overnight was the fact that Sarah copied Brunelli's secret hard drive to a server in Iceland. Erik understands immediately. They learned what she'd done.

Erik is less than a mile from the Rockledge exit, where he can get off the Beltway and reverse course, but in this traffic, it might take him ten minutes.

He says, "Where are you now?"

"In the car. On my way home."

"I have an idea. Let's go somewhere for a few days. Just drive south."

"You know, I had the same thought. I already picked up Óskar at school. I'm going to grab a few things from the house."

"Let me do that. You keep driving. I'll meet you at that pancake house in Virginia Beach."

"I just pulled up. It'll take five minutes."

"Please." Erik is trying very hard to pretend not to be scared to death. "Let me. You keep going."

"Erik, I've got this." He hears the slam of a car door, then another. "Óskar, honey, we're going on a little trip. Mommy's going to pack a quick bag. Should we take your LEGO guys?"

Signal on, Erik cuts through traffic to the breakdown lane, where he accelerates toward the exit. "Sarah, don't hang up. Keep me on the phone, okay?"

She gives a short laugh, the one that tells Erik she's nervous. "I love it when you're a worrywart."

Erik hears her keys jangle as she unlocks the house. The slap of the storm door behind her. Their son reciting his numbers.

He's almost to Connecticut Avenue when he hears Sarah's footsteps going up the squeaky stairs. She says, "Óskar, put your LEGO guys and your book in your backpack, please."

"Mama, can I bring Bear-Bear?"

"Great idea, honey." Óskar's feet thump away. "Now, where did I put my swimsuit?"

Erik doesn't want to distract her, but there's more than one reason he wanted to go to the house himself. "Sarah, you know my fire safe in the closet?"

"Yes." Her voice is muffled. She's put the phone down. He hears the clatter of hangers.

"I need you to get something out of it."

"I've already got the emergency cash and our passports from the drawer." She's annoyed.

"Open the safe." Erik tells her the combination. "Look under the insurance folder. There's a gun."

"What?" Sarah doesn't like guns.

Erik bought the revolver years ago, but somehow never found the right time to tell Sarah. His work group goes to the range at lunch, once a month. Erik's become a pretty good shot.

"I'll explain later. Just take it."

"I am *not* comfortable—"

"Take the damn gun, Sarah."

"Okay," she mutters. "Fine. Is this thing loaded?"

"Yes." He knows he shouldn't, but it makes him feel better anyway. He keeps the gun locked away, after all.

"We are not finished with this topic." She sighs. "Is there anything else you want me to pack?"

"Just go." He is trying not to shout.

"Okay, okay." She calls, "Óskar, come on. Time for our adventure." Erik hears their feet hurry down the squeaky stairs. "I don't want to stay in Virginia Beach, though. How about—"

A loud triple rap interrupts her. A knock at the front door.

Erik's heart stops in his chest.

She says, "Erik, is that you?"

"No, I'm still in Chevy Chase. Don't go to the door. Go out the back. I'll pick you up at the Philz on Adams Mill."

"There's a man in the backyard. How the hell did he get in the backyard?" She's breathing a little hard now, moving fast.

The triple rap at the door again, louder.

"Óskar, buddy, get behind the couch." Her voice is low and steady. "Now. Like you're hiding in your fort, okay? Good boy. You stay there and stay quiet until I tell you it's okay. Here, take this. Daddy's on the phone, but you can't talk to him."

"Mama?"

Another triple rap, this time even harder.

Sarah's voice drops again. "This is stranger danger, honey." Stranger danger is what Óskar's school calls their active shooter drill. "You stay down and stay quiet. You are hiding from everyone, got it? Say, 'Yes, ma'am,' and then be very, very quiet."

"Yes, ma'am." Óskar's voice is a whisper, but Erik can hear him clearly now because the phone is in Óskar's hand.

The front door slams open. Sarah gives an involuntary *yip*.

Erik swerves into traffic, cutting off a line of cars. Everybody honks, and Erik realizes the sound will be heard from the phone in Óskar's hand. He hits Mute on the dashboard and flies past Military Road toward Nebraska, where he runs a red light.

"What the hell do you think you're doing?" Sarah is armored in outrage. "Get out of my house, all of you."

"Oh, Sarah." Jerry Brunelli's smooth baritone. Unworried, unhurried. "Silly, stupid Sarah. You stuck your fingers into things that are not your business. And after all I've done for you, too." Erik can hear the smile in Brunelli's velvet voice.

"I don't know what you're talking about."

"Fitz, take her bag."

"You can't—" Erik hears a muffled slap. "Give me that back."

"The thing is, Sarah, you're not my only cybersecurity contractor. We have a keylogger on the system. We have a record of every keystroke. We know where you've been. What I don't know is what you've done with my files." A rustling sound as Brunelli fishes through her bag. "Laptop password, please."

"Go to hell."

"Fitz."

Another slap, this time a sharp *crack*. It's Fitzsimmons, Brunelli's silent bodyguard.

Erik needs to go faster. He swerves into oncoming traffic and brushes against a pickup truck, clips off his side mirror. He squeezes the wheel too tightly. His hands are screaming.

"There's no coming back from this, Jerry. That's assault."

"Oh, Sarah." Brunelli chuckles, deep and rich, and lets it build into a laugh. Then his voice turns cold. "Where's young Óskar?"

"Don't you touch him, you disgusting—"

Another slap.

"Maybe I'll pick up Óskar from school, bring him home early. I know the headmaster. I'm on the board of directors. Can't you see that I do what I want, Sarah? Exactly what I want. I always have, and I always will."

The rustle of clothing, a grunt, a squeak. Sarah fighting to get free. Erik stays in the oncoming lane, weaving through traffic, but he's too slow. There are too many cars.

"I know you made copies of my files. But I don't know where they are. Tell me now and we're done. You and your son walk away." Brunelli's voice hardens into a hammer. "Now, Sarah."

Erik can practically see her face. Flushed red, furious, her hair flying free. Dear God, he loves her. He will do anything for her and Óskar both; he will give anything. He swerves around a city bus, the squeal of his tires gone silent as his ears strain to hear everything coming through the speaker. Please, Óskar, don't say anything. Just hide behind the couch and breathe.

"All right," she says. "I made a copy. I'll show you."

Erik imagines Fitzsimmons releasing her. Sarah straightening her jacket, pushing her hair out of her face.

More footsteps. "I better do it." A third voice. Tom Wetzel, Brunelli's deputy. "What's your password, Sarah?"

"Give me my bag," she says. "There's a flash drive in the bottom. You need that software to navigate to the server."

"No," Erik says, loud inside his car. "No, Sarah, no." He rides the horn and runs the light at Tilden. He knows there is no flash drive. Sarah didn't trust them.

"Give her the bag," Brunelli says.

Erik can see her taking the strap and reaching inside. He won't get there in time. He hears a familiar *snick* as she pulls the hammer back. Sarah always did have strong hands.

Everyone talks at once.

"Gun." Fitzsimmons.

"Don't—" Wetzel.

"Stop." Brunelli.

BANG.

For a moment, silence.

Then Brunelli's voice, cold as ice. "What a mess. You *idiots*. Tom, how hard can it be to take a gun away from a girl?"

Wetzel's baritone is quiet. "She was stronger than she looked."

"Now we'll never find our files," Brunelli says. He exhales loudly, recalculating. "Okay. Tom, finish it. Make it look good. Fitz, you call our friend with Metro, let him know what's coming. Maybe he can be in the neighborhood."

Softly over the speaker, Erik hears a faint keening sound. Óskar, hiding with the phone behind the couch. Trying not to cry.

Erik careens forward, desperate, out of his mind, too far away.

"Two more in the face," Fitzsimmons says. "Makes it personal."

BANG. BANG.

The padded *thump* of the gun hitting the carpet.

Brunelli sighs. "You really screwed this up, Tom. Better get started on fixing it."

"What about the gun?"

"You're wearing gloves, Tom. Leave it. But take the laptop."

Fitzsimmons says, "Hello, Phil? There's been an incident. Time to earn your retirement supplement. No, no siren. You were driving by and heard shots. The front door was standing open. You think the husband did it. Here's the address." The voices fade.

Oh, Sarah.

Erik passes the National Zoo. He is eight blocks away, now seven, now six. Óskar's keening gets louder and louder.

AT THE curb, Erik abandons the car and sprints up the steps.

"Óskar?" He runs through the front door, his voice rising. "I'm here, Óskar. I'm here."

He stops short in the living room. Sarah lies across the couch. Blood everywhere. His head spins.

He clutches his skull with both hands as if he could crush it. He wants to die, but he can't. For the boy's sake, he must live.

"Óskar? Óskar, where are you?" The boy has gone silent. Erik bends at the side table and sees his son's small huddled form behind the couch. "Come out, Ós. I've got you. Come out."

The boy crawls toward him. His face is pale and still. There are no tears, not yet.

"Don't look, Ós. Close your eyes." He lifts Óskar into his arms, presses the boy's face into his shoulder. "Keep them closed. I've got you. Hold me tight."

Óskar clings with arms and legs. Erik scoops up Sarah's two bags and Óskar's backpack and hauls them out the door. Carrying everything. Even when he throws the bags in the car, he knows he will carry it all until the end of his days.

He climbs into the driver's seat with Óskar's arms still locked around his neck. He puts the car in gear. "Time to go on an adventure. Time to be real Vikings. Ready?"

Óskar keens softly. Erik holds him tight. Everything he loves is broken beyond repair.

He can only think of Iceland, the last place he has left. It might still be a home for Óskar. In Iceland, he will know what to do.

Present Day

LYING hidden on the snowy hillside above the hotel, watching Ohio State and Spatula Woman through the binoculars, Peter asked the Norwegian, "How did you dig up info on Brunelli? I thought he kept a low profile."

"His online presence is minimal now, but the Deep Web has many artifacts. Do you know the Defense Intelligence Agency?"

"Yes." The DIA was the Defense Department's intelligence arm.

"Brunelli was on a White House task force there after nine-eleven. I found David Staple on that same task force."

"But Brunelli's Catherine's husband. Why would he want to keep me from looking for Erik and Óskar?"

"You will have to ask him," said Holm.

"Oh, I will," Peter said. "When did Brunelli leave the DIA?"

"In 2005, he started a lobbying operation with Catherine Price's husband, Ken, who was at the CIA at the time."

"But that's not what he's doing now, right?" Peter asked.

"It's difficult to know what he's doing now. All his work is secret. He can do anything he wishes without government oversight."

AFTER Peter got off the phone, he climbed the hill to the church parking lot, then retraced his steps to the main shopping street, where he walked toward the Kea Hotel. As he passed Ohio State and Spatula Woman, they detached from their stations to drift along in his wake.

They gave Peter plenty of room, enough for the lurker in the watch cap and gray utility jacket to slip into the gap. Peter figured him for the primary assaulter. As Peter walked into the hotel, the static crackled like a power surge.

Tom Wetzel stood at the window of the crowded hotel bar. He kept his eyes on the street, waiting for Ash. Somehow, the man had gotten much farther than Wetzel had expected.

He hadn't seen Ash in person since their deployment in Iraq, but Wetzel made a point to keep in touch. A regular background check helped fill in the details.

Ash was a classic example of the kind of man who thrived in combat but failed at life afterward. He showed no evidence of employment since he'd mustered out. He didn't own a home. His credit report showed no debt, but no income, either. Taken together, it painted a picture of sporadic day labor, post-traumatic stress, and likely drug addiction. A sad, sad story.

Of course, these same facts explained why Wetzel had chosen Ash for this particular job. A man without a home. A man who wouldn't be missed.

As Wetzel watched, a tall, gaunt figure appeared and angled toward the hotel entrance. He wore a hooded black coat, and Wetzel couldn't make the ID until the figure turned to look through the bar window. When he saw Ash's pale, grim face under the tangled beard, Wetzel felt the fear tighten like a noose.

Ash pushed back his hood, walked into the crowded bar, and surveyed the room. Beside the Euro-tourists with their well-bred cheekbones and flashy gear, the damaged marine stood out like a wolf at a thoroughbred dog show. Wetzel was glad to see Fitzsimmons approaching through the snow, reaching for the door handle.

"Hello, Tom." Ash put out his hand to shake. "Where's Brunelli?"

Ash's grip was strong, but Wetzel was pleased to see that he looked like hell, one eye bruised and swollen, face pale and glazed with sweat. Seamus had told Wetzel how bad things were, but his description hadn't conveyed the reality.

Wetzel smiled. "Sorry, I'm here by myself. Jerry's still in Reykjavík, stuck in a meeting."

Ash still held Wetzel's hand. His grip was getting tighter. Wetzel tried to pull his hand back, but Ash wouldn't let go. His grin was too wide and showed too many teeth.

Wetzel's fear had him now. He wanted to look for Fitzsimmons but didn't. Instead he reminded himself that he was a principal in a major international consulting firm with a current net worth of $6.6 million. He was winning, and he was going to keep on winning, no matter what.

Ash said, "What's so important we had to meet in person?"

"I'm just checking in," Wetzel said. "Making sure you have what you need to find the boy and deliver him to the police. So Catherine can take him home."

"What's the boy got, Tom? Something in his head, that's my guess. Something worth a lot to somebody. Óskar's got a photographic memory, but I'm sure you know that."

How had Ash come up with that? Wetzel didn't know, and it didn't matter. "Dude, what are you talking about?" He put on a sympathetic look and kept his focus on Ash as the door opened and Fitzsimmons slipped through. "Are you all right?"

Ash's bony grip only got stronger. His eyes had a strange light. "You were never a great marine, but I didn't think you'd turn into a total piece of garbage," he said. "What happened to you?"

Wetzel ignored the pain and put his free hand on Ash's shoulder to help lock him in place.

"Nothing happened, dude. Working for Jerry is no different from being a marine, except the pay is much, much better."

Fitzsimmons slipped easily through the crowd. Wetzel felt a flare of pain in his hand as Ash squeezed tighter. Behind him, the door opened again and the husband-wife team came in. They split up to flank Ash on both sides. In ten seconds, Wetzel would win again.

Fitz loomed closer, the syringe small and low in his fist, the uncapped needle gleaming. Ketamine was fast. The flankers were four steps away. Wetzel smiled wider.

Then Ash moved, and Wetzel understood the depths of his miscalculation. He'd thought Ash was crippled and broken, his postwar failures a result of permanent and significant damage.

Now he understood that Ash wasn't disabled at all, just different. Rewired, repurposed. Remade into something new.

PETER watched Wetzel's eyes. When they flickered over Peter's shoulder, Peter yanked him forward hard, propelling him through the now empty space where Peter had just been. As Wetzel passed, Peter spun and shoved him into the arms of the lurker in the watch cap, who held something delicate in his outstretched fist.

Peter saw a slim needle and a clear plastic plunger. Still in motion, he grabbed the lurker's thick wrist and used his momentum to force the needle into the meat of Wetzel's hip.

Peter released the wrist, and the tight fist jerked back in response, breaking the needle under Wetzel's skin.

Peter had no idea what had just gotten pumped into Wetzel, and he didn't care. He hoped it was no pleasure cruise.

Wetzel clearly knew what had happened, because he froze in place. The lurker in the watch cap was jammed up behind him, reaching for Peter around Wetzel's torso. He had bright nailhead eyes in a face like a gravedigger's shovel.

The static crackled a warning, and Peter turned to see Ohio State coming fast. Peter sidestepped right and threw out a hard arm to catch the man's neck in the crook of his elbow in a classic clothesline that left Ohio State's boots climbing the air and his shoulders dropping to the floor.

Two down. Peter spun again and saw Spatula Woman closing with a dreamy half smile on her face and her thumb unfolding an ugly knife. Behind her, Wetzel's knees were mid-buckle.

Wetzel tumbled into a waiter, who tipped his tray of drinks. In the crash of glass, the crowd erupted into chaos. Spatula Woman's dreamy smile sharpened as she advanced.

Peter slipped behind the careening waiter and fled around the bar and through the dining room, where he shouldered open a swinging door with one last look at the lurker in the watch cap, nailhead eyes shining as he bulldozed through the packed people.

The door flapped shut, and Peter was in a long, narrow kitchen. On the far end were stairs down into darkness and a steel door with a crash bar. Peter slammed through and found himself standing at the bottom of the steps to the church parking lot. He jogged upward, looking over his shoulder. When he saw the man in the watch cap bang through, followed by Spatula Woman and a wobbly Ohio State towing Wetzel by the collar, he picked up speed.

He made sure they got a good look at the Defender before he popped the clutch and roared away. But before he got to the main highway, he detoured into the big municipal parking lot.

The black Dacia and Bjarni's Škoda were gone, along with the police car. The pale Mitsubishi was there, though, diesel exhaust floating from the tailpipe. At the far end of the lot, Peter finally turned onto the Ring Road, but kept his speed under the limit of thirty kilometers per hour and one eye on his mirror.

After a minute, the Mitsubishi pulled out behind him.

Two minutes later, another pair of headlights bounced into view. The lurker and the grad students in the red Jeep, Peter hoped. He'd done all he could to let them catch up.

He passed the sign for the city limits and accelerated. The road ahead was dark and empty and mostly clear, despite the heavy snow falling. There would be a plow truck up ahead somewhere, rumbling through the night.

He wanted to find a spot to take them before he caught up to the plow. He needed speed and traction and a tight, blind curve.

THE road ran straight through kilometers of silent winter farms and homesteads. The headlights stayed steady in his mirror, a half kilometer behind him.

As the world turned white and empty, the static softened and the adrenaline began to fade. Peter unzipped his coat and peeled it off his shoulders with shaking hands.

Despite Spatula Woman's ugly knife, he didn't think they'd meant to kill him in the bar. If they'd wanted him dead, they'd have tried to take him on the patio outside. Fewer witnesses and more room to use a weapon. No, the syringe had a purpose.

Maybe it was meant to make him seem drunk. They could haul him out of the bar, laughing the whole time, and kill him later.

After they'd found Óskar. Because Óskar must be alive. Otherwise why go to all this trouble to stop Peter?

Suddenly Peter remembered the black credit card. Catherine had given it to him, but the card had Brunelli's company name on it. Brunelli had tracked every purchase Peter had made. His ticket to Iceland, the Defender he drove, even the Litla Guesthouse, where Seamus had found him again.

Peter fished it out of his wallet, cracked the window, and pushed the black card out into the darkness.

Wetzel the Pretzel had been playing him from the beginning.

The headlights crept up behind him. He thought of how the Mitsubishi had run the Norwegian's Volvo off the highway from behind. Then he stepped on the gas.

The headlights came up behind him again, following closer this time. He was running at 130 kilometers per hour, too fast for the narrow road and the falling snow, his wipers flapping frantically. He understood now that he might not get to choose the ground. He might have to fight them as they came, four on one.

In his rearview, the headlights came still closer. Ahead, the road curved sharply to the left. Screw it, he thought—there's more than one way to do this. He downshifted hard to shed speed. Behind him, the headlights bounced and lurched. They'd either slam into his bumper or steer away and fly off the curve. He was trusting the Defender to stay on the pavement.

As he felt his tires slip, he saw a car off the road on the right, a snow-covered sedan with a light bar and police markings. But the windshield was clear. Was that a shadow in the driver's seat?

He upshifted and found traction to power through the curve. The dark police car didn't move. In his rearview, both pairs of headlights had vanished. The night remained black in his wake.

Up front, he saw three big vehicles blocking the road a half kilometer ahead, showing amber on their fenders. Then, as if on cue, three bright sets of headlights came to life and three light bars flashed red and blue in the cold winter night.

A sedan, a station wagon, and a big SUV were parked in an aggressive wedge, blocking the narrow road. The land fell away on both sides so Peter couldn't drive around them. Snow blew in white ropes across the asphalt as the wind scraped the road clean.

He thought about turning around to run back the way he came, but the lighter, nimbler vehicles would have no trouble keeping up. Either way, they'd have his plate number. They'd call for reinforcements and chase him until he ran out of gas.

As Peter slowed, four figures got out of the vehicles, bulky in their cold-weather gear. They adjusted their equipment belts, and Peter was glad not to see the shapes of holsters and pistol grips. These four were likely local police, well trained and capable but equipped only with batons and pepper spray.

They held out their palms for him to stop.

One of the officers detached himself from the group and walked toward Peter. With the swirl of snow and headlights in his eyes, he couldn't make out the man's face. Staying well to the side of the heavy Land Rover, he made a throat-cutting motion with his hand, indicating that Peter should kill his engine.

Peter did, but he left his headlights on and his keys in the ignition. He stuffed his phones into the top pouch of his day pack.

Next, the officer held his hand out, palm up, and gestured to the side, a polite invitation for Peter to leave his vehicle. Peter opened his door and stepped out. The wind slammed it shut behind him and almost blew him off his feet. He hadn't put his coat back on, thinking he might need an excuse to get back to the truck. Now he zipped up the neck of his fleece.

The officer beckoned Peter forward with a curl of his gloved fingers. Peter walked toward him. The officer plucked a radio off his chest and held it to his mouth. He spoke briefly, refastened the radio, then moved forward with the other officers in his wake.

As he stepped into the glow of the headlights, Peter saw his face clearly. It was Hjálmar.

Peter had underestimated him again.

The three officers began to close the gap behind Hjálmar, who raised his voice over the wind. "Your eye is not looking well, Peter. Have you seen a doctor?"

Peter called back, "You know I didn't kill David Staple."

Hjálmar's smile was gentle. "You did knock him to the ground, however. You took his wallet and passport."

"True," Peter admitted. "But I think Staple was killed by an Irish national named Seamus Heaney. He drives a Mitsubishi Pajero with front-end damage. Its original color was silver. He ran Kristjan Holm off the road." Peter hooked a thumb over his shoulder. "He was behind me on that curve. He's after Óskar."

Hjálmar didn't say anything. Peter pressed on.

"The FBI investigated David Staple for laundering money for the IRA. Before that, he worked with Jerry Brunelli, Catherine's husband. Erik didn't kill Sarah Price—someone else did, maybe Brunelli or one of his people. You need to call the FBI."

"An excellent idea," Hjálmar said. "I will call your FBI." The three bulky cops flowed around him, closing in. "Come with me, and we will sit in my office and talk to them together."

Peter held up a warning hand. He was running on fumes. "Hjálmar, you know why I'm here. To save Óskar."

"Yes, I know." Hjálmar's face was kind. "But who will save you, Peter? You want to do the right thing. Let me help."

The officers edged closer. "I can't, Hjálmar. I just can't."

"I'm sorry, Peter. You must."

Hjálmar raised a hand, and the night grew suddenly brighter. A vehicle had come up behind the Defender, unseen and unheard in the snow and the wind, and only now had turned on its headlights. Peter threw a quick glance over his shoulder and saw the police sedan from the curve, the spotter now blocking his escape.

He whipped abruptly back to face Hjálmar, and a wave of dizziness hit him. It only lasted a few seconds, but when he could focus again, the two biggest officers were already on him.

With strong hands, they'd moved him off-balance, face-first against the side of his truck. "Sir, you are under arrest. Do not resist." One man held Peter's left wrist behind his back, preparing him for the cuffs. The other man stood to Peter's right, reaching for his free hand. The third man stood ready to jump in.

Peter struggled to contain himself. He could break free, he knew, but these cops were just doing their jobs. He didn't want to hurt them. He wasn't an animal.

Peter felt cold steel on his skin and heard the *click* of the pawl as the cuffs closed, first on one wrist, then the other.

The burly officers took Peter by the biceps and pulled him away. The third officer retrieved Peter's coat and day pack from the Defender. The spotter got out of his snowy sedan.

"Hjálmar," Peter called. "We need to talk."

The wind rose higher still. It smelled like a frozen sea. The commissioner shook his head. His face was hard, all kindness gone. His voice carried over the storm. "We are done here."

Then he turned and walked away.

THE cold steel cuffs bit into Peter's wrists as the officers ushered him down the snow-swept road. With every step away from the Defender, the static crackled higher, stronger. He'd never felt it like this, not while he was outside.

As the cops moved him toward the sedan, Peter looked inside. Like any American police cruiser, the white Volvo had a steel grate between the back seat and the front, making a man cage.

After the car, they'd move him to a holding cell.

His chest was tight. He had to work to breathe. Despite the cold, sweat soaked his clothes.

The two burly police pushed him chest-first against the police Volvo and kicked out his feet. The third man patted him down and emptied his pockets. He put Peter's wallet, keys, and the orange knife into a clear plastic bag and handed it to Hjálmar with Peter's passport. The spotter came up with Peter's coat and day pack from the Defender.

Hjálmar tucked the passport into his breast pocket and the plastic bag into the top pocket of Peter's pack. The wind whipped at Peter's face. One of the burly officers opened the car door, then put a rough tactical glove on the back of Peter's head, directly on the tender skin split by Dónaldur's bottle. The infected wound tore open. The cop bent him down and put him in the back seat.

The door closed beside him with a solid *thump*.

Breathe in, breathe out. Peter's hands were cuffed behind him.

The doors wouldn't open from the inside. The steel grate was bolted to the seat back, the roof, and the side pillars. The officers stood outside and talked. Inside, the static raged.

He tried to take a breath, but his lungs wouldn't expand. His chest was wrapped in steel bands that tightened by the second.

Outside, the police kept talking like they had all the time in the world. Peter put his hot face against the cool window. How long would he be in that holding cell? Days, at least. Maybe weeks. He was going to die inside. He might die right here.

He kicked heedlessly at the metal mesh of his cage. His wrists strained behind his back. Cut by the cuffs, he began to bleed. The mesh clattered and flexed but did not give way. He turned sideways in the seat, hyperextended his long arms, and forced his tearing wrists down around the narrow curve of his ass. He pulled his knees to his chin and pushed the cuffs past his ankles and around his toes. Hands now in front, he set his upper back to the steel cage and kicked at the rear windshield.

His heels hit hard. He heard shouting. A fragment of stone from the Reykjavík alley was stuck in the lugs of his boot, and it hit with a *crack*. The glass starred, then bowed outward.

He kicked the windshield from its frame. Unthinking, he scrambled toward the hole. His legs launched him through the opening and across the trunk onto the cold, hard pavement.

He gathered his feet beneath him.

The two closest men came with hands open and ready. The first one grabbed Peter's wrist to lock the joint and turn him. But Peter's wrists were slick with blood. Still in cuffs, he came around and slammed the back of his left elbow into the cop's temple. The cop flew sideways and pinwheeled to the asphalt.

Peter reached down and plucked the man's baton from the sheath on his belt. He flicked his wrist down and out to snap the telescopic baton to its full length, three sections of spring steel and a heavy striking tip.

The other burly cop was already coming fast on Peter's blind side, and Peter turned to meet him. The man dropped his shoulder and drove his fist toward Peter's gut.

Peter slid left, the baton raised, then whipped it into the other man's extended right forearm. He heard the *crack* of bone.

The man's eyes flared with the pain, but he didn't stop coming. Peter dropped his hips, snapped the baton down, and smashed the heavy steel tip into the man's leading knee. It gave way under the blow, and he landed on his side, broken arm held against his chest. In serious hurt, the man scrabbled backward, desperate to get out of the fight.

The two officers with Hjálmar had held back by the larger SUV, not wanting to get in the way. Now they glanced at each other, expressionless, and reached for their own weapons.

These two were a little older, with gray in their beards, but no less large or capable. They spoke to each other in Icelandic, then split their position, one circling to Peter's right to get behind him.

Before the two graybeards could get comfortable, Peter feinted at the man in front of him, who swung his baton sideways to parry the blow. But Peter pivoted to the second man and snapped the heavy steel tip into the fragile bones of the cop's hand.

He winced, and his weapon fell to the pavement.

Peter scooped up the dropped baton in his right hand, holding it backward along the length of his forearm. Now he had a shield.

The two cops began to circle again. One man had a baton, the other nothing but a hurt hand, but he was still in the game.

Peter attacked both at once.

He swung fast and hard, striking at hands, wrists, forearms, and knees, driving them back but not landing anything.

The cop with the baton stepped in, swinging hard. At the same time, the officer with the broken hand circled around on Peter's weak side, a distraction he couldn't afford to ignore.

When the cop with the baton swung to break Peter's ribs, Peter brought his elbow sharply back to slip the blow, then smashed the man's forearm hard enough to break bone. The baton flew away, and he went down hard.

The last cop standing had no baton and one good hand. He fumbled for his pepper spray, not that it would work in this wind. Peter smacked the cop's gloved hand with the steel striking tip, then whipped the baton around and rapped the man's ankle.

He yelped and fell. Peter knelt on the man's thrashing thighs and tore the keys off his belt ring, then got to his feet.

When the cuffs fell clattering to the asphalt, the four injured men scrambled away however they could. Peter stood erect on the snowy road in the wind and cold and dark, breathing hard. The crackle of static like something alive inside him.

The adrenaline would only last so long. Soon would come the shakes and the crash. Black depression, shame, and regret.

They were officers of the law, sworn to their duty.

And Peter had hurt them. Smashed them down like cheap toys.

At least he hadn't killed anyone. Not today, anyway.

He stalked toward Hjálmar, whose back was against the SUV, rear hatch wide open. Peter's pack held his new coat down on the road, but the sleeves flapped in the whipping wind. Peter could see Hjálmar's pain and anger over his fallen men.

"I'm sorry," Peter said.

"You will be." Hjálmar held something along the back of his leg, maybe a baton, hoping Peter wouldn't notice. Overmatched but still ready to step up. Peter liked that.

Hjálmar had surely called for reinforcements, although the roadblock was many kilometers from any town large enough to have resident police. The four battered cops were hunched together on the side of the road. Peter stood between them and their vehicles, facing Hjálmar.

"Step away." Peter had to raise his voice over the sound of the gale. "I just want my gear and I'll be gone." His pack held his keys and phones and wallet. He'd need the coat in the days to come.

Hjálmar moved his hand out from behind his leg. It held a flat black pistol, pointed down at his side. "Get on your knees."

"I thought Icelandic police didn't carry guns."

"Some have them in the car." Hjálmar raised the pistol two-handed, the muzzle now pointed at the road near Peter's feet. "On your knees. Hands behind your head. Now."

Peter stepped closer. "You know what that weapon will do to a man at close range, Hjálmar? You want to see that every time you close your eyes?"

The barrel rose to center on Peter's chest, Hjálmar's face pale in the dark night. Peter was four feet away, now two. The muzzle described a small circle in the air. Hjálmar was shaking.

Peter closed the gap. Arms down, hands bloody, he stood with the muzzle tight against his chest. "Harder than it looks, isn't it?"

Hjálmar's shaking got worse. Peter abruptly swept the pistol from the older man's hand and away.

Backing toward the rear of the SUV, Hjálmar seemed relieved.

Peter glanced after the pistol, now buried in the snow somewhere. He'd meant to keep hold of it, but his hands were clumsy in the cold. He'd never find it before they came for him.

Instead he stuck one arm into his snowy coat, then the other, while the still rising wind tried to tear it free. With fumbling fingers, he fished his keys from the top pocket of the pack as well as his orange-handled knife. The blade was very sharp. It sliced effortlessly through the sidewalls of the police tires, over and over. They wouldn't come after him without a tow truck.

As he walked past the open back of Hjálmar's SUV, he saw a small bag, faded blue with shoulder straps. Óskar's LEGO book bag. He shoved the bag under his arm and turned to go.

Then he remembered what Hjálmar had put in his breast pocket. He put out his hand. "Give me my passport."

The commissioner had recovered his dignity. "I will not." Now they had to shout to be heard over the wind. "You will be in an Icelandic prison for the next ten years, or twenty."

"My passport. Now."

Hjálmar reached inside his jacket and withdrew the small blue book. Looking Peter in the eye, he threw it straight up.

The wind caught the little booklet. The cover opened, and the pages fluttered like wings. The passport lifted high, rising into the night sky until it was lost in darkness.

Hjálmar raised his chin. "We are a nation of laws. We will find you. You will be punished."

"I don't doubt it," Peter said. "When you find me, I'll have Óskar." He looked the older man hard in the face. "Make sure you get him to a safe place. Do you understand me?"

Hjálmar stared back without an answer.

Peter climbed into the Defender and pushed through the road-block. Then he roared northeast toward the gap in the mountains.

HE LEFT the main highway just before Blönduós, headed north on a narrow road between jagged mountains and the raging sea. The storm was fully on him now, the snow coming fast and hard.

Past the turnoff for Skagaströnd, the road changed from asphalt to gravel. The few farms in the flatter places became even more distant. The land felt vast and wild.

As the road climbed a hill, the gravel turned to potholes, and the truck rocked with the full force of the blizzard roaring across the Greenland Sea. Peter stopped on the high ground and stood on the running board with his binoculars raised.

The snow brightened the land below, and the ambient light reflected off the clouds. The windswept plain lay before him, dark yet gleaming. To the east, a steep promontory rose up five hundred meters. In a semicircle around its base stood three clusters of buildings. The family farm, more than two hundred years old.

The family wouldn't be happy to see him.

But he wasn't going there just yet. When the tire tracks turned into the unmarked driveway, Peter kept driving. The blizzard would cover signs of his passage soon enough.

After twelve curving kilometers, he came to the place he was looking for, a derelict barn not far off the road. The structure's concrete walls were mostly intact, but the windows and doors were empty sockets, the wood rotted away long ago. It was the broken line of the collapsed roof that had caught his eye on the Norwegian's big satellite map. He'd needed a place to hide the Land Rover, and he didn't want to worry about visitors.

He eased across a ditch and found himself following deep frozen wheel ruts under the snow that led him around the side of the structure. Behind the building, he saw an opening where the barn door had once stood, but he realized there was something blocking the way. He pulled the Defender tight alongside the structure, hoping it was enough to get the truck out of sight from the road.

The storm roared, and the snow swirled madly. He had a moment of dizziness and had to wait for his vision to clear. He was sweating and very thirsty.

He peered through the passenger window at the shape in the barn. It was the back of an old camper, half hidden in dark drifts.

Suddenly Peter had a bad feeling. With a flashlight in his hand, he climbed out of the Defender and walked into the dark barn.

The camper was a boxy cream-colored Winnebago Minnie Winnie with the distinctive orange *W* on the side. From the late seventies, Peter guessed, and not treated kindly since.

There was no sign of life. The windows were frosted over. Peter looked up. Flakes fell through the barn's broken rafters, but the roof was still mostly intact over the vehicle. A searching aircraft would never see it. A good place to hide.

The Winnebago's side door was dented, the lock broken. When he pulled it open, he caught the faint scent of cold iron. His bad feeling got worse. Shining the light up through the open doorway, he saw a large, dark stain, thick on the threadbare carpet.

Peter knew old blood when he saw it.

Chapter 11

Twelve Months Earlier

IN THE PARKING LOT across from the Reykjavík bus station, Erik stands with his bags at his feet and Óskar heavy in his arms.

The day after his mother's murder, Óskar hasn't really stopped crying, even in his sleep. When awake, his arms and legs are wrapped around his father like a desperate octopus. He buries his face into Erik's neck and whispers numbers into the darkness.

When Bjarni rolls up in the ancient camper, Erik's heart sinks. It looks far worse than he expected. But he must remain positive.

"Isn't this great, Óskar? We're having a real Icelandic adventure."

Óskar lifts his head to regard the ragged beast, and Erik knows he is not fooled. Things are very bad.

On Erik's way to Dulles International the day before, his phone began to ring. The caller ID said Thomas Wetzel. When it went to voice mail, Wetzel called again. Then again and again.

Past Dupont Circle, Erik saw an open parking spot and pulled over to turn off his ringing phone. Then he realized he needed the phone to buy plane tickets. The only available seats were first class, but he bought them anyway. He wasn't going to be able to use that credit card much longer.

Everything he'd heard over Sarah's phone was burned on his brain, especially this: Brunelli had a D.C. police detective on his payroll. Erik couldn't go to the authorities. If the police put him in jail, even overnight, he wouldn't see morning.

With the tickets handled, he called his cousin, who listened to Erik's story in silence. Then said, "I'm so sorry. How can I help?" It was Bjarni who suggested the camper, for sale by a friend. He'd buy it that afternoon and "forget" to register it in his own name.

When the call ended, Erik's phone immediately began to ring again. Soon it wouldn't be Wetzel calling, he thought. It would be the police, tracking the signal. He needed to get rid of it.

As he pulled into traffic, he held the ringing phone out the window and let it slip through his fingers. The car behind him crushed it into a thousand tiny pieces.

Now Bjarni climbs down from the camper. "It's not pretty, but she'll take you where you need to go."

"It's wonderful, Cousin. Thank you so much." Erik takes out his envelope of emergency cash. "How much do I owe you?"

Bjarni waves away the money. "You're family. I filled the gas tank and bought the things you asked for." Groceries, coats and boots, a good map. "But better not to call, not for a while."

Erik understands. With the police on his trail, he is a danger to everyone he touches. But after Bjarni hugs them and walks away,

Erik feels the desolation wash over him like the tide. They are alone. Sarah is dead. He wishes he, too, could cry for her loss, but he can't, not yet. They aren't safe. He can feel it.

Still, with the camper rumbling beneath him and Óskar strapped into his passenger seat clutching his backpack, Erik feels something like hope for the first time since this all began. The familiar sound of his own language, the cold wind of home.

The weather is good, and the road is clear of snow. He considered going east to his uncles, and he may yet ask for their help to get him to England, but Erik is tired of exile. Without Sarah, he can imagine nothing better than raising Óskar in a crowd of cousins, mowing hay and shearing sheep for the rest of his days.

But he can't go to the farm, not yet. Not until he's sure the police have given up on finding him. His family will help him deal with Brunelli when the time comes. Sarah's death won't be for nothing. Óskar still carries the encryption code in his head.

For the last two hours of driving, he worries that the abandoned barn has collapsed in the dozen years since he's been there. But while more of the roof has fallen, he manages to nose the camper inside and out of sight without having to do more than clear away a few rafters. Now he worries about the forecast. Erik needs fresh snow to cover his trail. Because Brunelli will use every bit of his influence to find them. The police will come looking. And after them, Fitzsimmons.

What can Erik do? How can he protect his son?

With Óskar in his arms, he walks out into the darkness and looks up. The sky is filled with stars.

"Óskar, do you see that big hill, with that flat spot on top?" He points away from the road, where the narrow plain rises into a rocky saddle. It is not a hill. It is a small mountain.

Óskar raises his head to look, then nods.

"On the other side, down below, is *Amma* Yrsa's farm, where I was born. We were there two summers ago. You remember?"

Óskar gives his dad a look. Of course he remembers.

Back inside the little camper, Erik seats Óskar at the table and spreads out Bjarni's map. He puts his finger on the barn. "We are here." Then he puts his finger on the saddle. "Here is the flat spot we looked at. Here is the way across. And here is the way to *Amma* Yrsa's farm. Can you take a picture to keep it in your head?"

Óskar nods.

"Okay," Erik says. "If anyone comes, you run up this hill quick as you can. But here is the hard part. Are you ready?"

He locks eyes with his son. He doesn't want to say this, but must.

"You do not wait for me, Óskar. You do not stop, you do not look back. You *run*. When you get to the flat spot, you *keep* running, across the top and down to *Amma* Yrsa's farm." He retraces the route with his finger. "Do you understand me?"

His seven-year-old son stares at him without blinking.

"Ós, this is very important." Erik clears his throat. He can barely get the words out. "If anyone comes, you must do this. You must run without me. Say yes, that you understand."

Óskar's eyes fill as he launches himself into his father's arms.

With bottomless sorrow, Erik knows that his son understands.

THE snow falls while they sleep, and they wake to a softer world. After a breakfast of *skyr* and bread, Erik challenges Óskar to a Viking race up the hill. The rules are simple. Run flat out, no stopping, no looking back. Óskar doesn't stop, and he doesn't look back. Erik lets him win, but just barely. At the top, he points the way across the saddle toward Grandma Yrsa's house.

Ten days pass in the little camper. They eat *skyr* and bread for breakfast, cheese and bread for lunch, fish cakes and potatoes for dinner. They play every card game Erik knows. Erik tells stories he learned as a child, but now he gives every story a happy ending.

Each morning and each afternoon, they race up the hill. Like Vikings, Erik says. And with each trip, Óskar gets a little faster. He doesn't stop. He doesn't look back.

Aside from themselves, they see no other signs of human life. The camper's electric heater works well, but Erik uses it sparingly. To charge the batteries and warm themselves, they only run the engine for a half hour during meals, but soon it will need more gasoline. Soon they will need more food. Erik is worried about getting the boxy old camper back to the road.

But he needn't have worried.

On the eleventh morning, while they eat breakfast, while the engine runs and the battery charges, a gray plume of exhaust rises through the barn's broken roof. On the dark road, a silver SUV approaches. Its headlights illuminate the faint, swirling cloud.

The SUV stops. Two men get out.

Their doors close with a double *thump*.

They walk toward the barn.

ERIK has been hiding for more than a week, and his ears have learned to sift through the variable noise of the wind for other sounds. He recognizes this new double *thump* instinctively. He scrambles to kill the engine, but he's too late. He hears the crunch of boots in the snow, then a voice.

"What a lovely spot for a hideaway."

The boots crunch closer. Erik drops to the floor and gathers Óskar into his arms. At the camper door, a sharp knock.

The voice again, louder now. It sounds Irish.

"Begging your pardon, but I'm an investor from Ireland hoping to purchase land. Would you have a moment to chat?"

Erik says nothing, just puts a finger to his lips. Óskar buries his face in Erik's neck.

"I know you're inside. I saw your exhaust from the road."

Erik tries to think of a way to see the man without being seen. He detaches himself from Óskar, then creeps away from the door to peek out the window over the sink. A man stands directly outside, grinning up at him, a dark shadow of beard in a pale face.

Behind the man stands Fitzsimmons like a statue in the cold.

Erik jumps backward, but of course they have seen his face.

The camper's thin door rattles. The metal is not strong.

The Irishman says, "You had a good idea, hiding here. I've done the same thing myself, finding a place to wait out the coppers. I was a copper, too, so I know how they think. Or don't think. Most coppers don't understand a desperate man. But I do."

The door bangs in its frame under the force of a fist. Óskar attaches himself to his father. Erik says, "What do you want?"

THE WILD ONE | 127

"As you know, there was an unfortunate misunderstanding. Your wife took some video files that don't belong to her. If we get our files, and proof that no copies exist, you will walk away a free man."

More crunching of boots in the snow. Erik imagines Fitzsimmons prowling around the camper, looking for another way in.

Then he realizes they haven't seen Óskar. They don't know he's there.

"Sarah didn't take any files," Erik says.

"I'm afraid you're misinformed, lad. Our expert went through her laptop with a microscope. We know she uploaded the files to another server before deleting them."

Erik doesn't answer.

"We even have the URL of the server," the Irishman continues. "But not the encryption key for access. That's quite a large number, is my understanding."

"I never saw that."

On the other side of the door, the Irishman talks on. "I was informed that Óskar is good with numbers. Has a perfect memory. And he's gone away with his dad. You bought him a plane ticket."

Erik cannot speak. Óskar's grip tightens. He makes the high keening sound of profound distress.

The door bangs again, louder this time. They're hitting it with something, a stone or a fallen timber.

"Come on, lad. Open up. We're your only chance at livin'."

All Erik can think of is Óskar. What they might do to get those numbers out of his head. What they will surely do once they have what they want.

Erik doesn't have a weapon. Why didn't he think to get one?

He scrabbles through the kitchen drawers. In one, he finds their only knife, a short blade he's used for peeling potatoes.

Another bang against the door, harder this time. Can Erik kill a man? He doesn't know. To save his son, he will try.

He looks at Óskar. "Get your coat and go to the back." A curtain closes off the sleeping alcove, where a wide rear window looks out at the mountains. "When you hear me shout, you climb out the window and run. Just like we practiced. You run and you don't stop.

You don't look back. You run all the way to *Amma* Yrsa's house. I'll be right behind you, I promise."

Óskar's eyes are huge.

"I love you, son. Now go."

Blinking back tears, Óskar slips on his coat and picks up his LEGO backpack. He climbs on the couch and unlatches the sliding glass. Erik reaches back and tugs the curtain across the opening.

There is another bang, and the caravan door buckles at the lock. Then it peels open, and cold air floods in.

The small man bounds up the steps with a grin on his face and Fitzsimmons right behind him. Erik raises his little paring knife.

The pale man also has a knife.

His hand moves faster than anything Erik has ever seen.

He cries out in pain. The last thing he sees is the pale man turning to Fitzsimmons. "The kid is running. Go get him."

ERIK is not alive to see the two men run up the mountain after Óskar. Trailing only by the length of a football pitch, they crash through the snow in their low boots. Their coats are good, but their thin socks and city pants are soon wet, then turn to ice. The wind cuts right through. Their chests heave with effort. They're not gaining on the boy, but they're not falling back, either.

The men are reassured to see that the boy is also not dressed for this weather. He wears pajama bottoms and no hat, yet carries a small book bag on his back. But he is light enough to run on top of the crusted snow, and he runs full out.

He does not stop to rest. He does not look back.

The snow falls harder. The men's legs ache. Ahead of them, the boy fades to a ghostly shape. Then he disappears entirely.

The smaller man stops, hands on his knees, breathing hard, and looks over his shoulder. The clouds are so thick that he can no longer see the barn. His own footprints are disappearing.

He says, "I don't care to die in this godforsaken place."

The taller man stops to consider and catch his breath. The weather is only getting worse. "Think he'll come down?"

"Come down to us or freeze to death up there, he's dead regardless. There's no shelter for kilometers in any direction."

"We wait below," says the taller man. "Give it twelve hours. He won't last twelve hours."

"Agreed," says the smaller man. "Let's get out of here."

They make their way downslope, following their own fast-fading tracks. They move the silver Mitsubishi behind the barn, then return to the camper and step over the cooling corpse.

They make hot chocolate on the little stove. Their wet clothes steam by the heater. They take turns watching out the rear window. The boy never returns.

Present Day

"SIR, we're still on mission." Wetzel held the phone to his ear as he slumped in the back of the Jeep. He didn't feel well at all. Fitz's ketamine injection had kicked in, and Wetzel could tell that the size of the dose was going to be a problem.

"You said that last time." Brunelli's voice was razor-sharp. "Mistakes have consequences."

Wetzel felt a flutter of fear. "Yes, we missed him at the bar, but we know where he's headed. The new plan still holds."

"You said that last time, too."

They had been reactive from the start, Wetzel had to admit. First, Sarah Price's accidental discovery of the video records, and her resulting moral outrage, which forced Wetzel's hand. Then Erik's unexpected instinct for survival.

When Seamus and Fitzsimmons reported that Erik and the kid were dead, Wetzel thought he'd contained the problem. But then the backpack showed up in Reykjavík Harbour, and Catherine Price had driven them nuts with her renewed conviction that the kid might still be alive.

At her insistence, Brunelli had instructed Wetzel to put a plan in motion. He'd connected Catherine with Ash, then put David Staple on a plane to Iceland. It seemed easy enough to get Ash sent back to the States, where Fitz would cut him into pieces and bury him in a shallow grave.

When the customs police refused to cooperate, Brunelli dug into the details again. Under his grilling, Seamus and Fitz had admitted that they hadn't actually seen the kid die. Maybe, Seamus offered, the backpack had washed down to the ocean with the kid's body.

Brunelli had gone ballistic. If Fitz and Seamus hadn't been so useful, and so necessary at that stage of the operation, Wetzel was fairly certain Brunelli would have told him to kill them both. As it was, Wetzel was sure that order would come before too long. Brunelli didn't like witnesses, either.

The secondary plan, then, was for Seamus to follow Ash until he found the kid or determined that the kid was actually dead. When Seamus reported finding Ash in an alley beaten half to death, Wetzel worried whether Ash would be any use at all.

Ash had surprised everyone by confronting Staple at the embassy. In retrospect, it was a sign of how difficult Ash would be to control, but at the time, Wetzel had just considered Staple a poor tool that had outlived its usefulness. When he told Seamus to eliminate him, Seamus had performed perfectly. The next day, Staple was a news item, and Ash was a wanted man.

It would have been easier if they could have taken him at the bar, moved him to the farm, and kept him sedated until they got what they needed from the family. Then they'd sink him in the bathtub and slit his wrists. The evidence would show that Peter Ash, decorated but damaged combat veteran, had murdered an entire Icelandic family, then taken his own life in a fit of remorse.

Even with Ash still under his own power, Wetzel knew the plan would work.

"Sir, the mission is sound," he told Brunelli. "Ash is running on fumes. We'll take him at the farm and improvise the rest. I'll call you when it's done."

Chapter 12

As PETER CLIMBED into the little Winnebago, the static flared.

He aimed his pocket flash around the space. He found a single dark, crusted island on the carpet, but no second stain. A year after the murder, the smell of death was faint but clear.

He felt a wave of dizziness and flashed back to that hot, dusty street. He stood beside Big Jimmy Johnson and stared into a blue Toyota Camry, where a family of four lay destroyed at his orders.

Then the children blinked their eyes.

He knew they were dead. He could see their ruined bodies. But now they reached for him.

He crashed out of the camper. With shaking hands, he strapped the bentwood snowshoes to his boots, then hoisted his pack and started walking. He was nowhere near a hundred percent.

Headed upslope with the ruined barn and the ocean at his back, he concentrated on what he'd seen. That single stain on the floor.

Bjarni was telling the truth. Erik was dead.

But maybe not the boy, not yet. Not if Peter could help it.

As he climbed, the dizziness returned twice. He felt a sharp pain in his head, and the world faded to gray. He wasn't sure, but the spells seemed to be getting longer. Behind him, the storm was already erasing his tracks.

He skirted a rock ledge and arrived at a broad saddle where the land rose on two sides. He consulted his folded map, found a route forward, and walked on.

The world faded twice more as he worked his way toward the high promontory he'd seen when he first drove into the valley. Each time he emerged from the blankness, he found himself someplace he didn't quite recognize, walking ahead of marks in the snow that he didn't remember making.

He didn't understand why a simple infection would make him feel so funky. It didn't matter. He'd get over it. He kept moving.

Finally he arrived at the great knobby scarp that leaned out over the hayfields and farm buildings five hundred meters below. The arctic hurricane hurled itself across the dark abyss of the sea.

He used Bjarni's folding shovel to dig himself a sheltered observation post. He counted back and realized he'd only slept maybe five hours total in the last three days.

Through his binoculars, the farm jumped into focus. In the ambient glow, it looked like something out of a picture book. Bright strands of Christmas lights hung along the eaves of the main house. Half a dozen cars and trucks wore fluffy white hats, including Bjarni's Škoda and the uncles' Dacia.

Waiting, he munched trail mix. He pulled his tent from his pack, thinking to shelter further from the storm. A gust plucked it from his hand and wrapped it around a high outcrop, where the wind played it like a teenager with a new drum set.

Finally, as daylight seeped through the falling snow, a line of police cars streamed up the long driveway to the farm. Hjálmar had gotten new tires and mustered reinforcements. Officers leaped from their cars and ran to the house and barns. This would probably take a while.

Then the real world faded again, and he found himself on that hot, dusty street, Big Jimmy at his back. The faded blue Toyota was full of broken glass. The dead children blinked up at him, then climbed out of their mother's arms. They opened the car doors and stepped into the street, reaching for him.

Peter should have been hot, but instead he was cold. His fingers were numb, and the tip of his nose burned. He opened his eyes, and it was dark again. Hours had passed. His body shivered uncontrollably. The infected wound on his head was leaking down the back of his neck.

He raised the binoculars and glassed the farm. The police cars were gone. Good. He couldn't stay in the open any longer.

He clambered to his feet, fumbled into the snowshoes, and

hoisted his pack. Then began the descent into the ring of farm buildings arranged like a fortification against the outside world.

If the police were gone, Brunelli's people would be coming. Peter had to get there first. Other than that, he was out of options.

His plan was simple. Knock on the door. Start talking.

Hope for mercy.

HALF blinded by the storm but cushioned by drifted snow, Peter followed the course of a fast-falling stream. As he walked, the world came and went, again and again. Sweating and shivering at the same time, he realized his fever had spiked.

The land flattened, and the stream widened as it wandered toward the sea. He turned toward the farm buildings, walking the bank of a laser-straight drainage trench with steep-angled sides, maybe five feet wide and five feet deep.

From above, he'd seen the cars parked at the largest farmhouse, so he walked in that direction. Lights shone from the eaves, and a wall of windows glowed. He was looking for a place to cross the trench when the world vanished midstride.

It came back slowly. He lay face-first in a cold crust of white, snowshoes tangled behind him, his backpack weighing him down. The drainage ditch had turned the corner of the meadow, but he'd kept walking in a trance and fallen to the bottom. His limbs felt weak, and his head hammered. Judging by the snow accumulated on his coat, he'd been gone for a while. It occurred to him that if he passed out again, he might never wake up.

He heard a low noise and looked up.

At the rim of the trench, a dog peered down at him and growled.

This was a sheep farm. Of course there was a dog.

It was black, brown, and white, shaggy with its winter coat. One eye was dark, the other light. An Australian shepherd, maybe forty pounds but looking bigger with all that fur.

It bounced down to the trench bottom. A meter away, it dropped its shoulders slightly, intent and growling again.

Peter shed his pack and lurched upright. One of his snowshoes had already come loose, the strap broken. The dog waited patiently as Peter bent and freed himself with frozen fingers.

When he finally stepped out of the straps, he scrambled up the steep side of the trench and into the farmyard. The dog came after him, alternating growls and feints at Peter's heels.

The Aussie was a sheepdog, bred to herd livestock.

Now it was herding Peter.

The lit-up main house stood fifty meters away. A simple structure with a wide-gabled roof and concrete walls, big enough for a large family. Peter headed in that direction, but the Aussie didn't like that idea. It came at him sideways and bumped his leg with its shoulder, turning him toward a long, low metal barn.

Maybe the dog had a point. Peter was in no shape to meet Bjarni and the uncles. He'd never get a chance to explain things, to warn them of the danger that followed. The uncles would wrap him in duct tape, then let the river wash him to the sea.

No, the barn wasn't a bad idea. Brunelli's goons would wait until after midnight. Peter could sleep, let the fever run its course. Although he didn't like taking advice from a dog.

Inside the barn, the white static rose. Only a few dim bulbs shone in the high white ceiling, and the animal smell was strong. He stumbled down the aisle between rows of waist-high stalls, each big enough for several dozen sheep. They were fluffy and dirty and scared, with horns that curled back over their heads. None of them wanted to be anywhere near Peter.

He picked up a sharp-tined hayfork and kept moving away from the door, looking for a place to hide. At the rear of the barn, he found a stall with fresh hay and fewer sheep. When he stepped over the barrier, they fled, scrambling toward the farthest corner.

He forked more hay into the stall as the static rose higher. He shivered so profoundly that the tool trembled in his hands.

At the back of the stall, where the angled ceiling met the wall, he sat and scooped loose hay over his legs. He closed his eyes, but his heart hammered. He was afraid of the dreams.

He'd put the bottle of Valium in his coat pocket. Now with shaking hands, he battled the childproof cap. It finally popped off with a jerk, and his last four pills flew into the hay. He picked desperately through the brittle stalks, rescuing pills one by one.

He wiped them off with his dirty fingers and swallowed them dry. Despite everything, they tasted fine.

As the Valium took hold, his nerves began to unknot, and the static hushed. Then he fell into a bottomless void.

He woke bathed in sweat, the dog's nose cold in his good eye. A broad-shouldered young woman with dark hair falling from an ice-blue stocking cap stood at the edge of the stall.

When she saw Peter push the dog's nose from his face, she turned her head away and called out. She held a square-tipped shovel in one hand. She wore a brown jacket and rubber boots.

Someone turned on more lights, and the bulbs wore fuzzy halos that almost sparkled. The dog whined softly.

Peter tried to bring back his few words of Icelandic. His whole body ached. "*Gud dai, ungfrú.* My name is Peter."

She just stared at him. He didn't want to think about what she might see. A battered one-eyed man passed out in her barn.

A giant in an orange coat stepped into view. He scowled at Peter and spoke into his phone. He had a gold earring. Peter knew his name, but he couldn't remember.

He needed a weapon. Moving slower than he wanted, he scrabbled under the hay but found nothing.

The orange giant shook his head. Ingo, that was his name.

Peter's hand brushed something hard. The hayfork. He grabbed it and put his elbows back to lever himself up. Ingo called something over his shoulder and put a foot on Peter's chest, pinning him to the floor. The woman stepped in, knelt on his arm, and pulled off his hat. Peter thrashed, and she caught his chin with one hand and stared at his face.

Axel appeared in the aisle and stepped over the stall wall carrying a big sheet of dirty plastic. Bjarni stood behind him with a coil of rope hung over the cast of his broken arm.

"Óskar," Peter said. "They're coming."

Ingo and Axel closed in.

As the plastic covered his face, he fell into the void again.

HE WOKE ON A HARD FLOOR in a small, low-ceilinged room with the dirty plastic sheet beneath him. The broad-shouldered young woman knelt on one side, and a slim older woman, with hooded eyes and hair like a gull's wing, knelt on the other. They were cutting the clothes off his body with kitchen knives that slid through the seams like water.

He turned and saw his winter coat and bibs hanging on the wall. In the shadows stood the enormous uncles, crossed arms like tree trunks. Bjarni still wore his red coat. Peter tried to speak, but the words never got past his clattering teeth.

His fleece sweater and pants were gone. The thin fabric of his long underwear parted like gossamer under the women's blades. Naked and trembling with fever, Peter didn't need to understand Icelandic to know they wanted to put him out in the snow.

Ingo moved to Peter's head, and Axel to his feet. They gathered up the plastic sheet, and it bunched over his face like a dirty caul. They lifted and carried him, suspended and swinging, to a brighter place, where they laid him down on a hard surface.

When the plastic parted, he saw white tiles and felt water falling down all around him. The younger woman pulled on rubber gloves. The dog sat, watching. Peter fell back into the void.

WHEN he woke again, he lay on his stomach on a new sheet of plastic, this time on a low bed. He was naked and dizzy and burning hot. Behind him, the young woman ran an electric clipper across his scalp with crisp indifference. His severed hair fell across his face and onto the sheet.

They were back in the small room. His head thundered, and his mouth was dry as the desert.

He tried to turn. "Óskar," he said. "They're coming."

"Shhh." She held his cheek to the pillow with a strong hand and kept the clipper moving as if she'd done this every day of her life. When she was done, she took her hand off his neck and called out. Bjarni came in with a bowl and a cloth and a cup and set them on the floor by his head. Then he looked at Peter, took a straight razor from his pocket, and flicked it open with a grim smile. The blade shimmered in the lamplight. Peter tried again to rise, but she pushed his face into the bed and held him there.

He felt the odd sensation of a wet paintbrush on his stubbled scalp. Old-fashioned shaving cream. The scrape of the blade against his skin, then a cloth wiping away the remains.

Then Bjarni dropped to his knees and wrapped his good arm around the top of Peter's head, pressing his cheek firmly to the plastic.

He bucked on the sheet. The young woman called out and put her knee on his back. The older woman came in and sat on his naked thighs, and he was held helpless and frantic.

He felt a stab of pain where Dónaldur had hit him with the bottle, then long moments of agony as she scoured the raw flesh. Then the cold, hard spike again, which he now recognized as alcohol, followed by pressure as she applied a bandage and tape.

"Okay," she said. Bjarni stood away, and the women rose to their feet. The older woman sighed, raked her hair back again, then lifted a huge steel syringe and stabbed him in the butt cheek. When she depressed the plunger, it felt like she'd set him on fire.

They left him thrashing in a scalding puddle of his own sweat.

"Save Óskar," he said to the empty room. "They're coming."

Then Ingo and Axel came in, picked up the ends of the sheet, and carried him into a bathroom, where they dumped him into a steep-sided white bathtub. The young woman wrapped his shaved scalp in a trash bag, then patted his cheek roughly and stuck a thermometer in his mouth. Ingo and Axel came in with buckets of snow and dumped them onto his body, again and again, until he lay buried to the neck in Iceland.

When the void opened up, Peter tried to hold on, but he fell through anyway.

HE WOKE with a start in the small room, unexpectedly lucid. The older woman sat in a chair beside the bed. Her gull-wing hair was cut in line with her jaw, framing the kind of face that belonged on a coin. She stared at him with an alarming frankness, as if measuring him for a prosthetic limb, or perhaps a coffin.

He'd been dreaming of Baghdad, the hot dusty street and the bloody dead. He knew this meant that the Valium had finally worn off, the end of his pills. Sparks climbed his spine. The static pushed him upright, but he couldn't get free of the sheets.

"Stay," said the older woman. "You are not well." She put a long, bony hand on his chest and pushed him back down. Watching her face, he knew this was Erik's grandmother, Yrsa. The matriarch of the family.

"What's wrong with me?" His tongue was thick.

"Karina believes you have an infection," Yrsa said. "In your blood. There are indications."

Sepsis, he thought. "How bad?"

"Perhaps you will die," Yrsa said. "Perhaps not." She held out a large glass of water. "Who else is with you?"

He took the glass and drank. "I'm alone. But the ones who killed Erik, they'll come, too. They want Óskar."

Yrsa watched him. "Why did you kill the man from your embassy?" She'd seen his face on the news.

"I didn't," he said. "The ones who killed Erik, they did it."

Clearly, she didn't believe him. "And why are you here?"

"Catherine Price sent me," he said. "Óskar's American grandmother. She's afraid for his life." His tongue felt thick. It was getting hard to organize his thoughts. "Why am I still alive?"

"It is poor manners to turn away a traveler in need." She rose. "When you are well enough, we will decide. Karina?"

The young woman appeared with the syringe. The plunger had a thumb ring and a needle like an ice pick. Karina made a circular motion with her hand. "Show me your, ah, backside."

"What is that?"

"Antibiotics," Yrsa said. "For sheep. Karina is the best large animal veterinarian in Nordhurland Vestra."

PETER woke gasping in the small room, heart pounding. The door stood open a crack, and a sliver of light seeped through. He could hear several conversations at once, along with the cheerful squeal and thump of children.

Óskar. He pushed himself up but felt a sharp tug on his arm. He was connected to a clear IV bag that hung from the back of a chair. The best large animal veterinarian in Nordhurland Vestra. Fluids meant for sheep.

Lungs tight, he pulled the needle from his arm and tried to stand. His feet tangled in the blanket, and he fell out of bed, naked and sweating. Driven by static, he pulled the sheet around himself and stumbled from the dark toward the light.

At the end of the hall, in a vast room with two dozen people at a long dining table spread with the remains of a feast, he tried to explain. "They're coming," he said. "Óskar."

The dog whined under the table. Adults held forgotten forks or coffee cups halfway to their mouths. Children looked up from their books or drawings. He searched their faces but didn't see the boy from the picture. They stared back at him, a wild one-eyed monster, bruised and swaying in their home.

Then Karina pushed back her chair and spoke softly to them. She wore a knit sweater over dark pants, her hair in an elaborate plait. Peter thought of June with an ache that went bone-deep.

On the left, past couches and overstuffed chairs, he saw a wide wall of windows and a sliding door with a view of a blizzard. He got the door open and one bare foot in the snow before a hand caught his arm and pulled him back. An ancient man with a hawk nose, his face a map of wrinkles. Thorvaldur, Óskar's great-great-grandfather, who had stabbed his neighbor with a hayfork.

Peter struggled, but Thorvaldur was tall and sturdy despite his years. With little effort, he moved Peter back to his small room and put him in a chair while Karina made the bed. With the sheets in order, she put a hand under his overheated arm. "Now. Sleep."

"Wait." The static bloomed electric up his spine. "No!"

On his feet again, he shook off her hand and pushed Thorvaldur aside. Karina called out, and the uncles picked him up by the armpits and carried him to bed.

The Icelanders held him while he shouted and thrashed in his fever. But they held tight as if each limb were a lifeline and Peter were the raging sea.

Finally he lay spent and splayed across the bed. Thorvaldur watched thoughtfully while Karina poured the contents of some little plastic packets into a tall glass of water, lifted Peter's head, and poured the bitter brew down his thirsty gullet.

The uncles held him down until sleep dragged him under.

HE LURCHED upright in bed and saw Thorvaldur beside him in the chair. The old man poured water from a pitcher into a tumbler and put it in Peter's hand.

Breathe in, he told himself. Breathe out. Finally he drank and held out the glass for more.

"You were in war." Thorvaldur's accent was thick. Outside the room, Peter heard children playing and the *clink* of dishes.

"Yes." Peter felt strange, like a windowpane. "Iraq and Afghanistan. How do you know?"

Thorvaldur held up a slim computer tablet. "I read news. You killed American in Reykjavík."

"No," Peter said. "Not me." He remembered that Brunelli's people would come for Óskar, but he also felt Karina's drugs working, medical-grade chemicals calming the static.

Peter knew the raid would come in the deepest hours of night. "What time is it?"

"Before dinner," Thorvaldur said. "I was in war also. Many years past."

And in halting words, Thorvaldur told the history of his war. How, at fifteen, he had crossed the ocean to Edinburgh with his three brothers in an open fishing boat to enlist in the British army.

"We were children," Thorvaldur said. "We thought it would be an adventure. But my brothers, they all died. I dream of them still." Eighty years past, and still the war lived inside him.

"You dream also, yes?" Thorvaldur said. He grabbed Peter's shoulder with a gnarled hand, surprising him with its warmth. Something in the old man's face, a kinship. "Come. Tell me."

So Peter did. He told about that dusty Baghdad street and the blue Toyota with bad brakes, the family just trying to escape their own neighbors. He talked until he fell into a fitful sleep.

WHEN HE WOKE AGAIN, THE lamps shone plain yellow light. The swelling in his eye had gone down, and he had binocular vision again. He still felt the static, but in the background. The house was silent except for the sound of his own breathing.

What had woken him? Something he'd heard in his sleep, a noise he couldn't identify. He knew the sounds of the house, the children playing, the adults talking and washing up, the dog's nails ticking across the tile. But he didn't know this soft rasp.

His door was closed for the first time.

He pushed himself out of bed, still naked, and went to the door. The knob wouldn't turn. The Icelanders had locked him in.

He tightened his grip, then gave the hollow knob a short, sharp twist. There was a thin metallic snap; then the knob turned freely.

The hallway was dark. The big room was empty of people. To the left, snow shone through the wall of tall windows. Ahead, past the couches and chairs, a wall of bookshelves and an opening that would lead to more bedrooms. To the right, a row of coats on hooks, then the dining table and kitchen. A clock told him it was 3:00 a.m. He saw no source of the unfamiliar noise.

He reversed course. Past his sickroom at the end of the hall was a laundry room, its window showing the empty side yard and sheep barn. The snow had stopped, but the clouds were low and dark. Beside the washer and dryer was a long table with neatly folded clothes.

Peter found a pair of soft black gym pants that fit well enough and a dark blue long-sleeved T-shirt that felt strange pulled over his shaved scalp. Almost like having his jarhead haircut again.

Then he heard it, more faintly in the laundry room. The softest of rasps. No, not a rasp. A slow, soft crunch. Then another.

The sound stopped him. Slightly louder this time, the slow crunch that he now recognized as a cautious footstep in the snow. He turned to the wall of windows as a shadow came into view, silhouetted against the winter landscape. As it advanced toward the glass sliding door, another shadow followed silently in its footsteps. Behind that shadow, two more.

They were here.

Chapter 13

Tom Wetzel's stomach lurched as the *Valkyrja* heaved over the top of the wave, then fell and buried its nose in the sea. The windows showed only ocean for a moment, until the little tour boat rebounded skyward and water streamed from its high bow.

The *Valkyrja*'s captain, an elderly Icelander named Einar, grumbled to himself as he goosed the throttle. Fitzsimmons had to break the man's jaw before he'd agreed to leave the shelter of his home fjord. Fist tight on the grab rail, Wetzel suspected Einar was giving them a deliberately rough ride.

Cassie and Thad, in tactical black, whooped with every wave, while Fitzsimmons stared at the darkness. Seamus just grinned at Wetzel. "You won't die at sea, lad. I'm almost certain of it."

Wetzel clenched his jaws and swallowed hot acidic bile. It wasn't the waves but the fear rising. Fear of drowning, yes, but also fear of failure. He needed to finish this thing. As Brunelli had reminded him several times already, Wetzel was in this up to his eyeballs, and he'd better get it done.

Unfortunately, his team had lost several days. The accidental dose of date-rape tranquilizer was big enough to relax a rhinoceros, and the side effects got ugly. So Seamus had turned the team back to Akureyri to regroup.

Wetzel was glad he was the unit paymaster. Otherwise they might have dumped him in the snow and gone on without him.

The next morning, they'd made a second try at the highway. But the snow was worse, and the roadblock hadn't gone away—if anything, there were more cops, and it looked like they were searching every car and checking identification.

Wetzel knew the police were mainly looking for Ash, but the

stepped-up scrutiny was a problem. Wetzel was the only one there on his real name, and their papers wouldn't withstand an Interpol investigation. So again they headed back to Akureyri.

It took Wetzel most of the day to locate a charter captain who was available for a quick sightseeing cruise, and Fitzsimmons's fists convinced Einar to take them into the open ocean. A December trip across the north coast of Iceland in the aftermath of a hurricane was a bad idea in every way, but time was short.

CAPTAIN Einar turned the tour boat into the waves, using the engine to hold them in place offshore. Seamus dropped the six-man Zodiac down and pulled the bow close. "Off you go, then."

"I'm staying aboard," Wetzel said. "The rest of you can finally go earn your pay."

"You're trained on this North Sea boat, then?" Seamus asked, pale face pleasant under the dark beard. "You can read the navs, manage the heavy seas, bring her home to Akureyri? Because I came up fishing off Strangford in a boat much like this one. Or are we trusting wee Einar to keep his bloody mouth shut?"

Like every marine, Wetzel had trained on assault boats. He could manage a Zodiac just fine, but he was no North Sea pilot. He shouldered his pack and jumped down to the little inflatable.

He got the outboard started. Cassie jumped in next with Thad right behind her, the two ex-CIA killers sure-footed as hounds. Timing the wave perfectly, Fitzsimmons dropped in like a ghost.

Wetzel cranked the throttle and angled the Zodiac through the surf toward the sheltered beach across the road from the farm.

Thad gave a woo-hoo. "Time to kill some people and make some money, honey."

THE four figures stacked up at the glass sliding door, one behind the next. They wore black tactical gear and face masks against the cold.

Peter padded barefoot around the back of the dining table, where a few crumb-specked plates remained on the surface. He saw dessert forks and butter knives, not any kind of useful weapon. At least he'd borrowed dark clothing from the laundry. In the unlit room, they helped him melt into the shadows.

The lead man crouched at the latch with a pick in his hand. The lock wouldn't take long.

He would have to work fast, take them one by one as they came through the door. In the hand of the third figure, he saw the glint of a knife. But he didn't see any guns.

Peter had nothing. The orange-handled fishing knife was in his pack, along with the folding shovel and the ice axe, but he had no idea where his pack was. He looked over at the open kitchen. No knife block with handles sticking out. He couldn't afford the time to rifle the drawers, or the resulting rattle.

He considered shouting to wake the family, but quickly decided against it. The noise would remove his only advantage, and even the uncles would take a minute to gather themselves. Plus, there were too many children who could, in their panic, walk into the fight. So he'd remain silent for the moment.

Bare feet sure on the warm tile, he crept along the line of bookshelves, approaching the sliding door from the shadows.

The lock clicked. The lead man stood up, stowed his picks, took a blade from his belt, then reached for the door handle.

Peter slipped a hardback book from the shelf at his back. If he wanted a knife, he was going to have to take it.

With the faintest of rumbles, the door slid open, and a long-limbed shape stepped through. Peter recognized the swimmer's body. The man in the Ohio State sweatshirt, come to do harm.

Peter held the book with a loose grip, spine out. When Ohio State was fully inside, Peter stepped from the shadows with the book in his hand and punched the spine into the other man's larynx. The crunch of ruined cartilage was barely louder than the sound of the wind pouring cold through the open door.

Ohio State kept coming, but his mouth hung open as realization dawned. Peter kicked him in the side of the knee; he folded to the floor with a *thud*, and the knife flew away. Preoccupied with his asphyxiation, Ohio State was no longer a threat. He'd be brain-dead in ten minutes.

The second figure was small but fast with the knife leading the way. Peter recognized the black blade and Spatula Woman's quickness with it. If she took note of her fallen comrade, he didn't see it. He was too busy trying to read her eyes.

After a series of lightning feints and probing slashes, she came for the axillary artery just below his collarbone. But Peter's arms were longer than hers. He caught the tip of her knife in the cover of the book, and when she withdrew the blade, his arm was already cocked for the hard jab. He punched a corner of the book into her eye, breaking at least one bone in her face.

As she found her balance and raised the knife again, Peter brought the heavy book around backhand, slammed the spine into her temple, and knocked her to the floor. She was done.

The next attacker was already stepping through the doorway with a wide sheath knife in his hand. His nailhead eyes were bright behind his mask, and he was clearly the most dangerous of the crew. Peter knew this was the lurker from the hotel bar.

The man stood in an easy crouch and watched Peter's eyes, waiting to see fear and desperation. But Peter wasn't giving the lurker that pleasure. He still held the book in his left hand. With his right, he reached out to the bookshelves, blindly found another hardback, and flung it sidearm. It bounced off the other man's chest. A second book hit his knife arm with no apparent effect. Then two more, thrown simultaneously, opened midair like startled pigeons flying into the lurker's face.

For a brief moment, the man's view was blocked. He raised his left hand to brush the books aside. By then Peter was almost on him. He gave a short cry, and the man, still mostly blind, instinctively raised the big knife. Peter now held the book out and open, each hand gripping a cover and half of the pages, and met the tip of the knife with the inside of the spine. The sharp point punched through the folded paper and glue and cover. Peter slammed the book shut and twisted with both hands, tore the paper-trapped knife from the lurker's hand, and spun the whole thing across the room, where it clattered across the tile.

The dog barked, a muffled sound, as Peter stepped inside the other man's guard. He slammed the web of his hand up and under the man's jaw and popped him back into the wall of windows. Then Peter dipped his other arm down to scoop up Spatula Woman's black blade, and when the lurker lunged forward again, Peter buried the knife in the other man's throat.

The lurker was still falling when Peter turned toward the door. A fourth figure stood just outside, eyes wide. He held a knife, but it was down at his side. Then he turned and ran into the snow.

Shoeless, coatless, blood burning, Peter ran after him with everything he had. He followed the dark figure up the driveway toward the road, his bare feet cold in the snow.

The man ahead was too large to be the Irishman. He had to be Wetzel, who'd always taken up the rear anyway. Wetzel, who'd pulled Peter into this whole thing.

The subarctic air ached in his chest, but his lungs were open and sucking oxygen. Wetzel ran ahead, dressed in boots and gloves, a coat and thermal pants. He ran for his life. But Peter ran for something else. He ran for the lives of others, and that made all the difference. He drew closer, then closer still.

The driveway came to the road, but Wetzel continued straight across it, clearly visible as he ran overland toward the sea. Peter's frozen feet tore on the rocks beneath the snow, but they were too cold to feel pain. He left red tracks behind him. Ahead, the land ended in darkness. The wind threw salt spray into Peter's face.

He finally caught Wetzel on the edge of a rocky gray beach, where an orange Zodiac had been pulled into the shelter of a cluster of boulders. He got a hand on Wetzel's neck and rode him down to the gravel. Wetzel rolled and raised the knife, but Peter slammed the hand to the rocky ground, and the knife flew away. Peter tore off the mask to see Wetzel's face.

Wetzel shouted, but Peter couldn't hear his words over the wind and the waves. They didn't matter anyway. Wetzel twisted and made it to his knees, arms out toward the Zodiac, but Peter threw him into the icy surf, where he knelt on the man's biceps and clamped a hand on Wetzel's face, holding him under.

It only took a few minutes, but it felt like forever.

Finally, Peter rose to his feet and let the waves take the body. Shaking uncontrollably, he looked out across the darkness, where a dim light rose and fell, getting smaller as the waiting boat slipped out to sea.

His legs ached in the icy water. He filled his lungs with the glorious wind. He was alive and glad of it. He had no regrets at killing Brunelli's people, Wetzel least of all.

Peter looked over his shoulder. One-armed Bjarni splashed into the surf, eyes wide. "Are you all right?" he said.

Peter didn't have an answer. He felt Bjarni's hand on his arm. "You killed those people," he said. "But you saved all of us."

Peter still didn't speak. What would he say?

Bjarni gave a polite tug. "Come," he said. "Please. You need to get inside. Unless you want to freeze to death out here."

Peter had been prepared to die over there for the men he'd served with. More than prepared, he'd been willing, if that's what it took. But was that the same as wanting it?

No. It wasn't.

In that moment, he saw himself clearly, perhaps for the first time. War had made him. He was a trained hunter and killer of men, and damn good at it. He was still useful. There was work to be done. He might as well get on with it.

Bjarni shed his red coat, and Peter wrapped it around his shoulders. They waded from the water and walked toward the road, where the brown Škoda waited with the doors wide open and the heater going full blast.

AT THE farmhouse, Peter stripped and stood under the hot shower until he stopped shivering. Karina dressed his torn feet and the vodka-bottle wound with fresh gauze and tape. In the mirror, a hungry stranger with a bruised face and a bandage on his shaved head stared back at him. He looked like a mental patient, he thought. Which maybe wasn't so far off.

He found Yrsa in the great room with a mop and a bucket, scrubbing blood from the floor. He heard a murmur of conversation through the walls, the children awake but kept in their rooms, away from the carnage. Through the wall of windows, he saw Ingo and Axel lining up bodies on a dirty sheet of plastic. Maybe the same plastic they'd wrapped him in not long ago.

"I'm sorry about this," Peter said.

Yrsa wore high rubber boots and a striped flannel nightgown, her hair up in short pigtails. She looked at him with caliper eyes, then held out the mop handle. "Scrub," she said.

Peter rinsed the mop and wrung it. The water ran pink. "This isn't over. He'll just send more men."

"Who?" She put her hands on her hips. "Who threatens my family? Who murdered my grandson and his wife?"

"His name is Jerry Brunelli. He's Sarah's stepfather."

Her eyes blazed. "And why did he do this?"

"I'm not sure, exactly," Peter said. "Sarah was an IT security specialist. Brunelli is a power broker in Washington, D.C. My guess is Sarah found something that threatened him, and he killed her for it. Something that Brunelli hasn't found yet. Because if he'd found it, he wouldn't have sent those people here."

"That is all you know?"

"It's not much," Peter admitted. "Listen, I left my pack out in the snow. Do you have my boots somewhere so I can get it?"

Her mouth tightened. She waved her hand toward a closet.

He guessed this meant they would let him live.

It took him a while to find his pack, buried deep under fresh snow. When he returned, the bodies were gone and the floor was clean. Ingo, Axel, Bjarni, and Thorvaldur all sat at one end of the long dining table, drinking coffee.

The other end of the table was packed with children. He counted fifteen of them, ages two to maybe twelve, talking and eating pancakes with powdered sugar and jam. Like the morning after a sleepover, he thought. Maybe that's what this was, all the kids at Grandma Yrsa's house for the holiday.

Several children looked about the right size, including a quiet boy at the far corner, half hidden behind wavy blond hair that fell across his face. Peter crouched at the kids' end of the table.

"Who wants to play a game?" he asked. The kids didn't know

what to make of the stranger with the shaved head, but they did quiet down. They'd started learning English in kindergarten.

"The game is called, What number comes next?" He didn't look at the boy with the hair over his face. "I'll say some numbers. When I stop, you keep going. Got it? Here we go." Slowly and clearly, he said, "Three point one four one five nine."

Every child stared at him like he was crazy, then looked at each other to see if anyone else understood the game. Except for the quiet blond boy, whose lips moved silently with the next numbers in the sequence. He knew four thousand of them.

Yrsa strode from the kitchen, glaring daggers at Peter. "What is the point of this?"

"You know the point," Peter said quietly. "Someone came looking for something hidden. What's the best place to hide something you don't want anyone to find?"

Yrsa's face changed as she figured it out. She clapped her hands. "Children, time to go outside. Who wants to have a snowball war?" She pointed a bony finger at Ingo and Axel, who obediently abandoned their coffee to shepherd the children into their coats and boots.

Yrsa reached out to the quiet blond boy. "Why don't you stay with me for a minute, *saeti*." She pulled him gently onto her lap and wrapped her arms around him. He buried his face in her chest. "What else are you carrying in that fine mind of yours? Something your mom or dad told you?"

"It's a secret," Óskar whispered. He was no longer the wild, exuberant boy from Catherine's video. Peter wondered if the damage was permanent.

"You can tell me your secret." Yrsa kissed his forehead. "Grandmothers are very good at keeping secrets."

Óskar gave Peter a skeptical eyeball.

"I'll put my hands over my ears," Peter said.

Yrsa glared at Bjarni and Thorvaldur, who also covered their ears.

Óskar only spoke for a few seconds before Yrsa said, "*Saeti*, wait one minute." Then looked at Peter. "Pen and paper, top drawer by the refrigerator."

When Óskar was done and Yrsa had double-checked her

handwriting against Óskar's memory, she gave the boy a hug and a kiss and sent him outside, where miniature Viking raiders were staging a snowball war with Ingo and Axel as their opposing kings. The boy ran up to enormous Axel, jumped onto his back, and pumped his fist in victory. Maybe Óskar would be okay.

Yrsa sighed. "How did I not think to ask?"

"How would you know? Erik has been dead for a year. You had no idea they were coming for Óskar until four hours ago."

"Well, it's better that we all know the secret," Yrsa said. "That way they're not after Óskar. They're after all of us."

"Já, já," said Bjarni. Thorvaldur nodded, too.

Peter was really getting to like these Icelanders.

"That reminds me," he said. He went to his pack, opened the top compartment, and pulled out a LEGO book bag. "I thought Óskar might want this. It washed up in Reykjavík Harbour."

Yrsa unzipped it and examined the contents. Someone, probably Hjálmar, had put the stuffed bear through the wash several times. The LEGO guys were still safe in their plastic jar.

"I've been wondering," Peter said. "If Óskar made it here safe, how did his book bag end up in the ocean?"

"We gave it a Viking funeral," Yrsa said. "Sent it to sea on a toy boat. The end of one life and the beginning of the next."

"The bag made it all the way from here to Reykjavík Harbour?"

She shook her head. "From here, the ocean currents would take it to Norway. So we launched from Reykjavík. I wanted it to wash ashore in the city."

It took Peter a moment to understand. "You wanted the backpack found," he said. "You wanted the people who killed Sarah and Erik to come back."

Yrsa pulled the rubber bands from her pigtails and shook out her gull-wing hair. "It was the only way to learn who our enemies were," she said. "The only way to keep Óskar truly safe."

These damn Vikings.

WHILE Yrsa and Karina got on the computer to figure out where Óskar's secret led, Peter went to check the bodies, laid out behind the barn in the front loader of the big tractor. Bjarni and Thorvaldur stood silently while Peter searched the pockets.

The two grad students each carried a Ziploc bag with a stack of króna notes and a cheap Icelandic burner phone, along with a cargo pocket filled with zip ties. The lurker carried twice as much money, two spare knives, and an expensive, encrypted sat phone.

Peter tried to get them unlocked, but their facial recognition didn't work, until Thorvaldur reached out and rearranged the damaged faces. Even the lurker's sat phone unlocked, a combination of poor operational security and excessive confidence.

Only the lurker's phone had anything on it. Four numbers. Two rang the grad students' phones. The third number rang and rang but never went to voice mail. The fourth number was answered on the second ring.

"Where are you, laddie?" A certain tension in the voice.

Peter smiled. "Hello, Seamus."

A pause. "I'm sorry, boyo, you've got the wrong number."

"Tell him I'm coming," Peter said. "I'll send you a text so you know what to expect."

The connection died, but Peter knew the Irishman wouldn't dump his phone, not quite yet. Peter took pictures of three dead, ruined faces, then sent them with the words *You're next*.

Bjarni and Thorvaldur looked at the screen over his shoulder, then looked at each other. Thorvaldur said something in Icelandic. Bjarni raised his eyebrows.

"What did he say?" Peter asked.

"He says you must be a berserk, to defeat these three and the other one. A wild man, a fearless bear-warrior."

"Not fearless," Peter said. "Just motivated."

Back at the farmhouse, they found Yrsa and Karina sitting at the table with a laptop, watching grainy video with their hands over their mouths.

PETER had to move fast. But he didn't want to spook Brunelli.

On the lurker's encrypted phone, he typed in the server's address and passcode, triple-checking the long string of numbers, then sent it to June Cassidy's work email. The subject line read *LOOK AT THIS RIGHT NOW*.

More than anyone, he trusted June's ruthless journalistic dedication to the truth, along with her network at the nonprofit group Public Investigations, to get the information into the right hands.

Then he realized the unknown sender and the URL link might get his email dumped into her spam filter. He should just call her. Even if the idea scared the hell out of him.

Her reaction was roughly what he'd expected, although the volume was louder. "What the hell are you doing in Iceland?"

Of course she'd seen the news about the murder of a U.S. State Department lawyer in Iceland. She was an investigative reporter. Peter's name and photo would have been featured prominently.

"I'm sorry," he said. "It's a long story."

"Then you damn well better start talking, Marine." Her voice crackled, and it wasn't the line. "I was worried about you. Are you safe? Are you in jail?"

He liked that she didn't ask if he'd killed David Staple. "I'm good," he said. "I miss you. Listen, did you get an odd email?"

A pause while she checked. "That's you? What is this?"

"Do you still have contacts in the State Department?"

Shouting, she said, "I thought you were going to the desert."

"June," he said. "When trouble calls my name, you know I have to answer."

"You lied to me. I am really pissed off." He could hear the tears in her voice.

"I'm sorry," he said. "I am. But right now I have to deal with this. Will you get on the horn to your Washington contacts?"

"Yes," she said. And hung up.

Peter was grateful that his next call would be easier. He dug his Icelandic burner out of his pack, tore off the tinfoil, and found Catherine's number. He wanted to tell her that Óskar was alive.

A man's voice answered. "Catherine Price's phone."

"Who is this?"

The voice was cold. "No, who the hell is this?" It was Novak, Catherine's bodyguard.

"This is Peter. We met in Portland, after Catherine asked me to find her grandson. Can I talk to her?"

"No," Novak said.

"Why not?"

"She's dead."

Peter closed his eyes. "How did she die?"

"She was mugged. In the District."

"And where the hell were you?"

"Getting the car." Novak spoke without inflection, but Peter knew the ex-cop was furious. He held himself responsible.

Brunelli wasn't wasting any time.

Peter glanced at a television in the corner showing the Icelandic news. The top story was the murder of David Staple. Peter's face filled the screen, followed by shots of a series of police roadblocks on cold, snowy roads.

Getting back to the States was going to be problematic. Even if Peter could make his way to an airport and charter a plane, he had no passport.

He turned to Ingo and Axel, who had returned to the table with tall stacks of pancakes. "You boys want to go fishing?"

Chapter 14

Potomac, Maryland
Two Weeks Later

JERRY BRUNELLI PACED through his house, from his office to the kitchen to the dining room, hating how the ankle monitor chafed on his skin. As if he were a common felon.

The confidence of the U.S. attorney assigned to his case amused Brunelli no end. The very fact that the judge had granted him house arrest was evidence that the machinery of his liberation was already in motion. He'd planned for this contingency as he'd planned for every other.

The heels of Brunelli's loafers echoed on the polished floors as he walked from entry hall to living room to grand ballroom. The house had been built by a railroad baron and enlarged several times. Brunelli, to burnish his image and launder his reputation, had thrown lavish parties here, including an annual costume ball whose central conceit allowed anyone to talk to anyone.

To that end, the house was an investment that had paid off many times over. After all, it was at one of those costume balls that Brunelli had met a certain Russian businessman who had given him the speck of polonium that Brunelli had used to eliminate his business partner, Ken Price. Dropped in a cup of herbal tea, the radioactive isotope had lingered in Ken's system just long enough to give him metastatic cancer, leaving the widow Price and her inherited shares vulnerable to a sweetheart takeover and Jerry Brunelli in control of the firm.

Of course, he'd needed to remove Catherine's son from the equation first, but it was a small thing for a man of Brunelli's capacities to arrange for a brake failure on an icy mountain road. He'd also kept Sarah close first by hiring her fledgling business, then by sending her a steady stream of new clients. By biting the hand that fed her, Sarah Price had practically killed herself.

He'd even maneuvered Catherine into demanding, as a condition of marriage, that he get out of lobbying for "consulting," where the money was better and the oversight minimal. Brunelli had been her white knight, riding to her rescue in a time of need.

She hadn't even signed a prenup. With her unfortunate death in a mugging, actually a carefully planned murder at the hands of Detective Moore of the Metro PD, who had found a small gap in her bodyguard's vigilance, Brunelli now owned it all.

He was pleased to learn that Tom Wetzel and Fitzsimmons were missing and presumed dead, too. The ex-marine that Wetzel had recommended to Catherine had not performed as promised. Rather than provide the ribbon to wrap up the entire Sarah Price problem, the man had somehow escaped the noose tied around his neck. As a result, Brunelli's leverage had been leaked to the news.

Of course, Brunelli had immediately set his contingencies in motion. He had a telegenic academic expert asserting that the footage had been created from whole cloth with advanced technology. The prominent network personality was vigorously denying his sexual proclivities on social media, claiming that the video was a smear tactic to attack his credibility. Significant technical evidence of Wetzel's involvement, along with his mysterious disappearance, made him a fine candidate for the leader of the plot. Brunelli's lawyers were working hard behind the scenes to make his own role vanish entirely.

They had better, Brunelli thought as he completed the circle to his private office overlooking the pool and the Potomac. He knew where too many bodies were buried. They couldn't afford to have him talking to the press, or to Congress.

Time for a drink. As he surveyed the selection of liquors on his bar cart, Brunelli's mind returned to the ex-marine.

Brunelli's ankle monitor, along with his legal troubles and the small army of federal agents occupying the grounds of his estate, were all the fault of this troublesome person. The fact that he was still at large was only a modest cause of concern, however. Given that the man was wanted for murder, with warrants for his arrest issued in Europe, Canada, and America, rational self-interest dictated that he was almost certainly saving his own neck rather than seeking out Brunelli's own.

Not to mention the fact that Brunelli's extensive network was combing the earth for him at this very moment.

Brunelli lifted the antique crystal decanter and poured himself a substantial measure of the fifty-year-old bottle of Macallan he'd bought at auction the year before. He raised the glass and let the flavor fill his mouth. The Scotch truly did taste better because it was so expensive. It was worth every penny.

Soon this would be over, and he'd go back to business as usual. He looked out at the floodlit night, raised his glass, and smiled.

The chime of breaking glass was the last sound he ever heard.

THE ELDERLY FISHING BOAT rode the East Greenland Current toward Labrador, her high bow and narrow waist slicing elegantly through the waves. She carried extra fuel drums in her fishhold, and her cranes were pulled in and lashed down tight.

Inside, Peter and the others watched developments on the satellite feed. Things happened quickly after June Cassidy called her contacts. Her story went live twenty-four hours after that.

So far, all the blame was falling on Tom Wetzel. All the videos had been added to the server using his log-in and workstation.

Jerry Brunelli was turning out to have a world-class crap-proof umbrella.

In the four days it took Ingo and Axel to drive to Seydisfjordur and return with the *Freyja*, the Icelandic police had come back to the farm twice. Peter had taken a tarp and his new sleeping bag out into the snow to catch up on his sleep.

Once she lost the Labrador Current, the *Freyja* headed south past Newfoundland, Nova Scotia, and New England, staying far enough offshore to avoid the attention of the Coast Guard.

Ten days after leaving Iceland, Peter ran the orange Zodiac across twelve nautical miles of open water toward a small marina outside of Ocean City, Maryland. The waves were manageable, and the sun was warm on Peter's face. The mid-Atlantic coast felt like Bermuda after the icy run across the North Atlantic.

It was off-season, not to mention almost dark, so nobody saw four men climb out of the small inflatable dinghy at the tender's dock and walk across the boatyard into the parking lot, where Novak sat waiting in a black four-door Silverado pickup.

Even in jeans and a sweatshirt, he still looked like the D.C. Metro cop he'd been.

Peter said, "Did you get the stuff I asked for?"

"On the floor." Novak nodded at the paper bag at Peter's feet. Ingo and Axel opened the back doors and climbed inside, pushing Bjarni into the middle seat. The big truck sank on its springs.

Novak looked at Peter. "Who are these guys? What are you looking to do here?"

"They're Vikings," Peter said. "They came to see the Air and Space Museum. For myself, honestly, I'm still figuring it out." He dumped the contents of Novak's bag into his day pack. Zip ties, duct tape, nitrile gloves, a folding knife. "Let's just take a look around. What's the security setup?"

Novak put the truck in drive. "The place is huge," he said. "There are two U.S. marshals at the front and a pair of cars blocking the driveway. They have four more men watching the doors and two men patrolling the grounds."

"Only eight guys? For a five-acre property?"

"That's because they're focused on keeping Brunelli inside," Novak said. "Not keeping someone else out." His eyes flicked to the backpack, then at Peter. "Really. What are you thinking?"

Peter reminded himself that Novak had gone out on a limb, acting as the driver for a wanted man. That alone was a crime.

"What I'd like," Peter said, "is to find a way to put Brunelli in an orange jumpsuit for the rest of his life. But I'm worried he's going to weasel out of everything. Did you talk to that Metro detective, Phil Moore?"

Peter had suggested Novak reach out to the man who'd run the investigation into Sarah's death, who'd also identified Erik Gríms- son as the primary suspect. The Norwegian had turned up several overseas bank accounts in the name of Moore's first ex-wife.

"Moore wasn't at work, and he didn't answer his phone, so I went to his apartment. He didn't answer my knock, either." Novak kept his eyes on the road. "But I knew that smell coming from under his door. He wasn't going to be talking to anyone."

"How did he die?"

"I got the ME report two days ago. Tissue samples put the cause of death as alcohol poisoning. The tox report also showed traces of ketamine in his system. You know what ketamine is?"

"A club drug," Peter said. "Also a date-rape drug." He thought of the syringe in the hotel bar in Akureyri. "Someone's tying up loose ends. Which reminds me. When you were working with Catherine, did you ever run into an Irishman? Small guy, very pale, black hair, heavy beard? Maybe went by Seamus?"

"Brunelli's bodyguard is an Irishman named Fitzsimmons," Novak said. "But he's the opposite of small. He went to Iceland with Wetzel and vanished. What's the story with your guy?"

The Norwegian had finally tracked down Seamus from the photo Peter took in Iceland. His real name was Seamus Conner. A Belfast policeman until he was arrested for murdering four of his fellow officers for the IRA. He disappeared from police custody in 1995, surfacing later in South Africa and Russia, where he'd worked as an enforcer for various criminal organizations.

"I'd really like to get hold of him," Peter said. "Aside from Brunelli, Seamus is the only guy left standing."

They dropped the Icelanders at the Kimpton in Dupont Circle just after seven. They really did want to see the Air and Space Museum, along with the National Mall at night, and Peter really didn't want them crashing through the woods in his wake.

Peter and Novak arrived in Potomac after nine.

NOVAK cruised the neighborhood. Most houses stood on large, wooded lots. Many residents had thoughtfully planted evergreen trees for year-round screening from the neighbors and the road.

Peter had spent part of the drive with a good map. Now he directed Novak down MacArthur Boulevard, with the dark woods of the C&O Canal National Historical Park on the left. Past Falls Road and into the park, Novak continued until he came to VFW Post 5633, a low brick building. He turned into the circular driveway and paused just long enough for Peter to roll out of the truck and disappear into the trees.

The night was moonless, and Peter was effectively invisible in the narrow band of forest between the road and the iron fences of the houses. He had the map in his head now, and when the road veered left, he kept to the shoulder of an irregular slope, steps muffled in the soft winter loam. He carried his day pack with water and energy bars and the things Novak had bought.

He smiled in the dark, knowing he was home.

He went to the top of the slope with his binoculars and spotted Brunelli's place a half mile away, lit up like a museum on the night of a gala. Every window shone, and the terraces and formal gardens were bright with accent lighting. Peter marked a modest rise where he could set up for a better view, then set out again.

He hadn't lied to Novak. He had no plan of action other than a night of surveillance. On the other hand, if an opportunity presented itself, he would be ready.

Slow and silent, he worked his way upwind toward the rise. Then the breeze rose, carrying the faint tang of cigarette smoke.

Peter froze in place, ears straining for sound. He heard nothing. The smell of smoke faded. He held that way for several minutes before he moved on, marking each footfall. He didn't want to meet an armed U.S. marshal in the dark.

The rise turned out to be a cluster of ancient granite boulders too stubborn to wash down to the river. He stood still and silent at its base, eyes searching for a path up, when he heard a soft *phut* overhead and the distant tinkle of breaking glass.

Peter knew those sounds. He tucked himself into a fold in the granite and waited. The shooter would prize speed over quiet now. A faint mechanical rattle, above and to his left. He circled that way, face down and ears wide open. The brittle crack of a stick. He circled faster. Then the scrape of a boot directly above him. He reached up and got a hand around the man's ankle as he sidestepped, pulling him, face-first, six feet down to the ground.

The man hit without crying out, already gathering his feet under him, scooping up a scoped hunting rifle as he came. Peter kicked him in the head, and it was over.

His back to a tree, the Irishman's eyes fluttered open as Peter zip-tied his arms around the trunk. He cleared his throat and spat. "I'm a changed man, lad. On the side of the angels now."

"I can see that." Peter used another zip tie to cinch the man's neck to the tree. "You don't like your old boss anymore?"

"I didn't mind him," Seamus said. "But I've a new employer now, pays much better. Wants to clean up a big mess."

Peter smiled. "Me too." He pulled the clip knife from his pocket and flicked it open with his thumb.

Seamus dug his bootheels into the dirt to get away, but he was tied up tight. "Surely we can come to an arrangement. There's money enough for everyone."

Peter put the point of the knife to the underside of the Irishman's chin and murmured, "Everyone thinks it's about the money." He pressed the tip gently into the soft skin. Seamus held himself very still. A dark drop of blood welled against the steel.

Then Peter took the knife away and, without his hands touching the rifle, smeared the collected blood into the textured plastic of the butt, just where it would meet a sniper's cheek.

Seamus twisted against his bonds and got nowhere. "Ach, lad, you're killing me."

"Actually," Peter said, folding the knife back in his pocket, "I'm not. No matter how much I'd like to."

He heard the crackle of radios as the marshals moved across the estate's lower gardens. Soon enough they'd venture past the fence. The Irishman's fingerprints would tie him to his Interpol warrants. If he talked to the feds, he might avoid getting strangled in an Irish prison. Or maybe not.

"Peter," the Irishman called out. "Peter!"

Peter didn't answer. Instead he turned away and angled downslope toward the river. As he walked, the breeze came up again, carrying the smell of wet dirt and rotting leaves and the coming promise of spring.

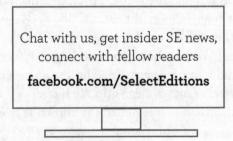

AfterWords

Setting has always been very important to author Nick Petrie. He approaches it almost as if he's creating a character. In *The Wild One*, Petrie succeeds in generating a powerful sense of place when he sends his series character, war veteran Peter Ash, to chilly Iceland to track down a missing child.

Petrie came up with the concept for *The Wild One* while on a backpacking trip to Iceland with his son. They traveled to remote northern regions close to the Arctic Circle, where there were no roads. "It was such a captivating and lonely place," says Petrie. "I really fell in love with it, and with the Icelandic people we met along the way."

While at the airport waiting to board their flight home, Petrie suddenly got the idea for *The Wild One*. "The book just appeared in my head, more or less fully formed, which has never happened to me before," he recalls. "I spent twenty minutes scribbling in my little notebook, trying to get everything down, before the book vanished again. I spent the next eighteen months trying to create that vision again in this novel."

Petrie did additional research for the story, including another trip to Iceland. This time, he drove the Ring Road, which features prominently in the book, and tried to soak up the desolate beauty of the country.

What's next for Peter Ash? All Petrie will say is that "Peter is a wanted man and things do not look good." We can't wait!

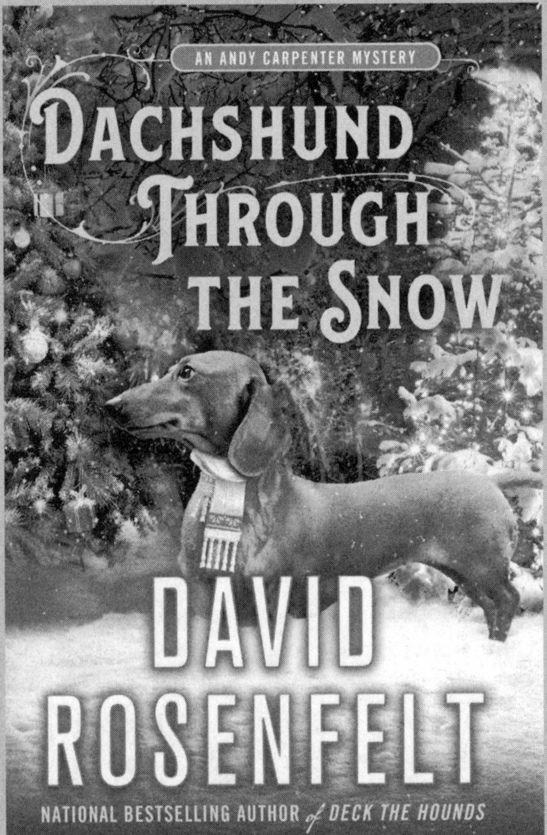
AN ANDY CARPENTER MYSTERY
DACHSHUND THROUGH THE SNOW
DAVID ROSENFELT
NATIONAL BESTSELLING AUTHOR of DECK THE HOUNDS

Prologue

It has been almost fourteen years since Kristen McNeil's body was discovered.

Her mother had called the police to say that Kristen had not come home one night, an uncharacteristic action for the eighteen-year-old. But not until thirty-six hours after that was Kristen found near Hinchliffe Stadium in Paterson, New Jersey.

Hinchliffe Stadium was a decayed relic of a time gone by in Paterson. In its day it was the scene of Minor League Baseball games, high school football, auto racing, and some important boxing matches. But it had fallen into terrible disrepair and wasn't designated as a historical landmark until eight years after Kristen had breathed her last.

So it wasn't exactly a high-traffic area back then, and had some kids not been playing there, it might have been much longer before her whereabouts became known.

The police immediately considered it an attempted sexual assault leading to the murder, since the victim's clothes were partially torn. The theory was that she had fought and scratched her killer, since traces of skin were under her fingernails.

The cause of death was strangulation, and in addition to the killer's leaving behind his DNA in the skin under Kristen's nails, the same DNA was found on a piece of discarded gum and a half-consumed beer can near the body. In the intervening years, no match had ever been made. The partial fingerprint on the beer can was not enough to yield a match.

Apparently the killer had had no other run-ins with the law, before or since, because his DNA was not in any database. Every few years, the Paterson Police ran it through the system, hoping for a match, but they were always disappointed.

The case was famous in Paterson, and occasionally the media would write stories revisiting it. It frustrated everyone that even though absolutely incontrovertible evidence existed to tie the killer to the crime, he was still out there, free.

Also, he might be dead, since it seemed unlikely that someone capable of such a cold-blooded murder would have kept his nose clean for the past fourteen years.

So all the authorities could do was wait for a break that seemed increasingly likely never to come.

Chapter 1

LAURIE COLLINS IS GREAT on the "giveth" . . . not so much on the "taketh away."

Every marriage should have a balance; I think I read that somewhere once. It works that way with me and Laurie Collins, as she represents the human-decency side of our marriage. It's not that I have inhuman decency, or human indecency; it's just that I am comparatively agnostic on the subject. Fortunately, Laurie has me covered.

Laurie's decency and spirit of giving last year-round but especially come out during Christmastime. Of course, that would depend on whether your definition of Christmastime coincides with hers. I doubt that it does. I'd be willing to bet that it doesn't.

For years she had viewed Christmas as starting with the conclusion of the Thanksgiving meal. On some level it seemed to make sense. Out with the old holiday, in with the new. And here in the Northeast, which is where our home in Paterson, New Jersey, is, the climate has a Christmassy chill in the air by then.

In her eyes, the end of Christmas has always been February 1, though she has never adequately explained the reason for that monthlong extension. I think it is just that she likes Christmas, so why not continue it?

Last February, when she retired her Christmas albums for the year and I could finally stop listening to "Jingle Bells," I made the mistake of mentioning that I was pleased that baseball season was about to get going, that "pitchers and catchers" had already reported for spring training. It got her to thinking that if baseball season could last seven months, it wasn't fair that Christmas season lasted less than half as long.

"It's only supposed to last three weeks," I made the mistake of pointing out, and in retaliation she decreed that this year Christmas in our house was going to be even longer.

So our son, Ricky, no sooner took off his Halloween costume last week than Laurie announced the start of Christmas. Which means the start of giving.

Laurie has never come across a charity she doesn't like. That's fine with me because we are quite wealthy as a result of my inheritance and some lucrative cases I have handled as a criminal defense attorney. She keeps searching for new ways to share our good fortune, and she keeps finding them.

Last year she added a new trick to her charitable repertoire. The local post office, as well as a couple of stores in town, puts a tree in their lobby. Children then fill out a small form asking for special gifts, and those are hung on the tree. Laurie takes a bunch of them and anonymously makes the wishes come true.

No place would think to install a Christmas tree the first week in November, so Laurie has approached the places and requested the wish lists of children who have already submitted them, in anticipation of the tree being set up. The stores know that Laurie is dedicated and totally reliable, so they are happy to give the wishes to her, and she is happy to fulfill them.

So that's what she is doing today, as a way to celebrate the start of her extended Christmas season. She's opening wish cards from our local pet store, occasionally laughing and more often crying. Some of them can be pretty heartbreaking, such as when children ask for a pair of shoes or a warm coat.

Laurie has a rule: if she opens a wish card, she will make it happen, no matter what. I cringe at the possibility that some kid is going to request a Porsche or a mail-order bride.

She generally does not include me in doing this, which I'm absolutely fine with. Occasionally she'll mention a wish that seems funny or maybe particularly sad, but basically it's her thing. So right now she is doing her thing, and I am fulfilling my own wish, which is to sit on the couch and watch ESPN.

"Andy, listen to this. It's from a boy named Danny Traynor." She starts reading the note, which starts with the traditional "Dear Santa." "'Santa, I know I always ask for stuff, but this time it's important. Can you please give us a coat for my mom and a sweater for my dog, Murphy? He's a dachshund, so it has to be a long one. And then I have a special request for my present. Please, Santa, please find my dad and bring him home. Thank you. Your friend, Danny.'"

"Uh-oh."

"We need to get into this, Andy."

"Get into it how? The kid's father might have run off with his secretary, for all we know."

"Maybe, and if it's something like that, we can back off. But we're investigators; let's find out."

"You're an investigator; I'm a lawyer. If the kid wants to sue his father, that's where I come in." Laurie was a lieutenant in the Paterson Police Department and has served as my chief case investigator ever since she left that job.

She nods. "Fair enough; I'll look into it myself. I have another job for you anyway. This one is right up your alley. It calls for a lawyer and dog lover, and you check both of those boxes."

"I do not like the sound of this." Laurie knows that I have been trying to get out of the lawyering business for a long time now. Unfortunately, I keep getting roped into taking on cases.

"This one is perfect for you. You might even have some fun."

"You know I don't like fun."

"I'll tell you what. Let's go interview your potential client. If you don't want to take on his case, then no problem."

"Now?" I point to the television. "While they're talking about the Giants?"

Instead of answering, she picks up her phone and dials. Someone must answer because she says, "Does now work for you?"

I assume the answer is yes since Laurie hangs up the phone, stands, and says, "Your client meeting is about to begin."

"Where are we going?"

"Eastside Park."

"Can we take Tara and Sebastian?" Tara is my golden retriever, widely recognized as the supreme living creature on all planets so far discovered. Sebastian is our basset hound. He doesn't aspire to such heights; all he wants to do is eat and sleep.

"Absolutely," Laurie says. "They will fit right in."

WE ENTER Eastside Park through the Park Avenue entrance. A police car is parked near the tennis courts, and we walk in that direction. Stands are always set up for spectators, maybe enough to hold forty people. That's more than sufficient; it's not like they play the U.S. Open in Eastside Park.

As we get closer, I see that a uniformed police officer is sitting in the first row of the stands, and with him is his partner, a beautiful German shepherd. I turn back toward the police car, and sure enough, on the side is writing identifying it as a K-9 unit. Nobody is playing tennis for them to watch, so it's a pretty good bet that this is who we are here to meet.

"You want to fill me in on what's going on?" I ask Laurie.

"Corey can do that."

I try to get a better look at the cop. "Is that Corey Douglas?"

"It is."

"He and I have an unpleasant history. I am not representing that guy. He's nuts."

About three years ago, I cross-examined Sergeant Corey Douglas about his actions on a case. I don't remember all the details, but the cross did not go well for him. I nailed him for not having probable cause to take the actions he took, and all the evidence he accumulated was ruled inadmissible.

It wasn't highly unusual, until he came at me in the parking lot afterward. He was furious with me, which in itself doesn't make him at all unique among police officers I encounter. What struck me was that his anger was on behalf of his dog.

The dog, whose name I believe is Simon, had performed great work in the operation, at some risk to his physical well-being. Douglas was outraged that Simon's success and the risks he had taken were now rendered worthless by the court.

He saw it as my fault. Which, I suppose, it was.

Douglas didn't attack me physically in the parking lot, which was lucky for me since he has me by forty pounds and four inches. But for a few minutes I thought he was going to lose it, so I got out of there fast, and I haven't seen him again until now.

We reach them, and Laurie says, "Corey, Andy . . . I believe you already know each other?"

He and I both nod, and I throw in a small sneer for effect. Tara and Sebastian, meanwhile, are not holding a grudge against Simon. They are sniffing away at each other.

Laurie smiles. "Good; this is a special moment. Corey, why don't you explain the situation to Andy?"

Instead of doing so, he says, "How about if we talk about the fee? If it's too high—"

Laurie interrupts, "There is no fee, Corey. If Andy does this, it's out of the goodness of his heart."

Are you out of your mind? is what I want to scream at Laurie. But when it passes through my wimp filter, it comes out as "I have a lot of heart goodness; I'm known for it."

Corey seems unappeased. Finally he says, "We can table that for now. I'm retiring next month; I've put in my twenty-five."

"Good luck with that," I say, staring my version of a dagger at Laurie. "I keep retiring, but it never seems to take."

"Simon—his full name is actually Simon Garfunkel—just turned nine." Corey points to him. "We've been together seven years; I want him to retire with me. But retirement age for police dogs is ten."

I know that the policy among police forces nationally in recent years is to let a dog live out his retirement years with his handler, should the handler want him. "So will they be giving Simon another handler for the next year?"

Corey nods. "Yes. They're planning to move Simon to the drug detail when I leave."

"What's the problem?" I ask.

"His hips are acting up, and those drug-detection dogs are on their feet all day. It won't be good for him. He's put in enough time and service; they should let him live out his years with me. He deserves that. He loves me, and I love him even more."

I see Laurie fight off a smile; she knows that's the kind of pitch that will get to me.

"Have you taken this up the ladder?"

"I talked to the captain and got nowhere. Then I took it to the Appeals Board and they blew me off. That's when Laurie suggested you."

"So you want me to represent you in court?"

He shakes his head. "Not me. Simon."

This time Laurie is unable to fight off the smile. "Simon would be your client, Andy."

"Can I talk to him privately?" I ask.

"Sure," Laurie says, and she leads Corey out of the stands, toward his car. Simon, Tara, Sebastian, and I are left alone.

"Simon, you've had enough of this working crap?"

He licks my arm as I scratch his neck, so I take that as a yes.

"And, Tara, you're good with this?"

I swear, she smiles at the prospect, so that's another yes. I don't ask Sebastian since it would involve waking him.

"All right, let's go for it." I get up and walk them all back to where Corey and Laurie are waiting.

"What was that about?" Corey asks.

"I can't tell you what we talked out because of lawyer-client confidentiality." Laurie rolls her eyes. "But I have decided to temporarily come out of retirement to represent Simon. Okay?"

Laurie gives me a kiss on the cheek. I take that as a yes.

Corey's reaction is slightly less heartwarming. "You know, I almost killed you in the parking lot that day."

"It's just as well that you didn't."

"Paperwork would have been ridiculous," he says. "Plus, I like Laurie."

"That's why I keep her around."

THIS one is not going to be easy.

I'm meeting at our house with Hike Lynch, the lawyer who works with me when I take on a case. Hike is a terrific researcher and has gathered a great deal of information both on animal law in general and police policy toward animals in particular.

Hike is by nature a total pessimist. He is positive that everything will turn out badly, and when it doesn't, he views it as proof that the next thing will turn out twice as bad.

But my concern about this case is not based on Hike's description of it as a "total, wall-to-wall loser." Considering his normal point of view, that could actually be described as almost upbeat. Unfortunately, I don't see much here to work on; no law limits police discretion in handling their working dogs.

There are laws against animal abuse, but in no way does this go anywhere near that standard. Simon is not being tortured or confined or starved; the police are simply insisting that he continue the job for which he has been trained.

While we're talking, I get a call from Dr. Dan Dowling, Tara's and Sebastian's veterinarian. I had asked Corey Douglas to take Simon in for a full medical examination, and Dowling is calling to give his report.

"I did a full workup, Andy. X-rays, blood work, all of it."

"What did you find?"

"For a dog his age, he's in good shape. Only abnormal test result was his thyroid level, and even that's not too far off. It's easily handled with Soloxine, which I gave Sergeant Douglas."

"What about his hips?"

"That's definitely an issue. He's got some arthritis. It's not overly dramatic, but it's there, and it's concerning."

"Is he in pain?"

"Definitely feeling some discomfort," Dowling says. "Shepherds are stoic, so it's not obvious, but it has to be there."

"If for the next year he is on his feet all day, every day, will that worsen the condition? Can he even do it?"

"I'm sure he can manage to do it, but it will take its toll on him later on, and it will certainly increase his discomfort."

I get off the phone and share the news with Hike, who of course says it works against us. "Arthritis is nothing; everybody's got arthritis."

"I didn't realize arthritis was nothing."

"Are you kidding? I've got arthritis that has arthritis."

The idea of Simon's possibly being in pain and moving with difficulty in his retirement annoys the hell out of me. "They're treating him like a dog."

"He is a dog," Hike points out.

"He's an employee; he's a cop. He has spent his life protecting your arthritis-ridden body. If he was human, they'd give him a gold watch and an early retirement with a pension."

"What are you saying? That they're discriminating against him because he's a dog?"

"Exactly. Simon is an employee, pure and simple, and the establishment is stepping on him because of who he is."

"So where exactly are you going with this?"

"We are about to sue the city for species discrimination."

WHEN Laurie gets home, I can tell she's upset.

Hike is still here, so I won't find out what's going on until he leaves. Laurie is not about to open up in front of Hike; she knows that whatever the problem is, he'll make her feel worse.

Since Hike and I are pretty much done anyway, I send him on his way with two assignments. One is to prepare the papers for a lawsuit we are going to file against the City of Paterson, and the other is to talk to Sam Willis.

Sam is my accountant and resident computer genius. He's capable of finding anything that can be accessed through the internet, legally and otherwise. The good news is that every single thing in the world can be accessed through the internet.

Before Hike leaves, he counsels me not to get my hopes up. "This is going nowhere. Simon is going to die on the job."

"Keep thinking the good thoughts," I say.

Once Hike leaves, I don't have to prompt Laurie to tell me what's on her mind. "I spoke to Mrs. Traynor."

"Ricky's teacher?" I regret the words as soon as they leave my mouth; I'm somehow not able to remember our son Ricky's third-grade teacher's name in the moment, but I know that Traynor is not on the list of possibles.

"No, Andy. Julie Traynor is Danny Traynor's mother. He's the little boy who left the wish on the tree."

I nod. "Got it."

"So I called her, told her that I had the gifts that Danny asked for. I asked if I could bring them over, and she hesitated but finally said it was okay.

"They live on Thirtieth Street, the upstairs apartment in a two-family house. Obviously not very well off financially, which explains the wishes. By the way, the dachshund is adorable."

"What about the missing father?"

"I'm getting there. She was grateful that I brought the stuff, especially since Danny was at school. She said that they've had to tighten their belts lately but didn't say why. She's going to hold on to it and give it to him at Christmas."

"They haven't started Christmas yet? Don't they realize that Halloween is over?"

"Andy . . . She seemed wary, like she was worried about talking to me. I told her that Danny asked if we would find his father, and it was like I shocked her with electricity. She told me her husband wasn't missing, that Danny had a wild imagination."

"You didn't believe her?"

"She didn't have to be hooked up to a poly for me to know that she was lying. I told her that I was an investigator and a former cop and that you were an attorney. She had heard of you. But she was more afraid of me than anything."

"Maybe she just considers the subject personal. Maybe their marriage is splitting up, or he's having an affair, or she's having an affair, or who knows what. It's not our business, Laurie."

"Maybe. But I was getting a weird vibe, Andy. This woman was scared, of her situation, of me, of the world. I think there is something going on there. I offered to help in any way I could, but she wanted none of it. She made that very obvious."

"Maybe there is something going on. But no matter what it is, it doesn't involve us, no matter what the kid wished," I say.

"I want to help her, and I really want to help that little boy."

We hear a noise outside.

Laurie glances quickly at her watch. "Ricky."

It's the school bus, and Laurie and I go outside to meet it. Laurie picks Ricky up and gives him a huge hug. She looks like she is going to crush him. Ricky looks at me as if to ask, *What the hell is going on?*

"Ricky, just go with the flow. It's Christmas."

Chapter 2

NOAH TRAYNOR WATCHED the end of his life through the window of his motel room.

It was not unexpected; far from it. On some level he found it relieving; it had been a while since he had had any kind of control over events, and this was sort of making it official.

For the better part of ten days, he had lived in this Paramus motel, leaving only to get his meals. His entire focus during that time had been on finding a solution to his predicament.

He had come up with absolutely nothing, and now it absolutely did not matter.

He could see the motel parking lot from his room, and farther in the distance the street behind it. That's where they parked so as not to call attention to themselves. The two cars were unmarked, but the four men that got out of them couldn't have been police officers more obviously if they had had their ranks tattooed on their foreheads.

Traynor knew that there must be others, parked outside his line of vision. Coming in force like this was understandable but ultimately unnecessary. He was not going to resist.

He watched the plainclothes officers coming toward the motel until they split up into pairs and went to each side. They would be taking the stairs to the second floor, where his room was.

He wasn't surprised that they'd found him; truly disappearing in this age of technology and information would take much more expertise and effort than Traynor had summoned. It didn't matter how they did it, but he figured they probably traced his calls to Julie and then used the GPS built into his phone.

Whatever. They were here.

Traynor wanted to avoid the drama and violence of their breaking into the room, so instead he went outside and waited for them just beyond the door. He raised his arms in the air.

Eight men appeared, the four in plainclothes and four in uniform. They drew their guns when they saw him and approached.

"Noah Traynor?"

"Yes."

They ordered him to put his hands against the wall and frisked him. Then they read him his rights.

"What are you charging me with?" he asked, though he knew.

"The murder of Kristen McNeil."

"I'm innocent," he said, knowing that they were probably the most meaningless words he had ever spoken.

"Everybody is, Traynor," said the arresting officer. "Everybody is."

"I NEED your help, Vince."

Vince Sanders is the editor of the local newspaper and one of the two people whom I share a regular table with at the wondrous establishment known as Charlie's Sports Bar. Our other tablemate is Pete Stanton, captain in charge of Homicide in the Paterson Police. They are here to eat, drink, and watch sports, in this case NBA basketball. Vince and Pete watch sports because they are fans; they eat and drink because I pay all the checks.

Life for Vince and Pete is simple.

"You want my help?" Vince says. "I'm sort of busy now, so I don't really like the sound of that."

"Really? Tell me if you like the sound of this." I call to the woman who has the misfortune to be our every-night waitress, "Sheila, from now on Vince is going to be running his own tab."

Vince sits up. "Andy is some kidder, huh, Sheila? Disregard anything this funny guy says." Then he turns to me. "I am a friend, and friends are here to help. Tell me what I can do."

"This is nauseating," Pete says.

I speak to Vince. "I want you to run a story about a dog."

"What's the story?" Vince asks.

"I don't want to tell you in front of Sergeant Schultz over here." I point to Pete. Since the story involves a lawsuit that we are filing in the morning against the police department, I don't want to give Pete a heads-up. "I'll come to your office in the morning to tell you the story and bring photos."

Vince nods. "Will you be bringing doughnuts?"

"I'll stop and pick up a dozen."

"I look forward to seeing you," Vince says. "Have I mentioned how much I cherish our friendship?"

While Vince pours it on, Pete takes out his phone and looks at it. "Good news. You can talk away, geniuses. I've got to run."

"Off to arrest another innocent person?" I ask.

"Dream on, Counselor."

Once he leaves, I tell Vince the story about Simon and describe what I want Vince to do. When I'm finished, he asks, "Are you still coming to my office in the morning?"

I shake my head. "No, not necessary anymore. I'll email you the photos."

"What about the doughnuts?"

"Not happening."

"This is very disappointing."

When I get home, Laurie sees me pull up and comes out on the porch to greet me. She's not smiling.

"Did you hear what happened?" she asks.

"I doubt it."

"They made an arrest in the Kristen McNeil murder."

"Good. That must be why Pete left Charlie's when he did." My reaction did not take into account that Laurie does not seem happy. Usually an arrest of a murder suspect would be considered good news. "Is there a problem connected to this?"

"The person they arrested is Noah Traynor."

The name sounds familiar, but I can't place it. I do know it's not Ricky's teacher. "Refresh my memory."

"He's the father of Danny Traynor, the boy who asked us to find his father."

"Poor kid. But his father appears to have been found."

"Technically speaking, he asked us to bring his father home. That has not been accomplished."

"Uh-oh."

We head into the house; I follow Laurie into the den, where she has two glasses of wine waiting for us. This is a disaster waiting to happen; nobody pours glasses of wine in advance of what is meant to be a casual conversation.

I usually play the role of counterpuncher in situations like this, and it rarely works out. It's time to be aggressive.

"What do you think the chances are that he's guilty?" I ask. As an ex-cop, Laurie always instinctively feels that the police would not make an arrest without a strong probability of guilt.

She thinks for a moment. "Without knowing the facts? Ninety-five percent."

"And if he did it, if he murdered that young woman, you think he should go home to his wife and kid and dachshund?"

"No. Of course not."

"Good."

She nods. "Then we agree. If we look into it and don't think he's innocent, we back off. You're the best, Andy."

How the hell did that happen?

VINCE must love his free food and beer.

The story in the paper is absolutely perfect. A photo of Corey Douglas's spectacular German shepherd accompanies it on page one, and it reads like the Paterson Police Department is trashing an American hero.

Which in my view they are.

Hike has filed a lawsuit on Simon's behalf seeking expedited relief, warning that a delay would result in immediate and irreversible harm to our client. Dr. Dowling has sent a letter, which we included in the filing, supporting that position.

I went one step further and enlisted the help of Rita Gordon, the chief clerk at the courthouse and a good friend. Rita has manipulated the system to make sure that our filed petition lands on the desk of Judge Seymour Markinson. Judge Markinson, though he shares his colleagues' disdain for me and my courtroom antics, loves dogs. If anyone would be willing to see past the irritation that I represent to protect Simon, he's the one.

I've taken a chance by going so public with this, especially so early. It will certainly generate the grassroots support that I want; no one living on the New Jersey section of Planet Earth would back the Paterson PD over a hero dog.

But it could definitely get the opposition's back up. They might resist simply to show that they cannot be intimidated and definitely not by an annoying defense attorney.

My being an annoying defense attorney, though, is why I took this approach. Corey had already gone about it the right way. He had spoken to his superiors, and when they'd refused his request, he had gone to the Appeals Board. They brushed him aside.

If these jerks can't find it in their hearts to let Simon retire a year early, then they deserve to be publicly humiliated.

Which is where I come in.

Hike and I are in my office going over the information that Sam

Willis has dug up, as well as deciding who we will call as witnesses. That's all dependent on Judge Markinson's granting the hearing that we've requested. If he doesn't, then we've gotten dressed up for a party that doesn't exist.

As we're wrapping up, Rita Gordon calls me on my cell. "The judge is pissed."

"How pissed?"

"He mentioned something about disemboweling you with a butter knife."

"Did he smile when he said it?"

"Andy, you didn't need to turn this into a public relations thing. You know that judges do not like to be pressured."

"Did we get the hearing?" I ask, since that is all that matters.

"Friday at ten a.m."

"Rita, you are fantastic."

"I am keenly aware of that."

So things are looking up. We've got the hearing we've been seeking and are pretty well along in our preparation. The other good news is that while Laurie has been looking into the arrest of Noah Traynor, she doesn't seem to have found anything that would call for us to intervene. It's possible that she is relaxing her self-imposed rules on being a Christmas-wish genie.

I head home to wait for Ricky to get home from school. Tonight there is both NBA and college basketball on television.

Life is good.

The first sign of life's possibly not being as good as I thought is a strange car in the driveway of our house. This isn't necessarily a problem, but I have a sense of foreboding.

When I get into the house, Laurie hears me and calls out, "Andy, we're in the kitchen." My keen sense of deduction tells me that "we're" refers to Laurie and the driver of that car.

When I get to the kitchen, I see that Laurie is having coffee with a woman I don't recognize.

"Andy Carpenter," Laurie says, "meet Julie Traynor."

I have a feeling life just took a turn for the worse.

"What's going on?" I ask after the requisite hellos.

"Julie called and asked if she could come over," Laurie says. "So we can hear what she has to say together."

Tara and Sebastian are lying at Laurie's feet, munching on chewies. Their expressions are impassive; they are obviously as much in the dark as Laurie and me.

"I'm sorry I was so cold when you came over," Julie says to Laurie. "But I was already so worried, and when I heard that you had been a police officer, I guess I was afraid to trust you."

"I understand," Laurie says, which makes one of us.

"But then when Noah was arrested . . . You know about that?"

Laurie nods. "We do."

"I didn't know where to turn," Julie says, then turns to me, meaning that she may have figured out where to turn. "My cousin is a lawyer; his name is Marvin Simmons. He's not a criminal attorney . . . he works for an insurance company. But when he heard that I had sort of a connection to you, he said that your reputation is that you're the best."

I don't know her cousin Marvin, but I already hope he and his company never win another case.

"Andy is definitely the best," Laurie says, obviously casting her lot with Cousin Marvin.

"We don't have much money," Julie says, "but I would pay whatever you charge no matter how long it takes me."

This is not getting better as we go along. "Why don't you tell us your story," I say.

"There is simply no way that Noah killed that girl. If you knew Noah, you would know that it is simply an impossibility."

"Why do the police think he did?"

"DNA. He had a brief relationship with her and was with her outside that stadium, just before it happened. He knew he must have left DNA that the police would have gotten. It was about two years before we met. He was just a kid. But they could never connect him to it because they didn't have his DNA on file.

"Then Noah's brother, who didn't know anything about this, sent his own DNA in to one of those genealogy sites. Once Noah heard about that, he knew this day was coming."

I know what she's talking about. People get their DNA results, then upload them to a website that tells them about possible relatives. Uploading the information removes the right to privacy, and the police can access those databases. Once they saw Noah's brother's DNA results and matched it up against the evidence from the murder, it was an easy next step to go after Noah.

"And you knew about his connection to the murdered woman all these years?"

"He told me about five years ago. I wanted him to go to the police, but he said that they would arrest him. It's not like he could direct them to the real killer. So we've lived in fear."

"What more can you tell us?" Laurie asks.

"I don't know all the details. But if you would talk to Noah. Please, if you would just talk to him."

"Of course we'll talk to him," Laurie says.

If I say, *No, we won't*, I don't think it will go over well. And the truth is that I feel sorry enough for Julie Traynor to at least want to do that much for her.

Ricky walks in, having just been dropped off by the school bus. Laurie introduces him to Mrs. Traynor, and his presence effectively ends the talk about murder.

Tara and Sebastian both go over to Ricky to get their expected petting, and he is only too happy to oblige.

"My son, Danny, is about your age," Julie says. "He loves dogs too."

"Do you have one?" Ricky asks.

"We do. His name is Murphy, and he's a dachshund."

She shows all of us a picture of Murphy that she has on her phone. He's adorable, which I admit grudgingly, because if not for Murphy, Danny would not have placed a wish on the pet store Christmas tree. And I wouldn't be going to the jail to talk to an accused murderer.

LAURIE comes with me to the jail to talk to Noah Traynor.

I register as his attorney, listing Laurie as my associate. That enables us to meet in a private room, outside the range of prison microphones.

Noah is brought into the room in handcuffs, as is customary, and the guard attaches those cuffs to the metal table. Then the guard takes a position outside the only door to the windowless room. It's a good bet Noah is not going to be able to use this meeting as an opportunity to escape.

He's about six feet tall, thin at maybe 160 pounds. Like all incarcerated people, he looks scared. But that's not the dominant aspect of his appearance. Trumping it all is that he looks tired.

"I've been running in place for fourteen years," he says after we introduce ourselves. Then, "Thank you for coming here. I'm very glad that Julie has not lost her power of persuasion."

"Just to be clear," I say, "we are here to listen and gather information. We have not committed to represent you."

"I understand. The public defender has been here and handled the arraignment. I pled not guilty."

I nod. "Why don't you tell us your story from the beginning."

"There isn't that much to tell. I was nineteen years old when I met Kristen McNeil in a bar. It was called the Moonraker and was on Route Four in Paramus. It's not there anymore."

"How long did you know her before her death?"

"About three weeks. But I only actually saw her three or four times. She was very secretive about it; she didn't want me to meet her friends or even spend time with me in public."

"Did she say why?"

"No. I asked her, but she sort of shrugged it off. I figured it must have had to do with some other relationship she had; as it turns out, she had an existing boyfriend, but I didn't know that then. I found her attractive, so I was fine with it."

"Did you have sex with her the day she died?" Laurie asks.

"No. I wanted to, and she said she wanted to. That was the reason we went out to that part of town."

"So describe what happened that day," I say.

"We met near the Falls, near Hinchliffe Stadium. I brought some beer, and we were drinking. Not too much; certainly neither of us was drunk.

"She had been acting strange, but I thought that just might be who she was, you know, high-strung and unpredictable. But then she started telling me that I had to take her with me when I left."

"Left for where?"

"College. I was leaving a few days later to go to the University of Maryland."

"Why did she want to go with you?"

"I don't know, but she said she couldn't live here anymore, that she had to leave. I asked why she couldn't just leave on her own, and she said she had no money. It was like she wanted to go with me and then live with me in secret. Really bizarre."

"What happened next?" I ask.

"When I didn't say she could come with me, she started to lose it, like she was panicking. I held her arms, trying to calm her down, and she scratched my face. I was bleeding. The whole thing was crazy."

"Were her clothes already torn when you left?" Laurie asks, since they were torn when she was found.

"No. Not by me, and not that I saw."

"What did you do after she scratched your face?" I ask.

"I left. I mean, the whole thing had blown up."

"Did she leave also?" Laurie asks.

"No. She was sitting there crying when I left. She had her own car, so I didn't think I had to worry about her. And the truth was, I wanted to get as far away from her as I could."

"What happened next?"

"I didn't think anything happened, at least at first. It wasn't until a couple of days later that I even heard about it. It was all over the news. They were calling it an attempted sexual-assault murder. Since she had scratched me like that, I thought they would think I killed her."

"So what did you do?" I ask.

"Nothing. Unless you consider panicking and freaking out doing something. I thought they'd come for me, but they never did. Gradually I began to believe that they had no way to connect the two of us. Over time I read up on things and realized that I wasn't in any DNA data bank. And since none of her friends knew me, I wasn't on the police radar."

"And you never told anyone?" I ask.

"I may have mentioned her by name to one or two people; I honestly can't remember. But I certainly never talked about it after she was killed; the first person I finally told was Julie."

"Didn't you want to help find the real killer?" I ask.

He nods. "Yes, of course, but I had nothing to offer. And then, as time went by, it would look worse and worse that I waited so long. So I did nothing; it was like I was frozen in place. I'm not proud of it, but I didn't see any other option at the time."

"And you saw nothing unusual as you were leaving?" I ask. "No people, no cars that seemed out of place?"

"Nothing. Why would I want to kill her? It doesn't make any sense. I'm not a violent guy. I've never even been in a fight."

He goes on to talk about the DNA test his brother took and how he realized that would eventually become his undoing.

"No one will believe me now," he says, probably accurately assessing his situation. "Not after all these years."

I tell him that Laurie and I will talk about this and get back to him. "In the meantime," I say, "I assume the public defender has instructed you not to talk about these matters to anyone."

"He has."

"It's excellent advice; follow it."

"So, DO you believe him?" I ask, once we're in the car.

Laurie thinks about it for a few moments. I'm not sure what to expect. As an ex-cop, she is always late to the party when it comes to believing protestations of innocence. But as a granter of Christmas wishes, she wants little Danny's to come true.

"I'm torn. If he's innocent, and I admit that is a very big if, I want him to have a chance. And while I know the public defenders are good, hardworking lawyers, they are overloaded. I just don't think they have the time or resources that would be necessary in a case like this."

I'm at a loss. I thought Laurie would have a strong point of view, since strong points of view are a specialty of hers. My role is traditionally to take the other side; if she was in favor of defending him, or against, I could simply take whatever the opposing position was and argue it. I'd lose, but at least I would be comfortable with the ground rules, and we would have talked it out. But Laurie's being unsure is disorienting and leaves me without a strategy.

"What do you think?" she asks.

"I'd like to talk to Billy." Laurie knows that Billy is Billy Cameron, nickname Bulldog, who is the head of the public defender's office. "He'll tell me the straight story."

"About what?"

"About Traynor's life in the intervening years since the murder. If he's lived a life on the straight and narrow ever since, then that would be compelling to me. I think it's rare that these things happen in isolation. If Noah Traynor strangled Kristen McNeil, then I doubt the incident turned him into a Boy Scout."

"So you'll talk to Billy tomorrow?"

I shake my head. "Tonight. Tomorrow I have a German shepherd to defend."

When we get home, I call Billy. I hope he'll tell me that while he's obligated to defend Noah, he's as evil as they come. He doesn't; he says that the limited background information they have gathered already shows the exact opposite.

"He could use you, Andy." While that may be true, Billy is thoroughly biased. He would like nothing better than to dump this off on me and thereby lower the workload on his exhausted staff.

"I'll get back to you," I say.

When I get off the phone, I tell Laurie about the conversation.

"The other thing to keep in mind is what Julie said about paying your fee," she says.

I nod. "Somehow I don't see myself collecting money every month from a poor woman with a son and dachshund."

Laurie smiles. "That is tough to picture."

"Maybe I can make up the difference by charging Simon the German shepherd double my normal fee."

"I think he'd be fine with it," she says. Then, "Does this mean you're taking the case?"

"Traynor said he's been running for fourteen years. One way or another we need to get him to the finish line."

"I love you, Andy."

"As well you should."

SIMON IS LOOKING GOOD THE next morning.

Corey must have taken him to the groomer yesterday in anticipation of his court appearance, because he's looking sharp and spiffy. Unfortunately, and the mistake is mine, I didn't want him looking sharp and spiffy.

We are arguing that he is not physically able to perform his job, so my preference would have been for him to look weak and haggard. But I failed to mention it to Corey, so that is on me.

A big crowd is on hand; the gallery is filled to overflowing. That is no doubt the result of the publicity campaign we engineered, and it could possibly annoy Judge Markinson, who Rita said was already pissed off. Nothing I can do about that now.

Sitting at the defense table beside me are Corey, Hike, and the aforementioned spiffy-looking Simon. He has his own chair and is sitting up on it attentively. I almost expect him to ask for a pen so he can take notes.

At the opposing counsel's table are three people. I only recognize one of them. She is Sara Hopson, a police department lawyer and, I am sure, the lead counsel. The other two people are either lawyers or paralegals.

Sara's presence is ironic since I know her to be a dog lover. She adopted a Lab mix from our Tara Foundation, the dog rescue organization that my former client Willie Miller and I run. Sara must not be happy to be here today, but it's her job.

Judge Markinson comes in and views the gallery with obvious displeasure before taking his seat at the bench. He sternly states that we are not conducting a "sideshow" and threatens to clear the courtroom if there are disruptions. It seems like a premature threat, but one that shows he is irritated by the publicity.

Which means he is mad at me.

Judge Markinson explains what is about to happen, that this is a hearing to determine whether our lawsuit has the merit to go forward. The Paterson PD has asked for a dismissal of our suit, and however the judge rules will indicate which way he thinks the ultimate verdict will be rendered.

Before we begin, Sara asks that Simon be removed from the courtroom, citing courtroom rules that only service animals are permissible inside. What she really wants is to eliminate the media eating all of this up and taking our side.

"Your Honor," I say, "Simon is the definition of a service animal; he has served this community for his entire life. He is also the petitioner in this action and should therefore be entitled to be present. Lastly, he is not being disruptive and is completely house-trained."

A slight titter from the gallery stops when Judge Markinson gives the room his fierce stare. "I'll allow Simon to remain, though I will revisit the decision if he becomes a distraction."

Since we have brought the action, we are up first. Our first witness is my vet, Dan Dowling.

"Have you examined Simon?" I ask.

"I have. A few days ago. I did a full workup, including blood work and a set of X-rays."

"Can you describe his physical condition?"

Dowling nods. "In many respects it is quite good for a dog his age. But his hips are a significant issue and concern." Dowling describes a deterioration and arthritis in the hips, a progressive condition, meaning it will become worse over time.

"His bosses are set on transferring him to drug enforcement and detection, which will mean he will be on his feet all day, every day. How will that affect him?" I ask.

"It will hasten the deterioration. I have no doubt he has discomfort now, and that will substantially worsen."

I introduce videos of Simon taken five years ago, running in the park with Corey. Then I show another video of him running last week and ask Dowling to point out the differences in Simon's gait, attributable to the hip issues.

"Is it likely that his seven years of service to the department has contributed to the deterioration?"

"I don't think there's any question about that. A German shepherd's hips have just so much wear and tear in them. His profession would have to have caused considerable stress on them."

I ask a few more questions, then turn the vet over to Sara.

"Dr. Dowling, is Simon capable of doing the job to which he is being assigned?"

"I'm quite sure he is, at least right now. German shepherds are stoic."

"Do you have any way to know how the alleged problems with his hips have progressed over time?"

"No, I've only examined him now." Dowling then drops a mini-bomb. "I requested previous X-rays from the department but was told they do not exist. That was disappointing."

She ignores that. "Are there medications that could help him?"

"Definitely there are meds that could help with the discomfort, though not with the deterioration. Checking through the records, I was struck by the fact that he has not been given that medication. It should be prescribed immediately." Dowling is killing Sara; I may have to nominate him as Witness of the Year.

"Isn't a sign of pain in a dog a reluctance to eat?" she asks.

"Often so, yes."

"Does Simon look malnourished to you?"

"No."

"Thank you. No further questions."

Chapter 3

THE PHONE HAD NOT RUNG in almost fourteen years.

Actually, it was the phone number that had not received any calls; the physical phone had been replaced six times. But its mission had never changed: it existed only to receive a call from one specific client.

The phone belonged to Charles Arrant, and although it had not rung in almost a decade and a half, Arrant was not surprised to see that streak come to an end. He devoured the news religiously, so he knew exactly what to expect.

That is not to say that there hadn't been other kinds of communication between the caller and Arrant. Arrant had been receiving money, substantial money, frequently. And he had been facilitating connections between the caller and many of Arrant's other clients. But everything had been done electronically, protected by encryption, not by personal contact.

Arrant was in the hotel gymnasium when the call came. He lived in hotels, a different one in a different city every month. He had not made a bed or cooked a meal in a decade. Other people served him, and he paid well for the privilege.

Arrant was known in his professional world as a specialist. He didn't agree with the characterization because while a specialist by definition focuses on one type of activity, Arrant was the master of many. He had few clients, but whatever they wanted him to do, it could accurately be said that he specialized in doing exactly that.

It should be noted that the name Charles Arrant no longer existed in any meaningful way in his life. He had not used it in more than a decade, ever since the first Red Notice had come out. Instead he used a series of identifications that were prepared by experts and virtually invulnerable to exposure as fakes.

He didn't say *Hello* when he answered the phone; he remembered with a small smile that this client considered it a wasted word. "You've been following the developments?" the client asked, starting the conversation as if they talked every day.

"I have."

"Get involved."

"I could use more specific instructions." Arrant thought he knew what the client meant, but it was prudent to be sure.

"Monitor the situation and report back to me."

"Understood."

There was no reason to discuss financial terms; money was never an object. There would not have been an opportunity to discuss them anyway, because as soon as Arrant said, "Understood," the client clicked off.

It was time for Arrant to get to work.

My next witness is Lieutenant Thomas Quinto. Quinto is in charge of the K-9 unit and is Corey's and Simon's boss.

"Lieutenant, can you please tell me department policy toward early retirement in the case of injury sustained on the job?"

He seems confused. "You mean for dogs?"

"I mean for police officers."

"If you're talking about humans, it's not really my area, but I believe that early retirement is often granted in cases like that. But dogs—"

I interrupt, "Thank you. Does this summarize department policy to your knowledge?" I offer into evidence a copy of a page taken from the *Paterson Police Administrative Policies and Guidelines*, handing copies to the court clerk, the judge, Sara, and Quinto.

"I believe it does, yes," Quinto says.

"Can you point out to the court where it is mentioned that it only applies to human officers?"

"Well, it just assumes."

"So it doesn't specify that it only pertains to humans?"

"Of course not. But they're definitely talking about humans."

"Are you admitting to the court that the department engages in species discrimination?"

"Come on . . ."

"Is that a yes?"

He shakes his head. "No."

"A canine is less of an officer than his human counterpart?"

"Let's just say he's different."

"Lesser?" I ask.

Quinto thinks for a moment. "In some ways."

"Has Simon performed his job well during his career?"

"Absolutely."

"Heroically?"

Quinto shrugs. "I guess, but that's what he has been trained to do. So . . ."

"Ah," I say, as if that clears it up. "It's not a big deal that he is a hero because he's had training. Wait a minute, don't human officers have training as well? Or do they just show up one day and grab a badge?"

"It's a different kind of training."

I nod. "Because they are different skills. But you see dogs as lesser officers with lesser rights?"

"In some ways."

"Do you remember an incident that took place three years ago involving a bank robbery at First Savings and Loan?"

"Yes," he says. "Simon trapped two of the thieves, and it resulted in their capture."

I ask for permission to play a short video clip on the courtroom monitor. It's a press conference being conducted by Richard Melnicker, the Paterson chief of police.

He is smiling as he answers a question from the press. Standing behind him is Lieutenant Quinto, who is nodding as Melnicker speaks. "And special thanks goes to Simon, without whom this operation would not have been so successful. We value our canines as much as we value any of our officers; they work tirelessly and are heroes, as Simon demonstrated today."

"You were nodding in agreement with what the chief was saying?" I say.

"I knew what he meant."

"Yes, it was fairly straightforward. Was the chief wrong?"

"No."

"Lieutenant, why are you taking the position that Simon has to work one more year?"

"It's not my position; it's department policy."

"There's the handbook; can you show me the policy?"

"It's based on long-standing precedent."

"So dogs have previously applied for early retirement before and been denied?"

"No, this is a first."

"Thank you."

Sara tries to rehabilitate him by pointing out differences in the way dogs and human officers are treated and dealt with. Basically, it is a recitation of what Quinto has always assumed to be department policy.

We break for lunch, and I will use the time to get ready to wrap up our case. I feel like it is going well, if only because not a single member of the general public will want to see Simon forced into a job that will contribute to his deteriorating health.

More important, not a single member of Paterson's elected government will want to see the public not get what they want.

By the time I get done with them, mobs will be in the street chanting their demand: *FREE SIMON GARFUNKEL!*

"HE's the best partner I've ever had, and I've had great ones."

Corey is on the stand talking about Simon, who sits on his chair staring straight at his friend, though able to avoid blushing at the praise. I had told him not to show emotion but said it was okay to wag his tail, and he's doing that now.

"Can you talk a bit more about that?" I ask.

"Sure. He is always there, totally present and in the moment, every day. He never has a bad attitude and never complains about anything. He is fearless; he would go through a brick wall to protect me and to do his job.

"But more importantly, he's my friend. He senses when I'm down, or upset, or scared, and he tries to make me feel better. And he does, every single time.

"I love that dog, and I don't want him to be hurting. He's done so much for me, for this department, for this city, that he deserves to live out his days in style and comfort. He's not a possession of the department; he lives and breathes and hurts and loves unconditionally. And anyone who says otherwise doesn't know what the hell they are talking about."

I don't say anything for a while; I don't ask a question or make a sound. I just let Corey's words settle into the courtroom; I would bet that not a person within the sound of his voice does not feel a clenching in their throat or moisture in their eyes.

Game, set, and match.

Sara has no questions for Corey and changes her plans to call an officer in the Paterson PD Administration. He was going to talk about department policy toward animals, which would now probably get him tarred and feathered by the gallery.

Judge Markinson gives us the opportunity to make a summation, sort of a closing argument. Because we went first in presenting our case, Sara gets to go first in this stage:

"Your Honor, I'm a lover of dogs; I have two of my own. I am also an admirer of them, and Simon is worthy of that admiration. I have seen canines in action, and I believe they love their job. We need them to do it, and they do it well.

"But we have rules and policies in place. They are not onerous, and they are not cruel. They balance care and compassion for the dogs with the needs of the community they protect.

"I recognize that this may not be the popular position to take. In a perfect world everyone, human and canine, could retire when they wanted to and live a life of leisure. But the world does not work that way, and it's in many ways good that it doesn't.

"Simon has a job and a purpose, and he should be allowed to finish his work. Then, God willing, he can spend his remaining years being doted on and fed biscuits. Thank you."

My turn. "I am sure that Ms. Hopson is sincere in what she says. But there is one important way she is wrong.

"She talked about policies that balance the needs of the community with compassion for the dog. But that is a fallacy. Those policies are rigid; that's why we are here today. And there is no planet on which inflexibility and compassion can coexist; they are by definition incompatible.

"I played for you an example of a high-ranking police official praising Simon and saying that he sees no fundamental difference between canine and human officers. I could have shown you ten other examples of the same statement made by other high-ranking officials.

"But they are talking the talk without walking the walk. Because a human officer in Simon's exact situation would get the compassion that Simon is being denied. He or she would get early retirement and a pension."

I smile. "As Simon's attorney, I can tell you that he is happy to forgo his pension. But he is not willing to give up his rights.

"I know something about dog rescue, and I know that there are many wonderful dogs, currently homeless and with bleak prospects, who could be trained to do this kind of work. There is no reason to work a dog like Simon until he hobbles in pain from deteriorated hips. We owe him much more than that.

"Let the next generation take over while we honor our elders.

"Simon and Sergeant Douglas and I thank you."

When I sit down, Corey leans over and says, "Great job. I'm glad I didn't kill you in the parking lot."

I expect Judge Markinson to retire to chambers to consider his ruling. But he surprises me.

"I will obviously issue a full, written opinion. But I can safely say that this matter will be allowed to proceed, and I think the plaintiffs have a substantial chance of prevailing on the merits. If the parties cannot arrive at an amicable solution, a trial date will be set." He stares directly at Sara when he refers to the possibility of a settlement; his meaning is clear.

He adjourns the hearing, and Corey asks me what this means.

"As much fun as it would be to take this to trial," I say, "I'm pretty sure that Simon is going to be sleeping in a lot."

"If you want me to, I will represent you."

I've come to the jail to inform Noah Traynor of my decision. I have second thoughts even as I'm saying it, but the die is cast.

"I want you to," he says without hesitation. "Thank you. But I also want to be straight; I can't imagine what your fee is, but right now I am unable to pay it."

"I understand. Let's not worry about that now."

"I will make good on this, as long as it takes." He describes what he does for a living: a freelance writer, he sells articles to magazines. Then, "Hopefully, I'll be able to write in here."

"Right now we need to focus on proving your innocence," I say, having absolutely no idea if he is innocent. "I want you to write down everything you remember about that incident. I want to know where you were the other times you saw Kristen, anything she ever said that in retrospect seems strange to you. If you remember it, I want to know about it."

"Okay."

"Anything else you want to tell me now?"

"This is going to sound a little weird, but I kept a scrapbook about the murder."

"A scrapbook?"

"Well, not a real scrapbook. I mean, I didn't paste articles down or anything. But I did follow all the media coverage because I was scared I'd be mentioned. I saved it all in an envelope. There might be some information in there that you can use."

"Where is it?"

"At my house. Julie can give it to you; it's at the top of the bedroom closet."

"Okay, I'll get it."

As I'm leaving, I call Laurie to tell her that I'm heading to the Traynor house, and she says that she'll meet me there.

When I arrive, Laurie is already there, as is Danny and the dachshund, Murphy. Danny is a cute kid, but humans as a species have a cuteness ceiling that they cannot exceed. Not so with dogs. Murphy is at a level beyond adorable.

I join them in a cup of coffee and briefly play a video hockey game with Danny. He destroys me, as Ricky always does.

I had told Laurie why I was coming by, so she goes over to Danny and Murphy to keep them occupied while I talk to Julie. "Noah said there is an envelope at the top of his closet. He wants me to have it."

She nods, clearly knowing what I'm talking about. She goes into the bedroom and comes out with a thick manila envelope that must weigh two pounds. "Here it is. I hope it helps."

"Me too," I say.

"I feel so much better with you on the case."

This time I don't say, *Me too.*

THE climb up Legal Mountain always begins with a meeting.

We get the staff together at the beginning of a case to prepare everyone. As always, we hold the meeting in my office on Van Houten Street in Paterson, on the second floor above the fruit stand owned by Sofia Hernandez, who is my landlord.

Present, besides Laurie, Hike, and me, are Sam Willis, Willie Miller, and Marcus Clark. Sam, my accountant, is the computer and technical guy for the team. Willie has no assigned role; he is my former client and current partner in the Tara Foundation dog rescue. But he is also incredibly tough and fearless and often comes in handy.

Marcus Clark is a top-notch investigator and the toughest person that was ever invented. He has functioned many times as my body-guard and protector, and if not for him, people would long ago have been talking about me in the past tense. But even though he is on my side, he scares the hell out of me.

Last to arrive is my assistant and self-described office manager, Edna. She likes working even less than I do. My taking on a client is enough to put her into a depressed funk that usually lasts until the jury reaches a verdict.

Edna looks and sees that the entire group has already assembled and says, "Sorry I'm here . . . I mean, sorry I'm late."

I open the meeting. "Our client is Noah Traynor. You've probably read about him in the newspaper; he has been charged with the murder of Kristen McNeil, fourteen years ago.

"We're just getting started, so there's not much for me to tell you yet. We have copies of media articles written contemporaneously with the crime and in the years since. It will at the least give you the bare bones until we receive the discovery.

"Sam, do what you can to supplement this. I'm sure you can find out plenty online, so just feed it to us when you have it."

While I am talking, Marcus gets up and looks outside the window. I don't know what he's doing and am afraid to ask. Even if I did, he would just grunt an answer that I would find incomprehensible. When I'm trying to have a conversation with him, I always find myself wishing I had a Google translator that I could set to "Marcus to English."

The group has a bunch of questions, few of which I can answer. It's just too early in the process to know much.

Marcus again gets up and looks out the window, but this time he turns and makes a slight head motion to Laurie. She stands, and the two of them go into the reception area to talk.

Moments later they come back, and Laurie says, "We may have a bit of a situation here."

There is dead silence in the room.

She continues. "I don't want anyone to look out the window, but Marcus had noticed when he arrived a man sitting in a gray Toyota 4Runner near the end of the block, across the street from the check-cashing place. He noticed it because he's Marcus and because there seemed to be no reason for the guy to be there.

"The guy and the car are still there, and he appears to be focused on this direction. It's possible that he's watching for a delivery of melons to the fruit stand downstairs or that he's doing one of a hundred other things that have nothing to do with us.

"But Marcus is suspicious, and I think we should accept that as serious. Marcus, have I left anything out?"

"Nunh," Marcus says, adding his typical light conversational wit to what might otherwise be a tense moment. But Marcus does have remarkable instincts in situations like this, so I will be surprised if he's wrong. Surprised but pleased.

"So here's what we are going to do," Laurie says. "Marcus is going to leave here first. If the guy downstairs follows him, then Marcus will successfully deal with him. If not, then Marcus will move into position where he can watch the watcher.

"Once Marcus is in place, we'll all leave gradually, either one at a time or in pairs. Just get in your cars and leave when it's your turn; if the guy follows you, then Marcus will be there to handle things. If not, you've got nothing to worry about.

"Andy, you and I will go last. We'll leave together, but since we each have our own car here, we'll obviously split up."

Everybody nods their agreement at the plan. Marcus leaves first, and about ten minutes later Laurie's cell phone rings. Marcus says that the guy did not follow him. Marcus is now in position, so we can start sending people down.

Edna and Hike go next. A few minutes later, Marcus calls and pronounces them free and clear. Sam goes next, then Willie. The calls come from Marcus: they have not been followed.

But the guy in the Toyota remains in place, apparently watching the office entrance. I know of no reason why Laurie or I would be subject to this kind of scrutiny, and possibly this is a false alarm, but we're about to find out.

Laurie and I go downstairs and out the front door together. Fortunately our cars are in different directions on the street, so we each go our own way once we're outside.

I start to drive home, and within three minutes my phone rings. Laurie says, "It's you."

"The guy is following me?" I ask.

"Yes."

"What should I do?"

"Just drive home as you normally would; Marcus is watching him. I'll see you at home."

The rest of the drive takes about fifteen minutes, all of which I spend unsuccessfully trying to figure out what this could be about. Situations like this are usually related to cases I handle, but I haven't exactly been a workaholic lately.

The obvious possibilities are the Noah Traynor case or my representation of Simon the police dog. It seems inconceivable that it could be the latter; my opposition was the police department, and I don't see any reason they would want to track me.

Even the Traynor case doesn't seem to make sense; it hasn't really begun. I haven't even read the discovery yet, no less started investigating. Who could I possibly be a threat to?

I get home and park next to Laurie's car in the driveway. I walk to the front door without looking around; I have faith that Marcus is doing his job. But it's still nerve-racking.

When I get inside, Laurie is just getting off the phone. "Ricky is sleeping over at Will Rubenstein's tonight," she says. Because we were going to be in the meeting, Will's mother had picked them both up at school and taken them to their house. "Until we get a better idea what's going on, it's best he not be here."

She no sooner says that than the phone rings again. She answers and says little, just a couple of *Right*s and *Okay*s, topping it off with "I agree."

"Marcus?" I ask when she hangs up.

She nods.

"What was it you agreed to?"

"That Marcus is not going to grab the guy now; he's going to watch him and not do anything until we can figure out who he is and what he's trying to do."

As much as I don't like the idea of being followed like this, it seems like a logical plan. "Please mention to Marcus that if the guy is about to shoot me, he should intervene."

She smiles. "If I think of it, I'll tell him."

Chapter 4

THE DISCOVERY DOCUMENTS have arrived, and they don't offer much.

The main connection tying Noah to the crime is DNA, proving he was with the victim close to the time of death. The skin under the fingernails also demonstrates that they had a physical altercation, so that is particularly damning evidence. The DNA evidence is all a jury would need, especially in light of Noah's actions, or inactions, after learning of the crime.

The value of these documents to us is that to some degree they give us an investigatory road map. The police conducted many interviews. They talked to all of Kristen's friends, her boyfriend, and even a few people they considered potential suspects.

But everybody had an alibi, and no one besides Noah left DNA and skin at the scene. That trumped everything.

The documents describe Kyle Wainwright as Kristen's boyfriend at the time of her death. Kyle's relationship with her, and that it had seemed to be ending, initially placed him dead center on the police radar. However, he was eliminated as a suspect, as he was on a college visitation trip at Tufts when she was killed.

Another interesting note is that Kristen had been acting a bit strangely in the days before her death, which is consistent with what Noah told us. Friends reported that she seemed nervous and even talked about going somewhere else to live, which is again what Noah described.

Significantly, at no point in the past fourteen years did Noah's name even come up. None of Kristen's friends mentioned him, nor did anyone else that was interviewed.

Starting right away, we will begin interviewing anybody and everybody who might have information helpful to our defense. We'll be coming at those talks from a different point of view than the police did. Their focus was that whoever was with Kristen was the killer. We will be assuming the opposite about Noah.

Of course, they might have been right.

I interrupt my reading to have an early dinner; Laurie has made her special-recipe fried chicken. It is fantastic; if I am ever able to successfully give up lawyering, I've got an idea to buy a million buckets and sell the stuff.

The doorbell rings while we're having coffee, and I tense up. I can't imagine Marcus would let some bad guy just walk up to the house, ring the bell, and shoot me, but you never know.

While I'm trying to figure out what to do, pretending to contemplate as I wipe the nonexistent fried-chicken crumbs from the side of my mouth, Laurie goes to the door.

"Corey, come on in," she says.

Both Corey and Simon are here, which delights Tara. She runs over to renew acquaintances with Simon, and the two furiously and simultaneously sniff and wag their tails. Sebastian deigns to lift his head up from his position on a dog bed.

"I bring news," Corey says.

"About the case?" I'm surprised if that's true; the proper thing would be for the lawyer to be informed of any developments.

He grins. "I heard from administration. I have a feeling they didn't want to tell you and give you the satisfaction."

"So it's good news?" Laurie asks.

"Simon and I now have the same retirement date, and that date is today."

"That's great!" Laurie says, raising her coffee cup in a toast.

Corey turns to me. "You did a great job; Simon and I are very grateful. I never thought you could pull it off."

"In any public fight between the bureaucracy and a dog, bet on the dog," I say.

"Maybe so, but you played it brilliantly. What do I owe you?"

"We've been through that already. Remember Laurie's goodness-of-my-heart speech? Besides, this one was fun."

He shakes his head. "No, I need to make this right. I'm serious about this. I'm going to start doing private work, and hopefully I'll be making good money."

"I've got an idea," Laurie says. "We're starting a case."

"The Traynor thing?"

"Right. You can work on it, and your fee will cover Andy's work."

He thinks about it. "Sounds fair. What do you want me to do?"

"Too soon to know," Laurie says. "You can be on retainer."

I nod. "Right. We pay for your availability. If we need you, it's covered. If not, the retainer money still goes to pay off my fee. At the end of the case, we're square."

He thinks about it more. "Okay, Simon and I are on call."

WE'RE going through the motions, but it's not really possible to visit the murder scene.

Kristen McNeil's body was discovered about a hundred yards from Hinchliffe Stadium in Paterson, right near the Great Falls, a truly impressive waterfall. Hinchliffe has a storied history and is one of only two stadiums still standing in which the old Negro League baseball games were played.

But "still standing" is probably the kindest way that Hinchliffe can currently be described. It has been out of use for more than two decades and was allowed to degrade badly. The area has changed enough that the scene has been substantially altered.

Laurie and I always go to the murder scene first; it helps us to get a firsthand feeling for what happened. Unfortunately, this scene is simply not what it was when the murder happened.

It's fairly easy to tell from the police sketches where the murder took place—on the far side of the stadium, with a clear view of the falls. To Kristen and Noah, it might have seemed like a romantic setting. But it was also desolate, and no one would have been there to help Kristen or hear her scream.

The parking lot is around at the front side of the stadium. "So they pulled up in separate cars," Laurie says. "Maybe they arrived at the same time, or maybe this was just the designated meeting place. After they argued, Noah said he left first, and he assumed she would follow."

"If she was alive when he left, then someone else must have been here the entire time. Unless she was waiting for someone."

"I think it's most likely someone came after Noah left. They could have seen his car drive off."

"I would tend to think the other way, that someone was here already," I say. "There are plenty of places they could have been hiding where they wouldn't be seen. If they waited for Noah's car to pull away before coming in, Kristen could have already been in her own car and leaving by then."

"But if they were here, they would have needed to leave their car somewhere. If it was in the parking lot, Noah would have seen it."

"They could have left it on the other side of the building. They could have been in place before Noah and Kristen arrived if they had advance knowledge of where they were going. Or they could have pulled up and left their car down the road; with the noise from the falls, they wouldn't have been heard."

I'm not sure that last theory is correct, because even as I'm saying it, we hear a car pulling up. Laurie reacts instantly, taking her handgun out of her purse. I just stand there, having neither of those items. I need to start carrying a purse.

But self-defense isn't needed; it's Marcus's car. He pulls up right near us and gets out, then walks around and opens the back door on the left side. He reaches in and pulls out a human being, dragging him out by the collar and resting him on the ground.

Laurie walks over to them and has a brief conversation with Marcus. I stand there like a jerk, waiting to hear what happened and hoping that the guy on the ground is still breathing.

Laurie comes back to me. "He's the guy that's been following you. His name is Freddie Siroka. Marcus got the name by having the license plate run. He was concerned that we'd be out in the open here and the guy might have taken a shot at us, so he decided to terminate the surveillance."

"Is he dead?"

"No. When Marcus grabbed him, Siroka took a swing at him. You can see how well it worked out for him."

I nod. "Siroka might not have been class valedictorian. Are we going to wait for him to wake up so we can question him?"

She shakes her head. "You need to go home and be there when Ricky gets home from school. Marcus and I will question him. Marcus is pretty good at it. I'll fill you in when I get home."

"Works for me." This is my favorite kind of plan.

When Ricky gets home, he joins me in taking Tara and Sebastian for a walk.

Laurie comes home just as we're about to leave, and she decides to come along as well. She says she wants to stretch her legs, but she's just spent hours at the stadium, so I've got a hunch her legs are already pre-stretched. I conclude that she wants to be around in case Siroka was not the only guy after me.

Our walk takes an hour, and when we get home, Marcus is waiting for us on the front porch. Ricky runs ahead to give him a hug, yelling for his "Uncle Marcus." Uncle Marcus smiles and twirls him in the air before putting him down.

Once we get in the house, Ricky goes to his room to pretend to do his homework while secretly watching television. Marcus, Laurie, and I go into the den so that they can update me on what they've learned. She'll be doing the updating, since she knows if Marcus does it I'd need subtitles.

Laurie reveals that she and Marcus succeeded in getting Siroka to talk. He said that he was hired by a sometime associate named George Taillon to keep an eye on Andy Carpenter and to report back on where he went. No more, no less.

At first he said he had no idea of the purpose of the surveillance and that under no circumstances was he instructed to have any encounter with me. He was to meet with Taillon every other night at Taillon's apartment to give a report. His sense was that Taillon would then forward that report to someone else.

Under prodding, Siroka admitted that it had to do with the McNeil case, though he wouldn't go so far as to say he had knowledge of who killed her. He might not be telling the truth and might be holding back other information, but Laurie doesn't think so. Marcus had apparently mentioned to him that if it turned out that Siroka was doing either of those things, he would pay him a visit. The prospect of that would not be appealing. I don't relish Marcus's visits, and he's working for me.

Marcus had also told Siroka not to give Taillon a heads-up that he'd spilled the beans to us, and Siroka promised not to. There is no way of telling if he will follow through on that promise. While he might not want Taillon to know that he had been busted, he'd have to tell him why he was discontinuing the surveillance.

We will commence finding out what we can about Taillon before we take our next step, but there is a good bet that he will at some point be paid a visit by me and Uncle Marcus.

"By the way," Laurie says, "I've got the whole thing on audiotape. Siroka didn't realize I was doing it; he was somewhat focused on Marcus. Will it be admissible?"

"You're worried if it's admissible?" I ask, amused.

She smiles. "You've got me thinking like a lawyer."

"That's a terrible thing to say. But we'll figure out a way to get it admitted, if we can't get Siroka to testify." It was brilliant of Laurie to tape it, and it was even legal for her to do so. New Jersey is a one-party consent state.

Our representation of Noah Traynor has obviously become a threat to someone.

Even though I am never thrilled to have enemies, in this case our discovery is potentially positive. It means another entity is out there that wants us to fail and wants Noah to be convicted.

Maybe, just maybe, that entity is the real guilty party.

PUBLICITY definitely can cut both ways.

Whereas Simon is experiencing the glories of retirement living at least in part because of the public outcry we created, Noah is on the wrong end of the media stick.

His arrest has sparked a deluge of stories about the Kristen McNeil murder. Now everyone is being reminded of what it was like back then, of the horror that Kristen and her family endured. Bearing the brunt of that public reeducation will be Noah. It's fair to say that not too many of the articles and televised pieces dwell on Noah's not having been convicted of anything.

Today I'm meeting with Jenna Silverman, the prosecutor assigned to put Noah away for the rest of his life. I've never gone up against her before, but I'm told she is young, competent, and fair, as prosecutors go. This will be her first murder trial.

The prevailing view is that Jenna's competence is unlikely to be severely tested by the upcoming trial. The prosecution's case is not complicated; Noah's DNA proves that he was there, and his not coming forward in the past fourteen years is evidence of his consciousness of guilt.

Jenna has called this meeting, and I know that the purpose is to discuss a possible plea bargain. Unfortunately, as is customary in situations like this, small talk has to come first.

"I'm an admirer of yours," she says. "I've studied quite a few of your cases."

"Stop it. I told myself I wouldn't cry."

"You're also a wiseass." She smiles. "I'm always surprised when I see how much judges let you get away with."

"It's because I'm extraordinarily charming. In fact, I'm about to flash my most winning smile, after which I expect you will dismiss the charges against Noah Traynor."

"Is that your way of saying I should get to the point?"

"You see right through me."

She nods. "Thirty years. No possibility of parole."

"You're way too kind."

"No, I'm not. He strangled an eighteen-year-old girl; if it were up to me, we wouldn't even be having this conversation."

I stand up. "I'll talk to my client. But a good guess is you're going to get to watch me charm another judge."

I decide to take the offer to Noah immediately, so I head for the jail. Thirty years without parole is a horrible sentence, but life in prison is even worse, and that's what he's facing if he loses at trial. It's his call to make, and as soon as we're settled in the lawyer visiting room, I present him with his options.

He doesn't hesitate. "I can't say I'm guilty. I can't give up thirty years of my life all for something that I didn't do."

"You do understand that there is a very real chance you will spend the rest of your life behind bars for something that you didn't do?"

It's like I slapped him in the face; he just about recoils from my words. "I know that. It's all I've been able to think about."

"You want some time to consider this? The offer will still be there next week."

"What are our chances of winning the case?"

"If the trial was starting today, it would be zero."

"But the trial is not starting today."

I nod. "Which is why I can't predict what is going to happen. We are just starting our investigation. The difficulty is that their evidence cannot be successfully challenged. You were there, it was your skin under her fingernails, and they can prove it.

"So while we can't prove that you didn't do it, we'll need to point to someone else who might have. We're just not anywhere near that yet, and there's no guarantee we're going to get there."

"But you're going to try? I mean, all out?"

"That I can guarantee."

"Okay," he says. "I'll think about the offer, but I know there is no way I am going to plead guilty to this."

"Fair enough."

CYNTHIA and Kevin McNeil have been grieving for fourteen years.

They are going to grieve for the rest of their lives; nothing that happens in this trial is going to change that. That's par for the course when parents lose a child, no matter how it happens.

But the manner of Kristen's death made it even more difficult, if that's possible. They've had to live with the knowledge that Kristen died in abject terror with no one there to help her. Parents cannot protect their child every minute of every day, but they can sure agonize when they don't.

While someone out there truly deserved the blame, they never knew who that someone was. Until now; now they are positive it is Noah Traynor.

All of this makes perfect sense from their point of view, and it is spelled out in an interview they did last night for a local news station. They said they would talk about this nightmare just the one time, then would have no more public comment.

They said they want Noah to get a fair trial, that they only want the real guilty party punished. But they also said that they had no interest in going to the trial because they didn't want to be in the same room as him.

Unfortunately, their claim that they would have no more public comments is actually extending to private comments, especially when it comes to us. Laurie called and asked them if we could talk with them, and they turned her down cold. They see us as the villains who are trying to prevent their daughter's killer from having to pay for his crime.

If I were them, I'd probably feel the same way.

Fortunately, not everyone in their family shares that point of view. Karen McNeil, Kristen's sister, took little convincing when Laurie called her. Karen is an ER nurse at Hackensack Hospital, and she suggested we meet in the hospital cafeteria at the end of her shift.

Laurie has come along just in case the situation requires any tact or human decency. We're sitting at a table when a woman in a nurse's uniform, probably in her early thirties, walks in and surveys the room. Having seen photos of Kristen, I have no doubt who this is. Karen looks like an older version of Kristen.

She comes over to us and asks, "Laurie?"

Laurie, always quick on her feet in conversational situations like this, answers, "Yes."

We do introductions all around, and I ask Karen if she wants anything to eat or drink. She asks for coffee, so I run off to get it. I am a vital cog in this operation.

By the time I come back, Laurie and Karen are smiling and chatting like reunited sorority sisters. We'd probably be better off if I didn't join them, but I promised her the coffee.

Laurie eventually steers the conversation toward the matter at hand. "Did Kristen ever mention Noah Traynor?"

A shake of the head. "Not to me, at least not directly."

"What do you mean, 'not directly'?"

"She said she met someone but never said his name. I assumed she was being secretive because of Kyle."

"Kyle Wainwright?" I ask. That's the name listed in the discovery documents as Kristen's boyfriend at the time.

Karen nods. "Right. They were together for quite a while, but something was going on."

"Going on how?" Laurie asks.

"I'm not sure. But whatever it was had Kristen really upset. I figured she was dating this new guy to get back at him."

"Was he the type to react badly?" I ask.

Karen shrugs. "I guess anyone would. But Kyle wasn't the violent type; at least he didn't seem to be. I always liked him well enough. And he always seemed crazy about Kristen."

"If something was bothering Kristen, something really important, would she have been likely to confide in you? I mean, something more significant than breaking up with a boyfriend?"

Karen smiles. "Back then nothing could have been more significant than breaking up with a boyfriend. But, yeah, I think so. I was only a year younger than her, so we were close."

"Did Kristen say anything to you about leaving home?"

"No, I'd remember that. But she was doing crazy things; it was like she was going through some kind of internal crisis."

"What kind of crazy things?" Laurie asks.

"Well, for one, she quit her job. And she really seemed to like that job."

"Where did she work?"

"Some tech company; I never understood what they do. Kyle's father owned it; I think he still does. Kyle got her the job; maybe that's why she quit."

"Are you still in touch with Kyle?"

She shakes her head. "No. It was pretty hard even to see him after Kristen died. I heard he took it really hard, and I still haven't gotten over it. I doubt I ever will."

"We understand," Laurie says. "There's so much she could have done."

Karen nods. "I might have had nieces and nephews by now." Then, "You think they have the wrong guy? How could that be?"

"We're trying to answer those questions," I say.

"It's your job to think he's innocent, right? I'm sorry, but I hope he's not; I hope he's guilty as hell."

"Why?"

"Because someone did it, and my parents need to know who that person is. So do I. Do you know they've never gone through her things? My mother cleans the room every day; she keeps it like a shrine. I'm hoping that once they know who took her away, they'll be able to move on, at least a little bit."

"They won't talk to us," Laurie says.

"I know," Karen says. "I told them they should but got nowhere with it. I told them we have to be sure; the worst possible outcome would be for the wrong person to go to prison."

"That's exactly how we feel," Laurie says. "We don't want to cause them more pain."

"That you couldn't do. Their life ended the same day Kristen's did. They were never the same. Do you know that someone broke into and robbed their house during the funeral? Took all my mother's jewelry. Can you imagine coming home from your teenage daughter's funeral and walking in to that?"

"No, I can't," Laurie says. "Thank you for talking to us."

As we're getting up to leave, Karen asks, "How old is your client?"

"Thirty-three," I say. "Why?"

"A couple of times . . . not too long before she died . . . she asked my opinion about dating older men. She said she had a friend who was involved with someone. It struck me as strange."

"Did she say anything else about it?" Laurie asks.

Karen shakes her head. "No. But if Traynor is thirty-three . . . Kristen would have been thirty-two now if she had lived."

Laurie nods. "Not much of a gap."

Chapter 5

CHARLES ARRANT TOOK PRIDE in not making strategic mistakes.

But on the rare occasions when it happened, he didn't whitewash it, deny it, or avoid confronting it. He knew that only made it worse. Instead, he fixed it. Every. Single. Time.

This time Arrant was particularly disappointed in himself. He'd overreacted to the phone call and did more than was necessary. He forced things rather than let the "game" come to him. And his move came back to bite him in the ass. That bad move could be reduced to four words: he hired a moron.

This particular moron's name was George Taillon. In Arrant's defense, he had employed Taillon before, and the results had been satisfactory. This was supposed to be a simple job, but Taillon, heretofore known in Arrant's mind as Moron Number One, had blown it by hiring Moron Number Two.

Arrant had told Taillon to watch the lawyer, Carpenter, from a distance. He was to report where he went; the information might come in handy down the road. But Taillon apparently felt the job was beneath him, and he hired Moron Number Two, Siroka. He, in turn, had blown it by allowing Carpenter to realize he was being watched. Carpenter reacted in an un-lawyer-like way by hiring muscle to deal with Siroka.

Siroka, to cement his status as a moron, had given up Taillon's name.

Then Siroka faced a choice. He decided that he had to tell Taillon what had happened since he could no longer do the surveillance. His dilemma was whether to admit he'd given up Taillon's name. He apparently decided, not without logic, that Taillon would find out anyway, since Carpenter was going to come after him. So Siroka told Taillon the truth.

Then Taillon faced a similar choice. He could tell Arrant what had happened or keep it from him and restart the surveillance himself, being more careful not to be detected. Keeping it to himself would have been the smart move, since Carpenter did not have Arrant's name. All of these events might never have gotten back to Arrant. But Moron Number One made the wrong choice. He told Arrant the truth.

The entire chain of events, Arrant knew, was not in any way devastating. Carpenter didn't know about Arrant; his knowledge stopped with Taillon. The problem, though, was that it opened up a new area of investigation for Carpenter. He would be smart enough to connect it to the Traynor case and would search for the reason that someone thought it important to follow him.

All of that is why Arrant summoned Taillon to a meeting to discuss the next steps. Arrant insisted that he bring Siroka with him so Arrant could know all the details of what had gone down.

Taillon and Siroka arrived at the Pennington Park baseball field at eight o'clock, as instructed. Arrant was already there waiting for them, and by 8:01 the two arrivals were dead.

Arrant left the bodies there so that they would be found and reported by the media. Carpenter would know that the new avenue of investigation had been decisively closed. And he'd also know without doubt the type of person that had closed it.

The type no one wants to cross.

IT'S way too early for me to have any suspects.

I really don't know any of the players yet, nor do I know enough about the victim's background and associations. But even with the little that I know, I'm interested in Kyle Wainwright, Kristen McNeil's "boyfriend of record" at the time of her death. She was clearly cheating on him with Noah, and while I don't know if Kyle was aware of it, if he was, then the rejection might have stung. He could have wanted revenge.

This brings me today to NetLink Systems, the company owned by Kyle's father, Arthur Wainwright. Arthur is what could be described as a leading citizen in North Jersey. He's politically influential nationally and is a wealthy philanthropist, donating to worthy causes through his Wainwright Foundation.

Kyle works here in the Paramus headquarters. No doubt he got the job as the result of a pressure-filled interview in which he impressed the hell out of his father. I've braved a steady rain to come here to speak to him, but I haven't called ahead. I find that people find it easier to refuse an interview over the phone than face-to-face.

I ask at the reception desk to speak with Kyle, and the young woman asks if I have an appointment. I say that I do not. I tell her that I am an attorney and that it is a personal matter.

She picks up the phone and tells someone that an attorney named Andy Carpenter is here asking to speak to Kyle. Ten minutes go by with nothing happening. The receptionist eventually apologizes and says, "Let me call back there again," but as she picks up the phone, I hear, "Mr. Carpenter?"

I look over and see someone who is unlikely to be Kyle Wainwright. This guy is probably in his early-to-mid-forties, which would make him a decade older than Kyle.

He approaches me with his hand extended. "My name is Jeremy Kennon. Why don't you come with me to my office?"

"I was looking for Kyle Wainwright."

He nods. "I know, but Kyle is at a meeting in the city." He smiles. "Come on back."

I follow him to his office. Kennon is obviously an important player here because he has an impressive corner office with glass walls providing an unimpeded view of the surrounding area.

"I'm head of technology here," Kennon says. "Kyle works for me; he's picked up the tech stuff very well. Obviously his father's kid."

"When will he be back?"

"Tomorrow morning. Not sure if he will want to talk to you, considering the circumstances. But he might."

"Which circumstances are you talking about?"

"You representing the guy accused of"—he hesitates—"killing

Kristen," he says uncomfortably. "We're all following it pretty closely. We cared about her a lot."

"You worked here then?"

He smiles. "Oh, yes. Fifteen years; I was one of the first employees hired."

"Has the company grown a lot over the years?"

He nods. "That's for sure. We only had two floors back then; now we have six. Every time we expand, they make me switch offices; by the time I'm unpacked, they're moving me again."

"Kristen McNeil worked here back then as well?"

"She did," he says. "Got here after me but didn't stay very long. She left a week or so before she died."

"Why did she quit?"

"I'm not sure; she never told me. I came in one day and found out she was gone. I was planning to talk to her about it but never got the chance. Something must have happened."

"What did she do here?"

"Just assistant stuff, nothing technical. She didn't work for me, so we didn't interact much. I think Arthur gave her the job as a favor to Kyle. But she was a hard worker and a good kid."

"Arthur Wainwright? Kyle's father?"

Another smile. "Also known as the Big Cheese."

"What does the company do, exactly?"

"We make hardware of various kinds. Our main product is routers. Are you familiar with this stuff?"

"Absolutely. I can even tell you what a router is. It's a device that routs things."

He laughs. "You're obviously accomplished in the field. All internet communications go through routers; it directs the data . . . tells it where to go. Even internally; if I send an email to someone in the next office, it goes out into the internet world and then comes back. And routers handle all that."

"Who do you sell them to?"

"We have corporate clients, but a lot of our router production has been subcontracted to us by the huge players in the field. We're a small fish, though a profitable one."

"Is Arthur Wainwright a tech guy or just a big-cheese guy?"

"He used to be at the top in the tech area, back when he started this company. But there are new developments every day, things change by the nanosecond, and one has to keep up with it. After a while Arthur chose to delegate to worker bees like me."

Back to the matter at hand. "Do you know what Kristen was worried about in the weeks before she died?"

He shakes his head. "No, but apparently she had good reason to worry. I just wish she had come to me, to any of us."

"Will you ask Kyle to call me?" I hand him my card.

"I'll do that. Like I said, he might, but he might not."

"I would think he'd want to find out the truth about what happened."

"I'm sure he would. But you and Kyle might have different truths."

"ANDY, come in here. Right away."

I'm in the den going over discovery documents. Laurie is up in bed; I thought she was reading, but based on her words, I'm hoping that she's yearning.

In any event, I've made it a lifelong habit to always obey when a beautiful woman calls me to bed, though for a lifelong habit it has happened remarkably few times.

As I reach the bedroom, I can hear that the television is on and Laurie is watching the news. The possibility of yearning being the reason for her calling me has just dropped off precipitously.

"Look at this." She points to the television screen.

Two photographs are on the screen, one of which I recognize immediately. Under the two photos are the names George Taillon and Fred Siroka. The bodies of the two men have been found in shrubbery in Pennington Park. They were believed to have been shot to death within the past twenty-four hours.

"The plot thickens," Laurie says.

"The chance that their getting shot has nothing to do with us is absolute zero," I say as Laurie nods her agreement. "And it's safe to say we can stop looking for George Taillon."

"There are a lot of layers to this."

"What do you mean?"

"Taillon paid Siroka to watch you, and it blew up in his face. A third party, we assume higher up on the chain of command, got rid of them. That's three levels, and we don't know if we reached the top yet."

"All because an arrest was made in a fourteen-year-old murder," I say.

"It's what happened as a result of the arrest. Let's say that there is someone out there who is the real killer. As long as no one was charged with the crime, and as long as the police assumed whoever left the DNA was the killer, then the real guilty person was safe.

"But once Noah was arrested, then the case was once again subjected to intense scrutiny. People, more specifically us, have a reason to look into the murder. We are trying to find the real killer, something the real killer seems not to be pleased about."

I nod. "Real killers do look at things like that negatively."

"They do. Which is why Marcus once again has to play the role of lawyer protector."

I shake my head. "No. Trying to put me out of commission would put an even more intense focus on our case, which is why they won't do it. We need Marcus investigating, not protecting."

She argues but finally agrees, at least for now. I call Sam and ask him to find out whatever he can about Taillon and Siroka.

"What are you looking for?" he asks.

"I won't know until you find it, so cast a wide net. I especially want to know if they've gotten their hands on any money recently and where it came from."

"I'm on it."

"Wait. Before you get off, tell me about NetLink Systems."

"What do you want to know?"

"What do they do? I know they make routers, and I know that all internet communications go through routers."

"Right. If not for routers, your computer would be a blank screen when you went online."

"And they sell these routers to who?"

"They're a relatively small company for the field, so I would imagine they have contracts to make them for bigger companies. I'm sure they also have companies that buy from them directly."

"What else do they make?"

"A whole bunch of stuff you've never heard of. Switches, hubs, WAPs, security cameras . . ."

"I've heard of security cameras."

"Congratulations. Can I go now?"

I let him off and call Pete Stanton on his cell phone. He answers with his customary warmth: "What the hell do you want?"

"Are you at Pennington Park?" I ask, assuming that the head of Homicide would be at a double-murder scene.

"Yeah. Why?"

"I'm coming down there."

"What do you think this is, Disneyland? It's a murder scene." Then, "Why would you come down here?"

"I have information for you about the two dead guys."

Pete knows me well enough to understand that I am serious about this. "Can it wait until tomorrow? I have a lot going on here, and the chief just showed up."

"I'll be in your office at ten a.m."

"That will give me something to look forward to."

The next day, Pete pushes our meeting back to 2:00 p.m.

I have no doubt that he's busy; a double murder is a big deal in cop-land. That he's seeing me at all today means he takes seriously that I have something important to say, as well as that he wants to continue to get free beer and burgers at Charlie's.

So I'm sitting in his office, alone, waiting for him to come back from a staff meeting. It's not until two fifteen when he walks in. "This better be good," he says. "And it better not be about the Kristen McNeil murder."

"No, you've already arrested the wrong guy in that case. I'm going to try and help you get the right guy in the double murder."

He sits behind his desk. "I can use all the help I can get."

"I'm going to want some information in return."

He frowns his disgust. "You have ten minutes."

"Siroka had been following me; I got lucky and Marcus noticed it. Marcus interceded in typical Marcus fashion, and they got together with Laurie and chatted. I guess Siroka just considered Marcus sort of a kindred spirit, because he opened up to him. He said that Taillon had hired him to follow me and that it had something to do with the Kristen McNeil murder."

"Interesting," Pete says. "So why were they killed?"

"Because whoever hired Taillon found out that we knew about him and Siroka. Taillon may have even reported that to his bosses, since he'd have to admit that the surveillance was over. Those bosses obviously didn't trust Taillon not to reveal their identities. They didn't want me digging any further."

"Why do you think Siroka was following you?"

"Do you have hearing issues? I already told you he said it related to my case. That is supported by the fact that I took over Noah Traynor's defense just before Siroka started tailing me."

"Or maybe somebody just doesn't like you."

"My turn," I say. "Have you found a connection between Siroka and Taillon?"

"They had worked together a few times; Taillon hired him for small jobs."

"Tell me about Taillon."

"He was sort of an independent contractor; gets hired on a case-by-case basis. Very good at his job."

"He worked alone?"

"That's difficult to answer. He had a loose arrangement with another guy with a similar résumé, but they were not partners."

"What do you mean by 'a loose arrangement'?"

Pete shrugs. "They'd back up each other when one couldn't handle something or when the situation required two people."

"What's the guy's name?"

"Mitch Holzer."

"Have you talked to him?"

"Yeah . . . nothing. Guys like that open up to the police all the time."

"You think he knows anything?"

"Hard to say. Following you is not exactly a job that requires an army, so I'm not sure why Taillon would have had to bring him in. But you never know."

I don't say anything, so Pete says, "If you're thinking of dealing with Holzer, think again. He is a dangerous guy."

I hold up both of my hands. "You want to know what dangerous is? These hands are registered with the bar association."

"Are we done here?"

"Two more questions. When you searched Taillon's house, did you find any money? And what about a cell phone?"

Pete looks at me strangely. "Twenty grand in cash. No cell phone either on the body or in his house." Then he stands. "Time's up . . . thanks for coming in. It's been a real treat."

WHEN I get home, our house is considerably more crowded than I remembered it.

That's because Ricky is having a rare, Laurie-endorsed, triple sleepover. Ricky's best friend, Will Rubenstein, is here. Also here is Danny Traynor, who seems to be fitting in quite well. Danny has brought along Murphy, his dachshund.

When I get to the kitchen, Laurie is on the phone. As soon as she gets off the call, she asks, "How did it go with Pete?"

I recount the conversation, and when I get to the part about Mitch Holzer, Laurie says, "I assume you're going to want to talk to him?"

"Might as well."

"Let me have Marcus do some homework on the guy to find out what we might be dealing with. But there is someone else for you to talk to first."

"Who?"

"That phone call I was on was from Kyle Wainwright. He's expecting you at his office at ten o'clock tomorrow morning."

"Good. Hopefully he'll confess."

She smiles. "I doubt it. You think he's a viable possibility?"

"Probably not. But I'll have a better feel for it after I talk to him. It's always possible that he lost control and killed his girlfriend for cheating on him. But with someone hiring guys like Taillon and Siroka, this doesn't feel like that kind of situation."

She nods. "I was thinking the same thing."

Just then Sam calls and tells me that he has tracked down the cell numbers for both Siroka and Taillon. That their phones are missing is not as significant to our investigation as it might seem. Everything done on a phone, and nowadays pretty much everything done in life, is recorded somewhere, by someone.

In the case of a phone, a record of all calls is stored for posterity on phone company computers. This is also true of the phone GPS records, meaning the phone company always knows where a phone is or was, even retroactively.

"I'll get right on it," Sam says. "Now that I have them."

By getting right on it, Sam means that he will hack into the phone company computers and retrieve all the information he needs. Technically, that's illegal. Nontechnically, it's also illegal. I've long ago come to terms with that.

In my view, the absolute best thing about sleepovers are the meals. I go out and get three pizzas, ensuring enough for everyone to have a satisfying dinner as well as leaving cold pizza for me in the morning.

These days I'm trying to appreciate the small pleasures.

I'M GETTING well-known here at NetLink Systems.

This time the receptionist gives me an enthusiastic hello and asks me how I am today. I decide to lie and tell her that I'm fine; it will shorten the conversation.

Once again she calls back to alert Kyle Wainwright that I'm here, and this time the wait is only two minutes. The door opens, and a man says, "Andy Carpenter? I'm Kyle Wainwright."

We shake hands and go back to his office. Kyle's office is two doors down from that of his boss, Jeremy Kennon. Like Kennon's and all the other offices on this hallway, the walls are glass, so anyone passing by can look in. Once we're seated, I notice someone walking by who stops and looks in at us. He's about sixty years old, and what little hair he has is gray. He seems to shake his head slightly and then continues walking.

"That's my father," Kyle says.

I don't see a need to respond to that, so I don't. Instead I ask, "So, you've had fourteen years to think about it. Any idea who killed Kristen McNeil?"

He shakes his head. "No, like everybody else, I've always assumed it was whoever left their DNA on the scene."

"I understand that she had broken up with you shortly before she died?"

"Not officially. She just wanted space, time to think, that kind of stuff. But, yeah, whatever the reason, the handwriting was on the wall. But it wasn't final, or at least I didn't think so."

"But she quit her job here; that seems somewhat final."

He nods. "I remember being surprised by that. We didn't work in the same department, and even if she dumped me, it wasn't like she was going to get fired. My father liked her, and I never would have been vindictive like that."

"You were away the day Kristen was killed?" I ask.

"Yeah . . . wait a minute, you think I might have killed her?"

"I don't have the slightest idea. Do the names Freddie Siroka or George Taillon mean anything to you?"

He thinks for a moment. "No . . . should they?"

I was searching for a reaction—and got none. Which of course means absolutely nothing. "Did you know Noah Traynor?"

"Your client? No, never met him, and Kristen never mentioned him to me. The first I heard of him was when they announced the arrest." Then, "Look, if you're trying to make a case that I killed Kristen, you're wasting your time."

"I'm just covering all the bases."

The door opens, and a young woman peers in. "Mr. Carpenter, Mr. Wainwright would like to talk to you before you leave."

"Uh-oh . . . that's my father," Kyle says. "You're going to get sent to your room without supper."

The woman smiles at what I guess is a common joke around here. "If you're ready, you could just follow me. . . ."

So I do. I follow her to the office all the way down the hall to the other corner office, on the opposite side of Kennon's. But Arthur Wainwright's office makes Kennon's and Kyle's look like telephone booths, if telephone booths still existed.

The woman knocks on the door, then opens it. Arthur Wainwright looks up from his desk as if annoyed. He calls me in with a hand motion, and in the reverse motion seems to dismiss the woman. This guy is good with his hands.

"I want you to leave my son alone," he says.

"Fine, thanks, how are you?"

"I mean it. He's been through enough."

"We had a conversation; no threats and no punches thrown. He seemed like he came out of it pretty well. But if you're worried, I'll send him some flowers. What's his favorite color?"

"I know all about you, Carpenter. Get out of here."

"You just asked me to come in."

"Leave now."

"Your son is a grown man. What are you so afraid of?"

"Would you like me to have you thrown out?"

"Believe me, I've been thrown out of better places by better people," I say as I leave. It's a pretty good exit line and would be even better if it weren't true.

GALE Halpern was Kristen McNeil's best friend.

At least that's how she was characterized in a number of media stories at the time of Kristen's death. She wasn't talking to the press in the weeks following the crime, but she's given a couple of interviews in recent years.

Laurie has tracked her down, and she agreed to talk to me. She asked that I come to her house in Fair Lawn. When I pull up, she comes out on the porch to greet me, shaking my hand with her right hand while cradling a baby in her left arm.

We go inside, and Gale points to a photograph on the mantel of two teenage girls, arms over each other's shoulders. "It's so hard to believe it's been fourteen years," she says. "That's how I'll always remember her because that's how she'll always be."

"Do you know why she was running away?"

"Who said she was running away?"

It's not a good sign that I know more about Kristen's mind-set than the person I'm interviewing. "People who knew her."

Gale shrugs. "She never told me that. But if it's true, then I would think she was getting away from Kyle."

"She was afraid of him?"

Gale nods. "I don't mean physically; he never hit her or anything. But he was taking over her life, and she was feeling confined. He wanted to know where she was all the time. I think that's why he got her the job at his father's company."

"Did you know Noah Traynor?"

"Not by name, but I knew there was somebody."

"Why?"

"I never said this before, but I think she was having an affair . . . although I guess at that age 'affair' sounds too sophisticated. She was fooling around, but she thought she was in love."

"But you don't know with who?"

"No, she wouldn't say, which was unlike her."

"Do you think Kyle knew about it?"

"I don't know for sure, but I'd bet he did. He knew every move she made. He was incredibly possessive."

"Were you surprised when she quit her job?"

"Very," Gale says. "She loved that job, and she really loved earning money. Kristen spent money faster than anyone I've ever known; she just loved to shop. She was making good money at her job but was still borrowing from me.

"Kristen always wanted to be older than she was; she was in a hurry to get somewhere, but I don't think she knew where. She seemed to think she'd know when she got there."

"Was she interested in dating older men?" Kristen's sister had said that Kristen might have been doing just that.

Gale almost does a double take. "How did you know that?"

"That's a yes?"

Gale nods. "She talked about it a lot. I don't know if she actually dated anyone older, but the idea certainly appealed to her."

"If she loved her job, why would she have quit?"

"I wish I could help you. Maybe you're right; maybe she was running away. But she had a life here, and family, and friends, and a job. If she was leaving all that, then something bad must have happened. Maybe the guy she was having the affair with dumped her. But I would say she was not running toward something; she was running away from something."

There's nothing more for me to learn from Gale, which is just as well, because she tells me that it's diaper-changing time.

All in all, nothing that Gale said to me is positive for us. If Kristen was having a secret affair, then the most likely person she was having it with would be the guy she rendezvoused with outside Hinchliffe Stadium.

My only suspect, and it's a stretch to even use that word, is Kyle Wainwright. Regardless of who Kristen might have been fooling around with, she was clearly separating from Kyle.

That would give him reason to be angry and lash out, particularly if he was as controlling as Gale makes him out to be. But he was out of town that day; that seems incontrovertible.

Do eighteen-year-old boys have the resources and connections to hire hit men? What about if they have rich fathers?

My next stop is the Coach House Diner on Route 4 to talk with Steven Halitzky, Kyle's college roommate at Tufts. I'm sitting in a booth having coffee when he walks in, looks around, and comes right over to me. "How ya doing?" he asks, smiling.

"How did you know who I was?"

"Are you kidding? I've seen you on television a bunch of times. You're a celebrity."

I like this guy already. He sits down and orders coffee and an English muffin. We chitchat a bit before I ask, "Have you stayed in touch with Kyle Wainwright?"

He shakes his head. "No, we see each other at get-togethers related to the school, but that's it. We were roommates as freshmen in the dorm, but then we both got apartments off campus. We weren't close, which is a nice way of saying I didn't like him very much. I don't think he was crazy about me either."

"Did he talk about the murder of his girlfriend?"

Halitzky nods. "A few times. He said she was his ex-girlfriend, that they had broken up."

"So he wasn't terribly upset?"

"If he was, he hid it well. And it sure didn't stop him from dating and partying. I'm talking about right out of the gate."

"Anything else you can tell me about him? I'm trying to get an accurate picture of who he is."

"I'll tell you one thing: I think it's hilarious that he wound up working for his father."

"Why?"

"He hated the guy. Talked about him like he was the worst father of all time; all he cared about was money and looking good. Apparently he used his high-priced lawyers to screw Kyle's mother in the divorce and left them with nothing."

"What brought Kyle and his father back together?"

Halitzky grins. "You tell me. You think money was involved? All I know is that Kyle said his father's whole public persona, the charity stuff, was a fake. That behind closed doors his father was . . . well, one time he called him a 'piece of garbage.'"

We talk some more, but I don't learn anything significant. I thank Halitzky for coming, pay the check, and we both go our separate ways. I got some information today, about both Kristen McNeil and Kyle Wainwright. Like all information that I acquire during an investigation, it might someday prove useful, or not.

I'll know when I know.

Chapter 6

As THANKSGIVINGS GO, this one is more crowded than usual.

Laurie has invited Julie and Danny Traynor to join us, and they've brought Murphy, the dachshund. Tara has definitely taken a liking to Murphy, and they sort of wrestle and sniff each other a lot. I think Sebastian likes him, too, because a couple of times he's summoned up the energy to blink.

Sam Willis comes over in time to watch the Lions play the Packers, and we eat the meal between games. It's so good that I don't even mind missing the first few minutes of the Redskins–Eagles game. Laurie has always been a great cook, but with Julie helping her, she has scaled new heights.

After dinner, Sam and I head to the game, and at halftime he asks, "Did you get my email?"

"No. What email is that?"

"I tried to call you, but you were out investigating something, and you had your phone off. So I emailed some stuff to you."

I shake my head. "I stopped in the office, but my computer was down; the wireless wasn't working."

"That's what happens when your internet provider owns a fruit stand."

Sam has long been on my case for using the wireless that Sofia Hernandez provides. I vow that I'll change the setup, but we both know that I won't. It's too much trouble.

"Should I open the email now, or can you summarize?"

"I can tell you the highlights. Taillon didn't use his cell phone much, so it wasn't hard to track down the calls. I went back twenty years; that's as long as the phone company keeps records. He kept the same number down through the years, so that made it even easier. He received twenty-one calls from eighteen different burner phones. As best I can tell, they were purchased, used a few times, and never used again. I can't trace who owned them."

"Makes sense. I'm sure he dealt with people that didn't want to be traced."

"Right," Sam says. "But two of the calls were made the day before Kristen McNeil's murder and one that night."

"Are you sure?"

"Yes. They were made from three different phones. If it's one person making the calls to him, he is a very careful guy."

This is stunning news, and it leads to a few conclusions. For one thing, Taillon's hiring Siroka to follow me clearly relates to the Noah Traynor case. Siroka had said that, but this confirms it. For another, Taillon was probably himself involved in Kristen McNeil's murder, whether directly or indirectly.

And last, it makes perfect sense that Taillon was killed, maybe by his own employer. He obviously knew a great deal, and we knew about him. He therefore presented an intolerable risk.

"This is significant stuff, Sam. Thanks."

"You want the other highlight?"

"There's more?"

He nods. "A week before Kristen McNeil was murdered, Taillon placed two calls to NetLink Systems."

THIS case is different from most.

In almost every situation in which a defendant is accused of murder, the defense has certain standard options. Alibis can be offered, prosecution theories can be attacked.

In this case? Not so much.

The prosecution will confidently offer their DNA evidence. They will say, without fear of contradiction, that Noah Traynor was at Hinchliffe Stadium with Kristen McNeil and that she had his skin fragments under her fingernails.

They will also say, again without fear of contradiction, that he could not have missed media reports about the murder yet did nothing. Did not come forward, did not explain himself, did not offer to help, did not submit to questions . . . nothing.

They don't have to offer theories; they simply have to present that evidence and let the jury decide.

With this fact pattern, there is no question how they would decide. Which means we cannot attack this head-on, so we have to come at it through a side door, and when we do, we had better have with us a person we can point to as the real murderer.

The only people I know that could possibly fit this description are Siroka and Taillon. The bad news is that they are not going to be walking through that door because they are both dead.

To make matters worse, it will be much harder to investigate Taillon and Siroka now that they have moved on to the great beyond. So while I am fairly certain that Taillon and maybe Siroka are directly connected to the McNeil killing, I am nowhere close to getting an impartial observer to believe it.

I can't even pin down who Taillon called at NetLink Systems. It could have been Kyle; maybe he hired Taillon to kill Kristen when Kyle was out of town and therefore had an alibi. Or it could have been any other employee there.

It is not even inconceivable that Taillon could have called Kristen herself. Her sister indicated that Kristen might have been having an affair with an older man; maybe she had taken up with Taillon. He was a dangerous guy, so something could have happened that made her scared and want to leave town.

Which brings us to Mitch Holzer. He's the guy that Pete Stanton said was a semi-associate of Taillon's, the person who would back up or fill in for Taillon when Taillon needed help or was unavailable. Pete described him as an independent contractor.

Laurie has had Marcus checking Holzer out and figuring out the best way to approach him. I already know that the best way to approach him is while standing behind Marcus, but I'm willing to listen to suggestions. He has just called to report in and is on the phone with Laurie offering those suggestions.

Laurie does almost no talking on the call, simply offering a few *Okay*s and *Right*s. When she finally gets off, she says, "Marcus is going to take you to see Holzer tonight."

This is not pleasant news. "Tonight? I have plans for tonight."

"What kind of plans?"

"I was hoping to have dinner with my family so that we could discuss family stuff."

"Family stuff?"

"Like how was your day, how was Ricky's day, how was my day. That's what families do; they talk at dinner about their day."

"Should I tell Marcus you don't want to talk to Holzer?"

She's got me; she knows I'll have to go. If I refused, I'd be letting down my client. This represents a perfect example of why I don't like to have clients in the first place.

"I'll go. But make sure Marcus knows that he has to stop Holzer from killing me."

MARCUS PICKS ME UP AT THE house at 10:00 p.m.

We drive to a bar on Market Street in downtown Paterson. The area is known for having its share of violent crime. The only way I would ordinarily come down here at this hour would be if I was accompanied by a Marine battalion, or Marcus.

Laurie said that Marcus told her that Holzer hangs out in this bar pretty much every night and actually uses an office in the back. I come up with a strategy on the way down there and share it with Marcus. He doesn't respond, but I assume he's heard me because I'm sitting three feet away and the radio is off.

The plan is not terribly complicated. Marcus is going to go in first and situate himself in a place from which he can observe. I'm then going to approach Holzer and try to talk to him, without his realizing that Marcus and I are together. I don't want Holzer to see me as an enemy, but good buddies don't bring Marcus Clark to a meeting.

We park a few stores down from the bar, and Marcus goes in while I wait in the car. I give him about three minutes, then take a deep breath and follow.

Probably fifteen people are in the bar. The first complication is that I have no idea what Holzer looks like. I go over to the bartender, who looks at me like I'm from another planet.

"I'm looking for Holzer," I say.

Without saying a word, the bartender turns and goes through a door to the back. About three minutes later, he returns and says, "He'll meet you in the back in five minutes."

"Through that door?" I point to the door he just used.

"No. Around the back. Through the alley."

I think I see the bartender make eye contact with a guy near the end of the bar. A large guy, by appearance he would fit the definition of goon. The combination of him and the word *alley* is worrisome. But I say, "Okay . . . thanks," to the bartender.

In the meantime, the goon gets up and goes outside. I walk over near Marcus and whisper, "He said to meet Holzer in the alley in five minutes. I think the guy that just left is involved."

Marcus doesn't say anything; he just gets up and leaves. I hope he's not going home; I wish I had kept the car keys.

I wait the five minutes; then I take a breath and go outside. The alley is to the right of the bar, and I instruct my legs to continue walking into the alley and toward the back of the building.

I am almost there when a figure appears next to me, walking at my side. It's Marcus, which is good news.

We turn the corner. Standing against the building are two men, the goon from the bar and another large guy I assume is Holzer.

The goon says to me, "Just you." Then, to Marcus: "Beat it."

Holzer, if that's who it is, says, "Oh, damn."

Marcus, in typical Marcus fashion, does not say anything and does not move.

"I told you to beat it," the goon says.

"That's Marcus Clark, right?" Holzer asks.

"I don't care who it is," says the goon, who will now and forever be known as the *idiot goon*.

The idiot goon makes a move toward Marcus, I assume to attempt to physically remove Marcus from the premises. The idiot goon reaches out with his arm, and Marcus takes that arm, sort of pivots around, and emulates an Olympic hammer throw, using the idiot goon as the hammer.

In the dim light, the result is a little hard to see, but the sound is crystal clear. The way Marcus performed the act, one can't say which part of the idiot goon's body hit the brick wall first. Based on the crunching sound and that he just crumples to the cement unmoving, I'm thinking it was his head.

"I tried to warn him," Holzer says.

"You and Marcus have met?" I ask.

Holzer nods. "Once, from a distance. But he's a known quantity. You I don't know."

"So why did you set up this scene back here?"

He shrugs. "Somebody comes looking for me, I'm careful. Especially after what happened to G."

Taillon's first name was George, so I assume that's who he's talking about. But I ask him, just to be sure, and he confirms it.

"Who killed him?" I ask.

"I still don't know who the hell you are."

"My name is Carpenter; you can call me C. I'm a lawyer, and Taillon hired someone to follow me. His name was Siroka, and they both got killed. I want to know who wanted me followed and why. I think that person is the same one that killed Taillon and Siroka."

"I don't know anything about why you were being followed."

"I didn't ask you that. I asked you who killed Taillon."

"I want to get the son of a bitch as much as you do. I got the word out on the street."

"Good. So what is the son of a bitch's name?"

Holzer thinks for a few moments, as if coming to a decision. The only sounds I hear are the small groans coming from the idiot goon. He seems to be at least partially awake and taking in the scene but doesn't seem inclined to get back in the action.

Finally Holzer says, "I'm just making a guess here. There's a name, a guy, that's hired G a few times in the past. I heard his name once. G wouldn't tell me anything about the guy; he let the name slip by accident. I guess he didn't want me to horn in on the action, which meant the guy paid big money."

"What was the name?"

"You didn't hear it from me, right?"

I nod; we could be getting close. "Right."

"Arrant. The guy's name is Arrant."

I'VE never heard the name Arrant, which is not significant. Plenty of bad guys are not on my radar, which is fine with me.

That might not even be the guy's name. Holzer said he only heard it once, so it could have been slightly different. And even if he got it mostly right, it could be spelled a few different ways.

But the good news is that I have a number of ways to check it out, the first one being Sam Willis. So Sam is the first call I make as soon as I get home, even though it's almost midnight. Sam is always awake.

Uncharacteristically, he sounds out of it when he answers the phone, so I ask, "Did I wake you?"

"No. I've got the flu; damn thing is wiping me out."

"Sorry to hear that. If you're up to it, call me tomorrow."

"Is this about a case? Tell me now. I need something to take my mind off how bad I feel."

I tell him about the name Arrant and how I need whatever information Sam can find.

"I'm on it. If I come up with anything, I'll email you a report."

Depending on what Sam can come up with, I might go to Pete Stanton to further dig up information on this Arrant guy. He's our only lead now, which doesn't say much for our investigation.

The morning starts on a decidedly down note; Hike comes over to go over pretrial preparation. We've filed a series of briefs, such as change of venue, request for bail, inadmissibility of certain evidence, et cetera. We're doing it now because we've come into the case late, and some of them basically duplicate efforts that the public defender had already made.

We've put a new twist on them, but it's not going to matter. Some of them have already been rejected, and the rest will be. If we're going to have any success in this case, it's going to have to be in front of the jury.

We've tracked down a few people we can use as character witnesses for Noah, but it's just fluff to pad our case. Our basic problem remains: we are not going to be able to prove Noah innocent; we must show that someone else is possibly guilty.

It's all depressing, so much so that Hike's leaving doesn't even make me feel better. I'm going to spend the rest of today rereading the discovery documents and reviewing witness statements. It looks like it's going to be a long and uneventful day.

Once again, I'm wrong. A major event happens in the form of a phone call from Sam Willis. His voice is still raspy from his illness as he says, "I can't believe you haven't called me."

"Why should I have called you?"

"Why? The email I sent after we talked last night."

"I just checked my emails. Didn't get anything."

"I sent it to your work email."

"Oh, I checked personal. You want to tell me about it?"

"You should look at it and call me back. But it's huge."

I hang up and open my business email account, which I almost never check. Sure enough, there's an email from Sam:

> *The guy Holzer was talking about is Charles Arrant. He was born in London but has lived all over the world. But get this . . . there's an Interpol Red Notice Alert out on him. In fact, there are three of them. I've attached a bunch of documents. Call me. Sam.*

Somehow Sam has gotten access to the actual Interpol documents, as well as media reports and other background information. But it all boils down to Arrant's having gotten Red Notices at the request of three countries: Great Britain, France, and Sweden. A number of photographs of him are also included.

What that means is that international arrest warrants are out on him. Any country that is part of the system can detain and arrest Arrant, after which he would be extradited to one of the three named countries.

But the background information makes it clear that Arrant's transgressions are not limited to those three countries. He is an international pariah, and the crimes he is alleged to have committed range from murder to financial fraud to espionage.

The real stunner is that these Red Notices are more than ten years old; Arrant has not been seen in all that time.

I keep reminding myself that he is connected to our case by the most fragile of threads. All we have on him is the name given to us by Holzer. Even if this is the same guy that Holzer was talking about, that Taillon was working for at one point, there is no guarantee that it has anything to do with Kristen's murder.

The question I ask is, Why would an international criminal want to kill an eighteen-year-old girl in Paterson, New Jersey?

And my answer, unfortunately, is, Beats the hell out of me.

Chapter 7

"You know anything about this?"

The voice asking the question belongs to Pete Stanton. He's calling at seven o'clock in the morning as I'm about to take Tara and Sebastian on their morning walk. I can hear the whirring sound of Laurie on the stationary bike in the exercise room.

"What are you talking about?"

"It's all over the news. Mitch Holzer is dead."

"Damn . . . murdered?"

"Unless you'd describe a bullet in his brain as natural causes."

This is stunning news, and it immediately registers in my brain as a confirmation of sorts that Arrant is our guy.

"Why are you calling me, Pete?"

"Because I told you about Holzer and now he's dead. I'm guessing you have information about it."

"I might." I'm not prepared to decide in the moment how much I want to share with Pete. I have to first calculate whether I would be helping or hurting my client's position by doing so. "But as you know, I am notoriously tight-lipped."

"Let's hear it."

"I'll come in later this morning."

He's not happy about it, but we arrange for me to be down at the precinct at eleven o'clock. Then I tell Laurie what has happened, and she finds the news important enough to cut her exercise bike ride short.

We turn on the television to learn what we can about Holzer's death. His body was found lying next to his car in a parking lot down the street from the bar where I spoke to him. He took one bullet in the back of the head, execution-style.

Holzer was no amateur; if Arrant took him out so easily, then Arrant's reputation is well justified.

"And he's obviously worried about something," Laurie says. "If he did this, and I would say it's likely that he did, then he killed Taillon, Siroka, and Holzer all to keep something quiet."

"Not necessarily. Taillon and Siroka, yes. But Holzer said that he was putting the word out about Arrant. Arrant has been invisible for ten years; he's got countries after him. Maybe he just didn't want any scrutiny. Although I don't know how Arrant could have such street connections in Paterson that he found out about Holzer. According to Holzer, they had no direct contact."

"So you think it's possible that Holzer's death could have nothing to do with our case?"

"All of it could have nothing to do with our case. We're just making educated guesses and hoping."

"You don't mean that."

I nod. "You're right, I don't."

We talk about how much I should be telling Pete about what I know, and then Laurie expresses concern for my safety, since I had spoken to Holzer and learned Arrant's name. Knowing Arrant's name seems to reduce one's life expectancy.

I tell Laurie that I'm not worried, that for Arrant to go after me would bring huge publicity and unwanted attention to him. Besides, I don't know anything of consequence, so I'm not a threat to him, at least not at this point.

I head downtown for my meeting with Pete, who starts the conversation by saying, "We've got a lot of people getting shot around here. And you seem to be hovering over all of it."

"I do what I can."

"So tell me about Holzer."

"After you mentioned him as being Taillon's backup, I went to talk to him."

"Where?"

"At the bar where he hangs out on Market Street."

"You went down there to talk to Holzer? You?"

An insult is implied there, but I ignore it. "Marcus," I say.

Pete nods. "We had a report that a muscle guy that worked for Holzer wound up in the hospital with a busted skull."

"I think Marcus happened upon him after he fell. He tried to catch him, but he was a moment too late."

"I'll bet. Go on."

"I asked Holzer if he had any idea who killed Taillon and Siroka because I think it is all about the Noah Traynor case. I believed that whoever had hired Taillon to have me followed also had him killed when I found out about it."

Pete frowns his disagreement at this, but doesn't interrupt, so I continue. "He didn't know, but he had an idea. And the idea had a name."

"And the name was?"

"Arrant. That's all he knew. Arrant. He said he had put the word out on the street to find the guy, but so far had no luck."

"Arrant," Pete repeats. "That's a last name?"

"It is; look him up. If it's the same guy, he's wanted by more countries than you could place on a map."

"What does that mean? Interpol?"

"You're not as dumb as you look."

"I'll check this out."

I hand Pete copies of the documents that Sam got for me, including the official ones from Interpol. He looks at me with suspicion. "Where did you get these?"

"From the international criminal fairy."

He looks at the documents. "What is this guy doing here?"

"He's covering up something big. And it's got to be more than just the murder of Kristen McNeil."

"Okay," Pete says, "you've given me the information. What's the quid pro quo?"

"What do you mean?"

"I mean what do you want from me?"

"I want you to catch him."

THE Paterson Police have no chance of getting Arrant. That's not even a criticism of them. If the entire world has been looking for him for a decade, he's not about to let himself get nabbed by a Jersey police department.

What I'm interested in is how Arrant came to view Holzer as a danger. I understand that Holzer had been asking around about him, but Holzer was a local street guy whose base of operations was a downtown bar. Somehow Arrant must have been tied into that world, enabling him to access information.

"Maybe we should call Cindy Spodek," Laurie suggests after dinner and after Ricky has gone to his room to do homework. Cindy is an FBI agent, number two in the Boston Bureau. She's a good friend of Laurie's and a semi-good friend of mine.

"Maybe . . . let me think about it," I say.

"What's the downside?"

"It could set off a chain reaction that would make Arrant aware that we know about him. I doubt he could know that Holzer mentioned his name to us, so he would have no reason to see us as a threat."

"I disagree. Remember, he's the one who most likely ordered Taillon to get you followed."

She has a point. "Okay. Maybe we'll call Cindy tomorrow. For now I need to walk and think."

She knows what I mean: I do my best thinking, such as it is, while walking Tara and Sebastian in the park. "I still think we should have you protected; just in case," she says.

I'm always torn in situations like this. I want to be protected because it feels very protective. But I never want to admit it, especially to Laurie. "I'll think about it," I finally say.

So Tara, Sebastian, and I head for Eastside Park. We're pretty far into the park and about to turn around when Tara tenses up and comes to a halt. I don't know what she has seen or sensed, but it has her on edge.

Then I see a glint of light come from behind a cluster of trees, and I go cold with panic. But the noise I hear is even more unexpected, a low, human voice. I think the word I hear is "Get."

Suddenly the noise changes and becomes louder. It starts as a rustling in the grass, then explodes into what seems like a combination of growling and yelling, some human, some canine.

The latest noise seems to come from the area where I saw the glint of light. In the moonlight, I can make out what is happening: a man is on the ground being attacked by a dog.

None of this makes sense to me, and I look to see if the dog is Tara. But it obviously can't be because I am still holding on to both Tara's and Sebastian's leashes. Tara is excited and pulling on hers. Sebastian seems bored with the whole thing.

Then I look to the side and see another human approaching the action. He leans over and picks something up, and I realize with some horror that he has picked up a gun. "Off," he says in a familiar voice, and the dog lets the guy go and backs off.

Finally it's all clear to me, even in this limited light. Corey Douglas and Simon have come to my rescue, even though I don't yet know who they have rescued me from.

Corey is holding his own gun; it could be the one he picked up, but I don't think so. "Turn around. Hands against the tree," he says to the man, who has just gotten to his feet.

The man does as he is told, but then whirls around, another gun having somehow appeared in his hand. But he doesn't get to use it because the deafening sound is Corey shooting him square in the chest. The impact of the bullet sends him backward, crashing into the tree; then he crumples to the ground.

Corey goes over to make sure the guy is not getting up. "He's dead," he says after feeling the guy's neck. Corey takes out his iPhone and activates the flashlight app, shining it in the dead guy's face. "You know who it is?"

I walk over and look. "I know who it is. Interpol has one less guy to find."

"Laurie told me to keep an eye on you," Corey explains. "She said definitely not to tell you. She didn't say why."

"I'm glad you and Simon were here."

"We owe you." I think he means he and Simon. "Remember?"

I nod. "Owed . . . past tense. We are more than even now."

"Who is he? What did you mean about Interpol?"

"He's an international criminal and a killer as well. The entire world is looking for this guy, and you nailed him."

Corey pats Simon's head. "We nailed him." Then, "I'll call in the department."

"I want to see what he has on him first."

"Hey." The cop in Corey thinks that I should not touch a thing.

"I'll replace it all exactly as I found it."

Using my iPhone flashlight, I take everything out of Arrant's pockets. His wallet has nothing in it to identify him by his actual name; instead he has two different sets of fake identification. I memorize the names, put the wallet back, and keep looking.

There is probably $3,000 in cash, which I have no interest in. There is also a hotel key, one of the magnetic kinds that slide into the door. It is from the Marriott in Saddle Brook, maybe ten minutes from where we are standing.

Corey is on the phone and doesn't seem to be looking, so I slip the key into my pocket. It doesn't make me feel great to deceive the guy who just saved my life, but I'll get over it.

Within five minutes, Eastside Park is lit up like it's daytime. At least ten police cars with lights flashing and two ambulances are here. Once the EMTs certify that Arrant is dead, which will be rather easy to do, they'll call in the coroner's van.

I call Laurie to tell her what happened, and while she's upset, that feeling is obviously offset by my being safe and talking to her. "You had Corey on me without telling me."

"Guilty as charged."

We decide that Laurie will get a neighbor to watch Ricky while she comes to the park to retrieve Tara and Sebastian. I'm going to be here for a long time, answering questions.

I get off the phone when Pete pulls up and comes over to Corey and me. "That's Arrant?"

"That's him," I say. "Try not to let him escape."

Pete turns to Corey. "I assume you did the shooting?"

Corey nods. "It was me. He drew a second weapon after Simon got him to drop the first one. Everything by the book."

Pete doesn't answer, but he doesn't have to. The scene speaks for itself; I was obviously walking the dogs in the park, and Arrant was there to take me down.

Finally Pete says, "Let's get this over with."

The "getting over with" part takes about three hours. We do it down at the precinct so the interviews can be recorded. It's all straightforward, and there will not be repercussions. It's made even easier for Pete that Corey is no longer on the force; "officer-involved" shootings are much more complicated.

We're done at around 1:00 a.m., and the cops drive us back to my house; Corey's car is parked just down the street. But Corey doesn't head for the car; instead he waits for me to go inside.

"You can go; I'm fine by myself."

"All evidence to the contrary. I do what Laurie tells me. I'm with you until you are in the house. Then she takes over."

"Are you going to kiss me good night?"

"Not a chance."

"Good. Corey . . . you saved my life. You and Simon. You both were amazing. So thank you."

"We did our job, just like you did when we were in court."

With that, I go into the house, and they turn and walk away. Laurie is waiting with some fresh coffee and a hug, not necessarily in that order. I go over the events of the night.

When I'm done, I take out the hotel key and show it to her.

"What's that?"

"A key to Arrant's hotel room."

"You took it off his body?"

I nod. "I did. I want to get a look in there."

"I would think that the police are all over it already."

"I don't think so. I'm sure he used one of two fake IDs, but by the time the cops make the connection and trace it to a hotel, we'll have been in and out of there."

"We?"

"I thought you might like to come along. Think of it as a morning adventure."

I call Sam, and he answers on the first ring, in typical Sam fashion. "Talk to me." His voice sounds less raspy.

"You feeling better?"

"Getting there. What do you need?"

"Can you get into the computer at the Saddle Brook Marriott? I need to know what room a particular guest is in."

"What's the name?"

I give him both names since I don't know which fake one Arrant used. I hope there's not a third name that I'm not aware of.

We get off the phone, and Laurie and I head to bed. I'm exhausted; almost getting killed can take a lot out of a person. I'm falling asleep when the phone rings. Caller ID tells me it's Sam.

"Hello?"

"Room 316, in the name of Edward Pruett. He was due to stay there another week."

IN THE morning, we drop Ricky off at school and head for the hotel.

Sam Willis meets us in the lobby. I asked him to come in case we find any electronic devices that we need help on. He's going to wait downstairs and come up if I call him; we don't want to look like an invading army heading for Arrant's room.

We walk to the elevator and take it to the third floor. We smile and chat on the way, trying to appear normal, even though appearing normal is not my specialty. Once we get off the elevator, we follow the signs to room 316, at the end of the hall.

I insert the key, and the light flashes green, always a good sign. Laurie goes in first. I opt not to carry her across the threshold.

"He had a suite," she says. "Crime pays."

She hands me a pair of skintight rubber gloves and puts a pair on herself. We go through the entire room, which is not difficult or time-consuming because he traveled lightly. Just some clothes and not much else, certainly not anything interesting.

A cell phone is in the night table drawer, so I call Sam and tell him to come up. He does, and Laurie hands him a pair of gloves. "This is so cool," he says.

He picks up the phone and examines it, pressing some buttons and looking like he knows what he's doing, which he does.

"Got to be a burner phone," he says. "There's no protection on it, no security."

"What does that mean?" I ask.

"Personal phones require a fingerprint, or facial ID, or at least a password. This has none of that; it's all there to be examined by anyone who wants to. I'd bet anything he was about to throw this one away. He must buy them by the truckload."

"What does he have on it?" Laurie asks.

"Not much. No emails, no downloads . . . none of that."

"What about phone calls?"

"He made three. Doesn't seem to have received any."

"So you can tell who he called?" Laurie asks.

"For now all I know are what numbers he called, but I can definitely attach names to it. Are we taking the phone with us?"

"No," I say.

"Then give me a second to write down the numbers." Sam does just that. Then, "We leaving together?"

"No, you head out, and then Laurie and I will follow once we make sure everything is the way we found it."

Sam leaves, and Laurie and I restore the few things we moved. As we leave, we wipe the outside doorknob clean. "I feel like a thief," she says.

"All for a good cause."

Once we're in the car, I call Pete. "What now?" he asks.

"I just got the weirdest anonymous tip. It said that Arrant was staying at the Saddle Brook Marriott in room 316 using the name Edward Pruett."

"An anonymous tip," he repeats, obviously skeptical.

"Yes. It was an anonymous tip left by a tipster who prefers to remain anonymous in order to retain his or her anonymity."

"The Feds were all over this early this morning. I'll relay this information."

"Do me a favor? Tell them you got it anonymously."

Chapter 8

I HATE JURY SELECTION.

Picking jurors, deciding which ones are most likely to buy the crap that we will be selling, is obviously crucial. What makes it so frustrating is that the reveal, the discovery of whether I made the right decisions, doesn't come until the end of the trial.

Then it's too late.

The only consolation is that the prosecutor, Jenna Silverman, has no clue either. She has a team of assistants and a jury specialist to consult with, but like me, she'll have to wait until the end to find out if she made the right calls.

We should be done by lunchtime, and Judge Calvin Stiller has said we would start with opening statements tomorrow.

This shouldn't be a long trial, but it will take quite a while to play out. That's because we are starting on Monday, but then we'll stop for Christmas on Friday, then stop again for New Year's Day. I only wish the court would adopt Laurie's three-month Christmas window. By then we might be ready to mount a decent defense.

Sam calls me during lunch with some news that seems bizarre. He's traced the three phone calls on Arrant's burner phone. One was to Taillon, which makes perfect sense. He might even have been calling him to arrange the Pennington Park meeting that resulted in Taillon's and Siroka's deaths.

The second call was to Gameday, a video-game company in Oklahoma. I have no idea why that call was made, and since it went through the company switchboard, there's no way to know who received it. The call could have been benign, though Arrant's profile doesn't seem to be that of video-game nerd.

The third call is even weirder. He called an assistant football coach at LSU named Ben Walther, who is the defensive coordinator. Walther has developed a national reputation and is said to be a leading candidate for some head-coaching jobs.

The call lasted ten minutes. LSU is playing Clemson in a national semifinal game in a couple of weeks, so Walther must be pretty busy. But he found time to take Arrant's call.

If I had to guess, based on Arrant's criminal history and ability to profit off of it, I would say that some illegal betting or fixing is going on. But that's a stretch; this is big-time college football with great scrutiny on it. Also, I am not aware of anything in Arrant's past that involved sports betting.

Unfortunately, I believe that Arrant died with the answers to all my questions. The key one is how an international criminal like Arrant became involved in the murder of Kristen McNeil.

Is it so simple that he had a client who was, for whatever reason, willing to pay to have her killed? Was he just a hired killer who farmed the job out to Taillon to literally execute? Or was there more to it? Did Kristen somehow represent a threat to Arrant or the people that paid him? I haven't found anything that would indicate this, and I'm running out of time.

But there's no opportunity to think about it now; I have a fun afternoon of guessing what a bunch of people who have no desire to serve on a jury will do once they get stuck on one.

THE jury has finally been chosen, and it's terrific, or awful.

So with the afternoon free before opening statements tomorrow, I go home and do what I do almost every day. I read through the discovery documents. After about an hour, my mind starts to wander to Kristen McNeil. Why was she killed?

The only people that come close to being suspects in my mind are the Wainwrights, father Arthur and son Kyle. Each brings his own issues to the suspect party. Kyle was Kristen's boyfriend, and she was dumping and cheating on him. Anger at rejection therefore becomes a possible motive.

Arthur Wainwright, as the father of Kyle, could also be involved. But what makes him intriguing is his wealth. Arrant did not come cheap, and he then turned around and hired Taillon, who hired Siroka. Money seems to be all over their actions and this case, and Arthur Wainwright has plenty of it.

One thing I have not focused on is NetLink Systems itself. It is a successful company, and Kristen worked there. She could have met someone else there who has some involvement in this case. NetLink could be described as Kristen's connection to the real world, and a high-stakes world at that.

Even more significant, we know that Taillon called NetLink twice just before Kristen was killed. I still don't know who he called—it could even have been Kristen herself—but the connection between Taillon and someone at NetLink is crucial.

I take out Sam's reports on Taillon's phone calls, but nothing more is to be learned there. I need to be aggressive and try to shake things up, so I decide to call Jeremy Kennon, the tech guy that Kyle works for. At least he didn't throw me out of his office, which is more than I can say for Arthur Wainwright.

The phone number for NetLink is in Sam's report. Assuming it's still the number, I dial it. It rings twice, and a woman answers, "Mr. Wainwright's office. How may I help you?"

I'm surprised by this; I thought I'd be reaching the switchboard. It sounds like I'm talking to the woman who brought me to Arthur Wainwright's office when I was there. "Hello, this is Andy Carpenter. We met last week, and—"

"Hello, Mr. Carpenter. How can I help you?"

"I was trying to reach Jeremy Kennon."

"Oh, let me switch you to the operator. This is Mr. Wainwright's private line."

"No, thank you. I've got another call coming, so I'll call back," I lie.

When we get off the call, I let the impact of what I've just learned sink in. Taillon didn't just call NetLink Systems twice the week of Kristen McNeil's murder.

He called Arthur Wainwright.

"I HAVE been through too many trials to minimize the importance of your job."

That's how Jenna Silverman begins her opening statement. With the first sentence, I can tell she is going to be a problem.

First of all, she looks the part. She's attractive but buttoned-down and professional, seeming to be serious and in control. She is someone you want to root for, whose side you want to be on.

She continues. "There really are very few tasks that you will do in your life that are more significant. You will go in a room, and you will decide the fate of another human being. Your decision will either send him to prison for most of the rest of his life, or free him, never to be bothered by these charges again.

"But I have also been part of enough trials to know that there is a difference between important and difficult. I'm going to be blunt here: your job is not difficult.

"Very often there are complicated issues involved in a trial, sometimes requiring a special expertise. This is not one of those cases. We will demonstrate through forensic evidence that cannot be challenged that Noah Traynor was with Kristen McNeil at the time and place of her death. That same evidence will prove that they had a violent confrontation.

"When I say that these facts cannot be challenged, I will predict that Mr. Carpenter will not even make the attempt. That's how irrefutable that evidence is.

"But Mr. Carpenter is an excellent attorney, and he is nothing if not resourceful. So he will parade a group of criminals before you, some dead and some alive. The one thing they will all have in common is that they are not relevant to this case.

"We will also show a consciousness of guilt that caused Mr. Traynor to avoid acknowledging these facts for fourteen years. If there was an innocent explanation, why not come forward with it? Why hide in the shadows for all this time?

"The answer will be crystal clear. Noah Traynor strangled Kristen McNeil and left her body lying in the dirt. After fourteen years, the truth is out, and Kristen will finally have her justice.

"Thank you for listening, and thank you for serving."

Judge Stiller gives me the floor, and I stand to give our opening statement. "Ladies and gentlemen, Ms. Silverman is correct in some of what she told you. She will present evidence saying that Kristen McNeil and Noah Traynor were together at the murder scene, and they had a disagreement that turned physical.

"We will not dispute any of that; we will acknowledge it and accept it as fact. We encourage you to do the same. But she will go on to say that those facts mean that Noah Traynor murdered Kristen McNeil, and we will vigorously dispute that, because they don't, and he didn't.

"Ms. Silverman describes Mr. Traynor's failure to come forward and tell his story as consciousness of guilt. It is not; it is consciousness of fear. The media was going crazy back then; they were buying the police theory that whoever left the DNA evidence behind was the guilty party.

"Mr. Traynor knew that if he was found to be the person with that DNA, he would be accused of the murder, no matter what he said. The fact that we are here today is evidence that he was right. Perhaps he should have come forward anyway, but his not doing so was out of fear, not guilt.

"But keep one thing in mind. While Ms. Silverman would have you believe that an innocent Mr. Traynor would have come forward to help the police find the killer, that simply is not true. He had no more idea who the real killer was than the police did.

"This tragic murder was not the result of a dispute among teenagers. Kristen McNeil was caught in a world that she could not handle, with evil people who cared nothing about her life. So they took her life and went on with theirs.

"You will meet those people, though some of them are no longer with us, additional victims of the violent world in which they lived. Noah Traynor has never been part of that world and never will be.

"Thank you."

JEREMY Kennon has agreed to meet me here, at my office.

He is doing so despite an obvious reluctance to meet with me at all. That he's come here is, I suspect, because he doesn't want to be seen with me at his office or in a public place.

It hurts my feelings, but I'll get over it.

Kennon shows up at ten after six, which is only ten minutes late. He makes no effort to apologize.

"Thanks for coming."

"No problem. Nice place you got, right above the fruit market. Do you pick up a cantaloupe when you drop off the rent check?"

"How did you know that? Get one when you leave, and get some peaches; they're unlike anything you've ever tasted."

He nods; I don't think he wants to continue a fruit-based conversation. "Anyway, better we meet here than at my office. You're not that well loved at NetLink right now."

"I'm really a joy, once you get to know me."

He grins. "So why am I here?"

"I need you to give me a road map. I think that Kristen McNeil may have been having a relationship with someone at NetLink."

"Kyle Wainwright. We've been over that."

"I'm talking about someone older."

"Can you be more specific?"

I shake my head. "I wish I could. That's why I need you to give me a road map, tell me who she had contact with while she was there. It doesn't have to be a current employee."

He pauses for a while. "I'd have to think about it. It's been a lot of years, and she wasn't in my department."

"She worked for Arthur Wainwright, didn't she?"

He nods. "As an intern-slash-assistant."

"Anything unusual about their relationship?"

"Come on. You can't possibly think that Arthur would—"

"I don't know Arthur. My only contact with him was when he threw me out of his office, and I thought he handled that with incredible charm and grace."

"He was being protective of his son."

"His son is not eighteen anymore, and why would he need protection in the first place?"

Kennon, instead of answering the question, says, "I owe everything to Arthur Wainwright. He's believed in me, he's mentored me, he's promoted me. You will not get me to say anything bad about him because I have nothing bad to say about him."

"I'm not trying to. What I'm trying to do is get a picture of what Kristen McNeil's work life was like fourteen years ago."

He nods. "I'll think about that, but I doubt I'll come up with much. I don't think your answer is at NetLink, but I know it is not in Arthur Wainwright's office."

I'm not going to push it with Kennon. He's clearly not going to give me any negative information on Wainwright, and I don't want Kennon warning Wainwright that he's on my radar. But he is dead center on it.

Taillon called Arthur Wainwright. That is a crucial piece of information, and while I'm not sharing it with Kennon, I'm going to share it with the jury.

What I need to focus on now is what Wainwright's motive could have been. A possibility is that Arthur was the older man Kristen spoke about. Maybe she was pressuring him, and he was afraid of the devastation to his life and reputation should it be revealed that he was having an affair with a teenage girl. So he killed her to keep her quiet, as a means of self-protection.

Another theory might be that she had learned something about Arthur's business life that would have been devastating to him and maybe NetLink should it have been made public. But NetLink has operated without a hint of scandal for the past fourteen years, which argues against its harboring an awful secret.

All I know for sure is that Taillon was in touch with Arthur Wainwright around the time of Kristen McNeil's murder.

If Noah Traynor is going to get his freedom back, I'm going to have to figure out why.

SERGEANT Theresa Swanson is Jenna's first witness.

She is here simply to set the scene, in this case the crime scene. Swanson and her partner, Luther Jackson, were the first officers there. Swanson was just a patrolwoman at the time; Jackson has since retired from the force.

"What brought you to Hinchliffe Stadium that day?" Jenna asks.

"There was a nine-one-one call reporting a body that was found there. A teenager named Douglas McCann had seen the body, ran home, and told his father, who called nine-one-one."

"Please describe what you saw when you arrived."

"A young female adult was lying in the shrubbery. She was wearing a blue blouse and a pair of jeans. The blouse was torn, and the jeans were unbuttoned. We determined that she was deceased. Her head and neck were bent at an unnatural angle."

"What did you do?"

"We called in the report, as well as bringing in EMS and the coroner, and secured the scene. Homicide detectives were there within seven minutes, and we turned the scene over to them."

"Did you examine Ms. McNeil's body?"

"We did not, other than to determine that she was deceased and could not be helped by CPR."

Jenna has photographs of the scene and body projected onto the screen set up in the courtroom. The jury seems to recoil in horror when they see Kristen's body, as she knew they would.

The tactic is powerful, and even though the pictures are not gory, they are devastating images. A young girl was lying in the dust and shrubs, her life and dignity taken from her. The jury is going to want to punish someone, and their only option is Noah.

I can get nothing from Swanson on cross-examination, so I decline to ask any questions.

The next witness Jenna calls is Lieutenant Stan Oglesby, of the Homicide Division. He is a direct report to Pete Stanton, who has often told me that Oglesby is an outstanding cop.

Oglesby arrived at the scene and took control of it, but the visual he describes is similar to how Swanson described it.

"Were you able to determine the time of death?" Jenna asks.

"I didn't try; that is better left to the coroner. But there were certain signs that she had been there for some length of time."

"Were you able to identify the body?"

He nods. "She still had her wallet in her possession, with her driver's license in it. Also, her car was in the parking lot, and it contained her registration and insurance card."

"What did the fact that her car was there tell you?"

"Again, I was just gathering information at that point, but it was clear that her killer had his own means of transportation."

When I get to question Oglesby, I say, "I'm going to ask you some questions. Please either answer them, or if you can't, just say, 'I don't know.'"

Jenna objects that I'm improperly instructing the witness, and Judge Stiller sustains. My first question for Oglesby is, "Let's start with your last comment about transportation. You said the killer had his own means of transportation. What type of transportation was it?"

"What do you mean?"

"Was it a car? A bicycle? Did he take a bus and walk to the stadium?"

"I can't say."

"Why can't you say?"

"Because I don't know the answer."

I nod. "Okay. Were the killer and Ms. McNeil the only two people present?"

"I can't say for sure."

"As to the exact place where you found the body, is that where she was killed?"

"I saw no evidence otherwise."

"So you're certain of it?"

"Not certain, no."

"Why was Kristen McNeil at Hinchliffe Stadium?"

"I can't be sure."

"Okay," I say. "Now that we know what you don't know, let's move on to what you do know. For most of the fourteen years since the murder, was Noah Traynor on a suspect list?"

"No."

"Had you ever even heard the name Noah Traynor before the DNA match came through?"

"No, I don't believe so."

"Did you interview many of Kristen's friends?" I ask.

"Yes."

"None of them mentioned him?"

"No."

"Once he became a suspect, did you check him out fully?"

"Of course."

"Did he have any convictions before the day Kristen McNeil was killed?"

"No."

"Any arrests, before or since?"

"No."

"Speeding tickets? Illegal parking?"

"No."

"Littering? Swearing in public?"

Jenna stands and objects, but before she can get it out, Oglesby has already answered, "No."

"Lieutenant, in your experience, is it unusual for a person to commit a vicious murder and yet live the entire rest of his life without doing anything wrong?"

"Every case is different."

I frown. "Thank you for sharing that. No further questions."

Chapter 9

THE CONVERSATION WITH Andy Carpenter left Kennon more than a little unsure about what to do.

Carpenter seemed to be coming after NetLink Systems in general and Arthur Wainwright in particular. Kennon wasn't sure how to react or if he needed to react at all.

Finally, he decided to talk about it with Kyle Wainwright. Not wanting to do so in the office, they met for a drink at a small bar in Englewood, not far from where Kyle lived.

They ordered drinks, and Kyle said, "Don't keep me in suspense; what did you want to talk about?"

"Andy Carpenter."

"Has he been around again?"

Kennon nodded. "He's asking questions about your father. I think he has the idea that he might have been having an affair with Kristen."

Kyle laughed. "Oh, come on . . . seriously?"

"He didn't say it, but that's the impression I got."

"My father barely even touched my mother. Maybe once, and they had me. My father figured that was plenty."

"You're missing the point, Kyle. If he thinks that Arthur was having an affair with Kristen, it's a short jump to thinking he killed her to cover it up. All Carpenter is interested in is blaming someone else for the murder."

"Let him try."

"You're not thinking about the company. If Carpenter winds up accusing Arthur in open court, it could spook our clients. Once a charge like that is out there, it never completely goes away, no matter what. Doesn't matter if it's true or not."

"You're not saying you think it could be true, are you?"

Kennon shook his head. "That's not the Arthur I know, but people do crazy things. It could have been an accident, but . . . no, at the end of the day I don't think it could be true."

"You think I should tell him what Carpenter is doing?"

"It might help him deal with this. Maybe he'd hire a lawyer to keep Carpenter off his ass."

"Why don't you tell him?"

Kennon laughed at the idea. "No chance. In a lot of ways, Arthur has been like a father to me, but he's not actually my father. That honor falls to you."

"I'll think about it. But that is not a conversation I would look forward to. He'd go absolutely crazy."

Kennon laughed again and stood up. "My work here is done." Then, "Seriously, I may be reading too much into this, but I thought you should know. I don't think your father is in any jeopardy, but if Carpenter makes public noises, it could be aggravating for him. That's all."

Kyle nodded. "I hear you."

I'M OF two minds about Janet Carlson.

Outside the courtroom she is a pleasure . . . smart, funny, and compassionate. She is also, without a doubt, the best-looking coroner on the planet.

But inside the courtroom, and particularly on the witness stand, I'm not a big fan of hers. By definition she always testifies for the prosecution, which makes her my enemy. Her intelligence, coupled with her calm and unruffled demeanor, make her someone I don't look forward to questioning.

Jenna has no such reservations. She starts by asking if Janet did the autopsy on Kristen McNeil.

"No, that was done by Dr. Paul Griffith, my predecessor."

"Dr. Griffith has since passed away, is that correct?"

Janet nods. "Yes. Six years ago."

Janet says that she has studied the autopsy results and is prepared to discuss them. "Dr. Griffith was meticulous in his work."

Under questioning, Janet says that Kristen died of asphyxiation as the result of strangulation. Janet repeats earlier testimony that her neck was broken and her larynx crushed.

"So this was done powerfully?"

"Yes. Very much so," Janet says.

"In your professional opinion, could it have been done accidentally, perhaps during rough sex?"

"No, I would say not, and Dr. Griffith specifically discounted that possibility. In addition to the nature of the strangulation, there was no evidence of sexual activity."

"Were there any other signs of a struggle?"

Janet nods. "Her blouse was torn, and she had skin tissue under her fingernails."

Jenna goes over the rest of the autopsy with Janet. The photographs come out again, just in case the jury has forgotten what the body and the scene looked like.

Once again I have no ammunition to attack the prosecution witness; everything they are saying is borne out by the evidence.

"Just to reconfirm what you said," I begin, "Kristen McNeil's blouse was torn, her jeans were unbuttoned, but there was no evidence of sexual activity, forced or otherwise?"

"Correct."

"Does that seem strange to you?"

"That is not within my purview."

"What about outside your purview? Does it seem strange there?"

"Somewhat."

"Let's talk about the skin fragments found under Kristen McNeil's fingernails. Did Dr. Griffith estimate when they arrived there?"

"What do you mean?"

"Well, he estimated a time of death within a four-hour window. Did he say when she got the skin fragments under her fingernails in relation to the time of death?"

Janet shakes her head. "No."

"Could it have been moments before death?"

"Certainly."

"How about ten minutes before?"

A slight shrug. "It's possible."

"An hour before? Two hours?"

"Dr. Griffith would have had no way of knowing that."

"When she got the skin under her nails, where was she?"

"Meaning . . . ?" Janet prompts.

"Meaning was it even at Hinchliffe Stadium? Could she have been somewhere else entirely?"

"Again, no way of knowing."

"Can you say with certainty that the person whose skin was under her nails was the killer?"

"I cannot."

"Thank you. No further questions."

CHRISTMAS Day at our house is traditionally a re-creation of the Thanksgiving Day experience, the only notable difference being that I watch NBA basketball instead of NFL football.

Once again, Laurie has invited Julie and Danny Traynor, and once again they have brought Murphy. The mood is more subdued than it was over Thanksgiving. Back then the trial hadn't started, so there was optimism that all would go well.

Julie has been in court every day, and it has not been fun for her. She can tell where this is going, as can pretty much everyone else, including the jurors. It hasn't been a barrel of laughs for me either. In any event, we do not discuss the trial whatsoever.

But Laurie has made sure that there are tons of presents to go around. Laurie has gotten me a pair of great seats to an upcoming Eagles concert. I like the Eagles, but she absolutely loves them, so she's thrilled with the gift.

Once the Traynor contingent has left, I head out for my walk with Tara and Sebastian. I haven't been through the park since the night Arrant came after me. Walking on the streets seems safer than the park, just in case.

Thinking back on that night, I still don't know why Arrant felt it necessary to come after Holzer and me in rapid succession. It's been bugging me ever since then how Arrant even knew that Holzer had given me his name.

The only person who knew about it, other than Laurie, Marcus, and me, was Holzer's "idiot goon." But he should have had absolutely no reason to be connected to Arrant.

I wish I knew the significance of Arrant's death. He could have been just one layer in a chain that went up from Siroka to Taillon to Arrant, with others above him. Or he could have been at the top of that chain.

I'm leaning toward the former theory. Taillon's phone calls to Arthur Wainwright around the time of the McNeil murder trump everything. It proves that Wainwright was involved.

Arrant worked for money, and Wainwright has plenty of it, so it makes sense that Arrant was a literal hired gun. But has he been replaced? That question, as does every other question in this case, depends on why Kristen McNeil was killed. If Arthur Wainwright was having an affair with Kristen and wanted to cover it up, then a person in Arrant's role is not necessary.

But I'm becoming less and less convinced that theory is credible. If Kristen's death was for a reason as simple as that, then Wainwright would have had no logical reason to order the deaths of Taillon, Siroka, and Holzer. He's gotten away with it for fourteen years, so why not just let the system run its course and convict Noah?

Far more likely is that Kristen McNeil had either been a part of, or a danger to, some ongoing conspiracy that Wainwright is desperate to keep operating and concealed. Then the scrutiny of a trial, and a lawyer like me investigating, would represent a problem worth killing to solve.

If there is an ongoing conspiracy, then somehow I need to un-cover its existence and its perpetrators. That is the kind of case we will have to build for this jury for us to have a real chance.

So midway through the trial, I am clear on a strategy. Executing it? That's another story.

I WISH I could have called in sick today.

Jenna's case can be summed up in one witness, and that's the one we're going to hear from in a little while. The jury seems to be sit-ting up a bit straighter in their chairs, which indicates to me that they know what's coming. Today is forensics day.

Jenna is going to heighten the anticipation by making everyone wait a bit longer. She calls as her first witness Arnie Pafko, who was a friend of Noah's back in the day.

Jenna establishes their relationship as high school buddies and fraternity brothers. She further gets him to say that they haven't talked in years, since she would know that I would bring that out on cross-examination. Then she gets down to the meat of it.

"Mr. Pafko, was there any time during which you were aware that Mr. Traynor knew Kristen McNeil?"

"Yes, he told me they were dating."

"How long before her death was this?"

"Maybe a couple of weeks. I had gone away to college, so I wasn't aware of the murder until a few weeks after it happened."

"What else did he tell you besides the fact that he and Kristen were dating?"

He hesitates. "They were going to have sex. He was sure."

"What was your response?"

He grins. "I told him he was crazy. We didn't get lucky too often back in those days."

"And when you told him that? What did he say?"

"That he guaranteed it. He was bragging, which wasn't so unusual.

But then he said, 'Believe me, she wants to.' So I said, 'She'll change her mind.' Then he said something that bothered me."

"What was that?"

"He said, 'Not if she knows what's good for her.'"

Jenna ends her examination on this dramatic note, which is a mistake, because I'm about to beat this witness with questions that she should have asked in a way that limited their impact.

"Mr. Pafko, why did the police ignore you when you told them you were concerned for Kristen McNeil's safety?"

"I didn't go to the police."

I feign surprise. "So you only told her parents?"

"I didn't tell them either. I didn't tell anybody."

"Why not?"

"I guess because I didn't really think Noah would do anything to hurt her. We did a lot of talking in those days."

"I'm confused. You thought he would hurt her, or you didn't?"

"I guess I didn't. Looking back, I should have taken action."

"Because she was killed," I say.

"Right."

"I can see that. Who at the Paterson Police Department did you talk to once you found out she was killed?"

"I didn't go to them. I should have."

"You just said that looking back, once she was killed, you should have taken action. But you actually didn't take action once you found out about it?"

"No; I feel guilty about that."

"This is the kind of guilt that doesn't kick in until fourteen years after the event? It's a slow-developing guilt?"

Jenna objects that I'm badgering him, but Judge Stiller overrules her and instructs him to answer.

"I'm not proud of my actions."

"That's the first thing you've said today that's believable."

Jenna jumps out of her seat to object, and before she even gets the words out, Judge Stiller sustains the objection, strikes my comment from the record, and instructs the jury to disregard it.

Good luck with that.

Jenna is pissed, which doesn't bother me in the least. Then she calls her last witness, which bothers me plenty.

SERGEANT Xavier Jennings is a major pain in the ass to defense attorneys.

Jennings has been in charge of forensics for the Paterson Police Department since about an hour after forensics was invented. He's seen everything, and not a defense attorney in New Jersey, yours truly included, can rattle or intimidate him.

He's also funny and self-effacing and smart. Outside the courtroom I like him; inside the courtroom I wish that he would spend an entire day stuck in an elevator with Hike.

As for juries . . . they eat him up with a spoon.

After Jenna establishes Jennings's credentials, she asks, "Sergeant Jennings, were you in charge of forensics fourteen years ago, when Kristen McNeil was murdered?"

He smiles. "Yes. My career hasn't exactly taken off."

She returns the smile. "Did you uncover any significant human DNA in the immediate area besides that of the victim?"

"Yes. We found DNA on a discarded beer can, on a chewed piece of gum, and most significantly, there were pieces of skin under the fingernails of the deceased."

"Did this DNA all belong to the same person?"

"Yes, it did."

"If that person is in the courtroom, can you point him out?"

Jennings points to Noah, and Jenna confirms the identification. She asks a few more questions, bringing out that traces of Noah's blood were under the fingernails as well.

Finally I get to ask my questions, none of which are going to make a dent in Jennings's testimony. "Sergeant, this crime took place fourteen years ago. You've had this DNA evidence all that time. Why did it take until now to identify who it belonged to?"

"The defendant's DNA was not included in any of the databases that we have access to."

"Are there any databases you don't have access to?"

"No."

"Had Mr. Traynor been arrested or convicted of a crime, either before or after the murder, his DNA would have been in one of these databases?"

"Yes."

"Sergeant, your work in this case demonstrates that Mr. Traynor was at some point at the scene of the crime, and that Ms. McNeil scratched Mr. Traynor in some fashion, correct?"

"Yes."

"Does it prove that he was on the scene when she was killed?"

"No."

"Does it prove that he committed the murder?"

"No."

"Thank you. No further questions."

Judge Stiller asks, "Ms. Silverman, do you have more witnesses to call?"

She stands. "No, Your Honor. The prosecution rests."

Judge Stiller adjourns for the day, telling me to be prepared to call our first witness in the morning.

Chapter 10

"The defense calls Laurie Collins."

Laurie stands up and walks to the stand. Every eye in the courtroom is on her, but she is used to that. When you look like Laurie, it's the rare eye that is not staring at you.

I briefly take Laurie through her work history, the highlights of which are as a lieutenant in the Paterson Police Department and as chief of police in her hometown of Findlay, Wisconsin. "What is your job now?" I ask.

"I'm a private investigator. Employed by you."

I introduce a photograph of Freddie Siroka and ask Laurie if she has ever met him. She confirms that she has and gives the date of that meeting.

"Where did this take place?"

"At Hinchliffe Stadium, in the area of where Kristen McNeil was killed. We were visiting the scene to gather information."

"Why was Mr. Siroka there?"

"We had determined that he had been following you. When we confronted him, he became violent. One of my fellow investigators subdued him, and then we detained and questioned him as to his motivation for doing the surveillance on you."

"Did he admit that he was in fact following me?"

She nods. "He did."

"Did he say why?"

"He said that he was hired by a Mr. George Taillon to do so, and that it was in reference to the Kristen McNeil case."

Jenna does not bother making a hearsay objection because she knows what's coming. She's heard the tape as part of discovery.

"Are you positive you are relating the substance of what he said accurately?"

"I am. I surreptitiously made a tape of it as he was talking."

I introduce the tape as evidence, in addition to an affidavit from our voice expert that it is in fact Siroka.

We play the tape, confirming all that Laurie had said.

"If you know, where is Mr. Siroka now?" I ask.

"He is dead. He was shot in the head."

Jenna starts her cross by asking if Laurie is familiar with Siroka's arrest and conviction history.

"Yes, I am."

"So you know about the nine arrests, four convictions, and three prison terms?"

"Yes."

"As a former police officer, did you find that you could rely on people with that kind of record to be truthful?"

"Sometimes they are, and sometimes they are not."

"I see," Jenna says. "I notice nowhere on that tape did Mr. Siroka say what the purpose was in following Mr. Carpenter. He just vaguely mentioned this case, but did not say what he or his employer had to gain by the surveillance. Is there something I missed?"

"I don't know what you missed or didn't miss," Laurie says, "but you are correct that Siroka did not say that."

"Did he have listening equipment with him?"

"No."

"Binoculars? Night-vision goggles?"

"No and no."

"So he was just watching Mr. Carpenter as he went through his day?"

"Apparently."

"If Mr. Carpenter went to the supermarket or the post office, Mr. Siroka would report that?"

"I don't know what he would report or not report."

"You said your other investigator subdued him, and then you questioned him. Is that correct?"

"That is correct."

"Is it possible that he feared being subdued even harder if he didn't come up with a story for you?"

"I don't know what was going through his mind. But as you heard on the tape, we did not threaten him."

"Thank you. No further questions."

KYLE Wainwright had gone back and forth since his conversation with Jeremy Kennon.

His decision was whether to tell his father that Carpenter might be coming after him. The lawyer might be intent on slandering Arthur Wainwright in a very public way, accusing him at least indirectly of having an affair with Kristen and maybe even being involved in her murder.

Kyle's relationship with his father had been checkered at best. Arthur had divorced Kyle's mother when Kyle was ten years old, a defining event in his life because of how bitter the divorce was and how little his mother was left with. She had since died, leaving Kyle with a lot of resentment toward his father.

Arthur took a penthouse apartment in a Fort Lee building, with a spectacular view of Manhattan. Kyle rarely came by; he had only visited three times in the two years Arthur had lived there. They saw each other in the office all the time, but their work life was much more interactive than their private life.

However, Kyle agreed with Kennon that a pressing business interest was here. Sliming Arthur's reputation, even if not proven, could be a major problem for NetLink with its clients. Kyle was someday going to inherit a controlling interest in the company, so he had a lot to protect.

So when Kyle called and said he was coming over to talk, Arthur knew that the subject was going to be significant. But he did not expect what was coming.

"Andy Carpenter is coming after you," Kyle said.

"Coming after me? What does that mean?"

"I'm not positive, but I think he's going to claim that you had an affair with Kristen, and—"

"That's insane!" Arthur screamed, showing more emotion than Kyle thought he had ever seen from him.

"I'm not finished. He might be pointing to you as the killer."

"Where are you getting this from?"

"Jeremy. He had a conversation with Carpenter, and this is the feeling he got. He's not sure, but we thought you should know so you can be prepared."

"Just let him try it. He has no evidence. I will sue him for every dime he's ever made. I will grind him into dust."

"He is a well-respected attorney; I don't think it's a good idea to underestimate him."

"Into dust. Into dust."

So Kyle left, having fulfilled his duty. He was not sorry he'd warned his father that Carpenter was going to be making the accusations.

He was also not sure that Carpenter wasn't right.

My next witness is Pete Stanton.

I know how much he hates testifying for the defense because he told me that if I made him do this, he would hunt me down after the trial, shoot me, and feed my body to a tank of piranhas.

Pete and I are really good friends.

"Captain Stanton, did you hear the tape that was played earlier in this courtroom? The one that testimony demonstrated was the voice of Freddie Siroka?"

"Yes."

"Did you hear him say that he was hired by George Taillon to follow me?"

"Yes."

"Were you familiar with Taillon? Could you describe what you knew about him?"

"He was a known criminal for hire. He had a lengthy arrest record but was a suspect in far more crimes than he was tried for. Witnesses had a way of disappearing or recanting."

"So a bad guy?"

Pete nods. "A bad guy."

"Did I come to see you to discuss both Taillon and Siroka?"

"Yes." Pete is testifying as if he is paying by the word.

"Why did I say I wanted to talk to you?"

"They had both been murdered the night before, and you said you had information about it that could be helpful to the police."

"Could you describe the circumstances of those murders?"

"They were each shot in the head in Pennington Park. Their bodies were discovered approximately twenty-four hours later."

"What information did I have for you?"

"You told me the circumstances of Siroka following you and his mentioning Taillon as his employer."

"Did you give me any information in return?"

"Yes. I told you that Taillon had an associate named Mitch Holzer, a known criminal who worked with Taillon. I warned you that he was dangerous and that you should be careful if you attempted to talk to him."

"Did we have another conversation two days later?"

"Yes. I was hoping you might have information regarding the murder of Mitch Holzer."

"The Mitch Holzer we spoke about two days earlier?"

"Yes," Pete says.

"He was murdered during the course of those two days?"

"Yes."

"What did I tell you in our second meeting?"

"That you had spoken to Holzer, and he had revealed to you that he believed that the person Taillon and Siroka were working for was a man named Arrant. Holzer believed that Arrant might have been the killer."

"Did you do any research into who Arrant might be?"

"Yes. His full name was Charles Arrant. He was wanted for a decade by Interpol, with arrest warrants in three European countries. He was wanted for murder and serious financial crimes."

"Also a bad guy?"

Pete nods. "A very bad guy."

"All of these murders we have been talking about . . . Siroka, Taillon, and Holzer. Is Noah Traynor a suspect in any of them?"

"No."

"Because he has been in jail this entire time, awaiting trial?"

"That is correct."

I turn Pete over to Jenna, who feigns boredom with the whole thing, as if this is just something we need to get through before the jury can vote to convict Noah.

Her questions are brief and to the point. "All of these people you are talking about, Siroka, Taillon, Holzer, and Arrant, they are all likely murderers?"

"It's a decent bet," Pete says.

"In your experience, are murderers violent people?"

"Yes."

"And sometimes they die violently?"

"Sometimes."

"Did any of them have their skin fragments under the fingernails of Kristen McNeil?"

"No."

"Thank you."

"The defense calls Corey Douglas," I say.

Corey comes to the stand. I take him through his work history, his recent retirement, and his work for us as an investigator. He also talks about Simon, and their work and personal life together.

Within ten minutes, I've turned Corey's attention to the night I was walking in the park with Tara and Sebastian. "You were there watching out for me? Protecting me?"

He nods. "Yes. You were not aware of it."

"Can you describe what happened?"

"An assailant was lying in wait for you in the park. He was preparing to shoot you, so I ordered Simon to attack him. Simon subdued him, and I was able to get his gun. I ordered him to stand and turn around so that I could handcuff him."

"Did he obey your orders?"

"He started to, but he had another concealed weapon that he revealed and attempted to fire at me. I shot him in self-defense, and the wound was fatal."

"Did you learn his identity?"

Corey nods. "Yes. His name was Charles Arrant."

"The Charles Arrant that Mitch Holzer mentioned to me? The Charles Arrant that was wanted by Interpol?"

Corey nods again. "One and the same."

I WOULD judge the first day of the defense case to be a modest success.

We have shown the jury that a lot of murders have been committed around here, none of which Noah Traynor is responsible for. We have not made an ironclad connection between those murders and this case, but we've established a strong inference.

We need to drive that home.

Laurie, Ricky, and I have a nice dinner, during which murders and trials are not mentioned. I'm feeling bad that I haven't been spending as much time with Ricky as I should; I rationalize it to myself that I am busy trying to prevent Danny Traynor from never spending time with his own father again.

After dinner, the phone rings and Laurie answers it. She tells me that it is Herbert Hauser on the phone. I've never met Hauser, but I know of him. He's a corporate attorney and litigator, probably the most successful in New Jersey.

I no sooner say hello than he starts to unload on me. "It has come to my attention that you are preparing to slander my client Arthur Wainwright in open court."

"Let me guess. You're calling to warn me against doing that."

"That is exactly correct. Mr. Wainwright has many options to deal with this kind of disgraceful behavior, and I will personally see to it that he uses them to maximum effect."

"Could you repeat that? I can barely hear you, what with my heart pounding and my knees knocking."

"You have been warned, Mr. Carpenter." Click.

When I get off, Laurie asks, "What was that about?"

"Wrong number."

I'M NOT worried about the threats from Arthur's lawyer.

I will simply be presenting evidence in open court, and every bit of it will be accurate. No one is going to perjure themselves. So I will not spend another moment thinking about that.

Much more concerning is that I don't have much to tie Arthur Wainwright or anyone else to the murder of Kristen McNeil. I've got to get at least one person on the jury to believe me.

Once I'm done doing what I can to provide reasonable doubt, I'm going to have to make the key decision of the trial, the key decision of every trial: whether to have the defendant testify.

I can't remember the last time I encouraged a defendant to testify. It brings with it enormous risks. Usually the potential upside doesn't nearly justify doing it, but this case might just be the exception to that rule.

We simply have to give the jury an explanation for the DNA evidence, especially the skin and blood under Kristen's fingernails. No matter what else we present, that evidence will ultimately carry the day if not explained.

So I am not going to make a recommendation until I have to, and as always it will be the defendant's choice, but right now I am leaning toward urging Noah to testify.

Today is "Laurie day" in that our next two witnesses are people that Laurie has found through diligent investigating. They won't make our case for us, but they might provide important building blocks.

The first witness, Marlene Simms, retired six years ago from her position as director of human resources at NetLink Systems.

I quickly establish the basics of Simms's career, with special attention on the twelve years she spent at NetLink. "So you were at NetLink Systems when Kristen McNeil was employed there?"

Simms nods. "Yes, sir."

"How did she come to get the job?"

"Well, it was an open secret that her boyfriend was Kyle Wainwright. Kyle's father, Arthur, is the founder and majority owner of NetLink. I'm assuming that's how the connection was made, though I can't say that for a fact."

"Did she have the kind of experience one would expect for the position?"

Simms thinks for a few moments. "That's hard to say. She had no experience whatsoever; she had just graduated high school. But the position had very little responsibility; she was an assistant who did relatively minor tasks."

"Who instructed you to hire her?"

"Arthur Wainwright."

I nod. "You said she was an assistant. Who did she assist?"

"Arthur Wainwright."

"Where was Kyle Wainwright during this time? Was he working at the company as well?"

"Yes, at least part-time. I think he was getting ready to go to college, and even then he worked at NetLink during vacations."

"So is it fair to say that Kristen and Arthur Wainwright spent a lot of time together?"

Simms nods. "Oh, yes. She had a desk outside his office. She took notes in his meetings, ran errands for him, those kind of things. He said it was a great way for her to learn the business."

"Did she seem happy there? Ever express any complaints?"

"She seemed very happy; it was a great opportunity for her and a nice place to work. But then suddenly she quit."

"She came to you and said she was leaving?"

"No, she just didn't show up for work one day and called me from home. Said she was not coming back. She seemed very upset. I remember being stunned by it; it was so sudden. As I said, she had seemed so happy. This came out of left field."

"Did she say why she was upset?"

Simms shakes her head. "No. I asked her if she wanted to come in and talk about it, but she was adamant that she did not want to do that. Usually when an employee leaves, we'd have an exit interview, but she wanted no part of that either."

"Had she told Arthur Wainwright of her decision?"

"I can't say for sure, but I told her that he might want to speak to her directly, and she said, 'No, I'm not talking to him.'"

"You were surprised by that?"

"Very. Especially the way she said it. She blurted it out but was decisive about it."

"As a professional who dealt with employees for many years, what was your impression of Kristen during that conversation?"

Simms pauses for a few moments. I'm about ready to prompt her when she says, "She was upset, worried. . . . I would say she seemed scared. I have no explanation for why."

Jenna objects that Simms couldn't know Kristen's state of mind. We argue the point, and Judge Stiller comes down on my side, but it doesn't matter. The jury heard that Kristen was upset and afraid, and that she was adamant she would not talk to the person she was closest to at NetLink, Arthur Wainwright.

Next up is Mike Greer, who also worked at NetLink. He started around the time that Kristen did but worked in finance.

"Did you have occasion to spend much time with her?" I ask.

He nods. "Some. We were both new there. We'd go to lunch and talk about what it was like, and other stuff."

"Did you two date?"

He smiles. "No, I wanted to, but she wasn't interested. She said her dating life was complicated enough. Then she said, 'Believe me, you have no idea how complicated.'"

"Did she seem happy at NetLink Systems?"

"Very. She wanted to make a career there. She even said she might take courses at night in the technical side of things."

"Do you know why she quit?"

He shakes his head. "I will never understand that. One day she just wasn't there. I called her because I was worried about her. She said she was never coming back but wouldn't say why. She didn't say she was scared, but she sounded like it."

I turn him over to Jenna, who again feigns indifference, as if this is all just a diversion from the conclusive DNA evidence.

Court is going to be closed for a couple of days, for New Year's Eve and New Year's Day. "Happy New Year," I say to Noah as the guard takes him away.

"That remains to be seen," he says.

He's right about that.

Chapter 11

IT WAS GOING TO BE an agonizing day for Cynthia and Kevin McNeil.

There was simply no getting around that. They had put it off for fourteen long years, but that didn't matter at all. If they waited twenty more, the pain would be just as fresh.

This was the day they would go through Kristen's room.

Karen, Kristen's sister, had come by to help get them through it. She thought they might back off at the last minute, but they were committed. The New Year was going to be the start of reclaiming their own lives.

Or at least that was the plan.

So they went into Kristen's room with their plastic bags for the items that they would throw away, give away, or keep. Cynthia assigned herself the task of going through Kristen's desk drawers. She didn't think Kristen kept a diary but wasn't sure if she was right. It would be painful to read, but it would bring Kristen back in some small way, through her words.

No diary was found, but in the bottom drawer was a sealed envelope. On the outside it simply said, "Mother and Father."

Cynthia experienced a quick intake of air and intense anxiety as she reached for it. She opened it quickly, wanting to get whatever was about to happen over as soon as possible.

She read it and said three words, to herself and to no one.

"Oh my God."

I HAVE a love/hate relationship with this holiday.

New Year's Eve is probably my least favorite day of the entire year, mainly because it leads into my least favorite night of the year. People all over the world get dressed up, drink too much, eat too much, and then play DUI roulette as they drive home. The funny thing is that no actual fun is involved.

Ricky has brought great joy to our lives in many ways, and New Year's Eve is just one of them. Laurie wants to spend the evening as a family, so we get to stay home and do family stuff. We play a board game or do a puzzle until Ricky falls asleep. Then Laurie wakes him to watch the ball drop.

The point is, we don't go out, which works well for me. And I have Ricky to thank for it.

New Year's Day is an entirely different animal. It is filled with college bowl games, six of them to be exact. But this weekend is nothing short of a football dream come true. That is because in addition to the great bowl games, Sunday brings an extraordinary NFL schedule. The Giants are playing the Redskins, and if the Giants win, they are in the playoffs.

Pinch me.

Of course, there is the trial to worry about, especially since our key witnesses are coming up. That means more trial prep today so that I can watch football tomorrow and Sunday.

Football and the trial have a puzzling intersection. One of the calls on Arrant's burner phone was to the LSU defensive coordinator, Ben Walther. I still have no idea why Arrant made that call. Maybe the Feds have found out, but if it has had any legal repercussions for that coach, news of it has not hit the media.

By three o'clock, I am sick of trial preparation. The phone rings, and I grab it. "Hello?" I say.

"Mr. Carpenter?" It's a young woman's voice that I don't recognize, but I do detect the anxiety.

"Speaking."

"This is Karen McNeil. We met and . . ."

"I know who you are, Karen. Is everything all right?"

"I'm not sure. Can you come over here? It's very important."

"Of course. Where are you?"

"My parents' house. There is something here. . . . You need to see it."

She gives me the address, which is in Teaneck, and I tell her I'll be there in a half hour. I leave immediately and beat my half-hour prediction by three minutes.

The McNeils live on a cul-de-sac in a neighborhood of comfortable homes with manicured lawns. As I pull up in front, the door opens and Karen McNeil stands there. Behind her are two people I'm fairly confident are her parents.

I walk up to the porch, and Karen thanks me for coming and introduces me to Cynthia and Kevin as we walk in. We go into the kitchen, and Cynthia offers me coffee or something else to drink. I decline, and I sense that they are grateful for that.

"How can I help you?" I say.

Kevin says, "Ever since Kristen left us, we haven't touched her things. Cynthia cleaned her room almost every day, but we left her possessions intact."

I nod and wait for Kevin to continue.

"We decided to do it for the new year, especially with the arrest and the trial ending soon. So today was the day."

"That must have been hard," I say.

He nods. "Maybe not for some people, but very hard for us. Anyway, in the bottom drawer of Kristen's desk, she had hidden this." He takes an envelope off the kitchen counter and hands it to me. "Please open it and read it."

So I do.

The next thing I do is email Hike instructions on what we need to get done in a hurry. I don't want to call him because I don't want the McNeils to hear the conversation.

My instructions are for Hike to start assembling the necessary experts we'll need first thing Monday morning. The timing is going to be all-important.

THE trial is about to be turned on its head.

I don't know if the letter that the McNeils found is real, but I have no reason to doubt it. The court and the prosecution may have plenty of reason to doubt it, though, so we have spent the past twenty-four hours dealing with experts in the field.

I don't have the results yet, but Hike is not in court this morning so that he can receive them. Even Hike is confident that they will turn out in our favor, which I have to admit gives me pause.

I call Sergeant Lucy Alvarez to the stand. She is one of the officers working the George Taillon murder. It's fair to say that the police are not mounting a full-court press to find the person who killed Taillon and Siroka since everyone believes that the guilty party is Charles Arrant, who is himself already dead.

As I stand, I notice that Herbert Hauser, the lawyer that threatened me on Arthur Wainwright's behalf, is in the courtroom. No doubt his presence is to send me a message.

Color me intimidated.

"Sergeant Alvarez, you are familiar with Charles Arrant and the fact that he was shot to death?"

"Yes, though it is not my case."

"Did I ask you to acquire some information about it so that you could offer it in your testimony?"

"You didn't ask me. You asked Captain Stanton, and he instructed me to do it."

I smile. "Thank you for the correction. What did Captain Stanton instruct you to get?"

"There was a burner cell phone that was found in Mr. Arrant's hotel room at the Saddle Brook Marriott."

"Where is that cell phone now?"

"I believe it remains in the custody of the FBI."

"Why the FBI?" I ask, pretending I don't know.

"There were three Interpol Red Notices out on Mr. Arrant, which makes it a federal case."

"Did they tell you what calls had been made on that phone?"

"Yes."

I introduce the document the FBI had sent the Paterson Police, detailing the calls. Then, "Can you tell the jury who was called from that phone?"

"One call was to a video-game manufacturer in Oklahoma named Gameday. It was answered by the switchboard, so there is no way to know who the call was routed to. The second call was to a man named Ben Walther, who is a football coach at Louisiana State University."

The gallery mumbles on hearing that name, possibly because it was unexpected, or maybe because LSU is playing tonight.

"And the third call?"

"He called George Taillon, who I believe you are familiar with."

"I am," I say, "but for those scoring at home, this is the George Taillon who ordered me followed and who was murdered?"

She nods. "That's him."

"Thank you, Sergeant. And since we're on the subject, are you working the Taillon murder case?"

"I am."

"I subpoenaed phone records of Mr. Taillon, and I asked the phone company to get you copies. Did you review them?"

"Yes."

I ask her to focus on the calls that Taillon received and direct her to the date of Kristen McNeil's death. She testifies that Taillon received two phone calls from burner phones the day before the murder and one the night of the murder.

"Is that suspicious to you?" I ask.

"Perhaps, but there could be innocent explanations."

I nod as if that is reasonable, which it is. "Now please turn to the phone calls Mr. Taillon made during that period of time."

She does so, and I ask her to identify two specific calls with the same phone number. "When were those phone calls made, in reference to the death of Kristen McNeil?"

"One was made seven days prior to the murder and the other five days prior."

"Who does that number belong to?"

"NetLink Systems."

"And did I ask you to call that number today?"

"You did, and I did so."

"Was it the NetLink switchboard?"

"No, it was the private line for Arthur Wainwright."

Just in case the jury is not paying attention, I hammer the point home. "George Taillon called Arthur Wainwright's private line twice within a week of Kristen McNeil's murder?"

"That is correct."

I think the jury and everyone else in the courtroom realize the significance of this. What they don't realize is that they ain't heard nothin' yet.

I MADE the decision not to prep my next witness.

I basically told her what I was planning to ask but did not request answers. I want the testimony to be completely spontaneous; it will be more powerful that way.

I spend the lunch hour going over the material Hike has come back with. He reveals that as both he and I expected, the information he's gotten fits exactly with what we hoped for. Now all I have to plan is how to introduce it to the judge and prosecution.

Before the jury is brought into the courtroom to take their seats, I ask the judge if we could briefly meet in his chambers, lead counsel only. He agrees, and Jenna and I follow him back there. Jenna looks warily at me, for good reason.

"Your Honor, these are copies of a letter, written by the victim in this case, that I am going to introduce into evidence. The witness who will be testifying is Karen McNeil, Kristen's sister."

The judge and Jenna take a few moments to read the letter, and Jenna is clearly stunned. "Your Honor, this is outrageous. The defense is claiming that this letter has existed for fourteen years, and they are springing it on us five minutes before the jury would hear it, without having shared it in discovery?"

"Your Honor," I say, "we have only had it for less than—"

Jenna interrupts, "And it is not even authenticated. Anyone could have written this at any time."

"Thank you for making my point for me," I say. "Your Honor, we had concerns about its authenticity as well, so we took great pains, at significant expense, to have its legitimacy confirmed by top experts. We are prepared to present their affidavits to that effect, and they are here in the courtroom available to testify.

"The salient point is that we literally received their verdicts within the last two hours, far too late to turn it over in discovery. I wish that were not the case, but we did everything by the book."

Judge Stiller has two options here. There is no chance he will disallow the letter. He could never prevent blockbuster evidence like this from reaching the jury. He'd be overturned on appeal before the ink on the verdict form was dry. His two choices are to let the trial move forward now or to grant a continuance to give the prosecution time to study it.

He surprises me by splitting the difference and coming up with a third choice. He says that we can move forward, but after the testimony, he will grant the prosecution a delay until tomorrow if they want the time to prepare for cross-examination. It seems to me like a reasonable compromise.

We head back into the courtroom, the jury is called in, and Karen McNeil takes the stand. "We're calling her?" asks Noah, surprised that the victim's sister is a witness for the defense.

I thought about giving him a heads-up on what is going to happen but decided against it. Let him enjoy it as it unfolds.

As I stand, I notice that Cynthia and Kevin McNeil are in the gallery for the first time.

I introduce Karen and have her talk briefly about her relationship to Kristen: "We were very close, in age and every other way. I still miss her every single minute of every single day."

"Did Kristen ever mention Noah Traynor to you?"

Karen shakes her head. "No, she didn't."

"What did you do this past Saturday?"

"I went to my parents' house."

"Why?"

"My parents haven't gone through Kristen's room in all these years. They cleaned it, but never moved or touched her things. They treated it like a shrine."

"Was Saturday significant in that regard?"

Karen nods. "They decided to do it, to start the new year fresh. This trial was going to be the turning point that would allow them to move on, or at least as much as was possible."

"And you were there to help?"

"And support them, yes."

"Please describe what happened."

"Well, we were going through her things, deciding what we wanted to give to charity, what to keep for sentimental reasons . . . that kind of thing. Then my mother started going through her desk drawers, and she found an envelope." Karen is starting to choke up; her emotion and distress are real and palpable.

"Do you want a minute?"

She shakes her head. "No, I want to get through this."

I go back to the defense table and pick up the envelope and introduce it as evidence. Then I hand it to Karen. "Is this it?"

"It certainly looks like it."

"Please open it and take out what is inside."

She does as instructed and unfolds the piece of paper.

"Please read it."

She looks at it and starts to read. " 'Mother and Father, if you're reading this . . .' " She stops and starts to sob softly.

"Would it be easier if the clerk read it for you?"

"No . . . I'll be okay." Karen starts to read again. " 'Mother and Father, if you're reading this, then you know I have left home. Please don't try to find me or contact me. It would put all of us in danger. I have saved a good amount of money, so don't worry. . . . I can take care of myself. I had an affair with Arthur Wainwright, but that is not why I left. It is because I have learned something terrible about him. He knows that I know, and I'm afraid of what he will do. I'm sorry . . . please try to understand.' " Then, "She signed it, 'Love you forever, Kris.' "

The silence in the courtroom is deafening. I turn and see that Cynthia and Kevin are quietly sobbing.

I introduce the affidavits certifying the authenticity of the letter. We have had a handwriting expert confirm that it is Kristen's writing and a carbon-dating expert confirm by analyzing the ink and paper that it was written well more than a decade ago.

Jenna opts not to delay her cross-examination until tomorrow. I think it's a correct decision; she wants this testimony over as soon as possible. She has no way to damage Karen and would look bad doing so even if she could.

All she can do is confirm that Karen and Kristen were close and get her to say that Kristen never revealed an affair with Arthur Wainwright to her. It is ineffective at best because Kristen never revealed anything about Noah Traynor to Karen either.

When I get back to the defense table, Noah obeys my pretrial admonition not to show emotion, good or bad. He must be jumping out of his skin with happiness, but he's hiding it.

I know the feeling. Defense attorneys don't get many days like this; if we did, I would like working more.

Chapter 12

I CAN'T GET OVERCONFIDENT about this.

We still have a major hill to climb. In our favor is that Kristen, in her own written words, said that she was having an affair with Arthur Wainwright and that she was running away because he presented a deadly danger.

That is incredibly compelling, but it doesn't prove that Arthur did anything. Kristen's fear could have been misplaced; maybe Arthur did not pose a real threat to her at all. Or maybe he did but never acted on it.

It is balanced by the fact that ironclad evidence shows Noah Traynor had been at the scene of the crime and had left his blood and skin under Kristen's fingernails. I think we still have to attack this evidence, to tell an alternative story about it. The only way to do that is to have Noah testify.

I have an instinctive revulsion at the idea of a defendant taking the stand, but that's what I am going to recommend here. Fortunately, I have had Hike prepping Noah on the testimony he will give. He wants to do it, and Hike says Noah should do okay. For Hike, that is a five-star review.

I cannot imagine what is going through Arthur Wainwright's mind tonight. Yesterday he was a well-respected businessman. Today he has been credibly accused of having an affair with an eighteen-year-old employee, then murdering her to protect some terrible secret that she learned about him.

Not a good day for old Artie.

The media is obviously covering the hell out of the day's events, but I am focused on something that they are not. Kristen said in her letter that Arthur was concealing a terrible secret. It wouldn't be just the affair; it had to be something else. But what? Whatever that is, it is most likely the same secret that Arrant has been murdering to protect.

THE next morning, the bailiff tells us to rise as the judge enters. Then he says whatever he thinks necessary and has the jury brought in. Judge Stiller is prompt and has never kept us waiting.

Until today.

Today, fifteen minutes go by with no Judge Stiller. When the fifteen-minute delay stretches to twenty-five, something significant must undoubtedly be causing this. Sure enough, the clerk comes out of the back where the judge's chambers are and walks over to first Jenna and then me.

"The judge wants to speak with you in chambers, immediately," the clerk says.

As we follow the clerk, Jenna and I make eye contact. The look on her face says she has no more idea what is going on than I do.

The judge is sitting at his desk in street clothes, which in itself is highly unusual. He looks positively somber.

"Sit down," he says. "Please."

Jenna and I sit down across from him and wait.

"I received some information about forty-five minutes ago," Stiller says. "I've attempted to confirm what I could, but some details are still unclear. But here is what we know for sure."

He takes a deep breath. "At some time during the night before last, probably between midnight and four a.m., Arthur Wainwright drove to a cemetery in Little Falls. He went to his former wife's gravesite, sat next to the headstone, put a handgun in his mouth, and fired it. He died instantly."

Judge Stiller's words just hang in the air, as Jenna and I sit in stunned silence. Neither of us knows what to say.

Judge Stiller picks up the slack. "The reason it took more than twenty-four hours to discover the body is due to the snow that fell on it, plus it was in a secluded area of the cemetery.

"You are going to have differing views on how this news will or should impact this trial. I suspect that you, Mr. Carpenter, will feel strongly that the jury hear about it. Ms. Silverman, I'm not going too far out on a limb to say that you will oppose that.

"So here is what I have decided to do. Court will not be in session today; we will resume tomorrow. I am going to sequester the jury, effective immediately.

"Depending on how we proceed, that sequestration will either be for one night or the duration of the trial. So prepare your arguments, file briefs before the close of business today, and I will see you back here tomorrow morning for oral arguments."

Holy crap.

I know I am going to spend the rest of the day preparing my arguments for getting this news in front of the jury and deciding whether, if I am successful, I'll still want Noah to testify.

But in the immediate aftermath of hearing the news, that's not what is dominating my mind. What I am feeling is . . . guilt.

Arthur Wainwright did not kill himself because of what I did in court yesterday. He died before Karen testified about the letter.

So either his decision was as a result of what I did in court prior to yesterday, or he somehow found out about the letter in advance of my presenting it.

Either way, I know intellectually that I did nothing wrong, and I also know that I only introduced evidence that was 100 percent true and accurate.

But the other fact that is 100 percent true and accurate is that I caused the death of Arthur Wainwright.

HIKE handed in our brief yesterday afternoon, moments before the prosecution submitted theirs.

The issue in front of us is whether to tell the jury about Arthur Wainwright's suicide. Obviously our defense position is that they should be told, but in addition to wanting that to happen, I also think it's the right thing to do.

We're about to be called into the judge's chambers for oral arguments, and I'm concerned about how Judge Stiller might rule. If he was leaning toward letting it in, I am surprised that he wouldn't have just done so yesterday. That he didn't and instead chose the major step of isolating those jurors indicates to me that he must be seriously considering leaving them in the dark.

As Jenna and I are walking toward the judge's chambers, Jenna asks me softly, "What do you think?"

"I think it's fifty-fifty. What about you?"

"Fifty-fifty sounds about right."

As soon as we're seated and the court reporter is ready, Judge Stiller says, "Let's hear from the prosecution first."

"Thank you, Your Honor. Our position is that this news is far more prejudicial than it is probative. The jurors will draw an inference that the suicide is related to this trial, and we do not know that to be the case. Even if we did know that for sure, we do not know why he did it. Maybe it was just the embarrassment of being accused or of it being revealed that he had an affair with an eighteen-year-old. Maybe he was dealing with unrelated stress or a health issue, and this development pushed him over the edge.

"Arthur Wainwright is not here to defend his actions with Ms. McNeil, assuming she was telling the truth in her note, or explain the reason that he took his own life. We don't have the knowledge or information to make the explanation for him.

"We would be entering uncharted waters here, and we cannot take a dead man with us. He cannot speak for himself, and we cannot speak for him. Attempting to do so would be prejudicial to the extent that it would far exceed the probative value."

Stiller nods and turns to me. "Mr. Carpenter?"

"Your Honor, with respect, Ms. Silverman effectively makes our point. There are a number of potential explanations for Mr. Wainwright's suicide besides the one that she fears, that he killed himself because he has been revealed as the person who murdered Kristen McNeil. Embarrassment, stress, medical issues . . . every one of those are conceivably correct, and she is free to make the jury aware of all of them. We can take our own position, and then the jury can decide. That is their proper role.

"As of two days ago, Arthur Wainwright was a person that we might well have called to the stand. Now he is the ultimate unavailable witness. We are therefore damaged by his absence; you would further damage us by denying us the ability to explain the reason for that absence.

"Jurors might wonder why we are not calling him. Are we afraid to confront him and hear his effective defense? Absent information, they will draw their uninformed conclusions.

"There is a significant precedent for our position, and—"

Judge Stiller interrupts, "Case law?"

"In a way. I am talking about this case, and the precedent that you have already set. You have admitted testimony about the deaths of four people, Siroka, Taillon, Holzer, and Arrant. I believe that those people are related to this case and that you were correct to admit that evidence.

"But Arthur Wainwright is far more clearly a factor in this case. He has arguably been accused of the murder by the victim herself. To admit that other testimony, and then to keep this out, would be totally inconsistent and I believe ill-advised.

"This is a search for the truth. To deprive them of this key fact is to set up an artificial barrier to arriving at that truth."

We argue it out a bit more, but the issues have been laid out. When we are finally finished, Judge Stiller says, "It comes in."

We go back into the courtroom, and I give a nod to Hike and Noah to let them know we have prevailed. Then I call Sergeant Stan Frazier of the Little Falls Police Department, whom I have arranged to have here in case the judge ruled in our favor.

I don't beat around the bush. I ask Frazier to describe what he found when he was called to the cemetery.

"A deceased male, age sixty-one. Cause of death was an apparently self-inflicted gunshot wound."

"Were you able to identify the deceased?"

Frazier nods. "Yes. It was Arthur Wainwright."

"Thank you."

It's decision time regarding Noah's possible testimony.

The advantage to his doing so is clear. His words are the only way to explain to the jury why he was at Hinchliffe Stadium that day, and more important, how his skin and blood wound up under Kristen McNeil's fingernails.

The jury is going to want to know that.

But the other factor is the manner in which I want to end the defense case. Frazier's testimony, brief as it was, was incredibly dramatic. The apparent importance of it was even inadvertently increased by Judge Stiller's decision to sequester the jury.

By doing so, he was saying to them that something important had happened, so important that they had to be protected from knowing it. Now they know it, and I don't see how they can look past it. The victim made the accusation from the grave, and the accused reacted by killing himself. Surely that would have to put a reasonable doubt about Noah's guilt in the mind of a juror.

The alternative to this dramatic ending would be to have Noah testify. No matter how well he held up, the last thing the jury would see would be Jenna pointing out holes in his story and reminding the jury that he kept quiet for fourteen years.

My assessment is that to end it here ensures us of at least a hung jury, with an outside chance for an acquittal. Noah's testimony would be a roll of the dice.

I lean across to Noah. "I don't think you should testify."

"Okay," he says.

"But as I've told you before, it's your call."

He nods. "My call is to trust your judgment."

"Call your next witness, Mr. Carpenter."

"Your Honor, the defense rests."

Laurie has been in the gallery today; we drove here together in the morning. On the way home, she says, "I think you made the right decision in not having Noah testify. Even though he'd be telling the truth, Jenna could have made him look bad."

"If you thought I made the wrong decision, would you tell me?"

"No chance."

I laugh for the first time in a while.

Tonight I'm going to prepare for my closing statement, which won't be hard to do. I never write out a speech like some lawyers do. I've long ago learned that I am best when I'm spontaneous.

That gives me plenty of time to think about Arthur Wainwright. It seems amazing to me that the testimony I brought out before revealing Kristen's letter could have pushed him over the edge. I'm starting to believe he must have found out about the letter well before Karen McNeil's testimony about it in court.

In any event, Arthur's suicide is an image I am not going to be able to remove from my imagination anytime soon, if ever.

At eight o'clock I am completely ready for court tomorrow and need to take my mind off things, so I head down to Charlie's. Vince and Pete are at our regular table.

"I am never testifying for you again," Pete says. "It's embarrassing. Nobody at the precinct will even talk to me."

"Arthur Wainwright found a way to avoid it," I say.

"Were you going to call him?" Pete asks.

"No, but he had no way of knowing that. Did he leave a note?"

"No."

"But you're sure it was a suicide?"

He nods. "Fingerprints on the gun; no indication anyone else was present. Nothing is ever definite, but the coroner didn't agonize over how to categorize it."

"Let me ask you a question," I say to Pete. "Charles Arrant, international criminal wanted by Interpol . . . what the hell was he doing in Paterson?"

"I have been asking myself that same question."

I nod. "Next question. Whatever he was doing here . . . with him gone, you think someone took his place?"

Pete answers with a question of his own. "Are you thinking that same someone killed Arthur Wainwright and made it look like a suicide?"

"Not really, but part of me hopes it's true."

"Why?"

"Because if someone else didn't kill Wainwright, then I did."

"Here's what we know beyond a shadow of a doubt," Jenna says.

She has spent most of the trial asking questions from a podium set up between the defense and prosecution tables, but now she is pacing around as she begins her closing argument.

"Noah Traynor was with Kristen McNeil outside of Hinchliffe Stadium, where she was brutally murdered. We know this because his DNA was on a piece of discarded gum and a beer can.

"We also know that Kristen and Noah Traynor had a violent confrontation; she scratched him so hard that she had his skin and blood under her fingernails. That could not have been done casually. That had to have been done in desperation.

"That would be less important if Kristen McNeil was shot from a distance, but she wasn't. Her killer wrapped his arms around her neck and squeezed so violently that he broke her neck and crushed her larynx.

"We don't have to have been there to imagine that while it was happening, she was clawing and scratching at her killer's arms, trying to get him off of her." Jenna pauses for effect. "Clawing and scratching . . . digging her nails into him.

"It's also important to remember another incontrovertible fact.

Noah Traynor hid from the police for fourteen years. He could have said, 'I was there. I want to help find the real killer. Ask me any questions you have.' But he did not. Do you think that is the way an innocent man would react?

"Mr. Carpenter responded to this evidence by basically leaving it unchallenged. Instead, he paraded unsavory characters in front of you, none of whom had anything to do with this case. All he was trying to do was distract you, plain and simple.

"That brings me to Arthur Wainwright. Kristen McNeil wrote a letter to her parents about him. You read it. It says that she had an affair with him and that she was running away because she was frightened of him.

"Let's assume she was telling the truth. Is it not possible she was afraid of him because he was wealthy and successful, a man capable of exercising tremendous influence in the community? Could she not have feared that he could hurt her and her parents, not physically, but financially or reputationally?

"But maybe not. Maybe she thought he might physically attack her. That is a huge leap from his actually doing it. It was not his skin under her fingernails, and there is absolutely no evidence that places him at Hinchliffe Stadium that day.

"And speaking of no evidence, there is no evidence that Arthur Wainwright, who was forty-seven years old at the time of Kristen's death, had ever committed a violent act in his life.

"But three nights ago, he did commit a violent act, the ultimate violent act, against himself. I am certain that Mr. Carpenter will tell you that he did so out of guilt, or shame, all as the result of his being exposed as a murderer. But maybe he was ashamed at being revealed as someone who had an affair with a teenager. Or maybe he had a crisis in his life, and this was the last straw?

"We can't get inside the mind of a tormented man. We have to focus on what we know. And we know, through evidence that cannot be refuted, that Noah Traynor killed Kristen McNeil.

"Thank you for listening, and thank you for your service."

My turn.

I also pace the room as I talk. I begin with "Freddie Siroka.

George Taillon. Mitch Holzer. Charles Arrant. These were all people that had violent criminal histories. You heard that from none other than the man in charge of the Homicide Division of the Paterson Police Department, Captain Pete Stanton.

"They were all connected to this case. You also heard that from Captain Stanton, and in one case you even heard it from Freddie Siroka, on audiotape. And they were all murdered, except for Mr. Arrant, who was killed while trying to murder yours truly. Noah Traynor is not a suspect in any of these murders. He has the perfect alibi; he was sitting in jail after being wrongly arrested for the death of Kristen McNeil.

"And then there is Arthur Wainwright. He was having a sexual relationship with a girl who was of an age where she could have been his daughter. In fact, she was the girlfriend of his son. You didn't have to hear this from me; you read it from Kristen McNeil's own hand.

"She feared him; she was petrified at what he might do. So much so that she quit the job that she loved, and she was running away, leaving friends and family behind. Again, those are not my words; they are hers.

"I want to talk for a moment about reasonable doubt. The judge will tell you that if you have a reasonable doubt as to whether or not Noah Traynor is guilty, then you must vote not guilty. That's the foundation on which this system is based.

"If you think it is possible that someone other than Noah Traynor committed this crime, then by definition you have reasonable doubt. So let me present you with a hypothetical situation: Supposing you heard from someone, maybe two or three people, that you trust that Arthur Wainwright killed Kristen McNeil. What would your reaction be? Would you say, 'That's crazy . . . absolutely impossible'? Would you tell them that they're nuts, that Wainwright could not have done it?

"I don't think you would. I think that after hearing the evidence, and especially the letter that Kristen McNeil wrote, that it would make sense to you. You might not be certain of it, but you'd certainly think it was possible.

"I believe what Kristen McNeil wrote, and I believe Arthur Wainwright killed himself because the truth was revealed. And if you think there is a chance that I am right, then you must have a reasonable doubt as to Noah Traynor's guilt.

"And if you have that reasonable doubt, you must vote to acquit. That is your responsibility.

"Thank you."

Chapter 13

I THINK THE LIKELY OUTCOME will be a hung jury.

I cannot imagine every single juror thinking there is not reasonable doubt as to Noah's guilt. On the other hand, I also cannot imagine every juror saying that it is a coincidence that Noah's skin was under the victim's fingers, but someone else killed her.

Because I think the jury will ultimately be hung, I think that they will take a long time to deliberate. I would think they will eventually tell the judge they're deadlocked, and he'll send them back to try harder. This could happen two or three times.

We're only in the third day of deliberations now, so while I don't think a verdict is imminent, I stay by the phone that I doubt will ring.

So of course it rings.

And of course it's Rita Gordon, the court clerk. "Judge Stiller wants you down here now."

"Is there a jury issue?"

She laughs a short laugh. "Yeah, you might say there's a jury issue, Andy. They've reached a verdict."

I'VE gotten to court too early.

When a verdict is about to be announced, I like to arrive late, just before the judge takes his spot behind the bench. Every minute sitting at the defense table feels like a minute on the treadmill, which is to say it is endless.

But this time I've arrived well in advance, and I just sit and watch as the gallery fills up. Laurie is here, and Sam Willis, and Willie Miller.

Julie Traynor comes in, and before she takes her seat, she comes over and squeezes my arm. "Thank you."

Hike comes in, sits down, and shakes his head from side to side. "Too soon. Way too soon."

Jenna comes in with her team. We make eye contact and both get up and walk toward each other. We shake hands, and she says, "I've enjoyed the battle."

"I wish I could say the same. I think I'm getting too old and cranky for this."

"I thought you were going to have your client testify."

I don't answer her; I just nod, and we go back to our respective corners. She didn't mean it in a negative way, but the comment cuts right through me. If we lose, I'm going to attribute it to that decision, and it's going to be hard to deal with.

Finally the court clerk arrives, and Noah is brought in. "Do you have a prediction?" he asks me, the strain evident on his face.

"Never. We wait and hope."

He nods. "I've been doing a lot of both."

Judge Stiller finally comes in; I feel like I've been sitting here since August. He calls the jury in and asks the foreman if they have reached a verdict. He says that they have.

Judge Stiller asks for the verdict to be brought to him, reads it to himself, and then tells the defendant to stand. I get up along with Noah and Hike; I can't even feel my legs.

This never gets any easier.

The judge gives the verdict back to the court clerk to read:

"We the jury, in the case of the *State of New Jersey versus Noah Traynor*, find the defendant, Noah Traynor, not guilty of the crime of murder in the first degree."

I'm pretty sure I've heard it correctly, and that is confirmed when

Noah hugs me. I look into the gallery and see the smile on Laurie's face as she hugs Julie Traynor, who is sobbing.

Life, at least for the moment, is once again good.

THIS is not the typical post-trial victory party.

We're doing it on Saturday afternoon, and rather than taking over Charlie's, we're located in an upstairs large private room there. The owners of Charlie's have made this accommodation because they are friends of mine and because on behalf of Vince, Pete, and myself, I have purchased about half a million beers over the years. And maybe two hundred thousand burgers.

The afternoon time and the special room are because of the unusual guest list. It includes Ricky and Danny Traynor, who would have trouble staying up if we had the gathering at night. But also present are Tara, Sebastian, Murphy, and Simon. While dogs are not allowed in New Jersey restaurants, Pete Stanton's presence has provided a tacit police department blessing.

The other celebrating humans, besides Laurie and me, are Vince, Julie and Noah Traynor, Sam, Hike, Willie, his wife Sondra, Edna, Marcus, and Corey Douglas.

Danny hasn't stopped smiling since we got here.

"Looks like your record as the Christmas-wish genie is intact," I say to Laurie.

"Admit it," she says. "It feels good."

"I admit it."

Noah and Julie walk over to thank Laurie and me.

"Time for me to get back to work," Noah says, smiling. "I wrote a lot in jail, but it isn't exactly upbeat stuff."

"There was a lot of media and public attention paid to this case and trial," I say. "Maybe a book might be a good idea?"

He nods. "I've already started to plan it. If I get an advance, I can start paying your fee."

"Read my lips," Laurie says. "There is no fee. Seeing Danny and his father together is all the fee Andy wants."

Laurie has clearly never been to law school; she has a fundamental misunderstanding of the economics of the profession.

Corey Douglas comes over, with Simon at his side. That dog is completely devoted to him. "Here are the reasons I am still alive and able to continue not collecting fees," I say.

Instead of acknowledging his saving my life in the park, Corey says to Laurie, "Did you tell him?"

"No. I was about to."

"Tell me what?" I ask.

Laurie, instead of answering, calls over to Marcus to join us, which he does. Then she turns back to me. "You seem to have a tendency to avoid taking on new cases."

"I try."

"But if you don't have clients, then we as investigators have nothing to investigate. Which means we have no work."

"So you're thanking me for giving you extended vacations?"

"I think I should just come out and say it. Corey, Marcus, and I . . . along with Simon, of course . . . we are going into business together. We are starting an investigation firm, and we even have a name. We're calling it the K Team, because of Simon."

"*Canine* starts with a *c*," I point out.

"I don't think you're seeing the big picture here. But if you are worried, don't be. When you take on cases, you will be our most important client. And if our work requires a lawyer, you will have first option."

"Yunhh," Marcus says, eliminating any confusion.

I'm not sure how I feel about this news. I'm sort of feeling left out, but I want to be left out.

"You guys will be a great team," I say, because they will be a great team. I raise my glass of Diet Coke. "To the K Team."

A TRIAL, at least for me, is about answering questions.

If I like the answers, I tell them to the jury. If I don't, I try to keep them to myself. But I like to have all the questions answered, even if just for my own peace of mind. When it comes to that, the Noah Traynor trial didn't end satisfactorily at all.

When no open issues are left in my mind after a trial, I would never consider looking at the trial documents again. Instead I would always pack them up and give them to Edna to file, and within a couple of years she'd get around to doing it.

In this case more issues are open than closed. I have tried to answer some questions from the very beginning and have just been unable to. Fortunately, the big one has been resolved. Arthur Wainwright is responsible for Kristen McNeil's death.

I don't believe he did it himself; the actual killer no doubt was one of the unsavory characters who have themselves since bitten the dust. If I had to guess, my vote would be on Taillon, but that doesn't matter now. Arthur willed it, and Arthur paid for it.

But the key question, the one I've been asking myself since the day I took the case, is why? Why was Kristen McNeil killed?

Everything else follows from that. What was Kristen so afraid of that she was running away? How did Charles Arrant, international criminal on the run from Interpol, wind up on a killing spree in Paterson, New Jersey? Had Arrant finished his mission, or is someone else here to take his place?

How did Arrant know that Mitch Holzer knew his name and told it to me, and why did that represent such a threat that he killed Holzer and tried to do the same to me? Arthur Wainwright killed himself before I unloaded the big guns in court . . . the phone calls he received from Taillon around the time of Kristen's death, and of course the letter that she left. How did Arthur know those revelations were coming?

The questions go on and on. The answers? Not so much.

So once again I turn to the dreaded trial documents.

Not surprisingly, I spend three hours learning absolutely nothing. It's unsettling to me in that Arrant and Wainwright seemed to know what we were doing, yet it's inconceivable that any member of our group did any leaking.

I discuss it with Laurie, and she says, "Let me get Roger Carrasco in here, just in case."

I know who she's talking about. Roger is a former colleague of Laurie's in the police department who now works in private surveillance. We've used him before to come in and make sure our home and my office were not being bugged. He does a full sweep for listening devices, phone taps, et cetera.

"You think we're being bugged?" I ask.

"I have no idea, but it would explain it. We talked about Holzer and Arrant in the house, and we certainly talked about the letter that Kristen McNeil wrote."

Laurie calls Roger, and he's at our house within an hour. Two hours go by before he determines that there are no signs of surveillance devices anywhere. He then goes through my office in less than an hour and calls with his report.

The place is clean.

Back to the documents.

Two things about the letter that Kristen wrote bug me.

One is that it appeared too conveniently; after fourteen years it was discovered just before I needed it at trial. I don't often get that lucky, and I distrust it when I do.

The other thing that bothers me is that in the letter Kristen mentions that she had saved money, and that therefore her parents shouldn't worry about her. Noah had told me that Kristen said she needed him to take her away because she had no money, and Kristen's friend Gale said that Kristen spent money faster than she made it. Gale even said that despite Kristen's earning a nice salary at NetLink, she was always borrowing from Gale.

This is not an earthshaking inconsistency. There are plenty of explanations. The most likely is that she was lying in the letter about having money so her parents would worry less about her.

But it's worth checking out.

I call Karen McNeil and get her voice mail. I leave a message for her to call me back. She does, about an hour later.

"How are you doing?" I ask.

"Okay. Better than my parents, but they're getting through it. I think things will get better, now that we know who did it. We're all grateful to you for making sure the real truth came out."

"I want to ask you a question about Kristen's letter. She mentioned that she had saved plenty of money, but other people have told me that she never saved a dime in her life, that she spent it as fast as she made it. Did that strike you as strange?"

"I guess it did, but I just thought she was saying it to ease my parents' mind."

"I thought of that as well."

"But . . ." Karen stops.

"But what?"

"There were a couple of things that were strange about that letter. Things were so emotional I hadn't focused on them, but I've thought about them since."

"Keep going."

"Well, for one thing, she called our parents 'Mother and Father.' Kristen just didn't talk like that; she wasn't nearly that formal. She called them 'Mom and Dad,' always."

"It was an unusual letter; maybe she felt the need to be more formal."

"I don't think so because of the other thing that bothers me. That was even stranger. She signed the letter 'Kris.'"

"So?"

"So Kristen hated the name Kris; she'd never let anyone call her that. She thought it made her sound like a boy."

"So you think she may not have written it?"

"No, she wrote it; I'm sure of that. I recognized her handwriting even before your expert confirmed it."

"You think she wrote it, but those aren't her words?"

Karen pauses before answering. "I can't say that. She was under tremendous stress. Maybe it made her talk differently."

"Here's a tough one for you. Would she be smart enough to change those words deliberately, to tip you off that she was being forced to write it?"

Karen thinks for a moment. "Maybe. One thing people never seemed to understand about my sister. She was really smart."

I HOPE that I'm seeing things that aren't there.

I hope that the letter from Kristen was written just as originally represented, in advance of her expecting to leave on her own, probably with Noah. Because if that isn't how it happened, if she was forced to write it, then nothing is as it seemed.

It would mean that Arthur Wainwright, the man who killed

himself because Andy Carpenter accused him of murder in open court, was innocent. Arthur, or a killer hired by Arthur, would not have forced Kristen to write a letter implicating Arthur in the murder. That would make no sense whatsoever.

But it physically can't have happened that way. The only way Kristen could have been forced to write that letter would be if she was under threat from her ultimate killer. But the letter was hidden in her desk drawer, waiting to be placed where her parents would find it, after she had run away.

If someone had forced Kristen to write it, someone who was set on implicating Arthur in the murder, they would have done a better job of it. They would have maneuvered a way to get the letter into the hands of her parents, not hidden in a place where it might not be discovered for fourteen years, if at all.

Besides, Arthur was wealthy, and Arrant, Taillon, and even Siroka were not in this for the thrill of the hunt. Whatever was going on, Arthur was in a unique position to finance it.

It has to be Arthur.

I am now in this all the way, which means I will bring Laurie back into it. She often sees things that I don't, but just talking it out is helpful and clears my mind.

Laurie thinks it unlikely that Kristen was forced to write the letter. "She was obviously under incredible stress. The fact that she might have used a few names or words that were uncharacteristic seems understandable."

"You're probably right, but let's follow it through." It's a technique I always use when a status quo is questioned. I assume the new scenario is correct, just to see where it leads.

Laurie nods. "The most obvious conclusion is that it would mean Arthur Wainwright was not involved in Kristen's murder. He wouldn't force her to write a letter accusing himself."

"No question," I say.

"And if he didn't do it, there would have been very little reason for him to commit suicide. Especially since he was dead before you introduced testimony about Taillon's phone calls to him, and before Karen read the letter in court."

"Something about the suicide bothers me," I say.

"What's that?"

"The location."

"The cemetery?"

"Yes, but more because it was at his ex-wife's gravesite. Kyle's college roommate told me that Kyle used to tell stories about their divorce, how bitter it was and how Arthur left her with almost nothing. Kyle hated him for it."

"You think it wasn't a suicide?"

"If Arthur didn't kill Kristen, which is the hypothetical we're currently working on, then I think it's very possible he was killed and it was set up to look like a suicide. If you wanted to do it in a place where you wouldn't be seen—"

She interrupts and finishes the thought. "What could work better than a secluded cemetery, in the middle of the night?"

"Right. And then there is the timing."

"What about the timing?"

"It's always been a little surprising that Arthur did what he did before the most damning evidence came out. I've assumed he somehow knew what was about to happen and bailed out rather than face it. But I never got the sense that Arthur was the type to back down; he was a fighter. He already hired a top lawyer in Hauser to go after me."

"So?"

"So maybe whoever was behind this knew what was going on and knew Arthur was about to come at me with both barrels. So he did what he had to do to stop him."

"How would the killer have known what was going to happen? We checked the place for bugs, so that couldn't be it."

"Beats the hell out of me. Sounds like a job for the K Team."

I've spent another two hours this morning getting nowhere.

Our theories about Karen's letter and Arthur's involvement are interesting and maybe even credible, but we have no way to confirm or refute them. Which in term renders them useless.

"I'm going for a ride," I say to Laurie.

"Where to?"

"I need to drop the rent check off at Sofia's." I'm talking about the fruit stand below my office, owned and operated by Sofia Hernandez.

"Are you familiar with the concept of mail?"

"I am. But you know that when I drop it off, she gives me a cantaloupe. I live for her cantaloupes."

I get in the car and head down to my office, still thinking about Arthur Wainwright. I park in front of the office, which means in front of Sofia Hernandez's fruit stand. She's behind the counter.

She lights up. "Mr. Andy, how are you today?"

"Very good, Sofia. How are you?"

"I'm good, family is good, but the fruit business is slow. I'm ready for summer."

We talk some more, and then I hand her the rent check.

"I forgot to tell you. I have PayPal now; you don't have to give me the checks. You can pay that way."

"That's okay. I like seeing you." The truth is that I wouldn't know how to use PayPal if you gave me a year to figure it out.

"You just want your cantaloupe." She smiles.

I return the smile. "You know me too well."

She gives me the cantaloupe. I have no idea how she gets ripe ones year-round, but I'm not complaining. We thank each other, and I head home, cherished cantaloupe on the seat next to me.

I'm on the way home, stopped at a light on Market Street. I'm smiling to myself over Sofia Hernandez using PayPal and, unlike me, trying to avoid becoming a technological dinosaur.

Then I wonder how many of my law school colleagues are paying rent to landlords who run fruit stands.

Then I say to myself, out loud, "Holy crap."

The first thing I do when I get home is call Sam Willis. "Sam, I've got some things I want you to do."

"We have a new client?"

"No. Same one."

"Oh." I can hear his disappointment. "What do you need?"

"Send me information on routers . . . how they work, general stuff. You can email it to me at the office."

"Routers? How technical do you want me to get?"

"Doesn't matter; I'm not going to read it. Also include whatever information about Kyle Wainwright you can find online. Doesn't matter what it is; I'm not going to read that either. Then I want you to talk to Sofia Hernandez and . . . hey, do you think you can hack into the computers of a university?"

"Why? You want me to change your grades?"

"Sam . . ."

"Of course I can get in. Those eggheads think they're so smart they never protect themselves well enough."

"Great." I tell him the situation and what I want him to do.

"I'm on it." The disappointment is gone from his voice.

As soon as I get off the phone with Sam, I call Pete Stanton. He gets on with "I don't like those midafternoon victory parties. By eight o'clock I was hungry again."

"Maybe if you'd stop arresting the wrong people, I wouldn't win so many cases, and we wouldn't need to have parties."

"Maybe I should arrest you for impersonating a jerk. What are you calling me for?"

"I know what's going on."

"Going on with what?"

"Kristen McNeil, Arthur Wainwright, everything."

He can tell by my voice that I'm serious. "I'm listening."

"You're going to have to do more than that. And you're not going to like it, but you're going to have to play by my rules."

Chapter 14

KYLE WAINWRIGHT FIGURED he had mourned long enough.

There was a business to run. NetLink Systems was now his business; his father's will clearly left it to him. There were other co-owners, but Arthur had 65 percent, which gave him full control. Which meant that Kyle was now in full control.

Kyle pretended to the outside world that he was upset about his father's death, but he didn't bother pretending it to himself. He could not stand the son of a bitch, ever since he'd bailed out on Kyle and his mother. But Kyle kept his eye on the financial ball, and now it had paid off.

Kyle was a smart guy, and he had carefully watched how his father ran things. Kyle had also watched Jeremy Kennon and the other tech guys and had learned from them. Kyle felt confident that he knew the business inside and out, and that he was ready.

But NetLink Systems was not quite the company it was a few days ago. The circumstances of Arthur's death carried with them a lot more than the whiff of scandal. NetLink's clients were going to be worried that they would be tainted by association, and they would need to be treated with kid gloves.

Countering that was that NetLink was an outstanding company that turned out an excellent product, and they had contracts in place with all of their important clients. By the time those contracts neared their end, the scandal would have faded.

Kyle would devote himself to making the clients comfortable; he was good at that. He would do whatever was necessary to ensure success.

He had waited too long. Nothing was going to stop him.

JEREMY KENNON IS NOT THERE when I call, so I leave a message. I've created a rather significant upheaval at NetLink Systems, to say the least, so I'm not sure if he'll call me back. But he's been willing to talk in the past, so I'm hoping he will.

He does . . . fifteen minutes later. "Haven't you caused enough damage already? What do you want now?"

"To talk."

"So talk." His tone makes it clear we're not buddies anymore.

"It has to be in person; I don't want to do it over the phone. And I have some theories to share with you that I need your input on. You have the expertise."

"What am I, on your staff? Tell me what this is about."

"Arthur and Kyle Wainwright. Not necessarily in that order."

"What about them?"

"Can we meet? There is something you need to hear, and some things for you to explain to me. You're the only one who can."

He thinks for a few moments. "You sure as hell can't come here to the office, not after what happened with Arthur."

"You pick the place."

"How about my house? I live in Ridgewood."

"No good. The place could be bugged. Surveillance is what we're going to be talking about."

"Come on, bugged? Who are you, James Bond?" Then, "So you pick the place."

"The Duck Pond in Ridgewood. Should be convenient."

"The Duck Pond? This is January."

"Dress warm . . . believe me, this is important. Eight o'clock? Near where the picnic tables are?"

"I should not be doing this. Eight o'clock."

I get off the phone and check my emails for the information on routers and Kyle Wainwright that Sam sent me. I skim it briefly. Then I call him to get the updates on the other areas he was checking into, and everything he says fits neatly into place.

Then I talk to Laurie about the arrangements I think we should make, all of which she agrees with.

And then all I can do is wait to meet with Jeremy Kennon.

I ARRIVE AT THE DUCK POND at ten before eight.

It's dark and cold here, not unexpected for a New Jersey night in January. I'm also not crazy about being in a dark place, all alone, but I have no reason to think I won't be safe.

Kennon pulls up right on time and parks near me. He walks over, arms folded. "This is nuts."

"I'll be as quick as I can. We can sit over there."

We sit at one of the picnic tables, across from each other. "Okay, let's hear it."

"Arthur Wainwright had been running an illegal operation out of NetLink Systems. He started it soon after he founded the company, and it's been ongoing ever since. He did it alone; there was no need to include anyone else. Ultimately, he brought in Kyle."

"What kind of illegal operation?" I've obviously got Kennon's attention.

"It has to do with the routers. There's a chip in there . . . at least I guess it's a chip. This really isn't my area; that's what I need you for. But when a router with that chip was placed in a company, or in a person's home, it allowed Arthur to monitor everything that came in on the internet into that network."

Kennon doesn't respond, so I continue. "They were spying on companies all over the world. They got intimate details of a company's operations, strategies, plans. You know how much that information would be worth to certain people? I'm sure you do.

"That's where Arrant came in. He was the conduit for all of it. He was international, so my guess is that there is spying involving a number of countries as well. There is no limit to what they might pay for industrial espionage. But that isn't for me to go through. That will be up to the authorities once we break this open."

"We?"

I nod. "You're the key player. You know the ins and outs of your systems. You can figure out how all this was done. This is the right time to get on the right side of this, Jeremy."

"What if you're wrong?"

"Fair enough. I'll give you an example. One of the routers Net-Link made is used in the athletic department at Clemson University.

A coach at LSU, going through Arrant, paid for their offensive game plan. I'm not sure if you saw the game, but LSU won, twenty-one to six."

"Arthur has been out of the tech area for a while."

I nod. "But Kyle hasn't. Kyle has been dealing with Arrant directly. The beauty of it is that no one else at NetLink had to know about it. All Kyle had to do was insert the chip, and no one could ever know that it was bad."

"Is that it?"

I nod. "Yes, except for one other thing. There's just one mistake in all I've told you so far."

"What's that?"

"Instead of using the name Kyle Wainwright, I should have used Jeremy Kennon."

The expression on his face is surprise. "What does that mean?"

"It means you've been conducting the operation, with Arrant. It means you killed Arthur Wainwright. It means that you were the older man Kristen McNeil was having an affair with. And it means you hired Taillon to kill Kristen McNeil, after he forced her to write the letter.

"Taillon didn't call Arthur's private line back then. He was calling you. You told me that the company was always changing offices, moving people around. I'm betting they didn't redo the phone system each time, so the private numbers stayed with the office."

Kennon lets this all sink in, then says, in a quieter, calmer voice than I would expect, "How did you figure it out?"

"It started with something you said. When you were at my office, you asked if I pick up a cantaloupe when I drop off my rent check. I didn't think anything of it, but looking back, I wondered how you possibly could have assumed that the person who ran the fruit stand was my landlord.

"So we talked to her. We asked her about the day last month when we lost wireless internet, and she said someone from the computer company had come by and installed newer equipment that day, without her even asking for it. And guess what? The new router was made by NetLink Systems.

"You were reading every email I got. That's how you knew about Mitch Holzer mentioning Arrant's name to me. And you read my email to my lawyer colleague about finding Kristen's letter. That's why you killed Arthur; you didn't want him defending himself. No telling what might have come out."

"Not bad," Kennon said. "But if you were looking to break this open, why are you telling me? Why not the police?"

"Did I mention the money that you must be making? I want some of it, and I want some for my client. Payment for the nightmare you put him through."

Kennon stands up, and somehow a gun has appeared in his hand. "I don't think so. You made a big mistake. You've set the whole thing up for Kyle to take the fall. It will look like he did all of this, including killing you." Kennon looks around. "You even picked a great location. Let's take a walk toward those trees."

Suddenly there is a sound I have now gotten familiar with, followed by a blur that runs across my line of vision and lands on Kennon. He screams and is on the ground, Simon ripping at his arm.

"Off," Corey says, and the ever-obedient Simon obeys. Freed from the crazy dog, Kennon tries to run, only to be grabbed by Marcus and tossed against a tree. He falls to the ground.

"Nicely done, boys," says Laurie.

Suddenly the area is lit up by floodlights; it's now daytime at the Duck Pond. Pete runs up, flanked by three officers.

I open my shirt, which does not feel good in the cold, and I rip the wire off my chest, which feels even worse. "You get it all?"

Pete nods. "Every word."

"Pete," I say, "have you met the K Team?"

I CAN'T sleep, so Laurie and I stay up late talking.

It's going to be August by the time the adrenaline wears off.

So we sit in the kitchen and try to figure out the parts of the conspiracy that we're not sure of. If Jeremy ever pleads guilty, maybe we'll have the last details confirmed.

"I think Kennon wanted to blame Arthur for Kristen's murder

all along," I say. "That's why he forced her to write the letter. She wrote it just before he killed her."

"How did they get it in the house?"

"Karen had told me that there was a break-in at the house while everyone was at the funeral. Jewelry was taken, but I think that was a cover. They were just planting the letter."

"But they never followed up to find another way to implicate Arthur. When the letter wasn't found, they let him off the hook."

"Right. Because of the skin under her fingernails. The police were set on the person with that DNA being the killer. So Kennon had to back off, especially when Kristen's parents didn't find the letter. It worked out for him because Arthur backed out of the tech area, giving Kennon free rein."

"So now what?"

"Now the government will have to track down all these routers. Sam says it will be an impossible task, but that's not our problem. My next step will be to do a public interview, letting everyone know that Arthur Wainwright was neither a murderer nor a suicide victim. It's the very least I can do."

"Poor Noah," Laurie says. "Talk about being in the wrong place at the wrong time."

"But it all worked out because of your three-month Christmas season. If you hadn't gotten Danny's wish list when you did, Noah would be heading to prison for the rest of his life."

We head up to bed. Ricky is sleeping at Will Rubenstein's, so Laurie puts on some romantic music.

"Jingle Bells."

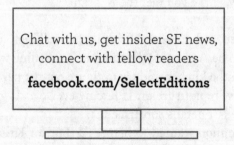

AfterWords

Dachshund Through the Snow is David Rosenfelt's nineteenth Andy Carpenter novel. By now, fans are affectionately familiar with Andy's wry humor, love of dogs, aversion to work, and history of solving tricky crimes.

Rosenfelt got the idea for Andy many years ago, when he was working as a screenwriter in Hollywood. He'd been writing TV movies, and Andy started out as a character in "Snapshot," one of his unsold scripts.

"The star was Andy Carpenter, a lawyer from Paterson, New Jersey," Rosenfelt recalls. Sound familiar? However, the networks weren't interested. The following year, Rosenfelt got a call from a producer. Apparently, "Tyne Daly wanted to do it if I made it a woman, and I put in jokes about being overweight, so it became Andrea Carpenter," says Rosenfelt. The networks still didn't bite.

About a year later, the actress Cheryl Ladd showed interest, but "she wanted to take out the overweight jokes." Andrea Carpenter became thin again, but the script didn't sell.

Eventually, Rosenfelt gave up on Hollywood and turned to novels. "I decided to write a courtroom drama," he says. "I took it out of the drawer, and that became the basis for the first novel, called *Open and Shut*, and I turned him back into a man. Andy has a little identity crisis going on here."

Clearly Andy has found his home in novels. Rosenfelt is currently at work on a new one.

She stopped to save a stranger.
Now only she can save herself . . .

NO
BAD
DEED

A NOVEL

"Sensational. . . .
Full of suspense
and quiet menace.
Don't miss it!"
—LEE CHILD

HEATHER
CHAVEZ

Chapter 1

IF MY KIDS HAD BEEN with me, it wouldn't have happened. I would have stayed in the minivan, doors locked, windows rolled up. Just like the 911 operator instructed.

But my husband, Sam, had the flu. He had picked up Audrey hours before, and Leo was studying at a friend's house, so I was alone in the van.

Driving in full dark, I felt alone in the world. Clouds thick with unshed rain drifted across a half-moon, drizzle seeping from them even as they threatened to split open completely. During commute, the two-lane road carried a steady stream of parents on their way to the elementary school up the road and nine-to-fivers headed to west Santa Rosa. Several hours post-commute, though, it was nearly deserted, owing equally to the time and the weather.

A couple of miles from home, my phone buzzed. A name popped onto the display: *Sam*. After ending a twelve-hour shift fishing coins out of a Labrador's stomach, I was too exhausted for another argument. Lately, all of our conversations seemed to start with the same four words: *I love you, but* . . .

Sam gave me only three rings to answer before ending the call.

In the sudden silence, my stomach grumbled. It was the third

time that week I had missed dinner, and it was only Wednesday.
I love you, but your patients see you more than me and our kids.
That was a popular one.

I popped open the energy drink sitting in the cup holder and took a sip. I grimaced. How did Leo drink this stuff? I drained half of it anyway. Caffeine was caffeine.

On the north side of the road, from among the oaks and evergreens, the old hospital slipped into view. Paulin Creek bordered the campus on the south. It had been vacant for years, so no one had reason to stop at the hospital. Still, I thought I saw movement between the buildings. A chill pricked the back of my neck.

I almost missed the shape that streaked across the road.

I jumped in my seat. A deer? No, it ran on two legs. A person.

When I reached to return the energy drink to the cup holder, my hand shook, so the can caught the lip of the console. It bounced onto the passenger seat, liquid pooling around my purse.

The expletives I let loose would've gotten my teen son grounded.

I pulled onto the shoulder, threw the car into park, and peeled off my cardigan to sop up the puddle. As I wiped my sticky hands, I squinted at a spot near the hospital's entrance.

It's probably a jogger.

In the rain.

In the dark without reflective gear.

The primitive part of my brain scoffed.

I switched on my brights to see better. I identified a second shape next to the first, just off the road.

I put the van in gear and pulled off the shoulder, driving slowly. With Halloween the next night, I thought it might be a couple of teenagers. What better place to stage a prank than an abandoned hospital? But as I drew close, my focus sharpened. A man and a woman stood in the spotlight of my high beams. They were arguing. No, *fighting*. This was balled fists, shoving, rage. The dark-haired woman in yoga pants didn't stand a chance.

The woman curled in on herself, dropping her chin and tucking behind her crossed arms. Making herself smaller, even as the man, bald and more than a foot taller, did the opposite.

Twenty feet away, I stopped the car, but left the engine running. My fingers were clumsy on the keypad as I dialed 911. The woman glanced in my direction. But the man in the jeans and white T-shirt never turned my way. He didn't so much as twitch.

"What's your emergency?" the dispatcher asked.

I startled at the voice. Double-checking that the doors were locked, I gave my location and then described the couple.

"They're fighting," I said.

"Is he armed?"

"I don't think so."

"What's he doing now?"

Before I could answer, the man picked up the woman and tossed her down the embankment toward the creek below.

A sudden weight pressed against my chest. The dispatcher's voice grew distant. My lungs seized, and my vision darkened around the corners. An urge to hide overwhelmed me. I wanted to crawl into the gathering void and disappear. It felt like a memory, though it couldn't have been. I had no memory like this. Suddenly I felt as vulnerable in my locked car as the woman on that trail.

Was I having a panic attack? My mouth was dry, my tongue a useless lump. I wasn't certain the dispatcher understood me.

What the hell is happening?

The man pulled something from his pocket. A cell phone? Something else? Then he was gone, maybe over the trail's edge.

Seeing him disappear was enough to snap me free of whatever had rendered me speechless. "He has something," I said.

"What's he doing?" The dispatcher's voice remained neutral.

"I don't know. I can't see them."

My hand dropped to the door handle. As if sensing the gesture, the dispatcher instructed, "Stay in the vehicle."

Before the dispatcher could ask any additional questions, I slipped my phone in my pocket and opened the door.

I'm NOT entirely sure why I got out of the van. It might have been because of that other girl. There was this brunette in my undergrad microbiology class. I'm ashamed to admit I didn't remember her name. I remembered *his* name, though—Dirk.

At an off-campus party, Dirk had openly berated the girl for over an hour. He wasn't her boyfriend but wanted to be, and until that night, maybe she had wanted the same thing. Then he had started grabbing her. When finally he had slapped her, only one guy grabbed Dirk's arm. But even that guy hadn't held on to Dirk's arm when he had followed the girl from the room.

Minutes later, she went over the balcony railing. She broke an arm and a couple of ribs and would have broken her skull if not for the hedge she bounced off before hitting the concrete.

Maybe it was that girl who made me get out of the van now, or maybe it was just that anger always made me do stupid things.

My heart tumbled in my chest. About fifteen feet away, halfway between the trail and the rushing water, the man stood over the woman, his hand clenched on a switchblade. He had a knife.

I could think of no way to be useful. It had been nearly twenty years since my last fist fight, and even back then, I hadn't been stupid enough to take on guys twice my size.

As the man's anger unspooled, his victim chose the defense often used by prey: She went limp. Her nose seeped blood.

I swallowed and shouted for him to stop as anger rose in me.

The man reached for the woman, his hands tightening on her sweatshirt. He yanked her toward him, so close her chest butted against his, the knife dangerously near her cheek.

I risked a few steps forward. "The police are coming."

The man stared up at me, through me, rain tracing a slick line from scalp to stubbled chin. At that moment, he was hardly human. He was an animal, body tensed, breath ragged.

"You should go," he said.

"I don't think I should," I said, even as I flashed to thoughts of Audrey and Leo. I couldn't leave this woman to him. My hand fell to my pants pocket and the outline my phone made there.

The man returned his attention to his victim, but his voice carried to where I stood. "Who do you love?" he asked. Though he looked at the woman, the way he raised his voice made me believe the question was for me. It startled me—not just his words, but the voice, which lacked any of the emotion that corrupted his face.

The man dropped his victim to the ground, holding her there with one of his muddy boots. He stared up at me. "Your life is already screwed up. You just don't know it yet." He kicked the woman's torso. Then he dropped into a squat and repositioned his blade so it faced downward, toward his prone victim.

I knew how to handle aggressive animals. If a dog attacked, you were supposed to kick it in the throat, nose, or back of the head. Break bones. I knew if it came to that, I would be the one broken and likely stabbed. I picked up a rock and threw it.

It caught him on the cheek. He rubbed his skin but remained focused on his prey. His shoulder cocked. The woman struggled.

The terror that had seized me in the van returned. I saw another woman, another time, imaginary but as real as the rain and the mud and the blood rushing in my ears.

I slid down the embankment and stumbled into the man, my trajectory a combination of clumsiness and luck, the blade grazing my arm. Barely a scratch, but I yelped, a sound I had heard many times from animals but that was unfamiliar in my own throat. He lost hold of the knife, and it tumbled into the water.

I fell backward onto the marshy creek bed. Perception became as slippery as the rain upon the rocks, the woman beside me still, the man's face warped with sick purpose.

Then, suddenly, he stopped. He dropped to a crouch beside me, grabbed my face between his hands. I had no doubt he could snap my neck with a single twitch. "Why the hell are you doing this?" he demanded. "Who are you?"

He was so close, his voice so thunderous, that my ears vibrated. I noticed a stain on his T-shirt that might have been blood.

He grabbed a handful of my hair, red and long, easily twisted around his fingers. He yanked it, pulling my face even closer.

Then—finally, thankfully—I heard sirens.

For only a second longer he studied my face, and I his. Broad nose, a bump along its bridge. A white worm of scar tissue that prevented stubble from growing along one patch of jaw. A man who liked to fight, and not just with women half his size.

He seemed unconcerned that I would be able to identify him. Testify against him.

"Let her die, and I'll let you live," he said.

He nudged the woman with his toe. "Probably not much of a choice anyway. She's close enough to dead."

Then he loped away, up the hill and toward the road where I had so helpfully left my minivan and its key.

He would get to my car first. My registration. My purse. In moments he would know my name, my address. And the names of my husband and children.

Chapter 2

MY TRAILSIDE EXAMINATION of the victim was brief, the moon providing the slightest of light. Her breathing was barely a whisper on my cheek, and her pulse was weak. No complaint of pain. Even when the paramedics moved her, she remained silent.

Half an hour after the ambulance took her away, I still waited for the police to release me. The rain had lightened to a mist that nevertheless glued my hair to my face and left my T-shirt sodden.

"You sure you don't want a jacket?" the officer asked again. I checked his name tag: Willis. That drew my attention to the body camera that had been recording for the past thirty minutes, making me second-guess my answers and wonder if the pitch of my voice or slope of my shoulders might later be interpreted as guilt.

"I'm not cold," I said. My nerves numbed, my damp clothes felt as warm as bathwater. That probably wasn't normal.

A man approached from the street, stopping to talk to the female officer who'd interviewed me first. The new arrival wore gray pants, a white shirt that reflected moonlight, and a pink striped tie.

I turned my attention back to Officer Willis, clasping my hands to stop them from shaking. "How's my family?"

I ran through the personal items in my van. Leo's football photos. A note from Audrey's first-grade teacher. Audrey's medication. The registration that bore my name and our address.

That man now had all of those things.

"Have you spoken with my husband?"

Officer Willis nodded. "We told him your van was stolen but you're okay."

"And they're fine? Sam? The kids? You still have a car there?"

"We still have a car there, and your family's okay."

I pushed. "You've checked recently?"

"He's not going anywhere near your house." I turned to the man who had spoken: the detective with the carefully pressed pants and bleached shirt. Now that he was closer, I saw that what I'd taken for stripes on his tie were actually strips of bacon.

"Cassie Larkin? Detective Ray Rico." He stood only an inch taller than me, his brown face broad, his smile wide. His black hair was cut short, his dark eyes sharp above thick creases.

"Willis, please bring Dr. Larkin a jacket," he said.

There was no choice in it for either of us, so when the officer returned with a sweatshirt, I accepted it.

Detective Rico turned on a recorder and flipped open his note-pad. He held a sheet of paper too, though I couldn't see what was on it. "Walk me through what happened."

When I finished my story, Rico acknowledged its end with a curt nod. "That was really . . . *brave* of you, to get out of your car."

"Anyone would've done the same."

"I don't know about that." Rico consulted his notebook. "You didn't know him, right? Not a patient or the parent of one of your kids' friends?" When I shook my head, he asked, "You're sure?"

I remembered the man's face, twisted in anger as he tossed the woman down the hill. "I've never seen him before."

"Would you be able to identify him?"

When I nodded, Rico held out the paper he was holding, face-down at first. "I'm going to show you some photographs."

He flipped the sheet over. On it were the photos of six men, all white, all bald or balding, all in their late forties to late fifties.

"The suspect might not be in this group," Rico said, his tone neutral. "So you're under no obligation to identify anyone."

My heart seized. It couldn't have been clearer if the photo had been ringed with fire. There, in the middle row, was the man with the ropy scar along his jaw and the once-broken nose.

"That's him." The finger I pointed shook as much as my voice.

"You sure?"

"Completely."

Rico held out a pen and asked me to sign the photo I had identified. He left for a moment, and when he returned, he asked: "Recognize the name Natalie Robinson?"

I shook my head. "Is that the victim's name?"

The detective's eyes were twin chips of granite. "How about Anne Jackson?"

"No. Who's Anne Jackson?"

Rico didn't answer. He jotted something in his notebook, then gestured toward my arm. "Tell me again how you got cut."

At the mention of the wound, I became aware of its throbbing. "He tried to stab her, but he got me instead. It's just a scratch."

"Carver Sweet's a big guy."

My heart pummeled my ribs. "You know who he is?"

"Now that you've identified him, we do." His expression remained stony. "So, Carver's a big guy, and he had a knife. You have kids, and you'd already called 911. Why risk a confrontation?"

I remembered how my sneakers lost purchase on the hillside, rocks and sticks threatening to twist my ankles. "I slipped."

"You slipped?"

"I'm clumsy, and the ground was wet."

Rico stared at me, letting the pause stretch. It reminded me of the times I had talked to clients who brought animals in with unexplained injuries or signs of malnourishment. It was the way you talked to someone you thought might be lying.

He consulted his notebook again. "You said Carver Sweet may have had blood on his shirt. At what point did you notice that?"

"Near the end."

"So when did you notice the victim was bleeding?"

"After he threw her down the slope. Her nose." Had there been other injuries? I strained to remember.

"So when you first pulled over, she wasn't bleeding?"

"I don't think so."

"He hadn't taken out the knife yet? When they were standing on the trail?"

"No." Rico's scribbling unnerved me. "Will she be all right?"

The detective looked up. "I don't know." He flipped to a new page in his notebook. "Did you notice any vehicles alongside the road?" When I shook my head, he explained, "We found two vehicles half a mile up. Crashed."

"If he forced her off the road, it wasn't random."

"What makes you say that?"

The attacker's question was fresh in my mind: *Who do you love?* And then: *Let her die, and I'll let you live.*

"It seemed personal."

Rico considered this. "Every crime is personal, even the random ones." His mouth settled into a grim line. "You say you didn't know the man, but did you know his victim?"

"I've never seen either of them before." It was only after I answered that the first two words registered: *You say.* As if he doubted what I said was true.

"So you say you were coming from work?"

There it was again. "Yes."

"And you left at what time?"

"Just after ten."

"Anyone able to verify that?"

"I was alone for the last hour, but before that, certainly."

"Any surveillance cameras at your clinic?"

"No." The chill from the rain that had soaked my clothes finally seeped into my skin. I shivered.

"The number three mean anything to you?" he asked.

I studied his face, but he hid his thoughts well. "No. Why?"

"Just something one of the officers found. Probably nothing."

Rico jotted something in his notebook and attempted a smile.

"Looks like someone may have spotted your vehicle in a grocery store parking lot, so we'll know more soon," he said. Then the smile disappeared. "Carver Sweet's not getting anywhere near your house, but you need to be careful. You're a threat to him."

The detective handed me his card, then called Willis over to drive me home. When Rico walked away, he wiped his palms on his slacks, as if trying to rid them of something unpleasant.

WE LIVED in a three-bedroom ranch-style house in Lomita Heights, a neighborhood that dated back to the 1960s. Our family had moved in sixteen years before when I was pregnant with Leo.

As I walked toward the door, Leo's face was wedged between the slats of the blinds, hair disheveled, eyes bleary.

He opened the front door. "What the heck, Mom?" A rumpled blanket on the couch suggested he had waited up for me. I hugged him fiercely. "The police came and talked to Dad, and now a cop brought you home? Where's the van?"

"Stolen."

"Really? Do they know who took it?"

"They do. I'll get it back soon." I trotted out my fail-safe distraction: "You hungry?"

Leo had eaten only an hour before, so of course he wanted a sandwich. I made two: turkey for him, veggie for me. Nerves roiled my stomach, but I forced down half of mine before grabbing a handful of batteries from the junk drawer and slipping them in my pocket. Leo ate and returned to bed, and after I tested the lock on his window, I checked on Audrey. My first grader had fallen asleep under a pile of blankets. I kissed her cheek, then felt her forehead. Damp, but not feverish. She hadn't yet caught her father's flu.

From Audrey's closet I pulled out her old baby monitor and switched the batteries. It still worked. I took the receiver with me.

Finally, in the hallway outside the master, I took a breath, braced for an argument, and pushed open the door. Sam was waiting on the bed in his pajama bottoms. My husband had the wiry build of an academic. He was also beautiful: dimpled smirk, messed hair that invited fingers, thick lashes that our children had inherited.

"I would've come out, but it seemed you needed some time with Leo," he said. "Tell me what happened."

I placed the receiver on the dresser next to a bottle of cold medicine and told him everything, omitting from my story the details that made me seem most reckless. As I talked, I removed my mud-streaked clothes and slipped on a sleeping shirt, one of Sam's.

When I stopped speaking, Sam sighed, his chest rattling with the effort. "Cassie." Part accusation, part concern.

He disappeared into the bathroom and returned with the first aid kit, switching on the light before sitting beside me on the bed.

"Give it here," he said, gesturing toward my arm. It was barely a scratch, but I extended my arm anyway.

"I'm a little irked with you," he said, the virus making his voice husky. He gently set to cleaning the wound with an antiseptic wipe.

"Irked, are you?"

"Yes, irked. Why did you risk your life like that? The kids—"

I recoiled as if pushed. "I was thinking of the kids," I said. "What kind of mother would I be if I let someone else's daughter be victimized? Besides, you would have done the same."

When Sam looked up from his task, his blue eyes intense, my breath caught in my throat. "It's not just the kids."

"I know."

He covered my cut with a bandage, then placed the first aid kit on the nightstand. "Next time you see a man with a knife, don't get out of the car. Promise me." His voice vibrated with more urgency than I had come to expect after seventeen years of marriage.

"I can't imagine it'll happen again. But I promise."

Sam's lips parted as if he were about to speak, but instead, he stretched past me to switch off the light.

We climbed into bed. Reaching for him, my fingers grazed his back just as he turned away from me, toward the wall. The cold medicine dragged him into sleep within minutes.

As I lay there listening to the monitor, the quiet that usually settled me instead seemed a presence, waiting, watching. Later, I would wonder if it was my intuition warning me of what was to come—of what, in fact, already had begun.

HAVING dreamed of large insects, even larger men, and bassinets filled with mud, I awoke groggy and with a headache.

I groaned when I saw the time. I had overslept.

When I swung my feet onto the carpet, I caught the glint of copper on the edge of the bed frame. I reached down and picked up the object that had drawn my attention, not metal at all, but paper. It was an origami dog no bigger than a business card.

The paper dog, with its folded ears and tiny legs, made me smile. It reminded me of the early days of my relationship with Sam, when he would leave gifts like this in unexpected places.

It had been a while since Sam had created art for me. Too busy, he said. We were both too busy—for art, for sex, for anything beyond the needs of our kids, his students, my patients.

I put the origami dog on my nightstand. Then I got up and followed the sound of chaos to the kitchen. I stopped in the doorway, watching, but had only a second before I was spotted. Leo, wearing a scowl, stood quickly. "Dad said we needed to let you sleep."

His backpack caught the edge of the bowl Sam had been using to scramble eggs. It clattered to the floor, its contents splattering the cabinets. Our Chihuahua mix, Boo, skittered over to investigate the puddle of slime. Sam nudged the dog aside with his foot.

I grabbed a roll of paper towels off the counter and started sopping up the mess, while Sam retrieved a fresh bowl and eggs. I turned my attention to Audrey, seated on a stool at the counter. "Did you take your medicine, Peanut?"

Before she could answer, Leo said, "I need to go to school now."

Audrey gasped, her eyes widening. "But you're not dressed."

"I'm dressed."

"Nooooooo." Audrey sighed as if her brother were the six-year-old. "You're normal dressed, not Halloween dressed."

She hopped down from the stool and twirled, showing off her black cat costume. "See. I'm a cat. What are you going to be?"

"Late for my workout. Can't someone drop me off and come back?"

"Yes, because that's reasonable," I said. "We'll rearrange our schedules because you've changed your plans at the last minute. Besides, we only have one car for the time being, remember?"

"So that's a no?"

I pointed at an empty stool. "That's a 'sit.' I'll take you after you eat." I slid three slices of sourdough in the toaster.

Sam's eyebrows furrowed as he studied me. "About the car, take mine. I'll grab a rental and a new booster seat for Audrey, after I call the locksmith."

"You're not going in?"

"Think I'll take another day." Sam hadn't missed work once the previous school year, but before I could think too hard on that, he said, "Audrey's medication is running low. I was going to stop by the pharmacy, unless you've already refilled it?"

I started to say that I had picked up the prescription the morning before, but then I remembered: my purse. Audrey's medication was one more thing I needed to replace.

"I can get it." After I canceled my credit card and stopped by the DMV. My headache intensified. I wasn't big on breakfast, and that morning I felt even less like eating than usual.

I returned to the bedroom to get dressed, my hands trembling as I buttoned my shirt. The night before, the man on the trail had been rabid and merciless. He had warned me: *Let her die, and I'll let you live.* Had the woman survived? I didn't know, but I had made every effort to save her, which I guessed would void his offer of mercy. And this man had my address. My keys.

The door swung open, and Sam walked in. He grabbed a small chunk of yellowed plastic from his dresser, then sat beside me on the bed. "You're sure you're okay?"

"I'm fine," I lied. "You seemed distracted last night."

"You had just been attacked."

"You sure that's it?"

Someone who hadn't been married to Sam wouldn't have noticed the pause, brief as it was before the familiar smirk shifted into place. "Of course," he said. I read his lie easily.

Sam slipped the piece of plastic he had been holding into his mouth.

"I wanted to give Audrey a preview of what I'll be wearing tonight."

"Wait. I thought Leo was taking her trick-or-treating?"

He fake-leered at me, exposing zombie teeth. When he went to kiss me, I pulled away.

"I thought the undead were sexy," he said.

I smiled. "Vampires are sexy," I clarified. "Zombies are . . . zombies. So why isn't Leo taking Audrey trick-or-treating?"

"He made plans with Tyler."

"When did he make these plans? Did he tell Audrey?"

"Yesss," Sam lisped. "He told Audrey. Now about this vampire favoritism . . . think about the poor, dentally challenged zombie. How much harder he has to work to lure a woman to his bed."

I had to admit it: Sam was a damned sexy zombie.

This time, I returned his kiss, flu be damned. Sam wrapped his arms around my waist and bent to kiss my neck.

"Mo-om," Leo yelled through the door. "Can we go?"

I yelled back, "Pretty impatient for someone who canceled trick-or-treating plans on his six-year-old sister."

On the other side of the door, Leo grunted.

"I think Leo might be part zombie," I said.

Sam's phone trilled. His attention snapped from me to his screen. "I'm sorry," he said, "but I have to take this."

I met his eyes—tried to read them.

He opened the door for me, waiting for me to walk through it before he answered the call.

AFTER dropping Leo off at Santa Rosa High, I had my vet tech, Zoe, also my closest friend, reschedule my morning appointments so I could call the bank and stop by the pharmacy and DMV.

When I finally pulled into my clinic's parking lot toward the end of lunch hour, my first thought was of Sam. I had met him here a month into my internship, when Princess Jellybean, his kindergarten class's guinea pig, had gotten sick. The vet I had been working with at the time had prescribed a special diet that required Sam to hand-feed Princess Jellybean. Even now, I smiled at the memory of him hunched over the rodent with a syringe.

It took him another month to get up the nerve to ask me out.

I thought of Sam now because of the phone call. After seventeen years of marriage, we didn't have secrets. Or so I had believed, until he had rushed me out that morning to take that call.

When I entered the clinic, Zoe was behind the front desk with Smooch, a one-eyed orange tabby, nestled in the basket beside her. Smooch blinked in greeting before returning to her nap. *Cats.*

Zoe jumped up, and I braced myself. My lavender-haired friend was six feet of muscled curves and bleached-smile exuberance. She was also a hugger. That morning, though, her embrace was tentative, as if she were afraid anything stronger would break me.

"You okay?" she asked. No smile for me today.

"I'm okay."

Zoe vibrated with curiosity but switched into business mode. "Daryl's on his way in with Lester."

Before I could ask why, the front door jerked open. Usually, Lester careened into a room, all crossed paws and thrashing tail. But that day, he stumbled in, dropping in a pile onto the floor. When I approached, the Labrador whimpered and peered at me from beneath the rim of his surgical collar but didn't move. I couldn't remember the last time I had seen slack in Lester's leash.

I knelt to scratch the Lab behind one floppy ear. "What's going on with our boy here?" I asked.

Daryl shared his dog's coloring and easy temperament.

"He's gotten worse since last night's surgery," he said.

I ushered Daryl and Lester into the exam room. We lifted the Labrador onto the stainless-steel table, and I checked the dressing on the wound. There were no signs of swelling or discharge.

"When was the last time he ate?" I asked.

"Breakfast. He was fine last night, then this morning he started acting like he'd scarfed down a whole plate of pot brownies."

"There's no chance he did?" This was Lester. I had to ask.

"Nah," Daryl said. "I thought it might be the anesthesia."

"So he was groggy, but he ate. Was his appetite normal?" When Daryl nodded, I asked, "He's been drinking water?"

It was cool in the exam room, but Lester began panting, drool dripping from his tongue onto the exam table. "Yeah, he's had water. What's wrong with him, Doc?"

Two sets of forlorn eyes pinned me. "I'm not sure," I said.

I checked Lester's gums and the inside of his cheek. Both were pale. Since he'd just had surgery, I worried his pale gums indicated a hemorrhage. He needed blood work immediately. An ophthalmic exam to check for pupil reactivity could also be useful in determining a toxicosis diagnosis.

"You kept him in his crate last night?" I asked.

"Yes, and took him into the bathroom when I showered. He was only out of my sight when some guy selling salvation knocked on my door, but even then, it was less than a minute."

"Not in the market for salvation, huh?" I placed my stethoscope to the dog's chest. One hundred and sixty beats per minute.

"Always. Something's wrong, isn't it?"

I got that familiar shiver in my gut, equal parts intuition and experience. "His heart's beating faster than normal, and his respiration's labored too. Has he vomited, or had diarrhea?"

"No."

I wondered at Lester's stumbling entrance earlier. "Tremors?"

Daryl's face clouded. "He *has* been a little shaky."

Lester cooperated when I took his temperature. Usually, he wiggled with enough vigor to require a second set of hands. When I palpated his stomach, he whined. Some pain there.

"His temperature's on the high end of normal," I said. "At any time, did Lester have access to any toxins?"

"You think Lester ate something he shouldn't have." It wasn't a question. We both knew the Lab's proclivity for eating unusual items, like the coins I had removed twenty-four hours before.

"It could be anything—moldy food from the garbage, antifreeze, medication, chocolate. Snail or gopher bait." I hadn't noticed any burns in Lester's mouth that would suggest the ingestion of chemicals, but such effects might not show for hours.

"I would've noticed," Daryl said, his voice tight.

Just then Lester heaved, the vomit thick and a brown that was nearly black. I had treated several dogs for chocolate toxicity, and all had survived. But something about this case disturbed me. I stared at the discharge, but saw nothing.

"Looks like chocolate," Daryl said. I detected relief and understood why. With the toxins I had named earlier, chocolate must have seemed the least of the potential dangers.

But I knew what Daryl didn't: There was no antidote to theobromine, the chemical sickening Lester now. I could give him diazepam for his tremors, or propranolol for any arrhythmia. I could administer activated charcoal for the chocolate that lingered in his stomach and intravenous liquids to prevent dehydration.

There was a lot I could do—except guarantee I could save him. And, of course, that was the only promise Daryl wanted.

As if reading my mind, Daryl asked, "Is he going to be okay?"

I started to give the only possible answer, that I would do everything I could, but then Lester vomited again, and I realized what had disturbed me a minute earlier. In the pan was a thick, dark liquid. Only that. No scraps of silver or plastic. In the other cases I had treated, there had always been bits of wrapper.

Even someone who hadn't gone to veterinary school knew enough about canines to know this: Dogs don't unwrap their food.

Chapter 3

I STABILIZED LESTER, then transferred him to a facility with twenty-four-hour care. I tried not to dwell on the missing wrapper. Daryl baked his special brownies at least a couple of times a week, and it was conceivable the Labrador had stolen unwrapped chocolate from Daryl's pantry.

I was distracted by a more immediate concern: Why wasn't my key unlocking the front door to my house?

For a second I wondered if this was how my marriage to Sam

ended: with a key stuck in a lock, preventing entry to the home we had shared for sixteen years. Exhaustion opened the way to doubt. No matter how strong our marriage was, Sam had always been a better person than me.

I had been a wild teenager who had morphed into a reckless and adrift young woman. But with Sam, I found mooring. I changed for the better. At least that's what I told myself. My father might have had a different opinion.

Still, there I was, doubting Sam because that morning he had preferred to take a phone call in private. In my place, Sam wouldn't have doubted me. Like I said, a better person.

I tried the key again. Still stuck. Then I remembered the envelope Sam had dropped off while I had been treating Lester, at the same time he had swapped his car for the rental I'd just driven home. The envelope contained a house key to fit the new locks.

I retrieved the new key, opening the door to a tiny dog bouncing at my feet. Other than Boo, the house was empty. Leo was spending the night at Tyler's, but where were Sam and Audrey?

Sam's blue Toyota Camry was still in the driveway, parked next to my rental sedan. He must have taken Audrey trick-or-treating.

We had agreed to leave at six, and it was now after seven. I was late getting home, again, and I knew how impatient six-year-olds could be. It was my fault that I had missed another family ritual.

I locked the door behind me and went into the kitchen. A pot of spaghetti sat on the stove, two jars of pasta sauce on the counter. The side of the pot was warm, so they hadn't been gone long.

I called Sam. It took a few rings for him to answer.

"Cassie." He said my name in that way only he did, his voice made huskier with the flu.

"I'm home."

"We shouldn't be out much longer. Audrey's starting to drag."

"I can meet you guys. I wouldn't want to disappoint Audrey."

Sam didn't point out I already had by being more than an hour late. "Like I said, we'll be home soon. We made spaghetti."

"I found it."

"Audrey insisted on making the sauce."

"I'm surprised she could open the jars."

"I helped with that and pouring it into the pan. But she's a heck of a stirrer."

In the background, I heard a chorus of "Trick or treat." I closed my eyes and pictured Audrey's face in a throng of children. Sam's voice was low when he next spoke. "We need to talk."

With that, the doubt sauntered back, like a cocky friend I was expecting but wasn't particularly happy to see. "About what?"

"We'll be home in half an hour," he said. "Love you, Cassie."

Sam hung up before I could say that I loved him too.

I ATE, then settled on the couch. Boo jumped up beside me. I covered myself with a fleece throw and sank back into the pillows, intending only a short rest. Just until Sam and Audrey got back.

My eyes burned, and sleep came quickly.

At some point, my vibrating phone woke me. That and the tickling on my foot. I answered, expecting Sam. It was Daryl.

"Sorry it's so late, Doc," he said. "Lester's still on an IV, but he's not vomiting anymore."

"I'm glad he's doing better."

"Thank you, Doc."

"You don't need to—"

Daryl interrupted me. "Yes, I do. That first time I came into your office, the incident with the sliding glass door . . ."

"Wasn't your fault."

"I know that, but I was high, and I was sure you would notice and make judgments. But you didn't."

That day, he couldn't have smelled more of skunk if he'd been sporting a white stripe down his back. "I noticed."

Daryl chuckled. "Oh, I know. What I meant is, you didn't judge."

Boo's fur brushed my toes, so I jiggled my foot. "Not my place."

"It's nobody's place, but that doesn't stop people from doing it," he said. "So thanks. Not just for today."

For a moment, neither of us spoke. Finally I asked, "Still no idea where Lester got the chocolate?"

"I've been thinking about it, a lot, but I have no idea."

Boo continued to graze my foot. Maybe it wasn't his fur. A paw? "I appreciate the update, Daryl."

"Yeah, well, sorry again it's so late, but I figured with kids, you'd still be up, since it's Halloween."

It wasn't until Daryl hung up that the full meaning of his apology registered: *Sorry again it's so late.*

I checked my phone. 9:07 p.m. It had been nearly two hours since I had talked to Sam. I punched in his number, but it went straight to voice mail. My heart beat faster.

Sam could have taken Audrey for a hamburger—except they had already eaten spaghetti.

Ice cream, then. But Sam wouldn't allow our daughter ice cream when she already had a bucketful of candy. Because of the liver transplant, we were both watchful of how much sugar she ate.

Concern became panic when I realized Sam couldn't have gone for burgers or ice cream. His car was at the house. *Wasn't it?*

I jolted from the couch, earning a yelp from Boo, who was tucked into the couch next to my hip. I pulled open the curtains even as my subconscious tingled: *Tucked into my hip?*

I didn't know which I had been hoping to see—the car or an empty driveway. Without a car, Sam would likely be in the neighborhood. If the car had been gone, it allowed the possibility that he had taken Audrey to a friend's house or stopped by work.

Sam's blue Toyota Camry was still parked in the driveway.

Suddenly the absence of options felt like a tangible void.

I flicked on the light. My subconscious drew my attention to the foot of the couch and to the tickling that couldn't have been Boo.

I screamed when I saw it. Black eyes were pinpricks in its large, round head. Stripes crossed its body, nearly two inches long. Mandibles jutted from its alien face, and it hopped on spiny legs. I jumped back, grateful no one witnessed my reaction.

Just a stupid Jerusalem cricket. Still, I shuddered to think that thing had been on my foot.

I grabbed an empty glass from the coffee table and trapped the bug beneath it, the insect's antennae testing the walls of its new prison. *Ping, ping.* Only a stupid insect, but in light of the events of the past twenty-four hours, it felt like something else. A reminder of how vulnerable we were. *Ping, ping, ping.*

My hand trembled as I texted Leo: *Heard from Dad?*

The response: *No. Why?*

He wanted to know what time your football game is tomorrow.

I could hear the eye roll in his reply: *Dad doesn't know the time?*

Leo saw through my lie. Understandably. Sam hadn't missed a game. I was the one who sometimes ducked in at halftime.

After another unsuccessful call to Sam, I grabbed my keys, stepped around the tiny monster encased in glass, and headed out to find my husband and daughter.

WITH its mature trees, older homes, and sidewalks sloping toward the sky, Lomita Heights had always felt like a monument. Some of the families had been living in their homes longer than I had been alive. It felt solid, entrenched. Safe.

But tonight, I felt none of the usual security. There were shadows in the trees, and the streets were nearly empty.

This lack of pedestrian traffic made the house a few blocks over stand out. With its over-the-top decorations, the two-story home could have passed for a commercial enterprise. Ghoulish heads streaked with stage blood impaled on fence posts. A reaper cast in the greenish glow of spotlights, skulls at its feet, bony hands protruding from freshly dug plots, all shrouded in dry-ice fog.

It was the only house that still had traffic. Among the stragglers was a black cat. *Audrey.*

I couldn't get to her fast enough, and when I reached her, I fell to my knees beside her. I pulled her into a hug so tight she might have melted into my ribs. Sam was nowhere in sight.

"I take it you're the mom?" I looked up and found myself staring into the face of a witch I didn't know.

"Mm-hmm," was all I managed. "Where's your dad, Peanut?"

My daughter's small shoulders lifted in a shrug. Her cheeks were smeared with tears. "I think he lost me," she said. "I saw Savannah from school. Tonight she was a cat too. I said hi to Savannah, and then Daddy was gone."

Her confusion was a gut punch. Sam was the reliable one. He was the parent who kept track of the kids' overbooked schedules. Remembered to reorder Audrey's medication, or buy Leo's cleats.

"Good of you to finally show up." I turned and saw that a short-skirted pirate in fishnets had joined the witch. I ignored the judgment, as thick as the smell of wine on the pirate's breath.

"Where do you remember seeing Dad last?"

"Before I saw Savannah." She grabbed some candy from her bucket and held out her hand, palm up, for inspection. "She gave me all her sour candies, and I gave her all of my purple ones."

I glanced up at the women. "How long has she been alone?"

The pirate pursed her lips. "She's not alone. *We're* with her. But *we're* not her parents."

The witch added, "Her dad's been gone for fifteen minutes. At least. We would've called, but your daughter doesn't know your number, and she doesn't have a cell phone."

I stood, pulling Audrey so she rested against my hip. "She's six. Of course she doesn't have a phone."

"I got my Clementine a phone for her fourth birthday."

The pirate's turn now. "Not that it's okay to dump a child on people you barely know."

I swallowed my irritation. "Sam left Audrey with you?"

The witch nodded. "He recognized me from carpool. We usually drop off around the same time."

"Then where did he go?"

"No clue. He said he wouldn't be gone long, but that was *fifteen minutes* ago."

"And neither of you have seen him since?"

The witch shook her head, but the pirate shrugged. "I saw him, but it was earlier. He looked like he was waiting for someone."

When Audrey burrowed closer to my hip, I wrapped my arm more tightly around her shoulders. "Why do you think that?"

"He kept checking his phone, looking around," the pirate said. "He was texting too. Then he must've connected with whoever, because he put his phone in his pocket."

"How long ago was that?"

"Longer than fifteen minutes," the pirate said.

We were going in circles, and I needed to get Audrey home. "Let me give you my number. In case you see him again."

I recited my number, which the pirate punched into her phone.

"Thanks for looking out for my daughter," I said. "I don't want to take you away from your kids any longer."

I took some pleasure in the women's sudden panic as they looked around and realized they had no idea where their children were. I would've probably taken more satisfaction if the same couldn't also be said of my husband.

I DROPPED off Audrey and Boo at Zoe's. I wanted to stay with her, to be at her bedside if she should awake, but Audrey didn't need my comfort. She needed me to find her dad.

Santa Rosa is about forty square miles, and I searched each one of them. Some twice. My husband hadn't come home, and one of the last things he had said to me had been: *We need to talk.*

Never good words to hear, less so under the circumstances.

As I drove, I called Sam's closest friend, Ozzy, several times. Straight to voice mail each time.

Midnight approached. I pulled into a grocery store parking lot and rested my forehead between my hands on the steering wheel.

Originally, I had considered that Sam had left to visit a friend. But that meant he had made the choice to leave our six-year-old daughter with a woman he only recognized from carpool. Besides, unless he was visiting someone within walking distance, he would have needed his car, and his car still sat in our driveway.

He might have left in someone else's car—either coaxed into it or carried. My mind churned like one of those farming combines— threshing possibilities, each more terrible than the last. Sam could have been shot, stabbed, or beaten. If his wallet and phone had been taken, how would the hospital know whom to call?

My hand trembled as I Googled hospital phone numbers. Each time I connected with the emergency department, I got the same response: No one matching Sam's description had been admitted.

That left the police and the morgue. I wasn't ready to call either.

There was another option. Sam's disappearance might be connected to the attack the night before. Carver Sweet would know we had kids if he had opened my wallet. It was Halloween . . . He could guess we would be out trick-or-treating. Easy prey.

Even as I cast aside a thousand explanations, one returned again and again: Sam might be having an affair. He might have left Audrey with a woman he barely knew because the alternative was to bring her to meet his lover.

His words hit me again: *We need to talk.*

Another possibility: Sam had intended to break it off with his lover, and she had reacted badly. That brought back the images of Sam unconscious, in a ditch, or in someone's trunk.

I gripped my cell phone tightly, scanning my contacts. Sam had no family except for cousins out of state. I didn't have the numbers of his coworkers, and I wouldn't have called them if I did.

I put the car in gear and headed to Ozzy's.

My husband's friend lived in Healdsburg, a small town twenty minutes north of Santa Rosa. Known for its wine, Healdsburg was surrounded by brewpubs, boutiques, and restaurants.

A short walk from downtown, Ozzy rented the upstairs granny unit of a century-old bungalow. Peeling blue paint. One window covered with plywood. Healdsburg property values being what they were, such a home wasn't labeled run-down, but *historic*.

I knocked on his door. Despite the hour, Ozzy answered quickly. His greeting was alert, if guarded.

"Hey, Ozzy." I tried to smile but had no stomach for it. "I was wondering if you've heard from Sam."

Ozzy Delgado had grown up in Austin, and the drawl crept into his voice when he was tired.

"I got your message, but I haven't seen him." He brushed a curl away from his face and opened the door just enough to show the left half of his body. He was wearing cargo pants and a floral-print, button-up shirt. He didn't invite me in.

"Seeing him and hearing from him aren't the same thing," I said, staring past him into the living room.

Ozzy closed the door a little. "Haven't heard from him either."

"No calls? No texts?"

"I'm aware what 'heard from him' means."

I pushed. "So, no contact?"

He swatted away another curl, his scowl and drawl deepening. "I'm sure Sam will be in touch."

"And I'm sure you're being evasive."

A few seconds passed, and my steady glare brought only a sigh.

"Sam took Audrey trick-or-treating," I said. "When they didn't come home, I went looking for them. I found her. Didn't find him."

His eyes widened slightly. "He left Audrey alone?"

"She was with two women I've never met."

His face relaxed. "Did Sam know them?"

"He recognized one of them from carpool," I admitted. I didn't like the way Ozzy looked at me when I said that. Like he felt sorry for me. Like he knew something I didn't.

"Well, there you go."

"It's odd timing, don't you think? For Sam to walk away from our daughter on Halloween."

"Would there have been a good time for him to leave?" Ozzy exhaled deeply. "It's late, Cassie. I'll let you know if Sam gets in touch. Anyway, I hope you guys work it out."

He shut the door, leaving me stunned. What the hell had he meant by that last part?

On my walk back to the car, I considered Ozzy's final comment. Sam despised confrontation—so much that he would avoid talking about his desire to divorce?

I rejected the thought as soon as it popped into my head. In high school, Sam had once stepped in when a group of guys was bullying a smaller, curly-haired teammate, ending up with a bloodied nose and Ozzy's friendship. Sam was also a fiercely protective husband and father, the kind of guy who dressed up like a zombie to take his six-year-old daughter trick-or-treating.

After considering everything, I couldn't believe Sam wasn't happy. The thought pricked at my consciousness before I could shoo it away: Maybe it wasn't that he wasn't happy with me, but that he was happier with someone else.

I started the car. Twenty-two minutes later, I turned onto Terra Linda Drive. In those twenty-two minutes I had reassured myself that Sam loved me, he loved our children, and he wouldn't have left without an explanation.

When the explanation came a minute later, it wasn't what I had been expecting: a text from Sam just as I was pulling up to our home. Two words. *I'm sorry.*

I parked in the middle of the driveway. There was no need to park on the right, the side usually reserved for me, because sometime in the past hour Sam's car had disappeared.

Chapter 4

WHEN I ENTERED THE HOUSE and flipped on the light, the first thing I noticed was the glass on its side in the middle of the floor. I puzzled over it a moment before I remembered: the Jerusalem cricket I had trapped. While I had been looking for Sam, he had entered our home, knocking over the glass, then had driven away.

Now freed, the insect had likely found a dark corner to hide in. I could picture its alien eyes watching me, its prickly feet—used to burrow into things moist and decaying—scuttling across my path. Though I knew it was irrational, that the insect's escape coincided with Sam's disappearance felt like an omen.

I grabbed a change of clothes for both kids before going into the master bedroom to pack my own bag.

I was still thinking of that insect and of Sam when I saw it: on the nightstand, the dog made of folded paper. It seemed less innocent in near darkness than it had in that morning's light.

With its ears folded downward, it reminded me of a Labrador. I lifted it to my nose and sniffed. I thought I caught a hint of chocolate. My hands jittered as I unfolded the origami into a sheet of foil-lined paper. Stamped on the coppery exterior was the brand name of the baking chocolate we sometimes bought.

On the other side, a number had been etched in pencil: 2.

I remembered what Rico had asked me after the attack: Did the number three mean anything to me?

Sometimes we step across life's thresholds without noticing. But this one came with blinking arrows and exclamation points. *2.*

I didn't know what the number meant, but I knew it meant something. Staring down at the paper, a question occurred to me: If Sam hadn't left the folded dog on my nightstand, how had the person who *had* left it gained access to our bedroom?

I folded the paper in quarters and slipped it into my pocket.

ZOE lived in a Mediterranean townhome with a tile roof and Juliet balcony. When I got there, my lavender-haired friend was on the couch, long legs tucked beneath her, the one-eyed Smooch draped around her shoulders. The stony set of her face told me avoiding her questions wasn't an option.

"How's Audrey been?" I asked.

"Didn't wake up once. Any word on Sam?"

I sank in the overstuffed chair facing her, hugging a throw pillow to my chest. "He texted that he's sorry."

"And . . . ?"

"That's it. He's sorry. Oh, and his car's gone now." I shifted in my seat and released my grip on the pillow. It slipped to the floor. "When I talked to Ozzy, he said he hoped we could work it out."

Zoe's face was red. "What the hell did he mean by that?"

"He didn't say."

"You guys are solid."

But was that true? I thought hard on this. When Audrey was a baby and needed a liver transplant, I hadn't handled it well. I worked longer hours so I could feel like I was actually of use to someone. As a medical professional, I had failed my daughter. It had taken jaundice setting in for me to recognize the symptoms, and by then she was sick. Really sick. And I was angry.

Sam, though—he carried our family through the crisis. I could always count on him, even when he couldn't count on me. But lately, I had been working longer hours again, and this time, Sam had pulled away. Just a little. Just enough for me to notice.

Part of me had been waiting for him to say: *I love you, but I can't do this anymore.*

"I think Sam was in the house," I said. "When I went inside to grab our things, the glass I'd used to trap a Jerusalem cricket had been knocked over. And there's something else." I took the chocolate wrapper from my pocket and showed it to Zoe.

"What's this?"

"I found it on my nightstand this morning. It was folded in the shape of a dog."

"Like origami?"

"Yeah. At first I thought it might be from Sam, but now . . ."

I waited to see if she would come to the same conclusion I had. I recognized the moment she did. She sniffed the wrapper.

"It smells like chocolate." Her eyes and mouth widened, her voice breathless as she asked, "Lester?"

"I thought so, but I have no idea what the number two means."

"Hmm. So it's a two."

"After I witnessed that attack, the detective asked if the number three meant anything to me."

"Does it?"

"I haven't a clue. But it feels like a threat, especially after what happened with Lester."

She paused, her face scrunching. "I thought you found it *before* Lester was poisoned?"

"I did."

"When you showed the wrapper to me, I didn't see a number." She turned it over and traced a section of raised foil, where the pencil mark on the other side had left it embossed with its mirror image. "Power of suggestion. You were thinking of that detective's question, so you saw a two. I was thinking leaving an origami dog seemed like something Sam would do. So I saw an S."

"But you agree it smells like chocolate."

"I've been to your house. It's a brand you use."

"You think it's a coincidence?"

"How would someone get into your house?"

"Carver took my van, which had my keys. We didn't get the locks changed until late yesterday morning." I thought of the bug freed from its jar. "If it's related to that night and he's done something with Sam—he'd have the new house key too."

"Isn't it more likely that Sam left it for you as some romantic gesture that only seems sinister now that he's gone?"

I took the wrapper back but said nothing.

"And isn't it more likely that, given that text you received, Sam left because . . ."

"Because?" But I knew where the sentence had been headed.

Zoe rested her hand on my knee. "Because he wanted to."

"Then it would seem an inappropriate time for romantic gestures."

"So what I'm saying doesn't make sense to you?"

I twisted my wedding ring. "I think Sam's been trying to tell me something for weeks, and I've missed it. Still, if there's even a chance that his absence isn't his choice . . ."

"You need to do whatever you can to find him."

Smooch slid from Zoe's neck onto her lap. Zoe's petting grew aggressive as she considered her next words. Finally she said, "I hope Sam's having an affair. I hope he's just taking time to figure everything out, because if that's what happened, he'll be back."

Even as the idea broke my heart, I thought: *I hope so too.*

I FELL asleep with my hand on my phone and woke up the same way. I checked the screen. No more texts from Sam.

From the kitchen I could hear Audrey making breakfast with Zoe. Laughing. The morning before, that had been the four of us, in our own kitchen, Sam scrambling eggs and none of us realizing it might be our last breakfast as a family.

I pulled the blanket around me and called my son.

Leo's voice held the usual hint of impatience. "What's up?"

"Just checking in." I forced a lilt in my voice. *Everything fine here.* "Did you and Tyler have fun last night?"

"Yeah, I guess. You and Dad coming to the game?"

It took a moment for my throat to clear. "I'm not sure if Dad's going to be able to make this one. I think you shouldn't go either."

"What?" If I'd told Leo we were moving to the Congo to live with the bonobos, he would've reacted with less incredulity.

"I was thinking you, Audrey, and I can go to dinner instead."

"Why would we do that?"

"Eating dinner is actually quite common."

He sighed, unimpressed. "But it's Monty." Montgomery High, Santa Rosa's rival. "No way. Coach would kill me."

I considered forcing Leo to miss the game. But then I thought: Tonight might be his last game. If Sam never returned, missing Monty would no longer top Leo's list of worst things.

"I just worry about you."

Leo caught the slight break in my voice. "Everything okay, Mom?" A pause. "Why isn't Dad coming to the game?"

The lie came quickly. "Dad's at a conference, and I'm fine. I think I'm still shaken up from the other night."

"Well, if everything's okay, I gotta go. See you at the game?"

"Audrey and I will be there."

ON THE ride to school, I glanced in the mirror to the back seat, where Audrey wriggled to get comfortable in her booster seat.

"Mommy, next year, can we have one of those pumpkins that looks like it's throwing up?" she asked. "You know, with the seeds and stringy parts coming out of its mouth?"

At last, a question I could answer honestly. Earlier, when Audrey had asked where her dad was, I told her the same lie I had told Leo. They both believed it without question.

I pulled alongside the curb near Hidden Valley Elementary.

"Sure. We can have a pumpkin like that next year."

Next year. What would that look like for our family?

Audrey grabbed her backpack, gave me a hug, then bounded toward a group of girls who squealed in greeting. Forget next year. I didn't even know what the next *day* would look like.

Earlier, I had canceled all my appointments. With no patients or kids to tend to, I considered my next step.

A dozen calls to Sam had gone unanswered. For the first time in months, I almost called my father, but it had been years since we had spoken. Six years. Our last conversation had been a stilted call a month after Audrey was born. What help could he be now?

The brick facade of the high school appeared in front of me before I fully realized where I was headed. I pulled into the staff lot and looked for Sam's blue Camry. When I didn't find it, I parked.

On my phone, I typed another text to Sam, hitting SEND before I could second-guess myself.

As I waited for his response, I reread the message: *Give me a reason not to file a missing person report. You've got five minutes.*

Sam needed only three: *I need time.*

Well, our kids need a dad. Call me.

Another text popped onto the screen: *I can't. Not yet.*

Why not?

It's complicated. And then: *I'm not alone.*

Despite my thought the night before that Sam might be cheating on me, what I pictured now was Sam hiding in a closet, or in the trunk of some stranger's car, bruised and bleeding.

Another possibility: Sam might not be the one texting me.

Who's with you? Are you hurt?

He answered only the second question: *I'll recover.*

Then call me.

When no response came, I dialed his number. It rolled into voice mail. His text came a second later: *I'm sorry.*

I summoned the courage to ask the question I didn't really want answered. *Are you having an affair?*

The bubbles signifying Sam was typing lasted several minutes, but the text that came was just four words: *Give me until tonight.*

I pushed: *You didn't answer me.*

I waited for the bubbles to appear again. Thirty seconds passed. A minute. Finally I typed: *How do I know this is really you?*

The reply came quickly this time. *Who else would it be?*

Another nonanswer.

Why did you leave Audrey with that woman?

The bubbles again, then: *The first time we met. Princess Jellybean.*

I inhaled sharply. *What?*
You asked if this was really me.

My hands trembled when I asked the question he still hadn't answered: *Are you having an affair?*

In the cold rental sedan, I waited for Sam's response, and when the bubbles popped on the screen, my heart's thundering grew so loud I half expected the windshield to flex. Then, for a moment, my heart stopped. The last text from Sam was a single word: *Yes.*

Clouds of pulled cotton hung above the skylight of the Santa Rosa Police Department, midmorning sun filtering in as I entered the station. Detective Ray Rico wasn't in, but the police technician at the counter said someone else would help me.

Five minutes later, a woman with a tight bun and heavily contoured cheeks introduced herself as Marisol Torres and ushered me into a room off the lobby. Despite the severity of her hairstyle, the officer's slight smile seemed sympathetic and genuine.

Torres gathered contact information, social media passwords, and a description of my husband. I scrolled through half a dozen photos before I found a photo that worked.

"This must be difficult for you," Torres said. "When's the last time you saw your husband?"

"Yesterday morning, shortly before seven."

"Any other contact yesterday?"

"We spoke on the phone at seven fourteen p.m." This I knew because I had checked my call log. Repeatedly. "When I got home just after seven, he had already left to take our daughter trick-or-treating."

"What did your husband say the last time you spoke?"

I had replayed our last conversation on a loop since Sam had disappeared. "He said he and Audrey would be home in about half an hour and that we needed to talk."

"About what?"

"He didn't elaborate."

She studied me intently. Though she tried to soften her eyes, I was no longer sure Officer Torres was on my side.

"What did you do then?" she asked.

"Waited for them to come home." I kept the fact I had fallen asleep to myself. Torres didn't need more reasons to doubt me.

I continued, "I got a call regarding a patient a few minutes after nine, and it hit me that Sam and Audrey hadn't come home yet."

"It didn't hit you that they hadn't returned until . . . what? . . . nearly two hours after talking to your husband?"

I kept my face as dispassionate as the officer's. "That's right."

"What did you do when you realized he hadn't come home?"

"I went looking for him." I told Torres about my search of the neighborhood and about finding Audrey with the two women.

"No other contact from Sam since?"

I hesitated. "There have been some texts," I said. "But I'm not sure they're from Sam." I showed them to her anyway.

"Why do you doubt these texts are from your husband?"

On the drive to the station, I had considered that question at length, so my response came easily. "Once you're in a relationship, people always ask how you met, right? At first, the Princess Jellybean reference threw me, but then I thought about all the times we've told that story. And . . . it didn't sound like him."

"How so?"

"For one thing, he didn't ask about the kids."

Torres's jaw clenched. "You don't think there's a chance your husband left voluntarily?"

I shook my head on reflex. Though she kept her expression neutral, I sensed she wasn't convinced. I couldn't blame her.

"Even if the texts are from Sam, he mentions right here that he's injured." I tapped the screen where I had asked Sam if he had been hurt. "If he's injured, you should follow up on that. And if the texts aren't from Sam . . ." I let my voice trail away. We both knew what might have happened if Sam hadn't sent those texts.

Torres stared for several seconds before saying, "Does Sam have any history of mental illness or substance abuse?"

"No."

"Financial problems?"

I started to say of course not, but I hadn't thought to check our bank balance or credit card receipts. I took care of the clinic's finances, and Sam handled the home accounts. "I don't think so."

Torres paused. "Mrs. Larkin, two women with no apparent agenda told you they saw Sam and he looked like he was waiting for someone. That he willingly left your daughter in their care. We'll stay open to all possibilities, but you should too."

Torres's slight smile now seemed more pity than sympathy.

Still, my husband's disappearance kept coming back to a single fact: "Sam wouldn't have left Audrey alone."

Torres's expression remained neutral. "She wasn't alone. Even if you didn't know that woman, your husband did."

Though her comment hadn't aimed to wound, it did. Sam knew the mom in the witch costume because he was the one who dropped Audrey off at school every day. He was the one who was there. Until now, when he suddenly wasn't.

"Why would he leave Audrey with someone else with our home only a few blocks away?" I asked. "Audrey was upset last night. Crying. If Sam had planned to be gone more than a few minutes, our daughter certainly wasn't aware of it."

"Do you have the numbers of these women?"

I shook my head. Another failure on my part.

Torres nodded, as if my oversight was understandable, but I sensed her judgment. Or maybe I was judging myself.

From my purse I pulled out the chocolate wrapper. I handed it to Torres. I told her about Lester being poisoned and about finding the wrapper folded into the shape of a dog on my nightstand.

She took the wrapper. "We'll look into this, and we'll enter the information about your husband into a national database. But unless we find something to indicate he is at risk, there's little we can do. Adults are allowed to come and go as they please."

Torres put down her pen and leaned forward. "Most missing adults return within a few days," she said. "Odds are Sam's safe."

I found no reassurance in the words.

"If there's any evidence he left involuntarily, we'll investigate it as we would any other crime. Just because the odds are that isn't what happened doesn't mean we won't consider it."

I nodded, signaling my acceptance that the interview was over.

"One other thing. By filing this report, you're entitled to know if we find your husband safe."

"Meaning?"

"That's all you have a right to know. If he doesn't want you to know where he is, we can't share his location."

She adjusted the clipboard in her lap. "You were involved in an assault case a couple of days ago, right?"

"It's been a hell of a week."

She straightened. "Cops look for patterns. The assault by itself could be bad luck, bad timing. But add to that a husband who disappears twenty-four hours later and the murder . . ."

When she didn't immediately finish her sentence, I pushed. "The woman he attacked died?"

"Wednesday was a busy day for Mr. Sweet. Before he assaulted that woman, he poisoned his wife," she said. "You're sure you don't know him?"

Since the attack, I couldn't escape the memory of Carver's face. Most of all, I remembered the scar—puckered flesh trailing his jaw like an albino snake. The mark of a predator.

"Never met him. But the woman he beat up—she survived?"

Torres's gaze sharpened, and I felt color bloom in my cheeks. "Ms. Breneman was released from the hospital yesterday."

"I'm glad to hear it," I said.

Torres nodded, standing. "We'll let you know if we hear anything, and when you can pick up your van."

I'd forgotten about that, and I nodded in thanks. "Your purse, though . . . It wasn't in the van when we found it. He either took it with him or threw it away." Neither option provided comfort.

Officer Marisol Torres walked away, all her original warmth replaced with an efficient brusqueness.

I thought of Sam, watched the officer depart, and considered that maybe I wasn't as good at reading people as I believed.

WHEN I left the police station, I paused outside. I should go home, check the computer, sift through phone records and credit card statements. But when I thought of home, I thought of Sam making tamales, or Sam tending to scrapes on Audrey's knees, insignificant injuries made instantly better with Dad's attention.

I couldn't go home.

Even though I hadn't yet decided on my next step, I walked with purpose toward the car. Keep moving, I told myself, just as I had the night before. Reflection could wait until tonight, when I spent another night on Zoe's sofa, or my first night alone in the bed I usually shared with Sam.

Struggling to come up with a plan, I drove past the police station—and saw it. A little metal box, its lens pointed at the street. I turned around at the next block and headed toward home after all.

THE cold sun stole the magic from the neighborhood where Sam had disappeared, ghosts now recognized as bedsheets, skeletons clearly plastic instead of bone.

It was not yet eleven a.m., and the street was deserted. I walked past yards accented with live oak and flowering pear trees. I scanned doorways, balconies, and rooftops for surveillance cameras.

I almost missed it, as focused as I was on the high points. But it wasn't a camera that drew my attention; it was a pumpkin. The jack-o'-lantern's eyes drooped, its eyebrows arched slits of dismay, its mouth downturned. Out of that mouth spilled a generous mound of stringy and seed-specked pumpkin guts.

As if it were throwing up.

This was exactly the kind of pumpkin Audrey had mentioned earlier, and it sat on the brick steps of the two-story home two doors down from the haunted house where I had found her.

Free newspapers were scattered on the front lawn. A side window was cracked, covered with cardboard.

Even though I expected no answer, I knocked.

"You looking for the Gardners?" I turned toward the voice, which belonged to an older woman in leopard-print glasses, a floral blouse, and periwinkle slacks. "Because if you're looking for the Gardners, they moved out the middle of this month."

If the house had been vacant for a couple of weeks, the porch light shouldn't have been on the night before. How had Audrey seen this pumpkin? I myself had nearly missed it in daylight.

The woman in the periwinkle slacks, hair just a shade lighter, took my pause as a sign I wanted to know more. "Stan, he's the husband, lost his job. The wife, Christina, couldn't support a family of five. Not in Sonoma County. They moved to Ohio." She held out her hand, and I shook it. "I'm Helen, by the way."

"Pleased to meet you. I'm Cassie." I pulled out my phone and displayed a photo of Sam. "Did you see this man last night?"

The older woman leaned in. "Is that your husband?"

When I nodded, Helen smiled. "He's a handsome young man. I've always been a sucker for dimples. My Bob had dimples."

"Do you remember seeing him?"

"Of course. Mainly because of the little girl. She sparkled and was so polite. Some of them don't say thank you, but she did."

My heart skipped. "You saw Audrey? What time was that?"

"I ran out of candy around eight, and they were one of the last. A quarter till?" She nodded. "Yes, that sounds about right."

That was thirty-one minutes after Sam had called me, promising to be home in thirty. "Was there anyone with them?"

The woman tilted her head, curiosity edging toward suspicion. "Are you two having trouble? Because I don't like to get involved."

I imagined the Gardners would disagree.

"My husband's missing." Saying it aloud, for the second time in an hour, made the stone I carried in my stomach heavier.

"And you think he might have gone off with someone?"

"He might have."

She considered this. "It was just him and the girl."

"If you don't mind me asking, which house is yours?"

Helen pointed to a yellow ranch across from where we stood.

I handed her one of my cards. "If you hear anything . . ."

Helen took the card and slipped it in the pocket of her slacks. "I hope you find your husband."

She patted me on the arm and walked away.

I HAD BEEN SO FIXATED ON the neighborhood where Sam had disappeared, at first, that I overlooked my own. Then I drove past Gino Baldovino's house.

Mr. Baldovino lived alone. Shortly after we had moved in, he crossed the street to tell me I was overwatering my strawflowers.

He had talked to us only once since, the previous autumn when a rake had disappeared from his front yard on the same day Leo had a couple of friends over. I could not convince my neighbor the boys weren't involved—rakes, as I pointed out, weren't high on the wish list of most teens—and he had left muttering in Italian.

The next day, Mr. Baldovino had installed a surveillance camera. Every day since, it had been pointed at our house.

My breath quickened as I crossed the street to the Baldovino home. My knock was only slightly louder than my heartbeat.

When the door opened, he snapped, "What do you want?"

Small talk would be wasted on him, so I opted for brevity: "Your surveillance from last night and this morning. Please."

His eyes narrowed. I guessed he was torn between his natural urge to shut the door and his desire to learn more about a possible crime in his neighborhood. Curiosity won out. "Why?"

Reluctant to share my story with him, I sought a lie. "A hanging planter on my side gate went missing."

"I don't remember a planter."

I cursed that I hadn't thought to say Audrey's bike or Leo's cleats. He wouldn't have cared about those items.

"I just hung it last night," I said.

"Were your sons' friends visiting?"

I sighed, refocusing my patience. "No."

"What was in the planter?" he asked.

"I don't know. Some tiny yellow flowers."

He snorted. "That narrows it down. Go buy another one."

"The flowers were new, but the planter was my mother's," I lied. Again. I had nothing of my mother's.

Mr. Baldovino considered this. "They're *my* DVDs."

Why else would I be here? I thought. "I can pay you."

His frown deepened. "You can return that rake your son stole."

"My son didn't steal your rake, Mr. Baldovino, but I can certainly buy you a new one."

"You wouldn't get the right kind."

I choked back another sigh. "Is there anything you want, Mr. Baldovino? How about some clippings from our garden?"

This interested him. "I want a tree. The Japanese maple."

"Of course. Now can I get the DVD?"

"I'll bring it to you after my nap."

I hadn't wanted to return home, but, forced to wait for the recording, I now had no choice.

Our house didn't have a dedicated office, so we had created a work space on one side of the dining room. Sam had found an old desk dumped curbside, then had spent a weekend sanding, sealing, and painting it a deep green. The family computer was positioned at its center, Leo's history book and piles of notebook paper shoving against it. And, perched on a shelf above the chaos, a picture of Sam and the kids at Sugarloaf Ridge State Park.

I settled in the chair and signed on to our bank's website, scanning the transactions for the past month. There were debits for groceries, gas, utilities, and restaurants, mostly the kind where meals were served in a bag. There were charges for a new phone case and sneakers for Leo, a couple of books for Audrey.

I went back another month, and still saw nothing suspicious: no large cash withdrawals, or a series of small ones. No flowers, romantic dinners, or lingerie had been purchased. But if Sam was having an affair, he was certainly smart enough to pay cash.

I found only one surprise. After combing through two months of transactions, I could find no mortgage payment listed.

I navigated to the mortgagor's website, which confirmed what I already suspected: The house payment was forty-five days late.

It had to be an oversight. If we had fallen behind on our bills, Sam would have told me. He wouldn't have risked the roof over our children's heads. We didn't have secrets like that.

I caught myself: Of course we had secrets. I just hadn't thought they were important ones. Last month when I bought Leo the

sneakers, to avoid an argument, I had lied that they were on sale.
I love you, but you spend too much money on the kids.

Maybe small secrets become larger ones until your husband goes missing and you discover your house payment is past due.

What else didn't I know about my husband?

I returned to the list of transactions and focused on the credits. I added up Sam's paychecks for the past two months. The total was lower than I expected. I went back six months and compared those to the current ones. The current deposits were significantly lower. Two weeks before, there had been no deposit at all.

I struggled to decipher what it all meant. Had Sam been getting cash back from his paychecks, squirreling it away until he could escape? Had he gotten a cut in pay he hadn't told me about?

Fury surged, bitter and sharp. *What the hell, Sam?*

I swept the framed picture of Sam and the kids from the shelf so that it fell facedown on the desk, painted that shade of green because Sam said it matched my eyes. I yanked open a drawer and lobbed the photo inside. The glass spiderwebbed.

Perversely satisfied, I slammed the drawer.

I gritted my teeth against angry tears. It wasn't just Sam. It was all of it. The attack on the trail. My patient's near-fatal poisoning. Finding Audrey with women I didn't know. My father. Myself.

Then there was Carver Sweet, a man who had killed his wife and knew where we lived.

I waited until my hands stopped shaking before turning my attention back to the computer, moving on to our cell phone records. I clicked on Sam's number, looking at his calls and texts.

Two numbers stood out: One I recognized, one I didn't.

Sam had texted only two numbers since his disappearance: mine and, apparently, Ozzy's. Sam's friend had lied to me.

The number I didn't recognize appeared three times on the day of his disappearance. None of the calls lasted longer than five minutes. One came in the morning, when Sam had excused himself to take that call. Another came only minutes before we spoke that final time.

Someone knocked, loudly, and I tensed. On the doorstep stood Mr. Baldovino, a shovel in one hand and a DVD tucked under his arm. He pulled it out and thrust it at me. "Here," he said.

When he saw me noticing the shovel, he added, "It's best to dig it out now since it's dormant."

It took me a second to realize he was talking about the Japanese maple. I leaned in to the doorframe for support.

"Thank you," I said as I took the DVD.

He grunted. "I don't like being lied to," he said. I was about to ask what he meant when he added, "There's no hanging basket."

Of course he had watched it.

"So," he asked, motioning to the DVD. "Who's the man taking your husband's car?"

WHEN I closed the door, the need for pretense gone, I slipped to the floor before my buckling knees could give way. I felt as if I had been hollowed and then refilled with an oily, sour blackness.

It had been easier to believe that Sam had left voluntarily. I had clung to it, the idea a raft in a vast and merciless ocean.

I told myself surveillance footage could be grainy. The man my neighbor thought was someone else could indeed be Sam, caught at an angle that made him appear unfamiliar.

Even as I placated myself with this, I knew I couldn't afford to. I needed to let go of the raft and see where this ocean carried me, even if I doubted my capacity to survive it.

I crossed the room to the DVD player and slid in the disc.

The footage was sharp. The slim hope I had harbored that Mr. Baldovino hadn't recognized Sam disintegrated instantly.

I fast-forwarded to the moments before I had returned home. I told myself there might exist a clue visible as Sam and Audrey left the house—perhaps he was carrying a bag, or the mystery woman followed. But in truth, I just needed to see him again.

When I did, my heart broke. The way he moved—hoisting Audrey over his shoulder, placing her on the sidewalk with an exaggerated twirl—was distinctly Sam. Lean, athletic, relaxed.

I focused on my breathing as I fast-forwarded past my own arrival home, then my hurried departure later. As I saw myself pull away from the house, I slowed the playback, my eyes intent on the blue Toyota Camry parked on the left side of our driveway.

It happened at twelve thirty-six a.m. The shape popped out of the right side of the TV screen and moved toward the car.

Mr. Baldovino was right. The man on the screen was not Sam. He was instantly recognizable: Huge, still wearing the same clothes he had been the night before, the attacker from the trail slipped into Sam's car and drove away.

The thief hadn't needed to break a window or force the lock. All he'd had to do was pull Sam's keys from his pants pocket.

Chapter 5

I MADE A COPY OF THE DVD and put it in my desk drawer. I slipped the original in my purse, along with a still I'd printed of the man who had taken Sam's car. The man I believed to be Carver Sweet.

At the police station, I asked for Detective Ray Rico.

Like the night we'd met, Rico wore a crisp white shirt, but this time instead of bacon, his tie was embellished with tiny hot dogs.

"Back to cured meats, I see." I handed Rico the DVD.

"This is the closest I get to them these days. Watching my sodium." He looked down at the DVD. "What's this?"

"You heard about Sam?"

"I got a copy of the report."

"Hear anything yet?"

"It's only been a few hours." I caught the hint of frustration in his voice. I knew how crucial these early hours were. "You okay?"

The question surprised me, and it required a longer answer than I had time to give. "That's footage from a neighbor's camera. I'm pretty sure Carver Sweet took my husband's car."

Rico motioned toward the back of the station, but I shook my head. "I have somewhere to be, but I wanted you to have that."

His eyes remained sharp. "You didn't answer my question."

I wanted to trust Rico, but I knew the first person the police looked at when a husband went missing was the wife.

"Only thing that will make me okay is finding Sam and Carver Sweet being arrested."

"We'll find them both, Dr. Larkin," he said. "Torres mentioned you found a wrapper folded into the shape of a dog. The number two written inside."

"A friend thought it might be an S."

"Looked like a two to me." A simple statement, but it was as if I had been carrying a heavy piece of furniture up a staircase and Rico had suddenly taken hold of one end.

"That night on the trail, you asked if the number three meant anything to me. Did you find something like that?"

"Not origami." Rico stared in that way he had, his eyes scraping my skin. If I'd had secrets, I would've confessed them all. "It was a rock. Painted with the number three. It's being analyzed."

"Where'd you find it?"

"In Carver's car."

I bit my tongue with enough force to draw blood.

Carver. I imagined him in a moldering basement hundreds of miles away, inflicting horrors on my captive husband.

"No news on where Carver might be?" I asked.

"Nothing yet, but we're looking."

I sensed I'd be getting no more information from Rico. Besides, I needed to get to the grocery store. Just thinking about my next stop stirred my irritation and thus my impatience.

"You'll reach out if you hear anything?" I asked.

Detective Rico gave a curt nod, then smoothed his hot-dog tie. "Of course," he said. I was twenty-five percent sure I believed him.

Ten minutes later, I pulled into the grocery store parking lot.

Inside, I approached the customer service desk and a blonde whose tag gave her name as Beth R. I asked for the manager.

Beth R. pushed her glasses up the bridge of her nose. "Is there something I can help you with?"

"Not unless my husband is texting you too."

Her eyebrows shot together. "I'm sorry?"

"The manager, please." She scurried away as if I'd kicked her.

Beth R. returned a moment later with the store manager, whose attempt at a grin faltered when he saw me.

"Hey, Ozzy," I said, my voice full of false cheer. "I figured you'd be working today."

Ozzy looked uncomfortable in his button-up shirt and tie, his usual curls restrained by hair gel.

"It's . . . uh . . . great to see you again, Cassie."

"I don't think you mean that, but that's fine. Right now, I'm not really glad to see you either."

Beth R. pretended to straighten something below the counter even as she leaned in to better hear our conversation.

Ozzy noticed and gestured toward an office behind the counter. "Do you want to talk somewhere quiet?"

"Oh, I'm good. So, I was going over Sam's phone records, and I noticed you guys have been texting. Which is weird, because last night you said you hadn't heard from him."

Beth R. dropped the pretense, staring openly now.

Ozzy brushed aside an errant curl, his dark eyes pleading. I sighed and headed toward the office.

He closed the door behind us. "Thanks for—"

I cut him off. "Why did you lie to me?"

"Sam's my friend, Cassie."

"You should have told me. If not for me, then for the kids."

He stuffed his hands in his pockets and looked away.

"After we spoke, Sam texted me too." I held out my phone. "But here's the thing—I don't think it was Sam. And if it wasn't, then Sam probably wasn't the person texting you either."

"You can't be sure."

"True." I took the picture of Carver Sweet from my purse and placed it on his desk. "But there's this. Two nights ago, I witnessed this man assaulting a woman. Last night, while I was on your doorstep, the same man took Sam's car from our driveway. He had Sam's keys. Why wouldn't he have his phone too?"

Ozzy still couldn't meet my eyes. "Sam texted you he wasn't alone. Maybe he knows this guy."

"Look, Ozzy, I don't care if Sam's having an affair." My voice was tight. "I need to know that my husband, the father of my children, isn't lying unidentified in a ditch on some rural road."

Ozzy sank into a chair behind the small, laminate-topped desk. When he spoke, his accent was thick. "He's having an affair."

My chest hitched, but I forced myself to say: "Tell me."

He loosened his tie. "I went to the school about a month ago to see if Sam wanted to grab coffee, and I saw them walking together. He told me she was a parent of one of his kids, and I believed him." He folded his hands. "I saw her again last week in his car."

"What were they doing?"

"Nothing like that. It just looked . . . suspicious. Then when he was at my house a few days ago, he left the room to take a call. I'm not going to judge, but I didn't want to see him throwing everything away, you know? So I called him on it. He denied it, told me he was trying to help a student of his. Hannah."

Ozzy looked embarrassed. "I believed him. But then he texted me later and asked me not to say anything to you, said you guys were just working through some crap."

"When was that?"

"A week ago."

Before Carver Sweet had access to Sam's phone.

"It was just those texts? You never again spoke about the affair in person?"

He smiled. I recognized the expression. It was the same one I had seen on Torres's face earlier. Pity.

"We spoke briefly. I told him whatever was going on with Hannah's mom needed to stop. He said, 'It's already gone too far.' That was it. I didn't push. He knew he'd screwed up."

"What's her name?"

Ozzy shook his head. "I don't know."

"Then what did she look like?"

"She had brown hair, or dark blond. She was short. Then again, Sam's tall. Most women look small next to him." He hesitated, trying to think of more details. "I think they met at a coffee shop downtown."

A coffee shop downtown. Yeah, that narrowed the options.

"Last night, what did Sam say in his texts?"

Ozzy looked down at his desk. "He said he was sorry."

My chest tightened. "For what?"

"For putting me in the middle, I guess."

When the silence stretched, I prodded, "What else?"

"He told me not to worry and that if I talked to you, I should tell you the same. Honestly, I thought he'd be back by now." Ozzy looked up, his expression hopeful. "It's been less than a day."

I pointed at the picture of the man taking Sam's car. "If he's taking time to work through his issues, how do you explain this?"

As Ozzy realized he had no explanation, the optimism drained from his face. My expression remained unchanged. I had started to lose hope the moment I had seen Carver Sweet on the screen.

THERE were no recent charges for coffee shops in our bank records—either Hannah's mom had paid or Sam paid cash.

Picturing Sam with another woman, *touching* another woman, I staggered on a memory: me as a teenager, punching a girl in the nose. Because she ridiculed me for not having a mother.

Another time, a boy, a knee to the groin. I hadn't wanted him to touch me.

You need to stop, my father had told me.

I can't stop, I'd said, even as I had realized how badly I wanted to. So my father had paid for kickboxing lessons. With the pads, I could hit harder and my opponent didn't get hurt. I wished I had kept up the sport, because I very much wanted to kick someone.

The closest coffee shop to the school was popular with students. Sam wouldn't have gone there. Not enough privacy.

The four spots most likely were a short drive away. I started with the one across from the bookstore. No one recognized Sam.

I got lucky at my second stop. A barista with a plug that stretched his earlobe nodded when I showed him Sam's photo.

"That's that teacher dude," he said. "Nice guy. Always tips."

The shop smelled of coffee and cinnamon rolls, and my stomach grumbled. I hadn't eaten since the spaghetti Sam and Audrey had made the night before. I grabbed a banana from a basket on the counter and a pesto-mozzarella sandwich from the rack.

As I paid, I glanced at the young man's name tag. Josh. "When's the last time you saw him?" I asked.

"He used to come in most days, first thing, but I haven't seen him for a couple of weeks," Josh said. "But I've been starting later, so he could be coming in before my shift." He added that the manager, Linda, worked most mornings.

When I asked to speak with Linda, the young barista tugged on his apron. "She had to run out, but she'll be back later."

Damn.

I gave Josh my contact information, then asked the question I'd purposely saved for last. "Did Sam ever meet anyone here?"

The chatty barista's eyes went flat. "He usually came in alone."

I had a teenage son. I was pretty good at recognizing the lies of young men. It was the older ones I apparently couldn't read.

"So who'd he meet when he did have company?"

Josh gnawed on his lip. "I said he was alone."

"You said *usually*. Which implies sometimes he wasn't."

The barista realized his slip. His knuckles went white.

Though I was sympathetic to Josh's situation, that didn't mean I wouldn't push. "I get it. I wouldn't want to tell a wife that her husband routinely had coffee with another woman either. But I already know Sam met someone here. Hannah's mom?"

"I don't know her name." The young barista's cheeks reddened. Another slip. I felt sorry for him. I'd seen Leo do the same.

"What did she look like?"

Josh fiddled with his earring. "I don't remember."

"Blonde? Brunette? Redhead?"

"She wasn't a redhead. Brunette maybe? They always sat on the patio, so they're probably on video."

He hadn't thought to lead with this? "You have video?"

Josh nodded. The door opened, letting in an older couple. Josh stood straighter and smiled. "I'm not sure if we can let you see it, but I'll check with my manager as soon as she gets back," he said.

He started to walk away, but on impulse, I reached out. "What do you get paid a week?"

He raised an eyebrow. "A couple hundred. Why?"

"You convince your manager to send me that video, and I'll return with a week's pay."

For the first time, Josh looked happy that I'd come in. He grinned. "Probably should've said five hundred, huh?"

Then he tightened the strings on his apron and hurried away to take the couple's order.

Time seemed to pull the sun through the sky at an alarming speed. It was already time to pick up Audrey.

Waiting alongside the curb, I had three minutes to inhale the sandwich before Audrey climbed into the car. I offered her the banana. She stuffed a third of it in her mouth. Though a tiny thing, my daughter had the appetite and eating habits of a piranha.

Around a mouthful, Audrey mumbled, "What's a peed-o-pill?"

I used a familiar trick. "Can you use it in a sentence?"

"Your dad is a peed-o-pill. P-E-D-O-P-H-H-I-L-E."

My shoulders tensed. She must have really studied the word to spell it so perfectly. "Did someone say that to you?"

I pulled into the heavy after-school traffic.

"I know I'm not supposed to talk to strangers." She sounded offended.

"Then why do you ask that?"

"'Cause of the note the man left in my backpack."

I pulled to the side of the road abruptly. "What man?"

"A man with a funny-looking shirt. It had a bear on it, smoking something. Bears can't smoke." Audrey smiled.

I tried to keep my voice calm. "Did this man say anything?"

Audrey shook her head. "I don't think he wanted me to see him, because he left the note when my backpack was still in the cubby. But I saw him because it was my day to water the plant."

I grabbed my daughter's backpack and reached inside, where I found a crinkled Post-it that read: "Your dad is a pedophile."

"I showed Ms. Dickerson the note, but I don't think she knew what the word meant. She had a funny look on her face when she read it."

I expected I would be getting a call from Audrey's teacher.

"Ms. Dickerson tried to keep it, but I wanted to show it to you so I took it back. That's why it's wrinkled."

Audrey fished a gummy worm from her pocket, picked off the lint, and popped it into her mouth. "Then I asked Bonnie, she's in third grade, and she said it means someone who likes little kids."

So I could probably expect a call from Bonnie's parents too.

"Did you see where the man went?" Audrey shook her head. "Do you remember anything else? Like, what color his hair was?"

Audrey's face scrunched in thought. I hoped I was wrong about what was coming. "I don't think he had any."

My grip on the steering wheel tightened.

"I don't understand what Bonnie meant," Audrey said. "Of course Daddy likes little kids. I'm a little kid, and Leo's not but he used to be, and he loves us."

"Yes, he does." I reached across the console to the back seat to squeeze Audrey's hand. "A pedophile isn't someone like Daddy. It's someone who says they like kids but who hurts them."

Audrey nibbled on the edge of her thumbnail. "Oh, and he put an envelope in my backpack."

"An envelope?"

"I know I'm not supposed to take anything from strangers, but he put it in my backpack, so that's different, right?"

"That's different. You didn't open it?" I had no idea what was inside, but I didn't imagine it would be anything I'd want her to see.

"No. Is Daddy home yet?"

I took the envelope from Audrey's backpack and stowed it in the glove box. I knew I had to tell my children that Sam was gone, but I wanted to break the news tonight, after Leo's game. So I told Audrey the lie I had been practicing, "Your dad has to be away at his conference a little longer than expected."

"Okay," she said. "Can we get ice cream?"

"I have to drop you at Zoe's so I can run an errand."

"After?"

Because of her transplant, I had always been careful about

my daughter's diet, but I found myself unable to deny her this.

"If there's time before Leo's game."

Audrey bounced in her booster seat, humming off-key. I dreaded the evening ahead, when I'd have to break my daughter's heart, and open the envelope, which might break my own.

As I drove, I realized there was one possible witness to Sam's disappearance who had received only a passing interrogation: our daughter. I turned down the radio and asked, "Did you and Daddy have fun trick-or-treating last night?"

"Mm-hmm. But where did Daddy go?"

I pulled in front of Zoe's house and parked. I turned to face Audrey. "I'm not sure. I thought we could figure it out together."

I kept my tone light, as if I were suggesting a game. "I saw that pumpkin you mentioned," I prompted. "It was cool."

"The puking one?" She smiled. "Do you think it would be hard to make? Daddy's good at art, so I bet he could do it."

A hand closed around my heart. "He could. Did he see it too?"

Audrey's shoulders rose, then fell. "He was talking to the lady."

The hand holding my heart squeezed. "What lady?"

"The one in the house."

I thought of the neighbor, Helen. I described her to Audrey and asked, "That lady?"

Audrey shook her head. "The lady in the house with the broken windows."

I forced my words out slowly to hide my surging anxiety. "Was she on the steps with you guys? Or inside the house?"

"Like I said, in the house."

"Was the porch light on?" Realizing it was starting to sound like an interrogation, I added, "Just tell me what you remember."

"I don't think the light was on. She didn't have candy."

"Do you remember what the woman looked like?"

At first, she didn't answer. Then she said, "Her hair was gray. Her face was gray too. Except for the black marks on her forehead. I think it was supposed to look like she was broken."

So she was in costume. A sudden thought chilled me: *If* she *was even a* she. "Was the woman big? Was she as tall as Daddy?"

"I don't think so. Daddy's tall."

"Did she go to the haunted house with you and Daddy?"

Audrey squirmed in her seat, turning away from me and toward the window. "I don't remember. That's when I saw Savannah."

I was certain my questions were making Audrey uncomfortable. Did she sense what might have happened?

"You seem sad."

Audrey's voice was small when she answered, "I don't like that Daddy left me."

My heart broke, and I leaned into the back seat to kiss the top of my daughter's head. "I don't like it either."

My daughter's face filled with the light of sudden clarity. "I know! Why don't we just call Daddy and ask him where he was?"

I squeezed her hand, and then told her a truth that nevertheless felt like a lie. "I don't think Daddy's available right now."

"It doesn't matter," Audrey said. "Daddy will call us. He always does when he goes away."

I thought, *Not this time.* But I said, "I bet you're right. Daddy loves you very much." The last part, at least, wasn't a lie.

PARKED outside the high school, I opened the glove box and pulled out the envelope. I tossed it on the passenger seat, took out my phone, and dialed. My father answered on the first ring.

"Cassie?" The excitement in his voice chipped at my heart.

"Hi, Red." It had been a long time since I had called him Dad.

"How've you been, sweetheart?"

How to summarize six years of life in less than thirty seconds? "The clinic's doing well, and the kids are pretty amazing."

"They would be. Audrey—she's okay?"

"She's okay," I confirmed. "Leo just got his permit."

He chuckled, a familiar rumbling. "Teaching you to drive . . . scariest months of my life."

My father wasn't exaggerating. In my teens, I had been a reckless driver. Back then, I had been reckless in most things.

"I got better once I had kids."

He sighed at that. "I'm sure you're a great mom."

"There's nothing I wouldn't do for them."

An uncomfortable silence followed. Then: "I should've been tested." It was the closest my father had ever come to an apology. "But you know how I hate needles." Apology ruined.

Audrey had been born without bile ducts in her liver, a condition known as biliary atresia. Not that we knew for the first few weeks. She seemed to have perfect health and a sunny personality.

Then her pink skin had started to yellow, and she had gotten cranky. At the doctor's appointment, I had known what I would hear: Our daughter needed a transplant. Audrey now carried a piece of Sam's liver inside her.

"There was no need," I said. "Sam was a match. Audrey's fine."

"Still, I should've been there for you, and for my granddaughter." Since he had never met Audrey, it was strange hearing him call her that. "Is everything okay, Cassie?"

I stared at the envelope. "I've had better weeks."

"Is there anything I can do?"

When Audrey had been a newborn, my father had asked this same question. When I had said yes, there was, he had changed his mind about the offer. After all these years, I should have been able to forgive him, but I had never been much good at that.

When I didn't respond, he asked, "What's wrong?"

Speaking to a man who had become almost a stranger to me, it was safe to say the words aloud. "I think Sam's left me."

"I'll get a flight. I can be there tonight, tomorrow at the latest."

"No," I said.

"Why'd you call, sweetheart?"

"I told you. Sam's gone."

His voice was gentle as he prodded, "But why me? We haven't talked since Audrey was a baby."

There it was. I closed my eyes and drew a deep breath. "When I was a child, did I have panic attacks?"

"Are you having them now?"

"I'm not sure."

I briefly described the sensations I'd experienced when Carver had thrown that woman over the embankment. The darkening vision. The way the air around me felt as if it had weight, grinding me into the ground and making each breath a chore.

A few seconds passed, no longer, before he answered, "Never." But the hesitation made me wonder if he was keeping something from me.

"It felt—*familiar.*"

No hesitation this time. "You were a colicky baby, a stubborn toddler, and living through your teen years nearly killed me," he said. "But you also had a generous heart and a smile that knocks me back every time I see it." He paused. "I miss that smile."

I didn't know what to say to that, but, fortunately, my father let me off the hook. "You've broken both your right arm and your left ankle. That doesn't include the sprains. But no, no panic attacks. Still, it's understandable why they'd be starting now."

"Thanks, Red," I said. "I— It was good talking to you."

I had already moved to disconnect when I heard his voice again. "Wait. I'll be there on the first flight that has an open seat."

Then he was gone.

I sat there for a couple of minutes, clutching my phone and eyeing the envelope on the passenger seat. Still not ready to open it. But there was something equally uncomfortable that I could do.

I hadn't written down the number, but that didn't matter. I had memorized it the moment I had seen it in Sam's phone records.

Uncertain what I would say, I dialed anyway.

On the third ring, a woman answered.

"Hello." She was out of breath.

I introduced myself and awaited her response. Would she recognize my name? And if she did, would she pretend not to?

She replied with a single word, "Yes." The woman recognized my name but didn't offer hers in return.

I wasn't sure what to say next. What was the protocol when speaking with a woman you suspected was sleeping with your husband? I settled on, "Do you have a daughter named Hannah?"

"I don't have kids, but I mentor a girl named Hannah."

Sunlight flooded the car's interior, but it was an illusion. The air was frigid. "Can we meet?" I asked.

In my head, I had a list of what I expected her to say. *Yes. No. Go to hell*. What she actually said wasn't on that list. Not even close. The woman with the unfamiliar number and unrecognizable voice sighed, deeply, then said, "We've already met."

Chapter 6

WE'VE ALREADY MET.

When I asked the woman to explain, she gave me her address and said she would be home in half an hour. When I pushed, she said, "Later." Then she hung up.

That wasn't at all how I'd expected that call to go.

With twenty-eight more minutes to kill, I got out of the car.

Santa Rosa High's hallways were nearly empty at that hour. Though this was Sam and Leo's domain, it wasn't a place I had visited more than a couple of times.

My sneakers squeaked as they led me to the door marked ADMINISTRATION. Before I entered, I adjusted the envelope tucked under my left arm. I hadn't been able to open it, or leave it behind.

Behind the counter sat a blonde wearing a green sweater and an expression of annoyance. It was directed at her computer screen, but she swiveled to share it with me.

I asked for Sam. When I mentioned his name, the woman's expression shifted, the edge of hostility unmistakable.

"Are you one of the parents?" she asked.

I felt suddenly reluctant to introduce myself, so instead, I repeated, "One of the parents?"

She motioned toward the envelope. "Is that for Mr. Diggs?"

She waited for me to speak, but I pressed my lips shut. Cranky Blonde seemed the type who liked to fill silences.

She said, "If you're one of the parents, you really should talk to Mr. Diggs. He's handling the situation."

Before I could ask what she meant by "situation," a man with an Adam's apple the size of a golf ball emerged from the office, shrugging into his coat. He stopped in front of me.

He smiled. "Did I hear you needed to speak with me?" he asked, extending his hand. His palm was slick. "I'm Charles Diggs, the principal here, but you can call me Chuck."

"Cassie Larkin."

His smile slipped, for no longer than a heartbeat. The office attendant's reaction was less subtle. Behind me, she snorted.

"My husband is a teacher here, though I suspect you've already made that connection." I gestured toward the blonde. "Your office attendant mentioned there's a *situation* involving Sam?"

Chuck Diggs shot a less-than-friendly look at the office attendant. "I can't discuss personnel matters, but it was a pleasure meeting you, Mrs. Larkin," he said, moving to leave.

I blocked his path. "Have you seen Sam today?"

"No, I'm sorry. But we have so many on staff, I can't keep track of all of their schedules. Have a great weekend, Mrs. Larkin."

He bid a quick goodbye to the woman—apparently, her name was Pam—before he stepped around me and out the door.

"So you're his wife and you don't know."

I turned toward the office attendant, the taint of hostility I had noticed earlier now mingled with something else. Pity?

"Know what?"

"I can tell you Sam didn't come in today. I can't tell you why."

"He's been sick, I know that."

She snorted again. "He hasn't been to work in weeks."

My mind stumbled on that. *Weeks?* My first thought: Why hadn't Sam told me? My second: Why hadn't Leo?

I flashed to what she had said a few minutes earlier. "Is this the thing with the students?"

My question was vague, but the woman grasped at the excuse to tell me more. "Wives don't always know," she said.

I guessed then that a relationship had ended badly for this woman. She hated me for what she perceived as my ignorance. But I couldn't argue with her preconceptions. I didn't know. If she hated me for blindly standing by Sam, I would play to that.

"The students are lying."

I expected outrage but got confusion. "You've talked to his students? I wasn't aware any of them had officially come forward."

I swore to myself before changing stories. "Of course I haven't spoken with any students. I only meant the rumors aren't true."

"It's more than rumor, Mrs. Larkin." She stood and hooked the strap of her purse over her shoulder. "People sometimes do stupid stuff, even teachers as respected as your husband."

"You've wanted to tell me something ever since you heard my name. So tell me."

Spots of red blossomed on her cheeks. "Sam has . . . a reputation. He's a bit of a flirt."

Sam had always been friendly, and on occasion, the dimpled smile had been misconstrued as something more. "You're claiming he's friendlier than he should be with colleagues."

"Not with staff. With his students."

When it came to Sam, my faith had been shaken lately, but cold certainty filled me now. "You're lying."

She hadn't expected that. The red spots on her cheeks darkened. "A couple of weeks ago, I heard two parents talking. They said he has favorites, usually pretty girls. They said one girl who's got a one-point-something GPA got an A in his class."

"I trust you contacted the licensing board?"

She scowled at the sarcasm. "I checked, and it's true. Some of his female students are getting A's in his class while others are failing."

As her voice rose, mine quieted. "I assume you checked to see if the same is true of his male students?"

She quirked an eyebrow. "Why would I do that?"

"Did you check to see if the reverse is true—girls failing in his class but excelling in, say, history or math?"

"That's really not the issue here."

"I disagree. Considering all the data is *exactly* the issue."

Pam crossed her arms, her lips puckering at my challenge. "Regardless, when I learned about Sam's . . . *issue* . . . I felt compelled to call it to Mr. Diggs's attention."

NO BAD DEED | 361

"I'm sure that was a difficult decision for you."

She stood taller. "Awfully judgmental for someone who doesn't know what her own husband is up to."

My voice was a whisper, but she heard each word when I said, "I'd advise you to stop spreading rumors about my husband."

Allegations like this could ruin careers, true or not.

"Or what? You'll sue me? Get me fired? With who as a witness?"

Heat settled into my balled fists, and my cheeks flamed. Still, I kept my voice low. "Witnesses aren't always a positive."

My eyes landed on her desk. A file, closed, rested on the surface. A student's last name on its tab was obscured by a sheet of paper. But I read the first name clearly enough.

Hannah.

I LEFT Pam there, my knees unsteady as I walked back to my car. I climbed in, and before I could lose my nerve, I ripped open the envelope some creep had given my six-year-old daughter.

The envelope contained a single photo, printed on copy paper. There was no misconstruing the activity depicted.

Two tangled bodies, one of them my husband's.

The picture showed Sam in bed with another woman.

If she was a woman at all. The female was thin and faced away from the camera. She easily could have been in her teens.

I searched for signs of photo-editing software. That was Sam's face, but was that his back? Was that his arm?

After a few seconds, I had to look away.

I understood why this envelope had been given to Audrey rather than me. Whoever was behind the photo wanted me to know how easily my children could be hurt. The monster had gotten to Audrey. What if, next time, the intent wasn't just to deliver a threat?

That's clearly what this was. A threat against my family.

What wasn't as clear was who was in the photo with Sam. Was it this mysterious Hannah? Someone else?

I flipped the photo over. On the back, written in black marker, was a number: 1.

THE ADDRESS SAM'S MAYBE-mistress had given me was a Craftsman downtown with peeling white paint.

A brunette with wide eyes answered the door. She wore yoga pants and a sweatshirt, her dark hair secured in a ponytail. I would have recognized her even if she hadn't been dressed the way she had been on the trail. The bruises, the worst of them the purple-black of a ripe avocado, took up nearly half of her face.

She greeted me by name, then introduced herself as Brooklyn Breneman. "I'd shake your hand, but pretty much every part of my right arm is broken or sprained," she said.

What did I say to that—*Sorry?* I settled on a silent nod.

She stepped aside so I could enter. Her hair color was right for the photo I'd been given, but I wasn't yet sure about her build. One thing of which I was certain: the faint smell of hard alcohol.

She gestured to a chair for me, while she took the couch. She winced as she settled into the cushions, cradling her arm.

"Tea?" she offered. On the table sat a teapot and two cups. One was filled with an amber liquid that definitely wasn't tea.

I declined. She sipped from the filled cup. "This is my friend's place," she said. "I can't go back to mine until they arrest Carver."

"He knows where you live?"

"He knows a lot about me. Probably about you too."

Of course it was true. He had stolen my wallet and van. Still, the way she said it made my flesh crawl. "What do you mean?"

Brooklyn placed a throw pillow on her lap, then her injured arm on top of the pillow. "We have a lot to talk about. I guess I should start by thanking you. If you hadn't been there, I'd be dead."

I was having trouble finding my voice. I had so many questions, but one was more urgent than all the others.

"Do you know what happened to Sam?"

She nodded. "I know part of it, at least. But it's complicated."

"I can handle complicated."

Her expression was one of doubt. When she didn't immediately start talking, I prodded: "How do you know Sam?"

"He was helping me with Hannah."

There was that name again: *Hannah.*

"Helping how?"

"Hannah's . . . troubled," she said. "You know, of course, that Sam was suspended a couple of weeks ago?"

Though I did now, thanks to chatty office attendant Pam, it bothered me that this woman had known longer.

When I nodded, she continued, "I'm Hannah's mentor, through one of those youth programs. Her foster mom is cool, but her biological mom—she's not a nice person."

"I don't need backstory. I need to find my husband." I might've emphasized the last two words more than necessary.

"I don't know where Sam is. But I know where he *was*." She sighed, then drained her mug. "I'll tell you a story about Hannah."

"I don't—"

She held up her hand. "Hannah's about four years old, and she doesn't come when her mom calls her for lunch. Her mom hated it when she or her sister hid, so Hannah expects to be punished. Instead, her mom tells her she's going to teach her to garden. She hands Hannah a pair of work gloves and a shovel. In their yard, there's this huge oak tree, and her mom makes her start digging in a spot underneath. The ground is hard, and Hannah's a child.

"As she digs, her mom asks her what she wants to grow. Roses? Snap peas? Goading her. When Hannah finally manages to dig a small hole, her mom drops this sack on the ground and says something like, 'I know. How about we plant this?' That's how Hannah finds out her dog got hit by a car. It's also her first real memory."

The story is horrible, but I've come for answers, not stories. Still, I feel a pang of guilt when I ask, "Why is this relevant?"

"Because you should understand what Hannah comes from before making judgments on what she might've done to Sam."

My guilt burned to ash and scattered. "And what was that?"

"Hannah was having problems in Sam's class. He reached out to me. He was trying to help her, and it worked. Her grades and attitude improved. Then Sam and I—"

"You're claiming you're sleeping with my husband."

"He never hid the fact he was married."

"*Is* married," I corrected.

Her eyes dropped to her lap. "He's attractive, but it was his sense of humor that got me, and his empathy. He's a great guy."

"Glad you think so."

When she spoke, it was in my husband's defense, not her own.

"Hannah's eighteen now, so even if she and Sam slept together, she was an adult," Brooklyn said. "I think it's more likely, though, that Hannah knew what was going on between Sam and me and that she was jealous. She started spreading rumors that Sam had pressed her for sex in exchange for an A. Those rumors came to the attention of the administration. You know the rest."

Was that why Sam had kept his suspension from me?

"You said you know what happened last night."

She gave a slight nod. "We met a few blocks from your house."

I felt sick. "You've been to our home?"

Brooklyn opened a drawer on the end table and pulled out a small bottle of tequila. She refilled her teacup.

"The night you and I met, I was leaving your house," she said. "I had dropped off a bottle of cold medicine. That's all."

If I had arrived home earlier, would I have met Brooklyn there instead of on the trail? As if I had asked the question aloud, she said, "I knew you were working late."

I had memorized the log of calls and texts to Brooklyn's number. She and Sam had spoken twice the night of the attack.

The police's suspicions of me suddenly didn't seem so unfounded: The wife is there when her husband's mistress is attacked, and twenty-four hours later, the husband disappears. In Detective Rico's place, I would have questions too.

"So you arranged to meet Sam in this neighborhood . . ."

"Near this abandoned house," she said, and my skin prickled. I easily pictured the rotting pumpkin on the stoop and the shattered window. "We were only supposed to be a few minutes."

"Romantic."

"It wasn't like that," she objected. "We met to talk about Hannah, and to come up with a plan. Find a way to salvage Sam's reputation while also protecting Hannah. Audrey was with a friend, and Sam and I didn't want to leave her for too long."

Each detail was a blow: their clandestine meeting; Brooklyn's casual use of "Sam and I" as if they were a couple; her show of concern over my daughter. Audrey was not hers to worry about.

Though I doubted she would answer, I asked anyway, "What's Hannah's last name?"

She shook her head firmly. "I'm only telling you as much as I am because you saved my life, and because I want to find Sam as much as you do. But you know I can't give you her last name."

"I'll find out."

"Maybe, but not from me." A sad smile played at the corners of her mouth. "You hate me, don't you?"

"I don't know you."

"I'm sleeping with your husband. You know that."

Brooklyn nursed her tequila and waited. Finally I said, "Not really."

"Not really, you don't hate me? Or you don't really know that Sam and I are sleeping together?"

"The affair part, but I suppose both are true." I had spent a lot of time hating as a teen, and I had no more energy for it. I was focused on a single task: finding my husband. "You said you and Sam met on Halloween. When did you last see him?"

"I'm not sure of the time, but we weren't together more than a few minutes when I saw Carver. He must've been tracking my car." Brooklyn paused. Her voice wavered as she said, "I ran."

"Did you call the police?"

"As soon as I was a safe distance, of course I did."

"You didn't warn Sam?"

"Why would I? Carver was after me, not him." Her tone became dismissive. "I'm still not sure Carver's the reason Sam disappeared. Sam's obviously dealing with his own problems."

The anger swelled suddenly, hot in my chest. Before this happened, I would never have left Sam behind, especially without warning him. I would have gone to my death protecting him. If I were being honest, I was pretty sure the same was true now.

"You should've warned him."

Brooklyn refreshed her drink. "I slept with him too. Carver." Her face flushed. "Just once. It's not like with—" She choked back my husband's name. "Anyway, I guess I have a type. Unattainable men. Just didn't think I'd also pick a homicidal one."

Then Brooklyn stood and left the room, her steps wobbly. She returned a few minutes later with a small stack of photos.

"I took these from him." She pressed the photos into my hand. "I knew he'd been in prison for killing a girl, but the way he told it, he was innocent. Plus he was only eighteen or nineteen when it happened, so I let myself believe him. Then I saw those."

The first picture—yellowed, the paper flaking—was of a girl in her teens, head tilted and smile wide. I flipped to the back. A rough hand had scribbled a name on it: "Natalie."

The second photo, of a woman in her forties, was newer. The subject wore a blue dress and had been captured in profile. On the back of the photo was written another name: "Anne."

While questioning me, Detective Rico had mentioned both those names: *Natalie* Robinson and *Anne* Jackson.

There was no name on the back of the third photo. Only a question mark. But I didn't need a name. It was a photo of me.

I traced the question mark, wondering if the same pencil had etched the number two on the chocolate wrapper.

Though Natalie, Anne, and I weren't related, we could have been. We were all redheads with light eyes.

There was one more photo, facedown.

As I flipped it over, she said, "I'm sorry. But you had to know."

The last photo was faded, obviously decades old. It was Natalie. Her eyes were slits. She had been wedged in a box, then lowered in the ground, a mound of dirt at the edge of the frame. Dead.

I dropped the stack on the table, hands shaking.

"That's a copy of the original, which I turned over to the police. There's no picture of it, but Anne's dead now too. So that just leaves me, who Carver tried to kill—and you."

My fingers burned where I had touched the photo of the dead girl. "I don't know him."

"That doesn't mean he doesn't know you," she said. "And in case you're thinking I'm not his type . . ." She slipped the case off her phone and pulled out her driver's license, which had been tucked inside. "This is how I looked when I met him."

The photo showed the same blue eyes, but the hair was a shade lighter than mine. At one time, Brooklyn had been a redhead.

"I know this is a lot to take in," she said.

I wasn't convinced of my part in any of this. "That night on the trail, he didn't seem to know me."

"You're sure?"

I considered this. He had asked who I was, but it had sounded less like an inquiry, more like an accusation: *Who* are *you?* Was that the same thing as asking for my name? "The situation on the trail didn't exactly lend itself to introductions."

"So what do you remember Carver saying that night?"

I remembered the threat about letting Brooklyn die, of course, and Carver asking whom I loved.

Mouth suddenly dry, I poured myself a cup of cold tea. I drained the cup. Carver had said my life was screwed up but I didn't know it yet. As if he had known it because he knew *me*.

She said, "What I remember is he could've killed you, easily, but he didn't. He seemed shaken that you were there."

I was skeptical. "You say Carver killed Natalie. He killed Anne. He tried to kill you. So why wouldn't he kill me?"

"I only know what I believe."

"Which is?"

She hugged a pillow to her chest with her good arm. "Before he killed Natalie and Anne, he loved them. I think that's his pattern. He identifies a woman who interests him, stalks her, woos her. Then he gets bored, or angry, and he fixates on someone new."

I studied her eyes, wide and blue. Innocent, or the illusion of it anyway. I looked for tells that she was lying, but I could find none.

She continued, "I think he fixated on you while he was following me, because of my relationship with your husband."

If I believed her, there was a question I needed answered. I braced myself and asked, "Was Sam planning to leave us?" Because it was *us*—me, Leo, and Audrey—that he had abandoned.

"If he was, it wasn't for me."

This was the first statement I was sure was a lie.

"Early on, I had illusions it might be something," she said. Too quickly. "But it was never that way for him."

I pulled the envelope from my purse. "There's a photo I'd like to share with you too." I slid it across the table. "Is this you?"

Her face blanched, but she recovered quickly. "No."

On this, I believed her. The woman in the picture was thin like Brooklyn, but taller, with longer arms and a narrower torso.

"Is it Hannah?"

Brooklyn remained silent, her eyes cemented to the photo.

"Is Hannah a brunette?"

She looked up then, and her nostrils flared.

"I'm tired," she said. "Call me if I can be of more help."

We both knew if I did call again, she wouldn't answer. Brooklyn had brought Sam cold medicine and worried over his children. She had just had a conversation with his wife about his disappearance. She had likely believed that when Sam returned there was a better than fifty percent chance he would choose her.

But seeing a photograph of someone else with the man she loved confirmed a truth Brooklyn hadn't wanted to face: She wasn't special.

I understood, because I knew exactly how that felt.

I WENT straight to my son's football game at Santa Rosa High. I chose a spot at the top of the bleachers and huddled in my fleece-lined sweatshirt, alone, until Zoe and Audrey joined me midway through the game. They had stopped for ice cream.

"Thanks for watching Audrey."

"I'd pay to watch her." Zoe's fingernails were painted with messy lavender polka dots. "Even got a free manicure out of it."

Audrey looked up at me, a smear of ice cream still on her cheek. She squirmed when I wiped it away with my sleeve. "I tried to paint Smooch's nails too, but she wouldn't let me."

"Smooch is independent like that," Zoe said.

Midway through the third quarter, Audrey noticed a classmate a few rows down and left to sit with her. I filled Zoe in on my conversation with Brooklyn. Then I handed her the envelope.

"At school today, a man slipped this in Audrey's backpack."

Zoe pulled out the photo, then angled it to get better light. She swallowed a gasp and worked to keep the shock from her face.

"That's horrible." I wasn't sure whether Zoe referred to the man slipping the picture into Audrey's backpack or the actual act photographed. Both were pretty horrible. "She looks—"

Zoe stopped, so I finished her thought. "Young."

She turned the photo facedown on her lap and pulled me into a hug that nearly crushed me. "I'm so sorry, Cassie. This sucks."

"It does indeed," I agreed. "But is it real?"

That was the main reason I had shared the photo with Zoe. My social media–obsessed friend had a gift: Even in the age of Photoshop, she could find the flaw in any picture.

Zoe returned her attention to the photo. "Lighting seems consistent," she said, aiming for neutral even as her voice broke. "No shadows or highlights where they shouldn't be."

She furrowed her brow. "If it's edited, there aren't any obvious artifacts left behind, and perspective's spot-on."

My heart plummeted. "So it's real?"

When her eyes settled on mine, I knew she believed the photo to be authentic. Still, she asked, "Do you mind if I take this? I'd be able to tell more easily with better lighting and a magnifier."

I held up my hands. "Take it," I said. "And Zoe—thank you."

She tucked it inside her jacket. "You showed this to Brooklyn?"

"I did."

"No chance it could be her in the photo?"

"Depends if it's been edited," I said. "There's a number on the back. Just like with the wrapper. So . . . three, two, one. Counting down?"

"To what?"

I shrugged and handed her Leo's yearbook. "On the way here, I picked this up too. I thought maybe we could research all the older girls named Hannah."

"Let me do it," she said. Zoe grabbed my arm, nearly crushing it. She pointed to the field. "He's going in."

When I shifted my focus toward the field, I could see Leo had indeed strapped on his helmet and taken his place behind the defensive line. I felt my lungs seize, at once proud and wary.

On the field, the quarterback passed off the ball to a running back, for a gain of five yards. Leo was minimally involved, sprinting forward but stopping short when a teammate got there first.

The next down was different. The Panthers lined up on their thirty-five-yard line. The ball spiraled high in the air, too high. A bad throw, it was anybody's to take. Black jerseys and white converged, all fighting to be first to snatch the ball from the sky.

Leo won the battle, catching the ball. A second later, he was tackled. A pile of white jerseys pinned down my breakable son.

The referee's whistle trilled, the pile cleared, and Leo emerged, unbroken. I let the oxygen back into my lungs.

As the Panthers defense switched with offense, I was surprised to see Leo stay in the game. Riding a wave of euphoria, I was unconcerned that the rival defenders towered over the Panthers. Though nearly the same height as my son, the largest of the defenders outweighed Leo by, I guessed, fifty pounds.

The quarterback threw the ball downfield, on the side opposite of Leo's, and the white jerseys swarmed the receiver.

Leo was the farthest Panther from the ball. Only one player was farther: the mountainous defender who, for some reason I couldn't fathom, raced away from the ball. Then I saw, and I understood.

Turned as he was toward the ball, Leo didn't brace himself. When the hit came, helmet to helmet, Leo was knocked in the air, crashing to the turf as the defender came down hard, with every pound of his extra fifty. This time, Leo didn't get up.

Chapter 7

MY PHONE BUZZED ONCE in my pocket, but I didn't reach for it. My eyes were fixed on the midfield, where my son lay unmoving.

I raced down the bleachers, grabbing Audrey as I passed. At the edge of the track, I hesitated, pulling her hard against my chest.

Leo was prone on the field, circled by a contingent of medical and coaching staff. So still, like a bird swatted from its nest. I zeroed in on his chest, and saw the rise and fall of his breathing.

"Mom, is Leo okay?" Audrey asked.

"He just got a little banged up, that's all." Because anything else was unthinkable.

My mind raced through the possibilities. The helmet-on-helmet impact made concussion likely. Then there were the bones. The force could have snapped any of them. I worried most about the neck. With that could come internal bleeding, paralysis—death.

Then I saw Leo's foot move. Though it was only a twitch, I imagined him walking off the field, stiffly, maybe even limping.

But that wasn't how Leo left the field. My son left on a stretcher, carried from the field to a waiting ambulance.

I checked my phone. A text, from Sam's number but, I was now certain, not from Sam.

Sorry about Leo.

ONLY hours earlier, I had believed nothing I saw that day would disturb me more than the photo of my husband with another woman. Then Leo was taken away on a stretcher. Seeing him like that rattled me in a way nothing had since Audrey was hospitalized as an infant.

I hadn't taken that number 1 on the back of that photo seriously enough. With Sam already gone and my children safely with me, what more could be taken? The answer, apparently, was everything.

Previously, I had considered that the numbers on the rock, the wrapper, and the photo might be a countdown of days. Maybe that wasn't it. The night Detective Rico had found the rock, there lived three people in my home that I loved beyond measure. Then Sam had disappeared, leaving two. If something happened to Leo . . .

Though the diagnosis of a concussion didn't require a CT scan, the doctor was concerned enough about the hit Leo had taken to request tests. Once he was rolled away, Zoe left for a while to see to Boo and Smooch. I declined her offer to take Audrey. Until I found Sam, I wanted both of our children near me.

While I waited in the padded chair outside the imaging room with Audrey, I turned my attention back to the text I had received from whoever had Sam's phone.

Sorry about Leo.

I typed: *Who are you?*

I'm Sam. Why don't you believe me?

Because you aren't Sam.

Of course I am. If I weren't Sam, how would I know about the fight Leo and I had the night before I disappeared?

This stopped me. What fight? I hadn't heard about any fight.

"Sam" typed over my silence: *I'm sure Leo didn't mean the things he said that night.*

The realization hit like a slap. *You've been eavesdropping.*

You sleep on the left side of the bed. Your bathrobe is green, the same shade as your eyes. The same shade as my favorite bra.

My blood froze, and I pulled Audrey closer. *Did you hurt Leo?*

How would I hurt Leo? I wasn't there. Really, Cassie.

I'm going to the police.

They didn't seem to believe you the last time.

So he had listened to me, even there, in the police station. Unless he knew someone who had passed along this information? Both choices left me chilled.

Did you hurt my husband?

I'm fine. I've found someone who doesn't work all the time.

The words brought back an argument about my long hours at the clinic. More than a month before.

I'm not sure if this new relationship will work out, so I hope you can leave us alone. I know how you can be when you're jealous.

With these words, I could suddenly see Brooklyn, or the young woman in the photo, brutalized and left for the police to discover. With evidence on her that would lead back to me.

But I was more afraid for Sam. My hands trembled as I typed: *If you hurt Sam, I'll end you.*

The taunt came quickly, and I sensed the sick joy in it: *And how exactly will you do that? I mean, if I weren't Sam. Which I am.*

I went to medical school. I'll come up with something creative.

I think I should go to the police.

If he did, this conversation would cast as much doubt on me as on him.

Then he typed: *Especially after what happened with Lester. I heard you actually poisoned him. Poor dog.*

Anger flooded me. I stabbed out a threat: *I've decided whatever I do to you will involve scalpels. Retractors and clamps too.*

I know you're hurting, but at least you have the kids. I pulled Audrey closer still. *I hope to see them soon.*

WITH the texts threatening my children and Leo getting an MRI, for his knee this time, I was well and truly pissed.

I spotted Zoe walking down the hospital corridor and waved her over. She handed me my laptop bag. "How's Leo?"

"Mild concussion. Perla's on her way?"

"Right behind me." She returned my house key. "She found something at the house, but I'll let her show you."

When Perla Anderson arrived five minutes later, Zoe took Audrey to another set of chairs halfway down the corridor.

Years before, I had treated Perla's Rottweiler for hip dysplasia. It had been a while since I had seen her, but she was nevertheless who I'd thought of after the latest string of texts.

Perla wore jeans and a T-shirt proclaiming: I'M NOT LAZY. JUST BUFFERING. She had a master's in computer science, and smelled of clove cigarettes and the coffee she sipped from her travel mug.

She put down her messenger bag and motioned to the bag Zoe had just given me. "Is that it?" she asked.

I pulled out the laptop, logged in, and handed it to her. I did the same with my phone.

She tapped at the keyboard, her nails jagged nubs.

"Zoe said you found something at our house?" I asked her.

She paused in her typing to reach into her pocket, then opened her palm. There rested three white circles, each the size of a penny.

"Someone has been eavesdropping on you. I found these on your ceiling in the living room, kitchen, and master bedroom."

Perla took a sip of coffee, then reached into her other pocket. This time, she hesitated. "I found this too." She pressed a small, hard object in my hand. It was a USB wall charger, also white, the kind everyone in our family used to charge our cell phones.

I studied it, not understanding at first. Then I noticed it: a small hole that shouldn't have been there.

"A camera?" She nodded, and I shivered. "Where'd you find it?"

"Your bedroom."

My stomach roiled. "You're sure that's all of them?"

"I swept for other devices, but that's it, at least as far as bugs." I didn't like the way she said that last part.

"Is there a way to tell who's texting with Sam's phone?"

She shrugged. "It may not even be Sam's phone. With caller ID spoofing, it would be easy enough for the texts to appear to come from anywhere."

"Can they be traced?"

"It's possible, but it's not easy. Plus, you have other issues."

Perla tapped the screen, clicking through a series of obscene social media posts and photographs about a football player named "JL" and JL's girlfriend.

"What's this?"

"I pulled those from Leo's social media."

Teenagers have lives and secrets and bad choices they hide from their parents. Of course they do. Still, it was with unshakable confidence that I said, "Leo wouldn't do this."

"I figured. Obviously, your security's been compromised."

I felt naked, exposed. "Why would someone target a child?"

"People are jerks."

In this case, true enough. "So someone has our passwords."

"Which is why you should change them."

"But how could this happen?"

Perla chewed on a hangnail. "Someone could've physically accessed one of your phones, or your computer, or gotten in some other way. Phishing emails, for instance."

"I wouldn't have opened an email like that."

She smiled, in the same way I did when Audrey mentioned

unicorns. "There are other ways to steal passwords too. Someone could've planted a keylogger into your keyboard. Any software you have scanning for an intrusion would miss hardware. Or say you find a USB drive you think contains patient files. Plug it in, and the malware does the rest."

I opened my mouth to say I wouldn't plug an unknown USB drive into my computer, but she stopped me. "A shared computer is only as safe as its least diligent user. Most of this isn't advanced stuff. Anyone with access to a search engine could pull it off."

The door from Imaging swung open, and the radiology tech pushed Leo's wheelchair through it. Slumped in his seat, hands folded in his lap, my boy looked so much like a younger version of himself that my heart ached.

Perla took this as her cue to leave. She downed her coffee and stowed her travel mug in her messenger bag. When she pulled her hand from the bag, she held two plastic-wrapped packages.

"I figured you might need these," she said.

I took the packages from her. They contained two prepaid cell phones. When Perla tried to hand me my laptop, I pushed it away.

"I don't want that."

She stowed it in my bag and slung it with hers over her shoulder. "I'll check it out further and get it back to you."

I moved toward my son, but Perla touched my arm. Her eyes flashed with an intensity I suspected mirrored mine.

"Remember: Sometimes people are jerks," she said. "If someone's messing with your kid, it's okay for you to be one too."

AUDREY rested in the chair beside Leo's hospital bed, curled into a ball, head propped on my folded sweatshirt. With Audrey asleep, Zoe headed home, leaving me alone with Leo.

The MRI had shown Leo had torn his meniscus. No surgery was needed, but he would be off football for the season. While we waited for the doctor to release him, Leo shifted in his bed, restless and sullen. "Where's Dad?" he asked.

I could have fallen back on the teachers' conference excuse I had given the kids earlier. But there had been enough lies.

I told Leo the parts I felt he could handle. But, really, what kid could be expected to handle any of it?

The flesh surrounding his swollen eye had shifted in color over the past few hours from pomegranate to plum. But the signs of physical suffering were shadows of the pain Leo displayed now.

I rested my hand over his, letting it linger before pulling it back. "I've filed a report with the police, so they'll be looking for him."

Leo's eyes widened at my mention of police. I backtracked, reciting the line given to me by Officer Torres: "Don't worry. Odds are your dad chose to leave and that he'll be back."

Was it any better for Leo to think his dad's absence was voluntary? Judging by my son's face, not by much.

Audrey adjusted in the chair but remained asleep. At least one of my children was at peace.

"Does she know?" Leo asked.

I shook my head. "I don't think he'd leave us forever. Maybe he just needed to do something alone, something important."

"What's more important than us?"

"Nothing." It was the truest answer. "But maybe there's something he needs to do before coming back to us."

Leo didn't ask what that might be, and I didn't know how I would have replied. The question he asked, though, was worse.

"Do you think something . . . *bad* . . . happened to him?"

I lied as easily as I had ever done anything. "Of course not."

Leo's face relaxed. Then I steeled myself and asked, "Have you seen your dad around school the past couple of weeks?"

My son's jaw tensed, and his eyes darted away. "I don't know."

I tried to keep my voice soft, reassuring. "You don't know, or you don't want to tell me?"

"I don't always see Dad."

I decided not to push. I knew Sam hadn't been at school, and judging by the way Leo squirmed in his bed, he did too.

The second question was more difficult. "Do you know a girl named Hannah?"

Leo smirked at that. It was Sam's smirk, reaching all the way to his eyes. "Half the girls at my school are named Hannah."

"Any of them students of your dad's?"

I had picked my words carefully, but any hope I'd had that the rumors hadn't reached Leo disappeared with his smirk.

"Is that her name?" he asked, his voice small and a little angry.

I didn't want to assume we were talking about the same thing, so I asked, "Whose name?"

"No one's." It seemed my son had the same idea.

I was exhausted. "I know it's hard, but you've got to tell me."

"It's nothing, Mom. Kids say stupid stuff all the time."

I realized how hard it must be for Leo, attending the school where his father taught. There would be the expectation of good grades and even better behavior. And in times like this . . .

I took Leo's hand and squeezed. Did I really need to know?

"It's okay, Leo," I said. "You don't have to tell me."

Relief flooded his face. Then I handed him his new phone and relief shifted to confusion.

"What's this?" he asked. "Where's my phone?"

"We need to use these until we find Dad."

"But how will Dad call us?"

"He'll find a way," I said. "You can't call him, though, okay? Actually, don't call anyone for a while."

He scowled. "Why not?"

I couldn't keep this from him. Not if I wanted him to be safe. So I told him that someone had stolen his dad's phone. I told him about the audio surveillance of our home. Then I described the social media posts Perla had discovered.

"JL? I'm pretty sure that's the guy who hit me."

"Do you know him?"

He scrunched his nose in distaste. "I've seen him around, but I don't really know him. He's an idiot."

"How so?"

Leo sighed. "After he hit me, he said something. I was out, but a couple of the guys said he was talking about his girlfriend."

I guessed it was related to the posts, but still I asked, "What about his girlfriend?"

"I don't know. I was unconscious, remember?"

I *did* remember. I would always remember.

I had to ask, "You didn't post those, right?"

"Of course not." With his answer, I knew the fabricated posts had been meant to provoke. They were likely the reason my son was laid up with a concussion and injured knee.

Leo's eyes suddenly glittered. "Dad wasn't at the game?"

"I haven't seen him since yesterday."

"You're sure? You would've seen him if he was there, right?"

I remembered the crowd, not so large that I hadn't scanned it thoroughly at least twice. I considered the question carefully.

"I probably would've seen him." I was no longer certain enough of anything to speak in absolutes.

When he answered, Leo's voice held equal parts excitement and confusion. "If Dad wasn't there, then why did I see his car?"

It took a moment to process my son's statement.

"You saw your dad's car?"

"It was definitely his car. It had that stupid bumper sticker."

Teach children how to think, not what to think.

My son spoke with a certainty that unnerved me, especially given that Sam wasn't the last person seen driving his Camry.

"If he was at the game, he might've seen what happened on the field. You should call him, tell him I'm okay."

His voice rang with so much hope that I had to turn away. I couldn't make that call, and a second later, Leo realized this too.

"Oh. Right."

Thinking of Sam made me glance down at my phone. I had missed a call, which didn't make sense. No one had this number.

Before I could check my voice mail, the doctor walked in. She gave discharge instructions, which I memorized with a zeal born from a desire to control one small part of our lives.

As soon as she was gone, I checked my voice mail. It was Perla.

Her message was brief: "Some woman has been calling your old phone. She seems pretty desperate to talk to you, but she didn't give her name. Just a number."

She recited it quickly before hanging up.

Reluctant to call back from my new phone, I figured I would get the kids to the car and then look for a pay phone.

Before heading to the car, I texted Zoe my new number and told her we were on our way to the house. Then I scooped up a sleepy Audrey. We walked in silence away from the hospital to the car.

Audrey's arms were slack around my neck, her body drooping with fatigue. I found comfort in the weight of her and her warm breath in my ear. The task felt familiar. Normal.

I suddenly tightened my grip, my heart seizing. There, in the hospital lot, two rows removed from where our own car was parked, sat a blue Toyota Camry. Just like Sam's.

Leo saw the car the second I did. Too late, I realized I had neglected to tell Leo about Carver Sweet taking Sam's Camry.

Leo ran toward the car, his injuries making his gait awkward.

No, Leo. My mind screamed, but I remained silent. The words would have been wasted. There was no stopping my son.

My own legs began pumping an instant after Leo's, Audrey bouncing against my chest as I ran.

Even with his injured knee, Leo covered the distance quickly. First, he checked the back of the Camry for the bumper sticker.

Next, he peered into the back driver's-side window. But his urgency had faded. I had already scanned the license plate. I knew.

He turned when I caught up with him. "It's not Dad's."

"I'm sorry, Leo," I said. And then, reluctantly: "But it's probably a good thing it isn't his."

I started to explain to my son why I was relieved the car wasn't Sam's, but my words stuck in my throat.

Because I noticed three things, almost simultaneously.

First, a dark stain on the back seat where someone had installed a car seat. Stolen, I guessed, to cover the blood.

The second thing I noticed was that the car was definitely Sam's. Someone had swapped the plates and scratched off the sticker. But there was no disguising the smudge of white paint on the bumper from when we had repainted the fence.

Then I noticed the most important detail: In the glass, I caught the reflection of the man who had been driving my husband's car. The man responsible for the bloodstain on Sam's back seat.

CARVER Sweet stood on a balcony less than twenty feet away, cast in the yellow glow of the parking lot lights.

Scanning a cluster of cars to the right, Carver didn't see us.

I handed Leo my purse and set Audrey on her feet. Then I nudged them toward our car. "Lock the doors. Call the police."

Leo hesitated, the concussion and late hour adding to his confusion. "Who is that guy, Mom?" Then he saw my face, and his own went pale. "You can't—"

I cut him off, my words a determined rush. "I'm not letting that bastard out of my sight this time until the police come." I pointed to where Carver stood. "He can't hurt me from there. Go."

"But what if—"

"If he moves, I'll get in the car and run him over."

Carver turned his head in our direction, and Leo ran, pulling Audrey with him. Behind me, I heard the car door open, then slam shut, but I kept my eyes on the man on the balcony.

Upon noticing me, Carver cocked his head and went still, observing me in the way I had often seen in cats with birds. Even from that distance I could see his mind puzzling over his options.

"You again." He sounded almost amused.

"What did you do to my husband?"

He laughed so softly I barely heard it. "You must've seen the blood in the back seat." He stepped to the edge of the balcony and peered down. Gauging how far a drop it would be to the sidewalk below? "Two nights ago I warned you that your life was already screwed up, but you didn't know it then. I guess now you do."

"Where's Sam?" I asked. "Why're you doing this?"

"Heard that boy of yours took a nasty hit tonight."

My breath quickened. There was a tremor in my voice when I spoke. "You won't get close enough to hurt my son again."

He surveyed the ground. "I'm pretty close right now."

"Why don't you jump down here so you don't have to shout?"

And so you can break your leg, or, better, your head?

He weighed my request to jump as if it had been a serious one. "I think I'd make it, but I do need my mobility," he said. "You know who can take a fall—that friend of yours, Brooklyn. I came here looking for her, but she's already been released."

"She isn't a friend, but I'm glad I was there that night."

He chuckled, but his eyes closed to slits. "I was less pleased," he said. "So how do you know Brooklyn?"

I remained silent, listening for sirens, or passersby.

"Your *friend* isn't here, and she isn't at her apartment. Do you know where she might be?"

I said nothing, but my face betrayed me. "You *do* know." His expression darkened. "I'm going to need the address."

"And I'm going to need you to screw yourself."

A car passed, but it wasn't the patrol car I waited for. Carver shifted, his face cast in full light now.

"You seem to have forgotten your first question," he said.

I hadn't forgotten. I had asked what he had done to Sam.

"I found your husband's photo in your wallet, so imagine how surprised I was to find him with her," Carver said. "She left him behind, of course, and so I took him. He was breathing then. I don't know about now. I placed him on a pile of feed sacks and watched as he rolled, facedown, on the burlap."

I didn't know if what Carver said was true, but I recoiled at the thought that Sam might be miles away from the life we had shared for nearly two decades, cold and alone and injured. Or worse.

"I can tell you where your husband is, if you tell me where Brooklyn is."

I had no allegiance to Sam's lover. I had already saved her once, and that was more than anyone could expect of me.

I almost gave Carver the information.

Instead, I invented an address. But my hesitation gave me away. He shook his head. "I don't believe you," he said.

Carver tensed. I recognized the coiled energy, and readied for it. As if connected by a wire, we acted at the same moment. He sprang, landing on the grass, while I took off in a sprint.

Had he cracked his skull? Shattered a tibia?

Then I heard him. Footsteps behind me keeping pace, even if one footfall landed with less certainty. A sprain, I guessed.

I cut sharply to the right, toward my car. Leo, bless him, had already started it.

I focused all my energy on reaching my car. With Carver only feet behind me, it seemed too great a distance to cover.

It took me a few seconds to realize the car was moving closer. Slowly. Twenty feet from us, then ten. Then my son stepped on the gas. Carver bounced off the hood and landed on the asphalt.

I jumped in the car as Leo scooted to the passenger seat. Carver got to his feet quickly, injured but still fueled by his rage. Then he ran, disappearing just as the police cruiser arrived.

The darkness absorbed Carver as if he belonged to it.

THE police didn't find Carver, or if they did, they didn't share the news with me. Sam's Camry had also disappeared.

I didn't mention how Leo had plowed down my assailant, and the officer didn't notice the small dent Carver had left on the hood.

Detective Rico wasn't there, and for that, I was grateful. I wouldn't have been able to lie to him so easily.

After the kids and I were in the car, I turned to face them.

"We should probably talk about what just happened," I said.

Audrey leaned over the console that separated the front seats. "You mean about how Leo hit that man with the car?"

"That's part of it, sure."

While I had been talking to Carver, then the police, Audrey and Leo had waited in the car. I wondered, *How much had they heard?*

"You didn't tell the police I hit that guy," Leo said. It was rare that I had my son's full attention, but I had it now.

"That's right."

"Why not?"

I had reasons. Earlier, the person texting me had mentioned a fight between Leo and Sam. Then Perla had shown me "evidence" of Leo's cyberbullying. I didn't like where this was headed at all.

"I'd rather the police focus their attention on me."

Audrey inched farther onto the console so that she leaned against me. "Does not telling them count as a lie?"

"It does."

"Did that guy do something to Dad?" Leo asked.

Audrey's eyes snapped fully open. "What do you mean? Daddy's at a conference for teachers."

I took a breath. Then I told my daughter that I had kept the truth from her. As I talked, I studied Audrey's face, confused but expectant, then Leo's, lips drawn tight in anger. Even if Carver was arrested and Sam found, my children's lives had permanently changed. The bedrock beneath them had shifted, split.

Leo cut in, impatient. "You didn't answer, Mom. Did that jerk hurt Dad?" Leo's face may have been a younger version of Sam's, but the edge in his voice he had inherited from me.

I wanted to reassure him and his sister that their father was fine, but I couldn't. "I think that man knows where your dad is."

"Then the police should find him and ask him," Audrey said.

I kissed my daughter's head. "That's what they're trying to do."

My children bought it. But I didn't. I knew no one would fight as hard to find Sam or protect my kids as I would.

WHEN I pulled the car to the curb in front of Zoe's townhome, Audrey ran ahead to knock. By the time Leo and I reached her door, it was already ajar, my daughter wrapped around Zoe's waist. Boo bounced around their ankles.

"I tried calling you," Zoe said, and it triggered a memory. The phone call I had meant to return before running into Carver.

I swore under my breath, then excused myself, leaving the kids with Zoe, and got back in the car. I found a pay phone outside a convenience store a few blocks away.

The woman who answered was warm in her greeting. "I'm glad you finally called, Cassie. It's Helen, from Lake Park Drive."

The neighborhood where Sam disappeared. "I remember. You saw Sam and Audrey on Halloween."

She got quickly to the point. "Remember the Gardners' house?"

After Brooklyn's story, I would never forget it. "Abandoned two-story, rotting jack-o'-lantern on the porch?"

"That's the one," she confirmed. "This evening, a neighbor mentioned he saw Sam go into the house on Halloween."

She paused, and I reflected that pauses were rarely followed by good news. Finally she said, "He wasn't alone. There was a woman. This neighbor said she and Sam seemed . . . intimate."

I gripped the handset until my knuckles lost color. "Did your neighbor mention anything about this woman's appearance?"

"Not much. He described her as attractive, a brunette, but otherwise unremarkable."

Helen's description bothered me. Brooklyn? Or the young woman in the photo? Both were brunettes. Something else was there, but it was like trying to catch smoke with a pool skimmer.

"My neighbor thinks Sam might have been back at the house earlier tonight."

My heart raced. "Is Sam there now?"

"I'm sorry, honey, he isn't. But if you want to take a look, I could meet you outside with a key. I used to water their plants, and I don't think they've changed the locks yet."

I asked her to call Detective Rico and tell him what she saw, then thanked her for the information.

"It's what I would do if it were Bob," Helen said. "In the meantime, I'll call this detective, after I see if my neighbor can give me a better description of that woman."

I BEAT Detective Rico to the abandoned house and tried the door. The handle moved freely in my gloved hand. I slipped the key Helen had given me into my pocket and moved into the house.

I pulled a small flashlight from my sweatshirt pocket. Outside, clouds shrouded the moon, but a streetlight in front of the home cut through curtainless windows, illuminating my path. I kept the flashlight in my hand but didn't bother switching it on.

The house was large but uncluttered by furniture. I finished checking the downstairs and attached garage in a few minutes.

I started up the staircase, each step hesitant. Halfway up, at the landing, the staircase angled to the left, thwarting the streetlight's glow. I turned on my flashlight and swept the beam up the stairs, toward the doors of the bedrooms. One door was open, but the beam died at the room's threshold. The other doors were closed.

I climbed the last few stairs and then walked through the open door first. A bathroom. I checked the drawers. Empty.

Next, I checked the bedrooms that, judging by the pastel zoo animals in one and glow-in-the-dark stars in the other, had probably belonged to the children.

I saved the master bedroom for last, and my heart thudded as I approached its closed door. I held my breath as I pushed it open.

A single pair of plaid curtains hung in the window that faced the street. A king-size bed remained, stripped of its linens. I stood there, frozen, staring at that bed. I tried not to think of a reason it alone would remain in the otherwise empty house.

I moved closer to the bed. The mattress sagged in the middle, and the right side bore a body-shaped yellow-brown stain.

I dropped to my knees and focused my flashlight under the bed.

Other than small tumbleweeds of dust and hair, the only items I could see were a sock and a plastic hanger. Nothing that would prove Sam had been here.

I suddenly felt vulnerable, my back tingling as if I were being watched. I bolted upright, hitting my head on the edge of the metal frame that held the box springs. I rubbed the back of my head.

No one watched me. At least as far as I could tell.

My hands were icy as I slid them under the corner of the mattress. I shimmied it sideways in an awkward series of stops and starts, until gravity pulled it the rest of the way to the floor.

My breath came in heavy bursts, not because of exertion.

A small plastic wedge of yellow and red sat at the corner of the box springs.

I picked up the zombie teeth Sam had modeled Halloween morning. The last time I had seen him.

I stared at the piece of plastic resting on my upturned palm. It was smeared with reddish brown paint.

But of course it wasn't paint. It was blood.

Chapter 8

THERE WAS NOW NO OUTCOME I could imagine that ended in anything other than tragedy.

I pulled my phone from my pocket and fumbled to dial Rico.

I heard a car and moved to the window. No need to make that call after all—the police were already there.

The police cruiser arrived first, then the tech who took my gloves as evidence.

I had wanted to run out the back door, or at least dispose of the gloves, but those were the choices of a guilty person. I was merely desperate. As I talked with Detective Ray Rico, I hoped that desperation didn't show.

"Heard you had a run-in with Carver at the hospital," he said.

"Surprised I didn't see you there."

"I thought I could catch a nap at the station." He motioned toward his wrinkled shirt. Despite his disheveled appearance, Rico's eyes remained sharp, and his questions came quickly.

"You entered through the front door?"

"Yes."

"And you borrowed a key from a neighbor?"

"From Helen."

"I thought you said the door was unlocked."

"I borrowed the key but ended up not needing it."

I uncrossed my arms. I had read somewhere that crossed arms made a person seem guilty, and I couldn't risk that. Especially since I had walked out to meet the police with my husband's blood on my hand.

"Explain again what brought you here." There was no malice in his voice, but his gaze remained pinned to mine.

"Another neighbor told Helen he'd seen Sam going into this house on Halloween, and again this evening. She called me."

"What's this neighbor's name?"

"I don't know."

"What's Helen's last name?"

I didn't know that either, so I pointed across the street to Helen's house. "She lives there, in the yellow one-story."

I slipped my hand in my pocket to retrieve my phone, intending to show proof of Helen's call. Then I remembered that Perla had my old phone—the one Helen had called—and my return call had been placed at a pay phone.

Fortunately, I'd memorized her number. I gave that to Rico, as well as Perla's contact information.

He made a note, then said, "Tell me what Helen told you."

As I recounted the brief conversation, I again wondered why the neighbor's description of the woman bothered me. Attractive, brunette, and unremarkable, he'd said. A doubt burrowed into my brain, too deep for me to grab.

Rico stopped taking notes. "Why didn't you call the police?"

"Helen called."

But my spine prickled, and I knew before Rico said it. "We didn't get a call from anyone named Helen. We did, however, get a call from someone reporting an intruder at this address. Do you own a gun, Cassie?"

His voice was soft, and this was the first time he hadn't addressed me as Dr. Larkin, but I took no comfort in his casual approach. "I don't," I said with a rough voice I barely recognized.

"The caller reported that the intruder had a gun. After what your family's been through, I understand why you'd carry one." I'd heard somewhere that detectives usually knew the answers to the questions they asked. Did Rico have "proof" I had a weapon?

"Will officers find a gun inside the house, Cassie?"

Would they? "If they find a gun, it isn't mine."

I tried to read Rico's eyes, but they gave away nothing. "The other thing is, the key you gave us doesn't fit this lock."

It didn't? Uncertain how to respond, I said nothing.

"You've never been here before, right?"

"I've been in the neighborhood when I was looking for Sam, but I've never been inside this house."

"You mean, before tonight."

"Of course." I realized I'd crossed my arms again.

"Where are your kids, Cassie?"

I felt the crease between my eyebrows deepen. Not a question I had been expecting. "With a friend."

"Both of them?"

"Of course. Why would you ask that?"

"I heard Leo was hurt pretty badly playing football."

"He has a mild concussion and a torn meniscus," I confirmed.

"He can walk, though? And drive?"

Had Rico learned that Leo had run over Carver? My eyes darted to my rental car for signs an evidence technician was examining the hood, but the car sat untouched under a streetlight.

Rico noticed. "Need to leave?"

My heart hammered. "Leo's injured, but he can walk. As far as driving, he's only fifteen."

"But he has his permit?"

"What are you asking, Detective?"

"Just making sure I've got the details right. Before you came here, you dropped Leo at his friend's house?"

"My friend," I clarified. "Why are you asking about Leo?"

My question hung in the air, unanswered. "Does this friend of yours have a car?"

"Of course she does."

"Leo would have access?"

"What does any of this have to do with finding Sam?"

Sympathy remained in Rico's expression, but it battled with something else—suspicion? "The kid who hurt your boy? I heard the play was dirty, and I can understand why that might make someone angry. Does Leo have a temper?"

I was suddenly terrified of saying the wrong thing. "No more than any teenager. Why?"

"That kid crashed about an hour ago, hit a tree, but there's also a dent on the opposite side of his car. I'm guessing when the investigation is done, we'll find that someone ran him off the road."

"Are you insinuating Leo's involved?"

"He and the boy *did* have history."

It left no room for doubt: Rico knew about the cyberbullying. I wondered what else he knew.

"What were Leo and Sam fighting about the night before your husband disappeared?"

The texts. The first had alluded to the fight. And then the second one: *I'm sure Leo didn't mean the things he said that night.*

I realized then that Rico knew everything. Not everything as in the truth. No, what Rico knew was all the "evidence" manufactured by the person targeting my family.

"I don't know anything about a fight," I said. "I wasn't home that night, remember?"

"You didn't hear about it afterward?"

"We had more important things to discuss." My cheeks burned. "You know about the social media posts. They were faked," I said. "There was a photo too," I said. "I'm guessing you know."

I paused to steady my breathing.

"The number one was written on the back—three days, three numbers. I should've told you about it, but if I'm being honest, I didn't feel much like sharing a photo of my husband with another woman. But I can get you that photo in the morning."

Rico asked, "How'd you get the photo?"

"My daughter found it in her backpack, in her cubby at school this afternoon."

Rico studied me through narrowed eyes. "Is there anything else you haven't told me?"

I sighed. "I'm sure there is. I can't think of anything right now."

He made a show of consulting his notebook. "I talked to the principal at the high school. Chuck Diggs. Principal Diggs said Sam might have been sleeping with his students."

"He wasn't."

"Sam's friend, Ozzy Delgado, said the same thing, that Sam would never touch a student."

"Because he wouldn't have."

"But Ozzy did say he was involved with someone. So a cheating husband disappears. Either Sam left to pursue this possibly illegal relationship, or you found out about the affair and there was a fight. In this scenario, we don't know where your husband is—but we have an idea what led to his disappearance."

Rico let his words settle. I couldn't move. I wanted to leave, but I also needed to hear where he was going with this.

"Then your son gets injured in a football game, and the guy who hit him ends up in the hospital too. The story line shifts. Leo has a temper. He fights with his dad; then Sam disappears. Leo bullies this boy online, and then that boy nearly dies in an accident."

"Do you really believe my son is capable of that?"

He shrugged. "I don't much like anonymous tips. I prefer when the person making the accusations is willing to stand behind them. That said, I don't really know your son."

"Then let me tell you: He's not."

Rico tucked his notebook inside the pocket of his jacket. "I'm married. Twenty-six years, three kids. I understand the impulse to protect your husband and kids," he said. "But I *am* going to need that photo as soon as possible. If I'm going to find Sam, I'm also going to need you to be straight with me."

The detective's tone sounded less sympathetic, and when he walked away, I got the unshakable feeling I had disappointed him.

After checking in with Zoe, I sat in the car and contemplated my next move. Helen's description of Sam's lover continued to trouble me. Attractive, brunette, and unremarkable.

It certainly sounded like Brooklyn, but I suddenly seized on the last of the descriptors—*unremarkable.*

Then it hit me. When I had asked Audrey to describe the woman she had seen with her dad on Halloween, Audrey had told me the woman had been wearing a costume. Gray wig. Painted face.

Hardly *unremarkable.*

Helen had lied. More than that, she had described Brooklyn as she normally was, not how she had appeared on Halloween. So Helen had seen more than she had admitted.

I got out of the car, taking the blazing lights on in her house as an invitation. Not that I required one.

With my fist, I knocked on the door. Immediately it opened—but instead of periwinkle hair and a creased brow, I was greeted by a middle-aged man wearing a knit cap, a thin robe, and a scowl.

"What do you want?" The man pulled his robe around him. At this hour, it likely offered inadequate protection against the chill.

"I'm looking for Helen."

The man's expression shifted to confusion. "Who?"

I repeated myself, this time describing Helen. Seeing no reaction, I added details as if the man wouldn't know a woman lived in his home unless I chose just the right word to describe her.

The man shook his head. "My wife and I have lived here for four years." His tone was apologetic.

It hit me that I had first met Helen on the street, and, earlier that night, on the doorstep of the abandoned house. I had never actually seen Helen leaving or entering the house she claimed as hers.

"Maybe she's a neighbor?" I asked.

"Never seen anyone like that." His eyes drifted across the street. "So—do you know what's going on over there?"

"They're looking for a man who disappeared last night."

"Oh, it's about that teacher? Yeah, the police were asking around about him earlier."

I gestured toward the house where Rico and his team still milled. "Do you know who lived there?"

The name he gave me was not Gardner.

WHILE talking to the man, I had missed a call from Zoe. When I called her back, she rushed through her first piece of news: Perla had texted Zoe asking that I stop by. *Nothing urgent,* she'd texted.

Zoe quickly moved on to her second announcement: She had found Hannah, or so she hoped. Zoe forwarded to my phone a photo from the yearbook and an address.

I checked the time. Though it was late, it was a Friday night. Hannah would likely be awake. That's if she was home.

First Hannah's house, then Perla's, I decided.

I stopped at an ATM; then I headed across town to confront a girl who had started rumors about sleeping with my husband.

A COUPLE of blocks from Hannah's house near a twenty-four-hour market, I spotted a teen couple on the sidewalk. The boy wore jeans and a sweatshirt, hood pulled over his head. The girl wore the same, though her sweatshirt fit more snugly.

The girl reminded me of a colorful moth as she flitted from streetlight to streetlight, laughing, weaving, casually flirting with the boy who walked beside her.

She was older than Leo. Legally an adult, but not by much. I recognized her from the yearbook photo. Hannah Zimmerman.

They seemed on a course for the market, so I pulled in the lot and waited. The couple stopped twenty or so feet from where I was parked. I got out of the car, preparing to call out Hannah's name in my best nonthreatening mom voice.

Before I could, the young woman approached me, turning up the wattage on her smile. Hannah was probably used to getting what she wanted. She nudged her boyfriend forward.

"We were wondering if, like, you could buy us some beer." The boy's face flushed, his words nearly lost in his mumbling.

The mom in me couldn't help it. "Do you think it's really a good idea to be approaching strangers in parking lots?"

The boy looked chastened—I got the feeling he wasn't as committed to this as his girlfriend—but Hannah looked irritated.

She switched off her smile. "Who are you, my mother?"

"Your name's Hannah, right?"

The girl draped a hand on her boyfriend's shoulder. She tried for flippant. "Buy us a twelve-pack, and I might answer that."

"Let me rephrase: Your name is Hannah Zimmerman, and you claim your art teacher pressured you to sleep with him."

I kept my tone as neutral as my mood allowed.

"Mr. Larkin? Yeah, that's what happened." Hannah seemed

unconcerned that her boyfriend was within earshot. "I was, like, failing, and Mr. Larkin asked me to stay after class. He said if I slept with him, he'd give me an A."

I allowed myself a second of relief. That she had called him Mr. Larkin made me doubt the rest of her story. "So, did you accept his offer?"

Hannah looked at the boy, while he stared at the pavement. "Mr. Larkin's hot for an old guy, so sure. He gave me an A."

I decided against punching her. "How much?" I asked.

Her face scrunched in on itself. "What?"

"Let's cut the crap. You didn't sleep with my husband. So you got something, and my guess would be money. How much?"

She aimed to look offended. "I'd never do that."

Coming here, I had intended to play to Hannah's conscience: *Mr. Larkin could lose his job. You wouldn't want that, would you?* But Hannah wasn't the kind of girl who had a conscience.

I reached into my purse and pulled out five twenty-dollar bills. "Was it more than that?"

I had her interest. "Hyperthetically, what if I had, like, been paid to make something up?"

Of course, she meant *hypothetically*. No wonder she was failing most of her classes. I pulled out two more twenties.

"Anything I give you would be like a bonus. I'll give you forty bucks for every *hyperthetical* detail I find useful."

I felt a little bad for mocking her.

Hannah thought it over. "Okay, maybe someone asked me to start the rumors, but I didn't mind. Like I said, Mr. Larkin's hot."

I remembered Brooklyn's story about Hannah digging a grave for her dead dog. That and a couple of deep breaths kept me from giving in to my anger.

I handed her forty dollars. "Who asked you to?"

She shrugged. "Some bald dude I met in the parking lot."

I kept my expression neutral even as the words settled against my eardrums like spikes: *Some bald dude.*

"He gave me a few hundred bucks," she said. "I told you two things, so is that worth eighty?"

I gave her forty. "Can you describe this man, other than bald?"

"He was a big guy. And old. Like forty or fifty."

I handed over two more twenties. "Do you remember anything else about this man? His car? His clothes?"

"No."

"Did he have a scar?"

She considered. "Maybe." When I didn't hand over any cash, she added, "Come on, I should get something for that."

I gave her another twenty. "Did he say anything about why he would want you to start the rumors?"

She shook her head. "He told me to start telling my friends I'd slept with Mr. Larkin. When I agreed, he told me he'd know if I didn't keep my end of the bargain." Hannah wrapped her arms around herself. "He looked kinda creepy when he said that. Then he walked away. I never saw his car, and he never came back."

"When was this?"

She held out her hand, palm up. I gave her another twenty.

"I don't know. About a month ago?"

So long before that night on the trail.

Unnerved, I got back into my car.

Perla lived in an apartment in Fountaingrove. I climbed the steps, rang the doorbell, then rapped softly on the door.

My knocks went unanswered. I called her several times, but my calls rolled to voice mail.

I weighed whether I should try the knob. Perla's lack of response worried me. It was likely locked anyway.

It wasn't. I pushed it open, just a little, and called her name.

I risked a single step over the threshold, into the living room.

"Perla?" I called again.

Still no response.

Concern drove me deeper into the apartment. I walked quickly through the other rooms—one bathroom, one bedroom, and the kitchen. On the kitchen counter rested a mug of coffee. I dipped my finger in, piercing the oily sheen to test the temperature. Cool.

The apartment was empty, but I really had no way to tell how long it had been that way. Nothing seemed out of place, so I left, making sure the door locked behind me.

ON THE way to Zoe's, I stopped at home to check messages on the landline. There was one from my father: "I just wanted to give you a heads-up . . . I'll be there early tomorrow." He gave the name of his hotel and his room number.

Stubborn man. I allowed myself a brief smile.

For the second night in a row, when I got to her home, Zoe waited. My friend offered me the use of her computer to check my email. Then she hugged me and said, "We'll talk in the morning."

I didn't like the way she said that.

I knew I needed sleep too, but instead, I logged on to the computer. Most of the messages were work-related, and I was preparing to log off when one email stopped me.

Linda? Who's Linda?

Then I remembered: Linda was the manager from the coffee shop. As I had requested of the barista, she had emailed me a video link with a one-word subject line: *Thursday.*

The day Sam disappeared.

It looked like I owed Josh two hundred bucks.

I inhaled deeply and tapped PLAY.

The manager had sent only the clip that interested me, so the couple walked immediately into the frame. A petite brunette wearing a ponytail and yoga pants, followed by a tall man with dark, close-cropped hair. I recognized the crooked grin even from a distance. I rested my fingertips on the screen, on his face. *Sam.*

In the video, Brooklyn took a seat at a table on the patio, her back to the camera. Sam sat opposite her, his face fully exposed. He leaned into the table, his grin slipping, his expression suddenly serious. He reached forward to place his hand on top of hers.

Brooklyn seemed to relax when Sam touched her, her erect back softening as she, too, leaned forward. She reached across the table, touching Sam's face, and my own cheeks burned as if slapped. Sam brushed her hand away, and, for a moment, I allowed myself to believe the gesture was driven by loyalty to our marriage. But then he smiled again, and his hand was back on hers.

I was so fixated on the images that I didn't at first notice the time and date stamp in the corner. It read October 24. The video wasn't from the day Sam disappeared at all, but from a full week before. The video may have corroborated Brooklyn's story that she knew Sam, but otherwise it was a dead end.

When Sam and Brooklyn stood to leave, I saw him: a man at the table behind theirs, obstructed until they moved off-screen. The man was in the corner of the frame, barely visible, except for a thin crescent of his hairless head.

Chapter 9

Despite my certainty that I would never sleep again, exhaustion had overwhelmed me. I had fallen asleep on Zoe's couch. As I shifted into a sitting position, my stiff limbs protested, my neck cracked. I popped and snapped like a bowl of crisped-rice cereal.

I checked the time on my phone: 5:48 a.m. I needed to go to my father's hotel once the kids woke up, but I wasn't going anywhere without at least a gallon of coffee. I moved into the kitchen and sat on one of the stools that butted up against the countertop.

I had watched the video many times the night before. The more I watched, the less certain I became the bald man was Carver Sweet. I forwarded the clip to Detective Rico anyway.

Zoe pushed an omelet in my direction and brought me a mug of coffee, a piece of wheat toast, and a small bowl of sliced apples.

"You're totally getting a raise," I said, alternating between bites of omelet and sips of coffee. "Have you heard back from Perla?"

"Not yet. But there's something I want to show you." When I arched an eyebrow, she added, "After you eat."

She arranged strips of bacon in the skillet. "Daryl texted. Lester's apparently doing well, and he's bringing in lemon bars on Monday."

Lemon bars were Zoe's favorite. "Better than his brownies."

Zoe flipped the bacon in the pan. Then she turned down the heat and faced me, arms crossed. "I love you, Cassie, but you need to stop. That man Carver Sweet could've killed you last night."

When I thought of all my family had been through, my cheeks flushed with repressed anger. "I won't give him the chance."

"Seems he had one last night."

"I'm still here, unscathed. Great omelet, by the way."

"You're not changing the subject. Listen, Cassie, I know you want to find Sam, but you're being reckless, and stubborn."

"Thank you."

"Not a compliment."

"You said you had something to show me?"

She sighed and retrieved an envelope from a drawer. I pushed my plate away. I knew what was in that envelope.

"I need to get that photo to Detective Rico," I said.

"First, you need to look at this." Zoe laid the picture on the counter, then pulled out a magnifier from the drawer. "Two things. Look at the edge of the mattress." She held the magnifier over the far right of the image, where the mattress met the edge of the carpet. "It's a little off. Not quite as straight as it should be."

Even under the magnifying glass, the mattress looked straight to me. I wondered if Zoe was finding flaws where none existed.

She read the skepticism on my face. "The second thing is more obvious." She moved the magnifying glass so it hovered over where Sam's arm crossed his lover's body.

"See the woman's hips here?" I appreciated that Zoe used the word woman, not girl. She slid the magnifier over the woman's midsection. "Now look at the spot right above her waist."

I could see it. Kind of. Something was off, but I couldn't name what it was. Zoe pointed. "The woman's waist doesn't quite blend with her hips." She traced a line, and though the difference was slight, I understood what Zoe was saying.

"Her top half's just a little smaller than her bottom half."

Zoe nodded. "As if someone wanted her frame to appear narrower.

Younger." She dragged her fingertip to the edge of the mattress. "That's also why this part curves slightly."

For a moment, I got caught up in Zoe's excitement. The photo was doctored. But then I realized what she hadn't said.

"So the photo was manipulated to make the woman in it appear younger. But she wasn't inserted entirely? Like a photo of Sam wasn't combined with a photo of the woman?"

"Probably not," she admitted. She quickly added, "That doesn't mean there aren't other explanations."

"Such as?"

"It could be old, from before you and Sam were together."

I looked at the photo, and traced a small scar above his hip, from when Sam had gotten hurt sledding a couple of years before.

"It isn't an old photo."

"It could be Brooklyn, right?" Zoe said.

"Hair color's right, I guess."

Leo shuffled into the kitchen, and Zoe and I both jumped.

"You're up early." I folded the photo and handed it back to Zoe, who slipped it back into the drawer.

"I smelled bacon." Leo grabbed a handful of the strips but stopped. He wrinkled his nose. "Is something burning?"

My eyes dropped to the pan, but the bacon sizzled half-cooked.

Zoe turned off the burner anyway, and we both scanned the room. The air remained still, clear.

Suddenly an icy finger trailed my backbone. "Wake your sister."

Because I smelled it. Smoke, subtle but acrid, the scent of smoldering wood corrupted by—something.

I turned to Zoe to ask her to call 911, but she already had the phone in her hand.

"Do you have a fire extinguisher?"

She pointed to the closet.

On legs that weren't entirely stable, I ran to the closet, grabbed the extinguisher, then leashed Boo.

"Where do you keep Smooch's crate?"

Zoe cradled the phone and pointed toward her bedroom.

As I crated Smooch, I identified the second scent. It was the smell of road trips and boat docks, benzenes and hydrocarbons, evil and intent. Gasoline.

Leo returned with a groggy Audrey at his side.

"Fire department's on its way," Zoe said. She grabbed her purse, keys, and the crate, while I lifted Boo, tucking him under the arm that didn't hold the extinguisher. A few quick strides, and I was at the front door, placing my palm against it. Warm. I gestured Zoe and the kids toward the back door. Cool to the touch.

"Got everything?" Leo and Zoe nodded, but Audrey peeled away from her brother and ran to me.

"Mommy?"

"We've got to leave, Peanut. Go with your brother."

But she buried her face in my stomach and her grasp tightened. This was her limit. The only way she was leaving was in my arms.

I handed Leo the dog and scooped up Audrey, tilting my chin toward the door. Zoe nodded and threw the door open.

Outside, the tang of gas was stronger. The flames weren't yet visible, but I knew they were there, waiting to trace the line of gasoline that led to a puddle on the back stoop.

I forced myself and my family forward.

As we approached the front yard, we could hear it. A soft crackling, like the snap of small bones. Still no flames.

When we turned the corner, we finally saw it: a small pile of what might've been rags had been set ablaze in front of the house, though the fire was spreading quickly beyond it. I caught the shimmer of gasoline, a pool on the front doorstep identical to the one in back. Then flames leaped into it. Dancing. Consuming.

I placed Audrey on the ground and pulled the extinguisher's pin, aiming the nozzle toward where fire licked the exterior wall, and squeezed, sweeping the extinguisher from side to side. It was like trying to stanch the flow from an artery with a cotton ball.

A crowd had gathered. I ignored them, finger on the trigger until the last of the spray dripped from the nozzle. A neighbor stepped in with a second extinguisher, another with a garden hose.

Together, we hobbled the fire. Firefighters were on their way. It was probably enough to keep the blaze from spreading.

I dropped the now empty extinguisher and walked toward the charred lump that had been the fire's source. Closer now, I saw it was a pile of clothing. A scrap of denim remained recognizable.

Jeans, the same wash Sam had been wearing the night he had disappeared.

I knelt down. On the jeans I smelled no gasoline, and they had been placed apart from the other items. There was no way for me to tell if the jeans really were Sam's, but the deliberate way they had been staged made me think they were.

At the least, they were a message. Shaking and reeking of smoke, I had a message of my own I was very eager to deliver.

AFTER extracting from Zoe an assurance that she and the animals would find someplace safe, someplace I didn't know about, I gathered the kids and headed to a hotel across town. Not to stay myself, but to meet a man I hadn't seen in six years.

On the way, I called Detective Rico. Dawn had just started to reach across the sky, but Rico answered on the second ring.

"Hello?"

"My friend Zoe's house was set on fire."

"Good morning. So it's a fire today, is it? Everyone okay?"

"We're fine." I gave him the address of Zoe's townhome. "After our conversation last night, I didn't want to be accused of keeping anything from you."

"No, we wouldn't want that." In the background, I heard the squeak of coils decompressing as he stood from a bed or a couch.

"I'm pretty sure Sam's jeans were left there for me to find. Near a pile of clothing used to start the fire."

"I don't suppose you're still at the scene?"

"Not right now, but you know how to reach me."

"You're currently number three in my contacts." I wasn't certain he was joking. "Just don't go changing it again."

The way things were going, I couldn't promise that. "Did you get that video I sent you from the coffee shop?"

"I did. You got that photo for me?"

"About that . . . It's at Zoe's house."

Though the photo was evidence, and I hoped the fire hadn't breached Zoe's threshold, part of me wanted the photo to burn.

"I think we need to talk in person."

"Probably, but it can't be now."

Somewhere in Rico's house, a child laughed. I was suddenly jealous, wanting that levity for my own children.

"Can you drop by the station at nine?" Rico phrased it as a request, but I could tell it wasn't one.

"I'll see you at nine." *If I can make it.*

He picked up on my hesitation. "I really need you to be there, Cassie." A pause, then, "And bring Leo."

I started to ask why he needed Leo, but Rico cut me off. "Gotta go." Suddenly distracted. "See you and your son at nine."

A FRIGID wind had started to blow. Despite the chill, I stood outside the door to my father's hotel room, unable to knock.

"I'm cold," Audrey said. She was still in her pajamas, and the jacket I'd grabbed for her was too thin for a November morning. She burrowed into Leo, using him as a windbreak.

I finally rapped on the door, and it swung open immediately. I stared into the face of my father.

Red McConnell's hair had thinned in the past six years, and the crevices under his eyes had grown more pronounced. He moved forward as if to hug me, but something in my face pinned his arms to his sides. He nodded in greeting instead.

Audrey stepped forward. "You're my grandpa," she said. "The other one. Not Daddy's. His name was Frank, but he's dead."

"I'm sorry to hear that."

"We went to visit him on his farm when I was little. Grandpa Frank had chickens. Can I watch your TV?"

"Of course."

Inside, Audrey grabbed the remote and jumped up onto the bed. Leo dropped himself in a chair, earbuds in, eyes attached to his phone. They both gave the appearance of normal, though I noticed the signs: Audrey's voice, an octave higher than usual, and Leo's distant stare. They hadn't cracked, but they were close.

"I tried calling your cell," Red said.

"I have a new number." I gave it to him, with instructions to call only in emergencies, and even then from a pay phone.

He raised his eyebrow at that, and I could tell he wanted to ask. I was grateful he didn't.

I spoke first. "You didn't have to come."

"You needed me. Where else would I be?"

I bit my tongue to keep from asking: *What about when Audrey needed you?*

He answered the unasked question. "I know there've been times I could've done more, and I'm sorry. You smell like smoke."

"Long story. Did Sue come?"

"She might have, if we hadn't broken up three years ago." Intended as a joke, the words served as a reminder of all the time lost.

"Seeing anyone new?"

"Not really."

Another pause in the conversation. Mentally, I prepared my best small talk—it's probably colder here than Arizona, right?—but before I spoke, Red said, "I didn't fly seven hundred and ninety-eight miles to talk about my failed relationships or the weather."

Parents were sometimes telepathic like that.

"Seven hundred and ninety-eight miles, huh?"

"I Googled it."

For the first time since entering the room, I smiled. "You would. You probably prepared a speech too."

"Wrote it on a napkin on the plane."

"Practiced it?"

"My seatmate pretended to be annoyed, but I think he really developed a secret crush on you. I might've shown him photos."

"I've changed a lot in the past six years."

"Not so much, and the photos were more recent than that." When I arched my eyebrow in query, Red said, "Sam emailed me photos of you and the kids at the beach last year."

Sam had been in contact with my father? Before I could ask him to elaborate, Red asked, "About Sam . . . do they know?"

"Some." For most of my childhood, it had been just the two of us. While it felt good to fall back into the familiar rhythms, talk of Sam's secret conversations with my father sobered me. It reminded me of how I had felt looking into an infant Audrey's jaundiced face after Red told me he wouldn't be tested because he hated needles and, besides, Sam or I would probably be a better match.

"I'm still angry with you."

"I know. But that doesn't mean I can't be here for you now."

I glanced at Audrey. "She was really sick." She had nearly died. But I couldn't add that last part. It seemed dangerous to release that thought into the universe.

"If you had been that sick as a baby, I wouldn't have survived it," he said. "You've always been stronger than me."

I didn't feel particularly strong.

"I miss Sam," I said, my voice low. "I've heard some horrible stuff about him in the past couple of days, but I still miss him."

"Whatever you've heard isn't true. Sam is a better father than I'll ever be, and I've never seen a man more in love with his wife."

I wanted to believe in the Sam he described.

"So are you going to tell me why the kids are still in their pajamas and you smell like a campfire?"

I led him outside and told him everything. I might have been angry at him, but there was no one I trusted more.

After I finished, I said, "I need to find him."

"Like the police said, most married men leave voluntarily." He was quieter now, less on Sam's side. Understandable.

"So you believe he was having an affair?"

"Don't you?" Though he had been certain of Sam's fidelity before hearing my story, he had doubts now.

"Even if he was cheating, that doesn't mean he left voluntarily."

"In which case, the police are looking for him."

"I know Sam better than they do." Did I? My father's doubt was contagious.

"I'm sure you do."

I couldn't be certain Red believed what he said, but the words nevertheless gave me comfort.

"If it had been Sam on the trail that night, he would've stepped in too," I said. "He wouldn't have hesitated."

"I know. Sam's a great guy." The admission came grudgingly.

"There's more to it. When Audrey needed a liver, Sam didn't ask about the risks to him. Not once." I touched Red's arm. I needed him to hear what I was saying. "That's not a jab at you. That's just how it went down.

"Having lived through my teen years, you may think I can be reckless. But I think before I act. Sam doesn't. He believes good people should prevent bad things from happening. A moral obligation, he calls it. In his mind, that's just the way things are."

Red nodded in understanding. "You think this *moral obligation* may have gotten him hurt."

"Yes."

"I admire Sam, but I live by a different code, and it has a single imperative: keep you and the kids safe."

"Like six years ago?"

Red's face went ashen, and I regretted my words. When I had imagined myself a pastry chef in middle school, my father had eaten pies made with too much sugar, cookies made with too little, and cakes swampy in the middle. He had swallowed every bite. This was a man I should've been able to forgive.

He grabbed my hand and squeezed it. "There's more to that story, more that I couldn't tell you then."

This surprised me. "Tell me now."

"Like I said, my main concern will always be keeping you safe, and distraction can be dangerous."

"It's a distraction not knowing what you're talking about."

"I know you're angry, but please—stay with me. Let me help."

"You used a credit card, right? Checked in under your own name?" When Red nodded, I continued, "It's not safe for us here."

"We can find another hotel," he said.

"They'll still keep records."

As much as I wanted to lean on my father, I couldn't.

He stepped closer and whispered, "Where are you going to go?"

Then the idea hit me. "I can't tell you," I said. "But thanks for coming. After I find Sam, I'd like to catch up and hear more about why you didn't want to help save your granddaughter's life."

Red cringed. "Isn't it enough to know I had a good reason?"

"Maybe. If you'd offered that explanation six years ago."

I gave my father a half-hearted hug and then went back inside the hotel room to gather my children.

My FATHER followed us to the car. After the kids climbed in, he told me to be careful. He started to say more, but the slamming of the car door interrupted him.

Leo had climbed out again, his voice shaky, his eyes wide as he asked, "Mom, why do you have a gun?"

That was an easy question to answer: I didn't.

I leaned into the car and saw the weapon resting on the passenger seat. Next to it, a Post-it, though not a number this time. A word, written in all caps, in red ink: "TODAY."

My mouth went dry. "It's not mine."

My father, who had been several feet away, started toward us. The hairs on the back of my neck prickled. I asked him to stop.

"Dad, get your stuff."

The edge of his mouth lifted at what I'd called him, but he climbed the stairs to his room without question.

Neck still prickling, I dropped to my knees beside the driver's-side door. Crawling, I swept my fingers along the metal.

Near the back bumper, I found what I'd been looking for: a small rectangle of magnetized metal. A GPS tracker.

Had Carver placed it there that first night, before I realized Sam was missing? Maybe later at the hospital, while I had been awaiting Leo's MRI results? Or perhaps it was Helen who had planted the tracker while I was distracted by the sight of my husband's blood. All I knew for certain was someone had tracked me to Zoe's to start that fire, then to the hotel to plant that gun.

Then another thought struck me: Had I been tracked for months? Had Carver's appearance near my home that first night been the random event I'd first believed it to be?

A strange number popped onto the caller ID of my phone. As I hit the connect button, I held my breath.

Zoe didn't spare time for a greeting. "I've been talking to the police. Cassie—" Her voice broke, and I caught the edge of what might have been a sob. "Perla's dead."

I placed my palm on the hood to steady myself.

"She was killed."

That couldn't be right. She'd been helping me. I'd just seen her. Only the night before.

"They found her body in her apartment late last night."

Each detail was a gut punch. Then the significance of it hit me: My phone and my laptop had been in Perla's possession. Either could've been used to track her to her apartment.

Zoe hadn't said how she'd been killed, but I saw the gun on my front seat and I knew. She had been shot to death, and then the gun used to kill her had been planted in my car. I felt sick.

"Cassie, the police are asking why you left before the firefighters came. What time you got to my place. Whether Leo was with me while you were gone. Why would they be asking about Leo?"

I grabbed the gun from my car, removed the bullets, then wiped it all with the hem of my sweatshirt.

"Who found her?" I asked. Had she been killed before I had visited? And if so, where had the body been?

"The police found her. They got a tip."

Of course they had. Just like they had been tipped to my presence inside the abandoned house—an intruder with a gun, Rico had said. They had probably been tipped to the gun in my car.

"One of the officers mentioned the key you gave them matched Perla's locks. And something about prints on a wrapper?"

Understanding seized me: I had been in Perla's home. I had locked her door as I left. I had given the police her key. And I had turned over a wrapper that likely had on it only my fingerprints, or the fingerprints of my son. I had never seen the rock with the number three that Rico had mentioned, but I was willing to wager that it had been as carefully manufactured as the rest of it. Had the rock come from my own backyard? The paint from our garage?

Suddenly I remembered the text I'd received while Leo had been hospitalized: *I know how you can be when you're jealous.* At the time, I had envisioned Brooklyn dead, evidence planted on her body for the police to discover. Right idea, wrong person.

I tossed the gun, bullets, and tracker into a dumpster. "Whose phone are you using?"

"A neighbor's. I didn't think you'd want me using my own."

"Get someplace safe."

I gave her Leo's number—I'd used my own burner to call Rico, and it would be easily traced. I powered down my phone—useless now—and took out the battery. I considered tossing it in the dumpster too, but it seemed too valuable a resource to discard.

I motioned for my dad to get in the car. I couldn't leave him behind after what had happened to Perla. We would have to abandon the car, but for now, we needed to get away from the hotel.

I told my dad: "Leave your phone."

He dropped it, stomped it, and kicked it across the asphalt. It skittered to a stop near the dumpster.

I pulled out of the parking lot just as I noticed the red and blue of a police cruiser's light bar reflected on the hotel's walls.

I WASN'T running from the police. Not with the kids in the car. But that didn't mean I had to make it easy for them.

I kept my foot light on the gas pedal and my eyes straight ahead as I pulled out of the lot, passing two police cruisers on their way in. As soon as I hit the street, I turned and pressed hard on the gas.

Okay, so maybe I *was* running from the police.

I ignored my father's panicked stare, my attention focused on the road ahead and my rearview mirror. I ended up at the convenience store pay phone I had used to call Helen the night before.

"Where are we going?" Audrey asked from the back seat.

I steadied my hands on the steering wheel as I pulled over. "I'm going to have Grandpa call a friend of mine," I said.

I glanced at my daughter's face. Definitely close to cracking.

"Dad, I need to leave you here, with the kids." I kept my voice light. "I'll be back in a few minutes."

He didn't ask. He had seen the tracker. He knew.

"Let me go instead."

I smiled at him, even as I wished I could accept his offer. "No offense, Dad, but I'm faster than you are."

But I wondered if I would be fast enough. What would be a safe enough distance away to ditch the car? And once I had, how many minutes would it take to run back to my family?

If the police were out looking for me, it wouldn't matter. Even an Olympian couldn't outrun a police car.

Before I left, I gave my father instructions and a number I had long since memorized.

"He'll help," I said, feigning confidence.

As I drove away, searching for a good spot to abandon the car, I wondered if I was making a mistake trusting a man who earned his living by baking pot-laced edibles.

DARYL lived on a four-acre lot between Santa Rosa and Sebastopol. The home was small and in need of paint, but the pot garden beside it was well tended.

Lester lumbered up the driveway to greet the car. Daryl's braking took the Lab by surprise, and he bounced off the driver's-side door. The cone around his neck kept his snout from being snubbed.

"Sorry, Doc," Daryl said. "I could've sworn I left him in his crate."

"I'm glad he's doing better. And thanks again for picking us up."

"No problem, Doc."

Daryl pulled the car alongside the front deck, killing the engine. Audrey immediately snapped off her seat belt and bounded out of the car with exuberance, all trauma temporarily forgotten.

Leo made no move to exit the car, so when my father climbed out, I whispered, "Watch them, okay? I need to talk to Daryl."

Inside, Daryl's living room wasn't what I had expected. The floors were stained concrete, and an abstract print played off the gray tufted chair and a purple rug I suspected was wool. An open laptop sat on the simple ottoman that served as a table.

Daryl lowered himself onto the couch.

"Nice place," I said.

"I inherited the furniture from my sister when she died last year in a motorcycle accident," he said. "She always had better taste than I did, and, unfortunately, a more reckless nature."

"I didn't realize you'd lost a sister. I'm sorry."

Daryl crossed his legs, resting one flip-flopped foot on the opposite knee. "So, Doc, why're you here?"

I had chosen Daryl because a pot dealer's home wouldn't be the obvious choice for my family's refuge. Maybe for good reason.

"My husband's missing, and a former patient who was helping me was shot to death." I watched Daryl's reaction to that second part. His face was stone, his eyes red, hooded orbs, so I told him the rest of it. By letting us into his home, he'd earned the full story.

When I finished, Daryl uncrossed his legs and leaned forward. "I've only met Sam once, but he seems like a stand-up guy. Besides, you're hot, you're smart, and you've saved Lester."

Lester was worth saving. "Not that I don't love a compliment, or several of them in this case, but . . . ?"

"Why would he leave you?"

"For another woman."

"Nah, I don't buy that. Like I said, you're hot, you've got kids and I'm guessing a decent paycheck." Daryl looked sheepish. "Sorry again for not being able to cover Lester's surgery, but since pot became legal, it's harder to make ends meet, you know?"

"It's fine, Daryl."

"Anyway, I think you need to strip everything away and focus on what you know to be true."

I wasn't sure what he meant, and my face must've shown that, because he added, "When you were telling your story, you told me you think Sam was having an affair."

"Based on evidence."

"But you don't *know* that." He settled back on the couch.

I got where Daryl was going. I thought about it.

"I know Sam disappeared while trick-or-treating with Audrey."

He nodded.

"I know he was suspended from work because of rumors he was having an affair with a student."

He nodded, more vigorously this time. "What else?"

"He may have been having an affair."

Daryl stopped nodding. "Nah. What you know is there's a photo, which someone messed with. You know that Sam's friend thinks he was having an affair, and this woman—" he paused.

"Brooklyn."

"You know Brooklyn says she and Sam were hooking up. But the video's the only undoctored, unbiased evidence you have, and it just proves they were tight. They could just as easily have been friends. Sam could've been helping this troubled girl—"

"Hannah. But she admitted she lied."

He smiled at me, in that indulgent way he might if I were Audrey's age. "Because liars wouldn't trade more lies for cash."

"True enough."

"Anyway, maybe Sam was helping Hannah. So Brooklyn and Sam are friends who're both concerned about this girl, and Brooklyn exaggerates the relationship. If Hannah's lie was convincing enough to get Sam suspended, couldn't Brooklyn be lying too? See . . . you don't *know*. So focus on what you do."

I thought of all the "facts" I'd taken for granted. Not just the affair. Sam's blood on those plastic teeth. Sam's jeans being used to set the fire at Zoe's. I knew we were being watched, and whoever was watching could fake either of those details.

"Perla's dead. I know that. Helen lied about living in that house. And I know that Carver Sweet killed at least one person, a girl named Natalie, and tried to kill Brooklyn."

"We'll see." Daryl pulled his laptop toward him. He typed Brooklyn Breneman's name in the browser. Apparently, she belonged to a couple of professional organizations and had been quoted in a news story on rising water rates.

Daryl faked a yawn. "Let's move on to Perla."

He didn't need more than her first name. Perla's photo was prominently displayed on the newspaper's website, above a headline: SANTA ROSA WOMAN SHOT TO DEATH. The three paragraphs that accompanied the picture didn't expand much on the headline.

Blackness pricked at the edges of my vision, so I closed my eyes.

"Sorry, Doc," Daryl said.

I could hear his fingers tapping the keyboard. When I opened my eyes, Perla's photo was gone. Just like Perla.

"How about Helen?" Daryl said. "Do you know her last name?"

I admitted I didn't, but I gave him the address where Helen had claimed to live. Thirty seconds later, Daryl pointed at the screen. "See, another thing you thought you knew but didn't really."

He nudged the computer toward me, and I read the information three times before I could convince myself of its truth. The property records showed the owner's name: Helen Staley.

"I don't understand," I said. "Helen didn't lie about living there?"

"We know only that she's listed as the owner of record."

"Which means the man who answered the door lied," I said. "So what was he doing in Helen's house?"

Daryl continued typing, more urgently now. "There's no way to tell, at least not with the information we have."

I took out my new phone, the one originally intended for Leo, to call Rico, to tell him about Helen, but then I realized he had access to the same information I did. Much more information than I did, in fact. He had likely already knocked on Helen's door.

When I returned my attention to the screen, Daryl was typing "Carver Sweet" into the search engine. The first hit linked to the local newspaper again. I skimmed the article over his shoulder.

Anne Jackson, 52, was found dead in her Cloverdale home late Wednesday, the victim of an apparent poisoning. Her husband, Carver Sweet, 58, is being sought in connection with the killing.

Sweet also attacked a second woman later that night, police say. Sweet fled after a passerby called 911.

The victim, whose identity is being withheld, was released from the hospital Thursday morning.

Near the end of the article came mention of Carver's previous conviction thirty-eight years earlier.

Sweet, 19 at the time, served 15 years at San Quentin for the 1980 murder of ex-girlfriend Natalie Robinson, 16. Robinson's body was found buried less than a mile from her Napa home. The girl's skull was fractured, and her ribs showed signs of earlier trauma, but the cause of death was listed as asphyxiation. Robinson was unconscious but alive at the time of her burial, according to police.

According to testimony from the girl's mother, Delphine "Dee" Robinson, Sweet was abusive, leading Natalie Robinson to end the relationship a month before she was killed.

Delphine Robinson died earlier this year at age 75.

Daryl tapped the screen. "Oh, great, Carver did his time at San Quentin," he said with genuine enthusiasm.

Still reeling from what we'd read, I asked, "Why's that great?"

"I know a guy. He can get information on anyone who's been in the system, but he's especially connected locally."

After several minutes more of searching and emailing, Daryl scrawled an address on a Post-it. "Carver's former cellmate, a pedophile named Ernesto Marino, goes by Ernie. My guy couldn't find a home address, but either Ernie or his girlfriend gets takeout from here nearly every afternoon." He handed me the Post-it. "Seems he has a real weakness for bacon-stuffed waffles."

Chapter 10

I GAVE AUDREY THE LAST immunosuppressant from the old bottle and left three pills from the refill with Daryl. Just in case.

After hugging Leo as tightly as he allowed me, I pressed a folded piece of paper into Audrey's hand.

"My new number," I explained. "Call me for any reason, even if it's just to tell me something silly Lester did."

"He *is* silly," she said, but she offered no smile.

I hesitated. "Do you want me to stay?"

"Are you going to find Daddy?" Her eyes burned with a faith I hadn't earned, and I pulled her closer to avoid that look. Still, I meant it when I whispered in her ear, "I will. Promise."

Daryl offered me the use of his ten-year-old Honda for the sixty-mile drive to San Francisco.

I entered the diner in the Mission District and asked the staff about Ernie. Daryl's intel was solid: Ernie was a regular—bacon-stuffed waffles with whipped cream, an extra side of syrup, and two maraschino cherries—and he never missed a weekend.

Though I wasn't hungry, I rented my prime spot facing the door by asking for a grilled cheese sandwich. The diner was packed.

Distracted by the crowd, I didn't notice the blonde in the blue cardigan until she was at the door, red takeout bag in her left hand.

I abandoned the grilled cheese and walked quickly to the register, slapping the check and a twenty on the counter.

"What did that woman order?" I asked, pointing toward the spot the blonde had occupied only seconds before.

The man behind the counter reached for my check. "Bacon-stuffed waffles, whipped cream, side of syrup, two cherries."

I left my change and hurried out the door.

The blonde was slow and easy to follow, but I stayed half a block back. I kept to the edge of the crowd, near storefronts that might provide refuge in case she looked over her shoulder.

The blonde turned a corner. A couple of seconds behind, I almost missed her as she climbed the steps of a Victorian row house. She didn't knock but instead used a key. This was her home.

In one of the windows on the second story, I saw the woman hand the red bag to a man fitting Ernie's description. He wore a baseball cap that he kept tugging over his forehead.

Beside him, a small boy pulled on a backpack before disappearing from view.

Seeing Ernie with that boy made me very angry.

A second later, the woman and the boy emerged and got in a car. I waited until it had crawled down the street before climbing up the steps and knocking on the door. When Ernie responded, I stopped short, my practiced speech forgotten.

"Oh," I said. "You're hurt."

The bill of Ernie's baseball cap had caught the edge of the door, slipping nearly off his head. I had seen a wad of gauze held in place by medical tape. At the border of the gauze, his skin was inflamed an angry pink. A wound, obviously infected.

I forced my eyes from his forehead. "Ernie, right?"

The man angled the brim of his hat over his forehead. He did a double take, but recovered quickly. "I ain't buying anything."

"I just need to talk to you for a couple of minutes."

His eyes went flat. "I was eating."

Strange, he hadn't asked for my name. "That's a nasty wound. I'm a veterinarian. I can look at it." There was little I could do for Ernie here—he needed antibiotics—but I wanted him to trust me.

Ernie's face flushed crimson. "I don't want no animal doctor messing with my head." He again tugged at his cap.

"You should see a doctor then."

Judging by the fraying sweat suit and bad haircut, Ernie looked like a man who didn't have a lot of cash to spare for health care.

"If you don't mind me asking, what happened?"

"I got in a fight." He puffed up his chest.

"Did you call the police?"

"Why would I call those jackasses?"

I fought the urge to step back, instead straightening my spine. "The guy you fought with—was it Carver Sweet?"

Ernie's eyes narrowed, and I saw recognition there. It had indeed been Carver who had messed him up. "You know Carver?"

"He's done some pretty horrible stuff to my family." I motioned at his forehead. "I'm guessing you can relate. When was he here?"

"Couple of days ago."

Carver couldn't know I would seek out Ernie, so why had he? "What did he want?"

Ernie shifted slightly. I stepped forward and put my foot on the threshold so he couldn't slam the door.

"I can see to that wound—in exchange for some information."

He dabbed at the sliver of gauze that peeked from beneath the bill of his cap. Whatever was festering there had to hurt. Finally he said, "I suppose I can let you in. For a minute."

THE air in the living room smelled faintly of infection, syrup, and processed meat. The waffles sat in their to-go container on a small table, but he pushed them to the side.

"First aid kit?" I asked. He directed me to the bathroom cabinet, and I returned a moment later. I sat at the other end of the sofa, the kit tucked in my lap. "Why did Carver come here?"

Ernie removed his baseball cap and placed it on the table, exposing gauze and its border of inflamed skin. When I leaned forward, he recoiled. "Gimme a minute," he said.

"Have you kept in touch with Carver since you were released?"

He shook his head. "Haven't talked to him in years."

"Then why did he come here?"

Ernie's eyes darted to the window. "He's crazy."

"Even crazy men have their reasons."

Sweat broke out on his cheeks. "He wanted to know about Dee."

That wasn't a name I'd expected to hear. "Natalie's mom?"

His eyes were slits. "You know about that?" When I nodded, Ernie continued, "So you know what happened to Natalie."

I flashed to the photos Brooklyn had shown me. The broken girl buried alive. "I know some of it."

"That was brutal, man. She nearly died giving birth."

"Natalie had a baby?"

Ernie shook his head. "Stillbirth. Carver's kid. Dee found Natalie when she was bleeding out, saved her, but it didn't matter. She ended up dead anyway."

It was a solid minute before I could speak. "What happened?"

"The police think she was hit in the head, but it took a while to find the body. She'd been buried, and whoever did it didn't wait until she was dead."

I'd read as much in the newspaper article. "You said *whoever did it*. You don't think it was Carver who killed her?"

Ernie looked away. "It could've gone down that way."

"But you don't think it did."

"I don't know, man." When Ernie returned his attention to me, his eyes blazed. "It could've been an accident, and he tried to cover it up. But whatever happened, Dee was angry, she'd just lost her daughter, and either way, Carver was gonna pay."

Ernie grimaced, then sighed. "My head really hurts, man. You think you can look at it now?"

I pulled a pair of latex gloves from the kit. "Why did Carver want to talk about Dee?"

"Is there aspirin or something in that kit?"

I paused to retrieve a foil pack of ibuprofen. He swallowed both capsules. "He knew Dee and I used to be tight, and he thought she might be behind some recent stuff he was going through."

"What kind of 'stuff'?"

"He was having problems with his wife. That's all he'd say."

I started removing the strips of medical tape that held the gauze in place. "Why would he think Dee had anything to do with that?"

"She set police on him about Natalie, so why wouldn't she mess with him again? That was his thinking anyway."

I began to gently peel the gauze away. "It would seem a long time for her to carry a grudge, especially since Carver already spent years in prison for something he might not have done."

"You didn't know Dee." He used his fist to wipe sweat from his cheek. "When Natalie was alive, Dee wanted her to be perfect. Entered her in pageants, like when she was three. Spray tan, false eyelashes. Once, when Natalie gained a couple of pounds, Dee had her eat nothing but celery, and when she snuck some crackers, Dee locked her in this box." He paused. "Makes me think of how Natalie died. If Carver didn't kill her, then Dee did."

Ernie jittered, tapping his foot. Finally he said, "Do you know about her other daughter?"

My hand froze. "Other daughter?"

"Megan. Carver was asking about her too."

"I wasn't aware Dee had another daughter."

"Most people weren't." Ernie drummed his foot against the floor.

"Dee enjoyed hurting Natalie and Megan. Sometimes she would leave Natalie in the box for days."

"Sounds like a good friend you had there."

Ernie's shoulders tensed. "We weren't friends."

I worked to keep my expression neutral. I knew how easily cornered animals could snap. "What happened to Megan?"

"I don't know."

"Did Dee kill her too?"

"I told you I don't know."

Ernie's darting eyes told me he was lying, but I let it go. He needed to believe I was on his side. "How did you and Dee meet?"

"When Carver and me were cellmates, she hired me to keep an eye on him."

I pulled the last of the bandage from his forehead and tried to mask my shock. The wound seeped, drainage thick and yellow.

I dabbed it with an alcohol swab, then opened a packet of antibiotic ointment and applied it to his forehead. He looked like he might pass out, a greasy sheen coating his face.

"Were you in touch with Dee in the months before she died?"

"Not really. Can I have more of those pills?"

I handed over another packet of ibuprofen. This time, I held on to them for a second before releasing them. "You're lying."

"No," he said, but his voice lacked conviction. "I mean, I didn't talk to her that much. Once in a while, she needed help with something . . . not illegal, really. It's hard for a convicted felon to get a job, you know?"

"What kind of *jobs* did you do for Dee?"

His face darkened. "Just stuff."

I took a square of gauze and secured it to his forehead with medical tape. I might have pressed harder than was entirely necessary. He winced. "I've got some pain pills," I lied. "Veterinary grade, but they'll work just fine. If I'm feeling generous."

"What does it matter?"

"I might have some antibiotics in the car too."

"That's cold. Aren't you legally required to give them to me?"

The tremor in his voice told me he wanted those pills, badly, but he wanted to keep his secrets more.

I pushed. "What kind of jobs did you do for Dee?"

Ernie crossed his arms across his chest, and his lips tightened.

I had one move left, and it was risky. "How old's the kid? The boy I saw in the window, putting on his backpack. He looks to be about eight or nine. Who is he, Ernie?"

He hesitated, suspicious. "My girlfriend's son."

"This is her place, isn't it? The three of you living together?"

When Ernie spoke, his tone was defensive. "Yeah, so?"

"You're a convicted pedophile, Ernie. You're living with a child. Does your girlfriend know?"

He squirmed. "She wouldn't care."

I very much doubted that. "What about Family and Children's Services—would they care? How about your parole officer?"

His face wavered between anger and fear. "What do you want?"

"Answer my questions, honestly, and I won't tell." It was a lie.

Ernie sighed and glared at me. "Dee hired me last year."

"To do what?"

Ernie's fingertips massaged one temple, his face settling into a scowl. "You got those pain pills? It really hurts, man."

I knew I would have to pay for additional information. I opened my purse, my attention falling on the lump in the zippered pocket.

I pulled out the bottle containing Audrey's medication and shook out two pills.

"These're strong, so it's better if you only take one now." They *were* strong, but the pills Audrey took so her body didn't reject her liver would do nothing for Ernie's pain.

He studied the pills. "What about the antibiotics?"

"I'll get those from the car when we're done."

Ernie swallowed both pills. I had minutes before he guessed they were fakes and realized I had no antibiotics in my car.

I pushed. "What did Dee hire you to do?"

"Can I have another pill, for later?"

I retrieved another tablet but kept it clasped in my hand.

"Dee wanted me to find someone."

I stretched out my hand and unclasped it, an offering. "Who?"

He snatched the pill from my palm and swallowed it immediately.

Something in the way Ernie looked at me now reminded me of the recognition I had seen on his face when I met him. Fear crushed my chest like a cheap paper cup. "You know who I am."

"I just met you, man."

"You haven't asked my name. Did Dee hire you to find *me*?"

His gaze grew wolfish. "Cassie Larkin, Terra Linda Drive. Husband Sam. Two kids. I gave Dee that information just before she died." Ernie grabbed my arm. "What about those antibiotics?"

I yanked my arm free, backed up out of his reach, and gestured toward his forehead. "You should seek medical attention."

His gaze dropped, and he reached for his baseball cap.

"Another piece of advice: You should move. If Carver comes around again, it could put your girlfriend and her son in danger."

I left Ernie slumped on the couch, his cheeks turning ashen. I made it as far as the porch before the screaming started.

I immediately recognized the screaming for what it was: an expression of intense pain, beyond what might be caused by an infected cut. Inside, I found Ernie curled up on the floor, legs twitching as he held his stomach with both hands.

He moaned. "I'm gonna be sick." I rolled him onto his left side, and he just missed vomiting on my shoes.

"Do you have a phone?" I asked.

Ernie managed to jerk a shoulder in the direction of the kitchen. I found his phone on the counter and used the emergency option on the lock screen to call 911. I didn't give my name, only the information that a man had been poisoned and that I would leave the bottle containing the suspected toxin on the coffee table.

When I hung up, I checked Ernie's pulse. It was weak, but his breathing was steady. I left the phone within his reach.

"The paramedics are on their way," I told him.

I couldn't stay, not with my daughter's name on the bottle that contained the poison. Because I had no doubt Ernie's distress was caused by the pills I had given him. Pills I could just as easily have given my daughter. Though I didn't know who, I knew someone had poisoned my daughter's medication—just as, according to the newspaper article, Carver might have poisoned his wife.

There were no words to describe the depths of my rage.

I put the bottle on the table and peeled off the label as best I could. I used a pen and paper from my purse to write the word "POISON" in all caps, and tucked the note underneath the bottle.

Then I stepped over the seizing pedophile and ran all the way back to where Daryl's Honda was parked several blocks away.

The sky had been scoured of fog by the time I crossed the Golden Gate, and the sun made its red towers glow.

Despite the view, I felt none of the usual amazement. Instead, I felt fear. Fear for Audrey and Leo that had been magnified a million times on seeing Ernie writhing on his living room floor.

I had called Red on my run back to the car. Between breaths, I had told him about the poisoned pills and had warned him not to let the kids eat anything or drink so much as a glass of water.

Everything was fine, he had assured me. The kids were fine. Daryl was fine. Heck, even Lester was fine.

I was right to be afraid. That became clear half an hour later when Leo called. I answered, putting my son on speaker.

"Everything okay?" I asked.

Leo was supposed to say what my father had: *Everything's fine.* Instead, he answered, "I don't think so."

And just like that, I turned to ice. "Explain."

"Audrey might've done something stupid."

I turned on the heater. "What did she do?"

"She tried to call Dad on Daryl's phone. A guy answered. He told Audrey he knew Dad and that Dad was trying to get a hold of you but couldn't because he didn't have your new phone number."

"Did she give it to him?"

"She's six." That was Leo's way of saying of course she had.

"Get your grandfather."

When Red came on the line, I rushed through an instruction. "Check with Daryl. I think he has a truck he uses for . . . work."

After I heard Red asking, and Daryl confirming, I added, "Get in the truck and head south. We'll meet at the dog park where Lester got attacked by bees. Daryl will know."

My father mumbled a quick "Okay" and disconnected.

So . . . the bastard who had Sam's phone also now had my number. I considered tossing my phone, but for now, I needed it, and besides, I was a moving target. A very angry moving target.

I pulled off the highway and called Detective Rico.

"You missed our meeting," he said when he answered.

I had remained steady when talking to my kids and father, but at the sound of Detective Rico's voice, I nearly lost it.

"How much have you heard?" I asked, my voice cracking.

"Pretend I don't know any of it."

I started with something he *did* know. "Perla's dead. That's why you had to get off the phone this morning."

"Yes." It was only one word, but I took comfort in his honesty.

"I didn't kill her, and neither did my son."

I could feel Rico weighing my guilt.

I steadied myself and took a chance. "There was a gun in my car. At the hotel. I threw it in the dumpster."

"We found it."

"Does it have my fingerprints on it?" *Or Leo's.*

"I'm guessing you wiped it down when you found it, but people rarely get everything."

I focused on the middle of that sentence: *when you found it.* I hoped that meant he believed me, at least a little.

"What do you think of me, Detective?"

"Are you asking if I think you killed your husband or Perla?" He paused, and my phone buzzed. I ignored the text as I awaited his judgment. Finally he said, "I don't."

It may have been a reckless question, but still I asked, "Why?"

"The *evidence,* the anonymous tips . . . it feels . . ."

"Manufactured?" I offered.

"Vengeful," he said. "Plus, while that neighbor Helen apparently left town, we found some curious deposits in her account."

First Hannah, now Helen. It seemed there was a long line of people willing to screw over my family for cash.

"Tell me the rest of it, Dr. Larkin."

I summarized my actions of the past few hours, starting with the poisoned pills and working back to most of what Ernie told me.

"He said Dee hired him to find you?"

"Yes." I chanced a quick look at my phone, at the text I'd missed a minute before, and I stopped breathing. I might've said goodbye to Rico but I probably didn't, my world suddenly reduced to the five inches of my cell phone screen. *Leo.*

There are few places darker than a parent's imagination. We fear our children will suffocate in their cribs, disappear from the playground, or take drugs and die in their best friend's bedroom.

While parents imagine such things happening, we don't expect them. But that doesn't mean we don't plan for them. We had a family password: *Xyz.* Quick to type, never used in casual conversation. Our deal was if our kids got in trouble, they could call or text those three letters, and we would be there. No questions.

I stared at the screen of my phone.

Xyz.

The first time either of my kids had used the code word. I called but got no answer. Despite my promises when making the pact, when it mattered, I hadn't been there to protect my children.

I HIT the highway well above the posted limit. The ringing in my ears was as sharp and insistent as the wind.

I tried Leo again, then Daryl, but both calls went unanswered. Next, I called Rico back and gave him Daryl's address.

I was nearly at Daryl's myself when the message came. I slowed before risking a quick glance down to see if it was Leo.

An image, too small to see clearly, had popped onto my screen.

Before I could pull over, my phone chimed again. I maneuvered the car onto the shoulder and picked it up.

A second photo was displayed beneath the first, both sent from a number I recognized: Helen's. I didn't know who had Helen's phone, or if her number had been spoofed.

The first photo was taken in Daryl's living room. Daryl was asleep on the couch, a blanket pulled up to his chin. Leo and Audrey were on the floor beside him, lying on their stomachs, their faces tilted just enough to afford them breath, and Audrey's right arm and Leo's left were extended, their fingertips touching. They weren't really sleeping. They were drugged. Posed.

I saw this immediately, in the stick-straight positioning of my children and, when I zoomed in for a closer look at Daryl's face, in the white orbs visible behind half-open lids.

Red wasn't in the frame. Where was Red?

The second photo was of Sam. This one was a close-up. Face ashen and bruised, his eyes were shuttered, his mouth agape.

I couldn't tell if he was alive or dead.

Sam lay against what might have been burlap. His lips still held a hint of pink, but I took little solace. Even if I found hints of life in the photo, I had no way to determine when it had been taken.

I read the message: *If no good deed goes unpunished, the consequences of the bad ones should be even worse, don't you agree? It's time to make a choice.*

A string of texts followed.

You can choose to save your children, or your husband.

My heart shattered, each piece heavier than the whole.

If you call the police again, all three will die.

If you try to negotiate, all three will die.

If you try to signal anyone, all three will die.

Pick now.

It became clear to me that it didn't matter if Sam was alive, because, depending on my choice, he might not be much longer.

Another text, a single number: *3.*

I couldn't choose, even though the choice was clear.

As a father, Sam had been puked on, lied to, yelled at. He had wounded his feet on misplaced toys and had weathered sleepless nights and illnesses, both terrifying and imagined. He had never ceased loving Audrey and Leo with unfaltering abandon.

2.

There was no question Sam would surrender his life to save his children. Without pause or regret.

1.

I had believed the greatest test in my life would be Audrey's illness. Now, with a single word, I would be sentencing my husband to death.

I made the only choice I could and typed: *Children.*

Chapter 11

ONCE OFF THE HIGHWAY, I approached Daryl's from a private road. The property owner might decide to take issue with my trespass, but that was the least of my concerns.

When the road veered toward a white ranch house with red shutters, I turned right sharply and carved my way across an uneven field, driving as fast as I was able.

Daryl's house grew on the horizon in the approaching dusk. I looked for police cars, but none had yet arrived.

A short wire fence separated the two properties. I slowed, intending to abandon the borrowed car and scale the fence. Daryl's truck was parked just a short jog away on the opposite side, its door open, closer to the main road. I could reach it in minutes.

As it turned out, I didn't have minutes. An unfamiliar white sedan pulled out of the carport and turned, approaching the road from the backside of the property.

I braced myself and then stomped on the gas. I hit the wire fence with a jolt, banging my knee, two of the three wire strands of the fence breaking on impact. The car screeched in protest as the third strand became entangled in the wheel well.

The sedan disappeared into a stand of oak and pine, but not before I saw a figure slumped against the front passenger window.

Leo.

Audrey was likely in the back seat, still unconscious.

I had chosen to save the kids. They were being taken anyway.

The wire wrapped itself around the drive shaft too, and the car shuddered to a stop. Despite the pain in my knee, I sprinted the few feet separating me from Daryl's truck.

The key was in the ignition. I threw the truck in gear, pressing the accelerator so it surged toward the driveway. I hit the road just in time to see the white sedan vanish around a bend in the road.

I reached for my phone to call 911 and realized my fatal mistake. I had left it behind in the disabled car.

I followed the sedan, beating the steering wheel with the palm of my hand. *Faster. I needed to go faster.*

The truck swallowed half of the gap between the two vehicles, but then the white sedan accelerated. I glanced down at my speedometer and cringed. Eighty. The road was posted at half that.

A crash at eighty would kill my children.

I reduced my speed. After a moment, the car slowed too.

I got a glimpse of a baseball cap as the car turned left, and the curve of a male jaw that seemed familiar, though in the fading light, it was impossible to see more.

I pursued, no longer plagued by fear or fatigue. The world had narrowed to the road ahead and the white sedan.

The car turned suddenly, back toward civilization, and I recognized where we were. Though I came from another direction, I drove this road nearly every day. A mile ahead was my clinic.

Suddenly brake lights flashed, and the car slowed nearly to a stop. It drifted toward the shoulder, and the door behind the driver jerked open. From the back seat, a figure tumbled onto the road. I braked, turning away from the sudden obstacle on the asphalt.

Audrey.

Having dumped half of his cargo, the driver of the white sedan pulled back onto the road. Without saying a word, he had given me another choice: I could pursue him, or I could save Audrey.

The other driver's leisurely retreat telegraphed how certain he was of my decision.

I pulled my daughter from the road, my heart breaking as I watched the white sedan carrying my son disappear.

AUDREY's arm had abraded against the road, angry slashes embedded with asphalt bits. Her bones appeared unbroken, and her head free of injury. I worried nonetheless. Her immunosuppressant drugs made her more vulnerable to infection.

That was when I noticed the note, tucked in Audrey's pants pocket: "Talk to the police and Leo dies."

The letters were hastily written, the scrawl just legible.

I transferred the note to my pocket. I secured Audrey in the back seat and headed for my clinic a few blocks away. With Leo's captor headed south and me headed north, each turn of the wheel felt like a betrayal of my son. I drove a little faster than was safe.

Audrey awoke with a whimper, which became a wail.

"Mommy, my arm hurts."

I pulled in front of the veterinary clinic and turned off the truck. I scooped her up, her body impossibly small against my chest.

At the door, I lowered Audrey to the ground.

"Damn it." The door was locked, and my keys were with my cell phone in the car I'd abandoned back at Daryl's.

Dusk was descending with alarming speed. Desperate, I looked around. I spotted a small stone with a sharp edge. It would do.

I wrapped my hand in my sweatshirt and swung the rock at the window closest to the door. The glass shattered. I knocked the shards clear before reaching inside to unlock the door.

Audrey stared at me, her eyes nearly as large as the moon.

I switched on the lights and glanced at the clock. How many miles had Leo's abductor traveled in the past couple of minutes?

As if sensing my thinking, Audrey asked, "Where's Leo?"

I moved quickly to gather what I needed in the exam room.

"I'll get Leo as soon as we take care of that arm." Audrey didn't notice the catch in my voice. I hoped she did notice the resolve.

Cradling her arm over the sink, I irrigated the wound with a syringe until it was free of dirt and the bits of asphalt. Every time she winced or cried out, her pain may as well have been mine. I gritted my teeth and applied an antiseptic wash.

"Almost done?" Audrey asked, biting her lip.

My brave girl. "Almost done." I slathered the wound with an antibiotic ointment and taped a dry dressing to Audrey's arm.

I looked up at the clock. The distance between me and Leo had grown another six minutes. In the heat of the chase, if I hadn't left my phone behind, I would've called 911. But that was before the note planted on my daughter: *Talk to the police and Leo dies.*

Would the person who pushed Audrey from that car even know if I made that call?

Who could I trust with Leo's life?

I returned my attention to my daughter. "What happened at Daryl's?" I said. It hit me then: I had no idea what had happened to Daryl, or to my father.

"I played with Lester," Audrey said.

"When I saw you in that car, I couldn't see who was with you. Was it Daryl?"

Audrey thought about it. "I don't think so. He took a nap."

"Did you take a nap too?" When Audrey nodded, I asked, "Were you tired?"

Audrey shrugged. My mind raced through the options.

A sedative? It wasn't easy to knock out three people simultaneously. Four if I counted my father.

"When I was in the car, the man mentioned ghosts."

My daughter's words caught me off guard. "What?"

"He was talking to someone. He mentioned whining ghosts."

Audrey was getting her words mixed up, probably because of the sedative, but I pushed. "He was talking on the phone?"

"Uh-huh."

"Did he say a name?"

"Uh-uh."

"Do you remember anything else?"

"Just the ghosts. Mommy, where's Leo?"

My head swam with thoughts so dark that for a moment I could see nothing else. But I forced myself back to the question I had asked myself moments earlier: *Who could I trust with Leo's life?*

I picked up the landline handset and dialed Detective Rico, but the call was interrupted by the bell attached to the front door. Though the clinic was closed, someone had entered the building.

I squeezed my daughter's shoulder with a hand gone suddenly clammy. "Stay behind me, okay?"

I grabbed a pair of bandage scissors and moved into the lobby, where I found Detective Rico standing near the pet food display.

He was wearing a tie covered in rubber ducks. He tried out a smile.

"I was just calling you," I said.

"Were you?" He gestured toward the scissors I held in my fist. "What are those for?"

"To stab someone in the neck, but apparently I won't need them." I slipped the scissors in my pocket. "Why're you here?"

"Your name's on the door." He motioned toward the broken window. "Plus, there's the alarm you triggered."

I leaned against the wall, weary. "How are they?" I asked.

Rico stared at me. "Your father and Daryl? They're okay."

So my father had been drugged too.

I hesitated. *Talk to the police and Leo dies.*

"What's going on here, Cassie?"

I wanted to trust him, but I knew that the moment I told Rico that Leo had been taken, the case would get loud, quickly: An Amber Alert would be issued; details about that white sedan would be flashed across billboards and cell phone screens.

Then there was Audrey, a witness. Would Rico be the one to interview her? A child psychologist? I didn't know.

But I *did* know that even if every law enforcement official between here and Canada mobilized, it wouldn't be enough. This was Leo. My son. He had been taken, and there was nothing I wouldn't do to get him back—and that included trusting Rico.

I took a breath and said, "Leo's been taken."

Though Rico didn't move, the pulse of the room quickened.

"I figured it was something like that," he said, his voice weary. At my look of surprise, Rico laid it out for me. "You got to Daryl's ahead of us. You were in his Honda, found disabled at the scene, and now you're driving his truck. I ran the plates. You wouldn't have walked away from Daryl and your dad, unconscious . . . unless someone took your children," he said, looking at my daughter, "and pushed one of them out of the car."

"I guess this means Leo's no longer a suspect?"

"I had to consider all the angles." A hint of an apology.

Then he excused himself to make some calls. I used the break to place my own call, to my father.

When Rico returned, his gaze dropped to my daughter, pinned to my side. "Audrey, right?"

She tucked herself behind my back. He motioned to her hidden arm. "With all that gauze, that must be a terrible injury."

"I fell," Audrey said. "I think I was pushed from a car."

Rico kept his tone neutral. "Who pushed you?"

My daughter shrugged with her uninjured arm.

Rico's eyes narrowed. "Why don't you draw a picture?"

I ushered my daughter to Zoe's desk, tucking her into a chair with a fistful of pens and a notepad.

With Audrey out of earshot, Rico continued, his voice quiet. "No chance Sam did this? Could this be a custody thing?"

"Of course not." A cold wind breached the shattered window, but I fought back the shiver. "If Sam were involved, he wouldn't have pushed Audrey from a moving car," I said.

I glanced at the clock again. In a blink, the minute hand had jumped from one number to the next. Five more minutes gone.

"We'll need to talk to Audrey more, find out as much as we can about what happened. You available to go to the station now?"

Another request that wasn't one.

I suddenly doubted my decision to involve the detective. There were reports to file, and interdepartmental cooperation to arrange. Leo didn't have that kind of time. The last note had said "today," and there weren't many hours left before today became tomorrow.

"Of course I'll come to the station," I lied.

He touched my arm briefly, and I met his gaze.

He pulled a folded square of paper from his pocket, unfolded it, then showed it to me. "Do you recognize this guy?"

My heart thundered. The man was bald like Carver, but that was where the similarities ended. Carver was older, all angles and scars, while this man had a long face, softer in the cheeks.

It was the man who had answered Helen's door. Was it also the driver of the white sedan?

"I saw him at Helen's house. Who is he?"

"Damon Kripke."

I swallowed. "What's his connection?"

"Helen and Hannah both ID'd Kripke as the guy who paid them. And there's the video you forwarded. It's hard to say, but he looks to be the guy who was following your husband and Brooklyn."

He paused, holding something back. "What else?" I said.

"I followed up on that name you mentioned—Megan. As far as I can tell, Delphine didn't have any other children."

I heard the hesitation in his statement. "But?"

"In the late seventies, a three-month-old girl with that name was abducted from a grocery store in Fresno."

Before I could push for details, Audrey rushed over to show us what she had drawn. I thought it might be a cat.

"Cool elephant," Rico said, and she beamed.

He noticed my look of surprise and shrugged. "My youngest is an artist too. Who do you think picks my ties?"

Audrey stood on her toes so she could see the paper Rico had shown me of Damon Kripke. She tugged on my sleeve and pointed. "That's him, Mommy," she said. "That's the guy who left the note about Daddy being a pedophile. Did I say that right?"

That was one part of the story I hadn't shared with Rico.

The detective's eyebrows knitted together. "You and your mom are going to come to the station with me. You okay with that?"

As Audrey nodded, I glanced away, guilt drawing my eyes to the glass fragments glinting on the tile beneath the window. I was in no hurry to fix it. What could a thief steal that I would miss? What I valued most had already been taken. "My dad and Audrey can ride with you, if that's okay. I'll follow in Daryl's truck."

"You sure you're fine to drive?"

My heart went from a careful plodding to a full-out sprint. "I'm not okay, but I'm capable of driving," I said.

I pushed open the door before the detective recognized the deception on my face.

A patrol car carrying my father pulled alongside the curb in front of the clinic. My father climbed out, but instead of heading toward me as I expected, he lingered at the curb, hands in his pockets. Even after the patrol car drove away, he avoided my eyes.

"You okay?" I asked.

He gnawed on his bottom lip, which was pressed into a thin, bloodless line. His eyes jerked away the moment they connected with mine. There was something there he didn't want me to see.

I took a step forward, my hand landing on his arm, but he moved away, rejecting my comfort.

"What happened at Daryl's?"

"I don't remember much," he said. "Any word on Leo?"

"I was hoping you could go with Audrey and Detective Rico to the station," I said.

"Happy to, but where will you be?"

"Right behind you."

"Let's not lie to each other anymore."

Voice low, I said, "I need to find Leo. At the station, I'd be useless, and if something happened to him while I was off . . ." I paused, studying him. "Is that what this is?"

"This?"

"You won't meet my eyes. You shouldn't feel guilty about Leo—"

"Of course I should, and I do, but this isn't about that."

The negative energy coming off my father could've been felt on the next block. "Whatever it is, tell me."

Our eyes locked. Finally he said, "I wish I'd been able to save Audrey's life. I understand why you were so angry. And still are."

At his words, I reached for the grudge I'd carried for six years like some parasitic twin. But the past seemed insignificant, and my reliance on old grudges petty and dangerous for my son.

"I'm sorry too," I said.

Red accepted my olive branch with a nod, but his mouth remained set in a grim line. Clearly the conversation wasn't over.

"The day you called to tell me Audrey was sick, my first impulse was to help." His voice cracked. "I've always wanted nothing more than to take care of you. From that first night."

Red squeezed my hand. His palm was slick, mine cold.

"There's something I need to tell you," he said.

RED TOLD HIS STORY IN A rush.

He started doing work on Dee's house in the Napa Valley in 1980, the spring Natalie Robinson turned sixteen.

Before it became a private residence, Dee's home had been a winery, one of hundreds operating in the state in 1920. Then Prohibition came, and the Depression, and everything changed.

The production of sacramental wines, exempt from the Eighteenth Amendment, saved some wineries, but most were shuttered. Over the ensuing decades, some abandoned sites, known as ghost wineries, found new life as restaurants, shops, or once again wine-producing facilities.

More than Prohibition, phylloxera, a sap-sucking pest, had doomed the winery that would become Dee's house. A creamery had been built, but bad business decisions doomed that too. So it became just a home for an eccentric woman and her two daughters.

Though renovations had made the main house livable, its stone walls had started to crumble and mold had crept into its cellar.

Dee recruited Red to restore the house to its historic glory.

The day Red met Dee's daughter Natalie, he made note of her boxy sweater and guessed the teen was pregnant. He also learned that such matters weren't discussed in Dee's house.

Outside the house, however, he heard rumors: Dee hadn't been able to bring pregnancies to term since Natalie's birth. Scar tissue, some said. Emergency hysterectomy, claimed others. Yet earlier that year, Dee had suddenly shown up in town with a baby in tow.

The baby's name was Megan. Her eyes glowed with intelligence, and despite her scratched skin and too-thin arms, she was quick to smile. Usually. Sometimes Red saw hints of a developing anger.

Red risked asking if Megan was adopted. Dee snapped, *She's mine,* which ended that conversation.

At least with Dee. When Red asked Natalie a couple of days later, the teen told him how earlier that year her mom had spotted an infant Megan in a Fresno grocery store. *Wouldn't it be nice to have another little girl?* Dee had asked. As if they had been car shopping and she had been deciding whether to upgrade to leather.

According to Natalie, Dee had stalked the baby through the

store, watching the girl whose mother called her Megan and who was only loosely strapped into the shopping cart. When Megan's mom had dropped a can of tomatoes and knelt to retrieve it, Dee had snatched the baby from the cart.

Natalie insisted on Red's silence, and he gave it to her. Too easily, since he had weeks before noticed bruises on Natalie's arm, and scratches even deeper than the ones on Megan.

He blamed cowardice. He knew what he would risk by taking Natalie and her sister from the house without Dee's consent: his photo on every newscast, the creepy contractor who abducted two girls, one a beautiful, very pregnant teen.

He could go to the police before he took the girls. Tell them about Megan, have them check their records for missing babies.

But what if the police didn't believe him? Red wasn't certain the children would survive an investigation.

There was also the possibility that Natalie had lied.

Still, there was no explaining those bruises.

Twenty-four hours later, Red stopped making excuses and made a decision: He would take Natalie and Megan from the house and work through the details later.

That night, Red noticed the sweat tracing Natalie's hairline, the intensity with which she gripped the edge of the dining room table, and he knew. Natalie was in labor.

Dee didn't realize it, so Red faked a distraction in the kitchen— the clatter of dropped tiles—to attract her attention. From there, he heard the squeak of the front door he had been meaning to fix.

While Dee didn't hear the squeak, eventually the silence pricked her ears. She felt Natalie's absence, and her expression darkened.

Outside on the porch, Dee spotted her daughter and yelled: *What have you done?* Her eyes blazed, twin strobes of crazy.

Beneath the magnolia tree, Red saw the girl too. Natalie was crawling, struggling to stand. She was pale as milk, her face slick. Was there too much blood? Red noticed Natalie no longer wore her sweater. Had it been used to wrap a newborn, then discarded along with the baby??

Dee walked the perimeter, calling out: *Baby, baby.* As if a newborn were capable of a response.

Red panicked over how to get Natalie and Megan to his truck, and how to find the baby. If it was even alive. Dee demanded Red leave, and he could tell she meant it. She herded Natalie inside.

I can help her, he said to Dee.

Dee returned with a gun. *This is our business. Get out.*

Red stalled, trying to come up with a new plan.

I have to get my wallet and my keys, he told her.

Just then, in the distance, Red heard what might have been a baby's cry. Dee cocked her head, and Red thought she heard it too.

But, reluctantly, Dee allowed him entrance into the house to retrieve the wallet that was already in his pocket.

Then Natalie screamed, and Dee shifted her full attention to her daughter. No trace of empathy on her face, only frigid resolve. She rested the gun on the ground next to where Natalie had fallen.

Red tried one last time. *I can take her to the hospital.* Dee refused his offer by placing her hand on the gun.

The realization came then, a blow to his gut: Three children needed his help, but he could save only one. Megan, who was inside asleep. Natalie, the teen likely beyond his help. Or the newborn whose cry he was now certain he could hear.

With Dee distracted, Red slipped farther into the house and grabbed Megan, still small enough to hold with one arm. He focused on her heartbeat, erratic but strong, and tried not to think of the two children he was forced by circumstance to leave behind.

After leaving Dee's that night, Red's only stop on his way out of town was at a pay phone, which he used to call 911. Red told the dispatcher about Natalie. He intended to share all of Natalie's story—the abuse, Dee's instability, the baby he left behind. But his new daughter started crying and, afraid of being caught with a stolen toddler, Red replaced the handset without saying more.

The police searched for Natalie. They found her two weeks later, but by then, she was in a box in the ground, dead.

THOUGH I knew it was a trick of shadow, Red's skin appeared to sag and his voice was weary when he ended his story.

"What happened to Megan?" I asked. But of course I knew. *I* was Megan. Which meant, "You're not my father."

Red grabbed my hand but released it just as quickly.

"I love you, Cassie. I'll die knowing my purpose in life was to raise you," he said. "But no, I'm not your father."

Chapter 12

RED'S GAZE WANDERED down the street, away from judgment. I sidestepped into his line of vision. I forced him to look at me.

"So Dee abducted me from that store in Fresno, and then *you* abducted me from her." My breath came in short, angry bursts.

"What else could I have done?"

"What about my parents?"

"It was only your mother, and she died twenty years ago."

Twenty years. "I could've known her. My mom."

"It took me years to find her, and by then—"

"You didn't want to lose me?" My voice broke as I considered what *I* had lost, not to mention the cost to my mom. "What happened to the baby you left behind? Natalie's child?"

Red cringed. "The police found only Natalie's body. No baby."

"But how can that be?"

He shrugged. "Dee was good at keeping secrets."

Not as good as the man who had raised me, apparently. "You're sure the baby survived that night?"

Red hesitated. "I want to believe it did."

I'm not sure I wanted the same thing. What would it have been like for a child to grow up in that house?

I seized on another detail. "Wait. Where was Dee's house?"

My father cocked his head. "Why?"

Audrey's comment. When I had been cleaning her wound. The

one I had dismissed too quickly. "Audrey heard her abductor talking about whining ghosts."

Red inhaled sharply. "Ghost winery."

"Still know the address?"

"I'll never forget that place." He stepped into the streetlight's glare and grabbed my hand. His skin was cold and damp. "Don't go. Let the police handle it."

"If I'd been taken, what would you do?"

He didn't hesitate. "Anything."

I gestured toward the inside of the clinic, where Audrey sat at the reception desk. "Take care of her."

"I haven't given you the address." His voice wavered.

"You will. You owe me."

He shook his head. Then he recited an address in Napa.

"We'll need to talk about this," he said. "After you find Leo."

"And Sam."

Red looked away to spare me the doubt in his eyes.

"Tell Rico where I'm headed. But give me ten minutes."

I wanted him there, but only after I arrived.

I watched Rico's car pull away from the clinic, with Red and Audrey inside; then I climbed into the truck. From the heating vent a folded sheet of paper protruded.

As I reached for it, my hand shook. The note was scrawled with a heavy hand. "I warned you. Now I'll have to kill them both."

On the back was the same address Red had just given me.

I CUT the travel time to Napa by half. As I approached the property, I slowed. Like at Daryl's, I headed for an adjacent parcel rather than coming in straight on.

I rattled the rusted chain and padlock that secured the gate. The lock sprang with the movement. The mechanism hadn't been secured. With another shake, the lock tumbled onto the gravel.

Come on in, it seemed to say.

I drove without my headlights on, windows down. I heard the crunch of my tires on the gravel and felt the chill of the wind.

The road narrowed. I pulled the truck as far off the road as I could, parking it between two oak trees, killed the engine, and got out.

I walked toward the lights of the house on the hill, passing what might once have been a guest house. Now all that remained were two walls that tilted in the absence of a roof.

Nearer the main house, beneath an oak tree, I stumbled, landing on my knees. When I reached out for balance, I found the obstacle that had snagged my shoe: A single bone jutted from the hard-packed dirt. I shivered. I was in the right place.

I didn't dwell on the bone and its implications. I focused my attention on the rows of wine grapes that marched up the hill.

In the distance, a car's headlights bobbed. I tucked myself behind the trunk of the nearby oak and stood still, watching.

The car veered toward the main road, passing a hundred yards from where I stood. If the driver spotted me, he gave no sign.

I remembered the bandage scissors I had earlier slipped in my pocket. I pulled them out now for reassurance and started climbing toward the house at the top of the hill.

I DIDN'T make it to the house. When I turned the corner, another structure drew my interest. A cinder-block creamery, the rotted planks of its roof slumped in resignation.

My attention shifted to its neighbor, a storage shed. Old, abandoned. It was the kind of place that might hold piles of burlap sacks. Like the one in that texted image of an unconscious Sam.

I approached the shed and tried the door. Locked.

I planted my feet, palmed my scissors, then threw my shoulder against the door. The frame crackled, split. Another strike, and I was in, brushing aside cobwebs that laced the entrance.

My shoulder throbbed as I stood in the threshold, surveying the shed—apparently once used for the storage of empty feed sacks. Fading light seeped in through the four small windows high in the rafters, filtered through clouds of dust and spiderwebbing.

Carver's earlier words, from our meeting at the hospital, tortured me now: *I placed him on a pile of feed sacks and watched as he rolled, facedown, on the burlap.*

Thinking of Sam that way—unconscious on his stomach, arms

splayed to his sides—brought a sudden, sharp clarity. Images flipped through my head in quick succession: Daryl drugged with my kids beside him. Sam's arm draped across his lover.

I had been so focused on the ways the image might have been manipulated. But now I saw what I had missed before—in the picture of Sam and the woman, there had been no tension in his shoulders or in his arms. He had been posed in profile, the bruised side of his face hidden against his *lover's* chest.

The sound of a man clearing his throat made me jump.

"Finally, your timing doesn't suck," he said.

I immediately recognized the voice.

The scissors clenched in my fist, I found Carver in the corner, mostly hidden by a stack of boxes. In his current condition, Carver posed no threat: Ropes bound his ankles and wrists.

"Care to untie me?"

"Not particularly."

Through the windows near the rafters, the moon cast pale bands across Carver's face. His lip was swollen, and the ropy scar along his jaw had been scraped raw. Bits of gravel pebbled one cheek.

"Where's Leo?"

He grinned. "Shouldn't a mom know where her kids are?"

"Do *you* know where *your* child is?"

"You know about that?"

My intake of breath was sudden and sharp. So what Red told me about the baby was true, and Carver knew about it. I hadn't expected that. "My father, Red, worked here as a contractor."

"I knew Red, or of him." His words careful. "Through Natalie."

"He was here the night Natalie gave birth. To your child."

"And he didn't try to save her?"

Her. So the baby had been a girl.

Anger flared that he would blame Red. "As the father, wasn't it your job to protect your child? What happened to her?"

"Growing up here, I'm guessing terrible things." For a moment, Carver's eyes went soft, his face slack. "Did you know that whenever Natalie did something her mom didn't like, Dee would throw her in a box? And she *really* hated her daughter getting knocked up. Usually, Dee would let her out after a day or two, but that last time, she planted her in the ground and walked away."

The casual way he said this made me want to stab him in an eye with my scissors. "You knew about the abuse and did nothing?"

"I didn't know back then. Until recently, I thought Natalie had miscarried. It was Ernie who told me about the box. But Red was here that night. He could've prevented all this from happening."

My hands tightened around the scissors so that the tip gouged my palm. "Where's my son? And my husband?"

"Probably dead."

I jammed my scissors into his foot, and he screamed.

"What did you do to my son?"

"I'm not part of that. I'm only here because Damon drugged me." His face darkened. "You stabbed me in the foot."

"You're lucky it wasn't your carotid artery." Which it might have been if not for the information I still needed. "Why would Damon drug you?"

He grimaced and studied his foot. "You know the story: Guy meets girl. Guy realizes girl's trying to screw up his life. Guy tries to kill girl. Then girl gets her friend to stab guy in the neck with a needle and toss him in some crappy shed."

My skin turned cold. "So it's not just Damon," I said. "Brooklyn's involved in Leo's abduction too?"

"You still don't get it. Damon's just some guy she's manipulating, just like she manipulated me. You too, and your husband. Nothing about that night on the trail was an accident."

"I know. You ran Brooklyn off the road."

"*She* ran *me* off the road. She knew where you'd be, and when. She had a tracker on your car, right? She had one on mine too." The grin was back, and it was polar. "But her timing was off. I don't think she planned how close I'd come to killing her."

Carver's expression shifted then, a mix of hostility and confusion. "But I still haven't figured out why—why would my own daughter want to kill me?"

"You mean like you tried to kill her?"

"That was before I knew she was my daughter, and after everything she did."

"And now that you know, you aren't still planning to kill her?"

Carver remained silent, but I read the answer in his face.

I considered him and the ropes that bound him. If he set after Damon and Brooklyn, he would serve as one hell of a distraction.

He noticed me studying the ropes and growled, "Untie me."

"Because you asked so nicely, or because you tried to kill me?"

"I wasn't trying to kill you. I just wanted you to let Brooklyn die." When Carver saw I was making no attempt to free him, he leaned back against the wall. "Back at the hospital, I lied."

"I'm not surprised. About what?"

"I never brought Sam here."

I studied his face, but I no longer trusted myself to recognize deception. "I don't understand."

Carver squirmed against his bindings. "When Brooklyn and Damon ambushed Sam, I heard the tail end of their conversation. Damon mentioned dumping Sam here."

"But the blood on the back seat."

"Damon and I had a disagreement."

"Sam's keys?"

"He dropped them when those two ambushed him, and I took them. I needed a car." Carver's tongue darted across the cut on his lip. "Do you know how my wife died?"

"She was poisoned."

"That was Brooklyn. She poisoned my wife's tea and watched as I served her. Up until that point, we both thought Brooklyn was a friend. Invited her into our home. First, she posted stuff online that got me fired. Then she emptied our bank account. Killed our cat and posed it on our bed as if it were sleeping. Then—Anne."

His entire body convulsed at the memory. "Each day, I'd find a note with a number. Three. Two. One. That last day, on the bottom of the box of tea, Brooklyn had written a single word in Sharpie: *Today*."

At that, I felt as if I had been hollowed out with a dull knife and then scraped raw. Part of me had wanted to believe the threat was idle, that Sam and Leo would be allowed to live.

"And then—" Carver's voice caught in his throat. He cleared it and started again. "And then, Brooklyn knelt down and told my wife it was my idea. I don't care if she's my daughter. For making that lie my wife's last memory, I *am* going to kill her."

Then Carver slipped the rope from his wrists.

He grabbed me and wrapped his arm around my neck. I struggled, but he was twice my size. He put my scissors in his back pocket, beyond my reach, then dragged me from the shed.

I clamped down on his arm with my teeth. He flinched, but he didn't release me, instead squeezing harder. When the stars prickled my eyes, I released all the tension in my body. Though instinct screamed to fight, I let him lay my limp body, almost gingerly, on the ground.

I let Carver go, opening my eyes only when I could no longer hear his footsteps. Even then, I lay there for another minute.

My breath quickened when I finally stood. When I turned, intending to search for anything I might use as a weapon, I froze.

Carver was walking back toward me, and he wasn't alone. Damon walked behind him, moonlight illuminating purpled lumps on his face and a swollen lip. Before Damon had taken down Carver with that needle to the neck, Carver had gotten some punches in.

At first, I thought I'd gotten it wrong, that Carver had been working with Damon all along. Then I saw the gun in Damon's hand. Even with all the bruising, I recognized him as the man who had answered Helen's door and likely the man who had pushed Audrey from that white sedan.

Though Damon's gun wasn't trained on me, it would take only a second for that to change. I stood as still as I was able.

"You're early, Cassie," he said. "We weren't ready for you."

I tried to read in the bumpy patchwork of his face how deep his commitment was to Brooklyn's cause. "Why are you doing this?"

Damon's eyes darted between my face and Carver's. I recognized the desperation in his expression: He was bracing himself to carry out whatever horrible demand had been made of him.

"I'm doing this because I'm her friend, and she asked me to."

Damon pointed the gun barrel at Carver's chest. "She wanted

more time with you, Carver. But with Cassie here now, it's too risky to leave you both alive."

Carver opened his mouth to speak, but Damon stepped forward and fired, point-blank, three times. Carver's mouth went slack, death consuming whatever he had been about to say.

Damon gestured toward the house. "Let's get this over with."

INSIDE the house, a stone fireplace stretched two stories to a redwood-beamed ceiling. The two wings of the second story were connected by a catwalk that looked out over the living room, all in white linen and crimson leather.

I noticed all of this, but only until I noticed my son, propped and unconscious on the sofa, Brooklyn behind him with a revolver aimed at Leo's head. Once I saw Leo, I noticed nothing else.

I dared not move. All it would take was a quiver of Brooklyn's finger and the blast that followed would end me as certainly as if the weapon had been pointed in my direction.

Bruises still mottled Brooklyn's face.

She squinted, her head tilted as she studied me. She asked Damon, "You took care of Sam, right?"

I caught my breath. *No.* I forced all my will into that denial, as if it could become a tangible thing capable of holding me up.

"Yeah, I took care of Sam."

I flashed to Carver's rage that night on the trail. He had been beyond reason or thought. Brooklyn had deconstructed Carver's life, piece by piece, until all that remained was a husk empty of all but that limbic center of his brain that shouted, *Avenge.*

The thought hit me with such force, I nearly stumbled. *I will save Leo and then kill everyone else in this room.*

I shook off the thought. I saved lives, I didn't take them.

"I'm surprised you got here so quickly." Brooklyn smiled. "Ten minutes earlier, we wouldn't have had time to kill your husband."

My muscles tightened as I scanned the room for weapons.

"Don't forget, Sam's death is on you. I gave you a choice, and you chose the kids. Still, you *did* call the police, and that decision has to have consequences. So who dies here: you, or your son?"

As easy a decision as I could ever make. "I'd gladly trade my life for my son's." The obvious question hung between us: *What prevented Brooklyn from killing us both?*

Brooklyn turned to Damon. "Make sure the kid's secure, then get rid of Sam's body."

Damon did as he was told. I heard a car start. I tried not to imagine Sam's body in its trunk.

I let Brooklyn usher me out the door, leaving Leo alone in the house. She walked me back the way I had arrived on the property.

She sped up, forcing me forward, and I recognized her purpose. We were headed for the valley oak at the edge of the property.

On my death walk, I gulped the air, crisp and sweet, filling my lungs to the point of pain. I looked for an opportunity. I saw none.

At least every step I took with her was a step away from my son. With Brooklyn occupied with me, and Damon disposing of Sam's body, if Leo regained consciousness, maybe . . .

Brooklyn continued to herd me, reveling in a moment she had probably spent a long time imagining. I was no more in control than a zebra herded into ambush by a pair of hunting lions.

I hated being that zebra. What could I do now that would save me, and save Leo? Even if I managed to overpower her, even if I escaped, it would be pointless if I couldn't make it back to the house to save my son, or allow him the time to save himself.

"You won't hurt him?" The question caught in my throat.

"No," she said. We both recognized the lie.

Then in the shadows beyond the oak, a nightmare took form. On the ground, a hole, and a box. It was impossible to misconstrue its purpose—the rectangle stretched as long as a human body.

We stopped beside the hole facing one another. Comfortable with her leverage, she nevertheless put nearly ten feet between us, and between her and the edge of the grave. She wouldn't fall in.

"This is where we gardened," she said. "Dee and me." She kicked a clod of dirt in the direction of the grave. "You know why we're here, right? I'd hate for you not to know."

I thought of what Red had told me about the night he had taken me from this place.

"You're angry because I escaped this place and you didn't."

Her face tensed. "You didn't *escape*. You were *chosen*."

As a toddler, I had no role in what happened back then, but such arguments wouldn't serve me now.

"She made me bury my dog here," Brooklyn said.

"That story you told me about Hannah's abuse. That wasn't her story. It was yours." The photos of Natalie she had shown me too: Those had been hers, not Carver's.

"Dee was never very good at keeping her pets alive," Brooklyn said. "Did you know they found Jerusalem crickets in Natalie's grave? The newspapers never mentioned the bites. Dee used to joke that when the police pulled Natalie from the ground, it looked like she had a bad case of chicken pox."

"But even if Dee killed her, Carver deserved prison for abandoning her like that. He deserved worse."

I heard the scratching of a small animal. I thought of all the creatures my corpse would soon feed, and my stomach turned.

"I think it's time," she said. "We haven't dug Leo's grave yet, so I'll have to get Damon on that."

Yet? My mind stumbled on that word.

Too late, I realized a quick death had never been her plan, for me or my son. Pinned beneath the earth, I would die as Natalie had died, but only after Brooklyn killed Leo.

From behind, two hands shoved me, hard, on my back. I tumbled face-first into the perfectly sized grave.

Chapter 13

I WASN'T ALONE IN THE BOX. I felt them, even as I heard their scuttling against the wood.

I pushed against the lid, though I knew the earth piled on the box would hold it in place as certainly as concrete. A few small holes were plugged with dirt. I took inventory of my pockets, but apparently, I had left my coffin-opener in my other pants.

I felt them again—the bugs. Hard little shells grazed my calf as several of them breached my pant leg.

I closed my mouth and screwed my eyes shut.

But the bugs weren't the real threat here. I knew that as I breathed my limited oxygen, I expelled carbon dioxide, the buildup of which would soon make the air around me unfit to breathe. How long did I have? I guessed twenty minutes. Maybe less.

I suppressed the urge to scream. It would deplete precious air.

I summoned all the leverage I had to throw myself against the box's edges. I found patches of wood that had gone soft, but located as they were on the coffin's floor, they were of no use.

My head ached from the carbon dioxide. Soon I would get sleepy, and then I'd no longer be capable of making decisions. Next—death. For me and for Leo.

My lungs cramped. It was pitch-black, a night more complete than the one several feet above my head.

In my grave, the bugs weren't my only company. The bite of memories was just as sharp.

Red letting go of the back of my bike, releasing me. It had been like flying. Knowing he was there, I hadn't fallen.

Sam in his hospital gown, reassuring me that he and Audrey would be okay. Tears did me no good, but they spilled anyway.

Then: a woman yelling at me to shut the hell up, followed by a stinging slap that had cut the inside of my cheek.

Where had that come from?

I banged my fists on the wood above me until they throbbed.

I deserved this. I had saved the woman who had killed my husband and abducted my son. I had allowed myself to be pushed into this grave. The worst of it: I had doubted Sam.

A bug bit my arm, breaking skin.

I had been stupid. Reckless. But while I accepted my blame in this, Sam had paid the greater cost. Soon Leo would too, unless I stopped wallowing and got out of this box. When the bug bit again, I brought my elbow down on its carapace, crushing it.

My head pounded, but I was no longer resigned to what had moments earlier seemed inevitable.

I would not die in this box like Natalie had.

I wasn't leaving my son to Brooklyn.

In the darkness, my fingertips took stock of my coffin. It was constructed of old plywood. My hands wandered along the parts I could reach, searching for more soft spots. I worked one of my feet free of its shoe and probed against the seams.

On my second inspection of the lid, I found a soft patch. Water damage. The wood had dried, but it remained weaker in that spot.

I beat against the lid with my knees and heard a crack. Dust rained on my stomach. I shimmied upward, moving my knees as close to the middle as I could. Again, I rammed my knees against the lid. The wood creaked, threatening to split.

I paused. Once I breached the wood, earth would pour on top of me. But how much dirt? I was pretty sure it had been a shallow grave, but I couldn't be sure it still wasn't enough to smother me.

But I had no other options. I resumed my pounding. Finally a section of the board cracked, and I pushed it with my knee. I fought the impulse to force it completely free. I could easily be immobilized by the heavy earth upon my body.

With one knee acting as a fulcrum, I used my legs and hands to push the dirt toward the box's edge. I worked quickly, packing the corners with dirt, seeing moonlight now. I shimmied toward the opening, muscles pulling in directions they weren't meant to. My fingers found the hole I'd made with my knees. I held my breath, screwed shut my eyes, clods of dirt hitting my face as I reached through the hole. Fighting against the earth's weight, I pulled myself through the opening. Coughing. Spitting dirt. But free.

No longer entombed, I stood up and heard the same scratching I had before being pushed into the hole, though it was fainter now. I imagined the bodies of those buried here digging with hands of bone, intent on returning me to my rightful place among them.

With as much power as I had left in my burning legs, I ran toward the lights of the house, which seemed impossibly far away.

I ENTERED THROUGH THE kitchen. It was dark, but all the lights blazed in the living room. Damon's voice carried. "Carver was a piece of crap, but I'm not hurting a kid."

"You're an idiot."

By Brooklyn's sharp intake of breath, I guessed Damon had grabbed her. "Yeah, I think I am."

I risked a step forward to see into the living room. Leo sat on the couch. His hands were secured behind him with duct tape, a strip of it also covering his mouth, but his feet were free.

Brooklyn touched Damon's arm, but her tone was harsh. "His parents are dead anyway. What's he got to go home to?"

He pushed her away. "You're a monster. You're . . ." He couldn't finish the sentence, his face pale, his voice shaky.

"I'm not a monster. I'm a monster's granddaughter."

I chanced another step. I noticed Leo's eye had been blackened, and my mood darkened with it. I hoped that meant he would be ready to fight if it came to it. I caught a glimpse of myself in the mirror—face streaked with dirt, eyes feverish.

Damon turned away from her and walked toward the door. "You don't want to do that," she warned, but he kept walking.

When Damon crossed the threshold, Brooklyn followed, and I moved quickly, stepping from the shadows into full light. Their argument carried from the front porch, and I was near the couch when I heard it—a crack that split into a boom.

She must have shot Damon.

I grabbed Leo from the couch by his elbow and turned toward the kitchen to leave the way I had entered, but the screen slapped in its frame, and Brooklyn was again there. She held the gun in a relaxed grip at her side, but its barrel rose when she saw me.

She took a shot. The gunfire forced us into the hallway, moving fast. I yanked Leo's elbow to telegraph turns but that was our only communication. We both understood the need for silence.

I started testing doors. The first was locked, the second a walk-in linen closet. But the third door swung open into a bedroom.

I pulled the door closed behind us and locked it. I knew Brooklyn was out there, trying doors as we had, quiet now.

I opened the window and pushed out the screen. I untied Leo's wrists and yanked the tape from his mouth, then signaled for him to go first. He bounded through the empty frame and dropped to the ground in one fluid movement. My exit was less graceful, but with my son's help, I managed to land without my knees buckling.

I heard a door slam. We had to run. Leo glanced toward the field, and I knew he recognized this as the best option too.

I heard footfalls, and I whispered, with urgency, "Go," pointing Leo away from the sound.

Then my son was gone, but I stayed—making the same choice I had earlier, my life for my son's—and Brooklyn was there, holding her gun and looking very unhappy to see me.

She fired, the bullet tearing into my left shoulder. Before she could take a second shot, I barreled into her. I grabbed her, my arms rigid, then buried my teeth in her neck.

Brooklyn howled and lost her grip on the gun. It tumbled, but pressed together as we were, it became wedged between us. She clawed at my injured shoulder, but the pain wasn't as heavy as my rage. I took a step back, and the weapon clattered to the ground.

Brooklyn and I both lunged for the gun. She hadn't had to dig herself from the earth and she still had two good shoulders, but I had my fury. A second later, I also had the gun.

"Dee kept your picture on the wall even after you were taken. She spent thousands trying to find you. You weren't even hers. *I* was, by blood, and I was here. But it's you she wanted, *Megan*."

Buying time or eliciting sympathy, I didn't know. My compassion I saved for those she had hurt. Killed.

I pulled the trigger.

Nothing happened.

Shock dawned in Brooklyn's eyes, then a look I'd seen often enough in patients. I knew what her next move would be.

She turned from me and ran.

She stumbled through the field, and I pursued. She might have spent her childhood hiding, but I wouldn't let her hide now. I half expected her to stop at the shed where I'd found Carver, but she lurched past without slowing.

There was only one other place she could be headed. The old creamery. The paint had flaked off the long-abandoned building. Plywood blinded most of the windows.

Brooklyn raced through the open door seconds before I did.

Creatures dead and hidden fouled the air inside. I heard their live brethren scuttling inside the pipes nested on the walls. My lungs seared, dust coating my throat. The moon slanted in through cracks in the ceiling, everything washed in an eerie white light.

Brooklyn rounded a piece of machinery that looked like it had once been used for bottling, several rollers on its conveyor belt missing. Her footfalls became slow, and I pulled within inches.

We faced each other, and I could read her determination to kill me in the grim set of her mouth, the flare of her nose.

Brooklyn lunged, so fast I didn't see it coming, and slammed her fist into my temple. My vision clouded, and I rocked on my heels, but I remained upright. I struck back, aiming for kidneys.

She stepped back, planting her feet wide. Then she came at me again, and the punch landed on the right side of my face.

When she took another swing, I drove my fist into the side of her neck, toward her carotid artery. She tilted slightly, wobbly now, and I hit her again, this time in the base of her throat. She crashed against the conveyer belt.

She straightened and grabbed her neck, gasping. I swung for her kidneys again, my aim truer this time. Her body went slack, and she crashed onto the ground, her head landing hard.

She wiped away blood from a cut on her forehead. "You can fight, which kinda surprises me," she said, her words slurred, "since you've never had to fight for anything your whole life."

With that, she got up. How was she still able to stand?

Brooklyn charged, her shoulders squared to take the impact, but I twisted, throwing my elbow toward her throat. Missed. Stumbling but somehow still on my feet. Staring into the face of the woman who had killed my husband, I surrendered to rage.

Her eyes burned, her intensity matching mine, but I had the reach. When she swung, it fell short, leaving her exposed. I exhaled—one small, sharp breath—focusing all of my energy into my fist. I snapped my elbow. The blow landed with a crunch.

She stumbled backward, grabbing the machinery for balance.

I took a step, but her next question stopped me. "Did you know there was a second grave on the other side of the tree?"

She smiled then, a mirthless smirk as cool as the air but not nearly as cold as her eyes. A recent memory returned—at the grave, I remembered a scratching I thought came from animals.

"Even if Sam wasn't dead earlier, he certainly is now," she said.

My heart shattered into a thousand jagged pieces. The skittering I'd heard. The scratching I'd ignored. Had it been Sam?

It became a chore to breathe. But I wasn't done.

Brooklyn had meant to distract with her revelation, and it worked. Her arm shot out, a rusty knife nicking my right side.

So she hadn't been holding on to the machinery for balance. She had been looking for a weapon. Growing up as she had, it made sense she had weapons hidden here.

When Brooklyn came at me again, I grabbed the hem of her T-shirt, balling it in my fist and pulling her toward me.

She thrashed, fabric tearing, but I held on, trading shirt for arm, twisting until she dropped the knife. Something popped. Shoulder or elbow? Didn't matter. It was hers, not mine. We fell sideways, my shoulder ramming a stack of rotting crates.

But Brooklyn took a harder hit, her head bouncing off the metal edge of the machinery. She lay there, as she had that night on the trail. I had saved her then. My hand twitched. Even now, I wanted to offer it to her. But I couldn't. She might come for me, for my family. When Brooklyn started moving again, I kicked her, my side throbbing in unison with my shoulder, until she stopped.

I shouted for Leo as I stumbled from the creamery, but I was really just shouting into the wind. I could only hope he would hear me and follow to the valley oak at the property's perimeter. I wasn't certain I had enough strength to dig Sam up by myself.

I returned to the gardening shed, found a shovel, then set out across the property. As I ran, I prayed to find the second grave empty, mounds of dirt beside it, Sam waiting at its edge. But when I reached the grave, it remained undisturbed.

Beneath the tree, I started digging. Even with the meager shovelfuls of earth I managed, my arms burned. I prayed for sirens, but I didn't slow, even as my heart rattled inside my chest.

A hand pressed against my back, and I jumped, reminded of the last time I had been touched in the same way at this place.

This time, it wasn't a man pushing me into my grave. It was Leo. My beautiful boy.

His face was slicked with sweat as if he had been running.

"The police?" I asked, and he nodded.

I handed him the shovel and fell to my knees.

Though he didn't know for certain why he was digging, Leo worked with an intensity I could no longer match. I scraped dirt from the grave as best I could. My fingers were raw, but didn't hurt. My head was numb too, and I fought the urge to vomit.

Sam's grave was even shallower than mine had been, and Leo quickly expanded the hole I had made, exposing the wood.

I pointed at the box, too weak to strike the wood myself. Leo understood. He brought the shovel down on the makeshift coffin's lid, the wood splintering more with each whack.

I bowed my head over the rim of the hole to listen, but I heard nothing. Blackness bled into the edges of my vision, followed by flashes of light. Blue and red light. I thought I heard sirens too.

Was Sam alive? Or were we too late?

There were men and women surrounding us now, in uniform mostly but some, like Detective Ray Rico, wearing suits.

Red had told me how Natalie had nearly perished beneath a tree the night she'd given birth, saved only to die later in that grave. Now, they were all dead. Natalie. Dee. Carver. Probably Brooklyn. With so much blood soaked into this land, how could anything but tragedy come to those born here?

Detective Rico loomed beside me, his suit streaked with dirt as he helped Leo and a uniformed officer pry at the lid. Strange to see Rico disheveled like that. No tie, either.

Then together, they grabbed the lid and pulled. We could see him now—Sam.

I noticed Sam's left hand. His ring finger. That was the part of him that moved first. Then I saw the stretcher, and the paramedics who brought it, before finally succumbing to the void.

Chapter 14

LATER, RICO TOLD ME WHY Brooklyn did what she did.

While searching for Sam, I'd heard horrible stories of Dee's abuse, but others came out afterward. Almost all involved the boxes she made for Natalie and Brooklyn. Over years of abuse, the plywood became stained with blood, the lids marked with the scratches made by two desperate girls. Natalie was buried in her box, and Brooklyn tried to bury me in hers.

Usually, the girls would remain confined for three days. I got it now. The notes: *3. 2. 1.* A countdown, but also payback. We endured three days as horrible as the ones Brooklyn had suffered.

Brooklyn didn't find freedom until Dee's death in August. For someone whose liberty was so hard-earned, Brooklyn threw it away easily enough. She survived, but she's in prison now. I'm still not sure how I feel about that. Damon survived too, and I've heard they still communicate.

After Dee's death, Brooklyn found the photos of Natalie. She also found the notes Ernie had given Dee—notes that led Brooklyn to us: me, the woman who had been saved at her expense; and Carver, the man Brooklyn believed should've saved *her*.

In Dee's things, there was no mention of Red. Maybe Dee didn't know he took me. Likely she thought Carver had, since he had been at the house that night too. Either way, I'm grateful for that omission. After all, despite everything, he's still my dad.

THE DAY SAM CAME HOME, Audrey insisted on being in charge of the decorations, which is how the entryway wall had come to be filled with half-empty pink balloons.

Leo had been put in charge of the tape dispenser. Each time Audrey made him redo the design, he complained, as older brothers do, but his complaints lacked conviction. The balloon heart grew more crooked with each attempt. Sam would love it.

"This one needs more tape." Audrey pointed to a sagging balloon already secured with three strips.

"Yeah, 'cause that's gonna help," Leo said, but he pulled off a fresh piece.

My cake hadn't turned out any better, but it was handmade and it was chocolate, so even if it sloped, Sam would love that too.

The evil that had entered our lives hadn't made it over this threshold, and I would continue to force it back with pink balloons and chocolate cake and this. All of this.

"Done?" I asked, my voice cracking. "Because we've got a cranky patient waiting in the car."

"Mom's actually crying over some stupid balloons," Leo said.

"Of course she is," Audrey said. "She's Mom." As if that explained everything. I supposed, in the wake of what had happened, it did. But in this house, I only let the happy tears fall.

At the car, I helped Sam from the passenger seat. He made the prerequisite joke about sponge baths meant to distract me from the way he winced when he got to his feet.

Only happy tears, I reminded myself.

I continued to feel guilt over being so easily manipulated into doubting Sam. In the video of him at the coffee shop, placing his hand on Brooklyn's, I hadn't seen the tears she had manufactured to invite the gesture. But I should have known.

He assured me it was fine, as often as I needed to hear it.

Still a better person than me.

Sam leaned into me as we crossed into the house. I accepted his weight. We both recognized we were stronger together.

"Red coming?" Sam asked. I could tell he was surprised when

I said yes. The invitation didn't mean I had forgiven him, not yet, but it meant I was trying.

Boo bounded at Sam's feet, nearly tripping him.

"Daryl said he'd stop by too."

Audrey shrieked. "Does that mean Lester's coming?"

I smiled and nodded. "And Lester. And Zoe."

"Do we have to wait to have cake?" Audrey asked.

Leo chimed in with, "Mom made it. We're probably extending our lives by waiting."

"I think we should eat the cake now," Sam said.

We didn't bother with plates. I moved the cake to the kitchen counter, and Sam handed out forks. Audrey sat on a stool while the rest of us stood, with me close enough to Sam to feel his leg against me. He pressed his leg into mine, then covered my hand with his.

While we waited for our guests, we finished half the cake. Though a little dry, it was still the best food I had ever eaten. Despite Leo's grumbling, Audrey said she wanted that exact cake for her seventh birthday, which led to making plans for that.

Making plans. Something just a short time earlier I hadn't thought possible. Almost as impossible as the laughter that seemed to come so easily to the kids, and, once or twice, to me too. I leaned into Sam, his warmth, and the cake, but most of all the laughter, serving as sentry against the darkness that was there, always there, but no longer strong enough to intrude. Not unless I chose to let it.

AfterWords

Heather Chavez's debut novel was inspired by a real-life drama. Chavez was picking up her daughter from school one afternoon when the pair noticed a teenage boy being attacked by two others. While the incident ended quickly, for Chavez it led to a series of nerve-racking what-ifs.

"What if the attack had happened at night instead of in the middle of the day?" she asked herself. "What if something even more horrible had preceded the attack? And what if my daughter hadn't been in the car?"

Chavez admits that—unlike her novel's heroine, Cassie—she probably wouldn't have gotten out of the car, even if her daughter hadn't been with her.

In that way, she notes, Cassie is more reckless than she is. Yet the two share certain similarities. In creating Cassie's workaholic character, Chavez drew from her own experiences as a newspaper copy editor: working until midnight nearly every night, and feeling guilty about not spending enough time with her family.

Today, as a writer, it's important to Chavez to portray strong women and mothers. "That's what gelled for me when I was writing the book," she says about Cassie. "Once I found her voice and her strength, all of a sudden it made sense."

Chavez currently lives in Santa Rosa, California, with her family. She is at work on her second novel.

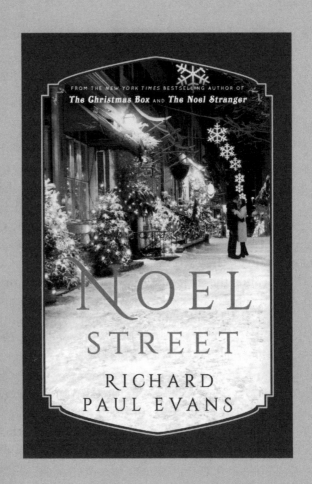

FROM THE *NEW YORK TIMES* BESTSELLING AUTHOR OF
The Christmas Box AND **The Noel Stranger**

NOEL
STREET

RICHARD
PAUL EVANS

Prologue

EVERY STORY IS A ROAD. And on all roads there are potholes and bumps, detours and unexpected encounters. This stretch of my story took place back in 1975 in a small mountain town you've never heard of—Mistletoe, Utah. It was a harsher than usual winter, and everything, it seemed, was frozen—including my life as a single mother working as a waitress at the Noel Street Diner.

Then, on one of those cold days, something came along that changed everything for me. More correctly, some*one*. It was the day I found William Smith lying under a truck on Noel Street.

Nineteen seventy-five seems both like just yesterday and a millennium ago. Gas was fifty-seven cents a gallon, and Foster Grant sunglasses set you back a five spot. Jimmy Hoffa disappeared, and the videocassette recorder appeared. Stylish women wore long print dresses and knits, and men wore polyester leisure suits in colors the fashion industry is still scratching their heads over.

New York City was on the verge of bankruptcy, while *Jaws,* *The Towering Inferno,* and *Funny Lady* reigned at the box office. The year's soundtrack was provided by the likes of the Eagles, Aerosmith, Elton John, and Queen, while a nation with just three television networks watched *The Six Million Dollar*

Man, All in the Family, M*A*S*H, and *The Carol Burnett Show.*

Just the year before, President Nixon had resigned in disgrace over the Watergate break-ins. America was a cauldron of social unrest, and demonstrations and riots were evening news staples. Some of those demonstrations were over the Vietnam War. Some were over racial or gender inequality. All concerned me. I was a single white mother with a Black child whose father had been killed in Vietnam. Dylan, my son, was now nearly seven years old. He knows his father only from my stories and the few photographs I have of him.

Mistletoe, Utah, was an unlikely place to raise a Black son. It was as homogeneous and white as a carton of milk. Dylan was not only the sole Black person in town, he was the only one some of the locals— mostly farmers and ranchers—had ever met. I know that seems hard to believe, but that's how many of these small western towns were.

Nineteen seventy-five was the year Saigon fell and the war ended. At least, historically. Parts of it would never die to me, not even now as I write this. But it was that footnote in history that, perhaps, played the most significant part of that winter's story.

While global chess pieces were being moved around the board by the forces that be, my little world was following its own rickety path, which took a major detour that holiday season, starting with, of all things, a burned-out clutch.

Will it ever stop snowing? I wondered as I walked to the car. The snow had piled up to almost six inches in the driveway of our duplex. I hadn't shoveled; I didn't have the time. Besides, it was just going to snow more. I pushed the snow off my car with a broom. "Come on, Dylan. We've got to go."

"Coming, Mama."

Dylan, who was tall for his age, came out of the house wearing a red-and-green stocking cap that one of the waitresses at the diner had knitted for him and his new winter coat that, in spite of his size, was still way too large. I had bought it that big out of necessity. He had grown out of his last coat in less than a year, and I didn't have the money to keep up.

"Is the door shut?"

"Yes, ma'am."

"Then hop in. We're late."

I laid the broom against the house and got in the car. As I backed out of our driveway, the Fairlane backfired, which made Dylan jump.

"Someone just shot at us!" Dylan shouted. He was imaginative.

"No one shot at us," I said. "It's just the car."

"It exploded."

"I'll give you that."

The Fairlane had been left to me in my grandfather's will. It had been a blessing and a curse. It was more than a decade older than Dylan, and things on it were starting to go, something I was financially not prepared to handle. I had just replaced the alternator two months earlier.

What now? I thought.

Chapter 1

I DON'T KNOW MUCH about cars, even my own—a '57 Ford Fairlane that collectors would die for today but that I couldn't give away back then. That morning as I started the car, something felt different, which from my experience—in both cars and relationships— was rarely good. And there was the smell of something burning, which was never good.

"Do you smell something?" I asked Dylan. He had sensory processing disorder—something we didn't know about back then— and was highly sensitive to smells.

"It smells like burnt toast," he said.

I sighed. "Looks like you're going to be late to school today. We need to see Mr. Renato again."

"I don't like Mr. Renato," Dylan said. "He smells funny."

"That's not nice," I said, even though it was true. "He just smells a little like garlic."

"What's gar-lick?"

"Garlic is something you put in Italian food, like spaghetti sauce and pizza. I know you like those."

"Yeah."

"Mr. Renato is Italian, like pizza. And if you say anything about how he smells in front of him, I'm going to ground you from watching TV for a whole week."

I looked over to see if he was getting it. He was frowning. "Can I tell him he smells like a garlic?"

"No!"

Mr. Renato owned Renato's Expert Auto Repair, but everyone just called it Renato's—a name that outsiders often mistook for an Italian restaurant.

Renato was of direct Italian descent, immigrating to America when he was nineteen. Like everyone else in town, including me, you had to wonder how he ended up in Mistletoe. It was a woman, of course. He met her in New York City and followed her back to a town so small that the McDonald's had only one arch. Actually, that's not true. We didn't have a McDonald's.

That was a joke. I had a whole repertoire of "our town is so small" jokes, mostly shared with me by truck drivers passing through. I've heard them all. *This town is so small that all the city limits signs are on the same post. A night on the town takes six minutes. The New Year's baby was born in September.*

The truth was, Mistletoe was so small that even people in the state of Utah didn't know it existed. Renato's love interest eventually left—both him and Mistletoe—but Renato stayed put. Unfortunately, my car kept us in frequent contact.

Renato's shop was on the way to Howard Taft Elementary, Dylan's school. The repair shop had three bays and a front office that perpetually reeked with the pungent scent of new tires.

"It smells in here," Dylan said as we walked in. I wasn't sure if it was a reference to the tires or the shop's proprietor.

I gave him a stern glance. "Remember what I said. I mean it."

"Yes, ma'am."

Just then a short olive-skinned man walked out of a back office holding a clipboard. He had a pen tucked behind his ear, partially concealed by his salt-and-pepper hair. He wore a long-sleeved, oil-stained cotton work shirt with an embroidered patch with his name on it. He smiled when he saw me.

"Ciao, bella." He walked over and kissed me on both cheeks. "You are too beautiful."

It was nice to hear, even from Renato, who was a living, breathing Italian caricature and pretty much said it to every woman he encountered.

I was pretty in a simple way. Or, at least, I used to be. I was raised in the small town of Cedar City, the only daughter of a military officer turned rancher, and looked as wholesome as my beginnings suggested. I had flaxen hair, a small mouth, but full lips and large brown eyes. I was trim, with curves. I wasn't tall, but at five feet five I was still taller than my mother. My height was something I got from my father, who was six one.

I didn't feel very pretty in those days. In the mirror of my self-image, I just saw a lonely, quietly desperate woman hidden behind a mask of exhaustion.

"Hi, Renato."

He smiled even more broadly. *"Mamma mia, sei troppo bella,"* he said, sighing dramatically. Pretty much everything he did was dramatic. "Every time I see you it reminds me that I was born twenty-five years too early."

"Maybe I like older men."

"Perché mi stuzzichi. How you tease an old man." He glanced down at Dylan. "How are you, *bambino?"*

"My name's not bambino," Dylan said.

Renato smiled. *"È vero."* He looked back up at me. "What brings you to my shop, *bella?"*

"The usual," I said. "My car's acting up again."

"Your curse, my blessing," he said. "Your naughty car brings you back to me. What is the problem this time?"

"Our car exploded this morning," Dylan said.

Renato looked out the door toward my car. "Exploded?"

"It backfired," I said. "But that's not the problem. I think it's the clutch. It feels loose. And it smells bad, like something is burning."

Renato frowned. "That is not good. Your clutch may be going out."

"That sounds expensive," I said anxiously. "Is that expensive?"

He nodded side to side, then raised his hand to explain. He always used his hands to speak. "The clutch plate is only twenty-five dollars."

"Thank goodness," I said. "I can almost afford that."

"It is not the part that is the problem," Renato said. "Replacing the part is the devil. That is what costs the money."

"How much?" I asked.

"Usually costs about five hundred."

My stomach fell. "Five hundred?"

"I'm sorry, but do not panic yet. I will have my man check it out first. You have your keys?"

"Right here." I fished my keys from my purse, which was a little embarrassing, since my key chain weighed about a pound and had two massive plastic key chains attached that Dylan had made for me at school that said WORLD'S BEST MOM.

Renato smiled at the bundle. "Good thing you have a big purse," he said.

"I wish it was to hold all the money I had."

"We should all have that problem," he said. "I'll have William check your car."

"Who's William?"

"He is my new guy."

"What happened to Nolan?"

"Nolan left."

"Left? He was here forever."

"Thirty-three years. He moved back to Montana to raise cattle on his brother's ranch. Fortunately, this man, William, showed up two days before he left. He used to be a mechanic in the army." He walked to the door to the garage and opened it.

"William."

A man about my age looked up from beneath the hood of a car. It was rare to see a new face in town outside the diner. He was tall, thin, with dark brown hair and dark features. Ruggedly handsome, I guess. At least, I thought that at first. It didn't last long. "Yes, sir," he shot back, like he was still in the military.

"I love it when he says that," Renato said to me. He turned back to his man. "I need you to check the clutch on a Fairlane."

"Yes, sir. Keys in the ignition?"

"I have them." He threw him my bundle. The man caught them.

The man, William, suddenly looked at me and Dylan with a strange expression. As the mother of a nonwhite child, I was used to this. "I'll need to take it around the block."

"Of course," I said, like I had any idea what he needed to do.

"He is going to take it for a drive so he can feel the clutch," Renato explained. The new guy opened a bay door and walked out to my car.

About five minutes later William pulled my car into one of the bays and climbed out.

"What do you think?" Renato asked.

"It's definitely slipping," he said. "I can smell it."

I frowned. "That's what I said."

I looked at Renato hoping for some good news, but he only frowned. "I am sorry, *bella*. It is going to need a new clutch."

My heart fell. It seems I was always paying for something. I had just finished paying off the alternator. Now this. And Christmas was coming. "Can you fix it?"

"Of course. I'll work with you on the price. I will give you the family discount. Can you make payments?"

"How much would you need?"

"I can do fifty dollars a month. I'll do the tune-up for free."

"Okay." I didn't have a choice. Dylan and I were barely making it as it was. I'd have to pick up an extra shift each month just for the clutch and pray something else didn't give out.

"Thank you," I said softly.

"*Prego, signorina.*"

"How long will it take to fix?"

"Maybe four to six hours. William is a fast worker. Can you leave it with me?"

"I kind of need a car. Will it last another day?"

"William, how much longer can she drive her car?"

"The clutch probably has a week or two left on it."

"Will I damage the clutch more?" I asked.

Renato shook his head. "The damage is done. But if it goes out completely, you could damage your engine."

Just then William shouted, "Hey! Get off that!"

I spun around. He was shouting at Dylan, who was standing on top of an oily machine next to a stack of tires. "That's not a toy."

Dylan was paralyzed with fear. He wasn't used to being yelled at. I walked over to him. "Sorry," I said to William. "He doesn't know better."

"You should keep an eye on him. This isn't a playground."

"I'm sorry," I said again. I turned to Dylan, who was still cowering. "Come on, Dylan. Let's go. Don't touch anything." So much for Mr. Rugged Good Looks, I thought.

"He's scary," Dylan said as I took his hand.

"Yeah," I said under my breath. "Very." I walked Dylan back into the front office. Renato was already there behind his counter writing on a pad.

"So here is the work order. We are going to replace your clutch and give you a free tune-up."

"So this new guy of yours. Mr. Personality."

Renato looked at me. "Mr. Personality?"

"How's he working out?"

"William is a hard worker. He is doing a very good job."

"But not much of a personality," I said.

Renato's expression didn't change. "Do not be quick to judge."

I wasn't sure how to handle Renato's uncharacteristic seriousness. And I was still reeling a little from his employee reprimanding my son and me, as well as the devastating financial news. "I'll see you tomorrow."

Renato nodded. "I am sorry for the bad news, *bella*. But I will give you the family discount."

"Thank you." As I left the place, it was all I could do not to cry. *Why couldn't I catch a break?*

As I pulled out of Renato's, the Fairlane seemed to drive even worse.

Dylan was still quiet as I pulled into the school parking lot.

"You okay?" I asked. "That was kind of scary to be yelled at."

He nodded. "I wasn't going to break anything."

"Maybe he was just afraid you were going to break yourself." I didn't believe it, but it didn't matter. I wasn't protecting the jerk; I was protecting my son. And he was probably just another bigot.

I parked the car in the vacant bus lane in front of the school. "Come on. School waits for no one."

Dylan was more than a half hour late for school, so I had to sign him in. I held his hand as we walked into the front office.

"Good morning, Elle Bell," the school secretary, Cheryl, said brightly. Much too brightly for where my mind was.

"Morning, Cheryl," I said, purposely leaving off the *good*.

"Late start?"

"Car problems."

She shook her head. "Again?"

"Different ailment, same car."

"I have the same problem with my husband," she said. "Dylan, please take this note to Mrs. Duncan." She handed him a pink slip of paper. Dylan turned to go.

"Wait," I said. "What about my kiss?"

Dylan looked embarrassed. "All right."

He quickly pecked my cheek. I pulled him into a big hug that he tried to escape from, then released him. As he backed away from me, I said, "Don't forget I'm working late tonight. Fran will be picking you up from school. You got that?"

"Bye, Mom." He ran out of the office.

"He's a good boy," Cheryl said.

"Probably the one thing in my life that's not going wrong."

"Well, if you had to choose something to not be broken, that's the thing."

I drove from the school to the diner. I could smell my burning clutch as I got out of the car. As usual, I parked behind the restaurant and walked in through the back door.

"Sorry I'm late," I said, shutting the door behind me.

Loretta, the diner's owner, looked at me. "Everything okay?"

"No. Another car problem."

She shook her head. "Is it serious?"

"Five hundred dollars serious."

She frowned. "I'm sorry. Pray for big tips."

"I already am," I said. "If they don't pick up, I'm going to be short on next month's rent."

"I'm sorry, baby," Loretta said. "Miracles happen."

"I could use a miracle right about now." I put on my apron. "But I won't be holding my breath."

IT WAS a normal day, as far as my days went, made up of the usual mix of regulars and strangers—elderly locals who were lonely or bored, as well as the occasional trucker. Like my clientele, my schedule was equally predictable. When I worked the late shift, I got home from work at ten—eleven on weekends. When I walked in that night, Fran, my sitter, was sitting at the kitchen table doing homework. Fran went to school at Weber State during the day to study music. She was lovely.

"How was he?" I asked.

"Amazing, as usual. He made this for you."

She held up a blue-green marbled ball of Play-Doh with tooth-picks sticking out, four on the bottom, two on top.

I took it from her. "What is it?"

"It's a reindeer," she said, grinning. "Can't you tell?"

I grinned back. "I love it."

"He loves you." She put her homework in a bag and then said, "I should probably tell you, Dylan asked me something tonight. He asked if Santa was a Negro."

It was the first time he'd used that word. "What did you say?"

"I said, 'Santa is a spirit. He's the color of giving.' Dylan seemed good with that. I hope that's okay."

My eyes watered. "Thank you. You said the right thing."

"He's a sweet boy."

I gave Fran a hug. She picked up her case and walked to the door. "See you tomorrow."

"Good night."

I walked to Dylan's room and opened the door. He was asleep. Fran was right; he was a sweet boy. He was also a beautiful boy. He had light mocha-colored skin and was lanky and handsome like his father, though with the more subtle facial features from my Swedish-Welsh heritage. He was exotic-looking, as he had blue eyes—something that people would sometimes stare at in disbelief.

I kissed his forehead. "I love you, little man." I shut his door, then went to my room and undressed.

Where had he heard the word Negro? I wasn't surprised that he'd asked. As the only Black person in an all-white farming town, it was only a matter of time.

The next morning, I got Dylan up, and while he ate breakfast, I made his usual sack lunch—a peanut-butter-and-jam sandwich, chips, and the donut I brought home every night from the diner. I checked my watch and said, "C'mon, sport. Time to go."

As we climbed into the car, Dylan asked, "Mom, what's a Negro? Marsha at school says I'm a Negro."

Take a deep breath. "Well, that means you're super smart and very handsome."

Dylan looked confused. "She said I'm a Negro because my skin is brown."

"That's part of it," I said. "Everyone has different colors on their body. Some have different color hair, different color eyes, and some have different color skin."

"She said I can't go to her house because I'm a Negro."

I bit down. "Well, there you go. People at Marsha's house must not be very smart or handsome, so they're intimidated by you."

"What's inti . . . date?"

"Intimidate. It means to be scared."

"Why are they scared?"

"Because they're not as smart or handsome. Did you even want to go to Marsha's house? It doesn't sound like a very fun place."

"She's having a birthday party."

I tried not to show my anger. "Some people are just—" I stopped short of calling her dumb. "They don't get out much," I finally said. I pulled up to the drop-off zone. "I love you, buddy."

"Love you too, Mom."

I watched him walk up to the front of the school and fall in with the other kids, all of them white. As I pulled away, I started to cry.

Chapter 2

I DROVE OVER TO RENATO'S and sat in the parking lot until I regained my composure. I wiped my eyes and then walked into the garage's office, a bell above the door announcing my entrance. To my dismay the new guy, William, was standing at the counter. I stiffened at the sight of him.

"Good morning, Elle," he said with surprising gentleness. Even more surprising was that he knew my name.

"Is Renato here?"

"No. He won't be in until this afternoon. But he told me you would be bringing your car in this morning. He has a loaner for you. It's that green-and-white Plymouth Valiant out there." He smiled. "I know what you're thinking. It's too sexy to drive."

I almost smiled too but didn't want to encourage him. "Thank you. How long will my car take?"

"I'll have it done by three," he said.

"What time do you close?"

"Five."

"I don't get off work until eight. Can I pick it up tomorrow?"

"No problem."

"Thank you."

He handed me the keys to the loaner. As I turned to go, he said, "I'm sorry I got mad at your son yesterday. The machine he was playing on could have hurt him. I'm just a little jumpy. I didn't mean to upset him. Or you. Please forgive me."

I looked at him. He was definitely sincere. There was also a vulnerability to him that I hadn't seen the last time.

"Thank you for watching out for my son. And the apology."

"You're welcome. One more thing. The driver's-side door on the Valiant sticks a little. You just need to give it a good tug. Oh, and the brakes are a little touchy. They're fine, just a little sensitive."

Like me, I thought. "Thanks for the warning."

I walked out to the Valiant. As warned, the door stuck. I yanked it open and climbed in. I adjusted the seat, put on my seat belt, then started the engine. It roared like an injured lion.

Some sexy, I thought.

As I drove to work, I prayed that the Fairlane's clutch wouldn't be as bad as they thought. I knew there was no hope for it, but I prayed anyway.

"How's it going, Jamie?" I said, walking into the diner. Jamie was the waitress I worked with most. She was five years older than me and off-and-on married so often that I sometimes forgot her marital status. She was born in Mistletoe and had worked at the diner since she was sixteen. She was now thirty.

"You know, different day, same problems. You got a new car? Those Valiants are crazy sexy."

I laughed. "It's a loaner Renato gave me while he fixes mine."

"Oh, right. Loretta told me your car was on the fritz. You can't catch a break, can you?"

"Not lately."

"Well, I'll pray for large tips. For both of us." As we walked out into the dining room, Jamie's eyes widened. "Oh, no."

"What?"

"Ketchup Lady is back."

I groaned. "I'm starting my shift with Ketchup Lady. Can this day get any worse?"

"I'd take her, but you know she's headed to your station."

"It's okay."

I watched as the Ketchup Lady, as usual, walked past the PLEASE WAIT TO BE SEATED sign and sat herself at the table she had claimed as her own.

No one knew the woman's name or where she lived. She had shown up at the diner the previous spring and had stopped by every week since. We called her Ketchup Lady because she put ketchup on everything, from pancakes to fried chicken and mashed potatoes. Her plate looked like a crime scene. None of the waitresses were fans, which had less to do with her culinary affinity than her personality, which was as nasty as her palate.

This morning she was wearing a red T-shirt that read: I LIKE KETCHUP ON MY KETCHUP.

I walked up to her table. "Good morning," I lied. "What can I get for you today?" *Besides ketchup.*

She looked at me as if she'd never seen me before. "What *may* you get for me? Learn proper grammar; you'll go further in life. I'd like the ham-and-cheese omelet smothered in ketchup. Also, a side of sausage—patties, not links—with ketchup. And your buttermilk biscuits with ketchup."

The biscuits were a new addition to her culinary repertoire. The idea of putting ketchup on a biscuit made me sick.

"We have a policy that we don't put things on our biscuits," I said. It was a policy I had made up on the spot. "But you're welcome to put anything on it you like."

She looked annoyed. "Then I'll need an extra bottle of ketchup. This one is nearly gone."

The plastic ketchup bottle on the table was more than half full. *Was she planning on drinking it?* I wouldn't have been surprised.

"Sure thing," I said. "I'll be right back with your meal."

I took her order to the kitchen. Our chef, Bart, looked it over. "So she's back," he said. "The First Lady of Ketchup."

"Back like a bad cough," I said.

I liked Bart—we all did. He had been with the diner since it opened, when he was young and still had a life or, at least, dreams. Now he was obese, old, and tired and lived alone in a Winnebago on the outskirts of Mistletoe near the town's landfill. The waitresses were the only family—male or female—he had.

As I left the kitchen, a group of men walked in. They were all wearing the same kind of trucking-company shirt. I walked over and greeted them, led them to a corner of my section, then got their menus and water. As I passed by Ketchup Lady, she said, "How long will it be?"

"Not long," I said.

"Check on my meal before you take that large table's order. I have a busy morning."

I bit my tongue. Literally. I wanted to empty the bottle of ketchup on her head. I went back to the kitchen. To my surprise Ketchup Lady's order was done.

I carried the woman's meal out along with an unopened bottle of ketchup, setting them down on the table in front of her. Ketchup Lady looked up at me with annoyance.

"I said *smothered.*"

The omelet was almost drowning in a pool of tomato. "You can add more ketchup yourself if you'd like."

"I didn't come here to make my own food," she said. "That's what I pay you for."

Again I bit down. "Here," I said. I took the opened bottle of ketchup and poured out the rest of its contents onto the plate, pretty much covering everything in a sea of red. "How's that?"

She looked at it for a moment and then said, "That will do."

I walked back to the kitchen, shaking my head. Fortunately, she didn't stay long. As I cleared her table, I noticed her plate was clean. Like it had been licked clean. And she left a tip with a note: *Here's your tip. I shouldn't have to ask for more ketchup.*

Around a quarter to five, a little before the dinner rush, Loretta came out of her office. "Elle, you've got a phone call. It's Renato," she said with unveiled enmity. Loretta knew Renato. Biblically, I mean. She'd once had a fling with him.

I wiped my hands on a dishcloth. "My car must be done." I walked back to her office. The receiver was sitting to the side of the telephone. "Hello."

"Elle," Renato said. "I have bad news."

My heart panicked. "It cost more than five hundred dollars?"

"No, it is something else. The reason your Fairlane backfired was because your timing belt is going out."

"The timing belt? What does that cost?"

"It is like the clutch. It is not the part; it is the labor. The belt is only fifty dollars, but there are a lot of engine parts that need to be removed to replace it."

"Can I drive without it?"

"No, *bella mia*. The car will not run without a timing belt."

I groaned, rubbing my eyes with my hand. "How much?"

From the length of his hesitation, I knew his answer would be bad. "Six hundred."

"Six hundred more. With the clutch, that's more than a thousand dollars." I breathed out heavily. "I don't even know if the car's worth that."

"Old cars do not become new," he lamented. "I checked the Blue Book on your car. It is worth almost two thousand. Maybe you should get a new car."

"But then I'd have a monthly payment . . ."

"Yes, but you have one now, anyway. If you sold the car, you could pay off the repairs and use the money toward a monthly payment. It would at least buy you a few months."

I pushed away my panic. "I'll think about it."

"So do you want me to fix it?"

I thought over my predicament. "I can't sell a car that doesn't run," I finally said. "I'll figure something out."

"I'm sorry, *bella*. I wish I could just do the work for you. But it is hard enough keeping the shop open as it is."

"I understand. I'd never ask that. When will it be ready?"

"We have to order the belt, but William is fast. It should be done by tomorrow night. You'll have it for the weekend."

"Thank you." I hung up and tried not to cry. Maybe I should have. I'm told that crying waitresses make more tips.

THE next morning, I dropped Dylan off, then hurried to the diner. Loretta was sitting at her desk counting receipts. "Good morning, honey."

"Not so good," I said, stopping at the door to her office. "I need to work more shifts."

Loretta looked up. "You got it, honey. You can start tonight if you like. Cassie just called in sick again. She's got that influenza that's going around. Trying to earn a little extra for Christmas?"

"Christmas is the least of my worries. I'm pretty sure the universe has conspired to bankrupt me before the year's out."

Loretta looked at me sympathetically. "I'm sorry, honey. Sometimes it feels like we're running just to stand still."

"I'm running and still going backward."

"Now that's depressing," Loretta said. "So I'm going to start putting out the Christmas decorations today."

"Don't do it all yourself," I said. "I want some fun."

"I'll have Bart bring down the boxes when he's got a minute."

I loved it when we decorated. The diner, like the street it was named after, was made for the holiday and wore it well.

"Hey, Elle," Jamie said, invading the back room. "Dennis is here. He's waiting for you."

"Thanks, doll."

I walked through the kitchen toward the front. Bart smiled when he saw me. "Elle."

"Morning, chef-man. Dennis is here. The usual."

"The Dennis usual," he echoed. "Eggs fried hard, side of ham, drizzle of mustard on the side."

"You got it."

Dennis was one of my regulars. He was an older gentleman—eighties, I guessed—a widower, tall, with a massive red nose and thick silver eyebrows. He wore a gray wool Irish flatcap that I'd never seen off his head, his silver hair peeking out from under it.

Dennis was sitting in his usual corner booth. He smiled when he saw me. "Hey, Elle."

"Good morning, Dennis."

His brows rose. "But is it?"

"Not really," I said. "But it's a pleasant fiction."

"Indeed," he said, and shut his menu. "I'll have the usual, with a drizzle of mustard on the side."

"I know. I already put your order in."

"You did, did you?"

"I thought I'd save you some time. Busy man like you."

"I'm about as busy as a sloth on sleeping pills. Who knows, I might mix things up on you sometime and order a short stack and hash browns just to keep you on your toes."

"I'll make you a deal. Change the hat and I'll wait for your order." He grinned. "Fair enough."

Outside the diner came a loud, prolonged honk, followed by a staccato chorus of others. The front of the diner was all windows, and I looked out to see what was happening. From what I could see, there was an older model olive-green Ford pickup parked in the street in front of the diner. The driver's-side door was open, and peculiarly, there was no one inside.

"What in tarnation?" Dennis said. "Looks like some fool just ditched his truck in the middle of the road."

Just then Lyle Ferguson, who owned the local hardware store, stormed through the door of the diner. "Someone call the police."

"What's going on?" Loretta asked, walking out from the kitchen.

"There's a man under that truck," Lyle said.

"He was run over?" Loretta asked.

"No, he just got out and crawled under it."

I walked to the door and looked out. I could see a man lying on his stomach underneath a truck. "What's he doing?" I asked.

"He's crazy," Lyle said. "He's shouting things in Chinese."

A blue-and-white police car with no siren but lights flashing pulled up to the curb next to the diner. Two officers got out. I knew both men, as they were diner regulars.

The driver of the police car, a lanky red-haired officer named Andy, knelt down beside the truck. Then the other officer, Peter, a stocky, thick man with a crew cut, did as well.

Pedestrians stopped on the sidewalk to watch as the drama unfolded.

"He's under his truck," Dennis said. "That crazy got under his truck. Probably on drugs. It's that LSD."

"He should be locked up in an asylum," Lyle said.

I had no idea what was going on, but my heart felt for the man. "Maybe he needs some coffee." I poured some coffee into a paper cup and walked out into the cold.

Andy and Peter were still crouched down next to the truck, which was still idling, the fumes of its exhaust clouding the air. Like Lyle had said, the man underneath the truck was shouting in a foreign tongue. I didn't understand what he was saying, but I understood the tone—he sounded angry. Or scared.

"Is everything okay?" I asked.

Officer Andy glanced up. "Stay back, Elle."

The man kept shouting, his voice growing in ferocity.

In spite of the warning, I moved a little closer and crouched down to see who it was. To my surprise I recognized him. It was William, the new guy at Renato's.

"I know him," I said.

Both officers looked at me.

"You know him?" Andy asked.

I nodded. Then I said, "William, can you hear me? It's me, Elle. Can you hear me? You're going to be okay."

His gaze met mine. He suddenly stopped shouting. The intensity left his face, replaced by a look of confusion.

"I brought you some coffee."

William looked to me like someone who had just woken from a dream. He wiped his eyes. Then he lay on his side and groaned a little, as if recovering from the outburst.

"Are you okay?" I asked.

"Yeah," he said, shielding his eyes.

"Sir," Andy said. "We need you to come out from under the truck."

William looked disoriented. Or maybe embarrassed. "Yes, sir," he said. He slid out from under the truck. The front of his sweatshirt was soaked and dirty. He put his head in his hands.

Andy turned to Peter. "I think we're okay. Go direct traffic."

Peter stood and walked around behind the truck.

Andy turned back to William. "Are you all right?"

"I'm sorry," he said. "I'm not sure what happened."

I moved in closer to William. "I brought you some coffee," I said again. I offered him the cup. "It's black."

William took the coffee. He drank the entire thing in two gulps, then handed me the cup. "Thank you."

"You're welcome."

"We need to get your truck out of here," Andy said to William. "Do you mind if I have Peter drive it?"

William rubbed his face. "The keys are inside."

"Thank you," Andy said, though he already knew. The truck was still idling. He turned and shouted, "Pete, move the truck."

"On it," Peter shouted back.

As Peter came back around, I said, "Can we get his coat?"

"Grab his coat," Andy said.

Peter grabbed William's thick army-green jacket and handed it to me, then climbed inside the truck.

"Where are you going to take it?" William asked.

"Not far," Andy replied. "Just down to the station. I'll drive you. We just need to ask you a few questions. Make sure you're all right."

William nodded. Andy stood, offered William his hand, and helped him up. "My car's right here," Andy said.

"Here's your coat," I said.

He took it from me and put it on. "Thank you."

William followed Andy to the police car. I just stood there watching as William climbed in. The police car drove off, followed by William's truck. I walked back inside the diner.

"What was that about?" Loretta asked.

"I honestly don't know," I said.

"It's that LSD," Dennis said. "Kids and drugs these days. I tell you, the world's coming apart at the seams."

THAT afternoon, I called Renato's. Renato answered the phone.

"Hi, it's Elle."

"*Ciao, bella.*"

"Did you hear what happened with your new guy?" I asked.

"*Si.* William told me. He did not look well, so I sent him home. That means your car is not going to be done by tonight."

"I understand."

"You can keep the Valiant for the weekend. It is a sexy car."

"Thank you," I said. "Is William okay?"

"I do not know," he said. "But he is a good man. We can hope."

Chapter 3

I woke the next morning to eighteen inches of new snow. Dylan wanted me to take him tubing and was upset when I told him that I had to work.

"But you don't work Saturday mornings," he said.

"I know. We just need a little more money right now."

"I hate money," he said.

I hugged him. "So do I. But I wish I had more of it."

Fran watched Dylan while I worked a double. Andy and Peter, the police officers, came in during the dinner shift.

"Hey, Elle," Andy said.

"Hey," I said. "Sit wherever."

"Thanks," Andy said.

I brought some water glasses over to the table. "Need a menu?"

"No," Andy said. "We know it by heart."

Peter shook his head. "I'm good too."

"What can I get you boys?" I asked.

Andy said, "I'll have the turkey sandwich smothered in gravy, with mashed potatoes, cranberry sauce, and mixed vegetables."

"One Thanksgiving come early," I said. "And what would you like to drink?"

"Ginger beer. And a piece of apple pie."

"I'll have the meat loaf special," Peter said. "Gravy on top *and* on the smashed potatoes."

"Smash the potatoes," I said. "Did you want some pie?"

"I'll have the apple."

I went back to the kitchen and put in the order. Then, while the chef was cooking, I took a short break to eat my own dinner. I was just through my meal when the kitchen bell rang.

"Order up, Elle."

"Thanks, Bart."

I carried the plates out to the police officers. "Here you go, gentlemen."

They both thanked me. Then Andy said, "Hey, I wanted to say, that was really nice of you to take that coffee out to that guy. He really appreciated it. He mentioned it several times."

"So are you guys friends?" Peter asked.

"No. I just met him a few days ago," I said. "He's a mechanic over at Renato's. He's working on my car."

"From under your car to his," Peter said, amusing himself.

"Why did he crawl under his truck?" I asked.

Andy cleared his throat. "I don't know the term for it, but that guy is a Vietnam vet . . ."

"Shell shock," Peter said. "It happened to a cousin of mine. His brain never really came back from the war. He ended up hanging himself."

Andy nodded. "Apparently, he saw bad stuff over there."

"He told us he lost half his patrol in an ambush," Peter said.

Andy continued, "So yesterday he was in front of your diner waiting for the light to change, when a song came on the radio that, like, triggered him. He suddenly thought he was under attack from the Vietcong."

Peter shook his head. "Down at the station, he told us he thought we were Vietcong soldiers. He shouted at us in Vietnamese."

"I didn't know soldiers had to learn Vietnamese," I said.

"They don't if they don't have to," Andy said.

"He was a POW for almost four years. He was in that famous Hanoi Hilton," Peter added.

"Oh, dear," I said.

"I can't imagine what that would do to your brain," Andy said. "He was with one of the last groups to come home."

I thought about how harshly I'd judged him. "Where's he from?"

"He moved here three weeks ago from Colorado, but originally he's from Indiana."

"Is he okay?" I asked.

"I think so," Andy said. "We took him over to the hospital in Ogden and let someone there check him out. They've got a psychiatric ward there."

"Hopefully they can help," I said.

"That was a tough thing, that war," Peter said, slowly shaking his head. "A lot of those boys never really came back."

Suddenly I teared up. Andy looked over at him. "You idiot."

Peter looked at me. "I'm sorry, Elle. I forgot."

"You *forgot* to plug in your brain this morning," Andy said. "So sorry, Elle. We shouldn't have brought it up."

"It's okay," I said, wiping my eyes. "I asked." I took a deep breath. "I'll stop bothering you boys and let you eat."

"You're never a bother, Elle," Andy said.

I started to go, then turned back. "What was the song that set him off?"

"Creedence Clearwater Revival," he said. "'Run Through the Jungle.'"

Sunday was the only day I had off all week. It was also my only day to spend with Dylan. The day began as it always did, with me making Dylan waffles with whipped cream and then taking him to church. We were nearing Thanksgiving, so the sermon was on gratitude and the power of thankfulness. I was grateful to hear it. It was nice to be reminded of all I had to be grateful for.

After church we came home and I made chili and homemade bread, using half the dough for fried scones. (In Utah the term scones is used for what the rest of the world calls fry bread or elephant ears.) My homemaking habits were more than economical. They were reminiscent of my own upbringing. Growing up in Cedar City, my mother made homemade bread every week. At least, she would when she wasn't on a bender.

After lunch Dylan asked if we could go outside and make a snowman. We made two: an effigy of each of us. Afterward we came back inside and made Christmas cookies. I had a collection of five Christmas cookie cutters: a star, a stocking, an angel, a Christmas tree, and a reindeer, the last being Dylan's favorite.

While waiting for the cookies to cool, I let Dylan eat an unfrosted one and watch TV while I took a forty-five-minute nap—by far, my greatest luxury of the week. Then we frosted the cookies and finished our night with our Sunday-evening tradition of lying on my bed and watching *The Wonderful World of Disney*.

I looked forward to this, as it was the one time that Dylan would still let me hold him. I knew it wouldn't always be that way—a fact I mourned. He was my little guy. My life. Even with the hardships of those days, I often thought that I would have loved to freeze that time of Dylan's life. But even then I knew it would be a mistake. To hold the note is to spoil the song.

MONDAY morning it was back to the usual grind. The diner's traffic was typical: the local regulars, a half-dozen truckers hopping off I-15, the odd salesman stopping by for breakfast.

Dennis came in at his usual time. He was wearing the same hat, of course. In spite of my earlier threat, I didn't put his order in.

"Morning, Elle."

"Good morning, Dennis. How's your day?"

"I'll let you know when it happens," he said. "I'll have the usual. If you didn't already have your guy back there make it."

"No, I waited. A drizzle of mustard."

"A drizzle of mustard."

A few minutes later I brought out his food.

"That was some excitement last week," he said. "Did you ever hear what happened to that guy who was run over by the truck? I looked in the obituaries this morning, but there wasn't anyone who had died in a truck-related accident."

Dennis's memory wasn't great. Somewhere over the weekend, he must have told himself a different story about the event. Dennis once told me he read the obituaries every day to see if he was in them. If he wasn't, he got dressed.

"He wasn't run over by the truck," I said. "He climbed under it."

Dennis's brow furrowed. "Why would he do that?"

"I guess he wasn't feeling well," I said.

"That makes no sense. Most of the time, I don't feel well, but I've never once crawled under my car." He shook his head. "He must still be alive. He wasn't in the obituary."

I WAS working a double shift, and the only time the diner could afford for me to be gone was between two and four, our slow time. I was eager to get my car back, but by the time the dinner rush ended, Renato's would be closed.

A little before noon I found Loretta in her office. "Loretta, I need to take a break after the lunch rush."

She looked up from her paperwork. "Did the school call?"

"No. I need to pick up my car before the shop closes."

"Fine with me, sugar plum. You hear that, Jamie?" she shouted. "You're pulling double duty this afternoon while Elle gets her car."

"Got it," Jamie said. She was putting on mascara in the bathroom outside Loretta's office. I don't know how Loretta even knew she was there. She had a sixth sense that way.

Before becoming a waitress, Jamie had worked a previous life as a hairstylist, and she saw her body, all six feet of it, as a blank canvas to be painted on—with makeup and hair dye being her preferred media.

Truthfully, I wasn't positive what color her hair was, though I guessed it was light brown on its way to gray. Since I met her, her hair had been platinum, dishwater blond, strawberry blond, lavender, umber, black, chestnut, and flaxen—pretty much the gamut of follicular possibility. Her color du jour was ginger.

"Thanks, honey," I said.

"Don't mention it. I'm praying for a miracle healing for your clutch."

I wasn't looking forward to getting my car back. I hated my car. And I was terrified to see the repair bill.

I drove over to Renato's a little before three.

"She's right there," Renato said, pointing. He handed me the keys with a sheet of yellow paper. "And here is the bill."

I took the paper from him. It hurt to see it. It was for seventy-seven dollars—twenty more than I hoped it would be.

"Seventy-seven?"

"Yes, *signorina*."

I looked into his eyes. "I know you're giving me a good deal, but right now that's a little steep for my monthly budget. Is it possible we could stretch it out a little more and make the monthly payment in the fifty-dollar range?"

"That is not a payment," Renato said.

I looked at him quizzically. "I don't understand."

"That is the whole bill. *Tutto il conto.*"

It took a moment for me to understand. "But you said it would be more than five hundred just for the clutch. And more for the broken belt."

"That bill is just for parts. There is no charge for labor."

"But . . ." I looked at him with gratitude. "You can't do that."

"Well, I didn't," he said. "William did. He repaired your car on his own time. It took him until four in the morning. You can thank me for the heating bill and him for the labor. *Un bacio* will be fine," he said, turning his cheek to me.

I kissed it, then said, "He fixed my car for free?"

"Except for the cost of parts," Renato said.

I couldn't believe it. "Is he still here?"

"No. He was sick over the weekend, so he's taking the day off."

"He was sick while he was working on my car?"

"Very sick. He was coughing like an old tractor. I think he has the influenza," Renato said. "I could barely understand him this morning." He leaned forward. "He sounded a little *pazzo.*"

"*Pazzo?*"

"A little delirious. Very sick."

I was speechless. Then I pulled my checkbook from my purse. "I'll pay this now." I wrote a check for seventy-seven dollars and handed it to Renato. "Why did he do that?"

"He said you were kind to him," Renato said.

"All I did was take him a cup of coffee."

"I told you, remember? Do not judge him too harshly."

"I'm sorry," I said. "That was foolish of me." I took a deep breath. "I would like to thank him. Do you know where he lives?"

He scrawled a number on the back of my receipt. "He lives in that apartment building on the end of Noel Street. The one with the *schifoso* yard, just three blocks down from the diner."

"I know the one," I said. "Thank you."

"*Prego, bella.*"

I got in my car and started it. It sounded beautiful. I suddenly began crying. *How could I have misjudged the man so badly?*

As I walked back into the diner, Jamie looked me over. "Oh, honey." My eyes must have been red, because she hugged me. "I'm so sorry. I've got a little stashed away. I can help."

Her response only made me cry more. "That's not why I'm crying. He fixed it for free."

"Renato fixed your car for free?" Loretta said, walking into the conversation. "That's a first. That man would charge a baby for diapers."

"It wasn't Renato," I said. "It was the new guy. William."

"The guy who stopped traffic the other day?" Jamie said. "The one you said was a beast?"

"I'm so sorry I said that. He worked on my car until four in the morning."

"Why would he do that?" Jamie asked.

"I don't know. All I did was take him a cup of coffee."

Loretta shook her head. "That must have been some coffee. Is he single?"

"Is he cute?" Jamie added.

"You two have a one-track mind."

"At least someone's on that track, baby girl," Loretta said. "You're derailed."

"I don't know if he's single."

"Well, you better find out. What did you say to him?"

"I didn't say anything. He wasn't there. Renato said he was sick. He was sick when he worked on my car."

"Maybe you should take him some chicken soup," Jamie said.

"That's a good idea," I said.

"I'll donate a crock of chicken noodle," Loretta said. "And whatever else you want to take him. We got pecan pie in today. A man fixes your car for free, you better take care of him."

"I'll take him dinner," I said. "But I don't get off until ten."

"I don't have anything tonight," Loretta said. "You can take off at seven thirty, after the rush."

"Thank you."

"You never answered me," Jamie said. "Is he cute?"

I thought a moment, then said, "Yes. He is."

Loretta nodded. "That always helps."

I was surprised to find myself growing excited about the prospect of seeing William, though frankly, I had no idea how the encounter would go. I'd seen the man three times. The first time, he yelled at my son and then scolded me; the second time, he apologized; and the third time, he was under a truck hiding from an imaginary enemy. Realistically, I should probably run. But he had blessed my life more than anyone in the last five years, and he didn't even know me. Who was this man?

Chapter 4

I DON'T KNOW IF IT'S TRUE of all small towns, but people generally eat early in Mistletoe, and by seven o'clock there were only eight customers in the diner.

Loretta came up behind me as I was filling a drink order. "You can go now, darlin'," she said. "Go see the man." She was carrying a paper bag and a large plastic container with its lid taped down. "I got him a few days' worth of soup." She had gotten more than just soup. She had filled the bag with the morning's pastries, a loaf of hard bread, and some pecan pie. "I threw a few bags of chamomile tea and some packets of sugar in the bottom of the sack. Nothing better for the system when you're sick."

"That's really kind of you."

"Whatever I can do. Now you have a good night and don't go catching anything. I already lost Cassie. I can't afford to have you sick too."

I carried the food out to my car. It wasn't lost on me that I was driving my car because of him. Instant karma.

I knew the apartment building. Everyone in Mistletoe did, as it was the only one in town. No one I knew had ever lived there, and, from all appearances, its only inhabitants were drifters, strangers, and men in trouble with their wives. The locals just called it "that apartment," but it had a name: the Harrison. It had once been a hotel, named after President William Henry Harrison, whose presidential run lasted a lackluster thirty-one days, as he died of pneumonia after giving his inaugural address in freezing temperatures without a coat. I have no idea why anyone would name a hotel after the man. You would think they would have chosen a president who had accomplished something while in office—or at least had the sense to wear a coat.

The hotel was built more than a hundred years back, when Mistletoe was a prosperous mining town. As usually happened, when the veins of ore ran dry, so did the town, leaving a few farmers and homesteaders and those too old to pick up and start their lives over again. The hotel passed into bankruptcy, and eventually the owner found a way to repurpose it.

It was dark out, and the Harrison apartments were near the south end of Noel Street in a run-down area. In a bigger town this might have been considered dangerous or scary, but this was Mistletoe, and its days of newsworthy crime were pretty much past.

There were no lights on this end of the street, and a sickle moon lit the area, sparkling off the recently fallen snow.

No one had shoveled the sidewalk in front of the apartments, and there was a single set of footprints that led into the building. William's olive-green pickup truck was parked around the side, visible from the street.

I parked my car at the curb out front of the building, got the food out of the back seat, and carried it up the snow-encrusted walkway to the front doors and into the apartment building's dimly lit lobby.

The inside of the building looked as derelict as its exterior. There was a bag of garbage, a bicycle with a flat tire leaning against one of the walls, and a pile of mail on the floor beneath an inset brass mailbox as if the building's residents, past and present, hadn't picked up their mail for a few months.

A spiderweb-covered bronze chandelier flickered a little but gave enough illumination to reveal a dirty black-and-white-checkered tile floor. The lobby still looked like it belonged to a hotel. There was a curved stairway with a carved wooden banister leading to a second-story landing with a spindled balustrade.

I was startled by a brindled brown-and-black cat that darted across the lobby and disappeared down the darkened hallway. From my pocket, I took the receipt where Renato had written the number of William's apartment. Number 205. I climbed one flight of stairs and walked down the hall to the third door on the right.

Curiously, the door to the apartment was already open a few inches. I rapped on the door with my hand. There was no answer—at least, not from *his* apartment. The door across the hall opened and quickly shut again before I could see who was there.

I rapped again. There was still nothing, though my knocking had opened the door a little more, wide enough to reveal the room's interior, lit by a single yellowish light from a brass floor lamp. I could hear the metallic ticking of a radiator.

"Hello?" I said. Then louder, "Is anyone home?"

There was no response.

"William?"

There was a spasm of coughing, followed a few moments later by heavy, slow footsteps. A hoarse voice asked, "Who is it?"

I swallowed. "It's Elle. From the diner." Then I added, "You fixed my car."

William staggered over to the door. I almost didn't recognize him. He wasn't wearing a shirt, just gray cotton sweatpants that hung loosely from his thin waist. He was lanky and lean in form but muscular. His right shoulder was covered in a tattoo. He looked sick; his face was pale and his hair matted to one side as if he'd been sleeping. His chin was covered in thick stubble. He leaned against the door for support.

"What can I do for you?" he asked, even though he clearly wasn't in a condition to do anything for anyone.

"I came to thank you," I said, feeling like getting him out of bed was doing more harm than good. "I heard you were sick, so I brought you something to eat." I squatted down and lifted the food. "I brought you some soup. It's still warm."

He coughed, covering his mouth with his forearm. He looked unsteady and in no condition to carry what I'd brought him.

"If you don't mind, I'll just put this on your counter."

He nodded slightly. "Thank you." He stepped back from the entrance, though still leaned against the door. I walked past him into the room.

The room smelled dank and musty, old like it was. The apartment still looked like a hotel room, boxy and curtly divided with a small coat closet near the front door. The front room included a small kitchen with a chin-high refrigerator and a small hot plate. The floral wallpaper was faded and torn in places.

What furniture there was looked to be remnants from the hotel days. There was a small table, two chairs, and a low couch upholstered in a threadbare green velvet from the fifties.

The bedroom door was open, and I could see the unmade bed he had just crawled out of. I set the food on the counter.

"Would you like me to pour the soup into a bowl?" I asked.

"No," he said softly. "Thank you."

I sensed that he wanted to be left alone. "I'll just leave everything here." I looked back at him. "I'm sorry you're so sick."

"Thank you," he said, the words sounding like they'd taken great effort. He was still leaning against the door, like it was holding him up. As I walked back toward him, he put his head down as if he were dizzy. Then he collapsed to the floor with a thud.

"William!"

He was unconscious. I put my hand on his forehead. He was burning with fever. I knelt at his side, my hand on his arm. "William," I said softly. "William."

Suddenly his eyelids fluttered open. He gazed at me with a confused expression. "Who are you?"

"I'm Elle. Remember? You fixed my car."

He closed his eyes for a moment, then said, "What are you doing here?"

"I brought you some food. I came to thank you."

He didn't respond.

"We should get you to the hospital," I said. "You're very sick."

"No," he said, squinting with pain. "No hospital. No doctor."

I wasn't sure what to do. I barely knew this man. Of course, he barely knew me, yet he had helped me. I couldn't help but feel somewhat responsible for his sickness, since he'd no doubt gotten sicker working through the night on my car.

"What can I do for you?" I asked.

He closed his eyes and breathed heavily but said nothing. He looked vulnerable and weak, nothing like the powerful, scary man I first encountered at the auto shop.

"Is there someone I can call?"

After a moment he said softly, "There's no one."

The words made my heart hurt. "Don't you have anyone to take care of you?"

"I don't need . . ." He didn't finish the sentence.

I sat there for a moment looking at him. His lips were dry and cracked. I guessed he was dehydrated. "I can help," I said. When he didn't object to my offer, I asked, "When was the last time you had something to drink?"

His response came haltingly. "I don't know."

"I'm going to get you some water."

I got up and began looking through his cupboards for a cup. There were only three, two coffee cups and a cheap plastic one. Then I looked inside his refrigerator to see if he had cold water. There was only a carton of milk, a half-empty jar of Miracle Whip, a small jar of mustard, and an opened package of hot dogs.

I filled the cup with water from the tap and brought it to him. I knelt down next to him and said, "Let me help you drink." I put my hand behind his head. His hair was matted and wet with sweat. "I'm going to help you lift your head."

He groaned a little as I lifted. Then I raised the cup to his lips, supporting the back of his head with my hand. He drank thirstily, though some of the water dribbled down the corner of his mouth, down his stubbled chin. When he had finished the water, he laid his head back. I dabbed the water from his face with my coat sleeve. He shivered.

"You have the chills," I said. "And your fever . . ." I touched his head again. I'd never felt a fever that hot. I wished I had a thermometer. The situation reminded me of a few months back when Dylan was running a fever and I had sat up with him through the night. "Do you have a thermometer?"

"No."

"I'm going to get a cold cloth for your forehead." I looked through his drawers until I found a dishcloth. I opened his freezer looking for ice. There was only a frosted package of peas. I wrapped them in the dishcloth and brought them over to him.

"Tell me if it's too cold."

He coughed again, then closed his eyes. I held the bag of peas to his forehead. I glanced down at my watch. It was past eight. Fran already would have put Dylan to bed. Fran rarely minded staying late, or even spending the night, but I needed to tell her. William shivered again.

"I need to go home and check on my son," I said. "But I'm going to come back. Okay?"

"You don't need to," he said.

"I think I do. Let me help you to your bed." I set my makeshift ice pack to the side and leaned over him. "Put your arms around my neck."

He lifted his arms around my neck, locking his fingers together. His breath was warm on my neck. It was strange to think it, but it was the first time in a long time that a man had put his arms around me.

"Let's sit you up first and let you get settled for a moment. I don't want all the blood rushing away from your head." I sat up, and he pulled himself to a sitting position.

A moment later I said, "Tell me when you're ready."

"Ready."

"All right. Up we go."

As I stood, he pushed himself up, using me more for balance than lift. I put my arm around his waist, and we walked to the bedroom. He sat down on the side of his bed, then lay back, groaning with the motion. I lifted his legs onto the bed.

490 | Richard Paul Evans

"You just rest. I'll be back in about a half hour."

"Thank you." He rolled his head to the side. For a moment I just looked at him. My heart hurt for his pain but equally for his loneliness. Lately I had obsessed over how hard my life seemed, but I didn't suffer from loneliness. I had friends. I had Dylan. For all I could see, he had no one.

I walked out of his bedroom, shutting the door behind me. I checked his apartment door to make sure it wouldn't lock behind me, then shut it and went down to my car. It had started snowing again, and the windshield was covered with white.

I turned on the windshield wipers and drove down the deserted Noel Street past the diner. I could see Jamie and Nora inside filling the salt and pepper bottles—one of the things we did before going home each evening.

My duplex was only eight minutes from the diner. I walked in to find Fran sitting on the couch reading a book. She jumped when I walked in.

"I scared you," I said.

"It's the book. It's a suspense novel."

"What is it?"

She held up the book so I could see its cover: *Where Are the Children?*

"That sounds scary. Who wrote it?"

"It's a new writer. Mary Higgins Clark. She's good."

"And how was Dylan?"

"He went right down," she said. "How was your night?"

"Different than I expected. Would you be okay staying a little longer? I'm taking care of someone."

"Who?"

"Just a friend," I said. "He's new in town. He's sick and doesn't have anyone else."

"No problem," she said. "Should I spend the night?"

"If you don't mind."

"I don't mind. Is it still snowing out?"

"A little."

"The weatherman said it was going to snow all night. All the more reason to stay put."

"Thank you. I just need to gather a few things."

I looked in on Dylan. He was sleeping soundly. I kissed his forehead, then went to my room and got a heating pad, a bottle of aspirin, a thermometer, and a couple of washcloths. I grabbed an ice pack and filled it with ice from the freezer, then put it all in a large canvas bag.

"I don't know when I'll be back," I said to Fran on my way out.

"Don't worry about a thing," she said.

"I never do when you're here."

The snow was already coming down heavier. I carried everything out to my car, then drove back to the Harrison. It was nearly ten o'clock when I opened the door to William's apartment. As I walked in, I heard a strange guttural noise that sounded more like a growl than a groan. Then I heard William shout out: "No!"

I slowly opened the door of his bedroom.

"William?"

His eyes were open, and he was looking at me, but *not* at me—like he was looking through me. He looked scared.

"Charlies are everywhere, Lieutenant! Let's Zippo it and get out of here."

I didn't know what to do. Was it dangerous for me to be here? He was powerfully built. What if he mistook me for something else?

Sympathy won out. "William, it's just me. Elle. You're in your bedroom. I'm the only one here. Everything's okay."

He stopped, breathed out slowly, then lay back down. My heart was still racing as I walked to the side of his bed and sat down.

"Hey." I put my hand on his forehead. He was still burning up. I took the thermometer from my bag. "William," I said softly. "I'm going to check your temperature."

He didn't open his eyes but turned back toward me.

"I'm going to put this thermometer under your tongue. Don't bite it." I held his bristled chin as I slid the thermometer between his lips and under his tongue. I held it there for a full minute and then pulled it out. A hundred four degrees. I had spent enough late nights in the ER with Dylan to know this wasn't good.

"You're a hundred and four," I said, setting the thermometer on the windowsill.

"I'm not that old," he said.

In spite of the circumstances, I grinned. "I really should take you to the hospital in Ogden. Would you let me?"

"No hospital. No doctors."

I sat there a moment as I thought what to do next. "Well, we need to do something. I brought you some aspirin. Let's at least get that in you."

I went back out to the kitchen and refilled his cup with water, then poured the aspirin into my hand.

"I've got some water and three aspirin. Open, please."

He opened his mouth and swallowed the pills with half the cup of water, then lay back.

"I brought you an ice pack," I said.

I pulled the ice pack from my bag. I propped his pillow up so it would hold the pack up to his forehead. It only took a minute for him to fall back asleep, his breathing taking on a calm, slow cadence. "I'm sorry you're so sick," I said. "I won't leave you."

I thought he was asleep—maybe he was—but a single tear rolled down his cheek.

THE lights were off, but it wasn't that dark. The moon reflecting off the snow lit the room in a brilliant blue. For nearly an hour I sat on the side of his bed watching him, his face half illuminated like a waning moon. He was so broken. Broken yet beautiful.

At one point he rolled over onto his stomach and the blanket came down from his shoulders. What I saw made my heart jump a little. There were rows of thick scars running vertically down his back. I pulled the blanket down to the small of his back. There were ten-inch scars, more than a dozen of them, raised and angry. I lightly touched one. "What did they do to you?" I asked softly.

Maybe half an hour later I sat down on the floor next to his bed with my back against the wall and closed my eyes but couldn't sleep, which was rare for me.

William got up once in the night to use the bathroom. He was disoriented, and I helped him to the toilet. When he came back to bed, he said, "Thank you, Nurse," which I think he believed.

I again put the ice pack on his head, then lay down on the floor. I think I fell asleep around one. William woke again around three thirty. He was tossing from side to side. He kept saying, "Don't. Don't. I don't know. I told you." I knelt at his side and gently touched his arm. "You're dreaming. You're okay. You're okay."

His eyes opened, and he breathed out heavily. Then he caught his breath and looked over at me. Even in the darkness, I could see the clearness and intensity of his gaze. This time he was looking directly at me. Then he said, "I see why he loved you."

I looked at him. "Who?"

He closed his eyes and went back to sleep. I watched him for a moment, then went back to the floor and fell asleep.

I woke a little before seven, the sun shining through the blinds, illuminating the room in golden stripes. I didn't know where I was at first, just that my back ached from sleeping on the floor. I sat up and yawned. William was still sleeping, lightly snoring.

I leaned over him just to make sure he was asleep; then I put my hand on his forehead. He was still feverish but not as hot as the night before. I pulled the covers up over him and was about to go when he slowly rolled over. His eyes were open. For a moment we just looked at each other.

"You're still here," he said in a raspy voice.

"I said I would be. I need to get my son off to school; then I'll come back." He just stared at me. I leaned over him and touched his forehead and said, "I'll be back."

Chapter 5

THE NIGHT'S STORM HAD blanketed my car in nearly a half foot of snow. I got a snow brush from my back seat and scraped off the windows, then drove home.

Fran was wearing one of my sweatshirts. She was in the kitchen making oatmeal.

"Morning, Florence Nightingale," she said.

"Good morning. Is Dylan still asleep?"

"He's taking a shower."

"How'd he sleep?"

"He doesn't even know you were gone. How are you?"

"Exhausted. I slept on the floor."

"That sounds painful." She brought me over a cup of coffee. I took a sip. "Thank you."

"Don't mention it. So who's your sick friend?"

"His name is William. Actually, he's not really a friend. I don't know him very well."

"But you spent the night . . ."

"It's not what you think," I said, drinking my coffee. "I went over to thank him for fixing my car, and he was so sick that he passed out. He was all alone. What was I supposed to do?"

"Is he cute?"

"That's not the issue."

Just then Dylan walked into the kitchen. He looked at me curiously—probably because I looked like I had slept in my clothes and my hair was a tangled mane. "Morning, honey."

He didn't say anything about Fran being there. "Hi."

"I've got some oatmeal for you, little man," Fran said.

Dylan walked to the refrigerator and took out a jar of strawberry jam and carried it over to the table.

"Thanks for staying," I said.

"You're welcome. If you're okay, I'll head on home."

"We're okay," I said. "Is it all right if I pay you Wednesday?"

"You know I'm good." She walked over and kissed Dylan on the forehead. "Have a good day, handsome man. I'll see you after school." She looked at me. "Would you like me to pick him up?"

"If you don't mind."

"No problem," she said. "Think you'll be late again?"

"I don't know."

"I'll bring my makeup just in case." She blew me a kiss, then walked out.

I got myself a bowl of oatmeal, put in brown sugar and raisins, then sat down across from Dylan. "How did you sleep?"

Dylan looked up from his bowl. "Good. Do you have to work tonight?"

"Yes."

He frowned. "You *always* have to work."

"Someone has to buy the oatmeal," I said. "I don't *always* work."

"It seems like it sometimes."

"I know. It does to me too. But I don't work this Saturday until three, so we can go somewhere."

"Where?"

"I don't know. Maybe tubing? If it's not snowing."

"Yeah!" Dylan pumped his fist. "And hot chocolate?"

"It's not tubing if you don't have hot chocolate after, right?"

He nodded. "Right."

"Now go brush your teeth. We need to get going."

Dylan ran off to the bathroom while I put our bowls in the sink to soak. He was right. It felt like I was always working.

I DROPPED Dylan off at school, then ran by the diner and grabbed some orange juice and a couple of oatmeal muffins.

"You're here early," Loretta said as I walked in.

"I'm just picking up some things for William. I'll put it on my tab."

"Ah. How did it go last night?"

"I ended up spending the night at his place."

Loretta clapped her hands. "There is hope yet!"

"It's not that," I said. "He was so sick that he passed out. I ended up taking care of him all night."

"Well, that's not bad either."

"I'm taking him something for breakfast. I'll be right back."

"Take your time, darlin'. You can't rush love."

"I'm not. I'm rushing breakfast."

I drove back down Noel Street to William's apartment. I rapped twice on his door and then let myself in. The apartment was still dark and quiet. Still carrying the juice and muffins, I walked to the door of his bedroom, lightly rapped on it, and then pushed it open. He was in bed but awake.

"Hi," I said.

"You came back."

"I said I would."

"Were you here all night?" he asked.

"Yes."

He looked at me with a curious expression. "Why'd you stay?"

"Because you needed me."

He smiled. It was only a slight smile, but it was the first smile I'd seen on him. It was like the sun rising after a cloudy day.

"Why did you fix my car?"

"Because you needed me," he said, using my words.

"You have no idea how much you helped." Suddenly the emotion of it caught up with me and my eyes welled up.

"I could say the same. You helped me when I was in the street."

"All I did was bring you coffee."

"You brought me more than coffee." He slowly shook his head. "You brought me back to reality."

I didn't know what to say to that. After a moment I said, "You must be hungry. I brought some orange juice and a muffin from the diner." I reached in the bag and took out the muffin. "Here."

He peeled the paper off the muffin and hungrily devoured it. He drank a cup of juice nearly as fast as he ate the muffin.

"You look a lot better than you did last night," I said.

"I felt like death."

"I brought another muffin." I handed it to him.

"Thank you." After he finished eating the second muffin, he said, "You're probably wondering why I climbed under the truck."

"I know why," I said. "The police officers who helped you are regulars at the diner. They told me what happened."

"You must think I'm a complete nutcase."

"I think you've been through some hard things." Then I said, "When I was taking care of you, I saw the scars on your back."

I could see that mentioning this brought him pain. "They're kind of hard to miss," he said.

"I'm sorry."

"You're not the one who should be sorry."

I sighed lightly. "I need to go to work." I stood. "I didn't get a chance to get groceries, but I can take a break from work later."

"You don't need to do that. You've done enough."

"It's my pleasure. I brought you some soup and bread last night. It's in the refrigerator. You can have that for lunch. Loretta sent you enough food to last a few meals."

"Loretta?"

"She's my boss. She owns the diner."

He nodded. "Please thank her for me."

"I will. There's also pecan pie. I don't know if you like that."

"I love pecan pie," he said. "Back in Indiana I used to buy those little Bama pies, you know the ones?"

"My husband used to like those," I said, softer. "I also brought some chamomile tea. It will help you feel a little better."

"You're making me feel better." For a moment he just looked at me; then he said, "May I ask you something?"

"Of course."

"Why are you being so good to me?"

"Why wouldn't I?"

"I could think of a hundred reasons," he said.

I smiled. "And I can't think of one."

THAT evening, I left work early again for William—this time so I could stop at the grocery store. I didn't know what he ate, so I bought some basics: oatmeal, bread, butter, milk, eggs, cheese, sandwich meat, and three cans of Campbell's soup. The bill came to almost twenty dollars, but when I thought about the hundreds of dollars he'd saved me, it seemed like a small price to pay.

I drove back to his apartment, knocked on the door, and let myself inside. His bedroom door was shut. "It's just me," I said.

As I set down the groceries, I noticed a saucepan in the sink with residue from the soup I'd left for him. At least he'd eaten something.

I quietly opened his bedroom door. He was sleeping, so I walked back to the kitchen and put everything away.

"Elle." His voice surprised me, not just because he was awake but because he had spoken my name. I liked the way he said it.

I walked back to his room and opened the door. "Hi."

"Hey," he said, smiling.

"How are you feeling?"

"Tired, mostly."

"I see you ate something."

"I had some of the soup you brought. It was good."

"Can I make you some chamomile tea?"

He nodded. "I'd like that."

"Do you have a kettle?"

"No. Just the pan I warmed the soup in."

"I can work with that."

I walked back to the kitchen, washed the pan in the sink, and filled it halfway with water. I set the pan on the hot plate. Once the water was boiling, I opened the cupboard and grabbed one of the coffee cups. One said WINCHELL'S DONUTS. The other was a glossy black mug with a white skull and the letters USMC. I chose the donut cup, as it seemed more life-affirming. I filled it with hot water and put in one of the tea bags.

"Do you like your tea with honey or sugar?"

"Sugar," he said.

I tore open a sugar packet and stirred it in. I let the tea steep for a minute, then took out the tea bag and brought the cup to him.

"There you go."

"Thank you." He blew on the drink, then took a sip.

I reached over and put my hand on his forehead. "You're not as hot as you were. You were a hundred and four last night."

"You took my temperature?"

I nodded. "You don't remember?"

"No." He looked at me, then said, "From my mouth . . ."

I laughed. "Yes. From your mouth."

"That's good to know. I was kind of vulnerable."

"Yes, you were."

We looked at each other, smiling. Was it chemistry?

"I can't stay late tonight," I said. "I've got to get back to my son. But I brought you some groceries."

"Thank you," he said. "How much do I owe you?"

"Nothing," I said.

"Come on. Let me pay you."

"After what you did, it would be embarrassing for me to take your money."

He looked at me gratefully. "Thank you."

"You're welcome."

"You don't have to stay. You've wasted enough time on me."

To my surprise I said, "I've enjoyed being with you."

"It's mutual," he said. He sipped his tea and then asked, "Do you know what day it is?"

"It's November eighteenth. Tuesday."

He looked confused. "I think I missed a few days."

"No doubt." I smiled. "Well, I better go." I started to leave, then stopped and turned back.

"Last night you said something peculiar."

"Yes?"

"You said, 'I see why he loved you.'"

He shook his head. "I must have been delirious."

"You were very sick." I breathed out. "Well, I better run." I looked at him again and then said, "Would you like to do something sometime, maybe get something to eat?"

"Thank you. That's a really kind offer, but . . ." He looked me in the eyes. "Could I say no?"

I flushed with embarrassment. "Of course. I didn't mean anything. I just . . ." I wasn't sure how to finish the sentence.

"I really appreciate all you've done for me."

"It's nothing compared to what you've done for me," I returned. The moment fell into awkward silence. Finally I said, "Well, I better go. If I can do anything for you . . ."

"I hope I didn't offend you."

"No," I said. "You didn't. Maybe bruised my ego a little."

He grinned. "Then I'm sorry for the bruises."

"Forgiven," I said. "I'll see you around." I walked out of his apartment. As I descended the stairs, my eyes welled up in embarrassment. It seemed that I was undesirable to everyone but old men and lonely truck drivers. My heart ached as I drove home.

THE next morning at work, Jamie asked, "How's your patient?"

"He's fine," I said.

"That wasn't very convincing."

"He's not my patient anymore. He's better."

"But you'll still be seeing him?"

"Apparently not. I asked him if he'd like to go out sometime. He turned me down."

"Loser," she said, shaking her head.

"He's not a loser," I said.

She looked at me with surprise. "Oh, my. You're defending him. Feelings, perhaps?"

"No," I said. "There are no feelings."

"Really?" she said. "So he's just another fish in the sea?"

"I don't have a sea," I said. "I don't have any bait, and I'm too tired to fish. I just want to get back to work."

"Oh, you got bait, girl," she said after me. "You just forgot how to use it."

It was a long day. I operated on little enough sleep as it was, but that late night caring for William had finally caught up to me. It was after the dinner rush when Jamie came to the break room to find me. "Elle, you've got to come see who just walked in."

"Who now?" I asked.

I followed her out. She pointed at the door. "That's him, right?"

William was standing inside the door next to the PLEASE WAIT TO BE SEATED sign. He still looked a little pale. "Yes, that's him."

"He's gorgeous."

"Then you should ask him out," I said. "Maybe he won't turn you down."

"No, he's yours," Jamie said. "Go get him."

I took a deep breath, then walked over to him. He smiled when he saw me.

"Dinner for one?" I asked, trying not to sound hurt.

"It's just me," he said. "As usual."

"You can sit wherever."

He looked around, then said, "Where are you serving?"

"That section," I said, gesturing to my zone with a menu, which I handed to him. "You can seat yourself. I'll get you some water."

"Thank you."

A moment later I brought him a glass. "Do you know what you want?"

"A chili cheeseburger and fries. And a Dr Pepper."

"Anything else?"

"I would like to apologize. You asked if I wanted to do something sometime and I said no."

It hurt just hearing it again. "Don't worry about it."

"I haven't stopped worrying about it since you left. I came to see if I could take you out to dinner."

"Why do I feel like you're doing this out of pity?"

"Because I am," he said.

"Oh, really?" I said.

"Not for you," he said quickly. "For myself. Any man who would turn down an offer like that from a beautiful woman like you is pretty pitiable. Or maybe he was just a recluse who was out of his head recovering from an illness."

"You were pretty sick," I said.

"Delirious," he said. "Totally out of my head."

"I might be able to cut you a little slack—being sick and all."

He grinned. "You are as merciful as you are beautiful."

I smiled.

"Are you busy tomorrow night?"

"I'm off," I said. "But I'll need to find a sitter for Dylan. Can I call you?"

"I don't have a phone, but you can call me at Renato's."

"You're already back at work?"

"I start back tomorrow. Renato needs the help."

"Apology aside, do you still want the food?"

"A man's got to eat."

"Yes, he does."

Back in the kitchen Jamie said, "How did it go?"

"He came to apologize and ask me out."

"Did you accept?"

"Of course."

Jamie smiled. "Smart girl."

William didn't stay long. He wolfed down his burger and was gone. He left me a ten-dollar bill for a four-dollar meal.

A few minutes after he left, I called Fran to see if she could watch Dylan. As usual, she was happy to help.

The next morning, I called William at Renato's. It took him a while to come to the phone.

"Sorry. I was under a car."

"Again?" I said.

He laughed. "It's getting to be a habit."

"So, I got a sitter."

"That's good," he said happily. "Can I pick you up at six?"

"Six is good."

"Do you like Italian food?"

"I love Italian food."

"Renato recommended a place in Ogden. DiSera's Italian. Have you been there?"

"No, but I've heard it's good."

"I'll make reservations," he said. "I'll see you at six."

"See you then."

I hung up. It had been years since I'd been out on a date. I couldn't wait.

Chapter 6

I FINISHED WORK AT TWO. I drove home, showered again, then went through my closet looking for something to wear. I didn't have many things to dress up in. I ended up in a long denim skirt and a high-necked blouse with ruffles on the cuffs that Loretta had given me the previous Christmas.

Fran arrived at a quarter to six. "You look nice," she said. "Love the blouse. Where are you going?"

"I'm going out on a date," I said proudly.

She looked at me like I was speaking a foreign language.

"Try not to look too surprised."

"Who's the lucky man?"

"William," I said. "The one I was taking care of this week."

"Ah," she said. "I wondered if there was a little flame there. I mean, you did spend the night."

"I didn't 'spend the night.' He was sick," I said.

Just then Dylan came out of his room. "Where are you going, Mama?"

"I'm going out to dinner with a friend."

A minute later the doorbell rang.

"That's him," I said. "I don't know when I'll be home. We're going to dinner in Ogden."

I opened the door. William stood in the doorway. He was dressed in bell-bottomed jeans and a knit sweater. His hair was nicely combed, and he was clean-shaven.

"You look nice," he said.

"Thank you. I was thinking the same about you. I just need to get my coat. Come in."

As I walked over to the closet, Fran approached William.

"I'm Fran," she said, looking a little too interested.

"I'm William. It's nice to meet you. Thanks for babysitting."

"It's cool," she said.

"All right," I said, walking between them. "I'm ready." I looked around. "Dylan? Where are you?"

Dylan was hiding behind the kitchen table. I forgot that Dylan and William had unresolved history.

"Dylan, come here."

"No."

"Dylan," I said more forcefully.

William raised his hand. "It's okay." He walked into the kitchen, crouching down a couple of yards from Dylan. "Dylan, my name is William. We got off to a rocky start, so I brought you something. It's a peace offering."

"What?"

"In this case, it's a candy bar." He brought a Hershey's chocolate bar from his jacket. "Do you like chocolate?"

Dylan nodded.

William turned to me. "Is this okay?"

"It's too late now," I said. "He's seen the goods."

He smiled, then turned back. He handed Dylan the candy bar. "I'm sorry I yelled at you. I promise I won't do that again."

Dylan took the chocolate. "It's okay."

William put out his hand. "Then we're cool?"

"We're cool," Dylan said, taking his hand.

"All right," William said, standing. "Big relief."

"Since you boys have it together," I said, "can we go?"

"Have a good time," Fran said to William.

I put on my coat and walked out with William into the cold.

"I'm in the Cadillac," he said, motioning to his green pickup.

"I remember."

He opened the door for me and helped me in; then he walked around and climbed in the other side. He started the truck and pulled out into the road.

"Good job with Dylan," I said. "You won him over."

"The magic of chocolate. Does wonders with kids."

"I've got news for you. It's not just kids. It's pretty much catnip for women."

He looked over and smiled. "That's good to know."

DISERA'S was one of the nicest restaurants in Ogden, evidenced by the full parking lot. I followed William into the lobby.

William walked up to the hostess, who looked a little frantic.

"May I help you?" she asked.

"We have reservations for seven," William said. "Under Smith."

She looked at her guest book. "William Smith for two?"

"Yes, ma'am."

"It will just be a few moments while they clear the table."

"Thank you."

I looked around the dimly lit restaurant. I watched the waiters and waitresses, wondering what it would be like to work in an environment where people dressed up to eat.

"Follow me, please," the hostess said.

William and I followed the hostess to a candlelit table in the corner. William pulled out the chair for me, and I sat down. The hostess unrolled our napkins and handed us menus.

"Charlotte will be right with you," she said.

William looked at me and smiled. "Does it feel different being on the other side of the menu?"

"It feels different sitting down to cloth napkins." I looked over the menu. The prices of the meals were triple those at the diner. I instinctively began looking for the cheapest item.

"I hear the lasagna is good," he said.

"I've heard that too," I said. "It's expensive. Everything on the menu is expensive."

"You're worth it," he answered.

I smiled at him. "I may be, but you don't know that."

"Maybe I do," he said. "You're the best nurse I've ever had."

"Maybe I missed my calling in life."

"Would you like some wine?" he asked.

"Yes." I loved wine, but with the exception of Loretta's Christmas party, I hadn't had any in two years. "I love red wine."

"They have some excellent Chiantis," he said.

"You've been here before?" I asked.

William shook his head. "No. Renato told me."

Our waitress came with a basket of breadsticks. "May I take your order?"

"Please," William said, deferring to me.

I ordered the lasagna. William ordered the spaghetti with clams and requested a wine list. A minute later the sommelier came out with their list and his recommendations. He returned with a bottle of a Ruffino Chianti Classico and poured our glasses.

I sipped the wine. "This is really nice. I don't want to know how much it cost."

"You don't need to worry about that. We're celebrating."

"What are we celebrating?"

"Whatever we want," he said.

We both took a drink of wine.

"That is good," he said.

"Heavenly," I replied.

He set down his glass. "Were you born in Mistletoe?"

"No. I'm from Cedar City."

"Where's that?"

"It's a town in southern Utah. It's not as small as Mistletoe."

"How did you end up there?"

"Now that's a story."

"I'm up for a story," he said.

"It may cost you another drink," I said.

William smiled as he refilled my glass.

I took another sip of wine. "So, how I ended up in Mistletoe. Basically, I ran away from home. My parents disowned me, or maybe I disowned them. It went both ways."

"What happened?"

"I married someone they didn't want me to marry."

"They didn't like him?"

"They never met him," I said. "He was Black."

He nodded knowingly. "Where did you meet?"

"In school. We fell in love. But I knew my parents would never approve of me marrying a Black man, so after a year of dating, we were secretly married and living a double life.

"I wish we had been more open, but neither of us had any money. Finally, he dropped out of school to work." I paused. "That's when he was drafted into the war." I took a drink, then a second.

"He didn't believe in the war. He said he had some friends moving to Canada to avoid the draft, but I wasn't going to do that. I couldn't leave my friends and family." I sighed heavily. "If only I'd known how things would turn out. I lost my family *and* him." I took another drink. William just looked at me sympathetically. I was drinking too much. It certainly loosened my tongue.

"The thing is, my family bleeds red, white, and blue. My great-grandfather served in World War One as a general, my grandfather was a colonel in World War Two, and my father served in the Korean War. I told my husband that if we ever hoped to have my father accept us, he'd have to serve. So he did, for me." My eyes suddenly moistened. "I asked too much. He never came back."

"I'm sorry."

"Me too," I said. I took another drink of wine. "But he left me something. We didn't know it at the time he was deployed, but I was pregnant. My parents, of course, were apoplectic. They thought I was an unmarried pregnant woman."

"You didn't correct them?"

"Not at first. When they finally learned that I was married and that my baby would be Black . . ." I shook my head. "Let's just say they weren't real pleased.

"I thought they'd change their mind after Dylan was born. I thought, who could reject a baby? But they did. About six months later we got in a big fight. My mother said he wasn't their grandson and never would be. I remember looking at my father, waiting for him to come to my defense, but he said nothing. I think that silence was worse than my mother's rejection." I breathed out. "That pretty much destroyed any chance of reconciliation. I told them that if they disowned their own grandson, then I was disowning them. That's when I left. I had a hundred and fifty dollars and the Fairlane my grandfather had given me.

"I drove north, looking for a job. I couldn't find anything. I wasn't exactly a stellar candidate—a single college dropout with a six-month-old baby. Dylan and I slept in the back seat of the car. After a week I was desperate, exhausted, and out of money.

"That's when I found Mistletoe. I was driving at night. It was snowing hard. Then I saw this light ahead. It was the diner. I was down to my last few dollars.

"I carried Dylan inside the diner. When I walked in, the place was almost deserted. There were Loretta, Jamie, and a couple of truckers. One of the truckers spun around in his chair, looked me over, and said, 'Well, look what the storm blew in.'

"Loretta was on him like sesame seeds on a bun. She got in his face and said, 'You say one more word like that and that's the last meal you'll eat at my place. You got me?'

"The man backed down like a scolded schoolboy. He said, 'Yes, ma'am.'

"Then Loretta came up to me and said, 'What's his name, darlin'?' I told her. She took Dylan from me and then said, 'Sit down, sweetie, before you fall down. What do you want to eat?' I said, 'Just some coffee and toast. I don't have much money.' She said, 'You're in luck, girl. We've got a special on dinner tonight. It's free ninety-nine.' She kept bringing me food; then, after I was done eating, she asked where I was spending the night. I said, 'We've been sleeping in the car.' She said, 'That's no place for a baby. Where are you headed?' I said, 'Wherever the road takes us.' She said, 'Well, honey, it's taken you here. And I have a room in back you can stay in. We've got plenty to eat.'"

"What a good woman," William said.

I smiled. "She saved my life. I found out later that her only son had committed suicide two months earlier and she was still raw."

William seemed to process this. Then he asked, "She offered you a job?"

"No, she never really hired me. It more or less just happened. At first I started helping out just to thank her. I did dishes, helped in the kitchen; then I started pouring water and bussing tables for the waitresses. They started sharing their tips.

"The other waitresses were sweet as can be. It was like Dylan had a plethora of mothers. They helped watch him, and I helped them all I could. I don't know where I'd be without them."

"What about your parents?"

"I haven't talked to them since I left home."

"What was your relationship like before you left?"

His question surprised me. "It was good, once. My father and I used to be really close. When I was sixteen, I didn't get asked to my first prom. That night, I was in bed, crying. He knocked on my door and then came in. He said, 'Why aren't you dressed? We have reservations.' He had bought me a corsage. He took me out to dinner and dancing." I looked down. "We used to be close."

"What about your mother?"

"We never really got along. My mother drank a lot. I used to ask my father why he stayed with her, but he just said, 'A soldier never leaves his post.'"

I swished what was left of the wine in my glass. "You have to give him credit. He was loyal. At least to her. Not so much to me. Maybe that's what makes it hurt so much."

"I'm really sorry," he said.

"So here I am. I always thought, once my husband gets back, everything will change. I might even finish school."

"What did you want to do?"

"I wanted to be a writer."

"Like . . . books?"

I nodded. "Maybe someday I'll write my story."

"I'd read it," he said.

"Thanks. I'll autograph it for you." I breathed out. "Enough about me. What about you? What brings you to Mistletoe?"

"My truck," he said.

"Something brought you here," I said. "No one arrives in Mistletoe by accident."

"I'm sure that's true," he said. He took a drink of wine, looked at me, then said, "I figured it was a nice place to die."

I wasn't sure if he was joking, but the moment was interrupted by our waitress. "Sorry for the wait. Here is your spaghetti alle vongole," she said, setting the plate in front of William. "And your lasagna, ma'am. *Buon appetito*." She walked away.

I picked up the conversation. "So, you won't tell me what brought you here, maybe you'll tell me where you came from."

"Denver. Most recently."

"What did you do there?"

"I worked at a car dealership for a while, maintaining cars."

"Did you always want to be an auto mechanic?"

"It was more something I did than aspire to. I was raised in Fort Wayne, Indiana. I guess being that close to the Indianapolis Speedway, cars got into my blood. I always wanted to race cars."

"But you moved to Denver?"

"After the war"—he hesitated—"things changed."

We ate a moment in silence. The lasagna was delicious.

"The thing about war is, everything you think you know about humanity, or about yourself, is challenged," William said. "Especially in a conflict like Vietnam. Did you know that Vietnam wasn't even a war? It was never approved by Congress, so technically it's considered a conflict." He shook his head. "Semantics and politics. When bullets are flying at you, it doesn't matter what you call it."

"Were you drafted?"

"Sort of," he said. "I'm what they call a two-or-ten."

"Two-or-ten?"

"The judge pounded his gavel and gave me a choice: two years in 'Nam or ten years in prison. I chose the former."

"What did you do?"

"Got in with the wrong crowd, mostly. I ended up spending time in prison anyway—the Hanoi Hilton. I would have done better at home." His voice fell an octave. "At least they're not allowed to torture you in U.S. prisons."

I let his words settle. "You served your country. That was an honorable thing."

"I wish it were that simple," he said. "I risked my life and had no idea what I was fighting for—a corrupt dictatorship that represented almost everything we're fighting against?" He took a drink of wine. "Needless to say, I'm pretty much a hot mess."

I had never before heard the term but liked it. "A hot mess. That sums us both up."

"The difference between you and me is that you can't afford chaos," he said.

"Why do you say that?"

"Because you care about your son more than yourself," he said. "You're a good person."

"So are you," I said.

He looked at me skeptically. "Now that's the wine talking."

I reached over and touched his hand. "No, it's my gratitude talking. What you did for me . . . Aside from Loretta, no one has ever helped me like that. Dylan and I are barely getting by. It would have taken me years to pay off that debt. You didn't even know me and yet you helped us. You have a good heart."

He went to pour more wine into my glass, but I put my hand over it. "That's enough. Are you trying to get me tipsy?"

"I'm just trying to make you feel good."

I looked at him for a moment, then said, "It's been a long time since anyone has tried to do that."

"Am I succeeding?"

I smiled. "Spectacularly."

We split a piece of tiramisu, and I confess, I had another glass of wine. It was the most relaxed I had felt in years.

Around nine he asked, "What time do you need to be back?"

"It doesn't matter."

"Can I show you something?"

"Sure."

"Come with me."

It was late, and the restaurant was only half full as we left the parking lot. William drove us about six miles up alongside a small canyon I'd never been to before. The canyon road was narrow and snow-packed. About four miles up the canyon, he stopped his truck next to a large snowbank. It was dark, and the granite walls were mostly concealed by snow-frosted pines.

"Is this it?" I asked.

"No, it's down that road a quarter mile. But there's more snow than I thought there'd be. I don't want to get the truck stuck. And you're not dressed for walking in snow."

"What is it that you wanted to show me?"

"It's just a place," he said. "A peaceful place."

I looked at him for a moment and then said, "I want to see it."

"Are you sure?"

I nodded. "I'm sure."

He got out of the truck and walked around to my door and opened it and helped me down. He took my hand. "If it gets too cold, just tell me and we'll come back."

"It's a deal."

Hiking through the snow was harder than I expected. We trudged along a narrow path surrounded on both sides by columnar trees, white and frozen, lining the path like marble pillars.

Suddenly we came to a clearing that overlooked the valley below. William stopped. "This is it."

"Oh, my," I said. In front of us was a waterfall, the exterior draped in an intricate lacework of ice. The sound of rushing water escaped the ice veil and fell below into a river whose banks were piled with snow. Everything around us was white, crystal, and blue, lit by a full moon that hung in the winter air.

"They call this Lace Veil Falls," he said.

"It's beautiful," I said. "How did you find this place?"

"I found it the day after I moved to Mistletoe," he said. "I sat up here one night and just looked out over the valley."

"Thank you for sharing this with me."

"You're welcome," he said softly. He turned and looked at me. I had my arms crossed at my chest, and I was shivering.

"You're freezing."

"I'm a little cold."

"Let's get you back." We walked about twenty yards when he looked at me and said, "Your feet must be frozen."

"It's not much farther," I said.

"I can carry you."

"Really, you don't have to—"

He reached down and lifted me, his muscular arms embracing me. "This is better."

I was thinking the same thing. It felt good to be in his arms as he effortlessly carried me all the way to his truck, set me down, opened the door, and then lifted me in. It was the most romantic thing I'd experienced in years. When he got back in the truck, he was quiet. Then I noticed that his eyes were wet.

"What is it?" I asked.

He didn't look at me. He just started his truck. "It's nothing."

I touched his arm. "Something just happened, didn't it?"

He took a deep breath, then said, "Thank you for sharing that with me. I wanted to share that with someone."

We drove in silence back to my duplex. It was almost midnight when we arrived. William walked me to the door.

"Thank you for tonight," I said. "It was really nice."

"Would you like to go out again?"

"I would love to."

He thought a moment, then said, "Is tomorrow too soon?"

I was happy that he was so eager. "I'd love to, but I work tomorrow night."

"How about Saturday?"

"I work at night, but during the day I could do something." I caught myself. "I'm sorry. I promised Dylan I'd take him tubing."

"We can do that," he said.

"You want to go tubing with us?"

"It sounds fun. I have inner tubes and an air compressor at the shop. The tubes will fit better in my truck than in your Fairlane."

"You talked me into it," I said. "Is nine good?"

"It's good for me."

Our words gone, we stood there quietly looking at each other. I wondered if he was going to kiss me. I was hoping he would. Instead, he put out his hand. "Thank you."

I took his hand. "You're welcome. Good night."

I opened the door and stepped inside. I couldn't wait to see him again.

Chapter 7

"How did the date go?" Jamie asked the next morning, pouring cream into a coffee cup.

I must have smiled. It was kind of automatic.

"That good, huh?"

"He was really sweet. And the restaurant was amazing."

"So, is there a sequel to this romance?"

"I wouldn't call it a romance."

"What would you call it?"

I smiled wider. "Fun."

"Even better," she said. "So when are you seeing him again?"

"We're going tubing with Dylan tomorrow."

"Getting in with the son. That's fast."

"It's not that. He asked me out and I'd already made plans with Dylan, so he offered to come along."

"Sounds like romance to me," Loretta said, walking past us to the kitchen.

"That woman should work for the CIA," Jamie said.

"Thought about it," she shouted back.

About an hour into my shift I got a call from Fran. She sounded awful. "Elle, I'm so sorry. I've come down with something. I'm so sick, I had to miss school."

"What do you have?"

"Everything. I've got a sore throat, chills, fever. I could feel it coming on last night. I don't think I should watch Dylan."

I wondered if I passed it on to her from William. "I'm sorry. I'll pick up Dylan and bring him here."

"Are you sure?"

"Of course. You get some rest. Get better."

"How was your date last night?"

"It was nice," I said. "You take care of yourself. I need you."

"I need you too. Bye."

It wasn't the first time I had to bring Dylan with me to the diner. Fortunately, Loretta was always good about it.

A little after two I picked Dylan up from school, stopped by home to get him something to do, then came back to work. Loretta was in her office when we walked through the back door.

"I'm sorry, Loretta. Fran's sick, so I had to get Dylan."

She smiled at Dylan. "Lucky us. How's my handsome man?"

"Good, Ms. Loretta. Can I have a hot chocolate?"

"Of course you can. With whipped cream?"

"Yes, ma'am."

"You have such nice manners that I'm going to get you a donut to go with that."

"Just sugar him up," I said.

"Someone's got to," Loretta said.

I said to Dylan, "Hang up your coat, then take your bag out to the corner table. You can do your Spirograph. Just don't bother anybody."

"I won't." He hung up his coat and walked out to the table in the farthest corner of the dining room. There's a reason I told him not to bother anyone. Dylan was well behaved, but he was naturally curious and liked talking to strangers. And, frankly, now and then there were people in the diner I didn't want him talking to.

I took him his hot chocolate and donut, then went back to work.

Around six I was taking an order when I noticed William walk through the door. He was wearing a green army jacket with his hands in his pockets. I waved, and he smiled and tipped his head. I finished taking the table's order and then walked over to him.

"Hi. What brings you here?"

"I just thought I'd come get something to eat."

"Oh," I said. "Your being here has nothing to do with me?"

He grinned "Maybe a little."

I felt like a smile was commandeering my face. "I had such a good time last night."

"Me too. You're good company. Sorry about the snow hike."

"Frostbite aside, it was my favorite part of the night," I said. "I'm serving this side, so just grab a table. Dylan's back there. Why don't you go on back and say hello?"

"Dylan's here?"

I nodded. "My sitter called in sick."

"I won't be eating alone, after all," he said. He headed back toward Dylan. Dylan looked up with a big smile.

A few minutes later I took William's order. It was interesting watching Dylan respond to being with him. He ordered the same thing William did—a tuna salad sandwich with fries. And a large dill pickle. I don't think I'd ever seen Dylan eat a pickle before.

A few minutes later Andy walked in. He was in uniform but alone this time. I sat him just a few tables from William before wondering if, considering their last encounter, that was such a great idea. As I walked back to the kitchen, I noticed that William got up and walked over to Andy's table and shook his hand.

It was twenty minutes later, when I was coming back to the kitchen after serving Dylan and William, that Jamie said, "Sorry, baby, she's baaaaack." I looked over. Ketchup Lady was there.

"Oh, no."

"My section's light. I can take her."

"No, I'm good, if you don't mind seating her."

"That woman seats herself, but I'll take her a menu." Jamie walked out to the woman while I grabbed a pitcher of water. I passed Jamie on the way to the dining room. "She sat herself at sixteen. Her usual."

She was seated just a few tables from Dylan and William. Honestly, I was kind of glad William was there. It would give us something to laugh about later.

"Thanks. Did you check the status of the ketchup at her table?"

"Yes. The bottle is half full."

"No, it's half *empty*," I said. I grabbed a full bottle of ketchup and, still carrying the pitcher, walked over to her. When I got to her table, Ketchup Lady looked more agitated than usual.

I set the water and ketchup down. "What can I get for you?"

"I can't sit here."

You seated yourself, I thought. "Is there a problem?"

"I would say so. Why is that nigger boy in here?"

My chest froze. I glanced over at Dylan, who was showing William how to use the Spirograph. "That boy is my son," I said, my face hot. "Don't you ever call him that again!"

The woman didn't flinch. "Well, I don't like him here."

I was so angry, I was shaking. "You get out of here right now before I shove this bottle of ketchup down your throat."

She looked at me in complete shock. "How dare you!"

"How dare *you!*" I shouted back.

She began looking around for support. I hadn't noticed, but Loretta was standing near the cash register within earshot of the altercation. "Did you hear that?" Ketchup Lady shouted to her. "Did you hear what this insolent *waitress* just said to me?"

Loretta walked over, glaring at the woman. "I heard what you said. You get out of my diner right now. And if I ever see you here again, I'll throw you out."

The woman's face was almost as red as the ketchup. "I . . . I . . ." She glanced over at Andy. "This woman just threatened me. Do your duty. This is our country!"

Suddenly William was standing next to me. He looked fierce. "This boy's father died protecting *your* country," he said slowly but forcefully. "Do you know how many Black brothers of mine died so you could fatten your face? Now get out before I drag you outside and throw you into the gutter where you belong."

Ketchup Lady looked terrified. She turned to Andy, who was watching. "He threatened my life, Officer. Arrest him."

Andy walked over. "No, all I heard was you threatening him. Get out now or I'll arrest you for causing a public disturbance."

The woman was trembling. She looked at Dylan. I sensed she was about to say something to him when William said, "You say one word to that child and you'll regret it for the rest of your life."

"How dare you threaten me! I have connections. You're going to see the inside of a jail, mister."

William almost looked amused. "You think that scares me? You have no idea what I've seen and what I'm capable of."

The woman looked faint. Loretta stepped forward and grabbed her by the arm. "Get out of here."

Ketchup Lady stood. She looked a little wobbly; then she stumbled toward the door. Jamie walked over to the table, grabbed the bottle of ketchup, and went to the door and threw it in the direction the woman had walked off in. I heard the bottle shatter.

"Take that, you gross slob," she shouted.

I broke down crying.

Loretta put her arm around me. "Come to the back, honey. Come back and sit."

"I can't," I said. "I've got to talk to Dylan." I looked over at him. He was visibly upset.

"Did he hear what she said?" I asked William.

He shook his head. "I don't think so."

Dylan ran over to me. "Why are you crying, Mama?"

I knelt down and hugged him.

William squatted down next to us. "Everything's okay," he said. "There was a mean lady, but we made her leave." William turned to me. "Elle, go back with Loretta. I'll take care of Dylan." Then he said to Dylan, "Would you like to share a milkshake?"

"No, I want my own."

"Even better," he said. "What flavor should we get?"

"Let's get strawberry."

"Perfect. I love strawberry."

Loretta smiled at him. "I'll get two strawberries. And thank you, sir, for your service."

"You're welcome."

She turned to me. "Your friend has things under control. Now come on back, darlin'."

As we walked back, she said to Andy, "Your dinner's on me, Officer. Dessert too."

"Always my pleasure," he said. "We don't need that kind of crazy in Mistletoe."

LORETTA let me go home early. Actually, she made me. William stayed with Dylan the whole time I was in the back with Loretta. They were arm wrestling when I came out, William pretending to lose.

I was wearing my coat and carrying Dylan's over my arm. "It's time to go, Dylan."

"Okay." He started stuffing all his toys back in his bag.

William sidled up to me. He asked softly, "Are you okay?"

I nodded. I was afraid if I opened my mouth I'd start crying.

"May I give you a hug?"

"Yes. Please."

He put his arms around me. For a moment he just quietly held me. He felt so good—his warmth, his strength.

"Can I drive you home?" he asked.

"I have my car."

"We can pick it up tomorrow after we go tubing. If you're still up for it," he said.

"I don't know."

"We should go. We can't let crazy people dictate our lives."

He squeezed me one last time, then released me and turned back to Dylan. "Hey, tough guy. Want to go home in my truck?"

"Yay!" he said.

I took Dylan's hand, and we walked out the diner's front door. I noticed that William seemed aware of the movement around him—every car and every human. He was still a soldier. When he pulled up to my house, he was just as vigilant, walking us to the door. I felt sorry for anyone who might think to cross him.

I opened the door. "Go inside, Dylan," I said.

He looked at William. "Can we play Rock 'Em Sock 'Em Robots?"

"It's too late tonight. But Mr. William is coming over tomorrow."

"I'll be over tomorrow morning," William said. "To take you tubing. I'll bring more chocolate."

"Yes!"

"But only if you go right to bed."

"Okay."

He ran inside. I looked up at William. Before I could thank him, he said, "Are you okay?"

"I'm still a little shaken up."

"There will always be people like that. Don't give them your time or your sanity."

I looked into his eyes. "Thank you for being there."

"You're safe now," he said. "You can trust me."

I looked at him. "I do. I don't know why—I barely know you— but I do." I leaned my head forward against his chest.

He put his arms around me and kissed my forehead. "You are an amazing, beautiful woman. No wonder . . ." He stopped.

I looked up at him. "No wonder what?"

He paused. "No wonder everyone loves you."

I didn't believe that was what he had been going to say. I took a deep breath and stepped back. "I'll see you tomorrow."

"Tomorrow," he said. "Lock your door."

"I will." Up until that day, I never had.

I woke the next morning feeling excited for the day. William arrived at my place at nine. He wore army boots, wool gloves, and his green army jacket. I figured it was the only coat he had.

Dylan answered the door. "Hi, Mr. William. Did you bring the chocolate?"

"Dylan," I said. "You don't just ask people for chocolate."

"No, he's just keeping me honest," William said. "I promised him." He brought a chocolate bar out of his jacket. "Did you go right to bed?"

"Yes, sir."

He held out the chocolate bar. "Then you've earned this amazing bar of chocolate."

Dylan took the candy and turned to me. "Can I?"

"Chocolate for breakfast?" I said. "Sure, why not?"

He quickly tore open the wrapper.

"Dylan, where are your gloves and hat?"

"I don't know."

"They're in your closet."

"If you knew, why did you ask?" Dylan said.

I breathed out. "Just get them."

William laughed. "He got you."

Dylan went to his room. When he returned, the bar of chocolate was gone and the corners of his mouth were stained with chocolate. We walked out to William's truck and climbed into it. The bed was filled with two large inner tubes, both dusted with snow.

"Where are we going?" he asked.

"There's a little park just before the canyon," I said. "It's not far from here. The hills are just the right size for Dylan."

"Just point the way."

Twenty minutes later we arrived at the park. There were maybe a dozen others, riding tubes and sleighs.

We picked a medium-sized hill, and William carried the two inner tubes up the incline while I walked up behind him holding Dylan's hand.

At the hill's summit we linked ourselves together with our legs and slid down, screaming and laughing. At least, I screamed. Dylan just laughed. I hadn't seen him that happy for some time. Falling snow limited our visibility, which added both to my fear and our general excitement. We tubed for about two hours, until we looked like animated snowmen. Our clothes soaked through and almost frozen, we drove back to my house.

"That was cool!" Dylan exclaimed, still excited from the day.

"That was a good place to tube," William said.

"It's not too steep or too crowded." I looked at him. "The county lets you cut Christmas trees there. Jamie and I cut one once, but we had trouble carrying it out."

"I could help with that," he said. "If you decide to do it again."

"I might take you up on that." I leaned over and whispered, "A tree is not in the budget this year."

William whispered back, "Does Dylan know?"

I glanced over at him and then shook my head. "Not yet. I'm still hoping something might work out."

He nodded. A moment later he said, "Do we have time to stop for a hamburger?"

"I just need to be at work by three."

"Plenty of time."

William drove us to the Arctic Circle, a hamburger joint a mile up I-15. As we walked into the restaurant, Dylan froze. There was a young Black man behind the counter. Seeing Black men in Mistletoe was rare enough, but a Black teenager was a first for him.

For a moment the two of them stared at each other. William approached the counter. "How's it going?"

The young man looked away from Dylan. "Not bad. What can I get for you?"

"I'd like two ranch burgers and an order of fries with your famous fry sauce." He turned to me. "What would you like?"

"I'll have half of what you're getting. Dylan will have a corn dog."

Dylan still just stood there staring at the young man. William turned to him. "Do you want fries with that?"

Dylan nodded.

"Got to have the fries," William said. "We'll also have two Cokes and a lime rickey. That will do it." He took his wallet from his back pocket. "Thank you."

"No problem," the young man said.

As we sat at the table, Dylan suddenly said, "He's a Negro."

William nodded. "There are Black people everywhere. In the army my best friends were Black. This is just kind of a different town. There aren't many Black people."

"How come?"

"Good question." William turned to me. "How come?"

"More are in the big cities than in small towns like ours," I said.

"Why?" Dylan asked.

"I'll have to think about that."

"Let us know when you figure it out," William said, grinning.

"So how's the corn dog?" William asked.

"Good," Dylan said.

"Where I used to live, sometimes they fed us fish heads."

I was surprised that he was talking about it.

Dylan stared at him, not sure if he was kidding. "Honest?"

"I'm telling the truth. I wish I wasn't."

"Did you eat them?"

"You'll eat anything if you're hungry enough. Even rats."

"Ooh," Dylan said.

William nodded. "Tastes like chicken."

ON THE way back to town, William said, "We still need to pick up your car."

I had forgotten that we had left it at the diner. "I'm glad one of us remembered."

A few moments later William stopped his truck behind the diner next to the Fairlane, which was covered with snow. "What time do you need to be back here?"

"Not until three," I said. "I have ninety minutes. Would you like to come over for some hot cocoa?"

"I would love to."

"Can Mr. William play Rock 'Em Sock 'Em Robots?" Dylan asked.

William turned to Dylan. "Are you good?"

"Yeah."

"We'll see," he said.

He turned to me, "Give me your car keys."

"How come?"

"So I can warm up your car while I clear off the snow."

I took my keys out. "You don't need to . . ."

He put his finger on my lips. "Let me be good to you."

It was the sweetest thing I had heard in months.

He got out, started my car, then cleared the snow off my windshield. Five minutes later he opened my door and offered me his hand. "It's ready. Your car's warm."

"Thank you," I said. "Meet you at my duplex?"

"I'll see you there."

"Can I ride with Mr. William?" Dylan asked.

"It's fine with me," William said.

"Sure."

Back at my duplex, we kicked off our boots and then went inside. Dylan led William into his room while I went to the kitchen and made hot cocoa. I poured three coffee cups full and dropped in marshmallows. I carried all three cups into Dylan's bedroom, something waitresses are good at. I gave them their drinks, then sat down on the floor next to William to watch them box.

"You're really good at this," William said to Dylan.

"You're not so good," Dylan said.

"Dylan," I said.

"He's right," William said. "I stink at this. He keeps knocking my block off."

They played a little longer, until I made Dylan get in the bathtub. While he was bathing, William and I sat at the kitchen table with our cocoa. "I like your place," he said.

"Thank you."

"Who lives in the other side of the duplex?"

"Mr. Foster."

"What's he like?"

"Old, mostly. He rarely comes out."

"But he's quiet?"

"Not really. His hearing's going, so he turns the TV all the way up. Fortunately, he goes to bed before Dylan does."

"Is he nice?"

"Yes, and he pays Dylan a dollar to take his garbage to the curb. That's like a nickel a foot."

"What does Dylan do with all that money?"

"I make him put it in his college fund."

We drank our cocoa.

"Today was a nice day," I said.

"Yeah, it was. Dylan's a great kid."

"He's my reason, you know? He's proof of God's love."

"He's proof of your love," William said.

"I worry about him. Like, maybe I'm going to ruin his life by living here."

"Why do you think that?"

"He's the only Black child in his school. He's the only Black child in this whole town. You saw how he reacted to that young man at the hamburger place. Then add to that the fact that he doesn't have a father."

"He has you. And you've done a great job with him."

"I just wish I could give him a better life."

"You give him love. That's better than anything material you could give him."

"I wish I could give him more time. I work so much." I shook my head. "I keep waiting for things to get easier, but they don't."

"Who watches Dylan when you're working?"

"Fran. She's like a second mother to him."

"How did you find her?"

"She worked at the diner for a while, but she didn't last long. She's in college now."

"Speaking of the diner . . ." He glanced down at his watch. "It's almost time for you to go to work. I better go."

I led William to the door. "Thank you for taking us tubing. And to lunch. We had a really good time."

"Good," he said.

"Before you go, I wanted to ask you something," I said.

"Yes?"

"I wanted to ask, what are you doing for Thanksgiving?"

"I've got a date with myself and a turkey-and-mashed-potatoes TV dinner. Hold the TV."

"Would you like to have dinner with Dylan and me? I can pretty much guarantee that the food will be better."

"Not to mention the company," he said. "What can I bring?"

"Just yourself," I said. "I get almost everything from the diner."

"Then how about I bring some wine," he said.

"I won't turn you down on that."

"I didn't think so. So do I have to wait until Thanksgiving to see you again?"

I smiled. "I'm off Tuesday at three. I'll get a sitter."

"I promise I'll make it worth your while."

Chapter 8

MONDAY NIGHT AFTER WORK, Fran met me outside the duplex, which is something she never did unless she was in a hurry to get somewhere. She stood in front of the door as if she were guarding it. "You'll never believe what happened," she said.

"I'm sure I won't," I replied. "Is it a good or bad thing?"

"Two things. First, Dylan is still up."

Bad thing, I thought. "It's a school night."

"I know, but I made a judgment call. Something special happened." She opened the door, and I walked in. In the middle of our living room was a six-foot Christmas tree. It was mostly decorated, and Dylan was laying strands of tinsel across its boughs. His smile was epic. "Look, Mama! We got a tree!"

I turned to Fran. "Where did it come from?"

"Well, we all went on an unexpected little field trip. William came by in his truck, and we went to a field and cut it down. He set it up, and Dylan and I did the decorations."

I glanced around. "Where's William?"

"He left a couple hours ago. He said 'Merry Christmas' and he'll see you tomorrow." She shook her head. "It's kind of a Christmas miracle."

"He's kind of a Christmas miracle," I replied.

I FOUND I was thinking about him all the time. I couldn't wait until Tuesday. How different my life felt having something to look forward to.

William wouldn't tell me what we were doing, as he wanted it to be a surprise. His only instruction was to dress for winter and wear warm boots. So I threw on a turtleneck sweater and jeans. He picked me up a little after four, and we drove north up I-15.

We were going for a sleigh ride. It was dusk when we arrived at Hardware Ranch, about an hour north of Mistletoe. The ranch was state-owned and encompassed nearly twenty thousand acres.

Dylan would have loved it, but I'm glad we went alone. William and I snuggled up together under a blanket for the hour-long ride, which took us through miles of pristine wilderness and past the largest herd of elk I'd ever seen.

After the ride we drove to the nearby town of Brigham City and had dinner at a little restaurant called the Maddox Ranch House. The restaurant had a reputation of having some of Utah's best fried chicken, bison steaks, and hot buttered rolls.

We both ordered comfort food. William ordered the breaded trout, while I had the chicken-fried steak with mashed potatoes.

"Thank you for the tree," I said again. "You should have seen how excited Dylan was."

"I did," he said.

"Of course. Was it hard getting the tree out?"

"A little. I could have used a horse to help pull it out," he said, buttering a roll. "Speaking of which, you seemed comfortable around the horses tonight."

"I grew up with horses," I said. "My father raises them. At least, he did. I have no idea if he still does."

"So your dad was a horse breeder."

"My dad was into a lot of things. He was in the military until he was thirty-five; then he retired and bought the ranch in Cedar City. He's an entrepreneur and an investor. We never wanted for anything.

"Growing up, we lived frugally—my father mowed his own lawn, drove an old car—but I realize now we were well off. My dad wasn't showy, and he's not obsessed with money; it just kind of flows with him." I looked at William. "Does that make sense?"

He nodded. "I knew people like that in the military."

"I certainly didn't inherit it from him. I've been poor since the minute I left home."

He grinned. "You mean, you're not getting rich at the diner?"

"No. Are you getting rich at Renato's?"

"Renato has been good to me," William said. "I'm not getting rich, but I don't really need much either. When I got back from the war, I had a lot of back pay from the military, so I've got savings. I'm doing okay."

"This is an odd question, but do you get paid as a POW?"

"It's considered time served. POWs also get a little extra—sixty-five dollars a month—for imminent-danger pay. Sounds absurd hearing it that way: I made an extra two dollars a day for putting my life in greater danger."

He took a bite of his fish, then said, "You also progress through the ranks, so your salary goes up." He smiled darkly. "I didn't get to do a lot of shopping in Hanoi, so the money just stacked up."

"You said you were sent to Vietnam by a judge."

He nodded. "I was facing hard jail time."

"That's hard for me to believe. You're one of the sweetest men I've ever met."

He smiled. "I put on a good show."

"I don't think so. I'm a pretty good judge of character," I said. "What's your family like?"

"Dead."

His reply stunned me. He noticed.

"Sorry," he said quickly. "That was . . . crass. The truth is, I had a great family and an idyllic childhood. I had both parents at home, two little sisters, Little League baseball on Saturday, church on Sundays. We were pretty much the Cleaver family—until they were killed in a car crash."

"Your whole family?"

He nodded. "Everyone but me. I was supposed to be with them, but I got in a fight with my mother before leaving and said I wouldn't go. I locked myself in my room. My dad wouldn't have put up with that nonsense. He would have knocked my door down and dragged me out, but he wasn't there. He was in Ohio on business. He was an auto parts salesman. My mother and sisters met up with him and were headed to Cincinnati for the week."

"What was the fight about?"

"I don't remember." William shook his head. "After they died, I had no one. My father didn't get along with his family, and my mother didn't have one. She was an only child and born late in her parents' lives. Her father was sixty-five when she was born. Her mother was fifty-two. Her father died when she was nine; her mother passed away the same year I was born.

"So with no family and since I wasn't yet eighteen, I became a ward of the state and was put in the foster-care system. It didn't go well. At that age, I was too old to assimilate into another family. Not to mention, I was pretty messed up. My family had just died, and the last thing I had said to my mother was that I hated her. The guilt and shame were eating me alive. I think some part of me blamed myself for their deaths."

"You know that's not true."

"I know—I knew it then—but I didn't *believe* it. I ended up as a foster child with a caseworker. I honor anyone who takes in a foster child, but the family I was put with was a mistake. They owned a dry-cleaning business and were basically looking for free labor. I was working sixty hours a week cleaning and pressing clothes. I told my caseworker that I was a slave, but she just thought I was exaggerating. After a year and a half I ran away.

"I couch-hopped for a while; then I got a job with one of my dad's old clients at a car dealership detailing cars. It was a good gig. Then one day at the dealership, I ran into a group of guys a few years older than me. I thought they were cool. They had hot cars and foxy girlfriends. They all shared an old home together. None of them worked; they just, like, hung out all day. One of them invited me to move into their place. They gave me cigarettes and beer. I thought I was pretty cool because they liked me.

"It never occurred to me how they were supporting their lifestyle. I didn't realize they made their money stealing or that they brought me in because they were grooming me for something. One night after a few months, they came to me and said, 'You've been living off us far too long. It's time you earned your keep.' They told me that if I didn't help them break into the car dealership I worked at, they were going to beat me up and then make me pay them back for food and beer and back rent.

"I offered them all the money I had, but they came up with some ridiculous amount I owed them, like five thousand dollars. So I helped them break in. They stole two cars. Then one of the security men walked in on us. One of the guys had a gun and shot him. It didn't kill him, but it was considered attempted murder.

"The security guard recognized me, and we were caught. I had just turned eighteen a week before, so I was tried as an adult. Those guys I thought were so cool showed their real colors; they told the court it was all my idea. Since I worked at the dealership, the judge believed them. It was their word against mine.

"That's when he gave me the option to go to Vietnam or prison. It was pretty much a no-brainer for me."

"And I thought I had it tough," I said.

"What I went through doesn't make your life any easier," he said. Then he forced a smile, saying, "That conversation turned heavy fast. Let's talk about something lighter."

I smiled back. "Like what?"

"Like, did you know your name is a palindrome?"

"What's a palindrome?"

"It's something that reads the same forward and backward. Like the words radar or racecar."

I worked it out in my head. "Racecar. That's kind of cool."

"They can be more than one word," he said. "My favorite palindromes are *Do geese see God?* and the world's first greeting: 'Madam, I'm Adam.'"

"You know, the man they named Noel Street for was a palindrome. His name was Leon Noel."

"I assumed they named it Noel Street because the town's name is kind of . . . Christmassy." He looked at me. "Is that a word?"

"Christmassy. Works for me," I said. "Mistletoe is definitely Christmassy. You arrived just in time for the Noel Street Christmas Market."

"I saw them putting up booths in the park," he said.

"Dylan and I look forward to the market every year. This year will be the best ever."

"Why is that?"

I looked at him and smiled. "Because you're here."

WILLIAM dropped me off at home a little before midnight. He walked me to the door. "So I'll see you on Thursday?"

He grinned. "Right. Thanksgiving. I'll come hungry."

"I promise you won't leave that way."

"I believe you." He looked into my eyes. The mood grew more serious. "I had a really good time tonight."

"Me too."

Then he leaned forward and we kissed. It was delicious.

After we separated, I said, "Thank you again for tonight."

"I'll see you Thursday."

He turned and walked back to his truck. I waved as he drove off, then went inside.

Chapter 9

THANKSGIVING WAS SPECIAL. For starters, I got the day off with pay. The diner was closed. It's not that there wasn't enough business. The opposite was true. Thanksgiving always provided a stream of travelers, truck drivers, and Eleanor Rigbys, but as a courtesy to her staff, Loretta shut the place down.

What made the day even better was a tradition started by our chef, Bart. The day before Thanksgiving, Bart made a meal for all of our families, which included his delectable corn-bread stuffing, pecan-crusted sweet-potato soufflé, Parker House rolls (just the dough so we could serve them hot), and mashed potatoes with turkey gravy. For dessert I purchased one of Loretta's famous Granny Smith apple pies. Instant Thanksgiving, just add turkey.

Or, in our case, chicken. Dylan liked chicken more than turkey, and since it was the right size for the two of us, that's what we usually had. But this year I opted for the larger species of bird.

WHAT I will always remember about that Thanksgiving is that the day started out good, ended good, and the dash between the two ends was a nightmare.

It was snowing again when William arrived at noon. I had just brought out the turkey, and the rolls were almost brown, so I asked him to carve the turkey, while I brought out the piping-hot rolls and saw to the rest of the meal. We set all the food out on the kitchen counter, then sat together around our tiny kitchen table.

"I'll pray," I said. "Let's hold hands." I cleared my throat. "God, we thank Thee for the remarkable abundance of our lives. We are grateful that William has chosen to spend this day with us. Please bless us to serve all thy children, especially those that are without. Amen."

"Amen," my men echoed.

I wondered if William had had a decent Thanksgiving since his childhood. He ate three plates of food and two helpings of pie.

"Remarkable," William said. "I don't think I've ever been this full. I might pop."

Dylan looked concerned. "Really?"

"No. But you should probably wear a raincoat just in case."

Dylan looked at me. "He's kidding," I said.

"Only about the popping part," he said. His face suddenly took on a softer expression. "How life can change. There was a time I was so hungry that I chewed on my shoe just to taste something."

"Yuck," Dylan said.

I looked at William sympathetically and took his hand.

"Why didn't you just go to the refrigerator?" Dylan asked.

He looked at Dylan, then suddenly smiled. "I should have thought of that."

After dinner Dylan went to his room to play, while I made William and myself some coffee.

"Cream and sugar?" I asked.

"Both, please."

I brought the cups over.

"This is good," he said.

"It's a special Kona coffee bean that Loretta buys."

"Membership at the diner has its privileges. Including this amazing dinner."

I looked at him happily. "What you said earlier, about chewing your shoe. Was that true?"

"Yes."

"How did you keep going?"

"Some say it's the survival instinct. But I don't think so. Nearly a million people take their lives each year. It's not about survival; it's about finding meaning in living. Even in our suffering."

"And you found meaning?"

"In a twisted way—I didn't want to let them win."

"It got you here," I said.

Just then there was a loud crash in the front room. William and I entered the living room. There was a grapefruit-size stone in the middle of the floor. Dylan came out of his room to see what the noise was. William said to Dylan, "Stay here." William ran to the window and looked out, but whoever had thrown it was gone.

We both walked over to the stone. Written on it in Magic Marker was one word: NIGGER.

William pushed the stone under the couch with his foot. "We're getting out of here," he said.

I think I was in shock. "Where?"

"My place," he said in a surprisingly calm voice.

WE DROVE in William's truck to the side of his building, walking through thick snow to the lobby. The brindled cat I'd seen the first day was sitting on the balustrade looking down on us.

"You have a cat?" Dylan asked.

"He's not mine," William said. "He doesn't belong to anyone. He just lives here. He might be the landlord."

"What's his name?"

"I've named him Ho Chi Minh. Because he likes to sneak up on you when you're not looking."

We walked up the stairs to William's apartment and went inside. I took Dylan's coat off and then my own. William left his on.

"Can I have the keys to your house?" he asked.

"Yes." I took them out of my purse. "How come?"

"I'm going to get some cardboard and patch up your window so the snow doesn't come in. I'll be back in an hour."

He walked out. "Where is Mr. William going?" Dylan asked.

"He just went to fix something," I said.

"How come someone threw a rock through our window?"

I didn't know that he had comprehended what had happened.

"I don't know. Sometimes people do strange things because they're afraid."

Dylan looked more puzzled. "What are they afraid of?"

"Things they don't understand," I said.

WHILE William was gone, I cleaned his apartment: washed the dishes, dusted, even mopped the floor with a cloth. An hour and a half later William returned. He looked around his apartment.

"You cleaned."

"I had to keep busy," I said. "How did it go?"

"I boarded up the window. I cleaned up the glass and then took the stone over to the police station. That one officer was there."

"Andy?"

"No, the short one with a crew cut."

"Peter," I said. "What did he say?"

"He asked if we saw anything. I told him we didn't, so he's going to check with your neighbors to see if they saw anything." He looked at me intensely. "He asked if you had any enemies they should know about."

The question angered me. "Not that I know of," I said.

"I told him about the Ketchup Lady."

"What did he say?"

"The other officer had already told him about what happened at the diner. He's driving over to her house later today."

"He knows who she is?"

"Loretta did. She looked her up once—just in case she ended up causing any problems."

My heart hurt. I looked over at Dylan, who was in the bedroom. "So what do we do now?"

"Let's go for a ride and not let this nastiness ruin our holiday."

"Where?"

"How about Salt Lake?" he said. "I heard that they turn the lights on at Temple Square on Thanksgiving night."

"Whatever you think," I said. The truth was, I was tired of always being in charge and having to figure out what to do. For once I just wanted to be looked out for. "When?"

"Now."

I walked back to the bedroom. "Come on, Dylan. We're going for a ride."

The drive to Salt Lake was slow. I-15 was slick, and we found ourselves following a caravan of snowplows. I didn't care. We weren't in any hurry.

When we arrived at the downtown area, we were surprised at how empty the square was. William stopped at the curb near the center and got out. He asked someone wearing a name tag what time they turned the lights on. He walked back to me. "Well, I messed that up. They turn them on the day after Thanksgiving."

"It's okay. It's still pretty. Let's walk around the grounds."

The truth was, I wasn't disappointed. In my state of mind, I wasn't really in the mood to fight crowds. It just felt good to be somewhere else. Mostly, it felt good to be with William.

We walked around the Temple grounds and then through one of the nearby indoor malls called the ZCMI Center. Our Thanksgiving gluttony had started to wear off, which we satiated with Chinese noodles, caramel apples, and saltwater taffy.

The evening was calm and pleasant, and by dusk I'd almost forgotten why we'd left Mistletoe to begin with. On the way back home, Dylan fell asleep on my lap.

"Looks like we wore him out," William said, glancing over.

"It's usually the other way around," I said.

"You can lean against me if you want."

I laid my head against his shoulder. We didn't speak much, because the silence was enough. We drove back to his apartment.

"I think you should stay at my place tonight," he said softly. "You and Dylan can sleep in the bed. I'll sleep on the couch."

I just nodded. William carried Dylan inside, and I tucked him into the bed that I had slept next to when I was taking care of William that first night.

"I don't have anything to wear," I said. In my hurry to leave, I'd only packed for Dylan.

"I might have something," William said. He opened a drawer and pulled out a T-shirt with the Harley-Davidson logo on it. "Try this. It might be long enough."

He stepped out of the room. I took off everything except my underwear and donned the long T-shirt. It fell to my knees. I opened the door. "It fits."

"You look cute." For a moment he just looked at me. Maybe longingly. Or maybe I just hoped.

"Is there anything else I can get for you?" he asked.

I walked over and hugged him. "Thank you for being so sweet. Today should have been awful. But I feel happy."

"So do I," he said. "Thank you for inviting me to dinner."

"Thank you for coming."

As I looked into his eyes, I felt drawn to him. Into him. We began kissing. It was several minutes before I pulled away. "I better go to bed," I said reluctantly.

"Good night," he said. He kissed me once more, then sat down on the couch. "Sleep well."

"You too," I said.

I went back inside the bedroom and shut the door behind me.

I couldn't sleep. I could still taste his lips on mine. For more than an hour I just lay in the dark thinking about him. Wanting him. I looked over at Dylan to make sure he was asleep; then I got out of bed. I opened the door, stepped out, and quietly pulled it shut behind me. William was asleep on the couch.

I knelt down on the floor next to him, then put my hand on his side. He slowly turned around, his eyes open. "I want to lay with you," I whispered.

His eyes gently studied my face. Then he moved back, giving me a small perch to rest my body next to his. I climbed onto the couch, our faces just inches apart. For a long time we just gazed into each other's eyes. Then I said, "I'm falling for you."

He just looked back at me with soft eyes. "Don't. I'm broken."

"I know."

His eyes suddenly welled with tears, which fell down his face. I gently touched the tears with my fingers. Then we kissed, softly, sweetly at first, then passionately. Everything dissolved around us. Only once before in my life had I felt that kind of love.

Chapter 10

Friday, November 28

I WOKE THE NEXT MORNING in William's bed next to Dylan. Somewhere in the night, William must have carried me back to his room. I was disappointed to not feel his body next to mine, but I was glad. It would have been confusing for Dylan had he come out of the room and found us together.

With Dylan still asleep, I got dressed and went into the living room. William was gone. I didn't know what that meant.

Ten minutes later I heard the front door open. William walked in. He was carrying a bag from the grocery store.

"I got us something for breakfast," he said.

I took the sack from him and set it on the counter. Then I helped him off with his jacket and put my arms around him. He wrapped his arms around me. I said softly, "I meant what I said last night."

He kissed the top of my head. "I know."

I knew he was having trouble saying how he felt about me. Of course, I wanted to hear it, but I didn't care right then. He had already said it, just without words. He had shown me he cared in a hundred ways. I would rather have someone show me love and not tell me than tell me and not show me.

"Is Dylan still asleep?" he asked.

"You'd know it if he wasn't," I said. "Do you have any eggs?"

"Maybe half a dozen."

"I can make French toast. Would you like that?"

"Yes."

I made coffee and cocoa and French toast, then took the remaining French toast batter and cooked it into a light scramble.

"I don't have syrup," he said.

"You have sugar," I said. "I can make that work." I dissolved brown sugar and water together, then buttered a couple of pieces of toast for Dylan and put the rest on a single plate and poured syrup over the top. Then I scooped up the egg and put it next to the toast. I brought the plate to the table. "Breakfast is served."

"Where's your plate?"

"I'll share yours."

He took a bite, then forked a bite for me. I opened my mouth, and he fed me. We ate the whole meal this way.

"Do you have to work today?" he asked.

"Tonight." I looked at him. "How about you?"

"Usual day."

"Could you drop by the diner after work? I'll feed you."

"I'll stay until closing if you want."

I smiled. "That would be nice."

He sat back. "Until we find out what happened, it would probably be best if Dylan didn't go back to your place." He added, "He could stay here."

"I think it would be better if he stayed with Fran. It would be more natural."

"Whatever you think is best."

I fed him the last bite of French toast. "Could you drive me to my car?"

"Your car's already downstairs. I got Sam at the grocery store to drive it over."

"Thank you."

He lifted our plate and stood. "I better get to work. Would you like me to find someone to repair your window?"

"No, I'll call the landlady. She's good about things like that."

"All right. I guess I'll go." He just looked at me as he breathed out slowly. "You make it hard to go."

I walked over to him, and we kissed. "Thank you for making me feel safe."

"Thank you for letting me."

DYLAN and I returned to our duplex a little after noon. Not only had William picked up the broken glass from the window and put cardboard over it but he'd cleaned up after the Thanksgiving meal as well. He had even vacuumed.

Gretchen, my landlady, was her typical efficient self and had someone there to repair the window even before it was time for me to leave for work. Fran arrived around two as the repairman was finishing up.

"Did they catch who did it?" she asked.

"Not yet," I said.

"People are sick."

I looked at her softly. "Some are."

I got Dylan off with Fran and then drove to work. Word about the stone being thrown through our window had already spread, and Loretta was eager to talk to me about it.

"I'm sure it's that vile Katherine woman," she said. "A.k.a. Ketchup Lady. You know I gave Andy her address. He and Peter went out to interrogate her."

"I don't know if it was her or not," I said. "I just don't ever want to see her again."

"You know you won't see her here. She steps one foot in here and she gets the boot. She can slurp her ketchup somewhere else."

"Thanks for the support."

"That's what I'm here for, baby girl."

William came in around seven. He sat himself in my section and got up and kissed me when I came out to him.

"Did you get your window fixed?" he asked.

"Yes. And the strangest thing, my house was sparkling clean."

"Christmas elves," he said.

"I think not." I grinned. "What are you doing tomorrow?"

"Working. Renato got backed up. I'm open Sunday, though. Do you have anything Sunday?"

"Church. But that's just until one." A thought crossed my mind. "Why don't you come to church with us?"

"I don't do church," he said.

"You might like it." I grabbed his hand. "I'll be there. Then I'll cook you a nice meal after."

"We could have Thanksgiving leftovers," he said.

"That sounds like a yes."

"Yes. What time?"

"Church starts at eleven, so if you're picking us up, ten thirty would be good."

"I'll be there."

"I have two more events to put on your calendar. The first is Saturday night, December sixth. It's the Noel Street Christmas Festival. The second is Friday, December twelfth, Dylan's Christmas concert at school."

"You're planning things two weeks out?"

"Of course. You have to plan things out," I said. "Don't you?"

"No, I just go with the wind," he said. "I'm a drifter."

"Would this drifter like to join us at the Christmas concert?"

"Absolutely. Sounds exciting."

"Don't get too excited," I said. "It's just the usual elementary school production. One of the teachers plays the piano while the kids sing. But Dylan's excited. This year he got chosen to be a bell ringer for 'Jingle Bells.'" I grinned. "It's a big honor."

"Sounds like it," he said.

"It's during the day. Can you miss an hour of work?"

"Renato doesn't care when I work, just that I get things done. I can go in a little early."

I smiled. "I'll let Dylan know. He'll be excited."

"That makes two of us," he said.

MY SUNDAY routine rarely varied, which is probably the biggest reason why I loved the day. It was truly a day of rest. I never worked on Sunday. I slept in almost an hour later than usual—a cherished extravagance. Then around nine, I made Dylan his traditional Sunday waffles for breakfast.

After doing the dishes, I laid out Dylan's Sunday clothes—jeans, a button-down shirt, and a clip-on bow tie—then got myself ready for church. I wore a long V-necked sage-green dress I'd bought three years earlier for one of Jamie's weddings.

I hoped William would think I looked pretty. Dylan did.

"Wow, Mama. You look beautiful."

I smiled. "Thank you."

William showed up at my apartment at ten thirty sharp. He was wearing jeans and a button-down shirt beneath a navy cardigan.

"Is this okay?" he asked, looking down at himself. "I wasn't sure how I was supposed to dress."

"You look nice."

"Thank you. Not as nice as you."

Dylan just stood there looking at William. "I don't want to wear a tie," he said.

"You look pretty debonair with a tie," William said.

"What's that mean?" he asked.

"It's an old word for handsome."

Dylan thought for a moment, then said, "I'll wear it."

The church Dylan and I attended was a nondenominational Christian church halfway between Mistletoe and the equally small town of Wilden, falling on the latter's side of the city line.

We walked into the chapel just a few minutes before the service began. The three of us sat together in the middle of a pew next to Fran, who had come early to save us seats.

The church was small and poor. Our pastor, Pastor Henderson, did yard care and blade sharpening on the side to make ends meet.

After Pastor Henderson made a few announcements, there was a song followed by prayer and then a Communion of grape juice and a Ritz cracker—always Dylan's favorite part of the service. This was followed by a sermon.

About ten minutes into the sermon, William handed me the keys to his truck and whispered in my ear, "I'll meet you at your apartment." He stood up and made his way out.

I turned to Fran. "Would you take Dylan home?"

"Got it," she said, watching William leave.

I stood up and walked out after him. When I got outside, William was walking briskly toward the main road. I couldn't believe he was walking home. It was at least seven miles to Mistletoe.

"William!" I shouted.

He stopped and turned around. When I caught up to him, I paused to catch my breath, then said, "Where are you going?"

"I just had to get out of there," he said. "I don't belong."

"Everyone belongs," I said.

"I don't," he said. "All that talk about grace and forgiveness." He looked at me. "I just couldn't handle it. There is no hope for me. Not after what I've done."

I pondered his words, then said, "Have you ever really shared what happened with anyone?"

"No."

I took his hand. "I want you to tell me about it."

He looked at me like I'd just asked him to jump off a cliff. Maybe I had. "I can't."

"What are you afraid of?"

"That you won't like me anymore."

I looked him in the eyes. "My husband wrote me about the war. I know he hid a lot from me, but I could still feel both the horror and shame he felt. You were put in a situation that wasn't your fault. Would you have done those things if you hadn't been taken from your home and ordered to kill?"

He shook his head. "No, of course not."

"The fact that you're suffering shows who you really are. You need to let it go. You don't need to worry about me not loving you. You can trust me."

"Not with this. I don't want to take that chance."

"You have to," I said softly. "Because if you believe that I couldn't love you if I knew the real you, then you will never believe in my love."

He slowly nodded. "Let's go someplace."

"Let's go to the frozen waterfall," I said.

"That would be appropriate."

We held hands as we walked back to the church and got in his truck. We drove up along the canyon to the waterfall. No one was there, but the wind was blowing hard, so we didn't get out of the truck. We just sat inside, the heater on high.

"Where do you want to begin?" I asked.

He took a deep breath. "Christmas Day." He went quiet. I reached over and took his hand.

"Tell me."

"The day started with a Christmas service put on by our chaplain. Everyone was melancholy or homesick. Everyone but me. I had no one back home. Then they opened their care packages while we listened to a broadcast Christmas message from President Johnson. After the service, the chaplain gave everyone a Bible. It was the only present I got."

He looked over at me. "Two days later we were called up to search a small village in Quang Tri. It was half an hour before dawn. We were moving in through a rice paddy when a dog started barking. An old man walked out of his hut. He looked around for a moment; then he saw one of our men. The old man and the soldier just stood there staring at each other. Then the old man started shouting.

"That's when all hell broke loose. Machine guns shredded everything in sight. Flamethrowers belched out hell. People were screaming and crying." He looked at me. "People were dying.

"Afterward I was counting casualties when I came across a Vietnamese woman huddled near the edge of the jungle. She was holding her son." William's voice choked with emotion. "He was no older than Dylan. He had been shot, and his life was bleeding out on his mother. For a moment we just looked at each other. Then she lifted her hand. I thought she had a grenade, so I shot her." His eyes welled up. "When I went to check her for weapons, I found that she was only trying to show me a prayer book."

"I'm sorry," I said.

"Four days after leveling that village, on New Year's Eve, we walked into an ambush. Half our platoon was killed. Friends of mine were killed." He looked into my eyes. "That's when I was taken captive."

"You've told me nothing that makes me respect you less," I said. I leaned over and kissed him on the cheek. "Tell me what it was like being a prisoner of war."

He rubbed his face. "There was constant physical and mental torture. The first year, I was tied up in a bamboo cage in the jungle with eleven other men. Six of them died of disease or starvation. After a year or so, those who had survived were moved to Hanoi.

"I spent the next few years lying on a bamboo mat on a concrete floor with my legs bound. There were meat hooks hanging from the ceiling above us." His voice softened with the recollection. "That's where I got those scars on my back."

I looked into his eyes. "Come here."

He leaned forward. I cupped the back of his head and pulled it against me and held him while he cried. "I love you," I said.

He pressed himself into me. "I love you too," he said softly.

WILLIAM and I arrived back at my duplex after dark. There were more snowmen in the yard. Nearly a dozen. Maybe more.

When we went inside, Fran was sitting at the table studying. Dylan was already asleep in bed.

"Did you have a good night?" I asked.

Fran nodded. "We watched Disney."

"And made snowmen," I added.

"Yes, we did," Fran said. "Hundreds."

I laughed. "Looks like it."

"Do you need anything else?"

I shook my head. "No. Thank you."

"You're welcome." She looked at William and smiled. "Have a good night."

"You too," William said.

After she left, I invited William to stay. He was vulnerable, and I didn't want him going home alone. I had him lie down on the couch. I put a warm washcloth on his face, then gently massaged his feet. He fell asleep in our front room around midnight.

Chapter 11

Saturday, December 6

FOR SOME STREETS, decorating for Christmas is like putting lipstick on a pig. But Noel Street didn't just share a holiday name, it was made for it. Dickens-era streetlamps with deep green patinas, hung with great pine wreaths, lined the cobblestone street. Silver tinsel wires were strung across the width of the road and wrapped with red-and-green ribbon.

The north end of Noel Street—the opposite end of town from the Harrison—circled Garfield Park, a grassy public square with an old wood pavilion and its centerpiece, a massive Norway spruce. The park was where the festival was held.

The Noel Street Christmas Festival was a complicated affair with rented booths, merchant stalls, choir stands, a public address system, and a printed program. Vendors sold everything from mulled wine and baked apples to funnel cake and roasted nuts.

There was a gingerbread house contest, a crèche display, a life-size nativity with a real donkey and oxen, a stall of reindeer, and, of course, a huge golden throne that Santa himself (accompanied by an enterprising local photographer) inhabited weekend evenings before Christmas.

Dylan had waited all week for the evening. William picked us up a little after sundown, and we drove downtown, parking in one of the reserved parking places behind the diner. Then the three of us wandered up and down the crowded sidewalks, stopping to watch street performers and carolers and peruse the vendors' booths and sample their wares. Christmas music blared from every corner.

We stopped at a booth selling German delicacies and ate bratwurst and sauerkraut sandwiches (something I could never have gotten Dylan to eat on my own) and spätzle (ditto) with large cups of cider served in plastic steins.

After we ate, we made our way to the crowded square, holding hands with Dylan in the middle. We stopped to take pictures by the Christmas tree and then walked to the main pavilion to listen to a barbershop quartet sing "God Rest Ye Merry, Gentlemen" followed by "It's Beginning to Look a Lot Like Christmas."

"This is impressive," William said. "There are a lot of people here. I wonder where they're coming from."

"It used to just be the locals and couples on dates," I said. "Now look at all the families. They're coming from all over."

We were standing near a large box wrapped in Mylar and tied with a bow to look like a Christmas present. We could see our reflection in the box. Just then Dylan looked up at me with a large smile. "Look, Mama. We're a family."

I smiled back at him, then looked at William. To my surprise he wasn't smiling. There was a peculiar look in his eyes. He suddenly released Dylan's hand. "Hey, buddy. Want some caramel corn?"

"Yeah."

Dylan hadn't noticed William's nuanced response, but I had. William left us for a moment, then came back with a large bag of caramel corn. From that moment on, William was different. Quieter and disconnected. He was also holding something so he couldn't hold hands. I puzzled to understand what had happened.

It was still early, just a little before nine, when William said, "We probably shouldn't keep Dylan up too late."

"You want to go already?" I asked.

"It would probably be best."

I hid my disappointment. "All right," I said. We walked against the flow of a still growing crowd back to his truck. It was a little after nine when we arrived back at my duplex. I sent Dylan inside to get ready for bed, remaining outside with William.

"Would you like to come in?" I asked.

"Thanks," he said. "But I'm a little tired."

I took his hand. "Are you okay?"

"I'm fine."

I looked into his eyes. "Are *we* okay?"

His pause was answer enough. "We're fine," he said.

I just looked at him, still unable to read what had happened. Whatever it was, he clearly didn't want to talk about it.

"All right. Good night." I stood on my toes to kiss him. He gave me just a light peck on the lips. "Good night."

He turned to go.

"Call me tomorrow?" I asked.

"Sure."

The next day, William didn't call or stop by the diner. I knew something had bothered him the previous night. As much as I wanted to see him, I didn't reach out to him. Whatever he was dealing with he needed to work out. But it wasn't easy. My heart ached. It didn't help that in the days leading up to the school Christmas concert, Dylan asked me at least a dozen times if William was going to be there. I wished I knew.

Friday, December 12

THE morning of the big program, my heart wrestled with the competing emotions of excitement and dread. *I still haven't heard from William since the festival. Where is he?*

Dylan was over-the-top excited about the concert and his debut performance as a first-grade bell ringer. It was a really big deal for him, which only made me more anxious about not hearing from William. Notwithstanding, I didn't want anything to take away from Dylan's day.

I put chocolate chips in his Cream of Wheat, something reserved for very special occasions, then dressed him in red corduroy pants with a long-sleeved white shirt and green suspenders.

"You, little man, look like Christmas personified," I said. "Santa would be proud."

"Is Mr. William going to be there?"

I deflected the question. "We'll see. Are you ready to ring that bell?"

He nodded. "I practiced."

As I put on his coat, Dylan asked, "Is Mr. William picking us up?"

"No. He's coming from work. We're going to meet him there."

His little forehead furrowed. "Is he coming for sure?"

My heart ached at the question. "I don't know for sure. He said he was coming. Unless there's an emergency, he'll be there."

"I hope there's not an emergency," Dylan replied.

Dylan and I got in the car. I started it up and turned on the heater. There was a huge burst of air, then nothing.

"No, no, no," I said.

"What's wrong, Mama?" Dylan asked.

I groaned. "This car hates me."

To my huge relief, William was waiting for us at the school when we got there. Dylan picked out his truck in the school parking lot the moment we drove in. I didn't know where he'd been but I was just glad he was there. I didn't want to see Dylan disappointed on such an important day.

William must have gotten there pretty early, because he'd secured front-row seats for us. As usual, most of those in attendance were mothers and grandparents with a sprinkling of fathers who could get off work. William looked a little out of place. He was taller and younger than most and decidedly male. He was also dressed nicely—nothing he'd be wearing to work at Renato's.

I sent Dylan to his classroom and then walked up to the front of the little auditorium. It had been decorated for the concert with a few hundred snowflakes the children had cut out.

William stood when he saw me. "Hi," he said. Noticeably, he didn't try to kiss me.

"Thanks so much for coming," I said. "Dylan asked me at least a half-dozen times if you were going to be here."

"I wouldn't miss it for the world," he said.

We sat down together. "How have you been?" I asked.

He avoided my gaze. "Just busy, you know?"

"I know," I said. I looked at him. "I've missed you."

"I've missed you too," he said softly.

"Did I do something wrong?"

He looked down, threading his fingers together. "No." Then he reached over and took my hand. For the moment, I let it go at that. I wanted his touch. I didn't want to spoil anything.

Fran arrived a few minutes before the concert. William hadn't known she was coming, and all the seats around us were taken, so she said hello, then went and sat near the back of the room.

The concert started promptly at nine thirty. Howard Taft Elementary School was small, with less than two hundred students in seven grades. The kindergarteners went first. They were singing "Rudolph, the Red-Nosed Reindeer" and someone had the bright idea of putting red noses—foam rubber clown noses, really—on each of the kids. Needless to say, the whole song was just an exercise in children chasing little red balls across the floor.

After the teachers had collected the noses, the next performance was Dylan's class with "Jingle Bells." The kids sang happily, and Dylan rang his bell with stoic concentration, his eyes not once leaving his teacher, Mrs. Duncan, who was directing.

We endured another four songs, and then William and I joined the rest of the parents in the cafeteria for milk and frosted Christmas tree–shaped sugar cookies.

I was looking for Dylan, when I saw him on the other side of the cafeteria with a group of children. He was pointing toward us.

"I'll be right back," I said to William. I crossed the room, smiling like only a proud mother could. "You were so great," I said when I got to him. "You really rang that bell."

Dylan just looked at me with a peculiar expression, the kind he wore when I caught him doing something he wasn't supposed to be doing.

Just then Mrs. Duncan walked up to me. "Hi, Elle."

"Congratulations," I said. "That was awesome."

"Congratulations to you," she returned.

I smiled. "For what?"

"Dylan tells us he's getting a father." She looked across the room at William. "Is that the lucky man?"

Dylan looked at me sheepishly.

"Mr. Smith is only a friend," I said. I looked at Dylan, torn between making him apologize and just holding him.

Just then one of the boys said, "I told you he was lying."

Dylan ran out of the room.

"Sorry," I said to his teacher. I chased after him. I found him hiding behind a row of coats in his classroom. I squatted down next to him. "Are you okay?"

He just looked at me with tears in his eyes.

"I'm not going to get mad at you." I sat down on the floor. "You know, it's hard not having a father, isn't it?"

He slowly nodded.

"You may not know it, but we're in the same boat, you and I. I don't have a father either. It doesn't seem fair, does it?"

He shook his head.

"You need to know something. You have a father. And he was a really great man. A special man. Your father is a hero. But you never got to see him, and that's not very fair to you. But he loved you very much, and he was so excited about coming home from the war and seeing you. He was excited about playing baseball and going tubing and taking you camping." My eyes welled up.

"But that didn't get to happen. I'm so sorry. And I know that he's sorry. But *you* have nothing to be sorry about. Because you're just a wonderful little boy, and none of this is your fault. Do you understand? You have nothing to be sorry or embarrassed about."

Dylan's eyes welled up too.

"Mr. William likes you very much. He's not your father, but he still cares about you and me. The other day he told me what a great kid you are. Do you know what I told him?"

Dylan shook his head again.

"I told him that he was right, that you're the best kid I know. Whether or not you have a father doesn't change that one bit.

"And you know what? Someday you might have the chance to *be* a father. And that little boy or girl will be the luckiest person in the world except for me, because I'll always be luckier. Because you're my son, and I'm glad I got to be your mother."

Dylan came out from behind the coats into my arms. I just held him.

After a few minutes I said, "Would you like to get a cookie?"

He nodded.

I leaned back and kissed his forehead. "Okay. Let's go."

I held his hand as we walked back down the hall to the cafeteria. The crowd had cleared a little, but there were still dozens of children swarming around the cookie table.

"Do you want me to go with you?" I asked.

"No, thank you."

"Okay. I'll be over here with Mr. William." I let go of his hand, and he ran over to the cookies where the other children were.

I looked around for William, hoping that he hadn't left. I found him standing alone on the south side of the cafeteria, leaning against the wall. I walked over to him.

"Where have you been?" he asked. Frankly, I wanted to ask him the same question.

"I had to talk to Dylan. He was telling some of the other children that you're his father."

William looked at me with a peculiar expression. "What?"

"Don't worry, I told him to stop."

William's expression turned still harder. He looked upset. "Why would he do that?"

The intensity of his response surprised me. "Why are you so upset by this? You should be flattered. Dylan looks up to you. He just wanted to be like the other kids whose dads are here."

William didn't say anything.

"Are you telling me that it's never even crossed your mind?"

"Has what crossed my mind?" he said angrily.

My eyes welled up. I covered them with my hand. "Oh my gosh." My pain turned to anger. I looked up at him. "What's going on? Why haven't you called?"

"I told you."

"You told me nothing!" I shouted. I noticed all the other parents looking at us. "Come outside."

William followed me outside the school. I turned on him. "What is this?"

"What is what?"

"This . . . us."

"What did you think this was?"

"Clearly not what you did," I said.

"Did I ever tell you that I was looking for a relationship?"

"Not in words."

"I didn't come to this place to fall in love."

I looked at him for a moment. "But you did, didn't you?"

He didn't answer.

"That's what it is, isn't it?" When he didn't answer, I said, "You fell in love and you got scared."

"What do you know about being scared?" he said.

My head was spinning. "Maybe nothing compared to you. But what I know is that you went through a hell that few people could understand, and you had every reason to die, yet you fought to live. And now that you're back, you're afraid of living."

"What do I have to live for?"

The question stung. "I thought I was something to live for. I thought Dylan was something to live for."

He didn't speak. The rejection that burned in me turned to anger. "You're a coward. You're not afraid of death, you're afraid that life might be worth living. You're afraid you might have to forgive yourself."

"There is no such thing as forgiveness."

"That's not true."

"Really? Have you forgiven your father?"

Again his words stung. I couldn't answer.

"Have you forgiven yourself for sending Isaac to fight in a war he didn't believe in and never came back from? Have you forgiven yourself for sending him to his death?"

His words sent a shock through me. My knees weakened. I began to tremble. "I didn't send him to his death."

"Are you sure?"

The words were like a spear through my heart. Suddenly Fran walked out of the school. She saw me breathless and heaving in pain and walked over. "Oh, honey. What happened?" She spun toward William. "What did you do to her?"

William just stood there.

"What did you do to her?!" she screamed.

He stood there, awkward and speechless. I looked up at him and said softly, "If I tell you you're right, will you leave me?"

"I'm so sorry," he said.

"You need to leave," Fran said. "You need to leave now."

His eyes welled. "I'm sorry." He turned and walked away.

After several minutes Fran said, "It's cold, Elle. Let's get you inside."

"I don't want to go in. I don't want Dylan to see me like this."

Fran took my hand. "I understand. Let me walk you to the car; then I'll get Dylan. I'll take him to my place."

"All right," I said softly.

We walked together across the wet pavement to my car. Fran opened my door, hugged me, and then helped me in.

"Just call when you want me to bring him back," she said. "He can spend the night if you want."

"Thank you."

She stood there with sympathetic eyes. Then she said, "What do you want me to tell Dylan if he asks about William?"

"Tell him he's gone."

Chapter 12

DYLAN SLEPT THAT NIGHT at Fran's. I couldn't sleep.

As I tossed in bed, somewhere in the middle of the night, something hit me. Something William had said at the school that stole any hope I had of sleep. *Did he really say what I thought he said?*

I waited until the sun came up; then, in just my sweats and a T-shirt, I put on my coat and drove to Renato's.

William's truck wasn't in the parking lot. I stormed into the repair shop's lobby. Renato was there talking to some man. "Where is he?" I asked Renato. "Where's William?"

"William quit," Renato said sadly. "Said he had to move on."

The words felt like a brick on my chest. "When?"

"He came by my house last night. He was very upset."

I ran back to my car. I drove to the Harrison with tears running down my cheeks. To my relief William's truck was still there.

I ran upstairs and pounded on his door. It was nearly a full minute before William opened it. He said nothing, his gaze on mine.

"I never told you my husband's name," I said. "I never told you his name was Isaac. You knew him, didn't you?"

William just looked at me.

"Tell me!" I shouted. "You knew my husband!"

William's face showed neither anger nor indifference. After a moment he said, "Come in."

His apartment looked even barer than before, if that was possible. There were two large green canvas duffel bags on the floor next to the couch. There was a gun on top of one of the bags.

William sat at one end of the couch. "Have a seat," he said.

I sat at the other end of the couch. I just sat there, trembling.

William rubbed his chin and said, "I knew Isaac. He was my best friend. I was with him when he died."

My eyes welled up.

"It was that New Year's Eve I told you about, right after the attack on Quang Tri. Our platoon walked into an ambush. Isaac got hit right off. I carried him to some rocks next to a waterfall, but he was bleeding badly. I kept telling him to hang in there, that we were going to make it. But we both knew otherwise." William swallowed. "His last thoughts were of you. He was afraid you would blame yourself for his death. He was afraid of his son growing up without a father. He asked me to find you and tell you that he loved you."

William's eyes welled up. "I was carrying him when I was captured." He looked into my eyes. "You wanted to know what kept me alive through that hell? It was that promise." He closed his eyes tight, forcing a tear down his cheek. "Actually, there were two promises. He made me promise to give you something." He breathed out slowly. "I was going to mail it to you after I left."

He reached into one of the duffel bags and brought out a black velvet pouch. "You have no idea what it took to get this to you." He handed it to me.

I opened the pouch and poured its contents into my palm. It was Isaac's wedding band. I looked up at William.

"I swallowed it at least a hundred times to keep them from finding it. If they'd seen me swallow it, they would have cut me open."

I caressed the ring between my fingers. It was just a simple gold band, all we could afford at the time. I remembered slipping it on Isaac's finger. William had risked his life to bring it to me.

"When I came back to America, I realized that the promise I made to Isaac was the only thing that kept me alive."

"Then he gave you a gift," I said.

He shook his head. "It was a curse." He looked at me. "You asked me why I came to Mistletoe. I came to fulfill a promise to my friend and then do what I should have done back in Vietnam."

"What's that?"

"Die."

The word echoed in my heart. "That place you took me," I said. "The falls . . ."

"That was where I was going to take my life."

"That's why you were crying?"

"I was crying because I was carrying Isaac like that when he died."

I let the words sink in. "Why did it take you so long to find me?"

"I was a mess. I was trying to make something stick. I couldn't."

"Maybe it was the wrong thing you were trying to make stick. Maybe God had something better for you."

"There is no God."

"Then why are you so angry at Him?"

He didn't answer. For a long time, there was only silence.

"I don't know why I didn't see it before, but I understand now," I said. "You were afraid because you finally found a family. You found what was taken from you all those years ago."

I reached out and touched his cheek.

"Can't you see it? Have you considered that maybe Isaac didn't ask you to make that promise for him? That promise was for *you*. It kept you alive through that hell. It brought you to us. He gave you a gift. He gave you back a family. He gave you us."

"That's what I'm afraid of."

"It's not what you're afraid of," I said. "It's what you're afraid of losing. Why else would you have taken an apartment and a job. You could have just found me at the diner and left the same day.

"William, God is giving you a second chance. But you have to have the courage to take it. You can have what you've always wanted. I know you're afraid of losing us. After all you've been through, who wouldn't be? But this time, this moment, is up to you. But if you don't take the chance, you've already lost us."

William was quiet for a long time. Then he looked up at me. I knew his answer before he spoke. All he said was "I'm sorry."

His words ended the conversation. My heart knew it was over. We were over. "Me too," I said. I felt nothing but darkness. "Are you going to take your life?"

"I don't know."

"Please don't. I love you, William. More than I could ever say." I swallowed. "And I know you love me."

He looked at me for a moment, then said, "More than I've ever loved anyone or anything." Then he said something I'll never forget. "It's the only thing more terrifying than death."

"That's the price of love," I said. "The risk of losing it. But it's worth the risk."

"Is it?"

"I guess that's for you to decide." I wiped my eyes and lifted the golden ring. "Thank you for this." I stood. "I guess I better let you get on with your life."

As he stood, I walked over and put my arms around him, my head against his chest. With his arms around me, he pulled me in close. For just a moment I pretended that this was something else, but my heart wouldn't allow it. I stepped back, kissed him, then turned and walked out of his life.

IT WAS ONLY A WEEK UNTIL Christmas. I was alone. Dylan had been with Fran for two days.

I couldn't stand the sound of my thoughts, so I turned on the radio to one of those all-Christmas-all-the-time stations.

My heart was broken.

Most of all, I was tired. Tired of loneliness and responsibility. And in spite of my exhaustion, I could see no respite, no reprieve, no way out, and Christmas was looming ahead of me like an iceberg in the path of a titanic meltdown.

Dylan would be back soon. I wished I had someone to send him off with for a while. Fran would have kept him, but she was leaving town for the holidays. I couldn't hide my brokenness.

My thoughts were interrupted by the doorbell. It was Gretchen, my landlady. She stood on the porch holding a plate of cookies. She looked at me, clearly shocked by my appearance. My hair was a rat's nest, and I had no makeup on.

"Elle, are you . . . okay?"

"I've been better," I said. "Come in."

She stepped inside. "Are you sick?"

"No. This has just been a hard month. It's been a hard year."

"I'm really sorry." Gretchen forced a smile. "But cheer up. I brought you my famous pepperkaker cookies."

"Thank you," I said. I took the plate and set it on the table. I turned back. "Look, I know I'm late on rent, but . . . is there any way we could split this month across the next three months?"

Gretchen looked confused. "You want to split up your rent?"

"Just for the next three months," I said.

"I don't know what you're talking about. Your rent's paid."

"I don't understand."

"Honey, there's nothing to understand. Your rent is paid up to the end of next year, which I am very grateful for."

"You must be mistaken. I didn't pay it."

"Not you, dear. It was the man you sent."

"What man?"

"The one you sent with your rent. I've never met him before. He told me he was paying the bill for you. He paid in cash."

I let the news sink in. "Was his name William?"

She bit her lip. "I'm sorry, he didn't give me his name. He was a nice-looking gent, older, maybe in his late fifties."

"Fifties? Are you sure?"

"Oh, yes. He had fabulous gray hair."

I honestly had no idea who it could be.

"I assumed you knew." She smiled. "Maybe it was someone you met at the diner. Maybe you have a secret admirer."

"I don't know anyone who could have done that."

She shrugged. "Well, someone paid it. Maybe it was an angel. I'm happy for you, Elle. You deserve a break. Maybe this news will brighten your day. Merry Christmas, my dear."

"Merry Christmas to you too," I said.

I shut the door after her. *Who had paid my rent?*

FRAN came by with Dylan a little after seven o'clock. She honked "Shave and a Haircut" as she pulled into my driveway—something Dylan always made her do. She was on her way to Texas to visit her family, and the back seat of her car was full of gifts and suitcases.

The passenger-side door opened, and Dylan practically sprang from it, running to me and shouting, "Mama! I missed you!"

I hugged him tight. "I missed you too, buddy."

He stood back. "Look!" He held out a wrapped box. "Fran gave me a present. But she says I can't open it until Christmas."

"Go put it under the tree," I said. "I'll be right there."

He ran into the house. Fran walked up, leaving her car idling.

"He's had a bath, and I fed him dinner." She looked at me. "Elle, I'm so sorry I can't keep him longer. You know I would."

"You've done more than enough. I'm worried about you driving at night. Are you sure you won't wait until morning?"

"I'll be okay. I'm just going to Green River tonight—maybe Laramie if the roads aren't too bad. That's not too far."

"I'm sorry I delayed your trip. But I don't know what I would have done without you."

"You're my family too. I'll be back January third, okay? I'll plan on getting right back into it." Fran leaned forward, and we hugged.

"Merry Christmas, Elle. Nineteen seventy-six will be a better year. I promise. You know I'm right about these things. It's the psychic in me."

"I'm going to hold you to that," I said. "Merry Christmas."

"I love you," she said.

"And I love you."

She walked back to her car. I shut the door behind her and went inside. I walked over to the tree. Dylan was sitting next to it. "How was your visit with Fran?" I asked.

"I can't wait to see what she got me. Is Mr. William coming for Christmas?"

"No. Mr. William had to go away."

"For . . . ever?"

"Yes."

Dylan looked sad. "But I like him."

A tear fell down my cheek. "Me too, buddy. Me too."

AN HOUR later there was a knock at my door. I had already sent Dylan to bed, and I guessed it might be Fran coming back. Maybe she had decided to wait to leave until tomorrow, after all. I opened the door, ready to give her a big hug.

My father stood in the doorway.

I didn't recognize him at first. He was older, of course, but he looked older than I would have thought after six years. He was completely gray, the hair at the top of his head thinning. He seemed smaller and softer somehow, even though he still held himself like a military man.

"Hi, Miche," he said. He pronounced it "Meesh." Michelle was my real name, but everyone except my father called me Elle.

I was speechless. Finally I asked, "How did you find me?"

"A mutual friend."

"We don't have mutual friends."

He cleared his throat. "Seeing me is probably a big shock."

"That's an understatement," I said.

Just then Dylan walked up behind me. "Mama." I didn't want him to see my father, but it was too late. He stood staring. Then he said, "I'm Dylan. Who are you?"

"Don't tell him," I said.

My father glanced at me, then Dylan. "You can call me Larry."

"Hi, Mr. Larry," Dylan said.

"Dylan, I need you to go back to your room."

Dylan frowned, then stomped back to his room.

"I'm sorry it's so late," my father said. "I tried to catch you earlier, but you weren't at the diner."

"How do you know where I work?"

"Same friend. May I come in? I promise I won't stay long."

I didn't move. I think I felt that letting him in was, in some way, symbolic of letting him back into my life.

"Just five minutes and I'll be gone," he said.

I thought over his request. "All right. But just five minutes."

I stepped back from the door and let him in. I walked to my kitchen and brought out an egg timer. I set it for five minutes, then put it on the table. My father watched my demonstration but said nothing about it.

"You have a nice place. May I sit down?"

I nodded. I noticed he was holding a manila envelope under his arm. For a moment we just looked at each other without speaking.

"You don't have much time."

"I know. . . . It's just been so long." He glanced at the egg timer, breathed in deeply, then sighed. "I came to tell you that I'm sorry. What I did to you, especially at such a difficult time, was unconscionable. I am ashamed of what I did. I don't expect you to forgive me, but I wanted you to know that I'm sorry. I was wrong."

It was the first time I had heard those words come out of his mouth. It should have felt good, but it didn't. I read somewhere that we always react angrily at people for finally doing what they should have done before. I wanted to punish him.

"Wrong about what?" I said.

"Pretty much everything," he said.

"What were you hoping would come from this? That after all this time I was just going to let you back into our lives? Is that what you expected?"

"Expected? No. But I was hoping."

I didn't respond.

"I believe that when you repent, you need to make restitution when possible. I wanted to see if you'd let me make up for what I should have done a long time ago."

"Is that what this is? Repentance?"

"In part."

I suddenly understood. "You paid my rent."

He nodded. The bell rang on the egg timer. I glanced at it and then back at him. "What made you think I wanted your help?"

"I didn't think you wanted my help. I just thought you probably needed it."

I wasn't sure how to respond to that. He glanced down at his watch. "Well, I've taken my five minutes. Thank you for hearing me out. I'm sorry to bother you. I just wanted to tell you in person how sorry I am." He slowly stood, his gaze catching mine. "And how much I've missed my girl." His eyes were moist. "I've made some big mistakes in my life, Miche, but none bigger than my mistake with you. Turning away my only daughter is unforgivable. I hope you can forgive me someday. Not for my sake—I don't deserve it—but yours. For your own peace."

William's words about forgiving my father echoed back to me.

My father began walking toward the door. "What I want doesn't matter, anyway. At least not for much longer."

"What do you mean by that?" I said.

He didn't answer but continued toward the door.

"What did you mean by 'much longer'?"

He turned back and looked at me as if he were trying to decide whether or not to answer. "I have cancer, Miche. The doctors say I won't be around much longer."

The words affected me more than I wanted them to. "That's why you came back now? Guilt? Dying regrets?"

He looked at me sadly. "No, the guilt and regret were there long before the cancer. Up until now I didn't know where you were." He gazed into my eyes. "I've looked for you for years. I even hired a private eye, but he failed. I had no idea where you went. I didn't even know what your new last name was. For all I knew, you had left the country." He sighed. "I'd given up hope of ever seeing you again, until your friend showed up."

"Who is this friend?" I asked.

"Second Lieutenant Smith."

It took me a moment to understand. "You saw . . . William?"

He nodded.

The revelation angered me. My life was none of William's business. "What did he tell you?"

"Much," he said softly. "He told me about Isaac—the kind of man he was, the kind of soldier he was. He told me how he was killed in action." My father's voice choked. "I'm so sorry you had to go through that alone. I'm sorry I wasn't there for you."

I could see the pain in his eyes.

"He told me he was ashamed of me."

"What did you say to that?"

"He didn't tell me anything I didn't already believe. I told him that I was ashamed of myself.

"Then he told me about you and Dylan. I asked him whether he thought you'd talk to me if I went to see you. He said he didn't know, but if I had any courage left in me, I should try." He cleared his throat, blinking away the tears. "I can't change what I've done, Miche. I can only try to change the future. I came to do the right thing, if that's possible." He looked into my eyes. "If you'll let me. I know I'm asking a lot, but it would be a true mercy."

As I looked into his pleading eyes, the man standing before me somehow changed. I no longer saw the rigid military man who had rejected my baby and me that painful night. I saw someone different. I saw a humble, broken man mourning the mistakes of his past. I saw a grieving, aging man trying to make something right. I saw through the veil of mistake and circumstance a man I'd once known, a man who had provided and cared for me. A man who had held my hand and carried me on his shoulders when I was tired. A man who, in his own, sometimes flawed ways, always did his best to protect me. In short, I saw my father again.

I couldn't speak for a long time. Then I nodded. "All right."

Those two simple words had a profound impact on him—more,

perhaps, than I could understand. He wiped his eyes with his forearm, then took the envelope from under his arm and handed it to me. "This is mostly just a lot of legal mumbo jumbo. I set up a college fund for Dylan. There's enough there for his education at a good school, also books and housing. He has several years before then, so the fund should grow a bit. It might even help him get a house someday."

"You paid for Dylan's college?"

"There's something else. I set up another fund. It's in that same envelope. It's called the Isaac Sheen Scholarship Fund. It's for one Negro student each year at Arizona State."

"Thank you."

"It's long past due," he said.

As I looked into his eyes, I suddenly started crying. He just stood there, almost at attention, his face full of emotion. "We once had a wonderful relationship, Miche. You were my life. My light. We had such fun." He grinned. "Well, maybe I was never much fun, but I tried."

I laughed through my tears. "You were fun. Sometimes."

He laughed as well. Then his gaze grew more serious. "My sins have brought their own punishment, Miche."

Hearing this made my heart hurt, not just for my loss but my father's as well. I thought of my love for Dylan and understood that my father loved me the same. For the first time I realized just how much he had suffered too.

I wondered if he'd gone through this alone or if my mother had changed as well. "Where's Mom?" I asked.

My father looked down. "She's gone. She tried, but . . ." He cleared his throat. "Two years ago her liver failed. We tried for a transplant, but it was too late."

I suddenly felt my own pain of loss. "I'm sorry I wasn't there for you."

"It was my own fault." His eyes welled up. "I can't tell you how many times I've looked through our photographs of us. The Christmases we spent. I've missed my daughter."

"I've missed you, Dad."

He swallowed. "May I hug you?"

"I would like that." I fell into him and we embraced. It felt so good to be held by him again.

"Thank you, Miche."

"Thank you, Daddy."

After we parted, his eyes were red. "Do you think I could see Dylan? I won't tell him who I am."

"Yes." I walked to Dylan's room and opened the door. As I expected, he wasn't asleep. He was always curious when someone new was in the house.

"Dylan. I want you to meet someone."

"Is it Mr. Larry?"

"Yes."

Dylan hopped out of bed. He walked directly up to my father. "Mr. Larry, why are you at my house?"

My father crouched down. "I came to see how you and your mother were doing. You are a handsome young man."

"I know," Dylan said. "Who are you again?"

My father just looked at him and then wiped his eyes.

"Why are you crying?" Dylan asked.

"Because I'm sorry you had to ask that."

I stepped forward. "Dylan, this is your grandpa. My father."

Dylan looked puzzled. "You said you didn't have a father."

"I was wrong," I said.

"I have a grandpa?"

"You do," my father said. "I'm right here."

Dylan still looked confused. "Where have you been?"

"I've been lost," he said. "Very, very lost."

"And someone found you?"

He smiled. "Yes. Someone found me. A soldier." He glanced at me, then back to Dylan. "If it's okay with you and your mother, I'd like to invite you to our house for Christmas. I'll even take you on a sleigh ride through the mountain with real horses."

"You have real horses?"

"Yes. And real cows, goats, and chickens."

"Are you a farmer?"

"Yes, I am. And I have a big farmhouse but no one to spend Christmas with."

Dylan looked at me. "Can we go for Christmas, Mama?"

I nodded. "Yes."

I looked over at my father. He didn't even try to stop his tears.

Chapter 13

TWO DAYS LATER Dylan and I made the three-hundred-mile drive south to Cedar City. I hadn't been there since I'd left six years earlier. It took us five hours. It's hard to believe that just five hours had separated so much.

I was wearing Isaac's ring on a gold chain around my neck. It was the gold chain my father had given me at my high school graduation. I hadn't worn it since I left, but even in the hard times, I hadn't been able to pawn it. Maybe, like William, I was still holding on to something I couldn't bring myself to admit I wanted. Or needed.

"The old Fairlane," my father said, walking out to greet us. "I'm a little surprised it's still running."

"Barely," I said. "I just replaced the alternator, clutch, and timing belt."

His brow furrowed. "What did that set you back?"

"Not as much as it should have," I said. "William fixed it for free. But it hasn't stopped the rest of it from falling apart." I grinned. "I think it has leprosy."

My father chuckled. "Old cars don't get new."

I smiled. "I've heard that."

CHRISTMAS Eve was a giant party. My father had cut his own tree from the forest behind his property. Unlike the small tree at home, his was massive and rose nearly fourteen feet high in his spacious living room. It was elaborately decorated with beautiful lights, ribbons, and ornaments.

"Who decorated your tree?" I asked.

He looked at me with surprise. "I did, of course. You know I'm a Christmasphile."

I smiled with remembrance. It was true. My father loved Christmas.

My father had a lot of friends whom he'd invited over to see his returned daughter and grandson. Probably close to a hundred people came by the house. I shouldn't have been surprised, but there were a lot of single, older ladies who spent a lot of time with us. Frankly, I didn't know there were that many single women in Cedar City. There were even a few handsome ranchers that my father, not so discreetly, informed I was single.

At the height of the party, my father walked to the center of the room with a glass of wine. He clinked on the glass with a spoon until the room was quiet. "I'd like to make a toast," he said. He turned to me. "As most of you know, Christmas is a special time of year for me. At least, it was. There hasn't been a tree in this house since my daughter left. I swore that there would be no tree until she came back. I had begun to lose hope that there would ever be a tree in this house again."

His eyes welled. "But Christmas is about hope. The Wise Men traveled far to find a mother with her child in a simple manger. The same is true for me. I may not be wise, but I was searching. And God sent me a star to find her. So I raise a toast to that star, a soldier who set me on the right path. I raise a toast to the season itself and its promise of hope. Most of all, I raise a toast to that mother and her beautiful, beautiful child. May Christmas forever live in our hearts." He raised his glass. "To Christmas."

I raised mine and said softly, "And to the Father."

All in all, it was a glorious celebration with food and music, laughter and joy. I think Dylan had more fun than the rest of us.

After everyone left, including a few of the women I practically had to shoo away, my father and I stayed up late and told stories of the old days, some true, some not so much. Mostly, my father just wanted to know all about my life since I'd left.

In the end he asked about William and what had happened between us. I was surprised at how much I was willing to share. Even though William had broken my heart, he'd given me a precious gift. He'd given me my father back. And he'd given Dylan a grandfather. Most of all, he'd given my heart something I didn't want to believe was lacking—forgiveness.

"He loves you," he said.

I nodded. "I know. But maybe not enough."

My father nodded, then said, "Don't underestimate the power of love over fear."

My father had prepared my old room upstairs for my return and one across the hall for Dylan. Being in a strange house, I asked Dylan if he wanted to sleep with me—something he often asked to do even in our house—but he turned me down. He was pretty excited to have his own room in the farmhouse.

The next morning, Dylan and I woke to the smell of coffee and Burl Ives's Christmas music playing from my father's television stereo. It was a powerful flashback for me, reminding me of many happy Christmases we had shared together.

Dylan and I walked downstairs to find the tree buried in a mountain of presents. There were more than twenty gifts for each of us. I don't know how my father knew what we wanted, but he did pretty well, though he later confessed that several lady friends had lent a hand in the purchasing and wrapping department.

Throughout the morning's unveilings, my father just sat in his old La-Z-Boy chair, the same one I remembered from my childhood, and watched the proceedings with a joyful smile.

The gifts he gave us were more than extravagant, and Dylan looked like he was living a dream he was afraid to wake up from. He got a cassette tape recorder, a phonograph player system with a built-in eight-track player, Jackson 5 and 5th Dimension albums, a pet rock, and a plethora of other amusements. There was even a new Atari Pong game, the expensive one Dylan sometimes talked about but knew I would never be able to afford. One of his favorite gifts was his own pair of leather cowboy boots.

"Look, Mama!" he said, holding them up. "I'm a cowboy."

"Put them on," I said.

"Can I?" he asked.

"Of course. That's what they're for."

Dylan pulled the boots on over his bare feet.

"Now you look like a real cowboy," I said.

"Except for a hat," my dad said. "Every cowboy needs a hat. Wait a second. I think I got one of those too." From behind the chair, he brought out a small felt cowboy hat. He threw the hat to Dylan, like it was a Frisbee.

"Wow!" Dylan said. He put it on. Backward.

"Other way, partner," my father said.

Dylan turned it around.

"It's a Stetson. That's the real McCoy."

"That's really too much, Dad."

"No," he said, winking at me. "It's not."

After we'd opened the last present, my father said, "I got one more thing for you, Miche."

"You got me enough already," I replied.

"Now don't be difficult," he said. "It's just one more thing. But try as I might, I couldn't get it through the door, so I left it outside. Come on, Dylan. I have something outside for you too."

"Is mine too big to come in the house too?"

"Well, yours can't come inside for other reasons," he said.

We followed my father out the side door. Sitting beneath the covered driveway was a brand-new cherry-red Valiant.

"It's the Valiant Regal sedan, six-cylinder, four-speed," he said, sounding almost like a TV commercial. "American made, of course. One of Chrysler's best new cars of the year."

"It's beautiful." I hugged my father. "Thank you so much, Dad."

"Is that our new car?" Dylan asked.

"It sure is," I said.

"Open the door, girl," my father said. "Nothing like the smell of a new car."

I opened the door and looked inside. It was gorgeous.

"Can I get in?" Dylan asked.

"Of course."

He jumped inside the front, falling back in the bucket seat. He turned to me. "It kind of stinks."

I smiled. "It's the new-car smell. You'll learn to like it."

"Have you ever seen a Valiant?" my father asked.

"Funny you should ask. I drove an older model a few weeks ago while they were fixing the Fairlane." I smiled. "Everyone kept telling me it was sexy."

"Well, I don't know about that, but it's a solid car and brand spanking new, right off the dealership floor."

"You bought it off the dealership floor? Whatever happened to 'Don't buy retail'?"

"You remembered," he said. "Well, I still hold to the maxim. I didn't buy it at retail. I bought it from my own dealership."

"You own a car dealership?"

"Two of them: one in Cedar, the other in St. George. Both Plymouth-Chryslers. They're doing well too. Some of those Japanese cars coming into the market have pilfered a few sales, but I don't think they'll last. They don't make them like we do here in America."

"Now what do I do with the Fairlane?"

"I'll take it off your hands. Maybe we'll keep it in the barn. Who knows, might be a collector's piece someday." He turned to Dylan. "Speaking of the barn, I got one more present to give."

The three of us walked out to the stable. My father walked up to one of the stalls. A quarterhorse mare put her head over the gate and nuzzled him.

"Oh, I love you too, Summer," he said, kissing her on the head. He turned around. "Dylan, come here for a second."

Dylan walked up behind my father. He'd never been near a real horse and was a little scared.

"No need to worry," my father said to Dylan. "This here is Summer. She's a mama horse, and just six months ago she gave birth to a baby colt. Can you see him back there?"

There was a beautiful bay roan colt with a black mane and a star on its nose. "What do you think of him?"

"He's cool," Dylan said.

"Well, I'm glad you think that, because he's yours."

"That's my horse?"

"He sure is."

Dylan turned to me. "Can I have him?"

"That's between you and Grandpa," I said. "He gave him to you."

"Yes!" Dylan said. He turned to my father. "What's his name?"

"He doesn't have one. He was waiting for you to name him."

"Can I call him Mr. William?" Dylan asked.

I swallowed. "You can call him anything you like."

My father winked at me. "You might want to think about it for a while," he said to Dylan. "A name is something you want to give a lot of thought to. Let's just call him Horse for now."

"Okay," Dylan said.

Thank you, I mouthed to my father.

"Well, let's get back inside before someone catches pneumonia. I've got breakfast to make." He said to Dylan, "Would you mind going with your mom to the henhouse and grabbing us a few eggs? A half dozen ought to do. There's a basket for the eggs right next to the door you walk in."

Dylan nodded. "Will you help me, Mama?"

"Of course."

It was my father's Christmas Day tradition to make us whatever we wanted for breakfast. He looked like he had bought out the local grocery store just to make sure he had everything we might ask for. He made waffles for Dylan, of course, with strawberries and whipped cream, two kinds of sausages, bacon, biscuits, ham-and-pepper omelets, and gravy. It was kind of obscene how much food he made. It was obscene how much I ate.

After breakfast my father started doing the dishes.

I walked up to his side. "I can do that, Dad. You've worked all morning."

"No. You play with your son."

"Trust me, he's played enough with me. I think he needs some Grandpa time."

As I was doing the dishes, the doorbell rang. "Miche, would you mind getting that?" my father shouted from the living room. "Dylan has me all tied up here. Literally."

"Sure, Dad," I said, wiping my hands with a dishcloth. "I can't believe how many friends you have."

"You know how it is. They're like crows. I try to scare them away, but they keep coming back."

"It's probably another one of your lady friends."

I walked to the front door and opened it.

William stood in the doorway. I looked at him for a moment, then said, "What took you so long?"

After kissing me soundly, William stood back and laughed.

"You were really expecting me to come back?"

"No, I didn't expect," I said, borrowing my father's words. "I hoped."

He looked in my eyes. "What gave you hope?"

"Two reasons. First, you talked with my father. My father's a smart man. He would have figured out pretty quickly that there was something between us." I smiled. "And if there's one thing about my father, the man's a fixer. He can fix anything. Tractors, dishwashers, windmills. Even relationships."

"I'll give him that," he said. "What's the second?"

"You love me."

New Year's Eve was the sixth anniversary of Isaac's death. The day was even more powerful to William. It was the day he had watched his friend die. It was the same day he'd been taken captive. Today it represented the opposite. It represented a new life and freedom.

It was shortly after midnight. My father had put Dylan to bed and then said good night and went to bed himself, leaving William and me alone on the couch.

I snuggled into his arms. "Do you believe in the spiritual law of restitution?" I asked.

He kissed me on the temple, then asked, "What's that?"

"It's the belief that everything we lose in this life will be returned to us in the next."

He pondered my question and then said, "I don't know." He pulled me in tighter. "But I know one thing about loss."

"What's that?"

"Whether we lose something or not, it's better to have had it."

Epilogue

ON WILLIAM'S AND MY first date I told him that I'd like to write a book someday. Here it is. At least, part one. My life isn't over.

In spite of my rent being paid for the year, less than a month later Dylan and I moved back home to Cedar City. Saying goodbye to Loretta, Fran, Jamie, and the rest of the regulars at the diner was excruciating, with an ocean of tears, even though I reminded them that I was just moving down the road. It was a long road, but the same one passed through both towns.

Loretta shut down the diner and threw a big going-away shindig for us. My dad and William were there. Against William's advice, I tried to hook Loretta up with my father. I figured it would be like having two people I love in the same house. It didn't take. William was right. She would have driven my father crazy. And vice versa.

William and I were married in April, the same month Isaac and I had been. He took a job in the service department of my father's Cedar City car dealership. In less than a year, he was managing the place. I believe that was my father's plan all along. I asked him if it was what he was expecting. He smiled and said, "Expecting, no. I just hoped."

As my father's health deteriorated, he turned more of the responsibility of running the dealerships over to William and me, opting to spend as much time with his grandson as he could.

My father taught Dylan to ride horses and motorcycles and tractors and pretty much anything else on his farm that moved. They went on many long rides on their horses, sometimes even overnighters with tents and packs. My father became as good a grandfather as a boy could hope for. Many times, at least when he was feeling sentimental, he told me how he regretted the years that he'd missed in our lives. But if you ask me, he made up for it and then some.

My father bravely fought his cancer like the soldier he was. The six months the doctors gave him ended up being almost six years. The doctors called it miraculous. I just think he finally had something to live for. That's something we can all understand.

My father passed away five years and thirty-five days after he found us that winter in Mistletoe. His death was Dylan's first real lesson in grief, and it was painful to watch. I suffered with him. But I was grateful for every one of those days I got with my father. Like I once told William, "The cost of love is the risk of losing it." But it's always worth it. After all, in the end what else is there?

My father willed everything to William and me. William was shrewd in business, and today we own six car dealerships—three in Utah, two in Nevada, and one in Colorado. It's hard to believe I was once so poor. Now we have the chance to help and bless others. It's nice being on that side of the menu too.

Dylan graduated from Arizona State, where he met a lovely woman and was married shortly after graduating with an MBA. Today he owns both a BMW and a Porsche dealership in Phoenix. He even likes the smell of new cars.

William and I have since retired. We have been traveling a lot. A year ago we took a vacation to Vietnam. It was a powerful experience for both of us. The "Hanoi Hilton," where William was held, was mostly demolished twenty years after the war, but not all of it. Today the existing structure operates as a museum and memorial. Propaganda inside the museum shows pictures of happy inmates shooting pool and playing cards, and claims that the term *Hanoi Hilton* was coined by happy, well-cared-for inmates. William said little as we walked through the site.

Two days later William took me to where Isaac fell, next to the waterfall. I was surprised that after all these years he could still find it, but I shouldn't have been. War is about logistics, and how do you forget what is unforgettable? I was wearing Isaac's ring as I knelt on the ground and wept for my love and thanked him for my new love. How different it must have seemed to me than to William. To an outsider the land was beautiful and full of life. I suppose time has changed and healed the country, just as it has us.

William and I now spend our winters in Arizona, blessed with our three beautiful grandchildren. William is restoring my grandpa's old Fairlane with Seth, our oldest grandson. Life is good. God is good.

As I look back over that year, it's amazing to me to see how so unexpectedly life can switch tracks to a new destination. But the complexity of those junctions is far too great to assign to the cogs and machinations of mere chance and circumstance.

Maybe that's why I've always thought of God less as an engineer than as an artist—one who uses our hopes, fears, dreams, and especially our tears to paint on the canvas of our souls, rendering something beautiful. The hardest part, I suppose, is waiting to see what He's up to.

AfterWords

Bestselling author Richard Paul Evans began his writing journey in the early 1990s, when he self-published *The Christmas Box,* a story he penned as an expression of love for his two eldest daughters. The book quickly caught the attention of major publishers and went on to make history, becoming simultaneously the number one hardcover and paperback book in the nation.

Since then, Evans has become something of a publishing phenomenon, with more than thirty million copies of his books in print, translated into more than twenty-four languages. Known for his holiday-themed stories, he's been hailed by the *New York Times* as the "king of Christmas fiction." In 2011, he also began writing the Michael Vey young adult series.

And yet, the author of forty novels still finds writing each one to be a unique experience. For *Noel Street,* which takes place in 1975, he watched eighteen hours of Vietnam documentaries as research. But the best part of his preparations, according the author, was listening to the music. "We had great music in 1975," he says fondly.

Over the years, Evans has been recognized for both his writing and his philanthropy, receiving the American Mothers Book Award and the *Washington Times* Humanitarian of the Century Award. He lives in Salt Lake City with his wife, Keri, not far from their five children and two grandchildren.

© 2020 by Trusted Media Brands, Inc.
Copyright © 2020 by The Reader's Digest Association (Canada) ULC

FIRST EDITION: Volume 374

Library of Congress Catalog Card Number: 98-640138
ISSN: 1541-0900

Printed in the United States of America

ACKNOWLEDGMENTS

Page 161: © Troye Fox 2016. Page 303: Brandy Allen. Page 455: Dave Hall. Page 575: Laurie Liss.
Jacket and title page image: Tim Graham/Getty Images.

The original editions of the books in this volume are published and copyrighted as follows:

The Wild One, published at $26.00 by G. P. Putnam's Sons,
an imprint of Penguin Random House LLC
© 2020 by Nicholas Petrie LLC

Dachshund Through the Snow, published at $24.99 by Minotaur Books,
an imprint of St. Martin's Publishing Group
© 2019 by Tara Productions, Inc.

No Bad Deed, published at $27.99 by William Morrow,
an imprint of HarperCollins Publishers
© 2020 by Heather Chavez

Noel Street, published at $21.99 by Gallery Books,
an imprint of Simon & Schuster, Inc.
© 2019 by Richard Paul Evans

The volumes in this series are issued every two months.
Readers may receive this service by contacting us by mail, email, or company website.

In the United States:
Reader's Digest Select Editions
PO Box 50005, Prescott, AZ 86304-5005
bookservices@rd.com
rd.com

In Canada:
Reader's Digest Select Editions
PO Box 970 Stn Main, Markham, ON L3P 0K2
bookservices@rd.com
rd.ca

Some of the titles in this volume are also available in large-print format.
For information about Select Editions Large Type, contact us at
PO Box 433031, Palm Coast, FL 32143-3031 or selt@emailcustomerservice.com.